ABOUT THE TRANSLATORS

RICHARD PEVEAR has published translations of Alain, Yves Bonnefoy, Alberto Savinio, Pavel Florensky, and Henri Volohonsky, as well as two books of poetry. He has received fellowships or grants for translation from the National Endowment for the Arts, the Ingram Merrill Foundation, the Guggenheim Foundation, the National Endowment for the Humanities, and the French Ministry of Culture.

LARISSA VOLOKHONSKY was born in Leningrad. She has translated works by the prominent Orthodox theologians Alexander Schmemann and John Meyendorff into Russian.

Together, Pevear and Volokhonsky have translated *Dead Souls* and *The Collected Tales* by Nikolai Gogol, and *The Brothers Karamazou, Crime and Punishment, Notes from Underground, Demons* and *The Adolescent* by Fyodor Dostoevsky. They were awarded the PEN Book-of-the-Month Club Translation Prize for their version of *The Brothers Karamazou*, and more recently *Demons* was one of three nor   e married and live in France.

D1513988

TRANSLATIONS OF DOSTOEVSKY
BY PEVEAR AND VOLOKHONSKY

The Adolescent (2003)
The Idiot (2002)
Demons (1994)
Notes from Underground (1993)
Crime and Punishment (1992)
The Brothers Karamazov (1990)

FYODOR DOSTOEVSKY

The Idiot

Translated from the Russian by
Richard Pevear and Larissa Volokhonsky

With an Introduction by
Richard Pevear

Granta Books
London

Granta Publications, 2/3 Hanover Yard,
Noel Road, London N1 8BE

First published in Great Britain by Granta Books 2003
This edition published by arrangement with Pantheon Books,
a division of Random House, Inc.
This translation has been made from the Soviet Academy of Sciences
edition (Izdatel'stvo 'Nauka'), volume 8 (Leningrad, 1973).

1 3 5 7 9 10 8 6 4 2

Printed and bound in Great Britain
by Mackays of Chatham PLC

CONTENTS

———

INTRODUCTION

On a house near the Pitti Palace in Florence there is a plaque that reads: "In this neighborhood between 1868 and 1869 F. M. Dostoevsky completed his novel *The Idiot.*" It is strange to think of this most Russian of writers working on this most Russian of novels while living in the city of Dante. In fact the author's absence from Russia can be felt in the book, if we compare it with his preceding novel, *Crime and Punishment* (1866), which is so saturated in place, in the streets, buildings, squares, and bridges of Petersburg, that the city becomes a living participant in events. Place has little importance in *The Idiot.* Petersburg and the residential suburb of Pavlovsk, where most of the action occurs, are barely described. There is little sense of a surrounding world or a wider human community. Russia is present in the novel not as a place but as a question – the essence of Russia, the role of Russia and the "Russian Christ" in Europe and in the world. It was precisely during the four years he spent abroad, from 1867 to 1871, that Dostoevsky brooded most intensely on the fate of Russia, as the exiled Dante brooded on the fate of Florence.

But it would be a mistake to think that this lack of an objective "world" makes *The Idiot* an abstract ideological treatise. On the contrary, it is perhaps the most physical and even physiological of Dostoevsky's novels. Its events seem to take place internally, not in a spiritual inwardness but within the body, within *a* body, rendered more by sensation than by depiction. With *Crime and Punishment,* as the philosopher Michel Eltchaninoff wrote recently,* Dostoevsky buried the descriptive novel; in *The Idiot* he arrived at a new form, expressive of "the inobjective body," which overcomes the dualities of interior and exterior, subjective and objective, physical and psychological. It is given in certain modes of

---

*In *L'Expression du corps chez Dostoevskij* ("The Expression of the Body in Dostoevsky"), Paris, 2000.

experience: sickness, for instance, is as much subjective as objective; so is violence, and so is life with others, the "invasive" presence of the other (hence the privileged place Dostoevsky gives to doorways and thresholds, to sudden entrances and unexpected meetings). And so, finally, are words spoken and heard, written and read aloud. Dostoevsky concentrates on these modes of experience in *The Idiot* to the exclusion of almost all else. The novel, broadly speaking, is an exploration of what it means to be flesh.

The idea of the "Russian Christ" is important in *The Idiot* (and was certainly important to his creator, who repeated Myshkin's words on the subject almost verbatim nine years later in his *Diary of a Writer*), but a much stronger presence in the novel is the painting that Dostoevsky significantly calls "The Dead Christ" (the actual title is *Christ's Body in the Tomb*), a work by Hans Holbein the Younger that hangs in the museum of Basel. Dostoevsky places a copy of the painting in the house of the young merchant millionaire Rogozhin. It is discussed twice in the novel, the second time at length and in a key passage. The shape of the painting is unusual: the narrator describes it as being "around six feet wide and no more than ten inches high." It is, in other words, totally lacking in vertical dimension.

Dostoevsky first read about Holbein's painting in Nikolai Karamzin's *Letters of a Russian Traveler* (1801), an account of the young author's travels in Europe, modeled on Laurence Sterne's *Sentimental Journey*. In a letter written from Basel, Karamzin mentions that he has been to the picture gallery there and "looked with great attention and pleasure at the paintings of the illustrious Holbein, a native of Basel and friend of Erasmus." Of this painting in particular (giving it yet another title) he observes: "In 'Christ Taken Down from the Cross' one doesn't see anything of God. As a dead man he is portrayed quite naturally. According to legend, Holbein painted it from a drowned Jew." That is all. But these few words must have made a strong impression on Dostoevsky. In August 1867, on their way from Baden-Baden to Geneva, he and his young wife made a special stop in Basel to see the painting.

INTRODUCTION

Dostoevsky's wife, Anna Grigorievna, wrote an account of their visit to the museum in her memoirs, published forty years later:

On the way to Geneva we stopped for a day in Basel, with the purpose of seeing a painting in the museum there that my husband had heard about from someone.

This painting, from the brush of Hans Holbein, portrays Jesus Christ, who has suffered inhuman torture, has been taken down from the cross and given over to corruption. His swollen face is covered with bloody wounds, and he looks terrible. The painting made an overwhelming impression on my husband, and he stood before it as if dumbstruck...

When I returned some fifteen or twenty minutes later, I found my husband still standing in front of the painting as if riveted to it. There was in his agitated face that expression as of fright which I had seen more than once in the first moments of an epileptic fit. I quietly took him under the arm, brought him to another room, and sat him down on a bench, expecting a fit to come at any moment. Fortunately that did not happen.

In a stenographic diary kept at the time of the visit itself, she noted: "generally, it looked so much like an actual dead man that I really think I wouldn't dare stay in the same room with it. But F. admired this painting. Wishing to have a closer look at it, he stood on a chair, and I was very afraid he'd be asked to pay a fine, because here one gets fined for everything."

Each of the three main male characters of the novel – the saintly "idiot" Myshkin, the passionate, earthbound Rogozhin, and the consumptive nihilist Ippolit – defines himself in relation to this painting. The question it poses hangs over the whole novel: what if Christ was only a man? What if he suffered, died, and was left a bruised, lifeless corpse, as Holbein shows him? It is, in other words, the question of the Resurrection. Dostoevsky, who was very careful about the names he gave his characters, calls the heroine of *The Idiot* Nastasya, a shortened form of Anastasia: *anastasis* is "resurrection" in Greek. Her last name, Barashkov, comes from the Russian word for "lamb."

The name of the novel's hero, Prince Lev Nikolaevich Myshkin, is also worth considering. It draws a pointed and oddly insistent comment from the clerk Lebedev on its first mention at the start of the novel: "the name's historical, it can and should be found in Karamzin's *History*." Karamzin's *History of the Russian State* was one of the most popular books of nineteenth-century Russia. In his *Diary of a Writer* (1873), Dostoevsky recalls: "I was only ten when I already knew virtually all the principal episodes of Russian history – from Karamzin whom, in the evenings, father used to read aloud to us." He could assume a similar knowledge among his contemporaries. But, as the literary scholar Tatiana Kasatkina pointed out in a recent lecture,* later commentators on *The Idiot* have generally failed to follow Lebedev's suggestion. Looking in Karamzin's *History*, we do indeed find the name Myshkin; it belonged not to a prince but to an architect. In 1471 Metropolitan Filipp of Moscow decided to build a new stone Cathedral of the Dormition of the Mother of God, and Myshkin was one of the two architects called in to build it. It was to be modeled on the Cathedral of the Dormition in Vladimir, the biggest in Russia. The architects went to Vladimir, took measurements, and promised to build an even bigger cathedral in Moscow. By 1474 the walls had reached vault level when the addition of a monumental stairway caused the entire structure to collapse. Dostoevsky twice wrote the words "Prince-Christ" in his notebooks for *The Idiot*. Readers have taken this to be an equation and, like Romano Guardini in *Der Mensch und der Glaube* (*Man and Faith*, subtitled "a study of religious existence in Dostoevsky's major novels"), have seen Prince Myshkin as a "symbol of Christ" or, in Tatiana Kasatkina's words, as a man upon whom "the radiance of Christ somehow rests," one who is "meant to stand for, or in some way even *replace*, the person of Christ for us." Karamzin's account of the architect Myshkin suggests a more ambiguous reading – as indeed does the prince's name itself, which is compounded of "lion" (*lev*) and "mouse" (*mysh*).

Dostoevsky began work on *The Idiot* in September 1867, a month after his visit to the Basel museum, but it was some time before he finally grasped the nature of his hero. His first

*Delivered at Chernogolovka, near Moscow, on May 15, 2000.

notes show the "idiot" as a proud and violently passionate man, a villain, even an Iago, who is to undergo a complete regeneration and "finish in a divine way." After working out a number of plans, he ended his notebook on November 30 with a final resolve: "Detailed arrangement of the plan and *begin* work in the evening." Four days later he threw everything out and started again. A new conception of the hero had come to him. He was to be a pure and innocent man from the beginning, a saintly stranger coming from elsewhere, and the drama would lie not in his own inner struggle but in his confrontation with people ("Now I am going to be with people," Myshkin thinks to himself on the train back to Russia) and in the effect of his innocence and purity on others. Instead of going on from the situation of Raskolnikov in *Crime and Punishment*, as Dostoevsky's early sketches suggested, he leaped to his diametrical opposite.

Dostoevsky described this new conception in a letter to his friend the poet Apollon Maikov: "For a long time now I've been tormented by a certain idea, but I've been afraid to make a novel out of it, because the thought is too difficult, and I'm not ready for it, though it's a thoroughly tempting thought and I love it. The idea is – *to portray a perfectly beautiful man*. Nothing, in my opinion, can be more difficult than that, especially in our time." He discussed the same idea in a letter written the next day (January 13, 1868) to his favorite niece, Sofya Ivanova. It is important enough to be quoted at length:

The main idea of the novel is to *portray a positively beautiful man*. There is nothing more difficult in the world and especially now. All writers, not only ours, but even all European writers, who have merely attempted to portray the *positively* beautiful, have always given up. Because the task is immeasurable. The beautiful is an ideal, but this ideal, whether ours or that of civilized Europe, is still far from being worked out. There is only one perfectly beautiful person – Christ – so that the appearance of this immeasurably, infinitely beautiful person is, of course, already an infinite miracle. (That is the sense of the whole Gospel of John: it finds the whole miracle in the *incarnation* alone, in the manifestation of the beautiful alone.) But I've gone on too long. I will only mention that of beautiful persons in Christian literature, the most fully realized is Don Quixote; but he is beautiful solely because he is at the same time ridiculous. Dickens's

Pickwick (an infinitely weaker conception than Don Quixote, but an immense one all the same) is also ridiculous and succeeds only because of that. Compassion is shown for the beautiful that is ridiculed and does not know its own worth – and so sympathy appears in the readers. This arousing of compassion is the secret of humor. Jean Valjean is also a strong attempt, but he arouses sympathy by his terrible misfortune and society's injustice towards him. I have nothing like that, decidedly nothing, and that's why I'm terribly afraid it will be a positive failure.

At that time he had written only the first seven chapters of part one. They were produced in a single burst of inspiration and sent to his publisher, Mikhail Katkov, who included them in the January 1868 issue of *The Russian Messenger*. The remaining nine chapters of the first part were finished by the end of February. But Dostoevsky was uncertain about what would follow, and he continued in that uncertainty all the while he was writing the novel. Only as he worked on the fourth and last part did he recognize the inevitability of the final catastrophe. And yet he could write to Sofya Ivanova in November 1868: "this fourth part and its conclusion is the most important thing in my novel, i.e., the novel was almost written and conceived for the novel's denouement."

This novel, which was to be filled with light, which was to portray the positively beautiful, ends in deeper darkness than any of Dostoevsky's other works. What happened here? Some remarks from another letter to Maikov may begin to suggest an answer. Speaking of his own poetic process, he says: "in my head and in my soul many artistic conceptions flash and make themselves felt. But they only flash; and what's needed is a full embodiment, which always comes about unexpectedly and suddenly, but it is impossible to calculate precisely when it will come about; then, once you have received the full image in your heart, you can set about its artistic realization." Dostoevsky's work was always "experimental" in the sense that, between the conception and the full embodiment, he allowed his material the greatest freedom to reveal itself "unexpectedly and suddenly." Despite his passionate convictions, he never imposed an ideological resolution on his work; he was never formulaic. But it is the special nature of *The Idiot* that the full image revealed itself as if with great reluctance and only towards the end of its artistic realization. René Girard was right to say that the failure of the initial idea is the triumph of another more profound idea, and that this prolonged uncertainty gives the novel "an existential density that few works have."* Much of Dostoevsky's distinctive quality as a writer lies in this living relation to his own characters.

Part one of *The Idiot* introduces most of the characters of the novel – the three central figures, Prince Myshkin, Rogozhin, and Nastasya Filippovna; the three families of the Epanchins, the Ivolgins, and the Lebedevs – and entangles them in various complex relations. Riddles and enigmas appear from the start, surrounded by rumors, gossip, attempted explanations, analyses by different characters (reasonable but usually wrong). The narrator himself is not always sure of what has happened or is going to happen. When he finished the first part, Dostoevsky still thought that the prince could go on to redeem Nastasya Filippovna and even to "regenerate" the dark Rogozhin. He wrote to Sofya Ivanova: "The first part is essentially only an introduction. One thing is necessary: to arouse a certain curiosity about what will follow . . . In the second part everything must be definitively established (but will still be far from explained)." But the second part was slow to come; it was finished only five months later, in July; and in it we immediately sense a change of tone and coloration. It begins under the image of Holbein's "Dead Christ," which appears here for the first time, and of Rogozhin's gloomy, labyrinthine house, a house associated with the castrates and old Russian sectarianism. The prince's humility and compassion acquire a strange ambiguity, and before long, the epilepsy for which he had been treated in Switzerland returns with a violent attack that throws him headlong down the stairs.

Critics have found this shift abrupt and puzzling. But there are hints of it even in the first part, not only in the name Myshkin, which "can and should be found in Karamzin," but in the prince's repeated accounts of executions he has

*Dostoevsky, *du double à l'unité*, Paris, 1963 (in English, *Fyodor Dostoevsky: Resurrection from the Underground*, New York, 1997).

witnessed or heard about, and above all in the story of his life in Switzerland, the befriending of the village children, and the death of poor Marie. This story, with its Edenic overtones, has deception at its center, and the deceiver is the prince himself, as he admits without quite recognizing. It is a first variation on one of the central themes of the novel: the difference between love and pity. The relation of the first part to the rest of the novel is one of question and answer, and the question was posed first of all for Dostoevsky himself, who did not know the answer when he started. It is essentially the same question implied in Holbein's painting: what if Christ were not the incarnate God but, in this case, simply a "positively beautiful man," a "moral genius," as a number of nineteenth-century biographers of Jesus chose to portray him, and as Leo Tolstoy was about to proclaim – "a Christ more romantic than Christian," in René Girard's words, sublime and ideal, but with no power to redeem fallen mankind? The prince cannot tell Nastasya Filippovna that her sins are forgiven. What he tells her is that she is pure, that she is not guilty of anything. These apparently innocent words, coming at the end of part one, unleash all that follows in the novel.

The Idiot is constructed as a series of outspoken conversations and exposures, beginning with the very first scene of the novel, the meeting of the prince with Rogozhin and Lebedev on the train to Petersburg, and continuing virtually unbroken till the final scene. The prince, being unguarded and guileless, blurts out things about himself that anyone else would conceal. This is such a winning quality in him that it even wins over the brutish Rogozhin. It also wins over, one after another, the whole procession of people he meets on his arrival in the city, from General Epanchin's valet to the general's private secretary, Ganya Ivolgin, to the general himself, his wife and daughters, to the whole of Ganya Ivolgin's family, and finally to the beautiful Nastasya Filippovna. He readily speaks of his illness and "idiocy," tells how he was awakened from mental darkness by the braying of an ass (at which the Epanchin girls make inevitable jokes), reveals his odd obsession with executions and the condemned man's last moments, and when one of the girls asks him to tell about when he was in love, he tells them at length about his "happiness" in Switzerland. His first words to Nastasya Filippovna, when he comes uninvited to her birthday party, are: "Everything in you is perfection." And his naïve directness prompts a similar directness in others, who speak themselves out to him, seek his advice, look for some saving word from him.

But this general outspokenness can also turn scandalous. Ganya Ivolgin repeatedly denounces the prince to his face and once even slaps him. At Nastasya Filippovna's party, a parlor game is played in which each guest (the ladies are excused) must tell the worst thing he has done in his life. On the prince's terrace in Pavlovsk, surrounded by almost the entire cast of characters, a vicious newspaper lampoon about the prince himself is read aloud. And on the same terrace Ippolit reads his "Necessary Explanation," which, among other things, is a direct attack on the prince for his "Christian" humility and meekness.

As one reads, however, and even rather early on, one becomes aware that, together with this outspokenness, there is a great reticence in *The Idiot*. For all its surprising frankness, there is much that goes unsaid, and what goes unsaid is most important. Olga Meerson has written a witty and penetrating study of this question,* showing how what is normally taboo in society is easily violated in Dostoevsky's work, but as a way of pointing to the greater significance of what his characters pass over in silence. This is a poetics of opening, but hardly of openness.

An ironic variation on the influence of the unsaid is the famous phrase "Beauty will save the world." These words are often attributed to Dostoevsky himself and have been made much of by commentators, but in fact he never said them. Both Ippolit and Aglaya Epanchin refer them to Prince Myshkin, but we never actually hear him say them either. The one time the prince comments on beauty is when he is giving his observations about the faces of Mrs. Epanchin and her daughters. He says nothing of the youngest, Aglaya. The

Dostoevsky's Taboos, published (in English) in Studies of the Harriman Institute, Dresden-Munich, 1998.

mother asks why, and he demurs: "I can't say anything now. I'll say it later." When she presses him, he admits that she is "an extraordinary beauty," adding: "Beauty is difficult to judge; I'm not prepared yet. Beauty is a riddle." This is the prince's first real moment of reticence in the novel. By the end he will have moved from naïve candor to an anguished silence in the face of the unspeakable.

Everything is a riddle in *The Idiot*, everything is two-sided, ambiguous. The structure of reality is double: there is the social world of Petersburg and Pavlovsk, and within it a world infinitely higher and lower, both personal and archetypal. Olga Meerson says in the conclusion of her book:

Dostoevsky . . . uses the language of social interactions for non-social purposes. Rather than depicting society, he borrows the sign system of literature – anthropological and fictional – that depicts society, in order to depict and address human conscience, conscious, unconscious, subconscious. Signs of verbal social decorum are transformed by having gained a new function; they no longer apply to the actual social decorum. The latter is constantly and scandalously violated in Dostoevsky precisely by those characters who are exceptionally sensitive to the new, *meta*-social functions of these signals of decorum.

The social world is relative, ambivalent, comic, "carnivalized," as the critic Mikhail Bakhtin preferred to say – a world in which a polite drawing room turns into a public square. The meta-social world is located in the deepest layers of consciousness, of memory, internal in each of us and at the same time transcending each of us. In this world, characters acquire the qualities of folk-tale heroes and villains, of figures in a mystery play, of angels and demons. There is a captive princess, there is a prince who is called upon to save her, and there is a dark force that threatens them both. The heavenly emissary must deliver the world's soul from bondage, Andromeda from her chains; if he betrays his calling, disaster will follow.

As if to underscore the distance between social realism and his own "realism of a higher sort," Dostoevsky refers to two other stories of fallen women: *La Dame aux camélias* by Dumas *fils*, and Flaubert's *Madame Bovary*, which the prince finds in Nastasya Filippovna's rooms near the end of the novel.

Nastasya Filippovna will hardly efface herself like Dumas's heroine; that sentimental resolution suits the taste (and the hopes) of her mediocre seducer, the "bouquet man" Totsky, whom she calls a *monsieur aux camélias*. Nor will she take her own life in despair, like Emma Bovary. Her fate is enacted in a different realm. The parallels serve to mark the difference. But, owing to the chasteness of his art (as opposed to its obvious scandalousness), Dostoevsky allows himself no direct statement of his idea, no symbolistic abstraction, no simple identification of the "archetypes" behind his fiction. He uses the methods and conventions of the social novel to embody an ultimate human drama.

Money, the most ambiguous of values, is the medium of the social world. Its fatal quality is treated in all tones, at all levels, in *The Idiot*. Totsky wants to "sell" Nastasya Filippovna to Ganya for seventy-five thousand roubles; Rogozhin offers a hundred thousand for her. In one of the greatest scenes in the novel, Nastasya Filippovna throws his hundred thousand into the fire with everyone watching and challenges Ganya to pull it out. There are many other variations: the prince's unexpected inheritance, and Burdovsky's outrageous attempt, spurred on by his nihilist friends, to claim part of it while maintaining his nihilist principles; General Ivolgin's theft of Lebedev's four hundred roubles and his subsequent disgrace; Ptitsyn's successful moneylending and his dream of owning two houses (or maybe even three) on Liteinaya Street; Evgeny Pavlovich's rich uncle and his embezzlement of government funds; Ippolit's story of the impoverished doctor; Ferdyshchenko's "worst deed"; the repeatedly mentioned newspaper stories of murders for the sake of robbery. The clownish clerk Lebedev, though a petty usurer himself, is also an interpreter of the Apocalypse: "we live in the time of the third horse, the black one, and the rider with a balance in his hand, because in our time everything is in balances and contracts, and people are all only seeking their rights: 'A measure of wheat for a penny, and three measures of barley for a penny . . .' And with all that they want to preserve a free spirit, and a pure heart, and a healthy body, and all of God's gifts. But they can't do it with rights alone, and there will follow a pale horse and him whose name is Death." His interpretation unwittingly reveals the twofold structure of reality in *The Idiot*.

Prince Myshkin has two loves, Nastasya Filippovna and Aglaya, one belonging to each "world" of the novel. He also has two doubles: Rogozhin and Ippolit. There is a deep bond between the dying consumptive nihilist thinker and the impulsive, unreflecting, passionate merchant's son, between the suicide and the murderer, and Ippolit recognizes it. "*Les extrémités se touchent,*" he says, quoting Pascal. As late as September 1868, Dostoevsky wrote in his notebook: "Ippolit – the main axis of the novel." The young nihilist belongs among Dostoevsky's "rebels against Creation," along with Kirillov in *Demons* and Ivan Karamazov. His "Necessary Explanation," as Joseph Frank has observed,* contains all the elements of the prince's worldview, but with an opposite attitude. Speaking of Holbein's *Christ*, he says that it shows nature as "some huge machine of the newest construction, which has senselessly seized, crushed, and swallowed up, blankly and unfeelingly, a great and priceless being." And he wonders how Christ's disciples, seeing a corpse like that, could believe "that this sufferer would resurrect," and whether Christ himself, if he could have seen his own image on the eve of his execution, would have "gone to the cross and died as he did." Ippolit is also a man sentenced to death by the "dark, insolent, and senselessly eternal power to which everything is subjected," but instead of meekly accepting his fate, instead of passing by and forgiving others their happiness, as the prince advises, he protests, weeps, revolts. If Ippolit is not finally the main axis of the novel, he poses its central question in the most radical and explicit way.

Rogozhin, on the other hand, tells the prince that he likes looking at the Holbein painting. The prince, "under the impression of an unexpected thought," replies: "At that painting! A man could even lose his faith from that painting!" "Lose it he does," Rogozhin agrees. But to Rogozhin's direct question, whether he believes in God, the prince gives no direct reply. That is another significant moment of reticence

Dostoevsky: The Miraculous Years, Princeton, 1995.

on Myshkin's part. Instead, he turns the conversation to "the essence of religious feeling" and says, "There are things to be done in our Russian world, believe me!" A moment later, at Rogozhin's request, they exchange crosses and become "brothers." Yet the exact nature of their brotherhood remains a mystery. From that point on, Rogozhin becomes the prince's shadow, lurking, menacing, hiding, yet inseparable from him, until the final scene finds them pressed face to face. Dostoevsky's doubles, which might seem images of personal division, are in fact images of human oneness.

The Idiot is Dostoevsky's most autobiographical novel. He gave Prince Myshkin many details of his own childhood and youth, his epilepsy, his separation from life and Russia (the author's years of hard labor and "exile" in Siberia corresponding to the prince's treatment in Switzerland), his return with a new sense of mission. More specifically, in Myshkin's story of the mock execution of an "acquaintance," Dostoevsky gives a detailed account of his own experience on the scaffold in the Semyonovsky parade ground, at the age of twenty-eight, when he thought he had only three more minutes to live. According to a memoir by another of the condemned men, Fyodor Lvov,* Dostoevsky turned to their comrade Speshnyov and said: "We will be together with Christ." And Speshnyov, with a wry smile, replied: "A handful of ashes." As Myshkin puts it: "now he exists and lives, and in three minutes there would be *something*, some person or thing – but who? and where?" *The Idiot* is built on that eschatological sense of time. It is the desolate time of Holy Saturday, when Christ is buried, the disciples are scattered and – worse than that – abandoned. "Who could believe that this sufferer would resurrect?" As it turned out, Dostoevsky had not three minutes but thirty-two years to think over Speshnyov's words and his own response to them. *The Idiot* marks an important step on that way.

Richard Pevear

*Published in *Literaturnoe nasledstvo* ("Literary Heritage"), vol. 63, p. 188; Moscow, 1956.

TRANSLATORS' NOTES

Russian names are composed of first name, patronymic (from the father's first name), and family name. Formal address requires the use of first name and patronymic. Diminutives are commonly used among family and intimate friends; they have two forms, the familiar and the casual or disrespectful; thus Varvara Ivolgin is called Varya in her family, but Varka by her little brother. A shortened form of the patronymic (i.e., Ivanych for Ivanovich, or Pavlych for Pavlovich), used only in speech, also suggests a certain familiarity. In the following list, stressed syllables are marked. In Russian pronunciation, the stressed vowel is always long, and the unstressed vowels are very short.

Mýshkin, Prince Lev Nikoláevich
Baráshkov, Nastásya Filíppovna (Nástya)
Rogózhin, Parfyón Semyónovich
Epanchín, General Iván Fyódorovich
_____, Elizavéta (Lizavéta) Prokófyevna
_____, Alexándra Ivánovna
_____, Adelaída Ivánovna
_____, Agláya Ivánovna
Ívolgin, General Ardalión Alexándrovich
_____, Nína Alexándrovna
_____, Gavríla Ardaliónovich (Gánya, Gánechka, Gánka)
_____, Varvára Ardaliónovna (Várya, Várka)
_____, Nikolái Ardaliónovich (Kólya)
Lébedev, Lukyán Timoféevich
_____,Véra Lukyánovna
Teréntyev, Ippolít (no patronymic)
Ptítsyn, Iván Petróvich (Vánka)
Radómsky, Evgény Pávlovich
Shch., Prince (no first name, patronymic, or last name)
Tótsky, Afanásy Ivánovich
Ferdýshchenko (no first name or patronymic)

Keller, Lieutenant, ret. ("the fist gentleman"; no first name
   or patronymic)
Pavlíshchev, Nikolái Andréevich
Dárya Alexéevna ("the sprightly lady"; no last name)
Burdóvsky, Antíp (no patronymic)
Belokónsky, Princess ("old Belokonsky"; no first name or
   patronymic)

A NOTE ON THE TOPOGRAPHY OF ST PETERSBURG

The city was founded in the early eighteenth century by a
decree of the emperor Peter the Great. It is built on the delta
of the river Neva, which divides into three main branches: the
Big Neva, the Little Neva, the Nevka. On the left bank of the
Neva is the city center, where the government buildings, the
Winter Palace, the Senate, the Summer Palace and Summer
Garden, the theaters, and the main thoroughfares such as
Nevsky Prospect and Liteiny Prospect (Liteinaya Street in
Dostoevsky's time) are located. Here, too, were the Semyonovsky and Izmailovsky quarters, named for army regiments
stationed there. On the right bank of the Neva before it divides
is the area known as the Vyborg side; on the right bank
between the Nevka and the Little Neva is the Petersburg side,
where the Peter and Paul Fortress, the oldest structure of the
city, stands; between the Little Neva and the Big Neva is
Vassilievsky Island. Further north are smaller islands such as
Kamenny Island and Elagin Island, which were then mainly
garden suburbs. To the south, some fifteen or twenty miles
from the city, are the suburbs of Tsarskoe Selo ("the Tsar's
Village") and Pavlovsk, where much of the action of *The Idiot*
takes place.

THE IDIOT

PART ONE

I

Towards the end of November, during a warm spell, at around nine o'clock in the morning, a train of the Petersburg–Warsaw line was approaching Petersburg at full steam. It was so damp and foggy that dawn could barely break; ten paces to right or left of the line it was hard to make out anything at all through the carriage windows. Among the passengers there were some who were returning from abroad; but the third-class compartments were more crowded, and they were all petty business folk from not far away. Everyone was tired, as usual, everyone's eyes had grown heavy overnight, everyone was chilled, everyone's face was pale yellow, matching the color of the fog.

In one of the third-class carriages, at dawn, two passengers found themselves facing each other just by the window—both young men, both traveling light, both unfashionably dressed, both with rather remarkable physiognomies, and both, finally, willing to get into conversation with each other. If they had known what was so remarkable about the one and the other at that moment, they would certainly have marveled at the chance that had so strangely seated them facing each other in the third-class carriage of the Petersburg–Warsaw train. One of them was of medium height, about twenty-seven years old, with curly, almost black hair, and small but fiery gray eyes. He had a broad, flat nose and high cheekbones; his thin lips were constantly twisting into a sort of impudent, mocking, and even malicious smile; but his forehead was high and well formed and made up for the lack of nobility in the lower part of his face. Especially notable was the deathly pallor of his face, which gave the young man's whole physiognomy an exhausted look, despite his rather robust build, and at the same time suggested something passionate, to the point of suffering, which was out of harmony with his insolent and coarse smile and his sharp, self-satisfied gaze. He was warmly dressed in an ample lambskin coat covered with black cloth and had not been cold during the night, while his neighbor had been forced to bear on his chilled back all the sweetness of a damp Russian November night, for which he was obviously not prepared. He was wearing a rather ample and thick sleeveless cloak with an enormous hood, the sort often worn by winter travelers somewhere far abroad, in Switzerland or northern Italy, for instance, certainly not reckoning on such long distances as from Eydkuhnen[1] to Petersburg. But what was proper and quite satisfactory in Italy turned out to be not entirely suitable to Russia. The owner of the cloak with the hood was a young man, also about twenty-six or twenty-seven years old, slightly taller than average, with very blond, thick hair, sunken cheeks, and a sparse, pointed, nearly white little beard. His eyes were big, blue, and intent; their gaze had something quiet but heavy about it and was filled with that strange expression by which some are able to guess at first sight that the subject has the falling sickness. The young man's face, however, was pleasant, fine, and dry, but colorless, and now even blue with cold. From his hands dangled a meager bundle made of old, faded foulard, containing, apparently, all his traveling possessions. On his feet he had thick-soled shoes with gaiters—all not the Russian way. His black-haired companion in the lambskin coat took all this in, partly from having nothing to do, and finally asked, with that tactless grin which sometimes expresses so unceremoniously and carelessly people's pleasure in their neighbor's misfortunes:

"Chilly?"

And he hunched his shoulders.

"Very," his companion replied with extreme readiness, "and note that this is a warm spell. What if it were freezing? It didn't even occur to me that it was so cold at home. I'm unaccustomed to it."

"Coming from abroad, are you?"

"Yes, from Switzerland."

"Whew! Fancy that! . . ."

The black-haired man whistled and laughed.

They got to talking. The readiness of the blond young man in the Swiss cloak to answer all his swarthy companion's questions was astonishing and betrayed no suspicion of the utter carelessness, idleness, and impropriety of some of the questions. In answering them he said, among other things, that he had indeed been away from Russia for a long time, more than four years, that he had been sent abroad on account of illness, some strange nervous illness like the falling sickness or St. Vitus's dance, some sort of trembling and convulsions. Listening to him, the swarthy man grinned several times; he laughed particularly when, to his question: "And did they cure you?" the blond man answered: "No, they didn't."

"Heh! Got all that money for nothing, and we go believing them," the swarthy man remarked caustically.

"That's the real truth!" a poorly dressed gentleman who was sitting nearby broke into the conversation—some sort of encrusted copying clerk, about forty years old, strongly built, with a red nose and a pimply face, "the real truth, sir, they just draw all Russian forces to themselves for nothing!"

"Oh, you're quite wrong in my case," the Swiss patient picked up in a soft and conciliatory voice. "Of course, I can't argue, because I don't know everything, but my doctor gave me some of his last money for the trip and kept me there for almost two years at his own expense."

"What, you mean there was nobody to pay?" asked the swarthy man.

"Mr. Pavlishchev, who supported me there, died two years ago. Then I wrote here to General Epanchin's wife, my distant relation, but I got no answer. So with that I've come back."

"Come back where, though?"

"You mean where will I be staying? . . . I don't really know yet . . . so . . ."

"You haven't decided yet?"

And both listeners burst out laughing again.

"And I supppose that bundle contains your whole essence?" the swarthy man asked.

"I'm ready to bet it does," the red-nosed clerk picked up with an extremely pleased air, "and that there's no further belongings in the baggage car—though poverty's no vice, that again is something one can't help observing."

It turned out to be so: the blond young man acknowledged it at once and with extraordinary alacrity.

"Your bundle has a certain significance all the same," the clerk went on after they had laughed their fill (remarkably, the owner of the bundle, looking at them, finally started laughing himself, which increased their merriment), "and though you can bet it doesn't contain any imported gold packets of napoleondors or fried-richsdors, or any Dutch yellow boys,[2] a thing that might be deduced merely from the gaiters enclosing your foreign shoes, but . . . if to your bundle we were to add some such supposed relation as General Epanchin's wife, then your bundle would take on a somewhat different significance, naturally only in the case that General Epanchin's wife is indeed your relation, and you didn't make a mistake out of absentmindedness . . . which is quite, quite human . . . well, say . . . from an excess of imagination."

"Oh, you've guessed right again," the blond young man picked up. "I am indeed almost mistaken, that is, she's almost not my relation; so that I really wasn't surprised in the least when they didn't answer me there. I even expected it."

"Wasted your money franchising the letter for nothing. Hm . . . but at any rate you're simple-hearted and sincere, which is commendable! Hm . . . and General Epanchin we know, sir, essentially because he's a generally known man. And the late Mr. Pavlishchev, who supported you in Switzerland, we also knew, sir, if it was Nikolai Andreevich Pavlishchev, because there were two cousins. The other one is still in the Crimea, but the deceased Nikolai Andreevich was a respectable man, and with connections, and owned four thousand souls[3] in his time, sir . . ."

"Just so, his name was Nikolai Andreevich Pavlishchev," and, having responded, the young man looked intently and inquisitively at Mr. Know-it-all.

These Mr. Know-it-alls are occasionally, even quite frequently, to be met with in a certain social stratum. They know everything, all the restless inquisitiveness of their minds and all their abilities are turned irresistibly in one direction, certainly for lack of more important life interests and perspectives, as a modern thinker would say. The phrase "they know all" implies, however, a rather limited sphere: where so-and-so works, who he is acquainted with, how much he is worth, where he was governor, who he is married to, how much his wife brought him, who his cousins are, who his cousins twice removed are, etc., etc., all in the same vein. For the most part these know-it-alls go about with holes at the elbows and earn a salary of seventeen roubles a month. The people whose innermost secrets they know would, of course, be unable to understand what interests guide them, and yet many of them are positively consoled by this knowledge that amounts to a whole science; they achieve self-respect and even the highest spiritual satisfaction. Besides, it is a seductive science. I have known scholars, writers, poets, political activists who sought and found their highest peace and purpose in this science, who positively made their careers by it alone. During this whole conversation the swarthy young man kept yawning, looking aimlessly out of the window and waiting impatiently for the end of the journey. He seemed somehow distracted, very distracted, all but alarmed, was even becoming somehow strange: sometimes he listened without listening, looked without looking, laughed without always knowing or understanding himself why he was laughing.

"But, excuse me, with whom do I have the honor . . ." the pimply gentleman suddenly addressed the blond young man with the bundle.

"Prince Lev Nikolaevich Myshkin," the other replied with full and immediate readiness.

"Prince Myshkin? Lev Nikolaevich? Don't know it, sir. Never even so much as heard it, sir," the clerk replied, pondering. "I don't mean the name, the name's historical, it can and should be found in Karamzin's *History*,[4] I mean the person, sir, there's no Prince Myshkins to be met with anywhere, and even the rumors have died out."

"Oh, that's certain!" the prince answered at once. "There are no Prince Myshkins at all now except me; it seems I'm the last one. And as for our fathers and grandfathers, we've even had some farmers among them. My father, however, was a second lieutenant in the army, from the junkers.[5] But I don't know in what way Mrs. Epanchin also turns out to be Princess Myshkin, also the last in her line . . ."

"Heh, heh, heh! The last in her line. Heh, heh! What a way to put it," the clerk tittered.

The swarthy man also smiled. The blond man was slightly surprised that he had managed to make a pun, though a rather bad one.

"And imagine, I never thought what I was saying," he finally explained in surprise.

"That's clear, that's clear, sir," the clerk merrily agreed.

"And say, Prince, did you do any studying there at your professor's?" the swarthy man suddenly asked.

"Yes . . . I did . . ."

"And me, I never studied anything."

"Well, I only did a little of this and that," the prince added, almost apologetically. "They found it impossible to educate me systematically because of my illness."

"You know the Rogozhins?" the swarthy man asked quickly.

"No, not at all. I know very few people in Russia. Are you a Rogozhin?"

"Yes, I'm Parfyon Rogozhin."

"Parfyon? You're not from those same Rogozhins . . ." the clerk began with increased importance.

"Yes, the same, the very same," the swarthy man interrupted quickly and with impolite impatience; he had, incidentally, never once addressed the pimply clerk, but from the very beginning had talked only to the prince.

"But . . . can it be?" The clerk was astonished to the point of stupefaction, his eyes nearly popped out, and his whole face at once began to compose itself into something reverent and obsequious, even frightened. "Of that same Semyon Parfyonovich Rogozhin, the hereditary honorary citizen[6] who died about a month ago and left two and a half million in capital?"

"And how do you know he left two and a half million in pure capital?" the swarthy man interrupted, this time also not deigning to glance at the clerk. "Just look!" he winked at the prince. "And what's the good of them toadying like that straight off? It's true my parent died, and I'm coming home from Pskov a month later all but bootless. Neither my brother, the scoundrel, nor my mother sent me any money or any notice—nothing! Like a dog! Spent the whole month in Pskov in delirium . . ."

"And now you've got a nice little million or more coming, and that's at the least—oh, Lord!" the clerk clasped his hands.

"Well, what is it to him, pray tell me!" Rogozhin nodded towards him again irritably and spitefully. "I won't give you a kopeck, even if you walk upside down right here in front of me."

"And I will, I will."

"Look at that! No, I won't give you anything, not even if you dance a whole week for it!"

"Don't give me anything! Don't! It serves me right! But I will dance. I'll leave my wife, my little children, and dance before you. Be nice, be nice!"

"Pah!" the swarthy man spat. "Five weeks ago," he turned to the prince, "I ran away from my parent to my aunt in Pskov, like you, with nothing but a little bundle; I fell into delirium there, and while I was gone he up and died. Hit by a stroke. Memory eternal to the deceased,[7] but he almost did me in before then! By God, Prince, believe me! If I hadn't run away, he'd have done me to death."

"Did you do something to make him angry?" the prince responded, studying the millionaire in the lambskin coat with some special curiosity. But though there might well have been something noteworthy in the million itself and in receiving an inheritance, the prince was surprised and intrigued by something else; besides, Rogozhin himself, for some reason, was especially eager to make the prince his interlocutor, though the need for an interlocutor seemed more mechanical than moral; somehow more from distraction than from simple-heartedness; from anxiety, from agitation, just to look at someone and wag his tongue about something. It seemed he was still delirious, or at least in a fever. As for the clerk, the man simply hovered over Rogozhin, not daring to breathe, catching and weighing every word as if searching for diamonds.

"Angry, yes, he was angry, and maybe rightly," Rogozhin replied, "but it was my brother who really got me. About my mother there's nothing to say, she's an old woman, reads the Menaion,[8] sits with the old crones, and whatever brother Senka decides, so it goes. But why didn't he let me know in time? We understand that, sir! True, I was unconscious at the time. They also say a telegram was sent. But the telegram happened to come to my aunt. And she's been widowed for thirty years and sits with the holy fools[9] from morning till evening. A nun, or not a nun but worse still. She got scared of the telegram and took it to the police station without opening it, and so it's been lying there ever since. Only Konev, Vassily Vassilyich, rescued me. He wrote about everything. At night my brother cut the gold tassels off the brocade cover on the old man's coffin: 'They cost a whole lot of money,' he says. But for that alone he could go to Siberia if I want, because that's a blasphemy. Hey, you, scarecrow!" he turned to the clerk. "What's the law: is it a blasphemy?"

"A blasphemy! A blasphemy!" the clerk agreed at once.

"Meaning Siberia?"

"Siberia! Siberia! Straight off to Siberia!"

"They keep thinking I'm still sick," Rogozhin continued to the prince, "but without saying a word, secretly, I got on the train, still sick, and I'm coming. Open the gates, brother Semyon Semyonych! He said things to the old man about me, I know it. And it's true I really irritated the old man then, on account of Nastasya Filippovna. That's my own doing. Sin snared me."

"On account of Nastasya Filippovna?" the clerk said obsequiously, as if realizing something.

"You don't know her!" Rogozhin shouted at him impatiently.

"Or maybe I do!" the clerk replied triumphantly.

"Well, now! As if there's so few Nastasya Filippovnas! And what a brazen creature you are, I tell you! I just knew some creature like him would cling to me at once!" he continued to the prince.

"Or maybe I do know her, sir!" the clerk fidgeted. "Lebedev knows! You, Your Highness, are pleased to reproach me, but what if I prove it? It's the same Nastasya Filippovna on account of whom your parent wanted to admonish you with a blackthorn stick, and Nastasya Filippovna is Barashkov, she's even a noble lady, so to speak, and also a sort of princess, and she keeps company with a certain Totsky, Afanasy Ivanovich, exclusively with him alone, a landowner and a big capitalist, a member of companies and societies, and great friends on that account with General Epanchin . . ."

"Aha, so that's how you are!" Rogozhin was really surprised at last. "Pah, the devil, so he does know."

"He knows everything! Lebedev knows everything! I, Your Highness, spent two months driving around with Alexashka Likhachev, and also after your parent's death, and I know everything, meaning every corner and back alley, and in the end not a step is taken without Lebedev. Nowadays he's abiding in debtor's prison, but before that I had occasion to know Armance, and Coralie, and Princess Patsky, and Nastasya Filippovna, and I had occasion to know a lot more besides."

"Nastasya Filippovna? Are she and Likhachev . . ." Rogozhin looked at him spitefully, his lips even turned pale and trembled.

"N-nothing! N-n-nothing! Nothing at all!" the clerk caught himself and quickly hurried on. "That is, Likhachev couldn't get her for any amount of money! No, it's not like with Armance. There's only Totsky. And in the evening, at the Bolshoi or the French Theater,[10] she sits in her own box. The officers say all kinds of things among themselves, but even they can't prove anything: 'There's that same Nastasya Filippovna,' they say, and that's all; but concerning the rest—nothing! Because there's nothing to say."

"That's how it all is," Rogozhin scowled and confirmed gloomily. "Zalyozhev told me the same thing then. That time, Prince, I was running across Nevsky Prospect in my father's three-year-old coat, and she was coming out of a shop, getting into a carriage. Burned me right through. I meet Zalyozhev, there's no comparing me with him, he looks like a shopkeeper fresh from the barber's, with a lorgnette in his eye, while the old man has us flaunting tarred boots and eating meatless cabbage soup. That's no match for you, he says, that's a princess, and she's called Nastasya Filippovna, family name

Barashkov, and she lives with Totsky, and now Totsky doesn't know how to get rid of her, because he's reached the prime of life, he's fifty-five, and wants to marry the foremost beauty in all Petersburg. And then he let on that I could see Nastasya Filippovna that night at the Bolshoi Theater, at the ballet, in her own box, in the baignoire, sitting there. With our parent, just try going to the ballet—it'll end only one way—he'll kill you! But, anyhow, I ran over for an hour on the quiet and saw Nastasya Filippovna again; didn't sleep all that night. The next morning the deceased gives me two five percent notes, five thousand roubles each, and says go and sell them, take seven thousand five hundred to the Andreevs' office, pay them, and bring me what's left of the ten thousand without stopping anywhere; I'll be waiting for you. I cashed the notes all right, took the money, but didn't go to the Andreevs' office, I went to the English shop without thinking twice, chose a pair of pendants with a diamond almost the size of a nut in each of them, and left owing them four hundred roubles—told them my name and they trusted me. I went to Zalyozhev with the pendants. Thus and so, brother, let's go and see Nastasya Filippovna. Off we went. What was under my feet then, what was in front of me, what was to the sides—I don't know or remember any of it. We walked right into her drawing room, she came out to us herself. I didn't tell her then that it was me, but Zalyozhev says, 'This is for you from Parfyon Rogozhin, in memory of meeting you yesterday. Be so good as to accept it.' She opened it, looked, smiled: 'Thank your friend Mr. Rogozhin for his kind attention,' she said, bowed, and went out. Well, why didn't I die right then! If I went at all, it was only because I thought, 'Anyway, I won't come back alive!' And what offended me most was that that beast Zalyozhev had it all for himself. I'm short and dressed like a boor, and I stand silently staring at her because I'm embarrassed, and he's all so fashionable, pomaded and curled, red-cheeked, in a checkered tie—fawning on her, bowing to her, and it's sure she took him for me! 'Well,' I say when we've left, 'don't you go getting any ideas on me, understand?' He laughs: 'And what kind of accounting will you give Semyon Parfyonych now?' The truth is I wanted to drown myself right then, without going home, but I thought: 'It makes no difference,' and like a cursed man I went home."

"Ah! Oh!" the clerk went all awry and was even trembling. "And the deceased would have hounded you into the next world for ten roubles, let alone ten thousand," he nodded to the prince. The prince studied Rogozhin with curiosity; the man seemed still paler at that moment.

"Hounded!" Rogozhin repeated. "What do you know? He found out all about it at once," he continued to the prince, "and Zalyozhev also went blabbing to everybody he met. The old man took me and locked me upstairs, and admonished me for a whole hour. 'I'm just getting you prepared now,' he said. 'I'll come back later to say good night.' And what do you think? The old gray fellow went to Nastasya Filippovna, bowed to the ground before her, pleaded and wept. She finally brought the box and threw it at him: 'Here are your earrings for you, graybeard, and now they're worth ten times more to me, since Parfyon got them under such a menace. Give my regards to Parfyon Semyonych,' she says, 'and thank him for me.' Well, and meanwhile, with my mother's blessing, I got twenty roubles from Seryozhka Protushin and went by train to Pskov, and arrived there in a fever. The old women started reading prayers at me, and I sat there drunk, then went and spent my last money in the pot-houses, lay unconscious in the street all night, and by morning was delirious, and the dogs bit me all over during the night. I had a hard time recovering."

"Well, well, sir, now our Nastasya Filippovna's going to start singing!" the clerk tittered, rubbing his hands. "Now, my good sir, it's not just pendants! Now we'll produce such pendants . . ."

"If you say anything even once about Nastasya Filippovna, by God, I'll give you a whipping, even if you did go around with Likhachev!" cried Rogozhin, seizing him firmly by the arm.

"If you whip me, it means you don't reject me! Whip me! Do it and you put your mark on me . . . But here we are!"

Indeed, they were entering the station. Though Rogozhin said he had left secretly, there were several people waiting for him. They shouted and waved their hats.

"Hah, Zalyozhev's here, too!" Rogozhin muttered, looking at them with a triumphant and even as if spiteful smile, and he suddenly turned to the prince. "Prince, I don't know why I've come to love you. Maybe because I met you at such a moment, though I met him, too" (he pointed to Lebedev), "and don't love him. Come and see me, Prince. We'll take those wretched gaiters off you; I'll dress you in a top-notch marten coat; I'll have the best of tailcoats made for you, a white waistcoat, or whatever you like; I'll stuff your pockets with money, and . . . we'll go to see Nastasya Filippovna! Will you come or not?"

"Hearken, Prince Lev Nikolaevich!" Lebedev picked up imposingly and solemnly. "Ah, don't let it slip away! Don't let it slip away!"

Prince Myshkin rose a little, courteously offered Rogozhin his hand, and said affably:

"I'll come with the greatest pleasure, and I thank you very much for loving me. I may even come today, if I have time. Because, I'll tell you frankly, I like you very much, and I especially liked you when you were telling about the diamond pendants. Even before the pendants I liked you, despite your gloomy face. I also thank you for promising me the clothes and a fur coat, because in fact I'll need some clothes and a fur coat soon. And I have almost no money at the present moment."

"There'll be money towards evening—come!"

"There will be, there will be," the clerk picked up, "towards evening, before sundown, there will be."

"And are you a great fancier of the female sex, Prince? Tell me beforehand!"

"N-n-no! I'm . . . Maybe you don't know, but because of my inborn illness, I don't know women at all."

"Well, in that case," Rogozhin exclaimed, "you come out as a holy fool, Prince, and God loves your kind!"

"The Lord God loves your kind," the clerk picked up.

"And you come with me, pencil pusher," Rogozhin said to Lebedev, and they all got off the train.

Lebedev ended up with what he wanted. Soon the noisy band withdrew in the direction of Voznesensky Prospect. The prince had to turn towards Liteinaya Street. It was damp and wet; the prince inquired of passersby—to reach the end of his route he had to go some two miles, and he decided to hire a cab.

II

GENERAL EPANCHIN lived in his own house off Liteinaya, towards the Cathedral of the Transfiguration. Besides this (excellent) house, five-sixths of which was rented out, General Epanchin owned another enormous house on Sadovaya Street, which also brought him a large income. Besides these two houses, he had quite a profitable and considerable estate just outside Petersburg; and there was also some factory in the Petersburg district. In the old days General Epanchin, as everyone knew, had participated in tax farming.[11] Now he participated and had quite a considerable voice in several important joint-stock companies. He had the reputation of a man with big money, big doings, and big connections. He had managed to make himself absolutely necessary in certain quarters, his own department among others. And yet it was also known that Ivan Fyodorovich Epanchin was a man of no education and the son of a common soldier; this last, to be sure, could only do him credit, but the general, though an intelligent man, was also not without his little, quite forgivable weaknesses and disliked certain allusions. But he was unquestionably an intelligent and adroit man. He had a system, for instance, of not putting himself forward, of effacing himself wherever necessary, and many valued him precisely for his simplicity, precisely for always knowing his place. And yet, if these judges only knew what sometimes went on in the soul of Ivan Fyodorovich, who knew his place so well! Though he did indeed have practical sense, and experience in worldly matters, and certain very remarkable abilities, he liked to present himself more as the executor of someone else's idea than as being his own master, as a man "loyal without fawning,"[12] and—what does not happen nowadays?—even Russian and warm-hearted. In this last respect several amusing misadventures even happened to him; but the general was never downcast, even at the most amusing misadventures; besides, luck was with him, even at cards, and he played for extremely high stakes, and not only did not want to conceal this little weakness of his for a bit of cardplaying, which came in handy for him so essentially and on many occasions, but even deliberately flaunted it. He belonged to a mixed society, though naturally of a "trumpish" sort. But everything was before him, there was time enough for everything, and everything would come in time and in due course. As for his years, General Epanchin was still, as they say, in the prime of life, that is, fifty-six and not a whit more, which in any case is a flourishing age, the age when *true* life really begins. His health, his complexion, his strong though blackened teeth, his stocky, sturdy build, the pre-occupied expression on his physiognomy at work in the morning, the merry one in the evening over cards or at his highness's—everything contributed to his present and future successes and strewed his excellency's path with roses.

The general had a flourishing family. True, here it was no longer all roses, but instead there were many things on which his excellency's chief hopes and aims had long begun to be seriously and heartily concentrated. And what aim in life is more important or sacred than a parental aim? What can one fasten upon if not the family? The general's family consisted of a wife and three grown-up daughters. Long ago, while still a lieutenant, the general had married a girl nearly his own age, who had neither beauty nor education, and who brought him only fifty souls—which, true, served as the foundation of his further fortune. But the general never murmured later against his early marriage, never regarded it as the infatuation of an improvident youth, and respected his wife so much, and sometimes feared her so much, that he even loved her. The general's wife was from the princely family of the Myshkins, a family which, while not brilliant, was quite old, and she quite respected herself for her origins. One of the influential persons of that time, one of those patrons for whom, incidentally, patronage costs nothing, consented to take an interest in the young princess's marriage. He opened the gate for the young officer and gave him a starting push, though he did not need a push but only a glance—it would not have been wasted! With a few exceptions, the couple lived the whole time of their long jubilee in accord. While still young, the general's wife, as a born princess and the last of the line, and perhaps through her own personal qualities, was able to find some very highly placed patronesses. Later on, with her husband's increasing wealth and significance in the service, she even began to feel somewhat at home in this high circle.

During these last years all three of the general's daughters—Alexandra, Adelaida, and Aglaya—grew up and matured. True, the three were only Epanchins, but they were of princely origin through their mother, with no little dowry, with a father who might later claim a very high post, and, which was also quite important, all three were remarkably good-looking, including the eldest, Alexandra, who was already over twenty-five. The middle one was twenty-three, and the youngest, Aglaya, had just turned twenty. This youngest was even quite a beauty and was beginning to attract great attention in society. But that was still not all: all three were distinguished by their cultivation, intelligence, and talent. It was known that they had a remarkable love for each other and stood up for each other. Mention was even made of some supposed sacrifices the elder two had made in favor of the common idol of the house—the youngest. In society they not only did not like putting themselves forward, but were even much too modest. No one could reproach them with haughtiness or presumption, and yet it was known that they were proud and knew their own worth. The eldest was a musician, the middle one an excellent painter; but almost no one knew of that for many years and it was discovered only quite recently, and that by accident. In short, a great many laudable things were said about them. But there were also ill-wishers. With horror it was told how many books they had read. They were in no rush to get married; they did esteem a certain social circle, but not too highly. This was the more remarkable as everyone knew the tendency, character, aims, and wishes of their father.

It was already around eleven o'clock when the prince rang at the general's apartment. The general lived on the second floor and occupied lodgings which, though as modest as possible, were still proportionate to his significance. A liveried servant opened the door for the prince, and he had to spend a long time talking with this man, who from the start looked suspiciously at him and his bundle. Finally, to his repeated and precise statement that he was indeed Prince Myshkin and that he absolutely had to see the general on urgent business, the perplexed servant sent him to another small anteroom, just before the reception room by the office, and handed him over to another man, who was on duty in this anteroom in the mornings and announced visitors to the general. This other man wore a tailcoat, was over forty, and had a preoccupied physiognomy, and was the special office attendant and announcer to his excellency, owing to which he was conscious of his worth.

"Wait in the reception room, and leave your bundle here," he said, sitting down unhurriedly and importantly in his armchair and glancing with stern astonishment at the prince, who had settled down right next to him in a chair, his bundle in his hands.

"If I may," said the prince, "I'd rather wait here with you. What am I going to do in there by myself?"

"You oughtn't to stay in the anteroom, being a visitor, that is to say, a guest. Do you wish to see the general in person?"

The lackey obviously could not reconcile himself to the thought of admitting such a visitor, and decided to ask again.

"Yes, I have business . . ." the prince began.

"I am not asking you precisely what business—my business is simply to announce you. And without the secretary, as I said, I am not going to announce you."

The man's suspiciousness seemed to be increasing more and more; the prince was too far from fitting into the category of everyday visitors, and though the general had rather often, if not daily, at a certain hour, to receive sometimes even the most varied sorts of visitors, especially on *business*, still, in spite of habit and his rather broad instructions, the valet was in great doubt; the secretary's mediation was necessary for the announcement.

"But are you really . . . from abroad?" he finally asked somehow involuntarily—and became confused; perhaps he had wanted to ask: "But are you really Prince Myshkin?"

"Yes, I just got off the train. It seems to me you wanted to ask if I'm really Prince Myshkin, but did not ask out of politeness."

"Hm . . ." the astonished lackey grunted.

"I assure you, I am not lying to you, and you won't have to answer for me. And as for why I've come looking like this and with this bundle, there's nothing surprising about it: my present circumstances are not very pretty."

"Hm. That's not what I'm afraid of, you see. It's my duty to announce you, and the secretary will come out, unless you . . . But that's just it, that unless. You're not going to petition the general on account of your poverty, if I may be so bold?"

"Oh, no, you may be completely assured about that. I have other business."

"Forgive me, but I asked by the look of you. Wait for the secretary; the general is busy with the colonel right now, and afterwards comes the secretary . . . of the company."

"In that case, if I'll have a long wait, let me ask you: is there someplace where I can smoke here? I have a pipe and tobacco with me."

"Smo-o-oke?" The valet raised his eyes to him with scornful perplexity, as if still not believing his ears. "Smoke? No, you can't smoke here, and moreover you should be ashamed of having such thoughts. Hah . . . very odd, sir!"

"Oh, I wasn't asking about this room. I know. I'd have gone wherever you told me, because I've got the habit, and I haven't smoked for three hours now. However, as you please, and, you know, there's a saying: when in Rome . . ."

"Well, how am I going to announce the likes of you?" the valet muttered almost inadvertently. "First of all, you oughtn't to be here at all, but in the reception room, because you're in the line of a visitor, that is to say, a guest, and I'm answerable . . . What is it, do you plan on living with us or something?" he added, casting another sidelong glance at the prince's bundle, which obviously kept bothering him.

"No, I don't think so. Even if they invite me, I won't stay. I've come simply to get acquainted, that's all."

"How's that? To get acquainted?" the valet asked in surprise and with trebled suspiciousness. "How is it you said first that you were here on business?"

"Oh, it's almost not on business! That is, if you like, there is one piece of business, just to ask advice, but it's mainly to introduce myself, because I'm Prince Myshkin, and the general's wife is also the last Princess Myshkin, and except for the two of us, there are no more Myshkins."

"So you're also a relation?" the now all but frightened lackey fluttered himself up.

"That's not quite so either. However, if we stretch it, of course, we're related, but so distantly it's really impossible to work out. I once wrote a letter to the general's wife from abroad, but she didn't answer me. All the same, I thought I should get in touch on my return. I'm telling you all this now so that you won't have doubts, because I can see you're still worried: announce that Prince Myshkin is here, and the announcement itself will contain the reason for my visit. If they receive me—good; if not—that also may be very good. Though I don't think they can *not* receive me: the general's wife will certainly want to see the eldest and sole representative of her family, and she values her origins very much, as I've heard specifically about her."

It would seem that the prince's conversation was the most simple; but the simpler it was, the more absurd it became in the present case, and the experienced valet could not help feeling something that was perfectly proper between servant and servant, but perfectly improper between a guest and a *servant*. And since *servants* are much more intelligent than their masters commonly think, it occurred to the valet that there was one of two things here: either the prince was some sort of moocher and had certainly come to beg for money, or the prince was simply a little fool and had no ambitions, because a clever prince with ambitions would not have sat in the anteroom and discussed his affairs with a lackey, and therefore, in one case or the other, might he not be held answerable?

"But all the same you ought to go to the reception room," he observed as insistently as possible.

"I'd be sitting there and wouldn't have told you all that," the prince laughed merrily, "which means you'd still be looking at my cloak and bundle and worrying. And now maybe you don't need to wait for the secretary, but can go and announce me yourself."

"I can't announce a visitor like you without the secretary, and besides, the general gave me a specific order earlier not to bother him for anyone while he was with the colonel, but Gavrila Ardalionych can go in without being announced."

"A clerk?"

"Gavrila Ardalionych? No. He works for the Company on his own. You can at least put your bundle down here."

"I already thought of that. With your permission. And, you know, I'll take the cloak off, too."

"Of course, you can't go and see him in your cloak."

The prince stood up, hastily took off his cloak, and remained in a rather decent and smartly tailored, though shabby, jacket. A steel chain hung across his waistcoat. The chain turned out to be attached to a silver Swiss watch.

Though the prince was a little fool—the lackey had already decided that—all the same the general's valet finally found it unsuitable to continue his conversation with the visitor, despite the fact that for some reason he liked the prince, in his own way, of course. But from another point of view, he provoked in him a decided and crude indignation.

"And when does the general's wife receive?" asked the prince, sitting down in his former place.

"That's none of my business, sir. She receives at various times, depending on the person. She'd receive the dressmaker even at eleven o'clock. Gavrila Ardalionych is also admitted earlier than others, even for an early lunch."

"Here it's warmer inside in winter than it is abroad," the prince observed, "but there it's warmer outside than here, while a Russian can't even live in their houses in winter unless he's used to it."

"They don't heat them?"

"No, and the houses are also built differently—the stoves and windows, that is."

"Hm! Have you been traveling long?"

"Four years. Though I sat in the same place almost the whole time, in the country."

"You're unaccustomed to things here?"

"That's true, too. Would you believe, I marvel at myself that I haven't forgotten how to speak Russian. Here I'm talking to you now and thinking to myself: 'I speak well enough after all.' That may be why I'm talking so much. Really, since yesterday all I've wanted to do is speak Russian."

"Hm! Heh! And did you live in Petersburg before?" (Try as he might, the lackey could not help keeping up such a courteous and polite conversation.)

"In Petersburg? Hardly at all, just in passing. And before I didn't know anything here, but now I've heard so much is new that they say anyone who knew it has to learn to know it all over again. There's a lot of talk about the courts."[13]

"Hm! . . . The courts. The courts, it's true, there's the courts. And do the courts there judge more fairly or not?"

"I don't know. I've heard a lot of good about ours. Then, again, we have no capital punishment."[14]

"And they have it there?"

"Yes. I saw it in France, in Lyons. Schneider took me there with him."

"By hanging?"

"No, in France they always cut their heads off."

"And what, do they scream?"

"Hardly! It's instantaneous. The man is laid down, and a broad knife drops, it's a special machine called the guillotine, heavy, powerful . . . The head bounces off before you can blink an eye. The preparations are the bad part. When they read out the sentence, get everything ready, tie him up, lead him to the scaffold, then it's terrible! People gather, even women, though they don't like it when women watch."

"It's not their business."

"Of course not! Of course not! Such suffering! . . . The criminal was an intelligent man, fearless, strong, mature, his name was Legros. And I tell you, believe it or not, he wept as he climbed the scaffold, he was white as paper. Is it possible? Isn't it terrible? Do people weep from fear? I never thought it was possible for a man who has never wept, for a man of forty-five, not a child, to weep from fear! What happens at that moment with the soul, what convulsions is it driven to? It's an outrage on the soul, and nothing more! It's said, 'Do not kill.' So he killed, and then they kill him? No, that's impossible. I saw it a month ago, and it's as if it were still there before my eyes. I've dreamed about it five times."

The prince even grew animated as he spoke, a slight flush came to his pale face, though his speech was as quiet as before. The valet watched him with sympathetic interest and seemed unwilling to tear himself away; perhaps he, too, was a man with imagination and an inclination to thinking.

"It's a good thing there's not much suffering," he observed, "when the head flies off."

"You know what?" the prince picked up hotly. "You've just observed that, and everybody makes the same observation as you, and this machine, the guillotine, was invented for that. But a thought occurred to me then: what if it's even worse? To you it seems ridiculous, to you it seems wild, but with some imagination even a thought like that can pop into your head. Think: if there's torture, for instance, then there's suffering, wounds, bodily pain, and it means that all that distracts you from inner torment, so that you only suffer from the wounds until you die. And yet the chief, the strongest pain may not be in the wounds, but in knowing for certain that in an hour, then in ten minutes, then in half a minute, then now, this second—your soul will fly out of your body and you'll no longer be a man, and it's for certain—the main thing is that it's *for certain*. When you put your head under that knife and hear it come screeching down on you, that one quarter of a second is the most horrible of all. Do you know that this isn't my fantasy, but that many people have said so? I believe it so much that I'll tell you my opinion outright. To kill for killing is an immeasurably greater punishment than the crime itself. To be killed by legal sentence is immeasurably more terrible than to be killed by robbers. A man killed by robbers, stabbed at night, in the forest or however, certainly still hopes he'll be saved till the very last minute. There have been examples when a man's throat has already been cut, and he still hopes, or flees, or pleads. But here all this last hope, which makes it ten times easier to die, is taken away *for certain*; here there's the sentence, and the whole torment lies in the certainty that there's no escape, and there's no greater torment in the world than that. Take a soldier, put him right in front of a cannon during a battle, and shoot at him, and he'll still keep hoping, but read that same soldier a sentence *for certain*, and he'll lose his mind or start weeping. Who ever said human nature could bear it without going mad? Why such an ugly, vain, unnecessary violation? Maybe there's a man who has had the sentence read to him, has been allowed to suffer, and has then been told, 'Go, you're forgiven.' That man might be able to tell us something. Christ spoke of this suffering and horror. No, you can't treat a man like that!"[15]

The valet, though of course he could not have expressed it all like the prince, nevertheless understood, if not all, at least the main thing, as could be seen by his softened expression.

"If you have such a wish to smoke," he said, "it might be possible, if you do it quickly. Because he may ask for you suddenly, and you won't be here. There, under the stairway, you see, there's a door. As you go through the door, there's a little room to the right: you can smoke there, only open the vent window, because it's against the rules . . ."

But the prince had no time to go and smoke. A young man suddenly came into the anteroom with papers in his hands. The valet began to help him out of his fur coat. The young man cocked an eye at the prince.

"Gavrila Ardalionych," the valet began confidentially and almost familiarly, "this gentleman here presents himself as Prince Myshkin and the lady's relation, come by train from abroad with a bundle in his hands, only . . ."

The prince did not hear the rest, because the valet started whispering. Gavrila Ardalionovich listened attentively and kept glancing at the prince with great curiosity. Finally he stopped listening and approached him impatiently.

"You are Prince Myshkin?" he asked extremely amiably and politely. He was a very handsome young man, also of about twenty-eight, a trim blond, of above average height, with a small imperial, and an intelligent and very handsome face. Only his smile, for all its amiability, was somewhat too subtle; it revealed his somewhat too pearly and even teeth; his gaze, for all its cheerfulness and ostensible simple-heartedness, was somewhat too intent and searching.

"When he's alone he probably doesn't look that way, and maybe never laughs," the prince somehow felt.

The prince explained all he could, hurriedly, almost in the same way as he had explained to the valet earlier, and to Rogozhin earlier still. Gavrila Ardalionovich meanwhile seemed to be recalling something.

"Was it you," he asked, "who sent a letter to Elizaveta Proko-fyevna about a year ago, from Switzerland, I believe?"

"Exactly so."

"In that case they know you here and certainly remember. You wish to see his excellency? I'll announce you presently . . . He'll be free presently. Only you . . . you must kindly wait in the reception room . . . Why is the gentleman here?" he sternly addressed the valet.

"I tell you, he didn't want to . . ."

At that moment the door of the office suddenly opened and some military man with a portfolio in his hand came through it, speaking loudly and bowing his way out.

"Are you there, Ganya?" a voice called from the office. "Come in, please!"

Gavrila Ardalionovich nodded to the prince and hastily went into the office.

About two minutes later the door opened again and the affable voice of Gavrila Ardalionovich rang out:

"Please come in, Prince!"

III

GENERAL IVAN FYODOROVICH EPANCHIN was standing in the middle of his office, looking with extreme curiosity at the entering prince, and even took two steps towards him. The prince approached and introduced himself.

"So, sir," replied the general, "what can I do for you?"

"I don't have any pressing business; my purpose was simply to make your acquaintance. I wouldn't want to disturb you, since I don't know anything about your day or your arrangements . . . But I just got off the train . . . I've come from Switzerland . . ."

The general was about to smile, but thought better of it and stopped; then he thought more, narrowed his eyes, looked his guest over once again from head to foot, after which he quickly motioned him to a chair, sat down himself somewhat obliquely, and turned to the prince in impatient expectation. Ganya stood in the corner of the office, by the desk, sorting papers.

"In fact, I have little time for making acquaintances," said the general, "but since you, of course, have some purpose of your own . . ."

"I did anticipate," the prince interrupted, "that you would not fail to see some special purpose in my visit. But, by God, apart from the pleasure of making your acquaintance, I have no particular purpose at all."

"For me, too, of course, it is certainly an extreme pleasure, but amusement isn't all, you know, one sometimes happens to be busy . . . Besides, so far I'm unable to see between us any common . . . any, so to speak, reason . . ."

"There's no reason, indisputably, and, of course, very little in common. Because if I am Prince Myshkin and your spouse is from our family, that, naturally, is no reason. I understand that very well. But nevertheless, my whole pretext consists only in that. I haven't been in Russia for four years or so; and what was I when I left— all but out of my mind! I knew nothing then, and know still less now. I'm in need of good people; there's even one piece of business I have, and I don't know who to turn to. When I was in Berlin, I thought: 'They're almost my relations, I'll start with them; we might be useful to each other—they to me, and I to them—if they're good people.' And I'd heard you were good people."

"Much obliged, sir," the general was surprised. "Allow me to inquire where you're staying."

"I'm not staying anywhere yet."

"So you came to me straight from the train? And . . . with your luggage?"

"All the luggage I have is a little bundle of linen, and nothing else; I usually carry it with me. I'll have time to take a room in the evening."

"Then you still intend to take a room?"

"Oh, yes, of course."

"Judging by your words, I was of a mind that you had come straight to me."

"That could be, but not otherwise than by your invitation. Though, I confess, I wouldn't stay even then, not that there's any reason, but just . . . by character."

"Well, that makes it opportune that I did not and do not invite you. Excuse me, Prince, but to clarify it all at once: since you and I have just concluded that there can be no talk between us of being related—though, naturally, I'd find it very flattering—it means that . . ."

"It means that I can get up and leave?" the prince rose slightly, laughing even somehow merrily, despite all the apparent embarrassment of his situation. "There, by God, General, though I have absolutely no practical knowledge either of local customs or of how people normally live here, things went with us just now as I thought they were certain to go. Well, maybe that's how it should be . . . And you also didn't answer my letter then . . . Well, good-bye and forgive me for bothering you."

The prince's gaze was so gentle at that moment, and his smile was so free of the least shade of any concealed hostility, that the general suddenly stopped and somehow suddenly looked at his visitor in a different way; the whole change of view occurred in a single instant.

"But you know, Prince," he said in an almost totally different voice, "after all, I don't know you, and Elizaveta Prokofyevna might want to have a look at her namesake . . . Perhaps you'd like to wait, if your time will keep."

"Oh, my time will keep; my time is all my own" (and the prince immediately put his round, soft-brimmed hat on the table). "I confess, I counted on Elizaveta Prokofyevna maybe remembering that I had written to her. Your servant, when I was waiting for you earlier, suspected that I had come to beg from you out of poverty; I noticed it, and you must have given him strict instructions about that; but I really didn't come for that, I really came only so as to get to know people. Only I have a slight suspicion that I've disturbed you, and that troubles me."

"I'll tell you what, Prince," the general said with a cheerful smile, "if you are indeed the way you seem to be, it might very well be pleasant to become acquainted with you; only, you see, I'm a busy man and presently I'll sit down again to look something over and sign it, and then I'll go to see his highness, and then to my department, and the result is that though I'm glad to meet people . . . I mean, good people . . . still . . . However, I'm so convinced of your perfect upbringing that . . . And how old are you, Prince?"

"Twenty-six."

"Hah! And I thought you were much younger."

"Yes, people say I have a youthful face. But I'll learn not to disturb you and figure it out quickly, because I myself don't like to disturb . . . And, finally, it seems to me that we're such different people, by the look of it . . . in many ways, that we perhaps cannot have many points in common, only, you know, I personally don't believe in that last notion, because it often only seems that there are no points in common, when there really are a lot . . . it comes from people's laziness, that they sort themselves out by looks and can't find anything . . . But, anyhow, maybe I've begun to bore you? It's as if you . . ."

"A couple of words, sir: do you have some property at least? Or perhaps you intend to take something up? I apologize for being so . . ."

"Good heavens, I understand your question and appreciate it very much. So far I have no property, nor any occupation either, and I should have, sir. And the money I now have isn't mine, it was given to me by Schneider, the professor who treated me and taught me in Switzerland, for the trip, and he gave me just enough, so that now, for instance, I have only a few kopecks left. I have one bit of business, it's true, and I'm in need of advice, but . . ."

"Tell me, how do you intend to subsist meanwhile, and what were your intentions?" the general interrupted.

"I wanted to do some sort of work."

"Oh, so you're a philosopher! But still . . . are you aware of having any talents, any abilities, at least of some sort, that could earn you your daily bread? Again, I apologize . . ."

"Oh, don't apologize. No, sir, I don't think I have any talents or special abilities; even the contrary, because I'm a sick man and have had no regular education. As for daily bread, it seems to me . . ."

The general interrupted again, and again began to ask questions. The prince told him once more all that has already been told. It turned out that the general had heard of the late Pavlishchev and had even known him personally. Why Pavlishchev had concerned himself with his upbringing, the prince himself was unable to explain—however, it might simply have been out of old friendship for his late father. The prince, at his parents' death, was left still a little child; all his life he lived and grew up in the country, since his health also called for village air. Pavlishchev entrusted him to some old lady landowners, his relations; first a governess was hired for him, then a tutor; he said, however, that though he remembered everything, he was hardly capable of giving a satisfactory account of it, because he had been unaware of many things. The frequent attacks of his illness had made almost an idiot of him (the prince actually said "idiot"). He told, finally, how one day in Berlin, Pavlishchev met Professor Schneider, a Swiss, who studied precisely such illnesses, had an institution in Switzerland, in canton Valais, used his own method of treatment by cold water and gymnastics, treated idiotism, insanity, also provided education, and generally attended to spiritual development; that Pavlishchev had sent him to Schneider in Switzerland about five years ago, and had died himself two years ago, suddenly, without making any arrangements; that Schneider had kept him and gone on with his treatment for another two years; that he had not cured him but had helped him very much; and that, finally, by his own wish and owing to a certain new circumstance, he had now sent him to Russia.

The general was very surprised.

"And you have no one in Russia, decidedly no one?" he asked.

"No one right now, but I hope . . . besides, I received a letter . . ."

"At least," the general interrupted, not hearing about the letter, "you have some sort of education, and your illness won't hinder you from occupying, for example, some undemanding post in some branch of the service?"

"Oh, certainly not. And concerning a post, I'd even like that very much, because I want to see for myself what I'm able to do. I studied constantly for four years, though not quite in a regular way but by his special system, and I also managed to read a great many Russian books."

"Russian books? So you're literate and can write without mistakes?"

"Oh, indeed I can."

"Splendid, sir. And your handwriting?"

"My handwriting is excellent. That's perhaps where my talent lies; I'm a real calligrapher. Let me write something for you now as a sample," the prince said warmly.

"Kindly do. And there's even a need for it . . . And I like this readiness of yours, Prince, you're really very nice."

"You have such fine handwriting accessories, and so many pencils, pens, such fine, thick paper . . . And it's such a fine office you have! I know that landscape, it's a view of Switzerland. I'm sure the artist painted it from nature, and I'm sure I've seen that spot: it's in canton Uri . . ."

"Quite possible, though I bought it here. Ganya, give the prince some paper; here are pens and paper, sit at this table, please. What's that?" the general turned to Ganya, who meanwhile had taken a large-format photographic portrait from his portfolio and handed it to him. "Bah! Nastasya Filippovna! She sent it to you herself, she herself?" he asked Ganya with animation and great curiosity.

"She gave it to me just now, when I came to wish her a happy birthday. I've been asking for a long time. I don't know, I'm not sure it's not a hint on her part about my coming empty-handed, without a present, on such a day," Ganya added, smiling unpleasantly.

"Ah, no," the general interrupted with conviction, "and really, what a turn of mind you've got! She wouldn't go hinting . . . and she's completely unmercenary. And besides, what kind of presents can you give: it's a matter of thousands here! Your portrait, maybe? And say, incidentally, has she asked you for your portrait yet?"

"No, she hasn't. And maybe she never will. You remember about this evening, of course, Ivan Fyodorovich? You're among those specially invited."

"I remember, I remember, of course, and I'll be there. What else, it's her birthday, she's twenty-five! Hm . . . You know, Ganya— so be it—I'm going to reveal something to you, prepare yourself. She promised Afanasy Ivanovich and me that this evening at her place she will say the final word: whether it's to be or not to be! So now you know."

Ganya suddenly became so confused that he even turned slightly pale.

"Did she say it for certain?" he asked, and his voice seemed to quaver.

"She gave her word two days ago. We both badgered her so much that we forced her into it. Only she asked us not to tell you meanwhile."

The general peered intently at Ganya; he evidently did not like Ganya's confusion.

"Remember, Ivan Fyodorovich," Ganya said anxiously and hesitantly, "she gave me complete freedom of decision until she decides the matter herself, and even then what I say is still up to me . . ."

"So maybe you . . . maybe you . . ." The general suddenly became alarmed.

"Never mind me."

"Good heavens, what are you trying to do to us!"

"But I'm not backing out. Maybe I didn't put it right . . ."

"I'll say you're not backing out!" the general said vexedly, not even wishing to conceal his vexation. "Here, brother, it's not a matter of your *not* backing out, but of the readiness, the pleasure, the joy with which you receive her words . . . How are things at home?"

"At home? At home everything's the way I want it to be, only my father plays the fool, as usual, but it's become completely outrageous; I no longer speak to him, but I keep him in an iron grip, and, in fact, if it weren't for my mother, I'd have shown him the door. My mother cries all the time, of course, my sister's angry, but I finally told them straight out that I'm the master of my fate and at home I want to be . . . obeyed. I spelled it all out to my sister anyway, in front of my mother."

"And I, brother, go on not understanding," the general observed pensively, heaving his shoulders slightly and spreading his arms a little. "Nina Alexandrovna—remember when she came to us the other day? She moaned and sighed. 'What's the matter?' I ask. It comes out that there's supposedly some *dishonor* in it for them. Where's the dishonor, may I ask? Who can reproach Nastasya Filippovna with anything or point at anything in her? Is it that she was with Totsky? But that's such nonsense, especially considering certain circumstances! 'You wouldn't let her meet your daughters, would you?' she says. Well! So there! That's Nina Alexandrovna! I mean, how can she not understand it, how can she not understand . . ."

"Her position?" Ganya prompted the faltering general. "She does understand it; don't be angry with her. Besides, I gave them a dressing-down then, so they wouldn't poke their noses into other people's business. And anyhow, so far things are holding together at home only because the final word hasn't been spoken; that's when the storm will break. If the final word is spoken tonight, then everything will be spoken."

The prince heard this whole conversation, sitting in the corner over his calligraphic sample. He finished, went up to the desk, and handed over his page.

"So this is Nastasya Filippovna?" he said, gazing at the portrait attentively and curiously. "Remarkably good-looking!" he warmly added at once. The portrait showed a woman of extraordinary beauty indeed. She had been photographed in a black silk dress of a very simple and graceful cut; her hair, apparently dark blond, was done simply, informally; her eyes were dark and deep, her forehead pensive; the expression of her face was passionate and as if haughty. Her face was somewhat thin, perhaps also pale . . . Ganya and the general looked at the prince in amazement . . .

"How's that? Nastasya Filippovna! So you already know Nastasya Filippovna?" asked the general.

"Yes, just one day in Russia and I already know such a great beauty," the prince answered and at once told them about his meeting with Rogozhin and recounted his whole story.

"Well, that's news!" The general, who had listened to the story with extreme attention, became alarmed again and glanced searchingly at Ganya.

"It's probably just outrageous talk," murmured Ganya, also somewhat bewildered. "A merchant boy's carousing. I've already heard something about him."

"So have I, brother," the general picked up. "Right after the earrings, Nastasya Filippovna told the whole anecdote. But now it's a different matter. There may actually be a million sitting here and . . . a passion, an ugly passion, if you like, but all the same it smacks of passion, and we know what these gentlemen are capable of when they're intoxicated! . . . Hm! . . . Some sort of anecdote may come of it!" the general concluded pensively.

"You're afraid of a million?" Ganya grinned.

"And you're not, of course?"

"How did it seem to you, Prince?" Ganya suddenly turned to him. "Is he a serious man or just a mischief maker? What's your personal opinion?"

Something peculiar took place in Ganya as he was asking this question. It was as if some new and peculiar idea lit up in his brain and glittered impatiently in his eyes. The general, who was genuinely and simple-heartedly worried, also glanced sidelong at the prince, but as if he did not expect much from his reply.

"I don't know, how shall I put it," replied the prince, "only it seemed to me there's a lot of passion in him, and even some sort of sick passion. And he seems to be quite sick himself. It's very possible he'll take to his bed again during his first days in Petersburg, especially if he goes on a spree."

"So? It seemed so to you?" the general latched on to this idea.

"Yes, it did."

"And, anyhow, that kind of anecdote needn't take several days. Something may turn up even today, this same evening," Ganya smiled to the general.

"Hm! . . . Of course . . . So it may, and then it all depends on what flashes through her head," said the general.

"And you know how she can be sometimes?"

"How do you mean?" the general, who by now was extremely disturbed, heaved himself up. "Listen, Ganya, please don't contradict her too much tonight, and try, you know, to . . . in short, to humor . . . Hm! . . . Why are you twisting your mouth like that? Listen, Gavrila Ardalionych, it would be opportune, even very opportune, to say now: what's all this fuss about? You see, concerning the profit that's in it for me, I've long been secure; one way or another I'll turn it to my benefit. Totsky's decision is firm, and so I, too, am completely assured. And therefore, if there's anything I wish for now, it's your benefit. Judge for yourself—or don't you trust me? Besides, you're a man . . . a man . . . in short, a man of intelligence, and I've been counting on you . . . and in the present case that is . . . that is . . ."

"That is the main thing," Ganya finished, again helping out the faltering general, and contorting his lips into a most venomous smile, which he no longer cared to hide. He fixed his inflamed gaze directly on the general's eyes, as if he even wished to read the whole of his thought in them. The general turned purple and flared up.

"Well, yes, intelligence is the main thing!" he agreed, looking sharply at Ganya. "And what a funny man you are, Gavrila Ardalionych! You seem to be glad, I notice, of that little merchant, as a way out for yourself. But here you precisely should have gone by intelligence from the very beginning; here precisely one must understand and . . . and act honestly and directly on both sides, or else . . . give a warning beforehand, so as not to compromise others, the more so as there's been plenty of time for that, and even now there's still plenty of time" (the general raised his eyebrows meaningfully), "though there are only a few hours left . . . Do you understand? Do you? Are you willing or are you not, in fact? If you're not, say so and—you're welcome. Nobody's holding you, Gavrila Ardalionych, nobody's dragging you into a trap by force, if you do see this as a trap."

"I'm willing," Ganya said in a low but firm voice, dropped his eyes, and fell gloomily silent.

The general was satisfied. The general had lost his temper, but now apparently regretted having gone so far. He suddenly turned to the prince, and the uneasy thought that the prince was right there and had heard them seemed to pass over his face. But he instantly felt reassured: one glance at the prince was enough for him to be fully reassured.

"Oho!" cried the general, looking at the calligraphy sample the prince presented. "That's a model hand! And a rare one, too! Look here, Ganya, what talent!"

On the thick sheet of vellum the prince had written a phrase in medieval Russian script:

"The humble hegumen Pafnuty here sets his hand to it."

"This," the prince explained with great pleasure and animation, "this is the actual signature of the hegumen Pafnuty, copied from a fourteenth-century manuscript. They had superb signatures, all those old Russian hegumens and metropolitans, and sometimes so tasteful, so careful! Can it be you don't have Pogodin's book,[16] General? Then here I've written in a different script: it's the big, round French script of the last century; some letters are even written differently; it's a marketplace script, a public scrivener's script, borrowed from their samples (I had one)—you must agree, it's not without virtue. Look at these round *d*'s and *a*'s. I've transposed the French characters into Russian letters, which is very difficult, but it came out well. Here's another beautiful and original script, this phrase here: 'Zeal overcometh all.'[17] This is a Russian script—a scrivener's, or military scrivener's, if you wish. It's an example of an official address to an important person, also a rounded script, nice and *black*, the writing is black, but remarkably tasteful. A calligrapher wouldn't have permitted these flourishes, or, better to say, these attempts at flourishes, these unfinished half-tails here—you notice—but on the whole, you see, it adds up to character, and, really, the whole military scrivener's soul is peeking out of it: he'd like to break loose, his talent yearns for it, but his military collar is tightly hooked, and discipline shows in the writing—lovely! I was recently struck by a sample of it I found—and where? in Switzerland! Now, here is a simple, ordinary English script of the purest sort: elegance can go no further, everything here is lovely, a jewel, a pearl; this is perfection; but here is a variation, again a French one, I borrowed it from a French traveling salesman: this is the same English script, but the black line is slightly blacker and thicker than in the English, and see—the proportion of light is violated; and notice also that the ovals are altered, they're slightly rounder, and what's more, flourishes are permitted, and a flourish is a most dangerous thing! A flourish calls for extraordinary taste; but if it succeeds, if the right proportion is found, a script like this is incomparable, you can even fall in love with it."

"Oho! What subtleties you go into!" the general laughed. "You're not simply a calligrapher, my dear fellow, you're an artist—eh, Ganya?"

"Astonishing," said Ganya, "and even with a consciousness of his purpose," he added with a mocking laugh.

"You may laugh, you may laugh, but there's a career here," said the general. "Do you know, Prince, which person we'll have you write documents to? I could offer you thirty-five roubles a month straight off, from the first step. However, it's already half-past twelve," he concluded, glancing at the clock. "To business, Prince, because I must hurry and we probably won't meet again today! Sit down for a moment. I've already explained to you that I cannot receive you very often; but I sincerely wish to help you a bit, only a bit, naturally, that is, with regard to the most necessary, and for the rest it will be as you please. I'll find you a little post in the chancellery, not a difficult one, but requiring accuracy. Now, as concerns other things, sir: in the home, that is, in the family of Gavrila Ardalionych Ivolgin, this young friend of mine here, whose acquaintance I beg you to make, there are two or three furnished rooms which his mother and sister have vacated and rent out to highly recommended lodgers, with board and maid services. I'm sure Nina Alexandrovna will accept my recommendation. And for you, Prince, this is even more than a find, first, because you won't be alone, but, so to speak, in the bosom of a family, and, as far as I can see, it's impossible for you to take your first steps on your own in a capital like Petersburg. Nina Alexandrovna, Gavrila Ardalionych's mother, and Varvara Ardalionovna, his sister, are ladies whom I respect exceedingly. Nina Alexandrovna is the wife of Ardalion Alexandrovich, a retired general, my former comrade from when I entered the service, but with whom, owing to certain circumstances, I have ceased all contact, though that does not prevent my having a sort of respect for him. I'm explaining all this to you, Prince, so that you will understand that I am, so to speak, recommending you personally, consequently it's as if I'm vouching for you. The rent is the most moderate, and soon enough, I hope, your salary will be quite sufficient for that. True, a man also needs pocket money, at least a small amount, but you won't be angry, Prince, if I point out to you that it would be better for you to avoid pocket money and generally carrying money in your pocket. I say it just from looking at you. But since your purse is quite empty now, allow me to offer you these twenty-five roubles to begin with. We'll settle accounts, of course, and if you're as candid and genuine a man as your words make you seem, there can be no difficulties between us. And if I take such an interest in you, it's because I even have some intention concerning you; you'll learn what it is later. You see, I'm being quite plain with you. Ganya, I hope you have nothing against putting the prince up in your apartment?"

"Oh, on the contrary! And my mother will be very glad . . ." Ganya confirmed politely and obligingly.

"I believe only one of your rooms is taken. That—what's his name—Ferd . . . Fer . . ."

"Ferdyshchenko."

"Ah, yes. I don't like this Ferdyshchenko of yours: some sort of salacious buffoon. I don't understand why Nastasya Filippovna encourages him so. Is he really related to her?"

"Oh, no, it's all a joke! There's not a whiff of a relation."

"Well, devil take him! So, how about it, Prince, are you pleased or not?"

"Thank you, General, you have acted as an extremely kind man towards me, especially as I didn't even ask—I don't say it out of pride; I didn't know where to lay my head. Though, it's true, Rogozhin invited me earlier."

"Rogozhin? Ah, no. I'd advise you in a fatherly, or, if you prefer, a friendly way to forget about Mr. Rogozhin. And in general I'd advise you to keep to the family you're going to be with."

"Since you're so kind," the prince tried to begin, "I have one bit of business here. I've received notification . . ."

"Well, forgive me," the general interrupted, "but right now I don't have a minute more. I'll tell Lizaveta Prokofyevna about you at once: if she wishes to receive you now (and I'll try to recommend you with a view to that), I advise you to make use of the opportunity and please her, because Lizaveta Prokofyevna may be of great use to you; you're her namesake. If she doesn't wish to, don't take it badly, she will some other time. And you, Ganya, look over these accounts meanwhile; Fedoseev and I already tried earlier. We mustn't forget to include them . . ."

The general went out, and so the prince had no time to ask about his business, which he had tried to bring up for perhaps the fourth time. Ganya lit a cigarette and offered one to the prince; the prince accepted, but did not start a conversation, not wishing to interfere, but began looking around the office; but Ganya barely glanced at the sheet of paper all covered with figures that the general had indicated to him. He was distracted: in the prince's view, Ganya's smile, gaze, and pensiveness became more strained when they were left alone. Suddenly he went up to the prince; at that moment he was again standing over the portrait of Nastasya Filippovna and studying it.

"So you like such a woman, Prince?" he asked him suddenly, giving him a piercing look. And it was as if he had some exceptional intention.

"An astonishing face!" replied the prince. "And I'm convinced that her fate is no ordinary one. It's a gay face, but she has suffered terribly, eh? It speaks in her eyes, these two little bones, the two points under her eyes where the cheeks begin. It's a proud face, terribly proud, and I don't know whether she's kind or not. Ah, if only she were kind! Everything would be saved!"

"And would *you* marry such a woman?" Ganya continued, not taking his inflamed eyes off him.

"I can't marry anybody, I'm unwell," said the prince.

"And would Rogozhin marry her? What do you think?"

"Why, I think he might marry her tomorrow. He'd marry her, and a week later he might well put a knife in her."

He had no sooner uttered these words than Ganya suddenly gave such a start that the prince almost cried out.

"What's wrong?" he said, seizing his arm.

"Your Highness! His excellency asks that you kindly come to her excellency's rooms," the lackey announced, appearing in the doorway. The prince followed the lackey out.

IV

ALL THREE EPANCHIN girls were healthy young ladies, tall, blossoming, with astonishing shoulders, powerful bosoms, strong, almost masculine arms, and, of course, owing to their strength and health, they liked to eat well on occasion, something they had no wish to conceal. Their mama, Lizaveta Prokofyevna, sometimes looked askance at the frankness of their appetite, but since some of her opinions, despite all the external deference with which her daughters received them, had in fact long lost their original and unquestionable authority among them, so much so that the harmonious conclave established by the three girls was beginning to gain the upper hand on most occasions, the general's wife, mindful of her own dignity, found it more convenient not to argue but to yield. True, her character quite often did not heed and obey the decisions of her good sense; with every year Lizaveta Prokofyevna was becoming more and more capricious and impatient, she was even becoming somehow eccentric, but since in any case a submissive and well-trained husband remained at hand, all superfluous and accumulated things usually poured down on his head, and then the family harmony was restored again and everything went better than ever.

The general's wife herself, however, never lost her own good appetite, and at half-past twelve usually partook, together with her daughters, of a copious lunch, which more resembled a dinner. Earlier, at exactly ten o'clock, while still in bed, at the moment of waking up, the young ladies had a cup of coffee. That was how they liked it and how it had always been arranged. At half-past twelve the table was laid in the small dining room, near the mother's rooms, and occasionally the general himself, time permitting, joined them at this intimate family lunch. Besides tea, coffee, cheese, honey, butter, the special pancakes the lady herself was particularly fond of, the cutlets, and so on, they were even served a strong, hot bouillon. On the morning when our story begins, the whole family was gathered in the dining room in expectation of the general, who had promised to come by half-past twelve. If he had been even a minute late, he would have been sent for at once; but he arrived punctually. Going over to greet his spouse and kiss her hand, he noticed this time something all too peculiar in her face. And though he had anticipated even the day before that it would be precisely so, on account of a certain "anecdote" (as he was accustomed to put it), and had worried about it while falling asleep the previous night, all the same he now turned coward again. His daughters came up to kiss him; here there was no anger against him, but here, too, all the same there was also something peculiar, as it were. True, the general, owing to certain circumstances, had become overly suspicious; but as he was an experienced and adroit father and husband, he at once took his measures.

Perhaps we will do no great harm to the vividness of our narrative if we stop here and resort to the aid of a few clarifications in order to establish directly and more precisely the relations and circumstances in which we find General Epanchin's family at the beginning of our story. We said just now that the general, though not a very educated but, on the contrary, as he himself put it, a "self-taught man," was nevertheless an experienced husband and adroit father. Among other things, he had adopted a system of not rushing his daughters into marriage, that is, of not "hovering over" them and bothering them too much with his parental love's longing for their happiness, as involuntarily and naturally happens all the time, even in the most intelligent families, where grown-up daughters accumulate. He even succeeded in winning Lizaveta Prokofyevna over to his system, though that was normally a difficult thing to do—difficult because it was also unnatural; but the general's arguments were extremely weighty and based on tangible facts. Besides, left entirely to their own wishes and decisions, the brides would naturally be forced to see reason at last, and then things would take off, because they would do it eagerly, casting aside their caprices and excessive choosiness; all the parents would have to do would be to keep a watchful and, if possible, inconspicuous eye on them, lest some strange choice or unnatural deviation occur, and then, seizing the proper moment, step in with all their help and guide the affair with all their influence. Finally, the fact alone, for instance, that their fortune and social significance increased every year in geometrical progression meant that the more time that passed, the more advantageous it was to his daughters, even as brides. But among all these irrefutable facts another fact occurred: the eldest daughter, Alexandra, suddenly and almost quite unexpectedly (as always happens) turned twenty-five. And at almost the same time Afanasy Ivanovich Totsky, a man of high society, with high connections and extraordinary wealth, again showed his old desire to marry. He was a man of about fifty-five, of elegant character and with extraordinary refinement of taste. He wanted to marry well; he was an exceeding connoisseur of beauty. Since he had for some time maintained an extraordinary friendship with General Epanchin, especially strengthened by a joint participation in certain financial undertakings, he therefore asked the general—looking for friendly counsel and guidance, so to speak—whether it would or would not be possible to think of him marrying one of his daughters. In the quiet and beautiful flow of General Epanchin's family life, an obvious upheaval was coming.

The undoubted beauty in the family, as has already been said, was the youngest, Aglaya. But even Totsky himself, a man of exceeding egoism, understood that he was not to seek there and that Aglaya was not destined for him. It may be that the somewhat blind love and all too ardent friendship of the sisters exaggerated the matter, but among them, in the most sincere way, they determined that Aglaya's fate was to be not simply a fate, but the most ideal possible earthly paradise. Aglaya's future husband would have to be endowed with all perfections and successes, to say nothing of wealth. The sisters even decided among themselves, and somehow without any special superfluous words, on the possibility, if need be, of making sacrifices on their own part in favor of Aglaya: the dowry allotted to Aglaya was colossal and quite out of the ordinary. The parents knew of this agreement between the two elder sisters, and therefore, when Totsky asked for advice, they had little doubt that one of the elder sisters would not refuse to crown their desires, the more so as Afanasy Ivanovich would make no difficulties over the dowry. As for Totsky's offer, the general, with his particular knowledge of life, at once valued it extremely highly. Since Totsky himself, owing to certain special circumstances, had meanwhile to observe an extreme prudence in his steps and was still only probing into the matter, the parents, too, offered only the most remote suggestions for their daughters' consideration. In response to which they received from them a reassuring, if not very definite, statement that the eldest, Alexandra, would perhaps not decline. Though of firm character, she was a kind, reasonable girl and extremely easy to get along with; she might even marry Totsky willingly, and if she gave her word, she would honestly keep it. She cared nothing for splendor, and not only threatened no fusses or abrupt upheavals, but might even sweeten and soothe one's life. She was very good-looking, though not in a spectacular way. What could be better for Totsky?

And yet the matter still went ahead gropingly. It was mutually and amicably agreed between Totsky and the general that for the time being they would avoid any formal and irrevocable steps. The parents had still not even begun to speak quite openly with their daughters; some dissonance seemed to set in: Mrs. Epanchin, the mother of the family, was becoming displeased for some reason, and that was very grave. There was one circumstance here that hindered everything, one complex and troublesome occurrence, owing to which the whole matter might fall apart irrevocably.

This complex and troublesome "occurrence" (as Totsky himself put it) had begun very far back, about eighteen years ago. Next to one of Afanasy Ivanovich's rich estates, in one of the central provinces, an impoverished petty landowner was living an impoverished life. This was a man remarkable for his ceaseless and anecdotal misfortunes—a retired officer, from a good noble family, and in that respect even better than Totsky, a certain Filipp Alexandrovich Barashkov. Buried in debts and mortgages, he succeeded at last, after hard, almost peasant-like labors, in setting up his small estate more or less satisfactorily. The smallest success encouraged him extraordinarily. Encouraged and radiant with hopes, he went for a few days to his district town, to meet and, if possible, come to a final agreement with one of his chief creditors. On the third day after his arrival in town, his warden came from the village, on horseback, his cheek burned and his beard singed, and informed him that the "family estate burned down" the day before, at noon, and that "his wife burned with it, but the little children were left unharmed." This surprise even Barashkov, accustomed as he was to the "bruises of fortune," could not bear; he went mad and a month later died in delirium. The burned-down estate, with its peasants gone off begging, was sold for debts; and Barashkov's children, two little girls aged six and seven, were taken out of magnanimity to be kept and brought up by Afanasy Ivanovich Totsky. They were brought up together with the children of Afanasy Ivanovich's steward, a retired official with a large family and a German besides. Soon only one girl, Nastya, was left, the younger one having died of whooping cough. Totsky, who was living abroad, soon forgot all about them. One day, some five years later, Afanasy Ivanovich, passing by, decided to have a look at his estate and suddenly noticed in his country house, in the family of his German, a lovely child, a girl of about twelve, lively, sweet, clever, and promising to become a great beauty—in that regard Afanasy Ivanovich was an unerring connoisseur. That time he spent only a few days on his estate, but he had time to arrange things; a considerable change took place in the girl's education: a respectable, elderly governess was called in, experienced in the higher upbringing of girls, an educated Swiss woman, who, along with French, taught various other subjects. She settled into the country house, and little Nastya's upbringing acquired exceptional scope. Exactly four years later, this upbringing came to an end; the governess left, and a certain lady came to fetch Nastya, also a landowner of some sort, and also Mr. Totsky's neighbor, but in another, distant province, and on the instructions and by the authority of Afanasy Ivanovich, took Nastya away with her. On this small estate there also turned out to be a small but newly constructed wooden house; it was decorated with particular elegance, and the little village, as if on purpose, was called "Delight." The lady landowner brought Nastya straight to this quiet little house, and as she herself, a childless widow, lived less than a mile away, she settled in with Nastya. Around Nastya an old housekeeper and a young, experienced maid appeared. There were musical instruments in the house, an elegant library for girls, paintings, prints, pencils, brushes, paints, an astonishing greyhound, and two weeks later Afanasy Ivanovich himself arrived . . . After that he somehow became especially fond of this little village lost in the steppes, came every summer, stayed for two, even three months, and thus a rather long time, some four years, passed peacefully and happily, with taste and elegance.

Once it happened, at the beginning of winter, about four months after one of Afanasy Ivanovich's summer visits to Delight, which this time had lasted only two weeks, that a rumor spread, or, rather, the rumor somehow reached Nastasya Filippovna, that in Petersburg, Afanasy Ivanovich was about to marry a beauty, a rich girl, from the nobility—in short, to make a respectable and brilliant match. Later it turned out that the rumor was not accurate in all details: the wedding was then only a project, and everything was still very uncertain, but all the same an extraordinary upheaval took place in Nastasya Filippovna's life after that. She suddenly showed an extraordinary resolve and revealed a most unexpected character. Without further thought, she left her little country house and suddenly went to Petersburg, straight to Totsky, all on her own. He was amazed, tried to begin speaking; but it suddenly turned out, almost from the first phrase, that he had to change completely the style, the vocal range, the former topics of pleasant and elegant conversation, which till then had been used so successfully, the logic—everything, everything! Before him sat a totally different woman, not at all like the one he had known till then and had left only that July in the village of Delight.

This new woman, it turned out, first of all knew and understood an extraordinary amount—so much that it was a cause of profound wonder where she could have acquired such information, could have developed such precise notions in herself. (Could it have been from her girls' library?) What's more, she even understood an exceeding amount about legal matters and had a positive knowledge, if not of the world, then at least of how certain things went in the world; second of all, this was a completely different character from before, that is, not something timid, uncertain in a boarding-school way, sometimes charming in its original liveliness and naïvety, sometimes melancholy and pensive, astonished, mistrustful, weepy, and restless.

No: here before him an extraordinary and unexpected being laughed and stung him with a most poisonous sarcasm, telling him outright that she had never felt anything in her heart for him except the deepest contempt, contempt to the point of nausea, which had followed directly upon her initial astonishment. This new woman announced to him that in the fullest sense it would make no difference to her if he married any woman he liked right then and there, but that she had come to prevent this marriage of his, and to prevent it out of spite, solely because she wanted it that way, and consequently it must be that way—"well, so that now I can simply laugh at you to my heart's content, because now I, too, finally feel like laughing."

At least that was how she put it, though she may not have said everything she had in mind. But while the new Nastasya Filippovna was laughing and explaining all this, Afanasy Ivanovich was thinking the matter over to himself and, as far as possible, putting his somewhat shattered thoughts in order. This thinking went on for some time; for almost two weeks he grappled with it and tried to reach a final decision; but after two weeks his decision was taken. The thing was that Afanasy Ivanovich was about fifty at that time, and he was in the highest degree a respectable and settled man. His position in the world and in society had long been established on a most solid foundation. He loved and valued himself, his peace, and his comfort more than anything in the world, as befitted a man decent in the highest degree. Not the slightest disturbance, not the slightest wavering, could be tolerated in what had been established by his entire life and had acquired such a beautiful form. On the other hand, his experience and profound insight into things told Totsky very quickly and with extraordinary sureness that he now had to do with a being who was completely out of the ordinary, that this was precisely the sort of being who would not merely threaten, but would certainly act, and above all would decidedly stop at nothing, the more so as she valued decidedly nothing in the world, so that it was even impossible to tempt her. Here, obviously, was something else, implying some heartful and soulful swill—like some sort of romantic indignation, God knows against whom or why, some insatiable feeling of contempt that leaps completely beyond measure—in short, something highly ridiculous and inadmissible in decent society, something that was a sheer punishment from God for any decent man to encounter. To be sure, with Totsky's wealth and connections, it was possible to produce some small and totally innocent villainy at once, so as to be rid of this trouble. On the other hand, it was obvious that Nastasya Filippovna herself was scarcely capable of doing any harm, for instance, in the legal sense; she could not even cause a significant scandal, because it would always be too easy to limit her. But all that was so only in case Nastasya Filippovna decided to act as everyone generally acts in such cases, without leaping too eccentrically beyond measure. But it was here that Totsky's keen eye also proved useful: he was able to perceive that Nastasya Filippovna herself understood perfectly well how harmless she was in the legal sense, but that she had something quite different in mind and . . . in her flashing eyes. Valuing nothing, and least of all herself (it took great intelligence and perception to guess at that moment that she had long ceased to value herself and, skeptic and society cynic that he was, to believe in the seriousness of that feeling), Nastasya Filippovna was capable of ruining herself, irrevocably and outrageously, facing Siberia and hard labor, if only she could wreak havoc on the man for whom she felt such inhuman loathing. Afanasy Ivanovich had never concealed the fact that he was somewhat cowardly or, better to say, conservative in the highest degree. If he knew, for instance, that he would be killed at the foot of the altar, or that something of that sort would happen, extremely improper, ridiculous, and socially unacceptable, he would of course be frightened, but not so much at being killed or gravely wounded, or having his face publicly spat in, and so on and so forth, as at it happening to him in such an unnatural and unacceptable form. And this was precisely what Nastasya Filippovna foretold, though so far she had been silent about it; he knew that she understood and had studied him to the highest degree, and therefore knew how to strike at him. And since the wedding was indeed only an intention, Afanasy Ivanovich humbled himself and yielded to Nastasya Filippovna.

Another circumstance contributed to this decision: it was difficult to imagine how little this new Nastasya Filippovna resembled the former one in looks. Formerly she had been merely a very pretty girl, but now . . . For a long time Totsky could not forgive himself that he had looked for four years and not seen. True, it means much when an upheaval occurs on both sides, inwardly and unexpectedly. However, he recalled moments, even before, when strange thoughts had come to him, for instance, while looking into those eyes: it was as if he had sensed some deep and mysterious darkness in them. Those eyes had gazed at him—and seemed to pose a riddle. During the last two years he had often been surprised by the change in Nastasya Filippovna's color; she was growing terribly pale and—strangely—was even becoming prettier because of it. Totsky, who, like all gentlemen who have had a bit of fun in their time, at first looked with scorn on this untried soul he had obtained for himself so cheaply, more recently had begun to doubt his view. In any case, he had already resolved that past spring to arrange a marriage for Nastasya Filippovna before too long, in an excellent and well-provided way, with some sensible and respectable gentleman serving in a different province. (Oh, how terribly and wickedly Nastasya Filippovna laughed at that now!) But now Afanasy Ivanovich, charmed by the novelty, even thought he might again make use of this woman. He decided to settle Nastasya Filippovna in Petersburg and surround her with luxurious comfort. If not the one thing, then the other: he could show Nastasya Filippovna off and even boast of her in a certain circle. And Afanasy Ivanovich cherished his reputation along that line.

Five years of Petersburg life had already gone by, and, naturally, in such a period many things had become clear. Afanasy Ivanovich's position was ungratifying; worst of all was that, having once turned coward, he could never afterwards be at peace. He was afraid— and did not even know why—he was simply afraid of Nastasya Filippovna. For some time, during the first two years, he began to suspect that Nastasya Filippovna wanted to marry him herself, but said nothing out of her extraordinary vanity and was stubbornly waiting for him to propose. It would have been a strange pretension; Afanasy Ivanovich scowled and pondered heavily. To his great and (such is man's heart!) rather unpleasant amazement, he had occasion suddenly to become convinced that even if he had proposed, he would not have been accepted. For a long time he could not understand it. Only one explanation seemed possible to him, that the pride of the "insulted and fantastic woman" had reached such frenzy that she found it more pleasant to show her contempt once by refusing than to define her position forever and attain an unattainable grandeur. The worst of it was that Nastasya Filippovna had gained the upper hand terribly much. She also would not yield to mercenary interests, even if the interests were very great, and though she accepted the offered comfort, she lived very modestly and in those five years saved almost nothing. Afanasy Ivanovich risked another very clever means of breaking his fetters: he began inconspicuously and artfully to tempt her, being skillfully aided, with various ideal temptations; but the incarnate ideals—princes, hussars, embassy secretaries, poets, novelists, even socialists—nothing made any impression on Nastasya Filippovna, as if she had a stone in place of a heart, and her feeling had dried up and died out once and for all. She lived a largely solitary life, read, even studied, liked music. She had very few acquaintances; she kept company with some poor and ridiculous wives of officials, knew two actresses, some old women, was very fond of the numerous family of a certain respectable teacher, and this family was very fond of her and received her with pleasure. In the evening she quite often had gatherings of five or six acquaintances, not more. Totsky came very often and punctually. More recently General Epanchin, not without difficulty, had made Nastasya Filippovna's acquaintance. At the same time, quite easily and without any difficulty, a young clerk named Ferdyshchenko had made her acquaintance—a very indecent and salacious buffoon, with a pretense to gaiety and a penchant for drink. She was also acquainted with a strange young man by the name of Ptitsyn, modest, neat, and sleek, who had risen from destitution and become a moneylender. Gavrila Ardalionovich, too, finally made her acquaintance . . . It ended with Nastasya Filippovna acquiring a strange fame: everyone knew of her beauty, but only that; no one had anything to boast of, no one had anything to tell. This reputation, her cultivation, elegant manners, wit—all this finally confirmed Afanasy Ivanovich in a certain plan. And it was at this moment that General Epanchin himself began to take such an active and great part in the story.

When Totsky so courteously turned to him for friendly advice concerning one of his daughters, he at once, in the noblest fashion, made a most full and candid confession. He revealed that he had already resolved to *stop at nothing* to gain his freedom; that he would not be at peace even if Nastasya Filippovna herself declared to him that henceforth she would leave him entirely alone; that words were not enough for him, and he wanted the fullest guarantees. They came to an understanding and decided to act together. At first they determined to try the gentlest ways and to touch, so to speak, only on "the noble strings of the heart." They both went to Nastasya Filippovna, and Totsky began straight off with the unbearable horror of his position; he blamed himself for everything; he said frankly that he was unable to repent of his initial behavior with her, because he was an inveterate sensualist and not in control of himself, but that now he wanted to marry, and the whole fate of this most highly respectable and society marriage was in her hands; in short, that he placed all his hopes in her noble heart. Then General Epanchin began to speak in his quality as father, and spoke reasonably, avoiding emotion, mentioning only that he fully recognized her right to decide Afanasy Ivanovich's fate, deftly displaying his own humility, pointing out that the fate of his daughter, and perhaps of his two other daughters, now depended on her decision. To Nastasya Filippovna's question: "Precisely what did they want of her?"—Totsky, with the same perfectly naked candor, admitted to her that he had been so frightened five years ago that even now he could not be entirely at peace until Nastasya Filippovna herself had married someone. He added at once that this request would, of course, be absurd on his part, if he did not have some grounds in this regard. He had noted very well and had positive knowledge that a young man of very good name, and living in a most worthy family, Gavrila Ardalionovich Ivolgin, whom she knew and received in her house, had long loved her with all the force of passion and would certainly give half his life just for the hope of obtaining her sympathy. Gavrila Ardalionovich himself had confessed it to him, Afanasy Ivanovich, long ago, in a friendly way and out of the purity of his young heart, and it had long been known to Ivan Fyodorovich, the young man's benefactor. Finally, if he was not mistaken, Nastasya Filippovna herself had known of the young man's love for a long time, and it even seemed to him that she looked indulgently upon that love. Of course, it was hardest for him of all people to speak of it. But if Nastasya Filippovna would allow him, Totsky, apart from egoism and the desire to arrange his own lot, to wish her at least some good as well, she would understand that he had long found it strange and even painful to contemplate her solitude: that here there was only uncertain darkness, total disbelief in the renewal of life, which could so beautifully resurrect in love and a family, and thereby acquire a new purpose; that here were ruined abilities, perhaps brilliant ones, a voluntary reveling in her own sorrow, in short, even some sort of romanticism unworthy both of Nastasya Filippovna's common sense and of her noble heart. After repeating once again that it was harder for him to speak than for anyone else, he ended by saying that he could not give up the hope that Nastasya Filippovna would not reply to him with contempt if he expressed his sincere wish to secure her lot in the future and offer her the sum of seventy-five thousand roubles. He added by way of clarification that in any case this sum had already been allotted to her in his will; in short, that this was in no way a compensation of any sort . . . and that, finally, why not allow and excuse in him the human wish to unburden his conscience at least in some way, and so on and so forth—all that is usually said on the subject in such cases. Afanasy Ivanovich spoke long and eloquently, having appended, in passing so to speak, the very curious piece of information that he was now mentioning the seventy-five thousand for the first time and that no one knew of it, not even Ivan Fyodorovich himself, who was sitting right there; in short, *no one* knew.

Nastasya Filippovna's answer amazed the two friends.

Not only was there not the slightest trace to be observed in her of the former mockery, the former hostility and hatred, the former laughter, the mere recollection of which sent a chill down Totsky's spine, but, on the contrary, she seemed glad that she could finally speak with someone in an open and friendly way. She admitted that she herself had long wanted to ask for some friendly advice, that only pride had prevented her, but that now, since the ice had been broken, nothing could be better. At first with a sad smile, then with gay and brisk laughter, she confessed that the previous storm would in any case not be repeated; that she had long ago partly changed her view of things, and though she had not changed in her heart, she was still bound to allow for many things as accomplished facts; what was done was done, what was past was past, so that she even found it strange that Afanasy Ivanovich could go on being so frightened. Here she turned to Ivan Fyodorovich and, with a look of the profoundest respect, told him that she had long since heard a great deal about his daughters and was long accustomed to having a profound and sincere respect for them. The thought alone that she might be of at least some use to them would for her be a cause of happiness and pride. It was true that she now felt oppressed and bored, very bored; Afanasy Ivanovich had divined her dreams; she would like to resurrect, if not in love, then in a family, with the consciousness of a new purpose; but of Gavrila Ardalionovich she could say almost nothing. True, he seemed to love her; she felt that she herself might come to love him, if she could trust in the firmness of his attachment; but, even if sincere, he was very young; it was hard to decide here. Incidentally, she liked most of all the fact that he worked, toiled, and supported the whole family by himself. She had heard that he was an energetic and proud man, that he wanted a career, wanted to make his way. She had also heard that Nina Alexandrovna Ivolgin, Gavrila Ardalionovich's mother, was an excellent and highly estimable woman; that his sister, Varvara Ardalionovna, was a very remarkable and energetic girl; she had heard a lot about her from Ptitsyn. She had heard that they endured their misfortunes cheerfully; she wished very much to make their acquaintance, but the question was whether they would welcome her into their family. In general, she had nothing to say against the possibility of this marriage, but there was a great need to think it over; she did not wish to be rushed. Concerning the seventy-five thousand—Afanasy Ivanovich need not have been so embarrassed to speak of it. She understood the value of money and, of course, would take it. She thanked Afanasy Ivanovich for his delicacy, for not having mentioned it even to the general, let alone to Gavrila

Ardalionovich, but anyhow, why should he not also know about it beforehand? She had no need to be ashamed of this money on entering their family. In any case, she had no intention of apologizing to anyone for anything, and wished that to be known. She would not marry Gavrila Ardalionovich until she was sure that neither he nor his family had any hidden thoughts concerning her. In any case, she did not consider herself guilty of anything, and Gavrila Ardalionovich had better learn on what terms she had been living all those years in Petersburg, in what relations with Afanasy Ivanovich, and how much money she had saved. Finally, if she did accept the capital now, it was not at all as payment for her maidenly dishonor, for which she was not to blame, but simply as a recompense for her maimed life.

By the end she even became so excited and irritated as she was saying it all (which, incidentally, was quite natural) that General Epanchin was very pleased and considered the matter concluded; but the once frightened Totsky did not quite believe her even now and feared for a long time that here, too, there might be a serpent among the flowers.[18] The negotiations nevertheless began; the point on which the two friends' whole maneuver was based—namely, the possibility of Nastasya Filippovna being attracted to Ganya—gradually began to take shape and justify itself, so that even Totsky began to believe at times in the possibility of success. Meanwhile Nastasya Filippovna had a talk with Ganya: very few words were spoken, as if her chastity suffered from it. She admitted, however, and allowed him his love, but said insistently that she did not want to hamper herself in any way; that until the wedding itself (if the wedding took place) she reserved for herself the right to say no, even in the very last hour; exactly the same right was granted to Ganya. Soon Ganya learned positively, by an obliging chance, that the hostility of his whole family towards this marriage and towards Nastasya Filippovna personally, which had manifested itself in scenes at home, was already known to Nastasya Filippovna in great detail; she had not mentioned it to him, though he expected it daily. However, it would be possible to tell much more out of all the stories and circumstances that surfaced on the occasion of this engagement and its negotiations; but we have run ahead of ourselves as it is, especially since some of these circumstances appeared only as very vague rumors. For instance, Totsky was supposed to have learned somewhere that Nastasya Filippovna, in secret from everyone, had entered into some sort of vague relations with the

Epanchin girls—a perfectly incredible rumor. But another rumor he involuntarily believed and feared to the point of nightmare: he had heard for certain that Nastasya Filippovna was supposedly aware in the highest degree that Ganya was marrying only for money, that Ganya's soul was dark, greedy, impatient, envious, and boundlessly vain, out of all proportion to anything; that, although Ganya had indeed tried passionately to win Nastasya Filippovna over before, now that the two friends had decided to exploit that passion, which had begun to be mutual, for their own advantage, and to buy Ganya by selling him Nastasya Filippovna as a lawful wife, he had begun to hate her like his own nightmare. It was as if passion and hatred strangely came together in his soul, and though, after painful hesitations, he finally consented to marry "the nasty woman," in his soul he swore to take bitter revenge on her for it and to "give it to her" later, as he supposedly put it. Nastasya Filippovna supposedly knew all about it and was secretly preparing something. Totsky was so afraid that he even stopped telling his worries to Epanchin; but there were moments when, being a weak man, he would decidedly feel heartened again and his spirits would quickly rise: he felt exceedingly heartened, for instance, when Nastasya Filippovna at last gave the two friends her word that on the evening of her birthday she would speak her final word. On the other hand, a most strange and incredible rumor concerning the esteemed Ivan Fyodorovich himself was, alas! proving more and more true.

Here at first sight everything seemed utterly wild. It was hard to believe that Ivan Fyodorovich, in his venerable old age, with his excellent intelligence and positive knowledge of life, and so on and so forth, should be tempted by Nastasya Filippovna—and that, supposedly, to such an extent that the caprice almost resembled passion. Where he placed his hopes in this case is hard to imagine; perhaps even in the assistance of Ganya himself. Totsky at least suspected something of the sort, suspected the existence of some sort of almost silent agreement, based on mutual understanding, between the general and Ganya. As is known, however, a man too carried away by passion, especially if he is of a certain age, becomes completely blind and is ready to suspect hope where there is no hope at all; moreover, he takes leave of his senses and acts like a foolish child, though he be of the most palatial mind. It was known that for Nastasya Filippovna's birthday the general had prepared his own present of an astonishing string of pearls, which had cost an enormous sum, and was very concerned about this present, though he knew that Nastasya Filippovna was an unmercenary woman. The day before Nastasya Filippovna's birthday he was as if in a fever, though he skillfully concealed it. It was precisely these pearls that Mrs. Epanchin had heard about. True, Elizaveta Prokofyevna had long ago begun to experience her husband's frivolity and was somewhat used to it; but it was impossible to overlook such an occasion: the rumor about the pearls interested her exceedingly. The general had perceived it just in time; certain little words had already been uttered the day before; he anticipated a major confrontation and was afraid of it. That was why he was terribly reluctant, on the morning on which we began our story, to go and have lunch in the bosom of his family. Before the prince's arrival, he had resolved to use the excuse that he was busy and get out of it. To get out, for the general, sometimes simply meant to get away. He wanted to gain at least that one day and, above all, that evening, without any unpleasantnesses. And suddenly the prince came along so opportunely. "As if sent by God!" the general thought to himself as he entered his wife's rooms.

V

THE GENERAL'S WIFE was jealous of her origins. Imagine her feelings when she was told, directly and without preliminaries, that this Prince Myshkin, the last of their line, whom she had already heard something about, was no more than a pathetic idiot and nearly destitute, and that he took beggar's alms. The general was precisely after that effect, in order to draw her interest all at once and somehow turn everything in another direction.

In extreme cases his wife usually rolled her eyes out exceedingly and, with her body thrown slightly back, stared vaguely ahead of her without saying a word. She was a tall, lean woman, of the same age as her husband, with much gray in her dark but still thick hair, a somewhat hooked nose, hollow yellow cheeks, and thin, sunken lips. Her forehead was high but narrow; her gray, rather large eyes sometimes had a most unexpected expression. She had once had the weakness of believing that her gaze produced an extraordinary effect; that conviction remained indelible in her.

"Receive him? You say receive him now, this minute?" and the general's wife rolled her eyes out with all her might at Ivan Fyodorovich as he fidgeted before her.

"Oh, in that respect you needn't stand on ceremony, my friend, provided you wish to see him," the general hastened to explain. "A perfect child, and even quite pathetic; he has fits of some illness; he's just come from Switzerland, straight from the train, strangely dressed, in some German fashion, and besides without a penny, literally; he's all but weeping. I gave him twenty-five roubles and want to obtain some scrivener's post for him in the chancellery. And you, *mesdames*, I ask to give him something to eat, because he also seems to be hungry . . ."

"You astonish me," Mrs. Epanchin went on as before. "Hungry, and some sort of fits! What fits?"

"Oh, they don't occur too often, and besides, he's almost like a child, though he's cultivated. I'd like to ask you, *mesdames*," he again turned to his daughters, "to give him an examination; it would be good, after all, to know what he's able to do."

"An ex-am-i-na-tion?" Mrs. Epanchin drew out and, in deep amazement, again began to roll her eyes from her daughters to her husband and back.

"Ah, my friend, don't take it in that sense . . . however, as you wish; I had in mind to be nice to him and receive him in our house, because it's almost a good deed."

"In our house? From Switzerland?!"

"Switzerland is no hindrance. But anyhow, I repeat, it's as you wish. I suggested it, first, because he's your namesake and maybe even a relation, and second, he doesn't know where to lay his head. I even thought you might be somewhat interested, because, after all, he's of the same family."

"Of course, *maman*, if we needn't stand on ceremony with him; besides, he's hungry after the journey, why not give him something to eat, if he doesn't know where to go?" said the eldest daughter, Alexandra.

"And a perfect child besides, we can play blindman's buff with him."

"Play blindman's buff? In what sense?"

"Oh, *maman*, please stop pretending," Aglaya interfered vexedly.

The middle daughter, Adelaida, much given to laughter, could not help herself and burst out laughing.

"Send for him, *papa*, *maman* allows it," Aglaya decided. The general rang and sent for the prince.

"But be sure a napkin is tied around his neck when he sits at the table," Mrs. Epanchin decided. "Send for Fyodor, or let Mavra

. . . so as to stand behind his chair and tend to him while he eats. Is he at least quiet during his fits? Does he gesticulate?"

"On the contrary, he's very well brought up and has wonderful manners. A bit too simple at times . . . But here he is! Allow me to introduce Prince Myshkin, the last of the line, a namesake and maybe even a relation, receive him, be nice to him. They'll have lunch now, Prince, do them the honor . . . And I, forgive me, I'm late, I must hurry . . ."

"We know where you're hurrying to," Mrs. Epanchin said imposingly.

"I must hurry, I must hurry, my friend, I'm late! Give him your albums,[19] *mesdames*, let him write something for you, he's a rare calligrapher! A talent! He did such a piece of old handwriting for me: 'The hegumen Pafnuty here sets his hand to it . . .' Well, good-bye."

"Pafnuty? Hegumen? Wait, wait, where are you going? What Pafnuty?" Mrs. Epanchin cried with insistent vexation and almost anxiously to her fleeing husband.

"Yes, yes, my friend, there was such a hegumen in the old days . . . and I'm off to the count's, he's been waiting, waiting a long time, and, above all, it was he who made the appointment . . . Good-bye, Prince!"

The general withdrew with quick steps.

"I know which count that is!" Elizaveta Prokofyevna said sharply and turned her gaze irritably on the prince. "What was it!" she began, trying squeamishly and vexedly to recall. "What was it! Ah, yes. Well, what about this hegumen?"

"*Maman*," Alexandra began, and Aglaya even stamped her little foot.

"Don't interrupt me, Alexandra Ivanovna," Mrs. Epanchin rapped out to her, "I also want to know. Sit down here, Prince, in this chair, facing me—no, here, move closer to the sun, to the light, so that I can see. Well, what about this hegumen?"

"Hegumen Pafnuty," the prince replied attentively and seriously.

"Pafnuty? That's interesting. Well, who was he?"

Mrs. Epanchin asked impatiently, quickly, sharply, not taking her eyes off the prince, and when he answered, she nodded her head after each word he said.

"The hegumen Pafnuty, of the fourteenth century," the prince began. "He was the head of a hermitage on the Volga, in what is now Kostroma province. He was known for his holy life. He went to the Horde,[20] helped to arrange some affairs of that time, and signed his name to a certain document, and I saw a copy of that signature. I liked the handwriting and learned it. Today, when the general wanted to see how I can write, in order to find a post for me, I wrote several phrases in various scripts, and among them 'The hegumen Pafnuty here sets his hand to it' in the hegumen Pafnuty's own handwriting. The general liked it very much, and he remembered it just now."

"Aglaya," said Mrs. Epanchin, "remember: Pafnuty, or better write it down, because I always forget. However, I thought it would be more interesting. Where is this signature?"

"I think it's still in the general's office, on the desk."

"Send at once and fetch it."

"I could just as well write it again for you, if you like."

"Of course, *maman*," said Alexandra, "and now we'd better have lunch; we're hungry."

"Well, so," Mrs. Epanchin decided. "Come, Prince, are you very hungry?"

"Yes, at the moment I'm very hungry and I thank you very much."

"It's very good that you're polite, and I note that you're not at all such an . . . odd man as we were told. Come. Sit down here, across from me," she bustled about, getting the prince seated, when they came to the dining room, "I want to look at you. Alexandra, Adelaida, offer the prince something. Isn't it true that he's not all that . . . sick? Maybe the napkin isn't necessary . . . Do they tie a napkin around your neck when you eat, Prince?"

"Before, when I was about seven, I think they did, but now I usually put my napkin on my knees when I eat."

"So you should. And your fits?"

"Fits?" the prince was slightly surprised. "I have fits rather rarely now. Though, I don't know, they say the climate here will be bad for me."

"He speaks well," Mrs. Epanchin observed, turning to her daughters and continuing to nod her head after each word the prince said. "I didn't even expect it. So it was all nonsense and lies, as usual. Eat, Prince, and go on with your story: where were you born and brought up? I want to know everything; you interest me exceedingly."

The prince thanked her and, eating with great appetite, again began to tell everything he had already told more than once that morning. Mrs. Epanchin was becoming more and more pleased.

The girls also listened rather attentively. They discussed families; the prince turned out to know his genealogy rather well, but hard as they searched, they could find almost no connection between him and Mrs. Epanchin. There might have been some distant relation between their grandmothers and grandfathers. Mrs. Epanchin especially liked this dry subject, since she hardly ever had the chance to talk about her genealogy, despite all her wishes, so that she even got up from the table in an excited state of mind.

"Let's all go to our gathering room," she said, "and have coffee served there. We have this common room here," she said to the prince, leading him out. "It's simply my small drawing room, where we gather when we're by ourselves, and each of us does her own thing: Alexandra, this one, my eldest daughter, plays the piano, or reads, or sews; Adelaida paints landscapes and portraits (and never can finish anything); and Aglaya sits and does nothing. I'm also hopeless at handwork: nothing comes out right. Well, here we are; sit down there, Prince, by the fireplace, and tell us something. I want to know how you tell a story. I want to make completely sure, so that when I see old Princess Belokonsky, I can tell her all about you. I want them all to become interested in you, too. Well, speak then."

"But, *maman*, it's very strange to tell anything that way," observed Adelaida, who meanwhile had straightened her easel, taken her brushes and palette, and started working on a landscape begun long ago, copied from a print. Alexandra and Aglaya sat down together on a small sofa, folded their arms, and prepared to listen to the conversation. The prince noticed that special attention was turned on him from all sides.

"I wouldn't tell anything, if I were ordered to like that," observed Aglaya.

"Why? What's so strange about it? Why shouldn't he tell a story? He has a tongue. I want to see if he knows how to speak. Well, about anything. Tell me how you liked Switzerland, your first impressions. You'll see, he's going to begin now, and begin beautifully."

"The impression was a strong one . . ." the prince began.

"There," the impatient Lizaveta Prokofyevna picked up, turning to her daughters, "he's begun."

"Give him a chance to speak at least, *maman*," Alexandra stopped her. "This prince may be a great rogue and not an idiot at all," she whispered to Aglaya.

"He surely is, I saw it long ago," answered Aglaya. "And it's mean of him to play a role. What does he want to gain by it?"

"The first impression was a very strong one," the prince repeated. "When they brought me from Russia, through various German towns, I only looked on silently and, I remember, I didn't even ask about anything. That was after a series of strong and painful fits of my illness, and whenever my illness worsened and I had several fits in a row, I always lapsed into a total stupor, lost my memory completely, and though my mind worked, the logical flow of thought was as if broken. I couldn't put more than two or three ideas together coherently. So it seems to me. But when the fits subsided, I became healthy and strong again, as I am now. I remember a feeling of unbearable sadness; I even wanted to weep; I was surprised and anxious all the time: it affected me terribly that it was all *foreign*—that much I understood. The foreign was killing me. I was completely awakened from that darkness, I remember, in the evening, in Basel, as we drove into Switzerland, and what roused me was the braying of an ass in the town market. The ass struck me terribly and for some reason I took an extraordinary liking to it, and at the same time it was as if everything cleared up in my head."

"An ass? That's strange," observed Mrs. Epanchin. "And yet there's nothing strange about it, some one of us may yet fall in love with an ass," she observed, looking wrathfully at the laughing girls. "It has happened in mythology.[21] Go on, Prince."

"Since then I've had a terrible fondness for asses. It's even some sort of sympathy in me. I began inquiring about them, because I'd never seen them before, and I became convinced at once that they're most useful animals, hardworking, strong, patient, cheap, enduring; and because of that ass I suddenly took a liking to the whole of Switzerland, so that my former sadness went away entirely."

"That's all very strange, but we can skip the ass; let's go on to some other subject. Why are you laughing, Aglaya? And you, Adelaida? The prince spoke beautifully about the ass. He saw it himself, and what have you ever seen? You haven't been abroad."

"I've seen an ass, *maman*," said Adelaida.

"And I've heard one," Aglaya picked up. The three girls laughed again. The prince laughed with them.

"That's very naughty of you," observed Mrs. Epanchin. "You must forgive them, Prince, they really are kind. I'm eternally scolding them, but I love them. They're flighty, frivolous, mad."

"But why?" the prince laughed. "In their place I wouldn't have missed the chance either. But all the same I stand up for the ass: an ass is a kind and useful fellow."

"And are you kind, Prince? I ask out of curiosity," Mrs. Epanchin asked.

They all laughed again.

"Again that accursed ass turns up! I wasn't even thinking of it!" Mrs. Epanchin cried. "Please believe me, Prince, I wasn't . . ."

"Hinting? Oh, I believe you, without question!"

And the prince never stopped laughing.

"It's very good that you laugh. I see you're a most kind young man," said Mrs. Epanchin.

"Sometimes I'm not," replied the prince.

"And I am kind," Mrs. Epanchin put in unexpectedly, "I'm always kind, if you wish, and that is my only failing, because one should not always be kind. I'm often very angry, with these ones here, with Ivan Fyodorovich especially, but the trouble is that I'm kindest when I'm angry. Today, before you came, I was angry and pretended I didn't and couldn't understand anything. That happens to me—like a child. Aglaya taught me a lesson; I thank you, Aglaya. Anyhow, it's all nonsense. I'm still not as stupid as I seem and as my daughters would have me appear. I have a strong character and am not very shy. Anyhow, I don't say it spitefully. Come here, Aglaya, kiss me. Well . . . enough sentiment," she observed, when Aglaya kissed her with feeling on the lips and hand. "Go on, Prince. Perhaps you'll remember something more interesting than the ass."

"I still don't understand how it's possible to tell things just like that," Adelaida observed again. "I wouldn't find anything to say."

"But the prince would, because the prince is extremely intelligent and at least ten times more intelligent than you, or maybe twelve times. I hope you'll feel something after that. Prove it to them, Prince, go on. We can indeed finally get past that ass. Well, so, besides the ass, what did you see abroad?"

"That was intelligent about the ass, too," observed Alexandra. "The prince spoke very interestingly about the case of his illness, and how he came to like everything because of one external push. It has always been interesting to me, how people go out of their minds and then recover again. Especially if it happens suddenly."

"Isn't it true? Isn't it true?" Mrs. Epanchin heaved herself up. "I see you, too, can sometimes be intelligent. Well, enough laughing! You stopped, I believe, at nature in Switzerland, Prince. Well?"

"We came to Lucerne, and I was taken across the lake. I felt how good it was, but I also felt terribly oppressed," said the prince.

"Why?" asked Alexandra.

"I don't understand why. I always feel oppressed and uneasy when I look at such nature for the first time—both good and uneasy. Anyhow, that was all while I was still sick."

"Ah, no, I've always wanted very much to see it," said Adelaida. "I don't understand why we never go abroad. For two years I've been trying to find a subject for a picture:

East and South have long since been portrayed . . .[22]

Find me a subject for a picture, Prince."

"I don't understand anything about it. It seems to me you just look and paint."

"I don't know how to look."

"Why are you talking in riddles? I don't understand a thing!" Mrs. Epanchin interrupted. "What do you mean, you don't know how to look? You have eyes, so look. If you don't know how to look here, you won't learn abroad. Better tell us how you looked yourself, Prince."

"Yes, that would be better," Adelaida added. "The prince did learn to look abroad."

"I don't know. My health simply improved there; I don't know if I learned to look. Anyhow, I was very happy almost the whole time."

"Happy! You know how to be happy?" Aglaya cried out. "Then how can you say you didn't learn to look? You should teach us."

"Teach us, please," Adelaida laughed.

"I can't teach you anything," the prince was laughing, too. "I spent almost all my time abroad living in a Swiss village; occasionally I went somewhere not far away; what can I teach you? At first I was simply not bored; I started to recover quickly; then every day became dear to me, and the dearer as time went on, so that I began to notice it. I went to bed very content, and got up happier still. But why all that—it's rather hard to say."

"So you didn't want to go anywhere, you had no urge to go anywhere?" asked Alexandra.

"At first, at the very first, yes, I did have an urge, and I would fall into great restlessness. I kept thinking about how I was going to live; I wanted to test my fate, I became restless especially at certain moments. You know, there are such moments, especially in solitude. We had a waterfall there, not a big one, it fell from high up the mountain in a very thin thread, almost perpendicular— white, noisy, foamy; it fell from a great height, but it seemed low; it was half a mile away, but it seemed only fifty steps. I liked listening to the noise of it at night; and at those moments I'd sometimes get very restless. Also at noon sometimes, when I'd wander off somewhere into the mountains, stand alone halfway up a mountain, with pines all around, old, big, resinous; up on a cliff there's an old, ruined medieval castle, our little village is far down, barely visible; the sun is bright, the sky blue, the silence terrible. Then there would come a call to go somewhere, and it always seemed to me that if I walked straight ahead, and kept on for a long, long time, and went beyond that line where sky and earth meet, the whole answer would be there, and at once I'd see a new life, a thousand times stronger and noisier than ours; I kept dreaming of a big city like Naples, where it was all palaces, noise, clatter, life . . . I dreamed about all kinds of things! And then it seemed to me that in prison, too, you could find an immense life."

"That last praiseworthy thought I read in my *Reader* when I was twelve years old," said Aglaya.

"It's all philosophy," observed Adelaida. "You're a philosopher and have come to teach us."

"Maybe you're even right," the prince smiled, "perhaps I really am a philosopher, and, who knows, maybe I actually do have a thought of teaching . . . It may be so; truly it may."

"And your philosophy is exactly the same as Evlampia Niko-lavna's," Aglaya picked up again. "She's an official's wife, a widow, she calls on us, a sort of sponger. Her whole purpose in life is cheapness; only to live as cheaply as possible; the only thing she talks about is kopecks—and, mind you, she has money, she's a sly fox. Your immense life in prison is exactly the same, and maybe also your four-year happiness in the village, for which you sold your city of Naples, and not without profit, it seems, though it was only a matter of kopecks."

"Concerning life in prison there may be disagreement," said the prince. "I heard one story from a man who spent twelve years in prison; he was one of the patients being treated by my professor. He had fits, he was sometimes restless, wept, and once even tried to kill himself. His life in prison had been very sad, I assure you, but certainly worth more than a kopeck. And the only acquaintances he had were a spider and a little tree that had grown up under his window . . . But I'd better tell you about another encounter I had last year with a certain man. Here there was one very strange circumstance—strange because, in fact, such chances very rarely occur. This man had once been led to a scaffold, along with others, and a sentence of death by firing squad was read out to him, for a political crime. After about twenty minutes a pardon was read out to him, and he was given a lesser degree of punishment; nevertheless, for the space between the two sentences, for twenty minutes, or a quarter of an hour at the least, he lived under the certain conviction that in a few minutes he would suddenly die. I wanted terribly much to listen when he sometimes recalled his impressions of it, and several times I began questioning him further. He remembered everything with extraordinary clarity and used to say he would never forget anything from those minutes. About twenty paces from the scaffold, around which people and soldiers were standing, three posts had been dug into the ground, since there were several criminals. The first three were led to the posts, tied to them, dressed in death robes (long white smocks), and had long white caps pulled down over their eyes so that they would not see the guns; then a squad of several soldiers lined up facing each post. My acquaintance was eighth in line, which meant he would go to the posts in the third round. A priest went up to each of them with a cross. Consequently, he had about five minutes left to live, not more. He said those five minutes seemed like an endless time to him, an enormous wealth. It seemed to him that in those five minutes he would live so many lives that there was no point yet in thinking about his last moment, so that he even made various arrangements: he reckoned up the time for bidding his comrades farewell and allotted two minutes to that, then allotted two more minutes to thinking about himself for the last time, and then to looking around for the last time. He remembered very well that he made precisely those three arrangements, and reckoned them up in precisely that way. He was dying at the age of twenty-seven, healthy and strong; bidding farewell to his comrades, he remembered asking one of them a rather irrelevant question and even being very interested in the answer. Then, after he had bidden his comrades farewell, the two minutes came that he had allotted to *thinking about himself*. He knew beforehand what he was going to think about: he kept wanting to picture to himself as quickly and vividly as possible how it could be like this: now he exists and lives, and in three minutes there would be *something*, some person or thing—but who? and where? He wanted to resolve it all in those two minutes! There was a church nearby, and the top of the cathedral with its gilded dome shone in the bright sun. He remembered gazing with terrible fixity at that dome and the rays shining from it: it seemed to him that those rays were his new nature and in three minutes he would somehow merge with them . . . The ignorance of and loathing for this new thing that would be and would come presently were terrible; yet he said that nothing was more oppressive for him at that moment than the constant thought: 'What if I were not to die! What if life were given back to me—what infinity! And it would all be mine! Then I'd turn each minute into a whole age, I'd lose nothing, I'd reckon up every minute separately, I'd let nothing be wasted!' He said that in the end this thought turned into such anger in him that he wished they would hurry up and shoot him."

The prince suddenly fell silent; everyone waited for him to go on and arrive at a conclusion.

"Have you finished?" asked Aglaya.

"What? Yes," said the prince, coming out of a momentary pensiveness.

"Why did you tell us about that?"

"Just . . . I remembered . . . to make conversation . . ."

"You're very fragmentary," observed Alexandra. "You probably wanted to conclude, Prince, that there's not a single moment that can be valued in kopecks, and that five minutes are sometimes dearer than a treasure. That is all very praiseworthy, but, forgive me, what ever happened to the friend who told you all those horrors . . . his punishment was changed, which means he was granted that 'infinite life.' Well, what did he do with so much wealth afterwards? Did he live 'reckoning up' every minute?"

"Oh, no, he told me himself—I asked him about it—he didn't live that way at all and lost many, many minutes."

"Well, so, there's experience for you, so it's impossible to live really 'keeping a reckoning.' There's always some reason why it's impossible."

"Yes, for some reason it's impossible," the prince repeated. "I thought so myself . . . But still it's somehow hard to believe . . ."

"That is, you think you can live more intelligently than everyone else?" asked Aglaya.

"Yes, I've sometimes thought so."

"And you still do?"

"And . . . I still do," the prince replied, looking at Aglaya, as before, with a quiet and even timid smile; but he immediately laughed again and looked at her merrily.

"How modest!" said Aglaya, almost vexed.

"But how brave you all are, though. You're laughing, but I was so struck by everything in his story that I dreamed about it later, precisely about those five minutes . . ."

Once again he looked around keenly and gravely at his listeners.

"You're not angry with me for something?" he asked suddenly, as if in perplexity, and yet looking straight into their eyes.

"For what?" the three girls cried in astonishment.

"That it's as if I keep teaching . . ."

They all laughed.

"If you're angry, don't be," he said. "I myself know that I've lived less than others and understand less about life than anyone. Maybe I sometimes speak very strangely . . ."

And he became decidedly embarrassed.

"Since you say you were happy, it means you lived more, not less; why do you pretend and apologize?" Aglaya began sternly and carpingly. "And please don't worry about lecturing us, there's nothing there to make you triumphant. With your quietism[23] one could fill a hundred years of life with happiness. Show you an execution or show you a little finger, you'll draw an equally praise-worthy idea from both and be left feeling pleased besides. It's a way to live."

"Why you're so angry I don't understand," picked up Mrs. Epanchin, who had long been watching the faces of the speakers, "and what you're talking about I also cannot understand. What little finger, what is this nonsense? The prince speaks beautifully, only a little sadly. Why do you discourage him? He laughed at the beginning, but now he's quite crestfallen."

"Never mind, *maman*. But it's a pity you haven't seen an execution, there's one thing I'd ask you."

"I have seen an execution," the prince replied.

"You have?" cried Aglaya. "I must have guessed it! That crowns the whole thing. If you have, how can you say you lived happily the whole time? Well, isn't it true what I told you?"

"Were there executions in your village?" asked Adelaida.

"I saw it in Lyons, I went there with Schneider, he took me. I arrived and happened right on to it."

"So, what, did you like it very much? Was it very instructive? Useful?" Aglaya went on asking.

"I didn't like it at all, and I was a bit ill afterwards, but I confess I watched as if I was riveted to it, I couldn't tear my eyes away."

"I, too, would be unable to tear my eyes away," said Aglaya.

"They dislike it very much there when women come to watch, and even write about these women afterwards in the newspapers."

"Meaning that, since they find it's no business for women, they want to say by that (and thus justify) that it is a business for men. I congratulate them for their logic. And you think the same way, of course?"

"Tell us about the execution," Adelaida interrupted.

"I'd be very reluctant to now . . ." the prince became confused and seemed to frown.

"It looks as if you begrudge telling us," Aglaya needled him.

"No, it's because I already told about that same execution earlier."

"Whom did you tell?"

"Your valet, while I was waiting . . ."

"What valet?" came from all sides.

"The one who sits in the anteroom, with gray hair and a reddish face. I was sitting in the anteroom waiting to see Ivan Fyodorovich."

"That's odd," observed Mrs. Epanchin.

"The prince is a democrat," Aglaya snapped. "Well, if you told it to Alexei, you can't refuse us."

"I absolutely want to hear it," repeated Adelaida.

"Earlier, in fact," the prince turned to her, becoming somewhat animated again (it seemed he became animated very quickly and trustingly), "in fact it occurred to me, when you asked me for a subject for a picture, to give you this subject: to portray the face of a condemned man a minute before the stroke of the guillotine, when he's still standing on the scaffold, before he lies down on the plank."

"What? Just the face?" asked Adelaida. "That would be a strange subject, and what sort of picture would it make?"

"I don't know, why not?" the prince insisted warmly. "I recently saw a picture like that in Basel.[24] I'd like very much to tell you . . . Someday I'll tell you about it . . . it struck me greatly."

"Be sure to tell us about the Basel picture later," said Adelaida, "but now explain to me about the picture of this execution. Can you say how you imagine it yourself? How should the face be portrayed? As just a face? What sort of face?"

"It was exactly one minute before his death," the prince began with perfect readiness, carried away by his recollection, and apparently forgetting at once about everything else, "the very moment when he had climbed the little stairway and just stepped onto the scaffold. He glanced in my direction; I looked at his face and understood everything . . . But how can one talk about it! I'd be terribly, terribly glad if you or someone else could portray that! Better if it were you! I thought then that it would be a useful painting. You know, here you have to imagine everything that went before, everything, everything. He lived in prison and expected it would be at least another week till the execution; he somehow calculated the time for the usual formalities, that the paper still had to go somewhere and would only be ready in a week. And then suddenly for some reason the procedure was shortened. At five o'clock in the morning he was asleep. It was the end of October; at five o'clock it's still cold and dark. The prison warden came in quietly, with some guards, and cautiously touched his shoulder. The man sat up, leaned on his elbow—saw a light: 'What's this?' 'The execution's at ten.' Still sleepy, he didn't believe it, started objecting that the paper would be ready in a week, but when he woke up completely, he stopped arguing and fell silent—so they described it—then said: 'All the same, it's hard so suddenly . . .' and fell silent again, and wouldn't say anything after that. Then three or four hours were spent on the well-known things: the priest, breakfast, for which he was given wine, coffee, and beef (now, isn't that a mockery? You'd think it was very cruel, yet, on the other hand, by God, these innocent people do it in purity of heart and are sure of their loving kindness), then the toilette (do you know what a criminal's toilette is?), and finally they drive him through the city to the scaffold . . . I think that here, too, while they're driving him, it seems to him that he still has an endless time to live. I imagine he probably thought on the way: 'It's still long, there are still three streets left to live; I'll get to the end of this one, then there's still that one, and the one after it, with the bakery on the right . . . it's still a long way to the bakery!' People, shouting, noise all around him, ten thousand faces, ten thousand pairs of eyes—all that must be endured, and above all the thought: 'There are ten thousand of them, and none of them is being executed, it's me they're executing!' Well, that's all the preliminaries. A little stairway leads up to the scaffold; there, facing the stairway, he suddenly burst into tears, and yet he was a strong and manly fellow and was said to be a great villain. A priest was

with him all the time, rode in the cart with him, and kept talking—
the man scarcely heard him: he'd begin to listen and after three
words lose all understanding. That's how it must have been. Finally,
he started up the stairway; his legs were bound, so he could only
take small steps. The priest, who must have been an intelligent man,
stopped talking and kept giving him the cross to kiss. At the foot
of the stairway he was very pale, but when he went up and stood on
the scaffold, he suddenly turned white as paper, absolutely white as
a sheet of writing paper. Probably his legs went weak and numb,
and he felt nauseous—as if something was pressing his throat, and
it was like a tickling—have you ever felt that when you were
frightened, or in very terrible moments, when you keep your reason
but it no longer has any power? It seems to me, for instance, that if
disaster is imminent, if the house is collapsing on you, you want
terribly much just to sit down, close your eyes, and wait—let come
what may! . . . It was here, when this weakness set in, that the
priest hurriedly and silently, with such a quick gesture, put the cross
suddenly right to his lips—a small silver cross with four points[25]—
and did it frequently, every minute. And the moment the cross
touched his lips, he opened his eyes and seemed to revive for a few
seconds, and his legs moved. He kissed the cross greedily, hurried
to kiss it, as if hurrying to grasp something extra, just in case, but
he was hardly conscious of anything religious at that moment. And
so it went till he reached the plank . . . It's strange that people rarely
faint in those last seconds! On the contrary, the head is terribly alive
and must be working hard, hard, hard, like an engine running; I
imagine various thoughts throbbing in it, all of them incomplete,
maybe even ridiculous, quite irrelevant thoughts: 'That gaping one
has a wart on his forehead . . . the executioner's bottom button is
rusty . . .' and meanwhile you know everything and remember
everything; there is this one point that can never be forgotten, and
you can't faint, and around it, around that point, everything goes
and turns. And to think that it will be so till the last quarter of a
second, when his head is already lying on the block, and he waits,
and . . . *knows*, and suddenly above him he hears the iron screech!
You're bound to hear it! If I were lying there, I'd listen on purpose
and hear it! It may be only one tenth of an instant, but you're bound
to hear it! And imagine, to this day they still argue that, as the head
is being cut off, it may know for a second that it has been cut off—
quite a notion! And what if it's five seconds! Portray the scaffold so
that only the last step is seen closely and clearly; the criminal has

stepped onto it: his head, his face white as paper, the priest offering him the cross, he greedily puts it to his blue lips and stares, and— *knows everything*. The cross and the head—there's the picture. The priest's face, the executioner, his two assistants, and a few heads and eyes below—all that could be painted as background, in a mist, as accessory . . . That's the sort of picture."

The prince fell silent and looked at them all.

"That, of course, is nothing like quietism," Alexandra said to herself.

"Well, now tell us how you were in love," said Adelaida.

The prince looked at her in surprise.

"Listen," Adelaida seemed to be hurrying, "you owe us the story about the Basel picture, but now I want to hear how you were in love. You were, don't deny it. Besides, as soon as you start telling about something, you stop being a philosopher."

"When you finish a story, you immediately feel ashamed of having told it," Aglaya suddenly observed. "Why is that?"

"This is quite stupid, finally," Mrs. Epanchin snapped, looking indignantly at Aglaya.

"Not clever," Alexandra agreed.

"Don't believe her, Prince," Mrs. Epanchin turned to him, "she does it on purpose out of some sort of spite; she hasn't been brought up so stupidly; don't think anything of their pestering you like this. They probably have something in mind, but they already love you. I know their faces."

"I know their faces, too," said the prince, giving special emphasis to his words.

"How is that?" Adelaida asked curiously.

"What do you know about our faces?" the other two also became curious.

But the prince was silent and serious; they all waited for his reply.

"I'll tell you later," he said quietly and seriously.

"You decidedly want to intrigue us," cried Aglaya. "And what solemnity!"

"Well, all right," Adelaida again began to hurry, "but if you're such an expert in faces, then surely you were also in love, which means I guessed right. Tell us about it."

"I wasn't in love," the prince replied as quietly and seriously, "I . . . was happy in a different way."

"How? In what way?"

"Very well, I'll tell you," the prince said, as if pondering deeply.

VI

"HERE YOU ALL ARE NOW," the prince began, "looking at me with such curiosity that if I don't satisfy it, you may well get angry with me. No, I'm joking," he quickly added with a smile. "There . . . there it was all children, and I was with children all the time, only with children. They were the children of that village, a whole band, who went to school. It wasn't I who taught them; oh, no, they had a schoolmaster there for that—Jules Thibaut; or perhaps I did teach them, but more just by being with them, and I spent all my four years that way. I didn't need anything else. I told them everything, I didn't hide anything from them. Their fathers and relations all got angry with me, because the children finally couldn't do without me and kept gathering around me, and the schoolmaster finally even became my worst enemy. I acquired many enemies there, and all because of the children. Even Schneider scolded me. And what were they so afraid of? A child can be told everything—everything. I was always struck by the thought of how poorly grown-ups know children, even fathers and mothers their own children. Nothing should be concealed from children on the pretext that they're little and it's too early for them to know. What a sad and unfortunate idea! And how well children themselves can see that their fathers consider them too little and unable to understand anything, while they understand everything. Grown-ups don't know that a child can give extremely important advice even in the most difficult matters. Oh, God! when this pretty little bird looks at you trustingly and happily, it's a shame for you to deceive it! I call them little birds because nothing in the world is better than a little bird. However, they all got angry with me in the village mainly for a certain occurrence . . . and Thibaut simply envied me. At first he kept shaking his head and wondering how it was that with me the children understood everything and with him almost nothing, and then he started laughing at me when I told him that neither of us would teach them anything, but they might still teach us. And how could he be jealous of me and slander me, when he himself lived with children! The soul is cured through children . . . There was a patient at Schneider's institution, a very unhappy man. His unhappiness was so terrible, there could hardly be the like of it. He was placed there to be treated for insanity.

In my opinion, he wasn't insane, he just suffered terribly—that was the whole of his illness. And if you knew what our children became for him in the end . . . But I'd better tell you about the patient later; now I'll tell you how it all started. The children disliked me at first. I was so big, I'm always so clumsy; I know I'm also bad-looking . . . finally, there was the fact that I was a foreigner. The children laughed at me at first, and then even began throwing stones at me, when they spied me kissing Marie. And I only kissed her once . . . No, don't laugh," the prince hastened to stop the smiles of his listeners. "There wasn't any love here. If you knew what an unfortunate being she was, you'd pity her as I did. She was from our village. Her mother was an old woman, and in her tiny, completely decrepit house, one of the two windows was partitioned off, with the permission of the village authorities she was allowed to sell laces, thread, tobacco, and soap from this window, all at the lowest prices, and that was her subsistence. She was ill, her legs were swollen, so she always sat in her place. Marie was her daughter, about twenty, weak and thin; she had been consumptive for a long time, but she kept going from house to house, hiring herself out by the day to do heavy work—scrubbing floors, washing laundry, sweeping yards, tending cattle. A French traveling salesman seduced her and took her away, but after a week he abandoned her on the road alone and quietly left. She came home, begging on the way, all dirty, ragged, her shoes torn; she had walked for a week, slept in the fields, and caught a bad cold; her feet were covered with sores, her hands swollen and chapped. She had never been pretty anyway; only her eyes were gentle, kind, innocent. She was terribly taciturn. Once, before then, she suddenly began to sing over her work, and I remember that everybody was surprised and started laughing: 'Marie's begun to sing! What? Marie's begun to sing!' And she was terribly abashed and kept silent forever after. People were still nice to her then, but when she came back sick and worn out, there was no compassion for her in anyone! How cruel they are about that! What harsh notions they have of it all! Her mother was the first to greet her with spite and contempt: 'You've dishonored me now.' She was the first to hold her up to disgrace: when they heard in the village that Marie had come back, everybody ran to look at her, and nearly the whole village came running to the old woman's cottage: old men, children, women, girls, everybody, in such a hustling, greedy crowd. Marie was lying on the floor at the old woman's feet, hungry,

ragged, weeping. When they all rushed in, she covered herself
with her disheveled hair and lay facedown on the floor like that.
Everybody around looked on her as if she were vermin; the old
men denounced and abused her, the young ones even laughed, the
women abused her, denounced her, looked at her with contempt,
as at some sort of spider. Her mother allowed it all; she herself sat
there nodding her head and approving. Her mother was already
very sick then and nearly dying; in fact, two months later she did
die; she knew she was dying, but even so she never thought of
being reconciled with her daughter till her dying day, never spoke
a single word to her, chased her out to sleep in the front hall, gave
her almost nothing to eat. She often had to soak her ailing legs in
warm water; Marie washed her legs every day and took care of her;
the woman accepted all her services silently and never said a kind
word to her. Marie endured it all, and later, when I became
acquainted with her, I noticed that she approved of it herself and
considered herself the lowest sort of creature. When the old woman
took to her bed, the old women of the village took turns looking
after her, as they do there. Then Marie was no longer given anything to eat; everybody in the village chased her away and nobody
even wanted to give her work as they used to. It was as if they all
spat on her, and the men even stopped considering her a woman,
such vile things they said to her. At times, very rarely, when they
got drunk on Sundays, they amused themselves by tossing coins to
her, like that, right on the ground; Marie silently picked them up.
She had begun to cough up blood by then. Finally her ragged
clothes turned into real shreds, so that she was ashamed to show
herself in the village; and she had gone barefoot ever since she
came back. It was then that the schoolchildren, the whole band—
there were over forty of them—began especially to mock her and
even threw mud at her. She had asked the cowherd to let her tend
the cows, but the cowherd had chased her away. Then she herself,
without permission, began going out with the herd for the whole
day, away from the house. As she was very useful to the cowherd
and he noticed it, he no longer chased her away and sometimes
even gave her the leftovers from his dinner, some cheese and bread.
He considered it great charity on his part. When her mother died,
the pastor saw no shame in disgracing Marie before all the people
in church. Marie stood behind the coffin, as she was, in her rags,
and wept. Many people came to see how she would weep and walk
behind the coffin; then the pastor—he was still a young man and

his whole ambition was to become a great preacher—turned to them all and pointed at Marie. 'Here is the one who caused this respected woman's death' (which wasn't true, because she had been sick for two years), 'here she stands before you and dares not look up, because she is marked by the finger of God; here she is, barefoot and in rags—an example to those who lose their virtue! Who is she? She is her own daughter!' and more in the same vein. And imagine, almost everyone there liked this meanness, but . . . here a peculiar thing occurred; here the children stepped in, because by then the children were all on my side and had begun to love Marie. This is how it happened. I wanted to do something for Marie; she badly needed money, but I never had a penny while I was there. I had a small diamond pin, and I sold it to a certain peddler: he went from village to village trading in old clothes. He gave me eight francs, though it was worth a good forty. I spent a long time trying to meet Marie alone; we finally met outside the village, by a hedge, on a side path to the mountain, behind a tree. There I gave her the eight francs and told her to be sparing of them, because I wouldn't have more, and then I kissed her and said she shouldn't think I had any bad intentions, and that I had kissed her not because I was in love with her but because I felt very sorry for her, and that from the very start I had never regarded her as guilty but only as unfortunate. I wanted very much to comfort her right then and to assure her that she shouldn't regard herself as so low before everyone, but she didn't seem to understand. I noticed it at once, though she was silent almost all the while and stood before me looking down and terribly embarrassed. When I finished, she kissed my hand, and I took her hand at once and wanted to kiss it, but she quickly pulled it back. Just then the children suddenly spied us, a whole crowd of them; I learned later that they had been spying on me for a long time. They began to whistle, clap their hands, and laugh, and Marie ran away. I wanted to speak to them, but they started throwing stones at me. That same day everybody knew about it, the entire village; it all fell on Marie again: they now disliked her still more. I even heard that they wanted to condemn her and punish her, but, thank God, it blew over. The children, however, wouldn't let her alone, teased her worse than before, threw mud at her; they chased her, she ran away from them with her weak chest, gasping for breath; they kept at it, shouting, abusing her. Once I even picked a fight with them. Then I started talking with them, talking every day, whenever I had a chance.

They sometimes stood and listened, though they kept up their abuse. I told them how unfortunate Marie was; soon they stopped abusing me and would silently walk away. We gradually began to talk. I didn't hide anything from them, I told them everything. They listened very curiously and soon started to feel sorry for Marie. Some started greeting her kindly when they met; the custom there, when you met someone, whether you knew them or not, was to bow and say: 'Good day.' I can imagine how surprised Marie was. Once two girls got some food and brought it to her, gave it to her, then came and told me. They said Marie burst into tears and now they loved her very much. Soon they all began to love her, and at the same time they began to love me as well. They started coming to see me often, asking me to tell them stories; it seems I did it well, because they liked listening to me very much. And later I studied and read everything only so as to tell them afterwards, and for three years after that I told them all sorts of things. When everybody accused me afterwards—Schneider, too— of talking to them like grown-ups, without hiding anything, I replied that it was shameful to lie to them, they knew everything anyway, no matter how you hid it, and might learn it in a bad way, while from me it wouldn't be in a bad way. You only had to remember yourself as a child. They didn't agree . . . I kissed Marie two weeks before her mother died; when the pastor gave his sermon, all the children were already on my side. I told them about it at once and explained the pastor's action; they all became angry with him, some so much that they sent stones through the pastor's windows. I stopped them, because that was a bad thing; but everyone in the village learned all about it at once, and here they began to accuse me of having corrupted the children. Then they found out that the children loved Marie and became terribly frightened; but Marie was happy now. The children were even forbidden to meet her, but they ran in secret to see her with her herd, quite far, almost half a mile from the village; they brought her treats, and some simply ran there to embrace her and kiss her, saying: *'Je vous aime, Marie!'* and then rushed headlong home. Marie almost lost her mind from this sudden happiness; she had never dreamed of anything like it; she was embarrassed and joyful, and the children, especially the girls, wanted above all to run to her and tell her that I loved her and had told them a lot about her. They told her that they knew everything from me, and that now they loved and pitied her and always would. Then they came running to me and with

such joyful, concerned little faces told me that they had just seen
Marie and that Marie sent her greetings. In the evenings I used to
go to the waterfall; there was one place completely screened off on
the village side, with poplars growing around it; that was where
they would gather with me in the evening, some even in secret. It
seemed to me that my love for Marie delighted them terribly, and
that was the one thing, during all my life there, in which I deceived
them. I didn't disappoint them by confessing that I did not love
Marie at all—that is, was not in love with her—but only pitied
her; everything told me that they preferred it the way they had
imagined and decided it among themselves, and so I said nothing
and pretended they had guessed right. And those little hearts were
so delicate and tender: among other things, it seemed impossible
to them that their good Léon should love Marie so much, while
Marie was so poorly dressed and had no shoes. Imagine, they even
got shoes and stockings and linen for her, and even some sort of
dress. How they managed it I don't know; the whole band worked
on it. When I asked them, they only laughed merrily, and the little
girls clapped their hands and kissed me. I, too, occasionally went
in secret to see Marie. She was becoming very ill and could barely
walk; in the end she stopped helping the cowherd altogether; but
even so she left with the herd each morning. She sat to one side.
There was a sheer, almost vertical cliff there, with a ledge; she
would sit on a stone in a corner that was shielded from everyone
and spend the whole day almost without moving, from morning
till it was time for the herd to go. By then she was so weak from
consumption that she mostly sat with her eyes closed, leaning her
head against the rock, and dozed, breathing heavily; her face was
thin as a skeleton's, and sweat stood out on her forehead and
temples. That was how I always found her. I'd come for a minute,
and I also didn't want to be seen. As soon as I appeared, Marie
would give a start, open her eyes, and rush to kiss my hands. I no
longer withdrew them, because for her it was happiness; all the
while I sat there, she trembled and wept; true, she tried several
times to speak, but it was hard to understand her. She was like a
crazy person, in terrible agitation and rapture. Sometimes the children came with me. On those occasions, they usually stood not far
away and set about guarding us from something or someone, and
they were extraordinarily pleased with that. When we left, Marie
again remained alone, motionless as before, her eyes closed and
her head leaning against the rock; she may have been dreaming of

something. One morning she was unable to go out with the herd and stayed in her empty house. The children learned of it at once and almost all of them went to visit her that day; she lay in her bed all alone. For two days only the children looked after her, taking turns in coming, but afterwards, when they learned in the village that Marie really was dying, the old women of the village began coming in turns to sit by her bedside. It seemed they started to feel sorry for Marie in the village, at least they no longer stopped or scolded the children as before. Marie dozed all the time, her sleep was restless: she coughed terribly. The old women chased the children away, but they came to the window, sometimes just for a moment, only to say: '*Bonjour, notre bonne Marie.*' And as soon as she saw or heard them, she would become all animated and, not listening to the old women, would at once try to prop herself on her elbow, nod to them, and thank them. They went on bringing her treats, but she ate almost nothing. Because of them, I can assure you, she died almost happy. Because of them, she forgot her black woe, as if she had received forgiveness from them, because till the very end she considered herself a great criminal. Like little birds, they fluttered with their wings against her window and called to her every morning: '*Nous t'aimons, Marie.*' She died very soon. I thought she would live much longer. On the eve of her death, before sunset, I stopped to see her; she seemed to recognize me, and I pressed her hand for the last time—how emaciated her hand was! Then suddenly in the morning they come and tell me that Marie is dead. Here there was no holding the children back: they decorated the whole coffin with flowers and put a wreath on her head. In church this time the pastor did not heap shame on the dead girl, and anyway there were very few people at the funeral, only some who came out of curiosity. But when it was time to carry the coffin, the children all rushed to do it themselves. As they couldn't really carry it, they helped, they ran after the coffin, all of them crying. Since then Marie's little grave has been constantly venerated by the children; every year they decorate it with flowers, and they've planted roses all around it. But with this funeral also began my great persecution by the whole village on account of the children. The main instigators were the pastor and the schoolmaster. The children were absolutely forbidden even to meet me, and Schneider even undertook to see to it. But we met all the same, we exchanged signs from a distance. They sent me their little notes. Later on it all settled down, but at the time it was very nice: I became even closer to the children because of this persecution. During my last year I even almost made peace with Thibaut and the pastor. But Schneider talked to me a lot and argued with me about my harmful 'system' with the children. What system did I have! Finally Schneider told me one very strange thought of his. This was just before my departure. He told me he was fully convinced that I was a perfect child myself, that is, fully a child, that I resembled an adult only in size and looks, but in development, soul, character, and perhaps even mind, I was not an adult, and I would stay that way even if I lived to be sixty. I laughed very much: he wasn't right, of course, because what's little about me? But one thing is true, that I really don't like being with adults, with people, with grown-ups—and I noticed that long ago—I don't like it because I don't know how. Whatever they say to me, however kind they are to me, still I'm always oppressed with them for some reason, and I'm terribly glad when I can go quickly to my comrades, and my comrades have always been children—not because I'm a child myself, but simply because I'm drawn to children. When I'd meet them, back at the beginning of my life in the village—it was when I used to go and be sad alone in the mountains—when I'd be wandering alone and sometimes met the whole band of them, especially at noontime, when they were out of school, noisy, running, with their satchels and slates, shouting, laughing, playing— my whole soul would suddenly begin to yearn for them. I don't know, but I began to feel some extremely strong and happy feeling each time I met them. I'd stop and laugh with happiness, looking at their flashing and eternally running little feet, at the boys and girls running together, at their laughter and tears (because many of them had managed to have a fight, to cry, and to make peace again and play together on their way home from school), and then I'd forget all my sadness. Afterwards, for all those three remaining years, I was unable to understand how people can be sad and what makes them sad. My whole destiny went to them. I never intended to leave the village, and it never occurred to me that I might someday return here, to Russia. It seemed to me that I would always be there, but I saw, finally, that it was impossible for Schneider to keep me, and then something turned up which seemed so important that Schneider himself hurried me on my way and wrote a reply for me here. I'll have to see what it is and consult with someone. Maybe my fate will change completely, but that's all not it and not the main thing. The main thing is that my whole life has changed already. I left a lot there, too much. It's all vanished. I sat on the train thinking: 'Now I'm going to be with people; maybe I don't know anything, but the new life has come.' I decided to do my duty honestly and firmly. Maybe it will be boring and painful for me to be with people. In the first place I decided to be polite and candid with everybody; no one can ask more of me. Maybe I'll be considered a child here, too—so be it! Everybody also considers me an idiot for some reason, and in fact I was once so ill that I was like an idiot; but what sort of idiot am I now, when I myself understand that I'm considered an idiot? I come in and think: 'They consider me an idiot, but I'm intelligent all the same, and they don't even suspect it . . .' I often have that thought. When I was in Berlin and received several little letters they had already managed to write to me, it was only then that I realized how much I loved them. Receiving the first letter was very hard! How sad they were as they saw me off! They began a month ahead: '*Léon s'en va, Léon s'en va pour toujours.*'* Every evening we gathered by the waterfall as before and kept talking about our parting. Sometimes it was as joyful as before; only when we broke up for the night, they started hugging me tightly and warmly, which they never did before. Some came running to see me in secret from the rest, singly, only in order to hug me and kiss me alone, not in front of everybody. When I was setting out, all of them, the whole swarm, saw me off to the station. The railway station was about half a mile from the village. They tried to keep from crying, but many failed and cried loudly, especially the girls. We hurried so as not to be late, but one or another of the crowd would suddenly rush to me in the middle of the road, put his little arms around me, and kiss me, for which the whole crowd also had to stop; and though we were in a hurry, everybody stopped and waited for him to say good-bye to me. When I got on the train and it started off, they all shouted 'Hurrah!' to me and stood there for a long time, until the train was quite gone. I kept looking, too . . . Listen, when I came in here earlier and looked at your dear faces—I'm very attentive to faces now—and heard your first words, I felt light at heart for the first time since then. I thought maybe I really am one of the lucky ones: I know it's not easy to meet people you can love at once, yet I met you as soon as I got off the train. I know very well that it's shameful to talk about your feelings with everyone,

---

*Léon is going away, Léon is going away forever!

yet here I am talking with you, and with you I'm not ashamed. I'm unsociable and may not visit you for a long time. Don't take it as thinking ill: I'm not saying it because I don't value you, and you also mustn't think I've been offended in any way. You asked me about your faces and what I observe in them. I'll tell you with great pleasure. Yours, Adelaida Ivanovna, is a happy face, the most sympathetic of the three. Not only are you very pretty, but one looks at you and says: 'She has the face of a kind sister.' You approach things simply and cheerfully, but you are also quick to know hearts. That's what I think about your face. Yours, Alexandra Ivanovna, is also a beautiful and very sweet face, but you may have some secret sorrow; your soul is no doubt very kind, but you are not joyful. There is some special nuance in your face that reminds me of Holbein's Madonna in Dresden.[26] Well, that's for your face— am I a good guesser? You yourselves consider me one. But about your face, Lizaveta Prokofyevna," he suddenly turned to Mrs. Epanchin, "about your face I not only think but I'm certain that you are a perfect child, in everything, in everything, in everything good and in everything bad, despite your age. You're not angry that I say it? You do know my regard for children? And don't think it's out of simplicity that I've just spoken so candidly about your faces; oh, no, not at all! Maybe I, too, have something in mind."

VII

WHEN THE PRINCE fell silent, they all looked at him gaily, even Aglaya, but especially Lizaveta Prokofyevna.

"Quite an examination!" she cried. "So, my dear ladies, you thought you were going to patronize him like a poor little thing, and he barely deigned to accept you, and that with the reservation that he would come only rarely. We've been made fools of—Ivan Fyodorovich most of all—and I'm glad. Bravo, Prince, we were told earlier to put you through an examination. And what you said about my face is all completely true: I am a child, and I know it. I knew it even before you said it; you precisely expressed my own thought in a single word. I think your character is completely identical to mine, and I'm very glad; like two drops of water. Only you're a man and I'm a woman, and I've never been to Switzerland, that's all the difference."

"Don't be in a hurry, *maman*," cried Aglaya, "the prince said he had something special in mind in all his confessions, and he wasn't simply saying it."

"Yes, oh, yes," the others laughed.

"Don't tease him, my dears, he may be cleverer than all three of you put together. You'll see. Only why have you said nothing about Aglaya, Prince? Aglaya's waiting, and I am, too."

"I can't say anything now. I'll say it later."

"Why? She's noticeable, I believe?"

"Oh, yes, she's noticeable. You're an extraordinary beauty, Aglaya Ivanovna. You're so good-looking that one is afraid to look at you."

"That's all? And her qualities?" Mrs. Epanchin persisted.

"Beauty is difficult to judge; I'm not prepared yet. Beauty is a riddle."

"That means you've set Aglaya a riddle," said Adelaida. "Solve it, Aglaya. But she is good-looking, isn't she, Prince?"

"Extremely!" the prince replied warmly, with an enthusiastic glance at Aglaya. "Almost like Nastasya Filippovna, though her face is quite different . . ."

They all exchanged astonished looks.

"Like who-o-om?" Mrs. Epanchin drew out. "Like Nastasya Filippovna? Where have you seen Nastasya Filippovna? What Nastasya Filippovna?"

"Gavrila Ardalionovich was just showing Ivan Fyodorovich her portrait."

"What? He brought Ivan Fyodorovich her portrait?"

"To show him. Today Nastasya Filippovna presented Gavrila Ardalionovich with her portrait, and he brought it to show."

"I want to see it!" Mrs. Epanchin heaved herself up. "Where is this portrait? If she gave it to him, he must have it, and, of course, he's still in the office! He always comes to work on Wednesdays and never leaves before four. Send for Gavrila Ardalionovich at once! No, I'm hardly dying to see him. Do me a favor, my dear Prince, go to the office, take the portrait from him, and bring it here. Tell him we want to look at it. Please."

"He's nice, but much too simple," said Adelaida, when the prince had gone.

"Yes, much too much," agreed Alexandra, "so that he's even slightly ridiculous."

It was as if neither had spoken her whole mind.

"However, with our faces he got out of it nicely," said Aglaya. "He flattered everyone, even *maman*."

"Don't be witty, please!" cried Mrs. Epanchin. "It was not he who flattered me, but I who was flattered."

"Do you think he was trying to get out of it?" asked Adelaida.

"I don't think he's so simple."

"Well, there she goes!" Mrs. Epanchin became angry. "And in my opinion you're even more ridiculous than he is. He's a bit simple, but he keeps his own counsel, in the most noble fashion, to be sure. Just as I do."

"Of course, it was bad of me to let on about the portrait," the prince reflected to himself on his way to the office, feeling some remorse. "But . . . maybe it's a good thing I let on . . ." A strange idea was beginning to flash in his head, though not a very clear one as yet.

Gavrila Ardalionovich was still sitting in the office and was immersed in his papers. Evidently he did not get his salary from the joint-stock company for nothing. He became terribly embarrassed when the prince asked about the portrait and told him how they had found out about it.

"A-a-ah! Why did you have to blab!" he shouted in angry vexation. "You don't know anything . . . Idiot!" he muttered to himself.

"I'm sorry, I said it quite unthinkingly, just by the way. I said that Aglaya was almost as good-looking as Nastasya Filippovna."

Ganya asked for more detail. The prince complied. Ganya again gave him a mocking look.

"You do go on about Nastasya Filippovna . . ." he muttered, but lapsed into thought without finishing.

He was obviously alarmed. The prince reminded him about the portrait.

"Listen, Prince," Ganya said suddenly, as if an unexpected thought had dawned on him. "I have a huge request to make of you . . . But I really don't know . . ."

He became embarrassed and did not finish; he was venturing upon something and seemed to be struggling with himself. The prince waited silently. Ganya studied him once more with intent, searching eyes.

"Prince," he began again, "right now they're . . . owing to a completely strange circumstance . . . ridiculous . . . and for which I'm not to blame . . . well, in short, it's irrelevant—they're a bit angry with me in there, it seems, so for the time being I'd rather not go there without being sent for. I need terribly to talk with Aglaya Ivanovna now. I've written a few words just in case" (a small, folded note appeared in his hand), "and I don't know how to deliver it. Would you take it upon yourself, Prince, to deliver it to Aglaya Ivanovna, right now, but only to Aglaya Ivanovna, that is, so that nobody sees—understand? It's not such a great secret, God knows, there's nothing to it, but . . . will you do it?"

"It's not altogether pleasant for me," said the prince.

"Ah, Prince, it's of the utmost necessity for me!" Ganya began to plead. "Maybe she'll answer . . . Believe me, only in the utmost, the very utmost case, would I turn to . . . Who else can I send it with? . . . It's very important . . . It's terribly important for me . . ."

Ganya was terribly afraid that the prince would not agree and kept peering into his eyes with cowardly entreaty.

"Very well, I'll deliver it."

"But only so that nobody notices," the now joyful Ganya pleaded. "And another thing, Prince, I'm relying on your word of honor, eh?"

"I won't show it to anybody," said the prince.

"The note isn't sealed, but . . ." the much too flustered Ganya let slip and stopped in embarrassment.

"Oh, I won't read it," the prince replied with perfect simplicity, took the portrait, and walked out of the office.

Ganya, left alone, clutched his head.

"One word from her, and I . . . and I really may break it off! . . ."

He started pacing up and down the office, too excited and expectant to sit down to his papers again.

The prince pondered as he went; he was unpleasantly struck by the errand, and unpleasantly struck by the thought of Ganya's note to Aglaya. But two rooms away from the drawing room he suddenly stopped, seemed to remember something, looked around, went over to the window, closer to the light, and began to look at Nastasya Filippovna's portrait.

It was as if he wanted to unriddle something hidden in that face which had also struck him earlier. The earlier impression had scarcely left him, and now it was as if he were hastening to verify something. That face, extraordinary for its beauty and for something else, now struck him still more. There seemed to be a boundless pride and contempt, almost hatred, in that face, and at the same time something trusting, something surprisingly simplehearted; the contrast even seemed to awaken some sort of compassion as one looked at those features. That dazzling beauty was even unbearable, the beauty of the pale face, the nearly hollow cheeks and burning eyes—strange beauty! The prince gazed for a moment, then suddenly roused himself, looked around, hastily put the portrait to his lips and kissed it. When he entered the drawing room a minute later, his face was completely calm.

But as he was going into the dining room (one room away from the drawing room), in the doorway he almost ran into Aglaya, who was coming out. She was alone.

"Gavrila Ardalionovich asked me to give you this," said the prince, handing her the note.

Aglaya stopped, took the note, and looked at the prince somehow strangely. There was not the least embarrassment in her look, perhaps only a glimpse of a certain surprise, and even that seemed to refer only to the prince. With her look Aglaya seemed to demand an accounting from him—in what way had he ended up in this affair together with Ganya?—and to demand it calmly and haughtily. For two or three moments they stood facing each other; finally something mocking barely showed in her face; she smiled slightly and walked past him.

Mrs. Epanchin studied the portrait of Nastasya Filippovna for some time silently and with a certain tinge of scorn, holding it out in front of her at an extreme and ostentatious distance from her eyes.

"Yes, good-looking," she said at last, "even very. I've seen her twice, only from a distance. So that's the sort of beauty you appreciate?" she suddenly turned to the prince.

"Yes . . . that sort . . ." the prince replied with some effort.

"Meaning precisely that sort?"

"Precisely that sort."

"Why so?"

"There's so much suffering . . . in that face . . ." the prince said, as if inadvertently, as if he were talking to himself and not answering a question.

"You may be raving, however," Mrs. Epanchin decided, and with an arrogant gesture she flung the portrait down on the table.

Alexandra picked it up, Adelaida came over to her, and they both began to study it. Just then Aglaya came back to the drawing room.

"Such power!" Adelaida cried all at once, peering greedily at the portrait over her sister's shoulder.

"Where? What power?" Lizaveta Prokofyevna asked sharply.

"Such beauty has power," Adelaida said hotly. "You can overturn the world with such beauty."

She went pensively to her easel. Aglaya gave the portrait only a fleeting look, narrowed her eyes, thrust out her lower lip, and sat down to one side, her arms folded.

Mrs. Epanchin rang.

"Send Gavrila Ardalionovich here, he's in the office," she ordered the entering servant.

"*Maman!*" Alexandra exclaimed significantly.

"I want to say a couple of words to him—and enough!" Mrs. Epanchin snapped quickly, stopping the objection. She was visibly irritated. "You see, Prince, we now have all these secrets here. All these secrets! It's required, it's some sort of etiquette, a stupid thing. And that in a matter which requires the greatest openness, clarity, and honesty. Marriages are in the works, I don't like these marriages . . ."

"*Maman*, what are you saying?" Alexandra again tried to stop her.

"What's wrong, daughter dear? Do you like it yourself? And so what if the prince can hear, since we're friends. I am his, at least. God seeks people, good people, of course, he doesn't need the wicked and capricious—especially the capricious, who decide one thing today and say something else tomorrow. You understand, Alexandra Ivanovna? They say I'm odd, Prince, but I have discernment. Because the heart is the main thing, the rest is nonsense. Brains are also necessary, of course . . . maybe brains are the main thing. Don't smile, Aglaya, I'm not contradicting myself: a fool with a heart and no brains is as unhappy a fool as a fool with brains but no heart. An old truth. I am a fool with a heart but no brains, and you are a fool with brains but no heart; and we're both unhappy, and we both suffer."

"What are you so unhappy about, *maman*?" Adelaida, who alone of the whole company seemed not to have lost her cheerful disposition, could not help asking.

"First of all, about my learned daughters," Mrs. Epanchin snapped, "and since that is enough in itself, there's no point in expatiating on the rest. There's been enough verbosity. We'll see how the two of you (I don't count Aglaya), with your brains and verbosity, are going to find your way and whether you, my much esteemed Alexandra Ivanovna, are going to be happy with your honorable gentleman . . . Ah! . . ." she exclaimed, seeing the entering Ganya. "Here comes one more matrimony. How do you do!" she responded to Ganya's bow without inviting him to sit down. "Are you embarking upon matrimony?"

"Matrimony? . . . How? . . . What matrimony? . . ." Gavrila Arda-lionovich murmured in stupefaction. He was terribly bewildered.

"Are you getting married, I'm asking, if you like that phrasing better?"

"N-no . . . I'm . . . n-not," Gavrila Ardalionovich lied, and a flush of shame spread over his face. He glanced fleetingly at Aglaya, who was sitting to one side, and quickly looked away. Aglaya was looking at him coldly, intently, calmly, not taking her eyes off him, and observing his confusion.

"No? Did you say no?" the implacable Lizaveta Prokofyevna persistently interrogated him. "Enough! I'll remember that today, Wednesday afternoon, you said 'No' to my question. Is today Wednesday?"

"I think so, *maman*," replied Adelaida.

"They never know what day it is. What's the date?"

"The twenty-seventh," replied Ganya.

"The twenty-seventh? That's good, for certain considerations. Good-bye. I suppose you have many things to do, and for me it's time to dress and be on my way. Take your portrait. Give my respects to the unfortunate Nina Alexandrovna. Good-bye, Prince, my dear boy! Come more often, and I'll be sure to call on old Belokonsky and tell her about you. And listen, my dear: I believe God brought you to Petersburg from Switzerland precisely for me. Maybe you'll have other things to do, but it was mainly for me. That's precisely how God reckoned. Good-bye, my dears. Alexandra, stop by for a minute."

Mrs. Epanchin left. Ganya, overturned, confused, spiteful, took the portrait from the table and turned to the prince with a crooked smile:

"Prince, I'm going home now. If you haven't changed your inten-tion of living with us, I'll take you there, since you don't know the address."

"Wait, Prince," said Aglaya, suddenly getting up from her chair, "you still have to write something in my album. Papa said you're a calligrapher. I'll bring it to you right now . . ."

And she left.

"Good-bye, Prince, I'm going, too," said Adelaida.

She firmly shook the prince's hand, smiled at him affably and tenderly, and left. She did not look at Ganya.

"It was you," Ganya rasped, suddenly falling upon the prince once everyone had gone, "you blabbed to them that I'm getting married!" he muttered in a quick half whisper, with a furious face, flashing his eyes spitefully. "You shameless babbler!"

"I assure you that you are mistaken," the prince replied calmly and politely, "I didn't even know you were getting married."

"You heard Ivan Fyodorovich say earlier that everything would be decided tonight at Nastasya Filippovna's, and you told it to them! You're lying! How could they have found out? Devil take it, who could have told them besides you? Didn't the old lady hint to me?"

"You ought to know better who told them, if you really think she was hinting to you. I didn't say a word about it."

"Did you deliver my note? Any answer?" Ganya interrupted him with feverish impatience. But at that very moment Aglaya came back, and the prince had no time to reply.

"Here, Prince," said Aglaya, putting her album on the little table. "Choose a page and write something for me. Here's a pen, a new one. Does it matter if it's steel? I've heard calligraphers don't write with steel pens."

Talking with the prince, she seemed not to notice that Ganya was right there. But while the prince was testing the pen, selecting a page, and preparing himself, Ganya went over to the fireplace where Aglaya was standing, to the right of the prince, and in a trembling, faltering voice said almost in her ear:

"One word, only one word from you—and I'm saved."

The prince turned quickly and looked at the two. There was genuine despair in Ganya's face; it seemed he had uttered these words somehow without thinking, as if headlong. Aglaya looked at him for a few seconds with exactly the same calm astonishment as she had looked at the prince earlier, and it seemed that this calm astonishment of hers, this perplexity, as if she totally failed to understand what had been said to her, was more terrible for Ganya at that moment than the strongest contempt.

"What am I to write?" asked the prince.

"I'll dictate to you right now," said Aglaya, turning to him. "Are you ready? Write: 'I don't negotiate.' Now put the day and the month. Show me."

The prince handed her the album.

"Excellent! You've written it amazingly well; you have a wonderful hand! Thank you. Good-bye, Prince . . . Wait," she added, as if suddenly remembering something. "Come, I want to give you something as a memento."

The prince followed her; but having entered the dining room, Aglaya stopped.

"Read this," she said, handing him Ganya's note.

The prince took the note and looked at Aglaya in perplexity.

"I know you haven't read it and you cannot be in this man's confidence. Read it, I want you to."

The note had obviously been written in haste.

Today my fate will be decided, you know in what manner. Today I will have to give my word irrevocably. I have no right to your sympathy, I dare not have any hopes; but you once uttered a word, just one word, and that word lit up the whole dark night of my life and became a beacon for me. Say another such word to me now—and you will save me from disaster! Only say to me: *break it all off*, and I will break it all off today. Oh, what will it cost you to say it! I am asking for this word only as a sign of your sympathy and compassion for me—only, *only*! And nothing more, *nothing*! I dare not think of any hope, because I am not worthy of it. But after your word I will accept my poverty again, I will joyfully endure my desperate situation. I will meet the struggle, I will be glad of it, I will resurrect in it with new strength!

Send me this word of compassion (of compassion *only*, I swear to you!). Do not be angry at the boldness of a desperate man, at a drowning man, for daring to make a last effort to save himself from disaster.

G. I.

"This man assures me," Aglaya said sharply, when the prince had finished reading, "that the words *break it all off* will not compromise me or commit me in any way, and, as you see, he gives me a written guarantee of it by this very note. See how naïvely he hastened to underline certain words and how crudely his secret thought shows through. He knows, however, that if he broke it all off, but by himself, alone, not waiting for a word from me, and even not telling me about it, without any hope in me, I would then change my feelings for him and would probably become his friend. He knows that for certain! But his soul is dirty: he knows and yet hesitates; he knows and still asks for a guarantee. He's unable to make a decision on faith. Instead of a hundred thousand, he wants me to give him hope in me. As for the previous word he talks about in his letter and which supposedly lit up his whole life, there he's lying brazenly. I simply felt sorry for him once. But he's bold and shameless: the thought of a possible hope immediately flashed in him; I realized it at once. After that he began trying to trap me; he does it still. But enough. Take the note and give it back to him, right now, when you've left our house, naturally, not before."

"And what shall I tell him in reply?"

"Nothing, of course. That's the best reply. So you intend to live in his house?"

"Ivan Fyodorovich himself recommended it to me earlier," said the prince.

"Beware of him, I'm warning you; he won't forgive you for giving him back the note."

Aglaya pressed the prince's hand lightly and left. Her face was serious and frowning, she did not even smile as she nodded good-bye to the prince.

"One moment, I'll just fetch my bundle," the prince said to Ganya, "and we can go."

Ganya stamped his foot in impatience. His face even darkened with rage. Finally the two men went outside, the prince carrying his bundle.

"The reply? The reply?" Ganya fell upon him. "What did she say to you? Did you give her the letter?"

The prince silently handed him his note. Ganya was dumbfounded.

"What? My note?" he cried. "He didn't give it to her! Oh, I should have guessed! Oh, cur-r-rse it . . . I see why she didn't understand anything just now! But why, why, why didn't you give it to her, oh, cur-r-rse it . . ."

"Excuse me, but, on the contrary, I managed to deliver your note at once, the moment you gave it to me and exactly as you asked me to. It ended up with me again, because Aglaya Ivanovna gave it back to me just now."

"When? When?"

"As soon as I finished writing in the album and she asked me to go with her. (Didn't you hear?) We went to the dining room, she gave me the note, told me to read it, and then told me to give it back to you."

"To re-e-ead it!" Ganya shouted almost at the top of his lungs. "To read it! You read it?"

And he again stood petrified in the middle of the sidewalk, so astonished that he even opened his mouth wide.

"Yes, I read it just now."

"And she, she herself gave it to you to read? She herself?"

"She herself, and, believe me, I wouldn't have read it without her invitation."

Ganya was silent for a moment, making painful efforts to figure something out, but suddenly he exclaimed:

"That can't be! She couldn't have told you to read it. You're lying! You read it yourself!"

"I'm telling you the truth," the prince replied in the same completely imperturbable tone, "and, believe me, I'm very sorry that it makes such an unpleasant impression on you."

"But, you wretch, did she at least say anything as she did it? Did she respond in any way?"

"Yes, of course."

"Speak then, speak—ah, the devil! . . ."

And Ganya stamped his right foot, shod in a galosh, twice on the sidewalk.

"As soon as I finished reading it, she told me that you were trying to trap her; that you wished to compromise her, in order to obtain some hope from her and then, on the basis of that hope, to break without losses from the other hope for a hundred thousand. That if you had done it without negotiating with her, had broken it off by yourself without asking her for a guarantee beforehand, she might perhaps have become your friend. That's all, I think. Ah, one more thing: when I had already taken the note and asked what the reply would be, she said that no reply would be the best reply—I think that was it; forgive me if I've forgotten her exact expression, but I'm conveying it as I understood it myself."

Boundless spite came over Ganya, and his rage exploded without restraint.

"Ahh! So that's how it is!" he rasped. "She throws my notes out the window! Ahh! She doesn't negotiate—then I will! We'll see! There's a lot about me . . . we'll see! . . . I'll tie them in little knots! . . ."

He grimaced, turned pale, frothed, shook his fist. They went a few steps like that. He was not embarrassed in the least by the prince's presence, as if he were alone in his room, because he regarded him as nothing in the highest degree. But he suddenly realized something and came to his senses.

"How did it happen," he suddenly turned to the prince, "how did it happen that you"—"an idiot!" he added to himself—"have suddenly been taken into such confidence, after being acquainted for two hours? How is it?"

With all his torments he only lacked envy. It suddenly stung him to the very heart.

"I'm unable to explain it to you," replied the prince.

Ganya looked at him spitefully:

"Was it her confidence she wanted to give you when she called you to the dining room? Wasn't she going to give you something?"

"I can't understand it in any other way than precisely that."

"But why, devil take it! What did you do there? What was it they liked? Listen," he was fussing with all his might (just then everything in him was somehow scattered and seething in disorder, so that he was unable to collect his thoughts), "listen, can't you somehow recall and put in order precisely what you were talking about, all the words, from the very beginning? Didn't you notice anything, can't you recall?"

"Oh, I recall very well," the prince replied. "From the very beginning, when I went in and was introduced, we started talking about Switzerland."

"Well, to hell with Switzerland!"

"Then about capital punishment . . ."

"About capital punishment?"

"Yes, apropos of something . . . then I told them how I'd lived there for three years, and also the story of a poor village girl . . ."

"To hell with the poor village girl! Go on!" Ganya tore ahead impatiently.

"Then how Schneider gave me his opinion of my character and urged me . . ."

"Blast Schneider and spit on his opinion! Go on!"

"Then, apropos of something, I started talking about faces—that is, about facial expressions, and I said that Aglaya Ivanovna was almost as good-looking as Nastasya Filippovna. It was here that I let slip about the portrait . . ."

"But you didn't repeat, you surely didn't repeat everything you'd heard earlier in the office? Did you? Did you?"

"I tell you again that I didn't."

"Then how the devil . . . Bah! Maybe Aglaya showed the note to the old lady?"

"About that I can fully guarantee you that she did not show it to her. I was there all the while; and she also didn't have time."

"Or maybe you didn't notice something . . . Oh! cur-r-rsed idiot," he exclaimed, now completely beside himself, "he can't even tell anything!"

Once he began to swear and met no resistance, Ganya gradually lost all restraint, as always happens with certain people. A little more and he might have started spitting, so enraged he was. But, precisely because of that rage, he was blind; otherwise he would long since have paid attention to the fact that this "idiot," whom he mistreated so, was sometimes capable of understanding everything all too quickly and subtly, and of giving an extremely satisfactory account of it. But suddenly something unexpected happened.

"I must point out to you, Gavrila Ardalionovich," the prince suddenly said, "that formerly I was indeed unwell, so that in fact I was almost an idiot; but I have been well for a long time now, and therefore I find it somewhat unpleasant when I'm called an idiot to my face. Though you might be excused, considering your misfortunes, in your vexation you have even abused me a couple of times. I dislike that very much, especially the way you do it, suddenly, from the start. And since we're now standing at an intersection, it might be better if we parted: you go home to the right, and I'll go left. I have twenty-five roubles, and I'm sure I'll find furnished rooms."

Ganya was terribly embarrassed and even blushed with shame.

"Forgive me, Prince," he cried hotly, suddenly changing his abusive tone to extreme politeness, "for God's sake, forgive me! You see what trouble I'm in! You know almost nothing yet, but if you knew everything, you would probably excuse me at least a little; though, naturally, I'm inexcusable . . ."

"Oh, but I don't need such big excuses," the prince hastened to reply. "I do understand that you're very displeased and that's why you're abusive. Well, let's go to your place. It's my pleasure . . ."

"No, it's impossible to let him go like that," Ganya thought to himself, glancing spitefully at the prince as they went. "The rogue got it all out of me and then suddenly took off his mask . . . That means something. We'll see! Everything will be resolved, everything, everything! Today!"

They were already standing outside his house.

VIII

GANECHKA'S APARTMENT was on the third floor, up a rather clean, bright, and spacious stairway, and consisted of six or seven rooms, large and small, quite ordinary, incidentally, but in any case not at all what the pocket of an official with a family, even on a salary of two thousand roubles, could afford. But it was intended for keeping tenants with board and services, and had been taken by Ganya and his family no more than two months earlier, to the greatest displeasure of Ganya himself, on the insistent demand of Nina Alexandrovna and Varvara Ardalionovna, who wished to be useful in their turn and to increase the family income at least a little. Ganya scowled and called keeping tenants an outrage; after that it was as if he began to be ashamed in society, where he was in the habit of appearing as a young man of a certain brilliance and with prospects. All these concessions to fate and all this vexatious crowding—all of it deeply wounded his soul. For some time now, every little thing had begun to annoy him beyond measure or proportion, and if he still agreed for a time to yield and endure, it was only because he had already resolved to change and alter it all within the shortest space of time. And yet this very change, this way out that he had settled on, was no small task—a task the imminent solution of which threatened to be more troublesome and tormenting than all that had gone before it.

The apartment was divided by a corridor that started right from the front hall. On one side of the corridor were the three rooms that were to be let to "specially recommended" tenants; besides that, on the same side of the corridor, at the very end of it, near the kitchen, was a fourth room, smaller than the others, which housed the retired General Ivolgin himself, the father of the family, who slept on a wide couch and was obliged to go in and out of the apartment through the kitchen and the back door. The same little room also housed Gavrila Ardalionovich's thirteen-year-old brother, the schoolboy Kolya. He, too, was destined to be cramped, to study and sleep there on another very old, narrow, and short couch, covered with a torn sheet, and, above all, to tend to and *look after* his father, who was more and more unable to do without that. The prince was given the middle one of the three rooms; the first, to the right, was occupied by Ferdyshchenko, and the third,

to the left, was still vacant. But first of all Ganya took the prince
to the family side. This family side consisted of a large room that
was turned, when needed, into a dining room, of a drawing room,
which was, however, a drawing room only during the daytime, but
in the evening turned into Ganya's study and bedroom, and, finally,
of a third room, small and always closed: this was the bedroom of
Nina Alexandrovna and Varvara Ardalionovna. In short, everything in this apartment was cramped and squeezed; Ganya only
gritted his teeth to himself; though he may have wished to be
respectful to his mother, it was evident the moment one stepped
into the place that he was the great tyrant of the family.

Nina Alexandrovna was not alone in the drawing room, Varvara
Ardalionovna was sitting with her; they were both busy knitting
as they talked with a visitor, Ivan Petrovich Ptitsyn. Nina Alexandrovna seemed to be about fifty, with a thin, pinched face and a
deep darkness under her eyes. She looked sickly and somewhat
woebegone, but her face and gaze were quite pleasant; her first
words betokened a serious character and one filled with genuine
dignity. Despite her woebegone look, one could sense firmness and
even resolution in her. She was dressed extremely modestly, in
something dark and quite old-womanish, but her ways, her conversation, her whole manner betrayed a woman who had seen better
society.

Varvara Ardalionovna was a young lady of about twenty-three,
of average height, rather thin, with a face which, while not really
beautiful, contained in itself the mystery of being likable without
beauty and of attracting to the point of passion. She resembled her
mother very much, and was even dressed almost like her mother,
from a total indifference to dressing up. The look of her gray eyes
could on occasion be very gay and tender, though it was most often
grave and pensive, sometimes even too much so, especially of late.
Firmness and resolution could be seen in her face, too, but one
sensed that this firmness could be even more energetic and
enterprising than in her mother. Varvara Ardalionovna was rather
hot-tempered, and her brother sometimes even feared that hot-
temperedness. Ivan Petrovich Ptitsyn, the visitor who was now
sitting with them, also feared it. He was still a rather young man,
under thirty, modestly but finely dressed, with pleasant but somehow much too staid manners. His dark blond beard indicated that
he was not in government service.[27] He was capable of intelligent
and interesting conversation, but was more often silent. Generally

he even made an agreeable impression. He was clearly not indifferent to Varvara Ardalionovna and did not hide his feelings. Varvara Ardalionovna treated him amiably, but delayed in answering some of his questions, and even disliked them; Ptitsyn, however, was far from discouraged. Nina Alexandrovna was affectionate with him, and lately had even begun to trust him in many things. It was known, however, that his specific occupation was making money by giving short-term loans at interest on more or less sure pledges. He and Ganya were great friends.

After a thorough but curt introduction from Ganya (who greeted his mother rather drily, did not greet his sister at all, and immediately took Ptitsyn somewhere out of the room), Nina Alexandrovna said a few kind words to the prince and told Kolya, who peeped in at the door, to take him to the middle room. Kolya was a boy with a merry and rather sweet face, and a trustful and simple-hearted manner.

"Where's your luggage?" he asked, leading the prince into his room.

"I have a little bundle; I left it in the front hall."

"I'll bring it right away. All we have for servants are the cook and Matryona, so I have to help, too. Varya supervises everything and gets angry. Ganya says you came today from Switzerland?"

"Yes."

"Is it nice in Switzerland?"

"Very."

"Mountains?"

"Yes."

"I'll lug your bundles here right away."

Varvara Ardalionovna came in.

"Matryona will make your bed now. Do you have a suitcase?"

"No, a bundle. Your brother went to get it; it's in the front hall."

"There's no bundle there except this little one; where did you put it?" asked Kolya, coming back into the room.

"But there's nothing except that," announced the prince, taking his bundle.

"Aha! And I thought Ferdyshchenko might have filched it."

"Don't blather," Varya said sternly. She also spoke quite drily with the prince and was barely polite with him.

"*Chère Babette*, you might treat me a little more gently, I'm not Ptitsyn."

"You still ought to be whipped, Kolya, you're so stupid. You may address all your needs to Matryona. Dinner is at half-past four. You may dine with us or in your room, whichever you prefer. Let's go, Kolya, stop bothering him."

"Let's go, decisive character!"

On their way out they ran into Ganya.

"Is father at home?" Ganya asked Kolya and, on receiving an affirmative reply, whispered something in his ear.

Kolya nodded and went out after Varvara Ardalionovna.

"A couple of words, Prince, I forgot to tell you, what with all these . . . doings. A request: do me a favor—if it's not too much of a strain for you—don't babble here about what just went on between me and Aglaya, or *there* about what you find here; because there's also enough ugliness here. To hell with it, though . . . But control yourself, at least for today."

"I assure you that I babbled much less than you think," said the prince, somewhat annoyed at Ganya's reproaches. Their relations were obviously becoming worse and worse.

"Well, I've already suffered enough on account of you today. In short, I beg you."

"Note this, too, Gavrila Ardalionovich, that I was not bound in any way earlier and had no reason not to mention the portrait. You didn't ask me not to."

"Pah, what a vile room," Ganya observed, looking around disdainfully, "dark and windows on the courtyard. You've come to us inopportunely in all respects . . . Well, that's none of my business; I don't let rooms."

Ptitsyn looked in and called Ganya. He hastily abandoned the prince and went out, though he had wanted to say something more, but was obviously hesitant and as if ashamed to begin; and he had also denounced the room as if from embarrassment.

The prince had just managed to wash and to straighten his clothes a bit when the door opened again and a new figure appeared in it.

This was a gentleman of about thirty, rather tall, broad-shouldered, with an enormous, curly, red-haired head. His face was fleshy and ruddy, his lips thick, his nose broad and flattened, his eyes small, puffy, and jeering, as if constantly winking. The whole of it made a rather insolent picture. His clothes were on the dirty side.

At first he opened the door just enough to thrust his head in. This thrust-in head surveyed the room for about five seconds, then the door slowly began to open, the whole figure was outlined on the threshold, but the visitor did not come in yet, but squinted and went on studying the prince from the threshold. Finally he closed the door behind him, approached, sat down on a chair, took the prince firmly by the hand and seated him at an angle to himself on the sofa.

"Ferdyshchenko," he said, peering intently and questioningly into the prince's face.

"What about it?" the prince replied, almost bursting into laughter.

"A tenant," Ferdyshchenko spoke again, peering in the same way.

"You want to become acquainted?"

"Ehh!" said the visitor, ruffling up his hair and sighing, and he started looking into the opposite corner. "Do you have any money?" he asked suddenly, turning to the prince.

"A little."

"How much, precisely?"

"Twenty-five roubles."

"Show me."

The prince took a twenty-five-rouble note from his waistcoat pocket and handed it to Ferdyshchenko. The man unfolded it, looked at it, turned it over, then held it up to the light.

"Quite strange," he said, as if pondering. "Why do they turn brown? These twenty-fivers sometimes get terribly brown, while others, on the contrary, fade completely. Take it."

The prince took the note from him. Ferdyshchenko got up from the chair.

"I came to warn you: first of all, don't lend me any money, because I'm sure to ask."

"Very well."

"Do you intend to pay here?"

"I do."

"Well, I don't, thank you. Mine's the first door to your right, did you see? Try not to visit me too often; I'll come to you, don't worry about that. Have you seen the general?"

"No."

"Heard him?"

"Of course not."

"Well, you will see and hear him. Besides, he even asks me to lend him money! *Avis au lecteur.** Good-bye. Is it possible to live with a name like Ferdyshchenko? Eh?"

---

*Warning to the reader.

"Why not?"

"Good-bye."

And he went to the door. The prince learned later that this gentleman, as if out of duty, had taken upon himself the task of amazing everyone by his originality and merriment, but it somehow never came off. He even made an unpleasant impression on some people, which caused him genuine grief, but all the same he would not abandon his task. In the doorway he managed to set things right, as it were, by bumping into a gentleman coming in; after letting this new gentleman, who was unknown to the prince, enter the room, he obligingly winked several times behind his back by way of warning, and thus left not without a certain aplomb.

This new gentleman was tall, about fifty-five years old or even a little more, rather corpulent, with a purple-red, fleshy and flabby face framed by thick gray side-whiskers, with a moustache and large, rather protruding eyes. His figure would have been rather imposing if there had not been something seedy, shabby, even soiled about it. He was dressed in an old frock coat with nearly worn-through elbows; his shirt was also dirty—in a homey way. There was a slight smell of vodka in his vicinity; but his manner was showy, somewhat studied, and with an obvious wish to impress by its dignity. The gentleman approached the prince unhurriedly, with an affable smile, silently took his hand and, holding it in his own, peered into his face for some time, as if recognizing familiar features.

"Him! Him!" he said softly but solemnly. "As if alive! I heard them repeating the familiar and dear name and recalled the irretrievable past . . . Prince Myshkin?"

"That's right, sir."

"General Ivolgin, retired and unfortunate. Your name and patronymic, if I dare ask?"

"Lev Nikolaevich."

"So, so! The son of my friend, one might say my childhood friend, Nikolai Petrovich?"

"My father's name was Nikolai Lvovich."

"Lvovich," the general corrected himself, but unhurriedly and with perfect assurance, as if he had not forgotten in the least but had only made an accidental slip. He sat down and, also taking the prince's hand, sat him down beside him. "I used to carry you about in my arms, sir."

"Really?" asked the prince. "My father has been dead for twenty years now."

"Yes, twenty years, twenty years and three months. We studied together. I went straight into the military . . ."

"My father was also in the military, a second lieutenant in the Vasilkovsky regiment."

"The Belomirsky. His transfer to the Belomirsky came almost on the eve of his death. I stood there and blessed him into eternity. Your mother . . ."

The general paused as if in sad remembrance.

"Yes, she also died six months later, of a chill," said the prince.

"Not of a chill, not of a chill, believe an old man. I was there, I buried her, too. Of grief over the prince, and not of a chill. Yes, sir, I have memories of the princess, too! Youth! Because of her, the prince and I, childhood friends, nearly killed each other."

The prince began listening with a certain mistrust.

"I was passionately in love with your mother while she was still a fiancée—my friend's fiancée. The prince noticed it and was shocked. He comes to me in the morning, before seven o'clock, wakes me up. I get dressed in amazement; there is silence on both sides; I understand everything. He takes two pistols from his pocket. Across a handkerchief.[28] Without witnesses. Why witnesses, if we'll be sending each other into eternity in five minutes? We loaded the pistols, stretched out the handkerchief, put the pistols to each other's hearts, and looked into each other's faces. Suddenly tears burst from our eyes, our hands trembled. Both of us, both of us, at once! Well, naturally, then came embraces and a contest in mutual magnanimity. The prince cries: 'She's yours!' I cry: 'She's yours!' In short . . . in short . . . you've come . . . to live with us?"

"Yes, for a while, perhaps," said the prince, as if stammering slightly.

"Prince, mama wants to see you," cried Kolya, looking in at the door. The prince got up to leave, but the general placed his right hand on his shoulder and amiably forced him back down on the couch.

"As a true friend of your father's I wish to warn you," said the general, "I have suffered, as you can see yourself, owing to a tragic catastrophe—but without a trial! Without a trial! Nina Alexandrovna is a rare woman. Varvara Ardalionovna, my daughter, is a rare daughter! Owing to certain circumstances, we let rooms—an unheard-of degradation! I, for whom it only remained to become a governor-general! . . . But we're always glad to have you. And meanwhile there's a tragedy in my house!"

The prince looked at him questioningly and with great curiosity.

"A marriage is being prepared, a rare marriage. A marriage between an ambiguous woman and a young man who could be a kammerjunker.[29] This woman will be introduced into the house in which my daughter and wife live! But as long as there is breath in me, she will not enter it! I'll lie down on the threshold, and just let her step over me! . . . I almost don't speak with Ganya now, I even avoid meeting him. I'm warning you on purpose, though if you live with us you'll witness it anyway without that. But you are my friend's son, and I have the right to hope . . ."

"Prince, be so kind as to come to me in the drawing room," Nina Alexandrovna called, appearing in the doorway herself.

"Imagine, my friend," cried the general, "it appears I dandled the prince in my arms!"

Nina Alexandrovna looked reproachfully at the general and searchingly at the prince, but did not say a word. The prince followed her; but they had only just come to the drawing room and sat down, and Nina Alexandrovna had only just begun telling the prince something hastily and in a half-whisper, when the general himself suddenly arrived in the drawing room. Nina Alexandrovna fell silent at once and bent over her knitting with obvious vexation. The general may have noticed her vexation, but he continued to be in the most excellent spirits.

"My friend's son!" he cried, addressing Nina Alexandrovna. "And so unexpectedly! I'd long ceased imagining. But, my dear, don't you remember the late Nikolai Lvovich? Wasn't he still in Tver . . . when you . . . ?"

"I don't remember Nikolai Lvovich. Is that your father?" she asked the prince.

"Yes. But I believe he died in Elisavetgrad, not in Tver," the prince observed timidly to the general. "I heard it from Pavlishchev . . ."

"In Tver," the general confirmed. "Just before his death he was transferred to Tver, and even before the illness developed. You were still too little and wouldn't remember either the transfer or the trip. And Pavlishchev could have made a mistake, though he was a most excellent man."

"You knew Pavlishchev, too?"

"He was a rare man, but I was a personal witness. I blessed him on his deathbed . . ."

"My father died while he was on trial," the prince observed

again, "though I could never find out precisely for what. He died in the hospital."

"Oh, it was that case to do with Private Kolpakov, and without doubt the prince would have been vindicated."

"Really? You know for certain?" the prince asked with particular curiosity.

"What else?" cried the general. "The court recessed without any decision. An impossible case! A mysterious case, one might say: Staff-captain Larionov, the commander of the detachment, dies; the prince is assigned to perform his duties temporarily. Good. Private Kolpakov commits a theft—of footgear from a comrade— and drinks it up. Good. The prince—and, mark you, this was in the presence of a sergeant-major and a corporal—reprimands Kolpakov and threatens him with a birching. Very good. Kolpakov goes to the barracks, lies down on his bunk, and a quarter of an hour later he dies. Splendid, but it's an unexpected, almost impossible case. Thus and so, Kolpakov is buried; the prince makes a report, after which Kolpakov is struck from the rolls. What could be better, you might think? But exactly six months later, at a brigade review, Private Kolpakov turns up, as if nothing had happened, in the third detachment of the second battalion of the Novozemlyansky infantry regiment,[30] same brigade and same division!"

"How's that?" cried the prince, beside himself with astonishment.

"It's not so, it's a mistake!" Nina Alexandrovna turned to him suddenly, looking at him almost in anguish. "*Mon mari se trompe.*"*

"But, my dear, *se trompe* is easy to say, but try and decide such a case yourself! They were all deadlocked. I'd be the first to say *qu'on se trompe*. But, to my misfortune, I was a witness and served personally on the commission. All the confrontations showed that this was the very same, absolutely the very same Private Kolpakov who had been buried six months earlier with the routine ceremony and to the roll of drums. The case is indeed a rare one, almost impossible, I agree, but . . ."

"Papa, your dinner is ready," Varvara Ardalionovna announced, coming into the room.

"Ah, that's splendid, excellent! I'm really hungry . . . But this case, you might say, is even psychological . . ."

"The soup will get cold again," Varya said impatiently.

*My husband is mistaken.

"Coming, coming," the general muttered, leaving the room. "And despite all inquiries . . ." could still be heard in the corridor.

"You'll have to excuse Ardalion Alexandrovich a great deal if you stay with us," Nina Alexandrovna said to the prince, "though he won't bother you very much; and he dines by himself. You must agree, each of us has his own shortcomings and his own . . . special features—some, perhaps, still more than those at whom fingers are habitually pointed. There's one thing I want very much to ask you: if my husband ever addresses you concerning the payment of the rent, tell him you have given it to me. That is, whatever you might give to Ardalion Alexandrovich would go on your account in any case, but I ask you only for the sake of accuracy . . . What is it, Varya?"

Varya came back into the room and silently handed her mother the portrait of Nastasya Filippovna. Nina Alexandrovna gave a start and began studying it as if in fright, but then with an over-whelmingly bitter feeling. In the end she looked questioningly at Varya.

"She made him a present of it herself today," said Varya, "and this evening everything is to be decided."

"This evening!" Nina Alexandrovna repeated in a half-whisper, as if in despair. "So, then? There are no more doubts here, nor any hopes: she has announced it all by the portrait . . . And what, did he show it to you himself?" she added in surprise.

"You know we've hardly said a word to each other for a whole month now. Ptitsyn told me about it all, and the portrait was lying there on the floor by the table. I picked it up."

"Prince," Nina Alexandrovna suddenly turned to him, "I wanted to ask you—in fact, that's why I invited you here—have you known my son for a long time? He told me, I believe, that you arrived from somewhere only today?"

The prince explained briefly about himself, omitting the greater part. Nina Alexandrovna and Varya heard him out.

"I'm not trying to ferret out anything about Gavrila Ardaliono-vich in asking you," observed Nina Alexandrovna, "you must make no mistake on that account. If there is anything that he cannot tell me himself, I have no wish to try and find it out behind his back. What I mean, in fact, is that earlier, in your presence and after you left, Ganya said in answer to my question about you: 'He knows everything, no need for ceremony!' Now, what does that mean? That is, I'd like to know to what extent . . ."

Suddenly Ganya and Ptitsyn came in; Nina Alexandrovna at once fell silent. The prince remained in the chair next to her, and Varya stepped aside; the portrait of Nastasya Filippovna lay most conspicuously on Nina Alexandrovna's worktable, directly in front of her. Ganya saw it, frowned, vexedly took it from the table, and flung it onto his desk, which was at the other end of the room.

"Today, Ganya?" Nina Alexandrovna suddenly asked.

"Today what?" Ganya gave a start and suddenly fell upon the prince. "Ah, I understand, you're into it here, too! . . . What is it with you, some sort of illness or something? Can't help yourself? But understand, finally, Your Highness . . ."

"I'm to blame here, Ganya, and nobody else," Ptitsyn interrupted.

Ganya looked at him questioningly.

"But it's better, Ganya, the more so as the matter's concluded on one side," Ptitsyn murmured and, stepping away, sat down at the table, took some sort of scribbled-over paper from his pocket, and began studying it intently. Ganya stood in gloom, waiting uneasily for a family scene. He did not even think of apologizing to the prince.

"If it's all concluded, then, of course, Ivan Petrovich is right," said Nina Alexandrovna. "Don't frown, please, and don't be vexed, Ganya, I won't ask about anything that you don't want to talk about yourself, and I assure you that I am completely resigned, kindly don't worry."

She said this without taking her eyes from her work and, as it seemed, quite calmly. Ganya was surprised, but remained warily silent and looked at his mother, waiting for her to speak her mind more clearly. Family scenes had already cost him much too dearly. Nina Alexandrovna noticed this wariness and added, with a bitter smile:

"You still doubt and don't believe me. You needn't worry, there will be no tears or entreaties, as before, at least not on my part. All I want is for you to be happy and you know that; I am resigned to fate, but my heart will always be with you, whether we stay together or must part. Of course, I can only answer for myself; you cannot ask the same of your sister . . ."

"Ah, her again!" cried Ganya, looking mockingly and hatefully at his sister. "Mama! Again I swear to you something on which you have my word already: no one will ever dare to mistreat you while I am here, while I am alive. Whoever it may concern, I shall insist on the fullest respect, whoever crosses our threshold . . ."

Ganya was so overjoyed that he looked at his mother almost conciliatingly, almost tenderly.

"I wasn't afraid for myself, Ganya, you know that. It's not myself I've worried and suffered over all this time. They say it will all be concluded tonight? What will be concluded?"

"Tonight, at her place, she has promised to announce whether she gives me her consent or not," replied Ganya.

"For almost three weeks we've avoided speaking of it, and it was better. Now, when everything's already concluded, I will allow myself to ask just one thing: how could she give you her consent and even present you with her portrait, when you don't love her? Can it be that she, being so . . . so . . ."

"Experienced, you mean?"

"That's not how I wanted to put it. Can it be that you could blind her eyes to such a degree?"

Extraordinary irritation suddenly rang in this question. Ganya stood, reflected for a moment, and, not concealing his derision, said:

"You've gotten carried away, mama, and again could not restrain yourself, and that's how everything always starts and flares up with us. You said there wouldn't be any questions or reproaches, yet they've already started! We'd better drop it, really, we'd better; at least you had the intention . . . I will never leave you, not for anything; another man would flee from such a sister at least—see how she's looking at me now! Let's leave it at that! I was already rejoicing so . . . And how do you know I'm deceiving Nastasya Filippovna? But, as for Varya, it's as she wishes and—enough! Well, now it's quite enough!"

Ganya was getting more and more excited with every word and paced the room aimlessly. Such conversations instantly became a sore spot in all members of the family.

"I said, if she comes in here, then I go out of here—and I'll also keep my word," said Varya.

"Out of stubbornness!" cried Ganya. "And it's out of stubbornness that you don't get married! What are you doing snorting at me! I spit on it all, Varvara Ardalionovna; if you like, you can carry out your intention right now. I'm quite sick of you. So! You've finally decided to leave us, Prince!" he shouted at the prince, seeing him get up from his place.

In Ganya's voice that degree of irritation could be heard in which a man almost enjoys his irritation, gives himself over to it without restraint and almost with increasing pleasure, whatever may come of it. The prince turned around at the door in order to make some reply, but, seeing from the pained expression on his offender's face that with one more drop the vessel would overflow, he turned again and silently went out. A few minutes later he heard, by the noises coming from the drawing room, that in his absence the conversation had become more noisy and frank.

He went through the large room to the front hall, in order to get to the corridor and from there to his room. Passing by the door to the stairs, he heard and saw that someone outside the door was trying very hard to ring the bell; but something must have been wrong with the bell: it only jiggled slightly but made no sound. The prince lifted the bar, opened the door, and—stepped back in amazement, even shuddered all over: before him stood Nastasya Filippovna. He recognized her at once from the portrait. Her eyes flashed with a burst of vexation when she saw him; she quickly came into the front hall, pushed him aside with her shoulder, and said wrathfully, flinging off her fur coat:

"If you're too lazy to fix the doorbell, you should at least be sitting in the front hall when people knock. Well, there, now he's dropped my coat, the oaf!"

The coat was indeed lying on the floor; Nastasya Filippovna, not waiting for the prince to help her out of it, had flung it off into his arms without looking, but the prince had not managed to catch it.

"You ought to be dismissed. Go and announce me."

The prince wanted to say something, but he was so much at a loss that nothing came out, and, holding the coat, which he had picked up from the floor, he went towards the drawing room.

"Well, so now he goes with the coat! Why are you taking the coat? Ha, ha, ha! Are you crazy or something?"

The prince came back and stood like a stone idol looking at her; when she laughed, he also smiled, but he was still unable to move his tongue. In the first moment, as he opened the door for her, he was pale; now color suddenly suffused his face.

"Ah, what an idiot!" Nastasya Filippovna cried indignantly, stamping her foot at him. "Well, what are you doing? Who are you going to announce?"

"Nastasya Filippovna," murmured the prince.

"How do you know me?" she asked quickly. "I've never seen you before! Go and announce . . . What's that shouting?"

"They're quarreling," the prince replied and went to the drawing room.

He came in at a rather decisive moment: Nina Alexandrovna was ready to forget entirely that she was "resigned to everything"; she was, however, defending Varya. Ptitsyn, too, was standing beside Varya, having abandoned his scribbled-over paper. Varya herself was not intimidated, nor was she the timid sort; but her brother's rudeness was becoming more and more impolite and insufferable. On such occasions she usually stopped talking and merely looked at her brother silently, mockingly, not taking her eyes off him. This maneuver, as she knew, was apt to drive him to the utmost limits. At that very moment the prince stepped into the room and said loudly:

"Nastasya Filippovna!"

IX

A GENERAL HUSH FELL: everyone looked at the prince as if they did not understand him and—did not wish to understand. Ganya went numb with fright.

Nastasya Filippovna's arrival, especially at the present moment, was a most strange and bothersome surprise for them all. There was the fact alone that Nastasya Filippovna was visiting for the first time; until then she had behaved so haughtily that, in her conversations with Ganya, she had not even expressed any wish to meet his relations, and lately had not even mentioned them at all, as if they did not exist. Though he was partly glad that such a bothersome conversation had been put off, in his heart Ganya had laid this haughtiness to her account. In any case, he had expected sneers and barbs at his family from her sooner than a visit; he knew for certain that she was informed of all that went on in his home to do with his marital plans and what views his relations had of her. Her visit *now*, after giving him her portrait and on her birthday, the day when she had promised to decide his fate, almost signified the decision itself.

The perplexity with which everyone gazed at the prince did not last long: Nastasya Filippovna herself appeared in the doorway of the drawing room and again, as she came in, pushed the prince slightly aside.

"I finally managed to get in . . . why did you tie up the bell?"

she asked gaily, holding out her hand to Ganya, who rushed to meet her. "What is this overturned look on your face? Introduce me, please . . ."

Completely at a loss, Ganya introduced her to Varya first, and the two women exchanged strange looks before offering each other their hands. Nastasya Filippovna laughed, however, and put on a mask of gaiety; while Varya had no wish to put on a mask and looked at her sullenly and intently; not even the shade of a smile, something required by simple politeness, appeared on her face. Ganya went dead; there was nothing to ask and no time to ask, and he shot such a menacing glance at Varya that she understood, from the force of it, what this moment meant for her brother. Here, it seems, she decided to yield to him and smiled faintly at Nastasya Filippovna. (They all still loved each other very much in the family.) Things were improved somewhat by Nina Alexandrovna, whom Ganya, utterly thrown off, introduced after his sister and even led up to Nastasya Filippovna. But Nina Alexandrovna had only just managed to start something about her "particular pleasure" when Nastasya Filippovna, without listening to the end, quickly turned to Ganya and, sitting down (though she had not yet been invited to) on a small sofa in the corner by the window, said loudly:

"Where's your study? And . . . and where are the tenants? Don't you keep tenants?"

Ganya blushed terribly and tried to mutter some reply, but Nastasya Filippovna immediately added:

"Where can you keep tenants here? You don't even have a study. Is it profitable?" she suddenly asked Nina Alexandrovna.

"It's a bit of a bother," Nina Alexandrovna began. "Of course, there should be some profit. Though we've just . . ."

But again Nastasya Filippovna was no longer listening: she was looking at Ganya, laughing and saying loudly to him:

"What's that face? Oh, my God, what a face you've got right now!"

This laughter continued for several moments, and Ganya's face indeed became very distorted: his stupor, his comical, cowardly bewilderment suddenly left him; but he turned terribly pale; his lips twisted convulsively; silently, with a fixed and nasty look, not tearing his eyes away, he stared into the face of his visitor, who went on laughing.

There was yet another observer who also had not yet rid himself of his near stupefaction at the sight of Nastasya Filippovna; but though he stood "like a post" in his former place, in the doorway to the drawing room, he nevertheless managed to notice Ganya's pallor and the malignant change in his face. This observer was the prince. All but frightened, he suddenly stepped forward mechanically.

"Drink some water," he whispered to Ganya, "and don't stare like that . . ."

It was evident that he had said it without any calculation, without any particular design, just so, on the first impulse; but his words produced an extraordinary effect. It seemed that all of Ganya's spite suddenly poured out on the prince; he seized him by the shoulder and looked at him silently, vengefully, and hatefully, as if unable to utter a word. There was general agitation. Nina Alexandrovna even gave a little cry. Ptitsyn took a step forward in alarm, Kolya and Ferdyshchenko appeared in the doorway and stopped in amazement, Varya alone watched as sullenly as before, but observed attentively. She did not sit down, but stood to one side, next to her mother, her arms folded on her breast.

But Ganya came to his senses at once, almost at the moment of his reaction, and laughed nervously. He recovered completely.

"What are you, Prince, a doctor or something?" he cried as gaily and simple-heartedly as he could. "He even frightened me. Nastasya Filippovna, allow me to introduce this precious specimen to you, though I myself met him only this morning."

Nastasya Filippovna looked at the prince in perplexity.

"Prince? He's a prince? Imagine, and just now, in the front hall, I took him for a lackey and sent him to announce me! Ha, ha, ha!"

"No harm, no harm!" Ferdyshchenko picked up, approaching hastily and delighted that they had begun to laugh. "No harm: *se non è vero . . .*"*[31]

"And I all but scolded you, Prince. Forgive me, please. Ferdyshchenko, what are you doing here at such an hour? I thought I'd at least not find you here. Who? Prince what? Myshkin?" she repeated to Ganya, who, still holding the prince by the shoulder, meanwhile managed to introduce him.

"Our tenant," repeated Ganya.

Obviously, the prince was being presented as something rare (and useful to them all as a way out of a false situation), he was

*If it's not true . . .

almost shoved at Nastasya Filippovna; the prince even clearly heard the word "idiot" whispered behind him, probably by Ferdyshchenko, in explanation to Nastasya Filippovna.

"Tell me, why didn't you undeceive me just now, when I made such a terrible . . . mistake about you?" Nastasya Filippovna went on, scrutinizing the prince from head to foot in a most unceremonious manner. She impatiently awaited the answer, as if fully convinced that the answer was bound to be so stupid that it would be impossible not to laugh.

"I was astonished, seeing you so suddenly . . ." the prince murmured.

"And how did you know it was me? Where have you seen me before? In fact, it's as if I have seen him somewhere—why is that? And, allow me to ask you, why did you stand there so dumbstruck just now? What's so dumbstriking about me?"

"Well, so? so?" Ferdyshchenko kept clowning. "Well, and so? Oh, Lord, what things I'd say to such a question! Well, so . . . What a booby you are, Prince, after this!"

"And what things I'd say, too, in your place!" the prince laughed to Ferdyshchenko. "I was very struck by your portrait today," he went on to Nastasya Filippovna. "Then I talked about you with the Epanchins . . . and early in the morning, still on the train, before I arrived in Petersburg, Parfyon Rogozhin told me a lot about you . . . And at the very moment when I opened the door, I was also thinking about you, and suddenly there you were."

"But how did you recognize me?"

"From the portrait and . . ."

"And?"

"And also because that was precisely how I imagined you . . . It's as if I've also seen you somewhere."

"Where? Where?"

"As if I've seen your eyes somewhere . . . but that can't be! I'm just . . . I've never even been here before. Maybe in a dream . . ."

"Bravo, Prince!" cried Ferdyshchenko. "No, I take back my *se non è vero* . . . But anyhow, anyhow, it's all just his innocence!" he added with regret.

The prince had spoken his few phrases in an uneasy voice, faltering and stopping frequently to catch his breath. Everything about him betrayed extreme agitation. Nastasya Filippovna looked at him with curiosity, but was no longer laughing. Just then a loud new voice was suddenly heard from behind the crowd that closely surrounded the prince and Nastasya Filippovna, parting the crowd, as it were, and dividing it in two. Before Nastasya Filippovna stood the father of the family, General Ivolgin himself. He was wearing a tailcoat and a clean shirtfront; his moustache was dyed . . .

This was more than Ganya could bear.

Proud and vainglorious to the point of insecurity, of hypochondria; seeking all those two months for at least some point on which he could rest with a certain dignity and show himself nobly; feeling himself still a novice on the chosen path, who might fail to keep to it; finally, in despair, having resolved to become totally insolent in his own house, where he was a despot, but not daring to show the same resolve before Nastasya Filippovna, who went on confusing him until the last moment and mercilessly kept the upper hand; "an impatient pauper," in Nastasya Filippovna's own phrase, of which he had been informed; having sworn with all possible oaths to exact painful recompense for it later, and at the same time occasionally dreaming childishly to himself of making all ends meet and reconciling all opposites—he now had to drink this terrible cup as well and, above all, at such a moment! One more unforeseen but most awful torture for a vainglorious man—the torment of blushing for his own family in his own house—fell to his lot. "Is the reward finally worth it?" flashed in Ganya's head at that moment.

What, for those two months, he had dreamed of only at night, as a nightmare which had made him freeze with horror and burn with shame, was taking place at that very moment: a family meeting was finally taking place between his father and Nastasya Filippovna. Occasionally, teasing and chafing himself, he had tried to imagine the general during the wedding ceremony, but he had never been able to finish the painful picture and had hastily abandoned it. Perhaps he had exaggerated the disaster beyond measure; but that is what always happens with vainglorious people. In those two months he had had time to think it over and decide, promising himself that he would try at all costs to cancel his father at least for a time, and even to efface him from Petersburg, if possible, whether his mother agreed to it or not. Ten minutes ago, when Nastasya Filippovna came in, he had been so stricken, so stunned, that he had completely forgotten the possibility of Ardalion Alexandrovich's appearance on the scene, and had not made any arrangements. And so, here was the general, before them all, solemnly prepared and in a tailcoat besides, precisely at the moment when Nastasya Filippovna "was only seeking a chance to shower him and his household with mockery." (Of that he was convinced.) And what, in fact, did her present visit mean if not that? Had she come to make friends with his mother and sister, or to insult them in his own house? But by the way both sides placed themselves, there could no longer be any doubt: his mother and sister sat to one side as if spat upon, while Nastasya Filippovna seemed to have forgotten they were even in the same room with her . . . And if she behaved like that, she certainly had her purpose!

Ferdyshchenko rushed to support the general and led him forward.

"Ardalion Alexandrovich Ivolgin," the bowing and smiling general said with dignity, "an old and unfortunate soldier, and the father of a family happy in the hope of receiving into itself such a lovely . . ."

He did not finish. Ferdyshchenko quickly offered him a chair from behind, and the general, somewhat weak in the legs after dinner, simply flopped or, better to say, collapsed into it; however, that did not embarrass him. He sat directly facing Nastasya Filippovna and, with a pleasant little grimace, slowly and dramatically brought her fingers to his lips. On the whole, it was rather difficult to embarrass the general. His appearance, apart from a certain slovenliness, was still quite decent, as he knew very well himself. In the past he had occasionally been received in very good society, from which he had been definitively excluded only two or three years ago. It was then that he gave himself over all too unrestrainedly to some of his weaknesses; but he still retained his adroit and pleasant manner. Nastasya Filippovna, it seemed, was exceedingly delighted by the appearance of Ardalion Alexandrovich, of whom she knew, of course, by hearsay.

"I've heard that this son of mine . . ." Ardalion Alexandrovich began.

"Yes, this son of yours! And you're a fine one, too, papa dear! Why don't I ever see you at my place? What, are you hiding, or is your son hiding you? You, at least, can come to me without compromising anybody."

"Nineteenth-century children and their parents . . ." the general tried to begin again.

"Nastasya Filippovna! Please let Ardalion Alexandrovich go for a moment, someone is asking for him," Nina Alexandrovna said loudly.

"Let him go! Good heavens, I've heard so much, I've wanted to see him for so long! And what sort of business can he have? Isn't he retired? You won't leave me, General, you won't go?"

"I give you my word that he'll come and see you himself, but now he's in need of rest."

"Ardalion Alexandrovich, they say you're in need of rest!" Nastasya Filippovna cried, making a wry and displeased face, like a flighty, foolish little girl whose toy is being taken away. The general did his best to make his own position all the more foolish.

"My friend! My friend!" he said reproachfully, turning solemnly to his wife and putting his hand to his heart.

"Won't you leave here, mama?" Varya asked loudly.

"No, Varya, I'll sit it out to the end."

Nastasya Filippovna could not help hearing both the question and the answer, but it seemed to increase her gaiety still more. She immediately showered the general with questions again, and after five minutes the general was in a most triumphant mood and was oratorizing to the loud laughter of those present.

Kolya pulled the prince's coattail.

"You at least take him away somehow! Can't you? Please!" Tears of indignation even scalded the poor boy's eyes. "Oh, damn you, Ganka!" he added to himself.

"Ivan Fyodorovich Epanchin and I were actually great friends," the general effused to Nastasya Filippovna's questions. "He and I, and the late Prince Lev Nikolaevich Myshkin, whose son I embraced today after a twenty-year separation, the three of us were inseparable, a cavalcade, so to speak: Athos, Porthos, and Aramis.[32] But, alas, one lies in his grave, struck down by slander and a bullet, another stands before you now and is still fighting against slander and bullets . . ."

"Bullets!" cried Nastasya Filippovna.

"They're here, in my breast, received at Kars,[33] and in bad weather I feel them. In all other respects I live like a philosopher, go about, stroll, play checkers in my café, like a bourgeois retired from business, and read the *Indépendence*.[34] But since that story of the lapdog on the train three years ago, my relations with our Porthos, Epanchin, have been definitively terminated."

"A lapdog? What was that?" Nastasya Filippovna asked with particular curiosity. "With a lapdog? And on the train, if you please! . . ." She seemed to be remembering something.

"Oh, a stupid story, not even worth repeating: because of Mrs.

Schmidt, Princess Belokonsky's governess, but . . . it's not worth repeating."

"No, you absolutely must tell it!" Nastasya Filippovna exclaimed gaily.

"I haven't heard it either!" observed Ferdyshchenko. "*C'est du nouveau.*"*

"Ardalion Alexandrovich!" Nina Alexandrovna's pleading voice rang out again.

"Papa, somebody's asking for you!" cried Kolya.

"A stupid story, and briefly told," the general began self-contentedly. "Two years ago, yes! or a bit less, just when the new —— railway line was opened, I (already in civilian dress), seeing to some extremely important matters to do with handing over my job, bought myself a first-class ticket: I got in, sat down, smoked. That is, I went on smoking, because I had lit up earlier. I was alone in the compartment. Smoking was not prohibited, but neither was it permitted; sort of half permitted, as usual; well, and depending on the person. The window's open. Suddenly, just before the whistle, two ladies with a lapdog place themselves just opposite me; late-comers; one is most magnificently dressed in light blue; the other more modestly, in black silk with a pelerine. They're not bad-looking, have a haughty air, talk in English. I, of course, just sit there smoking. That is, I did have a thought, but nevertheless, since the window's open, I go on smoking out the window. The dog reposes in the light blue lady's lap, a little thing, the size of my fist, black with white paws—even a rarity. Silver collar with a motto. I just sit there. Only I notice that the ladies seem to be angry, about the cigar, of course. One glares through a lorgnette, tortoiseshell. Again I just sit there: because they don't say anything! If they spoke, warned, asked—for there is, finally, such a thing as human speech! But they're silent . . . suddenly—without any warning, I tell you, without the slightest warning, as if she'd taken leave of her senses—the light blue one snatches the cigar from my hand and throws it out the window. The train flies on, I stare like a half-wit. A wild woman; a wild woman, as if in a totally wild state; a hefty one, though, tall, full, blond, ruddy (even much too ruddy), her eyes flashing at me. Without saying a word, with extraordinary politeness, with the most perfect politeness, with the most, so to speak, refined politeness, I reach out for the dog with two fingers, take it delicately by the scruff

*It's something new.

of the neck, and whisk it out the window in the wake of my cigar! It let out a little squeal! The train goes flying on . . ."

"You're a monster!" cried Nastasya Filippovna, laughing and clapping her hands like a little girl.

"Bravo, bravo!" shouted Ferdyshchenko. Ptitsyn, for whom the general's appearance was also extremely disagreeable, smiled as well; even Kolya laughed and also shouted, "Bravo!"

"And I'm right, I'm right, three times right!" the triumphant general went on heatedly. "Because if cigars are prohibited on trains, dogs are all the more so."

"Bravo, papa!" Kolya cried delightedly. "Splendid! I would certainly, certainly have done the same thing!"

"And what about the lady?" Nastasya Filippovna went on questioning impatiently.

"Her? Well, there's where the whole unpleasantness lies," the general continued, frowning. "Without saying a word and without the slightest warning, she whacked me on the cheek! A wild woman, in a totally wild state!"

"And you?"

The general lowered his eyes, raised his eyebrows, raised his shoulders, pressed his lips together, spread his arms, paused, and suddenly said:

"I got carried away!"

"And painfully? Painfully?"

"Not painfully, by God! There was a scandal, but it wasn't painful. I only waved my arm once, merely in order to wave her away. But Satan himself threw a twist into it: the light blue one turned out to be an Englishwoman, a governess or even some sort of friend of the house of Princess Belokonsky, and the one in the black dress was the princess's eldest daughter, an old maid of about thirty-five. And we all know the relations between Mrs. Epanchin and the house of the Belokonskys. All the young princesses swoon, tears, mourning for their favorite lapdog, the six princesses shrieking, the Englishwoman shrieking—the end of the world! Well, of course, I went with my repentance, asked forgiveness, wrote a letter, was not received—neither me nor my letter—then a quarrel with Epanchin, expulsion, banishment!"

"But, excuse me, how it it possible?" Nastasya Filippovna suddenly asked. "Five or six days ago in the *Indépendence*—I always read the *Indépendence*—I read exactly the same story! But decidedly exactly the same! It happened on one of the Rhine railways, in a passenger car, between a Frenchman and an Englishwoman: the cigar was snatched in exactly the same way, the lapdog was tossed out the window in exactly the same way, and, finally, it ended in exactly the same way as with you. The dress was even light blue!"

The general blushed terribly; Kolya also blushed and clutched his head with his hands; Ptitsyn quickly turned away. Ferdyshchenko was the only one who went on laughing. There is no need to mention Ganya: he stood all the while enduring mute and unbearable torment.

"I assure you," the general mumbled, "that exactly the same thing happened to me . . ."

"Papa did actually have some unpleasantness with Mrs. Schmidt, the Belokonskys' governess," cried Kolya, "I remember."

"So! The very same? One and the same story at two ends of Europe and the very same in all details, including the light blue dress!" the merciless Nastasya Filippovna insisted. "I'll send you the *Indépendence Belge!*"

"But notice," the general still insisted, "that to me it happened two years earlier . . ."

"Ah, maybe that's it!"

Nastasya Filippovna laughed as if in hysterics.

"Papa, I beg you to step out for a word or two," Ganya said in a trembling, tormented voice, mechanically seizing his father by the shoulder. Boundless hatred seethed in his eyes.

At that very moment an extremely loud ringing came from the doorbell in the front hall. Such ringing might have torn the bell off. It heralded an extraordinary visit. Kolya ran to open the door.

X

THE FRONT HALL suddenly became noisy and crowded; the impression from the drawing room was as if several people had come in from outside and others were still coming in. Several voices talked and exclaimed at the same time; there was also talking and exclaiming on the stairs, the door to which, from the sound of it, had not been closed. The visit turned out to be extremely strange. Everyone exchanged glances; Ganya rushed to the large room, but several people had already entered it.

"Ah, here he is, the Judas!" cried a voice the prince knew. "Greetings, Ganka, you scoundrel!"

"Yes, it's him himself!" another voice confirmed.

The prince could have no doubt: one voice was Rogozhin's, the other Lebedev's.

Ganya stood as if stupefied on the threshold of the drawing room and gazed silently, allowing some ten or twelve people to enter the room one after another unhindered, following Parfyon Rogozhin. The company was extremely motley, and was distinguished not only by its motleyness but also by its unsightliness. Some came in just as they were, in overcoats and fur coats. None of them, incidentally, was very drunk; but they all seemed quite tipsy. They all seemed to need each other in order to come in; not one of them had courage enough by himself, but they all urged each other on, as it were. Even Rogozhin stepped warily at the head of the crowd, but he had some sort of intention, and he looked gloomily and irritably preoccupied. The rest only made up a chorus, or, better, a claque of supporters. Besides Lebedev, there was also the freshly curled Zalyozhev, who flung his coat off in the front hall and walked in casually and foppishly with two or three similar gentlemen, obviously of the shopkeeper sort. Someone in a half military coat; some small and extremely fat man, ceaselessly laughing; some enormous gentleman, well over six feet tall, also remarkably fat, extremely gloomy and taciturn, who obviously put great trust in his fists. There was a medical student; there was an obsequious little Pole. Some two ladies peeped into the front hall from the stairs, hesitating to come in. Kolya slammed the door in their noses and hooked the latch.

"Greetings, Ganka, you scoundrel! What, you weren't expecting Parfyon Rogozhin?" Rogozhin repeated, having reached the drawing room and stopped in the doorway facing Ganya. But at that moment, in the drawing room, directly facing him, he suddenly caught sight of Nastasya Filippovna. Obviously he had never thought to meet her here, because the sight of her made an extraordinary impression on him; he turned so pale that his lips even became blue. "So it's true!" he said quietly and as if to himself, with a completely lost look. "The end! . . . Well . . . You'll answer to me now!" he suddenly rasped, looking at Ganya with furious spite. "Well . . . ah! . . ."

He even gasped for air, he even had difficulty speaking. He was advancing mechanically into the drawing room, but, having crossed the threshold, he suddenly saw Nina Alexandrovna and Varya and stopped, slightly embarrassed, despite all his agitation. After him came Lebedev, who followed him like a shadow and was already quite drunk, then the student, the gentleman with the fists, Zalyozhev, who was bowing to right and left, and, finally, the short, fat one squeezed in. The presence of the ladies still restrained them all somewhat, and obviously hindered them greatly, only until it *began*, of course, until the first pretext to give a shout and *begin* . . . Then no ladies would hinder them.

"What? You're here, too, Prince?" Rogozhin asked distractedly, somewhat surprised to meet the prince. "Still in your gaiters, ehh!" he sighed, now forgetting the prince and turning his eyes to Nastasya Filippovna, moving as if drawn to her by a magnet.

Nastasya Filippovna also looked at the visitors with uneasy curiosity.

Ganya finally came to his senses.

"Excuse me, but what, finally, is the meaning of this?" he began loudly, looking around sternly at the people coming in and mainly addressing Rogozhin. "It seems you haven't come to a cow-barn, gentlemen, my mother and sister are here . . ."

"We see it's your mother and sister," Rogozhin said through his teeth.

"It's clear they're your mother and sister," Lebedev picked up to lend it countenance.

The gentleman with the fists, probably thinking the moment had come, also began grumbling something.

"But anyhow!" Ganya raised his voice suddenly and explosively, somehow beyond measure. "First, I ask you all to go to the other room, and then I'd like to know . . ."

"See, he doesn't know," Rogozhin grinned spitefully, not budging from where he stood. "You don't know Rogozhin?"

"I suppose I met you somewhere, but . . ."

"See, he met me somewhere! Only three months ago I lost two hundred roubles of my father's money to you. The old man died and had no time to find out. You got me into it, and Kniff cheated. You don't know me? Ptitsyn is my witness! If I was to show you three roubles, to take them out of my pocket right now, you'd crawl after them on all fours to Vassilievsky Island—that's how you are! That's how your soul is! I've come now to buy you out for money, never mind that I'm wearing these boots, I've got a lot of money, brother, I'll buy you out with all you've got here . . . if I want, I'll buy you all! Everything!" Rogozhin grew excited and as if more and more drunk. "Ehh!" he cried, "Nastasya Filippovna!

Don't throw me out, tell me one thing: are you going to marry him or not?"

Rogozhin asked his question like a lost man, as if addressing some sort of divinity, but with the boldness of a man condemned to death, who has nothing more to lose. In deathly anguish he waited for the answer.

Nastasya Filippovna looked him up and down with a mocking and haughty glance, but after glancing at Varya and Nina Alexandrovna, she looked at Ganya and suddenly changed her tone.

"Absolutely not, what's the matter with you? And what on earth made you think of asking?" she replied softly and seriously and as if with some surprise.

"No? No!!" cried Rogozhin, all but beside himself with joy. "So it's no?! And they told me . . . Ah! Well! . . . Nastasya Filippovna! They say you're engaged to Ganka! To him? No, how is it possible? (I tell them all!) No, I'll buy him out for a hundred roubles, I'll give him a thousand, say, or three thousand, to renounce her, he'll run away on the eve of the wedding and leave his bride all to me. So it is, Ganka, you scoundrel! You'll take three thousand. Here it is, here! This is what I came with, to get a receipt from you. I said I'd buy you—and so I will!"

"Get out of here, you're drunk!" cried Ganya, blushing and blanching by turns.

His exclamation was followed by a sudden explosion of several voices; Rogozhin's whole crew had long been waiting for the first challenge. Lebedev whispered something extremely assiduously into Rogozhin's ear.

"That's true, clerk," replied Rogozhin. "It's true, you drunken soul! Eh, come what may. Nastasya Filippovna!" he cried, looking at her like a half-wit, timid and suddenly taking heart to the point of insolence, "here's eighteen thousand!" And he slapped down on the table in front of her a packet wrapped in white paper, tied crisscross with string. "There! And . . . and there'll be more!"

He did not dare to finish what he was going to say.

"No, no, no!" Lebedev began whispering to him with a terribly frightened look; it was clear that he was frightened by the enormity of the sum and had suggested starting with incomparably less.

"No, brother, in this you're a fool, you don't know where you've got to . . . and I, too, must be a fool along with you!" Rogozhin caught himself and gave a sudden start under the flashing eyes of

Nastasya Filippovna. "Ehh! I fouled it up, listening to you," he added with profound regret.

Nastasya Filippovna, peering into Rogozhin's overturned face, suddenly laughed.

"Eighteen thousand, for me? You can tell a boor at once!" she added suddenly, with brazen familiarity, and got up from the sofa as if preparing to leave. Ganya watched the whole scene with a sinking heart.

"Forty thousand then, forty, not eighteen!" cried Rogozhin. "Vanka Ptitsyn and Biskup promised to produce forty thousand by seven o'clock. Forty thousand! All on the table."

The scene was becoming extremely ugly, but Nastasya Filippovna went on laughing and did not go away, as if she were intentionally drawing it out. Nina Alexandrovna and Varya also got up from their places and waited fearfully, silently, for what it would lead to; Varya's eyes flashed, but Nina Alexandrovna was morbidly affected; she trembled and seemed about to faint.

"In that case—a hundred! Today I'll produce a hundred thousand! Ptitsyn, help me out, you'll line your own pockets!"

"You're out of your mind!" Ptitsyn suddenly whispered, going up to him quickly and seizing him by the arm. "You're drunk, they'll send for the police. Do you know where you are?"

"Drunken lies," Nastasya Filippovna said, as if taunting him.

"I'm not lying, I'll have it! By evening I'll have it. Ptitsyn, help me out, you percentage soul, charge whatever you like, get me a hundred thousand by evening: I tell you, I won't stint!" Rogozhin's animation suddenly reached ecstasy.

"What is all this, however?" Ardalion Alexandrovich exclaimed unexpectedly and menacingly, getting angry and approaching Rogozhin. The unexpectedness of the hitherto silent old man's outburst made it very comical. Laughter was heard.

"Where did this one come from?" Rogozhin laughed. "Come with us, old man, you'll get good and drunk!"

"That's mean!" cried Kolya, all in tears from shame and vexation.

"Isn't there at least someone among you who will take this shameless woman out of here?" Varya suddenly cried out, trembling with wrath.

"It's me they call shameless!" Nastasya Filippovna retorted with scornful gaiety. "And here I came like a fool to invite them to my party! This is how your dear sister treats me, Gavrila Ardalionovich!"

For a short while Ganya stood as if thunderstruck by his sister's outburst; but seeing that Nastasya Filippovna was really leaving this time, he fell upon Varya like a man beside himself and furiously seized her by the hand.

"What have you done?" he cried out, looking at her as if he wished to reduce her to ashes on the spot. He was decidedly lost and not thinking well.

"What have I done? Where are you dragging me? Not to ask her forgiveness for having insulted your mother and come to disgrace your home, you low man!" Varya cried again, triumphant, and looking defiantly at her brother.

For a few moments they stood facing each other like that. Ganya was still holding her hand in his. Varya pulled it once or twice with all her might, but could no longer hold back and suddenly, beside herself, spat in her brother's face.

"That's the girl!" cried Nastasya Filippovna. "Bravo, Ptitsyn, I congratulate you!"

Ganya's eyes went dim and, forgetting himself entirely, he swung at his sister with all his might. The blow would certainly have landed on her face. But suddenly another hand stopped his arm in midair.

The prince stepped between him and his sister.

"Enough, no more of that!" he said insistently, but also trembling all over, as if from an extremely strong shock.

"What, are you always going to stand in my way!" Ganya bellowed, dropping Varya's hand, and, having freed his arm, in the utmost degree of rage, he swung roundly and slapped the prince in the face.

"Ah!" Kolya clasped his hands, "ah, my God!"

There were exclamations on all sides. The prince turned pale. With a strange and reproachful gaze, he looked straight into Ganya's eyes; his lips trembled and attempted to say something; they were twisted by a strange and completely inappropriate smile.

"Well, let that be for me . . . but her . . . I still won't let you! . . ." he said quietly at last; but suddenly unable to control himself, he left Ganya, covered his face with his hands, went to the corner, stood facing the wall, and said in a faltering voice:

"Oh, how ashamed you'll be of what you've done!"

Ganya indeed stood as if annihilated. Kolya rushed to the prince and began embracing him and kissing him; after him crowded

Rogozhin, Varya, Ptitsyn, Nina Alexandrovna, everyone, even old Ardalion Alexandrovich.

"Never mind, never mind!" the prince murmured in all directions, with the same inappropriate smile.

"He'll be sorry!" shouted Rogozhin. "You'll be ashamed, Ganka, to have offended such a . . . sheep!" (He was unable to find any other word.) "Prince, my dear soul, drop them all, spit on them, and let's go! You'll learn how Rogozhin loves!"

Nastasya Filippovna was also very struck both by Ganya's act and by the prince's response. Her usually pale and pensive face, which all this while had been so out of harmony with her affected laughter, was now visibly animated by a new feeling; and yet she still seemed unwilling to show it, and the mockery remained as if forcedly on her face.

"Really, I've seen his face somewhere!" she said unexpectedly, seriously now, suddenly remembering her question earlier.

"And you're not even ashamed! You can't be the way you pretended to be just now. It's not possible!" the prince suddenly cried out in deeply felt reproach.

Nastasya Filippovna was surprised, smiled, but, as if keeping something behind her smile, slightly embarrassed, she glanced at Ganya and left the drawing room. But before she reached the front hall, she suddenly came back, quickly went up to Nina Alexandrovna, took her hand, and brought it to her lips.

"He guessed right, in fact, I'm not like that," she whispered quickly, fervently, suddenly flushing and becoming all red, and, turning around, she went out so quickly this time that no one managed to figure out why she had come back. They only saw that she whispered something to Nina Alexandrovna and seemed to kiss her hand. But Varya saw and heard everything, and in astonishment followed her with her eyes.

Ganya came to his senses and rushed to see Nastasya Filippovna off, but she had already gone out. He caught up with her on the stairs.

"Don't see me off!" she called to him. "Good-bye, till this evening! Without fail, you hear!"

He came back confused, pensive; a heavy riddle lay on his soul, still heavier than before. The prince, too, was on his mind . . . He was so oblivious that he barely noticed how the whole Rogozhin crowd poured past him and even jostled him in the doorway, quickly making their way out of the apartment after Rogozhin.

They were all discussing something in loud voices. Rogozhin him-self walked with Ptitsyn, insistently repeating something very important and apparently urgent.

"The game's up, Ganka!" he cried, passing by.

Ganya anxiously watched him leave.

XI

THE PRINCE LEFT the drawing room and shut himself up in his room. Kolya immediately came running to comfort him. It seemed the poor boy was no longer able to leave him alone.

"It's a good thing you left," he said. "There'll be worse turmoil there than before, and it's like that every day, and it all started because of this Nastasya Filippovna."

"You've got many different hurts accumulated here, Kolya," the prince observed.

"Hurts, yes. There's no point talking about us, though. It's our own fault. But I have a great friend here who's even more unhappy. Would you like to meet him?"

"Very much. A comrade of yours?"

"Yes, almost like a comrade. I'll explain it all to you later . . . And Nastasya Filippovna is beautiful, don't you think? I never even saw her till today, though I tried hard to. Really dazzling. I'd forgive Ganka everything if he loved her; but why he's taking money, that's the trouble!"

"Yes, I don't much like your brother."

"Well, what else! For you, after . . . But you know, I can't stand these different opinions. Some madman, or fool, or villain in a mad state, gives a slap in the face, and the man is dishonored for the rest of his life and can't wash it off except with blood, or if the other one begs forgiveness on his knees. I think it's absurd and despotism. Lermontov's play *The Masquerade*[35] is based on it and—stupidly so, in my opinion. That is, I mean to say, it's unnatural. But he wrote it when he was almost still a child."

"I like your sister very much."

"How she spat in Ganka's mug! Brave Varka! But you didn't spit, and I'm sure it's not from lack of courage. Ah, here she is herself, speak of the devil. I knew she'd come: she's noble, though she has some shortcomings."

"You have no business here," Varya fell upon him first of all. "Go to your father. Is he bothering you, Prince?"

"Not at all, on the contrary."

"Well, big sister's off again! That's the bad thing about her. And, by the way, I thought father would be sure to go with Rogozhin. He's probably sorry now. In fact, I should go and see how he is," Kolya added, going out.

"Thank God, I took mama away and put her to bed, and there are no new developments. Ganya is confused and very pensive. And he has reason to be. What a lesson! . . . I've come to thank you once again, Prince, and to ask you: did you know Nastasya Filippovna before?"

"No, I didn't."

"Then what made you tell her to her face that she was 'not like that'? And it seems you guessed right. It appears that she may indeed not be like that. However, I can't make her out! Of course, her aim was to insult us, that's clear. I heard a great many strange things about her even before. But if she came to invite us, why did she start treating mama that way? Ptitsyn knows her very well; he says he couldn't figure her out just now. And with Rogozhin? A woman can't speak like that, if she has any self-respect, in the house of her . . . Mama is also very worried about you."

"It's nothing!" the prince said and waved his hand.

"And how is it she listened to you . . ."

"Listened to what?"

"You told her she was ashamed, and she suddenly changed completely. You have influence over her, Prince," Varya added with a slight smile.

The door opened, and quite unexpectedly Ganya came in.

He did not even hesitate on seeing Varya; for a moment he stood on the threshold and with sudden resoluteness went up to the prince.

"Prince, I acted meanly, forgive me, dear heart," he said suddenly, with strong emotion. The features of his face expressed strong pain. The prince stared in amazement and did not respond at once. "Well, so, forgive me, forgive me!" Ganya insisted impatiently. "Well, if you want, I'll kiss your hand right now."

The prince was extremely surprised and silently embraced Ganya with both arms. The two men kissed each other with sincere feeling.

"I never, never thought you were like this," the prince said at last, barely catching his breath. "I thought you were . . . incapable."

"Of apologizing? . . . And what made me think earlier that you were an idiot? You notice things that other people never notice. One could talk with you, but . . . better not to talk!"

"There's someone else here that you should apologize to," the prince said, pointing to Varya.

"No, they're all my enemies. Rest assured, Prince, I've tried many times; they don't forgive sincerely here!" Ganya burst out hotly and turned away from Varya.

"No, I will forgive you!" Varya said suddenly.

"And go to Nastasya Filippovna's tonight?"

"I will if you tell me to, only you'd better judge for yourself: is it at all possible for me to go now?"

"But she's not like that. See what riddles she sets! Tricks!" And Ganya laughed spitefully.

"I know myself she's not like that and has her tricks, but what tricks? And besides, look, how does she consider you yourself, Ganya? So she kissed mama's hand. So it's some kind of tricks— but she did laugh at you! By God, brother, that's not worth seventy-five thousand! You're still capable of noble feelings, that's why I'm telling you. No, don't go there! Be careful! It can't come to any good!"

Having said this, Varya quickly left the room in great agitation.

"That's how they always are!" said Ganya, smiling. "Can they possibly think I don't know it myself? I know much more than they do."

Having said this, Ganya sat down on the sofa, obviously wishing to prolong his visit.

"If you know it yourself," the prince asked rather timidly, "why have you chosen such a torment, knowing that it's really not worth seventy-five thousand?"

"I wasn't talking about that," Ganya muttered, "but, incidentally, tell me what you think, I precisely want to know your opinion: is this 'torment' worth seventy-five thousand or is it not?"

"To my mind, it's not."

"Well, no news there. And it's shameful to marry like that?"

"Very shameful."

"Well, be it known to you, then, that I am getting married, and it's now quite certain. Earlier today I was still hesitating, but not anymore! Be quiet! I know what you want to say . . ."

"It's not what you think, but I'm very surprised at your extreme assurance. . ."

"About what? Which assurance?"

"That Nastasya Filippovna is certain to accept you, and that it's all concluded, and, second, even if she does, that the seventy-five thousand will go straight into your pocket. Though, of course, there's much here that I don't know."

Ganya made a strong movement towards the prince.

"Of course you don't know everything," he said. "And what would make me take all this burden on myself?"

"It seems to me that it happens all the time: a man marries for money, and the money stays with the wife."

"No, no, it won't be like that with us . . . Here . . . here there are certain circumstances . . ." Ganya murmured in anxious pensiveness. "And as for her answer, there's no doubt about it now," he added quickly. "What makes you conclude that she'll reject me?"

"I know nothing except what I've seen. And Varvara Ardalionovna also said just now . . ."

"Eh! That's nothing, they just don't know what else to say. And she was making fun of Rogozhin, rest assured, that I could see. It was obvious. I was frightened earlier, but now I can see it. Or maybe you mean the way she treated my mother, and my father, and Varya?"

"And you."

"Perhaps. But here it's the age-old woman's revenge and nothing more. She's a terribly irritable, suspicious, and vain woman. Like an official overlooked for promotion! She wanted to show herself and all her contempt for us . . . well, and for me, too—it's true, I don't deny it . . . But she'll marry me all the same. You don't even suspect what tricks human vanity is capable of. Here she considers me a scoundrel because I'm taking her, another man's mistress, so openly for her money, but she doesn't know that another man could dupe her in a more scoundrelly way: he'd get at her and start pouring out liberal and progressive stuff, all drawn from various women's questions, and he'd have the whole of her slip right through the needle's eye like a thread. He'd convince the vain fool (and so easily!) that he's taking her only 'for the nobility of her heart and her misfortunes,' and marry her for her money all the same. She doesn't like me, because I don't want to shuffle; it would be fine if I did. And what's she doing herself? Isn't it the same? Why, then, does she go scorning me and playing all these games? Because I show my pride and don't give in. Well, we'll see!"

"Did you really love her before this?"

"In the beginning I loved her. Well, enough . . . There are women who are only fit to be mistresses and nothing else. I'm not saying she was my mistress. If she wants to live quietly, I'll live quietly, too. If she rebels, I'll drop her at once and take the money with me. I don't want to be ridiculous; above all I don't want to be ridiculous."

"I keep thinking," the prince observed cautiously, "that Nastasya Filippovna is intelligent. If she anticipates such torment, why should she walk into the trap? She could marry somebody else. That's what surprises me."

"But there's the calculation! You don't know everything, Prince . . . here . . . and, besides, she's convinced that I'm madly in love with her, I swear to you, and, you know, I strongly suspect that she also loves me, in her own way, that is, as the saying goes: 'The one I treat, I also beat.' She'll consider me a varlet all her life (that may be what she wants) and love me in her own way even so; she's preparing herself for that, it's her character. She's an extremely Russian woman, I tell you. Well, but I'm preparing my own surprise for her. That scene earlier with Varya happened accidentally, but it was to my profit: now she's seen and been convinced of my devotion and that I'll break all connections for her sake. Meaning we're no fools, rest assured. Incidentally, I hope you don't think I'm such a babbler? Indeed, my dear Prince, perhaps it's a bad thing that I'm confiding in you. I fell upon you precisely because you're the first noble person I've met—I mean, 'fell upon' with no pun intended. You're not angry because of what happened, eh? I'm speaking from the heart maybe for the first time in a whole two years. There are very few honest people here. Ptitsyn's the most honest. It seems you're laughing, or aren't you? Scoundrels love honest people—did you know that? And I'm . . . However, in what way am I a scoundrel? Tell me in all conscience. Why do they repeat after her that I'm a scoundrel? And, you know, I also repeat after them and her that I'm a scoundrel! That's the most scoundrelly thing of all!"

"I'll never consider you a scoundrel now," said the prince. "Earlier I took you altogether for a villain, and suddenly you overjoyed me so—it's a real lesson: not to judge without experience. Now I see that you not only cannot be considered a villain, but that you haven't even gone all that bad. To my mind, you're simply the most ordinary man that could be, only very weak and not the least bit original."

Ganya smiled sarcastically to himself but said nothing. The prince saw that his opinion was not liked, became embarrassed, and also fell silent.

"Did father ask you for money?" Ganya asked suddenly.

"No."

"He will. Don't give him any. And he even used to be a decent man, I remember. He was received by good people. How quickly they all come to an end, all these decent old people! Circumstances need only change, and there's nothing left of the former, it's gone up like a flash of powder. He didn't lie like that before, I assure you; he was just a much too rapturous man before, and—this is what it's come to! Drink's to blame, of course. Do you know that he keeps a mistress? He hasn't stayed simply an innocent little liar. I can't understand my mother's long-suffering. Did he tell you about the siege of Kars? Or how his gray outrunner began to talk? He even goes that far."

And Ganya suddenly rocked with laughter.

"Why are you looking at me like that?" he asked the prince.

"It surprises me that you laugh so genuinely. You really have a childlike laugh. When you came in to make peace with me and said: 'If you want, I'll kiss your hand,' it was like children making peace. Which means you're still capable of such words and gestures. Then suddenly you start reading a whole lecture about all this darkness and the seventy-five thousand. Really, it's all somehow absurd and cannot be."

"What do you want to conclude from that?"

"Mightn't it be that you're acting too light-mindedly, that you ought to look around first? Varvara Ardalionovna may have spoken rightly."

"Ah, morality! That I'm still a little boy, I know myself," Ganya interrupted him hotly, "if only in that I've started such a conversation with you. I'm not going into this darkness out of calculation, Prince," he went on, giving himself away like a young man whose vanity has been wounded. "Out of calculation I'd surely make a mistake, because my head and character aren't strong yet. I'm going out of passion, out of inclination, because I have a major goal. You must think I'll get the seventy-five thousand and right away buy a carriage and pair. No, sir, I'll go on wearing my two-year-old frock coat and drop all my club acquaintances. There are few people of self-control among us, and they're all usurers, but I want to show self-control. The main thing here is to carry it through to the end—that's the whole task! When he was seventeen, Ptitsyn slept in the street, peddled penknives, and started with a kopeck; now he's got sixty thousand, but after what gymnastics! Well, I'm going to leap over all the gymnastics and start straight off with capital; in fifteen years people will say: 'There goes Ivolgin, the king of the Jews.'[36] You tell me I'm an unoriginal man. Note for yourself, dear Prince, that nothing offends a man of our time and tribe more than to be told that he's unoriginal, weak of character, with no special talents, and an ordinary man. You didn't even deign to consider me a good scoundrel, and, you know, I wanted to eat you for that just now! You insulted me more than Epanchin, who considers me (and without any discussion, without any provocation, in the simplicity of his soul, note that) capable of selling him my wife! That, my dear, has long infuriated me, and I want money. Having made money, be it known to you—I'll become an original man in the highest degree. The meanest and most hateful thing about money is that it even gives one talent. And so it will be till the world ends. You'll say it's all childish or maybe poetry—so what, it's the more fun for me, but the main thing will be done all the same. I'll carry it through to the end and show self-control. *Rira bien qui rira le dernier.** Why does Epanchin offend me so? Out of spite, is it? Never, sir. Simply because I'm so insignificant. Well, sir, but then . . . Enough, however, it's late. Kolya has already poked his nose in twice: he's calling you to dinner. And I'm clearing out. I'll wander in to see you some time. It'll be nice for you here; they'll take you as one of the family now. Watch out, don't give me away. I have a feeling that you and I will either be friends or enemies. And what do you think, Prince, if I had kissed your hand earlier (as I sincerely offered to do), would it have made me your enemy afterwards?"

"It certainly would have, only not forever, later you would have been unable to keep from forgiving me," the prince decided after some reflection, and laughed.

"Aha! One must be more careful with you. Devil knows, you poured in some poison there, too. And, who knows, maybe you are my enemy? Incidentally—ha, ha, ha! I forgot to ask: is my impression right, that you like Nastasya Filippovna a bit too much, eh?"

"Yes . . . I like her."

*He who laughs last laughs best.

"In love?"

"N-no!"

"But he turns all red and suffers. Well, all right, all right, I won't laugh. Good-bye. And, you know, she's a virtuous woman, can you believe that? You think she lives with that one, with Totsky? No, no! Not for a long time. And did you notice that she's terribly awkward and was even abashed for a few moments today? Really. There's the kind that loves domination. Well, good-bye!"

Ganechka went out much more casually than he came in, and in good spirits. For about ten minutes the prince remained motionless and pondered.

Kolya again stuck his head in at the door.

"I don't want any dinner, Kolya. I had a good lunch at the Epanchins'."

Kolya came all the way in the door and handed the prince a note. It was from the general, folded and sealed. By Kolya's face it could be seen that it was painful for him to deliver it. The prince read it, got up, and took his hat.

"It's two steps from here," Kolya became embarrassed. "He's sitting there now over a bottle. How he got them to give him credit I can't understand. Prince, dear heart, please don't tell them later that I brought you the note! I've sworn a thousand times not to do it, but I feel sorry for him. Oh, and please don't be ceremonious with him: give him a little something, and there's an end to it."

"I had a thought myself, Kolya. I need to see your father . . . on a certain matter . . . Let's go . . ."

XII

KOLYA LED THE prince not far away, to Liteinaya, to a café and billiard parlor on the ground floor, with an entrance from the street. There, to the right, in the corner, in a private little room, Ardalion Alexandrovich had settled like an old-time habitué, a bottle on the table in front of him and, in fact, with the *Indépendence Belge* in his hands. He was expecting the prince. As soon as he saw him, he put the newspaper aside and began an ardent and verbose explanation, of which, however, the prince understood almost nothing, because the general was already nearly loaded.

"I haven't got ten roubles," the prince interrupted, "but here's twenty-five, have it broken for you and give me back fifteen, otherwise I'll be left without a penny myself."

"Oh, no question; and rest assured that this very hour . . ."

"Besides, I have something to ask you, General. Have you ever been to Nastasya Filippovna's?"

"I? Have I ever been? You say this to me? Several times, my dear, several times!" the general cried in a fit of self-satisfied and triumphant irony. "But I finally stopped it myself, because I did not wish to encourage an improper union. You saw it yourself, you were a witness this afternoon: I've done everything a father could do—but a meek and indulgent father; now a father of a different sort will come onstage, and then—we shall see whether the honored old soldier will gain the upper hand in this intrigue, or a shameless adventuress will get into the noblest of families."

"But I precisely wanted to ask you whether, as an acquaintance, you might not get me into Nastasya Filippovna's this evening? I absolutely must be there tonight; I have business; but I have no idea how to get in. I was introduced to her today, but all the same I wasn't invited: she's giving a party this evening. I'm prepared to overlook certain proprieties, however, and they can even laugh at me, if only I get in somehow."

"And you've hit squarely, squarely upon my own idea, my young friend," the general exclaimed rapturously. "I didn't summon you for a trifle!" he went on, picking up the money, however, and dispatching it into his pocket. "I summoned you precisely to invite you to accompany me on the march to Nastasya Filippovna, or, better, on the march against Nastasya Filippovna! General Ivolgin and Prince Myshkin! How will that seem to her! And I, in the guise of birthday courtesies, will finally pronounce my will—in a roundabout way, not directly, but it will be as if directly. Then Ganya himself will see what he must do: either an honored father and . . . so to speak . . . the rest of it, or . . . But what will be, will be! Your idea is highly fruitful. At nine o'clock we'll set out, we still have time."

"Where does she live?"

"Far from here: by the Bolshoi Theater, Mrs. Mytovtsev's house, almost there in the square, on the second floor . . . She won't have a big gathering, despite the birthday, and they'll go home early . . ."

It had long been evening; the prince was still sitting, listening, and waiting for the general, who had started on an endless number of anecotes and never finished a single one of them. On the prince's arrival, he had called for a new bottle and finished it only an hour later, then called for one more and finished that one. It must be supposed that in the meantime the general had managed to tell almost the whole of his story. Finally the prince got up and said he could not wait any longer. The general finished the last dregs of his bottle, got up, and started out of the room with very unsteady steps. The prince was in despair. He could not understand how he could have been so foolishly trusting. In fact, he had never trusted the general; he had counted on him only so as to get into Nastasya Filippovna's somehow, even if with a certain scandal, but he had not counted on an excessive scandal: the general turned out to be decidedly drunk, extremely eloquent, and talked nonstop, with feeling, with a tear in his soul. Things constantly came round to the fact that, owing to the bad behavior of all the members of his family, everything was about to collapse, and it was time finally to put a stop to it. They finally came out to Liteinaya. The thaw was still going on; a dismal, warm, noxious wind whistled along the streets, carriages splashed through the mud, iron-shod trotters and nags struck the pavement ringingly. A dismal and wet crowd of pedestrians wandered along the sidewalks. Some were drunk.

"Do you see these lighted second floors?" said the general. "That is where all my comrades live, while I, I, who served and suffered more than all of them, I trudge on foot to the Bolshoi Theater, to the apartments of a dubious woman! A man with thirteen bullets in his chest . . . you don't believe me? And yet it was solely for me that Pirogov telegraphed to Paris and left besieged Sevastopol for a time, and Nélaton, the court physician in Paris, obtained a safe conduct in the name of science and came to besieged Sevastopol to examine me.[37] The highest authorities know of it: 'Ah, it's that Ivolgin, the one with thirteen bullets! . . .' That's what they say, sir! Do you see this house, Prince? Here on the second floor lives my old comrade, General Sokolovich, with his most noble and numerous family. This house, with three more on Nevsky Prospect and two on Morskaya—that is the whole present circle of my acquaintance, that is, my own personal acquaintance. Nina Alexandrovna has long since resigned herself to circumstances. But I still go on remembering . . . and, so to speak, find repose in the cultivated circle of my former comrades and subordinates, who adore me to this day. This General Sokolovich (it's a rather long time, however, since I've been to see him and Anna Fyodorovna) . . . you know, my dear Prince, when you don't receive, you some-

how involuntarily stop visiting others as well. And yet . . . hm . . .
it seems you don't believe . . . Though why shouldn't I introduce
the son of my best friend and childhood companion to this charming family? General Ivolgin and Prince Myshkin! You'll meet an
amazing girl, and not just one but two, even three, the ornaments
of our capital and society: beauty, cultivation, tendency . . . the
woman question, poetry—all this united in a happy, diversified
mixture, not counting the dowry of at least eighty thousand in cash
that each girl comes with, which never hurts, whatever the woman
and social questions . . . in short, I absolutely, absolutely must
and am duty-bound to introduce you. General Ivolgin and Prince
Myshkin!"

"At once? Now? But you've forgotten," the prince began.

"I've forgotten nothing, nothing, come along! This way, to this
magnificent stairway. Surprising there's no doorkeeper, but . . . it's
a holiday, and the doorkeeper is away. They haven't dismissed the
drunkard yet. This Sokolovich owes all the happiness of his life
and career to me, to me alone and no one else, but . . . here we are."

The prince no longer objected to the visit and obediently followed the general, so as not to vex him, in the firm hope that
General Sokolovich and his whole family would gradually evapor-
ate like a mirage and turn out to be nonexistent, and they could
calmly go back down the stairs. But, to his horror, he began to lose
this hope: the general was taking him up the stairs like someone
who really had acquaintances there, and kept putting in biograph-
ical and topographical details full of mathematical precision.
Finally, when they reached the second floor and stopped outside
the door of a wealthy apartment, and the general took hold of
the bellpull, the prince decided to flee definitively; but one odd
circumstance stopped him for a moment.

"You're mistaken, General," he said. "The name on the door is
Kulakov, and you're ringing for Sokolovich."

"Kulakov . . . Kulakov doesn't prove anything. It's Sokolovich's
apartment, and I'm ringing for Sokolovich. I spit on Kulakov . . .
And, you see, they're opening."

The door indeed opened. A footman peeped out and announced
that "the masters aren't at home, sir."

"Too bad, too bad, as if on purpose," Ardalion Alexandrovich
repeated several times with the deepest regret. "Tell them, my dear
fellow, that General Ivolgin and Prince Myshkin wished to pay
their personal respects and were extremely, extremely sorry . . ."

At that moment another face peeped from inside through the open door, the housekeeper's by the look of it, perhaps even the governess's, a lady of about forty, wearing a dark dress. She approached with curiosity and mistrust on hearing the names of General Ivolgin and Prince Myshkin.

"Marya Alexandrovna is not at home," she said, studying the general in particular, "she took the young lady, Alexandra Mikhailovna, to visit her grandmother."

"And Alexandra Mikhailovna went with her—oh, God, what bad luck! And imagine, madam, I always have such bad luck! I humbly ask you to give her my greetings, and to remind Alexandra Mikhailovna . . . in short, convey to her my heartfelt wish for that which she herself wished for on Thursday, in the evening, to the strains of Chopin's ballade; she'll remember . . . My heartfelt wish! General Ivolgin and Prince Myshkin!"

"I won't forget, sir," the lady bowed out, having become more trustful.

Going downstairs, the general, his fervor not yet cooled, continued to regret the failure of the visit and that the prince had been deprived of such a charming acquaintance.

"You know, my dear, I'm something of a poet in my soul, have you noticed that? But anyhow . . . anyhow, it seems we didn't go to exactly the right place," he suddenly concluded quite unexpectedly. "The Sokoloviches, I now recall, live in another house, and it seems they're even in Moscow now. Yes, I was slightly mistaken, but that's . . . no matter."

"I'd only like to know one thing," the prince remarked dejectedly, "am I to stop counting on you entirely and go ahead on my own?"

"To stop? Counting? On your own? But why on earth, when for me it's a capital undertaking, upon which so much in the life of my whole family depends? No, my young friend, you don't know Ivolgin yet. Whoever says 'Ivolgin' says 'a wall': trust in Ivolgin as in a wall, that's what I used to say in the squadron where I began my service. It's just that I'd like to stop on the way at a certain house, where my soul has found repose these several years now, after anxieties and trials . . ."

"You want to stop at home?"

"No! I want . . . to see Mrs. Terentyev, the widow of Captain Terentyev, my former subordinate . . . and even friend . . . There, in her house, I am reborn in spirit and there I bring the sorrows of my personal and domestic life . . . And since today I precisely bear a great moral burden, I . . ."

"It seems to me that I did a very foolish thing anyway," the prince murmured, "in troubling you earlier. And besides that, you're now . . . Good-bye!"

"But I cannot, I cannot let you go, my young friend!" the general roused himself. "A widow, the mother of a family, and from her heart she produces chords to which my whole being responds. The visit to her is a matter of five minutes, in that house I behave without ceremony, I almost live there; I'll wash, do the most necessary brushing up, and then we'll take a cab to the Bolshoi Theater. You can be sure I shall have need of you for the whole evening . . . Here's the house, we've arrived . . . Ah, Kolya, you're already here? Well, is Marfa Borisovna at home, or have you only just arrived?"

"Oh, no," replied Kolya, who had run right into them in the gateway, "I've been here for a long time, with Ippolit, he's worse, he stayed in bed this morning. I went down to the grocer's just now for a deck of cards. Marfa Borisovna's expecting you. Only, papa, you're so . . . !" Kolya broke off, studying the general's gait and bearing. "Oh, well, come on!"

The meeting with Kolya induced the prince to accompany the general to Marfa Borisovna's as well, but only for a minute. The prince needed Kolya; as for the general, he decided to abandon him in any case, and could not forgive himself for venturing to trust him earlier. They climbed up for a long time, to the fourth floor, and by the back stairs.

"You want to introduce the prince?" Kolya asked on the way.

"Yes, my friend, I want to introduce him: General Ivolgin and Prince Myshkin, but what . . . how . . . Marfa Borisovna . . ."

"You know, papa, it would be better if you didn't go in. She'll eat you up! It's the third day you haven't poked your nose in there, and she's been waiting for money. Why did you promise her money? You're always like that! Now you'll have to deal with it."

On the fourth floor they stopped outside a low door. The general was visibly timid and shoved the prince forward.

"And I'll stay here," he murmured. "I want it to be a surprise . . ."

Kolya went in first. Some lady, in heavy red and white makeup, wearing slippers and a jerkin, her hair plaited in little braids, about forty years old, looked out the door, and the general's surprise unexpectedly blew up. The moment the lady saw him, she shouted:

"There he is, that low and insidious man, my heart was expecting it!"

"Let's go in, it's all right," the general murmured to the prince, still innocently laughing it off.

But it was not all right. As soon as they went through the dark and low front hall into the narrow drawing room, furnished with a half-dozen wicker chairs and two card tables, the hostess immediately started carrying on as if by rote in a sort of lamenting and habitual voice:

"And aren't you ashamed, aren't you ashamed of yourself, barbarian and tyrant of my family, barbarian and fiend! He's robbed me clean, sucked me dry, and he's still not content! How long will I put up with you, you shameless and worthless man!"

"Marfa Borisovna, Marfa Borisovna! This . . . is Prince Myshkin. General Ivolgin and Prince Myshkin," the general murmured, trembling and at a loss.

"Would you believe," the captain's widow suddenly turned to the prince, "would you believe that this shameless man hasn't spared my orphaned children! He's stolen everything, filched everything, sold and pawned everything, left nothing. What am I to do with your promissory notes, you cunning and shameless man? Answer, you sly fox, answer me, you insatiable heart: with what, with what am I to feed my orphaned children? Here he shows up drunk, can't stand on his feet . . . How have I angered the Lord God, you vile and outrageous villain, answer me?"

But the general had other things on his mind.

"Marfa Borisovna, twenty-five roubles . . . all I can do, with the help of a most noble friend. Prince! I was cruelly mistaken! Such is . . . life . . . And now . . . forgive me, I feel weak," the general went on, standing in the middle of the room and bowing on all sides, "I feel weak, forgive me! Lenochka! a pillow . . . dear!"

Lenochka, an eight-year-old girl, immediately ran to fetch a pillow and put it on the hard and ragged oilcloth sofa. The general sat down on it with the intention of saying much more, but the moment he touched the sofa, he drooped sideways, turned to the wall, and fell into a blissful sleep. Marfa Borisovna ceremoniously and ruefully showed the prince to a chair by a card table, sat down facing him, propped her right cheek in her hand, and silently began to sigh, looking at the prince. The three small children, two girls and a boy, of whom Lenochka was the oldest, came up to the table; all three put their hands on the table, and all three also began to gaze intently at the prince. Kolya appeared from the other room.

"I'm very glad to have met you here, Kolya," the prince turned to him. "Couldn't you help me? I absolutely must be at Nastasya Filippovna's. I asked Ardalion Alexandrovich earlier, but he's fallen asleep. Take me there, because I don't know the streets or the way. I have the address, though: near the Bolshoi Theater, Mrs. Mytovtsev's house."

"Nastasya Filippovna? But she's never lived near the Bolshoi Theater, and my father has never been to Nastasya Filippovna's, if you want to know. It's strange that you expected anything from him. She lives off Vladimirskaya, near the Five Corners, it's much nearer here. Do you want to go now? It's nine-thirty. I'll take you there, if you like."

The prince and Kolya left at once. Alas! The prince had no way to pay for a cab, and they had to go on foot.

"I wanted to introduce you to Ippolit," said Kolya. "He's the oldest son of this jerkined captain's widow and was in the other room; he's unwell and stayed in bed all day today. But he's so strange; he's terribly touchy, and it seemed to me that you might make him ashamed, coming at such a moment . . . I'm not as ashamed as he is, because it's my father, after all, not my mother, there's still a difference, because in such cases the male sex isn't dishonored. Though maybe that's a prejudice about the predominance of the sexes in such cases. Ippolit is a splendid fellow, but he's the slave of certain prejudices."

"You say he has consumption?"

"Yes, I think it would be better if he died sooner. In his place I'd certainly want to die. He feels sorry for his brother and sisters, those little ones. If it was possible, if only we had the money, he and I would rent an apartment and renounce our families. That's our dream. And, you know, when I told him about that incident with you, he even got angry, he says that anyone who ignores a slap and doesn't challenge the man to a duel is a scoundrel. Anyhow, he was terribly irritated, and I stopped arguing with him. So it means that Nastasya Filippovna invited you to her place straight off?"

"The thing is that she didn't."

"How can you be going, then?" Kolya exclaimed and even stopped in the middle of the sidewalk. "And . . . and dressed like that, and to a formal party?"

"By God, I really don't know how I'm going to get in. If they receive me—good; if not—then my business is lost. And as for my clothes, what can I do about that?"

"You have business there? Or is it just so, *pour passer le temps** in 'noble society'?"

"No, essentially I . . . that is, I do have business . . . it's hard for me to explain it, but . . ."

"Well, as for what precisely, that can be as you like, but the main thing for me is that you're not simply inviting yourself to a party, to be in the charming company of loose women, generals, and usurers. If that were so, excuse me, Prince, but I'd laugh at you and start despising you. There are terribly few honest people here, so that there's nobody at all to respect. You can't help looking down on them, while they all demand respect—Varya first of all. And have you noticed, Prince, in our age they're all adventurers! And precisely here, in Russia, in our dear fatherland. And how it has all come about, I can't comprehend. It seemed to stand so firmly, and what is it now? Everybody talks and writes about it everywhere. They expose. With us everybody exposes. The parents are the first to retreat and are ashamed themselves at their former morals. There, in Moscow, a father kept telling his son to *stop at nothing* in getting money; it got into print.[38] Look at my general. What's become of him? But, anyhow, you know, it seems to me that my general is an honest man; by God, it's so! All that is just disorder and drink. By God, it's so! It's even a pity; only I'm afraid to say it, because everybody laughs; but by God, it's a pity. And what about them, the smart ones? They're all usurers, every last one. Ippolit justifies usury; he says that's how it has to be, there's economic upheaval, some sort of influxes and refluxes, devil take them. It vexes me terribly to have it come from him, but he's angry. Imagine, his mother, the captain's widow, takes money from the general and then gives him quick loans on interest. It's terribly shameful! And, you know, mother, I mean my mother, Nina Alexandrovna, the general's wife, helps Ippolit with money, clothes, linen, and everything, and sometimes the children, too, through Ippolit, because the woman neglects them. And Varya does the same."

"You see, you say there are no honest and strong people, that there are only usurers; but then strong people turn up, your mother

*To pass the time.

and Varya. Isn't it a sign of moral strength to help here and in such circumstances?"

"Varka does it out of vanity, out of boastfulness, so as not to lag behind her mother. Well, but mama actually . . . I respect it. Yes, I respect it and justify it. Even Ippolit feels it, though he's almost totally embittered. At first he made fun of it, called it baseness on my mother's part; but now he's beginning to feel it sometimes. Hm! So you call it strength? I'll make note of that. Ganya doesn't know about it, or he'd call it connivance."

"And Ganya doesn't know? It seems there's still a lot that Ganya doesn't know," escaped the prince, who lapsed into thought.

"You know, Prince, I like you very much. I can't stop thinking about what happened to you today."

"And I like you very much, Kolya."

"Listen, how do you intend to live here? I'll soon find myself work and earn a little something. Let's take an apartment and live together, you, me, and Ippolit, the three of us; and we can invite the general to visit."

"With the greatest pleasure. We'll see, though. Right now I'm very . . . very upset. What? We're there already? In this house . . . what a magnificent entrance! And a doorkeeper! Well, Kolya, I don't know what will come of it."

The prince stood there like a lost man.

"You'll tell me about it tomorrow! Don't be too shy. God grant you success, because I share your convictions in everything! Goodbye. I'll go back now and tell Ippolit about it. And you'll be received, there's no doubt of that, don't worry! She's terribly original. This stairway, second floor, the doorkeeper will show you!"

XIII

THE PRINCE WAS very worried as he went upstairs and tried as hard as he could to encourage himself. "The worst thing," he thought, "will be if they don't receive me and think something bad about me, or perhaps receive me and start laughing in my face . . . Ah, never mind!" And, in fact, it was not very frightening; but the question: "What would he do there and why was he going?"— to this question he was decidedly unable to find a reassuring answer. Even if it should be possible in some way to seize an opportunity and tell Nastasya Filippovna: "Don't marry this man and don't ruin yourself, he doesn't love you, he loves your money, he told me so himself, and Aglaya Epanchin told me, and I've come to tell you"— it would hardly come out right in all respects. Yet another unresolved question emerged, and such a major one that the prince was even afraid to think about it, could not and dared not even admit it, did not know how to formulate it, and blushed and trembled at the very thought of it. But in the end, despite all these anxieties and doubts, he still went in and asked for Nastasya Filippovna.

Nastasya Filippovna occupied a not very large but indeed magnificently decorated apartment. There had been a time, at the beginning of those five years of her Petersburg life, when Afanasy Ivanovich had been particularly unstinting of money for her; he was then still counting on her love and thought he could seduce her mainly by comfort and luxury, knowing how easily the habits of luxury take root and how hard it is to give them up later, when luxury has gradually turned into necessity. In this case Totsky remained true to the good old traditions, changing nothing in them, and showing a boundless respect for the invincible power of sensual influences. Nastasya Filippovna did not reject the luxury, even liked it, but—and this seemed extremely strange—never succumbed to it, as if she could always do without it; she even tried several times to declare as much, which always struck Totsky unpleasantly. However, there was much in Nastasya Filippovna that struck Afanasy Ivanovich unpleasantly (later even to the point of scorn). Not to mention the inelegance of the sort of people she occasionally received, and was therefore inclined to receive, into her intimate circle, there could also be glimpsed in her certain utterly strange inclinations: there appeared a sort of barbaric mixture of two tastes, an ability to get along and be satisfied with things and ways the very existence of which, it seemed, would be unthinkable for a decent and finely cultivated person. Indeed, to give an example, if Nastasya Filippovna had suddenly displayed some charming and graceful ignorance, such as, for instance, that peasant women could not wear cambric undergarments such as she wore, Afanasy Ivanovich would probably have been extremely pleased with it. This was the result towards which Nastasya Filippovna's entire education had originally been aimed, according to Totsky's program, for he was a great connoisseur in that line; but alas! the results turned out to be strange. In spite of that, there nevertheless was and remained in Nastasya Filippovna something that occasionally struck even Afanasy Ivanovich himself by its extraordinary and fascinating originality, by some sort of power, and enchanted him on occasion even now, when all his former expectations with regard to Nastasya Filippovna had fallen through.

The prince was received by a maid (Nastasya Filippovna always kept female servants), who, to his surprise, listened to his request to be announced without any perplexity. Neither his dirty boots, nor his broad-brimmed hat, nor his sleeveless cloak, nor his embarrassed look caused the slightest hesitation in her. She helped him off with his cloak, asked him to wait in the front hall, and went at once to announce him.

The company that had gathered at Nastasya Filippovna's consisted of her most usual and habitual acquaintances. There were even rather few people compared with previous years' gatherings on the same day. Present first and foremost were Afanasy Ivanovich Totsky and Ivan Fyodorovich Epanchin; both were amiable, but both were in some repressed anxiety on account of the poorly concealed expectation of the promised announcement about Ganya. Besides them, naturally, there was Ganya as well—also very gloomy, very pensive, and even almost totally "unamiable"—who for the most part stood to one side, separately, and kept silent. He had not ventured to bring Varya, but Nastasya Filippovna made no mention of her; instead, as soon as she greeted Ganya, she reminded him of the scene with the prince. The general, who had not heard about it yet, began to show interest. Then Ganya drily, restrainedly, but with perfect frankness, told everything that had happened earlier, and how he had already gone to the prince to apologize. With that he warmly voiced his opinion that the prince, quite strangely and for God knows what reason, was called an idiot, that he thought completely the opposite of him, and that he was most certainly a man who kept his own counsel. Nastasya Filippovna listened to this opinion with great attention and followed Ganya curiously, but the conversation immediately switched to Rogozhin, who had taken such a major part in that day's story and in whom Afanasy Ivanovich and Ivan Fyodorovich also began to take an extremely curious interest. It turned out that specific information about Rogozhin could be supplied by Ptitsyn, who had been hard at work on his business until nearly nine o'clock that evening. Rogozhin had insisted with all his might that he should get hold of a hundred thousand roubles that same day. "True, he was drunk," Ptitsyn observed with that, "but, difficult as it is, it seems he'll get the hundred thousand, only I don't know if it will be today and the whole of it. Many people are working on it—Kinder, Trepalov, Biskup; he's offering any interest they like, though, of course, it's all from drink and in his initial joy . . ." Ptitsyn concluded. All this news was received with a somewhat gloomy interest. Nastasya Filippovna was silent, obviously unwilling to speak her mind; Ganya also. General Epanchin was almost more worried than anyone else: the pearls he had already presented earlier in the day had been received with a much too cool politeness, and even with a sort of special smile. Ferdyshchenko alone of all the guests was in jolly and festive spirits, and guffawed loudly, sometimes for no known reason, only because he had adopted for himself the role of buffoon. Afanasy Ivanovich himself, reputed to be a fine and elegant talker, who on previous occasions had presided over the conversation at these parties, was obviously in low spirits and even in some sort of perplexity that was quite unlike him. The remainder of the guests, of whom, incidentally, there were not many (one pathetic little old schoolteacher, invited for God knows what purpose, some unknown and very young man, who was terribly timid and kept silent all the time, a sprightly lady of about forty, an actress, and one extremely beautiful, extremely well and expensively dressed, and extraordinarily taciturn young lady), were not only unable to enliven the conversation especially, but sometimes simply did not know what to talk about.

Thus, the prince's appearance was even opportune. When he was announced, it caused bewilderment and a few strange smiles, especially as it was evident from Nastasya Filippovna's surprised look that she had never thought of inviting him. But after her surprise, Nastasya Filippovna suddenly showed such pleasure that the majority prepared at once to meet the unexpected guest with laughter and merriment.

"I suppose it comes of his innocence," Ivan Fyodorovich Epanchin concluded, "and to encourage such inclinations is in any case rather dangerous, but at the present moment it's really not bad that he has decided to come, though in such an original manner. He may even amuse us a bit, at least so far as I can judge about him."

"The more so as he's invited himself!" Ferdyshchenko put in at once.

"So what of it?" the general, who hated Ferdyshchenko, asked drily.

"So he'll have to pay at the door," the latter explained.

"Well, all the same, sir, Prince Myshkin isn't Ferdyshchenko," the general could not help himself, having been so far unable to accept the thought of being in the same company and on an equal footing with Ferdyshchenko.

"Hey, General, spare Ferdyshchenko," the latter said, grinning. "I'm here under special dispensation."

"What is this special dispensation of yours?"

"Last time I had the honor of explaining it to the company in detail; I'll repeat it once more for Your Excellency. Kindly note, Your Excellency: everybody else is witty, but I am not. To make up for it, I asked permission to speak the truth, since everybody knows that only those who are not witty speak the truth. Besides, I'm a very vindictive man, and that's also because I'm not witty. I humbly bear with every offense, until the offender's first misstep; at his first misstep I remember at once and at once take my revenge in some way—I kick, as Ivan Petrovich Ptitsyn said of me, a man who, of course, never kicks anybody. Do you know Krylov's fable, Your Excellency: 'The Lion and the Ass'?[39] Well, that's you and me both, it was written about us."

"It seems you're running off at the mouth again, Ferdyshchenko," the general boiled over.

"What's that to you, Your Excellency?" Ferdyshchenko picked up. He was counting on being able to pick it up and embroider on it still more. "Don't worry, Your Excellency, I know my place: if I said you and I were the Lion and the Ass from Krylov's fable, I was, of course, taking the Ass's role on myself, and you, Your Excellency, are the Lion, as it says in Krylov's fable:

> The mighty Lion, terror of the forest,
> In old age saw his strength begin to fail.

And I, Your Excellency, am the Ass."

"With that last bit I agree," the general imprudently let slip.

All this was, of course, crude and deliberately affected, but there was a general agreement that Ferdyshchenko was allowed to play the role of buffoon.

"But I'm kept and let in here," Ferdyshchenko once exclaimed, "only so that I can talk precisely in this spirit. I mean, is it really possible to receive somebody like me? I do understand that. I mean, is it possible to sit me, such a Ferdyshchenko, next to a refined gentleman like Afanasy Ivanovich? We're left willy-nilly with only one explanation: they do it precisely because it's impossible to imagine."

But though it was crude, all the same it could be biting, sometimes even very much so, and that, it seems, was what Nastasya Filippovna liked. Those who wished absolutely to call on her had no choice but to put up with Ferdyshchenko. It may be that he had guessed the whole truth in supposing that the reason he was received was that from the first his presence had become impossible for Totsky. Ganya, for his part, had endured a whole infinity of torments from him, and in that sense Ferdyshchenko had managed to be very useful to Nastasya Filippovna.

"And I'll have the prince start by singing a fashionable romance," Ferdyshchenko concluded, watching out for what Nastasya Filippovna would say.

"I think not, Ferdyshchenko, and please don't get excited," she observed drily.

"Ahh! If he's under special patronage, then I, too, will ease up . . ."

But Nastasya Filippovna rose without listening and went herself to meet her guest.

"I regretted," she said, appearing suddenly before the prince, "that earlier today, being in a flurry, I forgot to invite you here, and I'm very glad that you have now given me the chance to thank you and to praise you for your determination."

Saying this, she peered intently at the prince, trying at least somehow to interpret his action to herself.

The prince might have made some reply to her amiable words, but he was so dazzled and struck that he could not even get a word out. Nastasya Filippovna noticed it with pleasure. This evening she was in full array and made an extraordinary impression. She took him by the arm and brought him to her guests. Just before entering the reception room, the prince suddenly stopped and, with extraordinary excitement, hurriedly whispered to her:

"Everything in you is perfection . . . even the fact that you're so thin and pale . . . one has no wish to imagine you otherwise . . . I wanted so much to come to you . . . I . . . forgive me . . ."

"Don't ask forgiveness," Nastasya Filippovna laughed. "That will ruin all the strangeness and originality. And it's true, then, what they say about you, that you're a strange man. So you consider me perfection, do you?"

"I do."

"Though you're a master at guessing, you're nevertheless mistaken. I'll remind you of it tonight . . ."

She introduced the prince to the guests, the majority of whom already knew him. Totsky at once said something amiable. Everyone seemed to cheer up a little, everyone immediately began talking and laughing. Nastasya Filippovna sat the prince down beside her.

"But anyhow, what's so astonishing in the prince's appearance?" Ferdyshchenko shouted louder than everyone else. "The matter's clear, it speaks for itself!"

"The matter's all too clear and speaks all too much for itself," the silent Ganya suddenly picked up. "I've been observing the prince almost uninterruptedly today, from the moment he first looked at Nastasya Filippovna's portrait on Ivan Fyodorovich's desk this morning. I remember very well that already this morning I thought of something which I'm now perfectly convinced of, and which, let it be said in passing, the prince himself has confessed to me."

Ganya uttered this whole phrase very gravely, without the slightest jocularity, even gloomily, which seemed somewhat strange.

"I didn't make any confessions to you," the prince replied, blushing, "I merely answered your question."

"Bravo, bravo!" cried Ferdyshchenko. "At least it's candid—both clever and candid!"

Everyone laughed loudly.

"Don't shout, Ferdyshchenko," Ptitsyn observed to him disgustedly in a half-whisper.

"I didn't expect such *prouesse** from you, Prince," said Ivan Fyodorovich. "Do you know what sort of man that suits? And I considered you a philosopher! Oh, the quiet one!"

"And judging by the way the prince blushes at an innocent joke like an innocent young girl, I conclude that, like a noble youth, he is nurturing the most praiseworthy intentions in his heart," the toothless and hitherto perfectly silent seventy-year-old schoolteacher, whom no one would have expected to make a peep all evening, suddenly said, or, better, maundered. Everyone laughed still more. The little old man, probably thinking they were laughing at his witticism, looked at them all and started laughing all the harder, which brought on so terrible a fit of coughing that Nastasya Filippovna, who for some reason was extremely fond of all such original little old men and women, and even of holy fools, at once began making a fuss over him, kissed him on both cheeks, and

*Prowess.

ordered more tea for him. When the maid came in, she asked for her mantilla, which she wrapped around herself, and told her to put more wood on the fire. Asked what time it was, the maid said it was already half-past ten.

"Ladies and gentlemen, would you care for champagne?" Nastasya Filippovna suddenly invited. "I have it ready. Maybe it will make you merrier. Please don't stand on ceremony."

The invitation to drink, especially in such naïve terms, seemed very strange coming from Nastasya Filippovna. Everyone knew the extraordinary decorum of her previous parties. Generally, the evening was growing merrier, but not in the usual way. The wine, however, was not refused, first, by the general himself, second, by the sprightly lady, the little old man, Ferdyshchenko, and the rest after him. Totsky also took his glass, hoping to harmonize the new tone that was setting in, possibly giving it the character of a charming joke. Ganya alone drank nothing. In the strange, sometimes very abrupt and quick outbursts of Nastasya Filippovna, who also took wine and announced that she would drink three glasses that evening, in her hysterical and pointless laughter, which alternated suddenly with a silent and even sullen pensiveness, it was hard to make anything out. Some suspected she was in a fever; they finally began to notice that she seemed to be waiting for something, glanced frequently at her watch, was growing impatient, distracted.

"You seem to have a little fever?" asked the sprightly lady.

"A big one even, not a little one—that's why I've wrapped myself in a mantilla," replied Nastasya Filippovna, who indeed had turned paler and at moments seemed to suppress a violent shiver.

They all started and stirred.

"Shouldn't we allow our hostess some rest?" Totsky suggested, glancing at Ivan Fyodorovich.

"Certainly not, gentlemen! I precisely ask you to stay. Your presence is particularly necessary for me tonight," Nastasya Filippovna suddenly said insistently and significantly. And as almost all the guests now knew that a very important decision was to be announced that evening, these words seemed extremely weighty. Totsky and the general exchanged glances once again; Ganya stirred convulsively.

"It would be nice to play some *petit jeu*,"* said the sprightly lady.

"I know an excellent and new *petit jeu*," Ferdyshchenko picked

*Parlor game.

up, "at least one that happened only once in the world, and even then it didn't succeed."

"What was it?" the sprightly lady asked.

"A company of us got together once, and we drank a bit, it's true, and suddenly somebody suggested that each of us, without leaving the table, tell something about himself, but something that he himself, in good conscience, considered the worst of all the bad things he'd done in the course of his whole life; and that it should be frank, above all, that it should be frank, no lying!"

"A strange notion!" said the general.

"Strange as could be, Your Excellency, but that's what was good about it."

"A ridiculous idea," said Totsky, "though understandable: a peculiar sort of boasting."

"Maybe that's just what they wanted, Afanasy Ivanovich."

"One is more likely to cry than laugh at such a *petit jeu*," the sprightly lady observed.

"An utterly impossible and absurd thing," echoed Ptitsyn.

"And was it a success?" asked Nastasya Filippovna.

"The fact is that it wasn't, it turned out badly, people actually told all sorts of things, many told the truth, and, imagine, many even enjoyed the telling, but then they all felt ashamed, they couldn't stand it! On the whole, though, it was quite amusing—in its own way, that is."

"But that would be really nice!" observed Nastasya Filippovna, suddenly quite animated. "Really, why don't we try it, gentlemen! In fact, we're not very cheerful. If each of us agreed to tell something . . . of that sort . . . naturally, if one agrees, because it's totally voluntary, eh? Maybe we can stand it? At least it's terribly original . . ."

"A brilliant idea!" Ferdyshchenko picked up. "The ladies are excluded, however, the men will begin. We'll arrange it by drawing lots as we did then! Absolutely, absolutely! If anyone is very reluctant, he needn't tell anything, of course, but that would be particularly unfriendly! Give us your lots here in the hat, gentlemen, the prince will do the drawing. It's the simplest of tasks, to tell the worst thing you've done in your life—it's terribly easy, gentlemen! You'll see! If anyone happens to forget, I'll remind him!"

Nobody liked the idea. Some frowned, others smiled slyly. Some objected, but not very much—Ivan Fyodorovich, for example, who did not want to contradict Nastasya Filippovna and saw how carried away she was by this strange notion. In her desires Nastasya

Filippovna was always irrepressible and merciless, once she decided to voice them, capricious and even useless for her as those desires might be. And now it was as if she was in hysterics, fussing about, laughing convulsively, fitfully, especially in response to the objections of the worried Totsky. Her dark eyes flashed, two red spots appeared on her pale cheeks. The sullen and squeamish tinge on some of her guests' physiognomies perhaps inflamed her mocking desire still more; perhaps she precisely liked the cynicism and cruelty of the idea. Some were even certain that she had some special calculation here. However, they began to agree: in any case it was curious, and for many of them very enticing. Ferdyshchenko fussed about most of all.

"And if it's something that can't be told . . . in front of ladies," the silent young man observed timidly.

"Then don't tell it. As if there weren't enough nasty deeds without that," Ferdyshchenko replied. "Ah, young man!"

"But I don't know which to consider the worst thing I've done," the sprightly lady contributed.

"The ladies are exempt from the obligation of telling anything," Ferdyshchenko repeated, "but that is merely an exemption. The personally inspired will be gratefully admitted. The men, if they're very reluctant, are also exempt."

"How can it be proved here that I'm not lying?" asked Ganya. "And if I lie, the whole notion of the game is lost. And who isn't going to lie? Everybody's bound to start lying."

"But that's what's so enticing, to see how the person's going to lie. As for you, Ganechka, you needn't be especially worried about lying, because everybody knows your nastiest deed without that. Just think, ladies and gentlemen," Ferdyshchenko suddenly exclaimed in some sort of inspiration, "just think with what eyes we'll look at each other later, tomorrow, for instance, after our stories!"

"But is this possible? Can this indeed be serious, Nastasya Filippovna?" Totsky asked with dignity.

"He who fears wolves should stay out of the forest!" Nastasya Filippovna observed with a little smile.

"But excuse me, Mr. Ferdyshchenko, is it possible to make a *petit jeu* out of this?" Totsky went on, growing more and more worried. "I assure you that such things never succeed—you said yourself that it failed once."

"What do you mean, failed! Why, last time I told how I stole three roubles, just up and told it!"

"Granted. But it's surely not possible that you told it so that it resembled the truth and people believed you? And Gavrila Ardalionovich observed very correctly that it only needs to ring slightly false and the whole notion of the game is lost. Truth is then possible only accidentally, through a special sort of boasting mood in the very worst tone, which is unthinkable and quite improper here."

"Ah, what an extraordinarily subtle man you are, Afanasy Ivanovich! I even marvel at it!" cried Ferdyshchenko. "Just imagine, ladies and gentlemen, with his observation that I couldn't tell the story of my theft so that it resembled the truth, Afanasy Ivanovich has hinted in the subtlest fashion that in reality I also couldn't have stolen (because it's indecent to speak of it publicly), though it may be that in himself he's quite certain that Ferdyshchenko might very well steal! But to business, gentlemen, to business, the lots are all here, and even you, Afanasy Ivanovich, have put yours in, so nobody has refused. Draw the lots, Prince!"

The prince silently put his hand into the hat and took out the first lot—Ferdyshchenko's, the second—Ptitsyn's, the third— the general's, the fourth—Afanasy Ivanovich's, the fifth—his own, the sixth—Ganya's, and so on. The ladies had not put in any lots.

"Oh, God, how unlucky!" cried Ferdyshchenko. "And I thought the first turn would go to the prince and the second to the general. But, thank God, at least Ivan Petrovich comes after me, and I'll be rewarded. Well, ladies and gentlemen, of course it's my duty to set a noble example, but I regret most of all at the present moment that I'm so insignificant and in no way remarkable; even my rank is the lowest of the low. Well, what indeed is so interesting about Ferdyshchenko's having done something nasty? And what is the worst thing I've done? Here we have an *embarras de richesse*.* Maybe I should tell about that same theft again, to convince Afanasy Ivanovich that one can steal without being a thief."

"You also convince me, Mr. Ferdyshchenko, that it is indeed possible to feel an intoxicating pleasure in recounting one's foul deeds, though one has not even been asked about them . . . But anyhow . . . Excuse me, Mr. Ferdyshchenko."

"Begin, Ferdyshchenko, you produce a terrible amount of superfluous babble and can never finish!" Nastasya Filippovna ordered irritably and impatiently.

*Embarrassment of riches.

They all noticed that, after her latest fit of laughter, she had suddenly become sullen, peevish, and irritable; nevertheless she insisted stubbornly and despotically on her impossible whim. Afanasy Ivanovich was suffering terribly. He was also furious with Ivan Fyodorovich: the man sat over his champagne as if nothing was happening, and was perhaps even planning to tell something when his turn came.

XIV

"I'M NOT WITTY, Nastasya Filippovna, that's why I babble superfluously!" Ferdyshchenko cried, beginning his story. "If I were as witty as Afanasy Ivanovich or Ivan Petrovich, I'd be sitting quietly this evening like Afanasy Ivanovich and Ivan Petrovich. Prince, allow me to ask what you think, because it seems to me that there are many more thieves than nonthieves in the world, and that there does not even exist such an honest man as has not stolen something at least once in his life. That is my thought, from which, however, I by no means conclude that everyone to a man is a thief, though, by God, I'd sometimes like terribly much to draw that conclusion. What do you think?"

"Pah, what stupid talk," responded Darya Alexeevna, "and what nonsense! It can't be that everyone has stolen something. I've never stolen anything."

"You've never stolen anything, Darya Alexeevna; but what will the prince say, who has so suddenly blushed all over?"

"It seems to me that what you say is true, only it's greatly exaggerated," said the prince, who was indeed blushing for some reason.

"And you yourself, Prince, have you ever stolen anything?"

"Pah! how ridiculous! Come to your senses, Mr. Ferdyshchenko," the general stepped in.

"It's quite simply that you're ashamed, now that you have to tell your story, and you want to drag the prince in with you because he's so unprotesting," Darya Alexeevna declared.

"Ferdyshchenko, either tell your story or be quiet and mind your own business. You exhaust all my patience," Nastasya Filippovna said sharply and vexedly.

"This minute, Nastasya Filippovna; but if even the prince admits it, for I maintain that what the prince has said is tantamount to an admission, then what, for instance, would someone else say (naming no names) if he ever wanted to tell the truth? As far as I'm concerned, ladies and gentlemen, there isn't much more to tell: it's very simple, and stupid, and nasty. But I assure you that I'm not a thief; I stole who knows how. It was two years ago, in Semyon Ivanovich Ishchenko's country house, on a Sunday. He had guests for dinner. After dinner the men sat over the wine. I had the idea of asking Marya Semyonovna, his daughter, a young lady, to play something on the piano. I passed through the corner room, there was a green three-rouble note lying on Marya Ivanovna's worktable: she had taken it out to pay some household expenses. Not a living soul in the room. I took the note and put it in my pocket, why— I don't know. I don't understand what came over me. Only I quickly went back and sat down at the table. I sat and waited in rather great excitement; I talked nonstop, told jokes, laughed; then I went to sit with the ladies. About half an hour later they found it missing and began questioning the maidservants. Suspicion fell on the maid Darya. I showed extraordinary curiosity and concern, and I even remember that, when Darya was completely at a loss, I began persuading her to confess her guilt, betting my life on Marya Ivanovna's kindness—and that aloud, in front of everybody. Everybody was looking, and I felt an extraordinary pleasure precisely because I was preaching while the note was in my pocket. I drank up those three roubles in a restaurant that same evening. I went in and asked for a bottle of Lafite; never before had I asked for a bottle just like that, with nothing; I wanted to spend it quickly. Neither then nor later did I feel any particular remorse. I probably wouldn't do it again; you may believe that or not as you like, it's of no interest to me. Well, sirs, that's all."

"Only, of course, that's not the worst thing you've done," Darya Alexeevna said with loathing.

"It's a psychological case, not a deed," observed Afanasy Ivanovich.

"And the maid?" asked Nastasya Filippovna, not concealing the most squeamish loathing.

"The maid was dismissed the next day, naturally. It was a strict household."

"And you allowed it?"

"Oh, that's wonderful! Should I have gone and denounced myself?" Ferdyshchenko tittered, though somewhat astounded by the generally much too unpleasant impression his story had made.

"How dirty!" cried Nastasya Filippovna.

"Bah! You want to hear a man's nastiest deed and with that you ask him to shine! The nastiest deeds are always very dirty, we'll hear that presently from Ivan Petrovich; and there are all sorts of things that shine externally and want to look like virtue, because they have their own carriage. There are all sorts that have their own carriage . . . And by what means . . ."

In short, Ferdyshchenko was quite unable to stand it and suddenly became angry, even to the point of forgetting himself, going beyond measure; his face even went all awry. Strange as it might seem, it is quite possible that he had anticipated a completely different success for his story. These "blunders" of bad tone and a "peculiar sort of boasting," as Totsky put it, occurred quite frequently with Ferdyshchenko and were completely in character.

Nastasya Filippovna even shook with wrath and stared intently at Ferdyshchenko; the man instantly became cowed and fell silent, all but cold with fright: he had gone much too far.

"Shouldn't we end it altogether?" Afanasy Ivanovich asked slyly.

"It's my turn, but I shall exercise my privilege and not tell anything," Ptitsyn said resolutely.

"You don't want to?"

"I can't, Nastasya Filippovna; and generally I consider such a *petit jeu* impossible."

"General, I believe it's your turn next," Nastasya Filippovna turned to him. "If you decline, too, then everything will go to pieces after you, and I'll be very sorry, because I was counting on telling a deed 'from my own life' at the end, only I wanted to do it after you and Afanasy Ivanovich, because you should encourage me," she ended, laughing.

"Oh, if you promise, too," the general cried warmly, "then I'm ready to tell you my whole life; but, I confess, while waiting for my turn I've already prepared my anecdote . . ."

"And by the mere look of his excellency, one can tell with what special literary pleasure he has polished his little anecdote," Ferdyshchenko, still somewhat abashed, ventured to observe with a venomous smile.

Nastasya Filippovna glanced fleetingly at the general and also smiled to herself. But it was obvious that anguish and irritation were growing stronger and stronger in her. Afanasy Ivanovich became doubly frightened, hearing her promise of a story.

"It has happened to me, ladies and gentlemen, as to everyone, to do certain not entirely elegant deeds in my life," the general began, "but the strangest thing of all is that I consider the short anecdote I'm about to tell you the nastiest anecdote in my whole life. Meanwhile some thirty-five years have passed; but I have never been able, in recalling it, to break free of a certain, so to speak, gnawing impression in my heart. The affair itself, however, was extremely stupid: at that time I had just been made a lieutenant and was pulling my load in the army. Well, everybody knows what a lieutenant is: blood boiling and just pennies to live on. I had an orderly then, Nikifor, who was terribly solicitous of my livelihood: he saved, mended, cleaned and scrubbed, and even pilfered everywhere, whatever he could to add to the household. He was a most trustworthy and honest man. I, of course, was strict but fair. At some point we were stationed in a little town. I was quartered on the outskirts, with a retired lieutenant's wife, and a widow at that. The old hag was eighty or thereabouts. Her little house was decrepit, wretched, wooden, and she didn't even have a serving woman, so poor she was. But the main thing about her was that she had once had the most numerous family and relations; but some had died in the course of her life, others had gone away, still others had forgotten the old woman, and her husband she had buried forty-five years earlier. A few years before then her niece had lived with her, hunchbacked and wicked as a witch, people said, and once she had even bitten the old woman's finger, but she had died, too, so that for some three years the old woman had been getting along all by herself. My life with her was terribly boring, and she herself was so empty I couldn't get anywhere with her. In the end she stole a rooster from me. The affair has remained cloudy to this day, but no one else could have done it. We quarreled over that rooster, and considerably, but here it so happened that, at my first request, I was transferred to other quarters on the opposite side of town, with the numerous family of a merchant with a great big beard—I remember him as if it were yesterday. Nikifor and I are joyfully moving out, we're indignantly leaving the old woman. About three days go by, I come back from drill, Nikifor tells me, 'You shouldn't have left our bowl with the former landlady, Your Honor, we have nothing to serve soup in.' I, naturally, am amazed: 'How's that? Why would our bowl have stayed with the landlady?' The astonished Nikifor goes on to report that the landlady hadn't given him our bowl when we were moving because, since I had broken a pot of hers, she was keeping our bowl in exchange for her pot, and I had supposedly suggested doing it that way. Such baseness on her part naturally drove me beyond the final limits; my blood boiled, I jumped up and flew to her. By the time I reach the old woman I'm, so to speak, already beside myself; I see her sitting all alone in the corner of the front hall, as if hiding from the sun, resting her cheek on her hand. I immediately loosed a whole thunderstorm on her: 'You're this,' I said, 'and you're that!'—you know, in the best Russian way. Only I see something strange is happening: she sits, her face is turned to me, her eyes are popping out, and she says not a word in reply, and she looks at me so strangely, strangely, as if she's swaying back and forth. I finally calm down, look closely at her, ask her something—not a word in reply. I stand there irresolutely; flies are buzzing, the sun is setting, silence; completely bewildered, I finally leave. Before I reached home I was summoned to the major's, then I had to pass by my company, so that I got home quite late. Nikifor's first words: 'You know, Your Honor, our landlady died.' 'When?' 'This evening, an hour and a half ago.' Which meant that, just at the time when I was abusing her, she was departing. I was so struck, I must tell you, that I had a hard time recovering. It even made its way into my thoughts, you know, even into my dreams at night. I, of course, have no prejudices, but on the third day I went to church for the funeral. In short, the more time passed, the more I thought about her. Nothing special, only I pictured it occasionally and felt rather bad. The main thing is, how did I reason in the end? First, the woman was, so to speak, a personal being, what's known in our time as a human; she lived, lived a long time, too long finally. She once had children, a husband, a family, relations, everything around her was at the boil, there were all these smiles, so to speak, and suddenly—total zero, everything's gone smash, she's left alone, like . . . some sort of fly bearing a curse from time immemorial. And then, finally, God brings her to an end. At sunset, on a quiet summer evening, my old woman also flies away—of course, this is not without its moralizing idea; and at that very moment, instead of, so to speak, a farewell tear, this desperate young lieutenant, jaunty and arms akimbo, sees her off the face of the earth with the Russian element of riotous abuse over a lost bowl! No doubt I was at fault, and though, owing to the distance in time and to changes in my character, I've long regarded my deed as someone else's, I neverthe- less continue to regret it. So that, I repeat, I find it strange, the more so as, even if I am at fault, it's not so completely: why did she decide to die precisely at that moment? Naturally, there's some excuse here—that the deed was in a certain sense psychological— but all the same I never felt at peace until I began, about fifteen years ago, to keep two permanent sick old women at my expense in the almshouse, with the purpose of easing their last days of earthly life by decent maintenance. I intend to leave capital for it in perpetuity. Well, sirs, that's all. I repeat that I may be to blame for many things in life, but I consider this occasion, in all conscience, the nastiest deed of my whole life."

"And instead of the nastiest, Your Excellency has told us one of the good deeds of your life. You've hoodwinked Ferdyshchenko!" concluded Ferdyshchenko.

"Indeed, General, I never imagined that you had a good heart after all; it's even a pity," Nastasya Filippovna said casually.

"A pity? Why is that?" asked the general, laughing amiably and sipping, not without self-satisfaction, from his champagne.

But now it was Afanasy Ivanovich's turn, and he, too, was prepared. They could all tell beforehand that he would not decline like Ivan Petrovich, and, for certain reasons, they awaited his story with particular curiosity and at the same time with occasional glances at Nastasya Filippovna. With extraordinary dignity, which fully corresponded to his stately appearance, in a quiet, amiable voice, Afanasy Ivanovich began one of his "charming stories." (Incidentally speaking, he was an impressive, stately man, tall, slightly bald, slightly gray-haired, and rather corpulent, with soft, ruddy, and somewhat flabby cheeks and false teeth. He wore loose and elegant clothes, and his linen was of astonishing quality. One could not have enough of gazing at his plump white hands. On the index finger of his right hand there was an expensive diamond ring.) All the while he was telling his story, Nastasya Filippovna intently studied the lace on the ruffle of her sleeve and kept plucking at it with two fingers of her left hand, so that she managed not to glance at the storyteller even once.

"What facilitates my task most of all," Afanasy Ivanovich began, "is that I am duty-bound to tell nothing other than the worst thing I've done in my whole life. In that case, naturally, there can be no hesitation: conscience and the heart's memory straightaway prompt one with what must be told. I confess with bitterness that numbered among all the numberless, perhaps light-minded and . . . flighty deeds of my life, there is one the impression of which weighs all too heavily on my memory. It happened about twenty years ago. I had gone then to visit Platon Ordyntsev on his estate. He had just been elected marshal[40] and had come there with his young wife for the winter holidays. Anfisa Alexeevna's birthday also fell just then, and two balls were planned. At that time an enchanting novel by Dumas *fils* had just become terribly fashionable and made a great deal of noise in high society—*La Dame aux camélias*,[41] a poem which, in my opinion, will never die or grow old. In the provinces all the ladies admired it to the point of rapture, those at least who had read it. The enchanting story, the originality with which the main character is portrayed, that enticing world, so subtly analyzed, and, finally, all those charming details scattered through the book (for instance, about the way bouquets of white and pink camellias are used in turn), in short, all those enchanting details, and everything together, produced almost a shock. The flowers of the camellia became extraordinarily fashionable. Everyone demanded camellias, everyone sought them. I ask you: can one get many camellias in the provinces, when everyone demands them for balls, even though the balls are few? Petya Vorkhovskoy, poor fellow, was then pining away for Anfisa Alexeevna. I really don't know if there was anything between them, that is, I mean to say, whether he could have had any serious hopes. The poor man lost his mind over getting camellias for Anfisa Alexeevna by the evening of the ball. Countess Sotsky, from Petersburg, a guest of the governor's wife, and Sofya Bespalov, as became known, were certain to come with bouquets of white ones. Anfisa Alexeevna, for the sake of some special effect, wanted red ones. Poor Platon nearly broke down; a husband, you know; he promised to get the bouquet, and—what then? It was snapped up the day before by Mytishchev, Katerina Alexandrovna, a fierce rival of Anfisa Alexeevna's in everything. They were at daggers drawn. Naturally, there were hysterics, fainting fits. Platon was lost. It was clear that if Petya could, at this interesting moment, procure a bouquet somewhere, his affairs would improve greatly; a woman's gratitude on such occasions knows no bounds. He rushes about like crazy; but it's an impossible thing, no use talking about it. Suddenly I run into him at eleven in the evening, the night before the birthday and the ball, at Marya Petrovna Zubkov's, a neighbor of the Ordyntsevs. He's beaming. 'What's with you?' 'I found it. Eureka!' 'Well, brother, you surprise me! Where? How?' 'In Ekshaisk' (a little town there, only fifteen miles away, and not in our district), 'there's a merchant named Trepalov there, bearded and rich, lives with his old wife, and no children, just canaries. They both have a passion for flowers, and he's got camellias.' 'Good heavens, there's no certainty there, what if he doesn't give you any?' 'I'll kneel down and grovel at his feet until he does, otherwise I won't leave!' 'When are you going?' 'Tomorrow at daybreak, five o'clock.' 'Well, God be with you!' And I'm so glad for him, you know; I go back to Ordyntsev's; finally, it's past one in the morning and I'm still like this, you know, in a reverie. I was about to go to bed when a most original idea suddenly occurred to me! I immediately make my way to the kitchen, wake up the coachman Savely, give him fifteen roubles, 'have the horses ready in half an hour!' Half an hour later, naturally, the dogcart is at the gate; Anfisa Alexeevna, I'm told, has migraine, fever, and delirium—I get in and go. Before five o'clock I'm in Ekshaisk, at the inn; I wait till daybreak, but only till daybreak; just past six I'm at Trepalov's. 'Thus and so, have you got any camellias? My dear, my heart and soul, help me, save me, I bow down at your feet!' The old man, I see, is tall, gray-haired, stern—a fearsome old man. 'No, no, never! I won't.' I flop down at his feet! I sprawl there like that! 'What's wrong, my dear man, what's wrong?' He even got frightened. 'It's a matter of a human life!' I shout to him. 'Take them, then, and God be with you.' What a lot of red camellias I cut! Wonderful, lovely—he had a whole little hothouse there. The old man sighs. I take out a hundred roubles. 'No, my dear man, kindly do not offend me in this manner.' 'In that case, my esteemed sir,' I say, 'give the hundred roubles to the local hospital, for the improvement of conditions and food.' 'Now that, my dear man, is another matter,' he says, 'good, noble, and pleasing to God. I'll give it for the sake of your health.' And, you know, I liked him, this Russian old man, Russian to the root, so to speak, *de la vraie souche*.* Delighted with my success, I immediately set out on the way back; we made a detour to avoid meeting Petya. As soon as I arrived, I sent the bouquet in to Anfisa Alexeevna, who was just waking up. You can imagine the rapture, the gratitude, the tears of gratitude! Platon, yesterday's crushed and dead Platon, sobs on my breast. Alas! All husbands have been like that since the creation . . . of lawful wedlock! I won't venture to add anything, except that Petya's affairs collapsed definitively after this episode. At first I thought he'd put a knife in me when he

*Of the true stock.

found out, I even prepared myself to face him, but what happened was something I wouldn't even have believed: a fainting fit, delirium towards evening, fever the next morning; he cried like a baby, had convulsions. A month later, having only just recovered, he asked to be sent to the Caucasus: decidedly out of a novel! He ended up by being killed in the Crimea. At that time his brother, Stepan Vorkhovskoy, commanded the regiment, distinguished himself. I confess, even many years later I suffered from remorse: why, for what reason, had I given him this blow? It would be another thing if I myself had been in love then. But it was a simple prank, out of simple dalliance, and nothing more. And if I hadn't snatched that bouquet from him, who knows, the man might be alive today, happy, successful, and it might never have entered his head to go and get himself shot at by the Turks."

Afanasy Ivanovich fell silent with the same solid dignity with which he had embarked on his story. It was noticed that Nastasya Filippovna's eyes flashed somehow peculiarly and her lips even twitched when Afanasy Ivanovich finished. Everyone glanced with curiosity at them both.

"Ferdyshchenko's been hoodwinked! Really hoodwinked! No, I mean really hoodwinked!" Ferdyshchenko cried out in a tearful voice, seeing that he could and should put in a word.

"And who told you not to understand things? Learn your lesson now from intelligent people!" Darya Alexeevna (an old and trusty friend and accomplice of Totsky's) snapped out to him all but triumphantly.

"You're right, Afanasy Ivanovich, this *petit jeu* is very boring, and we must end it quickly," Nastasya Filippovna offered casually. "I'll tell what I promised, and then let's all play cards."

"But the promised anecdote before all!" the general warmly approved.

"Prince," Nastasya Filippovna suddenly addressed him sharply and unexpectedly, "these old friends of mine, the general and Afanasy Ivanovich, keep wanting to get me married. Tell me what you think: should I get married or not? I'll do as you say."

Afanasy Ivanovich turned pale, the general was dumbfounded; everyone stared and thrust their heads forward. Ganya froze in his place.

"To . . . to whom?" asked the prince in a sinking voice.

"To Gavrila Ardalionovich Ivolgin," Nastasya Filippovna went on as sharply, firmly, and distinctly as before.

Several moments passed in silence; the prince seemed to be trying hard but could not utter a word, as if a terrible weight were pressing on his chest.

"N-no . . . don't!" he whispered at last and tensely drew his breath.

"And so it will be! Gavrila Ardalionovich!" she addressed him imperiously and as if solemnly, "did you hear what the prince decided? Well, so that is my answer; and let this business be concluded once and for all!"

"Nastasya Filippovna!" Afanasy Ivanovich said in a trembling voice.

"Nastasya Filippovna!" the general uttered in a persuading and startled voice.

Everyone stirred and started.

"What's wrong, gentlemen?" she went on, peering at her guests as if in amazement. "Why are you all so aflutter? And what faces you all have!"

"But . . . remember, Nastasya Filippovna," Totsky murmured, faltering, "you gave your promise, quite voluntarily, and you might be a little sparing . . . I'm at a loss and . . . certainly embarrassed, but . . . In short, now, at such a moment, and in front . . . in front of people, just like that . . . to end a serious matter with this *petit jeu*, a matter of honor and of the heart . . . on which depends . . ."

"I don't understand you, Afanasy Ivanovich; you're really quite confused. In the first place, what is this 'in front of people'? Aren't we in wonderfully intimate company? And why a *petit jeu*? I really wanted to tell my anecdote, and so I told it; is it no good? And why do you say it's 'not serious'? Isn't it serious? You heard me say to the prince: 'It will be as you say.' If he had said 'yes,' I would have consented at once; but he said 'no,' and I refused. My whole life was hanging by a hair—what could be more serious?"

"But the prince, why involve the prince? And what, finally, is the prince?" muttered the general, now almost unable to hold back his indignation at such even offensive authority granted to the prince.

"The prince is this for me, that I believe in him as the first truly devoted man in my whole life. He believed in me from the first glance, and I trust him."

"It only remains for me to thank Nastasya Filippovna for the extreme delicacy with which she has . . . treated me," the pale Ganya finally uttered in a trembling voice and with twisted lips.

"This is, of course, as it ought to be . . . But . . . the prince . . . In this affair, the prince . . ."

"Is trying to get at the seventy-five thousand, is that it?" Nastasya Filippovna suddenly cut him off. "Is that what you wanted to say? Don't deny it, you certainly wanted to say that! Afanasy Ivanovich, I forgot to add: you can keep the seventy-five thousand for yourself and know that I've set you free gratis. Enough! You, too, need to breathe! Nine years and three months! Tomorrow—all anew, but today is my birthday and I'm on my own for the first time in my whole life! General, you can also take your pearls and give them to your wife—here they are; and tomorrow I'll vacate this apartment entirely. And there will be no more evenings, ladies and gentlemen!"

Having said this, she suddenly stood up as if wishing to leave.

"Nastasya Filippovna! Nastasya Filippovna!" came from all sides. Everyone stirred, everyone got up from their chairs; everyone surrounded her, everyone listened uneasily to these impulsive, feverish, frenzied words; everyone sensed some disorder, no one could make any sense of it, no one could understand anything. At that moment the doorbell rang loudly, strongly, just as earlier that day in Ganechka's apartment.

"Ahh! Here's the denouement! At last! It's half-past eleven!" Nastasya Filippovna cried. "Please be seated, ladies and gentlemen, this is the denouement!"

Having said this, she sat down herself. Strange laughter trembled on her lips. She sat silently, in feverish expectation, looking at the door.

"Rogozhin and the hundred thousand, no doubt," Ptitsyn murmured to himself.

XV

THE MAID KATYA came in, badly frightened.

"God knows what it is, Nastasya Filippovna, about a dozen men barged in, and they're all drunk, they want to come here, they say it's Rogozhin and that you know."

"That's right, Katya, let them all in at once."

"You mean . . . all, Nastasya Filippovna? They're quite outrageous. Frightful!"

"All, let them all in, Katya, don't be afraid, all of them to a man, or else they'll come in without you. Hear how noisy they are, just like the other time. Ladies and gentlemen, perhaps you're offended," she addressed her guests, "that I should receive such company in your presence? I'm very sorry and beg your pardon, but it must be so, and I wish very, very much that you will agree to be my witnesses in this denouement, though, incidentally, you may do as you please . . ."

The guests went on being amazed, whispering and exchanging glances, but it became perfectly clear that it had all been calculated and arranged beforehand, and that now Nastasya Filippovna—though she was, of course, out of her mind—would not be thrown off. They all suffered terribly from curiosity. Besides, there was really no one to be frightened. There were only two ladies: Darya Alexeevna, the sprightly lady, who had seen everything and whom it would have been very hard to put out, and the beautiful but silent stranger. But the silent stranger was scarcely able to understand anything: she was a traveling German lady and did not know a word of Russian; besides that, it seems she was as stupid as she was beautiful. She was a novelty, and it was an accepted thing to invite her to certain evenings, in magnificent costume, her hair done up as if for an exhibition, and to sit her there like a lovely picture to adorn the evening, just as some people, for their evenings, borrow some painting, vase, statue, or screen from their friends for one time only. As far as the men were concerned, Ptitsyn, for instance, was friends with Rogozhin; Ferdyshchenko was like a fish in water; Ganechka had not yet come to his senses, but felt vaguely yet irresistibly the feverish need to stand in this pillory to the end; the old schoolteacher, who had little grasp of what was going on, all but wept and literally trembled with fear, noticing some sort of extraordinary alarm around him and in Nastasya Filippovna, whom he doted on like a granddaughter; but he would sooner have died than abandon her at such a moment. As for Afanasy Ivanovich, he, of course, could not compromise himself in such adventures; but he was much too interested in the affair, even if it had taken such a crazy turn; then, too, Nastasya Filippovna had dropped two or three such little phrases on his account, that he could by no means leave without clarifying the matter definitively. He resolved to sit it out to the end and now to be completely silent and remain only as an observer, which, of course, his dignity demanded. General Epanchin alone, thoroughly offended as he had just been by such an unceremonious and ridiculous return of his present, could, of course, be still more offended now by all these extraordinary eccentricities or, for instance, by the appearance of Rogozhin; then, too, even without that, a man like him had already condescended too much by resolving to sit down beside Ptitsyn and Ferdyshchenko; but what the power of passion could do, could also be overcome in the end by a feeling of responsibility, a sense of duty, rank, and importance, and generally of self-respect, so that Rogozhin and his company, in his excellency's presence at any rate, were impossible.

"Ah, General," Nastasya Filippovna interrupted him as soon as he turned to her with this announcement, "I forgot! But you may be sure that I foresaw your reaction. If it's offensive to you, I won't insist on keeping you, though I'd like very much to see precisely you at my side now. In any case, I thank you very much for your acquaintance and flattering attention, but if you're afraid . . ."

"Excuse me, Nastasya Filippovna," the general cried in a fit of chivalrous magnanimity, "to whom are you talking? I'll stay beside you now out of devotion alone, and if, for instance, there is any danger . . . What's more, I confess, I'm extremely curious. My only concern was that they might ruin the rugs or break something . . . And we could do very well without them, in my opinion, Nastasya Filippovna!"

"Rogozhin himself!" announced Ferdyshchenko.

"What do you think, Afanasy Ivanovich," the general managed to whisper quickly, "hasn't she gone out of her mind? Without any allegory, that is, in a real, medical sense, eh?"

"I told you, she has always been inclined to it," Afanasy Ivanovich slyly whispered back.

"And the fever along with it . . ."

Rogozhin's company was almost the same as earlier that day; the only additions were some little old libertine, once the editor of a disreputable scandal sheet, of whom the anecdote went around that he had pawned and drunk up his gold teeth, and a retired lieutenant—decidedly the rival and competitor, in his trade and purpose, of the gentleman with the fists earlier—who was totally unknown to any of Rogozhin's people, but who had been picked up in the street, on the sunny side of Nevsky Prospect, where he was stopping passersby and asking, in Marlinsky's style,[42] for financial assistance, under the perfidious pretext that "in his time he himself used to give petitioners fifteen roubles." The two competitors had immediately become hostile to each other. The earlier gentleman with the fists even considered himself offended, once the "petitioner" was accepted into the company and, being taciturn by nature, merely growled now and then like a bear and looked with profound scorn upon the fawning and facetiousness of the "petitioner," who turned out to be a worldly and politic man. By the looks of him, the lieutenant promised to succeed in "the business" more by adroitness and dodging than by strength, being also of smaller stature than the fist gentleman. Delicately, without getting into an obvious argument, but boasting terribly, he had already hinted more than once at the advantages of English boxing; in short, he turned out to be a pure Westernizer.⁴³ At the word "boxing," the fist gentleman merely smiled scornfully and touchily, and without condescending, for his part, to an obvious debate with his rival, displayed now and then, silently, as if accidentally, or, better to say, exposed to view now and then, a perfectly national thing—a huge fist, sinewy, gnarled, overgrown with a sort of reddish fuzz—and everyone could see clearly that if this profoundly national thing were aptly brought down on some object, there would be nothing left but a wet spot.

Again, as earlier, none of them was "loaded" to the utmost degree, thanks to the efforts of Rogozhin himself, who all day had kept in view his visit to Nastasya Filippovna. He himself had managed to sober up almost completely, but on the other hand he was nearly befuddled from all the impressions he had endured on that outrageous day, unlike any other day in his life. Only one thing remained constantly in view for him, in his memory and in his heart, every minute, every moment. For this *one thing* he had spent the whole time from five o'clock in the afternoon till eleven, in boundless anguish and anxiety, dealing with the Kinders and Biskups, who also nearly went out of their minds, rushing about like mad on his business. And yet, all the same, they had managed to raise the hundred thousand in cash, which Nastasya Filippovna had hinted at in passing, mockingly and quite vaguely, at an interest which even Biskup himself, out of modesty, discussed with Kinder not aloud but only in a whisper.

As earlier, Rogozhin marched in ahead of them all, the rest advancing behind him, fully aware of their advantages, but still somewhat cowardly. Above all, and God knows why, they felt cowardly towards Nastasya Filippovna. Some of them even thought they would immediately be "chucked down the stairs." Among those who thought so, incidentally, was that fop and heartbreaker

Zalyozhev. But the others, and most of all the fist gentleman, not aloud but in their hearts, regarded Nastasya Filippovna with the profoundest contempt and even hatred, and went to her as to a siege. But the magnificent décor of the first two rooms, things they had never seen or heard of, rare furniture, paintings, an enormous statue of Venus—all this produced in them an irresistible impression of respect and even almost of fear. This, of course, prevented none of them from squeezing gradually and with insolent curiosity, despite their fear, into the drawing room behind Rogozhin; but when the fist gentleman, the "petitioner," and some of the others noticed General Epanchin among the guests, they were at first so taken aback that they even began retreating slowly into the first room. Lebedev alone was among the most emboldened and convinced, and marched in almost on a par with Rogozhin, having grasped the actual meaning of one million four hundred thousand in capital and of a hundred thousand now, right here, in the hand. It must be noted, however, that none of them, not even the all-knowing Lebedev, were quite certain in their knowledge of the extent and limits of their power and whether indeed everything was now permitted them or not. There were moments when Lebedev could have sworn it was everything, but at other moments he felt an uneasy need to remind himself, just in case, of certain encouraging and reassuring articles of the legal code.

On Rogozhin himself Nastasya Filippovna's drawing room made the opposite impression from that of all his companions. As soon as the door curtain was raised and he saw Nastasya Filippovna—all the rest ceased to exist for him, as it had in the afternoon, even more powerfully than in the afternoon. He turned pale and stopped for a moment; one could surmise that his heart was pounding terribly. Timidly and like a lost man he gazed at Nastasya Filippovna for several seconds, not taking his eyes off her. Suddenly, as if he had lost all reason and nearly staggering, he went up to the table; on his way he bumped into Ptitsyn's chair and stepped with his huge, dirty boots on the lace trimming of the silent German beauty's magnificent light blue dress; he did not apologize and did not notice. Having gone up to the table, he placed on it a strange object, with which he had also entered the drawing room, holding it out in front of him with both hands. It was a big stack of paper, about five inches high and seven inches long, wrapped firmly and closely in *The Stock Market Gazette*, and tied very tightly on all sides and twice crisscross with the kind of string used for tying sugar loaves. Then he stood without saying a word, his arms hanging down, as if awaiting his sentence. He was dressed exactly as earlier, except for the brand-new silk scarf on his neck, bright green and red, with an enormous diamond pin shaped like a beetle, and the huge diamond ring on the dirty finger of his right hand. Lebedev stopped within three steps of the table; the rest, as was said, gradually accumulated in the drawing room. Katya and Pasha, Nastasya Filippovna's maids, also came running and watched from under the raised door curtain with deep amazement and fear.

"What is this?" asked Nastasya Filippovna, looking Rogozhin over intently and curiously, and indicating the "object" with her eyes.

"The hundred thousand!" he replied almost in a whisper.

"Ah, so he's kept his word, just look! Sit down, please, here, right here on this chair; I'll tell you something later. Who is with you? The whole company from before? Well, let them come and sit down; there on the sofa is fine, and on the other sofa. The two armchairs there . . . what's the matter with them, don't they want to?"

Indeed, some were positively abashed, retreated, and sat down to wait in the other room, but others stayed and seated themselves as they were invited to do, only further away from the table, more in the corners, some still wishing to efface themselves somewhat, others taking heart somehow unnaturally quickly, and the more so the further it went. Rogozhin also sat down on the chair shown him, but did not sit for long; he soon stood up and did not sit down again. He gradually began to make out the guests and look around at them. Seeing Ganya, he smiled venomously and whispered to himself: "So there!" He looked without embarrassment and even without any special curiosity at the general and Afanasy Ivanovich, but when he noticed the prince beside Nastasya Filippovna, he could not tear his eyes from him for a long time, being extremely astonished and as if unable to explain this encounter to himself. One might have suspected that there were moments when he was actually delirious. Besides the shocks of that day, he had spent the whole previous night on the train and had not slept for almost two days.

"This, ladies and gentlemen, is a hundred thousand," said Nastasya Filippovna, addressing them all with some sort of feverishly impatient defiance, "here in this dirty packet. Earlier today he shouted like a madman that he would bring me a hundred thousand in the evening, and I've been waiting for him. He was bargaining for me: he started at eighteen thousand, then suddenly jumped to forty, and then to this hundred here. He has kept his word! Pah, how pale he is! . . . It happened at Ganechka's today: I went to call on his mother, on my future family, and there his sister shouted right in my face: 'Why don't they throw this shameless woman out of here!' and spat in her brother Ganechka's face. A hot-tempered girl!"

"Nastasya Filippovna!" the general said reproachfully. He was beginning to take his own view of the situation.

"What is it, General? Indecent or something? Enough of this showing off! So I sat like some sort of dress-circle virtue in a box at the French Theater, and fled like a wild thing from all the men who chased after me in these five years, and had the look of proud innocence, all because my foolishness ran away with me! Look, right in front of you he has come and put a hundred thousand on the table, after these five years of innocence, and they probably have troikas standing out there waiting for me. He's priced me at a hundred thousand! Ganechka, I see you're still angry with me? Did you really want to take me into your family? Me, Rogozhin's kind of woman! What was it the prince said earlier?"

"I did not say you were Rogozhin's kind of woman, you're not Rogozhin's kind!" the prince uttered in a trembling voice.

"Nastasya Filippovna, enough, darling, enough, dear heart," Darya Alexeevna suddenly could not stand it. "If they pain you so much, why even look at them? And do you really want to go off with this one, for all his hundred thousand? True, it's a hundred thousand—there it sits! Just take the hundred thousand and throw him out, that's how you ought to deal with them! Ah, if I were in your place, I'd have them all . . . no, really!"

Darya Alexeevna even became wrathful. She was a kind woman and a highly impressionable one.

"Don't be angry, Darya Alexeevna," Nastasya Filippovna smiled at her, "I wasn't speaking angrily to him. I didn't reproach him, did I? I really can't understand how this foolishness came over me, that I should have wanted to enter an honest family. I saw his mother, I kissed her hand. And if I jeered at you today, Ganechka, it was because I purposely wanted to see for the last time myself how far you would go. Well, you surprised me, truly. I expected a lot, but not that! Could you possibly marry me, knowing that this one here had given me such pearls, almost on the eve of the wedding, and that I had taken them? And what about Rogozhin? In your own house, in front of your mother and sister, he bargained for me, and after that you came as a fiancé all the same and almost brought your sister? Can it be true what Rogozhin said about you, that for three roubles you'd crawl on all fours to Vassilievsky Island?"

"He would," Rogozhin suddenly said quietly but with a look of great conviction.

"It would be one thing if you were starving to death, but they say you earn a good salary! And on top of it all, besides the disgrace, to bring a wife you hate into the house! (Because you do hate me, I know it!) No, I believe now that such a man could kill for money! They're all so possessed by this lust now, they're so worked up about money, it's as if they'd lost their minds. Still a child, and he's already trying to become a usurer. Or the one who wraps silk around a razor, fixes it tight, sneaks up behind his friend, and cuts his throat like a sheep, as I read recently.[44] Well, you're a shameless one! I'm shameless, but you're worse. I'll say nothing about this bouquet man . . ."

"Is this you, is this you, Nastasya Filippovna?" the general clasped his hands in genuine grief. "You, so delicate, with such refined notions, and all at once! Such language! Such style!"

"I'm tipsy now, General," Nastasya Filippovna suddenly laughed. "I want to carouse now! Today is my day, my red-letter day, my leap day, I've waited a long time for it. Darya Alexeevna, do you see this bouquet man, this *monsieur aux camélias*, he's sitting there and laughing at us . . ."

"I'm not laughing, Nastasya Filippovna, I'm merely listening with the greatest attention," Totsky parried with dignity.

"Well, then, why did I torment him for a whole five years and not let him leave me? As if he was worth it! He's simply the way he has to be . . . He's still going to consider me guilty before him: he brought me up, he kept me like a countess, money, so much money, went on me, he found me an honest husband there, and Ganechka here, and what do you think: I didn't live with him for five years, but I took his money and thought I was right! I really got myself quite confused! Now you say take the hundred thousand and throw him out, if it's so loathsome. It's true that it's loathsome . . . I could have married long ago, and not just some Ganechka, only that's also pretty loathsome. Why did I waste my five years in this spite! But, would you believe it, some four years ago I had moments when I thought: shouldn't I really marry my Afanasy Ivanovich? I thought it then out of spite; all sorts of things came into my head then; but I could have made him do it! He asked for it himself, can you believe that? True, he was lying, but he's so susceptible, he can't control himself. And then, thank God, I thought: as if he's worth such spite! And then I suddenly felt such loathing for him that, even if he had proposed to me, I wouldn't have accepted him. And for a whole five years I've been showing off like this! No, it's better in the street where I belong! Either carouse with Rogozhin or go tomorrow and become a washer-woman! Because nothing on me is my own; if I leave, I'll abandon everything to him, I'll leave every last rag, and who will take me without anything? Ask Ganya here, will he? Even Ferdyshchenko won't take me! . . ."

"Maybe Ferdyshchenko won't take you, Nastasya Filippovna, I'm a candid man," Ferdyshchenko interrupted, "but the prince will! You're sitting here lamenting, but look at the prince! I've been watching him for a long time . . ."

Nastasya Filippovna turned to the prince with curiosity.

"Is it true?" she asked.

"It's true," whispered the prince.

"You'll take me just as I am, with nothing?"

"I will, Nastasya Filippovna . . ."

"Here's a new anecdote!" muttered the general. "Might have expected it."

The prince, with a sorrowful, stern, and penetrating gaze, looked into the face of Nastasya Filippovna, who went on studying him.

"Here's another one!" she said suddenly, turning to Darya Alexeevna again. "And he really does it out of the kindness of his heart, I know him. I've found a benefactor! Though maybe what they say about him is true, that he's . . . *like that*. How are you going to live, if you're so in love that you'll take Rogozhin's kind of woman—you, a prince? . . ."

"I'll take you as an honest woman, Nastasya Filippovna, not as Rogozhin's kind," said the prince.

"Me, an honest woman?"

"You."

"Well, that's . . . out of some novel! That, my darling prince, is old gibberish, the world's grown smarter now, and that's all nonsense! And how can you go getting married, when you still need a nursemaid to look after you!"

The prince stood up and said in a trembling voice, but with a look of deep conviction:

"I don't know anything, Nastasya Filippovna, I haven't seen anything, you're right, but I . . . I will consider that you are doing me an honor, and not I you. I am nothing, but you have suffered and have emerged pure from such a hell, and that is a lot. Why do you feel ashamed and want to go with Rogozhin? It's your fever . . . You've given Mr. Totsky back his seventy thousand and say you will abandon everything you have here, which no one else here would do. I . . . love you . . . Nastasya Filippovna. I will die for you, Nastasya Filippovna. I won't let anyone say a bad word about you, Nastasya Filippovna . . . If we're poor, I'll work, Nastasya Filippovna . . ."

At these last words a tittering came from Ferdyshchenko and Lebedev, and even the general produced some sort of grunt to himself in great displeasure. Ptitsyn and Totsky could not help smiling, but restrained themselves. The rest simply gaped in amazement.

". . . But maybe we won't be poor, but very rich, Nastasya Filippovna," the prince went on in the same timid voice. "I don't know for certain, however, and it's too bad that up to now I haven't been able to find anything out for the whole day, but in Switzerland I received a letter from Moscow, from a certain Mr. Salazkin, and he informs me that I may have inherited a very large fortune. Here is the letter . . ."

The prince actually took a letter from his pocket.

"Maybe he's raving?" muttered the general. "This is a real madhouse!"

"I believe you said, Prince, that this letter to you is from Salazkin?" asked Ptitsyn. "He is a very well-known man in his circle, a very well-known solicitor, and if it is indeed he who has informed you, you may fully believe it. Fortunately, I know his handwriting, because I've recently had dealings with him . . . If you will let me have a look, I may be able to tell you something."

With a trembling hand, the prince silently gave him the letter.

"But what is it, what is it?" the general roused himself up, looking at them all like a half-wit. "Can it be an inheritance?"

They all turned their eyes to Ptitsyn, who was reading the letter. The general curiosity received a new and extraordinary jolt. Ferdyshchenko could not sit still; Rogozhin looked perplexed and, in terrible anxiety, turned his gaze now to the prince, now to Ptitsyn.

Darya Alexeevna sat in expectation as if on pins and needles. Even Lebedev could not help himself, left his corner, and, bending double, began peering at the letter over Ptitsyn's shoulder, with the look of a man who is afraid he may get a whack for it.

XVI

"IT'S A SURE THING," Ptitsyn announced at last, folding the letter and handing it back to the prince. "Without any trouble, according to the incontestable will of your aunt, you have come into an extremely large fortune."

"It can't be!" the general exclaimed, as if firing a shot.

Again everyone gaped.

Ptitsyn explained, mainly addressing Ivan Fyodorovich, that the prince's aunt, whom he had never known personally, had died five months ago. She was the older sister of the prince's mother, the daughter of a Moscow merchant of the third guild, Papushin, who had died in poverty and bankruptcy. But the older brother of this Papushin, also recently deceased, was a well-known rich merchant. About a year ago, his only two sons died almost in the same month. This so shocked the old man that soon afterwards he himself fell ill and died. He was a widower and had no heirs at all except for the prince's aunt, his niece, a very poor woman, who lived as a sponger in someone else's house. When she received the inheritance, this aunt was already nearly dead from dropsy, but she at once began searching for the prince, charging Salazkin with the task, and managed to have her will drawn up. Apparently, neither the prince nor the doctor he lived with in Switzerland wanted to wait for any official announcements or make inquiries, and the prince, with Salazkin's letter in his pocket, decided to set off in person . . .

"I can tell you only one thing," Ptitsyn concluded, addressing the prince, "that all this must be incontestable and correct, and all that Salazkin writes to you about the incontestability and legality of your case you may take as pure money in your pocket. Congratulations, Prince! You, too, may get a million and a half, or possibly even more. Papushin was a very rich merchant."

"That's the last Prince Myshkin for you!" shouted Ferdyshchenko.

"Hurrah!" Lebedev wheezed in a drunken little voice.

"And there I go lending the poor fellow twenty-five roubles today, ha, ha, ha! It's a phantasmagoria, and nothing else!" said the general, all but stunned with amazement. "Well, congratulations, congratulations!" and, getting up from his seat, he went over to embrace the prince. After him, the others began to get up and also made for the prince. Even those who had retreated behind the door curtain began to emerge in the drawing room. Muffled talk, exclamations, even calls for champagne arose; all began pushing, jostling. For a moment they nearly forgot Nastasya Filippovna and that she was after all the hostess of her party. But it graduallly dawned on everyone at almost the same time that the prince had just proposed to her. The matter thus looked three times more mad and extraordinary than before. Deeply amazed, Totsky shrugged his shoulders; he was almost the only one to remain seated, while the rest crowded around the table in disorder. Everyone asserted afterwards that it was also from this moment that Nastasya Filippovna went crazy. She sat there and for some time looked around at them all with a sort of strange, astonished gaze, as if she could not understand and was trying to figure something out. Then she suddenly turned to the prince and, with a menacing scowl, studied him intently; but this lasted only a moment; perhaps it had suddenly occurred to her that it might all be a joke, a mockery; but the prince's look reassured her at once. She became pensive, then smiled again, as if not clearly realizing why . . .

"So I really am a princess!" she whispered to herself as if mockingly and, happening to glance at Darya Alexeevna, she laughed. "An unexpected denouement . . . I . . . was expecting something else. But why are you all standing, ladies and gentlemen, please be seated, congratulate me and the prince! I think someone asked for champagne; Ferdyshchenko, go and order some. Katya, Pasha," she suddenly saw her maids at the door, "come here, I'm getting married, have you heard? The prince, he's come into a million and a half, he's Prince Myshkin, and he's taking me!"

"And God be with you, darling, it's high time! Don't miss it!" cried Darya Alexeevna, deeply shaken by what had happened.

"Sit down beside me, Prince," Nastasya Filippovna went on, "that's right, and here comes the wine, congratulate us, ladies and gentlemen!"

"Hurrah!" cried a multitude of voices. Many crowded around the wine, among them almost all of Rogozhin's people. But though they shouted and were ready to shout, many of them, despite all the strangeness of the circumstances and the surroundings, sensed that the décor was changing. Others were perplexed and waited mistrustfully. And many whispered among themselves that it was a most ordinary affair, that princes marry all kinds of women, and even take gypsy women from their camps. Rogozhin himself stood and stared, his face twisted into a fixed, bewildered smile.

"Prince, dear heart, come to your senses!" the general whispered in horror, approaching from the side and tugging at the prince's sleeve.

Nastasya Filippovna noticed it and laughed loudly.

"No, General! I'm a princess myself now, you heard it—the prince won't let anyone offend me! Afanasy Ivanovich, congratulate me; now I'll be able to sit next to your wife anywhere; it's useful to have such a husband, don't you think? A million and a half, and a prince, and, they say, an idiot to boot, what could be better? Only now does real life begin! You're too late, Rogozhin! Take your packet away, I'm marrying the prince, and I'm richer than you are!"

But Rogozhin grasped what was going on. Inexpressible suffering was reflected in his face. He clasped his hands and a groan burst from his breast.

"Give her up!" he cried to the prince.

There was laughter all around.

"Give her up to you?" Darya Alexeevna triumphantly joined in. "See, he dumps money on the table, the boor! The prince is marrying her, and you show up with your outrages!"

"I'll marry her, too! Right now, this minute! I'll give her everything . . ."

"Look at him, drunk from the pot-house—you should be thrown out!" Darya Alexeevna repeated indignantly.

More laughter.

"Do you hear, Prince?" Nastasya Filippovna turned to him. "That's how the boor bargains for your bride."

"He's drunk," said the prince. "He loves you very much."

"And won't you be ashamed afterwards that your bride almost went off with Rogozhin?"

"It's because you were in a fever; and you're in a fever now, as if you're delirious."

"And won't it shame you when they tell you afterwards that your wife was Totsky's kept woman?"

"No, it won't . . . You were not with Totsky by your own will."

"And you'll never reproach me?"

"Never."

"Well, watch out, don't vouch for your whole life!"

"Nastasya Filippovna," the prince said quietly and as if with compassion, "I told you just now that I will take your consent as an honor, and that you are doing me an honor, and not I you. You smiled at those words, and I also heard laughter around me. Perhaps I expressed myself in a funny way, and was funny myself, but I still think that I . . . understand what honor is, and I'm sure that what I said was the truth. You were just going to ruin yourself irretrievably, because you would never forgive yourself for that: but you're not guilty of anything. It can't be that your life is already completely ruined. So what if Rogozhin came to you, and Gavrila Ardalionovich wanted to swindle you? Why do you constantly mention that? Very few people are capable of doing what you have done, I repeat it to you, and as for wanting to go off with Rogozhin, you decided that in a fit of illness. You're still in a fit, and it would be better if you went to bed. You'd get yourself hired as a washerwoman tomorrow and not stay with Rogozhin. You're proud, Nastasya Filippovna, but you may be so unhappy that you actually consider yourself guilty. You need much good care, Nastasya Filippovna. I will take care of you. I saw your portrait today, and it was as if I recognized a familiar face. It seemed to me at once as if you had already called me. I . . . I shall respect you all my life, Nastasya Filippovna," the prince suddenly concluded, as if coming to his senses, blushing and realizing the sort of people before whom he had said these things.

Ptitsyn even bowed his head out of chastity and looked at the ground. Totsky thought to himself: "He's an idiot, but he knows that flattery succeeds best: it's second nature!" The prince also noticed Ganya's eyes flashing from the corner, as if he wanted to reduce him to ashes.

"What a kind man!" Darya Alexeevna proclaimed tenderheartedly.

"A cultivated man, but a lost one!" the general whispered in a low voice.

Totsky took his hat and prepared to get up and quietly disappear. He and the general exchanged glances so as to leave together.

"Thank you, Prince, no one has ever spoken to me like that," said Nastasya Filippovna. "They all bargained for me, but no decent person ever asked me to marry him. Did you hear, Afanasy Ivanych? How do you like what the prince said? It's almost indecent

. . . Rogozhin! Don't leave yet. And you won't, I can see that. Maybe I'll still go with you. Where did you want to take me?"

"To Ekaterinhof,"[45] Lebedev reported from the corner, but Rogozhin only gave a start and became all eyes, as if unable to believe himself. He was completely stupefied, like someone who has received a terrible blow on the head.

"Oh, come now, come now, darling! You certainly are in a fit: have you lost your mind?" the frightened Darya Alexeevna roused herself up.

"And you thought it could really be?" Nastasya Filippovna jumped up from the sofa with a loud laugh. "That I could ruin such a baby? That's just the right thing for Afanasy Ivanych: he's the one who loves babies! Let's go, Rogozhin! Get your packet ready! Never mind that you want to marry me, give me the money anyway. Maybe I still won't marry you. You thought, since you want to marry me, you'd get to keep the packet? Ah, no! I'm shameless myself! I was Totsky's concubine . . . Prince! you need Aglaya Epanchin now, not Nastasya Filippovna—otherwise Ferdy-shchenko will point the finger at you! You're not afraid, but I'd be afraid to ruin you and have you reproach me afterwards! And as for your declarations that I'd be doing you an honor, Totsky knows all about that. And you, Ganechka, you've missed Aglaya Epan-chin; did you know that? If you hadn't bargained with her, she would certainly have married you! That's how you all are: keep company with dishonorable women, or with honorable women—there's only one choice! Otherwise you're sure to get confused . . . Hah, look at the general staring openmouthed . . ."

"It's bedlam, bedlam!" the general repeated, heaving his shoulders. He, too, got up from the sofa; they were all on their feet again. Nastasya Filippovna seemed to be in a frenzy.

"It can't be!" the prince groaned, wringing his hands.

"You think not? Maybe I'm proud myself, even if I am shameless. You just called me perfection; a fine perfection, if just for the sake of boasting that I've trampled on a million and a princely title, I go off to a thieves' den! What kind of wife am I for you after that? Afanasy Ivanych, I've really thrown a million out the window! How could you think I'd consider myself lucky to marry Ganechka and your seventy-five thousand? Keep the seventy-five thousand, Afanasy Ivanych (you didn't even get up to a hundred, Rogozhin outdid you!); as for Ganechka, I'll comfort him myself, I've got an idea. And now I want to carouse, I'm a streetwalker! I sat in prison for ten years, now comes happiness! What's wrong, Rogozhin? Get ready, let's go!"

"Let's go!" bellowed Rogozhin, nearly beside himself with joy. "Hey, you . . . whoever . . . wine! Ohh! . . ."

"Lay in more wine, I'm going to drink. And will there be music?"

"There will, there will! Keep away!" Rogozhin screamed in frenzy, seeing Darya Alexeevna approaching Nastasya Filippovna. "She's mine! It's all mine! A queen! The end!"

He was breathless with joy; he circled around Nastasya Filippovna and cried out to everyone: "Keep away!" His whole company had already crowded into the drawing room. Some were drinking, others were shouting and guffawing, they were all in a most excited and uninhibited state. Ferdyshchenko began trying to sidle up to them. The general and Totsky made another move to disappear quickly. Ganya also had his hat in his hand, but he stood silently and still seemed unable to tear himself away from the picture that was developing before him.

"Keep away!" cried Rogozhin.

"What are you yelling for?" Nastasya Filippovna laughed loudly at him. "I'm still the mistress here; if I want, I can have you thrown out. I haven't taken your money yet, it's right there; give it to me, the whole packet! So there's a hundred thousand in this packet? Pah, how loathsome! What's wrong, Darya Alexeevna? Should I have ruined him?" (She pointed to the prince.) "How can he get married, he still needs a nursemaid himself; so the general will be his nursemaid—look how he dangles after him! See, Prince, your fiancée took the money because she's dissolute, and you wanted to marry her! Why are you crying? Bitter, is it? No, but laugh, as I do!" Nastasya Filippovna went on, with two big tears glistening on her own cheeks. "Trust in time—everything will pass! Better to change your mind now than later . . . But why are you all crying— here's Katya crying! What's wrong, Katya, dear? I've left a lot to you and Pasha, I've already made the arrangements, and now goodbye! I've made an honest girl like you wait on a dissolute one like me . . . It's better this way, Prince, truly better, you'd start despising me tomorrow, and there'd be no happiness for us! Don't swear, I won't believe you! And it would be so stupid . . . No, better let's part nicely, because I'm a dreamer myself, there'd be no use! As if I haven't dreamed of you myself? You're right about that, I dreamed for a long time, still in the country, where he kept me for five years, completely alone, I used to think and think, dream and dream—

and I kept imagining someone like you, kind, honest, good, and as silly as you are, who would suddenly come and say, 'You're not guilty, Nastasya Filippovna, and I adore you!' And I sometimes dreamed so much that I'd go out of my mind . . . And then this one would come: he'd stay for two months a year, dishonor me, offend me, inflame me, debauch me, leave me—a thousand times I wanted to drown myself in the pond, but I was base, I had no courage—well, but now . . . Rogozhin, are you ready?"

"Ready! Keep away!"

"Ready!" several voices rang out.

"The troikas are waiting with their little bells!"

Nastasya Filippovna snatched up the packet with both hands.

"Ganka, I've got an idea: I want to reward you, because why should you lose everything? Rogozhin, will he crawl to Vassilievsky Island for three roubles?"

"He will!"

"Well, then listen, Ganya, I want to look at your soul for the last time; you've been tormenting me for three long months; now it's my turn. Do you see this packet? There's a hundred thousand in it! I'm now going to throw it into the fireplace, onto the fire, before everyone, all these witnesses! As soon as it catches fire all over, go into the fireplace, only without gloves, with your bare hands, with your sleeves rolled up, and pull the packet out of the fire! If you pull it out, it's yours, the whole hundred thousand is yours! You'll only burn your fingers a little—but it's a hundred thousand, just think! It won't take long to snatch it out! And I'll admire your soul as you go into the fire after my money. They're all witnesses that the packet will be yours! And if you don't get it out, it will burn; I won't let anyone else touch it. Stand back! Everybody! It's my money! I got it for a night with Rogozhin. Is it my money, Rogozhin?"

"Yours, my joy! Yours, my queen!"

"Well, then everybody stand back, I do as I like! Don't interfere! Ferdyshchenko, stir up the fire."

"Nastasya Filippovna, my hands refuse to obey!" the flabbergasted Ferdyshchenko replied.

"Ahh!" Nastasya Filippovna cried, seized the fire tongs, separated two smoldering logs, and as soon as the fire blazed up, threw the packet into it.

A cry was heard all around; many even crossed themselves.

"She's lost her mind, she's lost her mind!" they cried all around.

"Maybe . . . maybe we should tie her up?" the general whispered to Ptitsyn. "Or send for . . . she's lost her mind, hasn't she? Lost her mind?"

"N-no, this may not be entirely madness," Ptitsyn whispered, pale as a sheet and trembling, unable to tear his eyes from the packet, which was beginning to smolder.

"She's mad, isn't she? Isn't she mad?" the general pestered Totsky.

"I told you she was a *colorful* woman," murmured Afanasy Ivanovich, also gone somewhat pale.

"But, after all, it's a hundred thousand! . . ."

"Lord, Lord!" was heard on all sides. Everyone crowded around the fireplace, everyone pushed in order to see, everyone exclaimed . . . Some even climbed onto chairs to look over the heads. Darya Alexeevna ran to the other room and exchanged frightened whispers with Katya and Pasha about something. The German beauty fled.

"Dearest lady! Queen! Almighty one!" Lebedev screamed, crawling on his knees before Nastasya Filippovna and reaching out towards the fireplace. "A hundred thousand! A hundred thousand! I saw it myself, I was there when they wrapped it! Dearest lady! Merciful one! Order me into the fireplace: I'll go all the way in, I'll put my whole gray head into the fire! . . . A crippled wife, thirteen children—all orphaned, I buried my father last week, he sits there starving, Nastasya Filippovna!!" and, having screamed, he began crawling into the fireplace.

"Away!" cried Nastasya Filippovna, pushing him aside. "Step back, everybody! Ganya, what are you standing there for? Don't be ashamed! Go in! It's your lucky chance!"

But Ganya had already endured too much that day and that evening, and was not prepared for this last unexpected trial. The crowd parted into two halves before him, and he was left face to face with Nastasya Filippovna, three steps away from her. She stood right by the fireplace and waited, not tearing her burning, intent gaze from him. Ganya, in a tailcoat, his hat and gloves in his hand, stood silent and unresponsive before her, his arms crossed, looking at the fire. An insane smile wandered over his face, which was pale as a sheet. True, he could not take his eyes off the fire, off the smoldering packet; but it seemed something new had arisen in his soul; it was as if he had sworn to endure the torture; he did not budge from the spot; in a few moments it became clear to everyone that he would not go after the packet, that he did not want to.

"Hey, it'll burn up, and they'll shame you," Nastasya Filippovna cried to him, "you'll hang yourself afterwards, I'm not joking!"

The fire that had flared up in the beginning between the two smoldering logs went out at first, when the packet fell on it and smothered it. But a small blue flame still clung from below to one corner of the lower log. Finally, a long, thin tongue of fire licked at the packet, the fire caught and raced along the edges of the paper, and suddenly the whole packet blazed in the fireplace and the bright flame shot upwards. Everyone gasped.

"Dearest lady!" Lebedev kept screaming, straining forward once more, but Rogozhin dragged him back and pushed him aside again.

Rogozhin himself had turned into one fixed gaze. He could not turn it from Nastasya Filippovna, he was reveling, he was in seventh heaven.

"There's a queen for you!" he repeated every moment, turning around to whoever was there. "That's the way to do it!" he cried out, forgetting himself. "Who among you rogues would pull such a stunt, eh?"

The prince watched ruefully and silently.

"I'll snatch it out with my teeth for just one thousand!" Ferdyshchenko offered.

"I could do it with my teeth, too!" the fist gentleman, who was standing behind them all, rasped in a fit of decided despair. "D-devil take it! It's burning, it'll burn up!" he cried, seeing the flame.

"It's burning, it's burning!" they all cried in one voice, almost all of them also straining towards the fireplace.

"Ganya, stop faking, I tell you for the last time!"

"Go in!" Ferdyshchenko bellowed, rushing to Ganya in a decided frenzy and pulling him by the sleeve. "Go in, you little swaggerer! It'll burn up! Oh, cur-r-rse you!"

Ganya shoved Ferdyshchenko aside forcefully, turned, and went towards the door; but before going two steps, he reeled and crashed to the floor.

"He fainted!" they cried all around.

"Dearest lady, it'll burn up!" Lebedev screamed.

"Burn up for nothing!" the roaring came from all sides.

"Katya, Pasha, fetch him water, spirits!" Nastasya Filippovna cried, seized the fire tongs and snatched the packet out.

The outer paper was nearly all charred and smoldering, but it could be seen at once that the inside was not damaged. The packet had been wrapped in three layers of newspaper, and the money was untouched. Everyone breathed more easily.

"Maybe just one little thousand is damaged a tiny bit, but the rest is untouched," Lebedev said tenderly.

"It's all his! The whole packet is his! Do you hear, gentlemen?" Nastasya Filippovna proclaimed, placing the packet beside Ganya. "He didn't go in after it, he held out! So his vanity is still greater than his lust for money. Never mind, he'll come to! Otherwise he might have killed me . . . There, he's already recovering. General, Ivan Petrovich, Darya Alexeevna, Katya, Pasha, Rogozhin, do you hear? The packet is his, Ganya's. I grant him full possession of it as a reward for . . . well, for whatever! Tell him that. Let it lie there beside him . . . Rogozhin, march! Farewell, Prince, I've seen a man for the first time! Farewell, Afanasy Ivanovich, *merci!*"

The whole of Rogozhin's crew, with noise, clatter, and shouting, raced through the rooms to the exit, following Rogozhin and Nastasya Filippovna. In the reception room the maids gave her her fur coat; the cook Marfa came running from the kitchen. Nastasya Filippovna kissed them all.

"Can it be, dearest lady, that you're leaving us for good? But where will you go? And on such a day, on your birthday!" the tearful maids asked, weeping and kissing her hands.

"I'll go to the street, Katya, you heard, that's the place for me, or else I'll become a washerwoman! Enough of Afanasy Ivanovich! Give him my regards, and don't think ill of me . . ."

The prince rushed headlong for the front gate, where they were all getting into four troikas with little bells. The general overtook him on the stairs.

"Good heavens, Prince, come to your senses!" he said, seizing him by the arm. "Drop it! You see what she's like! I'm speaking as a father . . ."

The prince looked at him, but, without saying a word, broke away and ran downstairs.

At the front gate, from which the troikas had just driven off, the general saw the prince catch the first cab and shout, "To Ekaterinhof, follow those troikas!" Then the general's little gray trotter pulled up and took the general home, along with his new hopes and calculations and the aforementioned pearls, which the general had all the same not forgotten to take with him. Amidst his calculations there also flashed once or twice the seductive image of Nastasya Filippovna; the general sighed:

"A pity! A real pity! A lost woman! A madwoman! . . . Well, sir, but what the prince needs now is not Nastasya Filippovna . . ."

A few moralizing and admonishing words of the same sort were also uttered by two other interlocutors from among Nastasya Filippovna's guests, who had decided to go a little way on foot.

"You know, Afanasy Ivanovich, they say something of the sort exists among the Japanese," Ivan Petrovich Ptitsyn was saying. "An offended man there supposedly goes to the offender and says to him: 'You have offended me, for that I have come to rip my belly open before your eyes,' and with those words he actually rips his belly open before his offender's eyes, no doubt feeling an extreme satisfaction, as if he had indeed revenged himself. There are strange characters in the world, Afanasy Ivanovich!"

"And you think it was something of that sort here, too?" replied Afanasy Ivanovich with a smile. "Hm! Anyhow, you've wittily . . . and the comparison is excellent. You saw for yourself, however, my dearest Ivan Petrovich, that I did all I could; I cannot do the impossible, wouldn't you agree? You must also agree, however, that there are some capital virtues in this woman . . . brilliant features. I even wanted to cry out to her just now, if only I could have allowed myself to do it in that bedlam, that she herself was my best defense against all her accusations. Well, who wouldn't be captivated by this woman on occasion to the point of forgetting all reason . . . and the rest? Look, that boor Rogozhin came lugging a hundred thousand to her! Let's say everything that happened there tonight was ephemeral, romantic, indecent, but, on the other hand, it was colorful, it was original, you must agree. God, what might have come from such a character and with such beauty! But, despite all my efforts, even education—all is lost! A diamond in the rough—I've said it many times . . ."

And Afanasy Ivanovich sighed deeply.

PART TWO

I

A COUPLE OF DAYS after the strange adventure at Nastasya Filippovna's party, with which we ended the first part of our story, Prince Myshkin hastened to leave for Moscow on the business of receiving his unexpected inheritance. It was said then that there might have been other reasons for such a hasty departure; but of that, as well as of the prince's adventures in Moscow and generally in the course of his absence from Petersburg, we can supply very little information. The prince was away for exactly six months, and even those who had certain reasons to be interested in his fate could find out very little about him during all that time. True, some sort of rumors reached some of them, though very rarely, but these were mostly strange and almost always contradicted each other. The greatest interest in the prince was shown, of course, in the house of the Epanchins, to whom he had even had no time to say good-bye as he was leaving. The general, however, had seen him then, even two or three times; they had discussed something seriously. But if Epanchin himself had seen him, he had not informed his family of it. And, generally, at first, that is, for nearly a whole month after the prince's departure, talk of him was avoided in the Epanchins' house. Only the general's wife, Lizaveta Prokofyevna, voiced her opinion at the very beginning, "that she had been sadly mistaken about the prince." Then after two or three days she added, though without mentioning the prince now, but vaguely, that "the chiefest feature of her life was to be constantly mistaken about people." And finally, ten days later, being vexed with her daughters over something, she concluded with the utterance: "Enough mistakes! There will be no more of them!" We cannot help noting here that for a long time a certain unpleasant mood existed in their house. There was something heavy, strained, unspoken, quarrelsome; everyone scowled. The general was busy day and night, taken up with his affairs; rarely had anyone seen him so busy and active—especially with official work. The family hardly managed to catch a glimpse of him. As for the Epanchin girls, they, of course, said nothing openly. It may be that they said very little even when they were by themselves. They were proud girls, arrogant, and sometimes bashful even among themselves, but nevertheless they understood each other not only from the first word but even from the first glance, so that sometimes there was no need to say much.

An outside observer, if there had happened to be one, could have come to only one conclusion: that, judging by all the afore-mentioned facts, few as they were, the prince had managed in any case to leave a certain impression in the Epanchins' house, though he had appeared there only once, and that fleetingly. It may have been an impression of simple curiosity, explainable by some of the prince's extraordinary adventures. Be that as it may, the impression remained.

Gradually the rumors that had begun to spread around town also managed to be shrouded in the darkness of ignorance. True, tales were told of some little fool of a prince (no one could name him for certain), who had suddenly inherited an enormous fortune and married some traveling Frenchwoman, a famous cancan dancer from the Château des Fleurs in Paris. But others said that the inheritance had gone to some general, and the one who had married the traveling Frenchwoman and famous cancan dancer was a Russian merchant, an enormously wealthy man, who, at the wedding, drunk, merely to show off, had burned up in a candle exactly seven hundred thousand worth of the latest lottery tickets. But all these rumors died down very quickly, a result to which circumstances contributed greatly. For instance, Rogozhin's entire company, many of whom could have told a thing or two, set off in its whole bulk, with Rogozhin himself at its head, for Moscow, almost exactly a week after a terrible orgy in the Ekaterinhof vauxhall,[1] at which Nastasya Filippovna had also been present. Some people, the very few who were interested, learned from other rumors that Nastasya Filippovna had fled the day after Ekaterinhof, had vanished, and had finally been traced, having gone off to Moscow; so that Rogozhin's departure for Moscow came out as being somewhat coincident with this rumor.

A rumor also went around concerning Gavrila Ardalionovich Ivolgin himself, who was also quite well known in his circle. But with him, too, a circumstance occurred which soon quickly cooled and ultimately stopped entirely all unkind stories concerning him: he became very ill and was unable to appear not only anywhere in society but also at his work. After a month of illness, he recovered, but for some reason gave up his job in the stock company, and his place was taken by someone else. He also did not appear even once in General Epanchin's house, so that the general, too, had to hire another clerk. Gavrila Ardalionovich's enemies might have supposed that he was so embarrassed by everything that had happened to him that he was even ashamed to go out; but he was indeed a bit unwell; he even fell into hypochondria, became pensive, irritable. That same winter Varvara Ardalionovna married Ptitsyn; everybody who knew them ascribed this marriage directly to the circumstance that Ganya refused to go back to work and not only stopped supporting his family but even began to need help and almost to be looked after himself.

Let us note parenthetically that Gavrila Ardalionovich was never even mentioned in the Epanchins' house—as if there had been no such person in the world, let alone in their house. And yet they all learned (and even quite soon) a very remarkable circumstance about him, namely: on that same night that was so fatal for him, after the unpleasant adventure at Nastasya Filippovna's, Ganya, having returned home, did not go to bed, but began waiting with feverish impatience for the prince to come back. The prince, who had gone to Ekaterinhof, came back after five in the morning. Then Ganya went to his room and placed before him on the table the charred packet of money, given to him by Nastasya Filippovna while he lay in a swoon. He insistently begged the prince to return this gift to Nastasya Filippovna at the first opportunity. When Ganya entered the prince's room, he was in a hostile and nearly desperate mood; but it seemed some words were exchanged between him and the prince, after which Ganya sat with him for two hours and spent the whole time weeping bitterly. The two parted on friendly terms.

This news, which reached all the Epanchins, was, as later events confirmed, perfectly accurate. Of course, it was strange that news of this sort could travel and become known so quickly; for instance, everything that had happened at Nastasya Filippovna's became known at the Epanchins' almost the next day and even in quite accurate detail. Concerning the news about Gavrila Ardalionovich, it might be supposed that it was brought to the Epanchins by Varvara Ardalionovna, who somehow suddenly appeared among the Epanchin girls and very soon was even on a very intimate footing with them, which for Lizaveta Prokofyevna was extremely surprising. But though Varvara Ardalionovna for some reason found it necessary to become so close with the Epanchins, she surely would not have talked with them about her brother. She, too, was a very proud woman, in her own way, despite the fact that she had struck up a friendship there, where her brother had almost been thrown out. Before then, though she had been acquainted with the Epanchin girls, she had seen them rarely. Even now, however, she almost never appeared in the drawing room, and came in, or rather, dropped in, by the back door. Lizaveta Prokofyevna had never been disposed towards her, either before or now, though she greatly respected Nina Alexandrovna, Varvara Ardalionovna's mother. She was astonished, became angry, ascribed the acquaintance with Varya to the capricious and power-loving character of her daughters, who "invent all kinds of things just to be contrary to her," yet Varvara Ardalionovna went on visiting them all the same, both before and after her marriage.

But a month passed after the prince's departure, and Mrs. Epanchin received a letter from the old Princess Belokonsky, who had left for Moscow some two weeks earlier to stay with her married elder daughter, and this letter produced a visible effect on her. Though she said nothing about what was in it either to her daughters or to Ivan Fyodorovich, the family noticed by many signs that she was somehow especially agitated, even excited. She kept starting somehow especially strange conversations with her daughters, and all on such extraordinary subjects; she obviously wanted to speak her mind, but for some reason she held back. The day she received the letter, she was nice to everyone, even kissed Aglaya and Adelaida, confessed something particular to them, but precisely what they could not tell. She suddenly became indulgent even to Ivan Fyodorovich, whom she had kept in disgrace for a whole month. Naturally, the next day she became extremely angry over her sentimentality of the day before and by dinnertime managed to quarrel with everyone, but towards evening the horizon cleared again. Generally, for the whole week she continued to be in very bright spirits, something that had not happened for a long time.

But after another week, another letter came from Princess Belokonsky, and this time Mrs. Epanchin decided to speak out. She solemnly announced that "old Belokonsky" (she never referred to the princess otherwise, when speaking in her absence) had told her some very comforting news about this . . . "odd bird, well, that is, about this prince!" The old woman had sought him out in Moscow, made inquiries about him, and learned something very good; the prince had finally called on her in person and made an almost extraordinary impression on her. "That's clear from the fact that she invited him to come every day from one till two, and the man drags himself there every day, and she's still not sick of him," Mrs. Epanchin concluded, adding that through "the old woman" the prince was now received in two or three good houses. "It's good that he doesn't sit in his corner feeling bashful like a fool." The girls, to whom all this was imparted, noticed at once that their dear mama had concealed a great deal of her letter from them. They might have known it from Varvara Ardalionovna, who could and certainly did know everything that Ptitsyn knew about the prince and his stay in Moscow. And Ptitsyn might have been even better informed than anyone else. But he was a man of extreme reticence in business matters, though he certainly shared things with Varya. Mrs. Epanchin at once began to dislike Varvara Ardalionovna still more for it.

But be that as it may, the ice was broken, and it suddenly became possible to talk openly about the prince. Besides that, the extraordinary impression and the exceedingly great interest that the prince had aroused and left behind him in the Epanchins' house once more clearly showed itself. Mrs. Epanchin even marveled at the impression made on her daughters by the news from Moscow. And the daughters also marveled at their mother, who had so solemnly announced to them that it was "the chiefest feature of her life to be constantly mistaken about people," and at the same time had recommended the prince to the attention of the "powerful" old Princess Belokonsky in Moscow, having, of course, to beg for her attention in the name of Christ and God, because on certain occasions the "old woman" was hard to get going.

But once the ice was broken and a fresh wind blew, the general also hastened to speak his mind. It turned out that he, too, was extraordinarily interested. He informed them, however, only of "the business side of the subject." It turned out that, in the interests of the prince, he had charged a couple of gentlemen, highly reliable and of a certain sort of influence in Moscow, to keep an eye on him and especially on his guide Salazkin. Everything that had been said about the inheritance, "about the fact of the inheritance, so to speak," turned out to be true, but the inheritance itself turned out in the end to be by no means as significant as had originally been spread about. The fortune was half entangled; there turned out to be debts; there turned out to be some sort of claimants, and the prince, in spite of all guidance, behaved in a most unbusinesslike way. "Of course, God be with him": now that the "ice of silence" was broken, the general was glad to declare this "in all the sincerity" of his soul, because, "though the fellow's a bit *like that*," all the same he deserved it. But meanwhile, all the same, he had made some blunders here: for instance, some of the dead merchant's creditors had appeared, with disputable, worthless papers, and some, having heard about the prince, even came without any papers—and what then? The prince satisfied almost all of them, though his friends pointed out to him that all these petty folk and petty creditors were completely without rights; and he had only satisfied them because it actually turned out that a few of them had indeed suffered.

To this Mrs. Epanchin responded that Belokonsky had written something of the same sort to her and that "this is stupid, very stupid; but there's no curing a fool"—she added sharply, but one could see from her face how glad she was of what this "fool" had done. In conclusion to all this the general noticed that his wife was as concerned for the prince as if he were her own son and that she had also begun to be terribly affectionate to Aglaya; seeing which, Ivan Fyodorovich assumed a very businesslike air for a time.

But once again all this pleasant mood did not exist for long. Only two weeks went by and something suddenly changed again, Mrs. Epanchin scowled, and the general, after shrugging his shoulders a few times, again submitted to the "ice of silence." The thing was that just two weeks earlier he had received undercover information, brief and therefore not quite clear, but reliable, that Nastasya Filippovna, who had first disappeared in Moscow, had then been found in Moscow by Rogozhin, had then disappeared again somewhere and had again been found by him, had finally given him an almost certain promise that she would marry him. And now, only two weeks later, his excellency had suddenly received information that Nastasya Filippovna had run away for a third time, almost from the foot of the altar, and this time had disappeared somewhere in the provinces, and meanwhile Prince Myshkin had also vanished from Moscow, leaving Salazkin in charge of all his affairs, "together with her, or simply rushing after her, no one knows, but there's something in it," the general concluded. Lizaveta Prokofyevna, for her part, also received some unpleasant information. In the end, two months after the prince's departure, almost all the rumors about him in Petersburg had definitively died out, and in the Epanchins' house the "ice of silence" was not broken again. Varvara Ardalionovna, however, still visited the girls.

To have done with all these rumors and reports, let us also add that a great many upheavals had taken place at the Epanchins' by spring, so that it was hard not to forget about the prince, who for his part never sent, and perhaps did not wish to send, any news of himself. Gradually, in the course of the winter, they finally decided to go abroad for the summer—that is, Lizaveta Prokofyevna and her daughters; the general, naturally, could not spend time on "empty entertainment." The decision was taken at the extreme and persistent urging of the girls, who had become completely convinced that their parents did not want to take them abroad because they were constantly concerned with getting them married and finding suitors for them. It may be that the parents also finally became convinced that suitors could be met abroad as well, and that one summer trip not only could not upset anything, but perhaps "might even contribute." Here it would be appropriate to mention that the intended marriage between Afanasy Ivanovich Totsky and the eldest Epanchin girl broke up altogether, and no formal proposal ever took place. It happened somehow by itself, without long discussions and without any family struggles. Since the time of the prince's departure, everything had suddenly quieted down on both sides. This circumstance was one of the causes of the then heavy mood in the Epanchin family, though Mrs. Epanchin said at the time that she would gladly "cross herself with both hands." The general, though in disgrace and aware that it was his own fault, pouted for a long time all the same; he was sorry to lose Afanasy Ivanovich: "such a fortune, and such a dexterous man!" Not long afterwards the general learned that Afanasy Ivanovich had been captivated by a traveling high-society Frenchwoman, a marquise and a *legitimiste*,[2] that a marriage was to take place, after which Afanasy Ivanovich would be taken to Paris and then somewhere in Brittany. "Well, the Frenchwoman will be the end of him," the general decided.

But the Epanchins were preparing to leave by summer. And suddenly a circumstance occurred which again changed everything in a new way, and the trip was again postponed, to the greatest joy of the general and his wife. A certain prince arrived in Petersburg from Moscow, Prince Shch., a well-known man, incidentally, and known from a quite, quite good point. He was one of those people, or, one might even say, activists of recent times, honest, modest, who sincerely and consciously wish to be useful, are always working, and are distinguished by this rare and happy quality of always finding work. Without putting himself forward, avoiding the bitterness and idle talk of parties, not counting himself among the foremost, the prince nevertheless had a quite substantial understanding of much that was happening in recent times. Formerly he had been in government service, then he began to participate in *zemstvo*[3] activity. Besides that, he was a useful corresponding member of several Russian learned societies. Together with an engineer acquaintance, he contributed, by gathering information and research, to correcting the planned itinerary of one of the most important railways. He was about thirty-five years old. He was a man "of the highest society" and, besides that, had a fortune that was "good, serious, incontestable," as the general put it, having met and become acquainted with the prince on the occasion of some rather serious business at the office of the count, his superior. The prince, out of some special curiosity, never avoided making the acquaintance of Russia's "businesspeople." It so happened that the prince also became acquainted with the general's family. Adelaida Ivanovna, the middle sister, made a very strong impression on him. By spring the prince had proposed. Adelaida liked him very much, and so did Lizaveta Prokofyevna. The general was very glad. Needless to say, the trip was postponed. A spring wedding was planned.

The trip, however, might have taken place by the middle or the end of summer, if only in the form of a one- or two-month excursion of Lizaveta Prokofyevna and her two remaining daughters, in order to dispel the sadness of Adelaida's leaving them. But again something new happened: at the end of spring (Adelaida's wedding had been delayed somewhat and was postponed till the middle of summer) Prince Shch. introduced into the Epanchins' house a distant relation of his, with whom, however, he was rather well acquainted. This was a certain Evgeny Pavlovich R., still a young man, about twenty-eight, an imperial aide-de-camp, strikingly handsome, "of a noble family," a witty, brilliant "new" man, "exceedingly educated," and—somehow much too fabulously wealthy. With regard to this last point the general was always careful. He made inquiries: "There is actually something of the sort—though, in any case, it must be verified." This young and "promising" imperial aide-de-camp was given a strong boost by the opinion of the old Princess Belokonsky from Moscow. In one respect only was his reputation somewhat ticklish: there had been several liaisons and, as it was maintained, "victories" over certain unfortunate hearts. Having seen Aglaya, he became extraordinarily sedentary in the Epanchins' house. True, nothing had been said yet, nor had any allusions been made, but all the same the parents thought that there was no need even to think about a trip abroad that summer. Aglaya herself was perhaps of a different opinion.

This happened just before our hero's second appearance on the scene of our story. By that time, judging from appearances, poor Prince Myshkin had been totally forgotten in Petersburg. If he had suddenly appeared now among those who had known him, it would have been as if he had dropped from the moon. And yet we still have one more fact to report, and with that we shall end our introduction.

Kolya Ivolgin, on the prince's departure, at first went on with his former life, that is, went to school, visited his friend Ippolit, looked after the general, and helped Varya around the house, that is, ran errands for her. But the tenants quickly vanished: Ferdyshchenko moved somewhere three days after the adventure at Nastasya Filippovna's and quite soon disappeared, so that even all rumors about him died out; he was said to be drinking somewhere, but nothing was certain. The prince left for Moscow; that was the end of the tenants. Afterwards, when Varya was already married, Nina Alexandrovna and Ganya moved with her to Ptitsyn's, in the Ismailovsky quarter; as for General Ivolgin, a quite unforeseen circumstance occurred with him at almost that same time: he went to debtors' prison. He was dispatched there by his lady friend, the captain's widow, on the strength of documents he had given her at various times, worth about two thousand. All this came as a total surprise to him, and the poor general was "decidedly the victim of his boundless faith in the nobility of the human heart, broadly speaking." Having adopted the soothing habit of signing vouchers and promissory notes, he never supposed the possibility of their effect, at least at some point, always thinking it was *just so*. It turned to be not so. "Trust people after that, show them your noble trustfulness!" he exclaimed ruefully, sitting with his new friends in Tarasov House[4] over a bottle of wine and telling them anecdotes about the siege of Kars and a resurrected soldier. His life there, however, was excellent. Ptitsyn and Varya used to say it was the right place for him; Ganya agreed completely. Only poor Nina

Alexandrovna wept bitterly on the quiet (which even surprised her household) and, though eternally ill, dragged herself as often as she could to see her husband in Tarasov House.

But since the "incident with the general," as Kolya put it, or, more broadly, since his sister's marriage, Kolya had gotten completely out of hand, so much so that lately he even rarely came to spend the night with the family. According to rumor, he had made many new acquaintances; besides that, he had become all too well known in the debtors' prison. Nina Alexandrovna could not do without him there; and at home now no one pestered him even out of curiosity. Varya, who had treated him so sternly before, did not subject him now to the least inquiry about his wanderings; and Ganya, to the great astonishment of the household, talked and even got together with him occasionally on perfectly friendly terms, despite all his hypochondria, something that had never happened before, because the twenty-seven-year-old Ganya, naturally, had never paid the slightest friendly attention to his fifteen-year-old brother, had treated him rudely, had demanded that the whole household treat him with sternness only, and had constantly threatened to "go for his ears," which drove Kolya "beyond the final limits of human patience." One might have thought that Kolya was now sometimes even necessary to Ganya. He had been very struck that Ganya had returned the money then; he was prepared to forgive him a lot for that.

Three months went by after the prince's departure, and the Ivolgin family heard that Kolya had suddenly become acquainted with the Epanchins and was received very nicely by the girls. Varya soon learned of it; Kolya, incidentally, had become acquainted not through Varya but "on his own." The Epanchins gradually grew to love him. At first the general's wife was very displeased with him, but soon she began to treat him kindly "for his candor and for the fact that he doesn't flatter." That Kolya did not flatter was perfectly right; he managed to put himself on a completely equal and independent footing with them, though he did sometimes read books or newspapers to Mrs. Epanchin—but he had always been obliging. A couple of times, however, he quarreled bitterly with Lizaveta Prokofyevna, told her that she was a despot and that he would not set foot in the house again. The first time was over the "woman question," the second time over what season of the year was best for catching siskins. Incredible as it might seem, on the third day after the quarrel, Mrs. Epanchin sent him a footman with a note asking him to come without fail; Kolya did not put on airs and went at once. Only Aglaya was constantly ill-disposed towards him for some reason and treated him haughtily. Yet it was her that he was to surprise somewhat. Once—it was during Holy Week[5]— finding a moment when they were alone, Kolya handed Aglaya a letter, adding only that he had been told to give it to her alone. Aglaya gave the "presumptuous brat" a terrible look, but Kolya did not wait and left. She opened the note and read:

> Once you honored me with your confidence. It may be that you have completely forgotten me now. How is it that I am writing to you? I do not know; but I have an irrepressible desire to remind you of myself, and you precisely. Many's the time I have needed all three of you very much, but of all three I could see only you. I need you, I need you very much. I have nothing to write to you about myself, I have nothing to tell you about. That is not what I wanted; I wish terribly much that you should be happy. Are you happy? That is the only thing I wanted to tell you.
>
> Your brother, Pr. L. Myshkin.

Having read this brief and rather muddle-headed note, Aglaya suddenly flushed all over and became pensive. It would be hard for us to convey the course of her thoughts. Among other things, she asked herself: "Should I show it to anyone?" She felt somehow ashamed. She ended, however, by smiling a mocking and strange smile and dropping the letter into her desk drawer. The next day she took it out again and put it into a thick, sturdily bound book (as she always did with her papers, so as to find them quickly when she needed them). And only a week later did she happen to notice what book it was. It was *Don Quixote de La Mancha*. Aglaya laughed terribly—no one knew why.

Nor did anyone know whether she showed her acquisition to any of her sisters.

But as she was reading this letter, the thought suddenly crossed her mind: could it be that the prince had chosen this presumptuous little brat and show-off as his correspondent and, for all she knew, his only correspondent in Petersburg? And, though with a look of extraordinary disdain, all the same she put Kolya to the question. But the "brat," ordinarily touchy, this time did not pay the slightest attention to the disdain; he explained to Aglaya quite briefly and rather drily that he had given the prince his permanent address,

just in case, before the prince left Petersburg, and had offered to
be of service, that this was the first errand he had been entrusted
with and the first note he had received, and in proof of his words
he produced the letter he had himself received. Aglaya read it
without any qualms. The letter to Kolya read:

> Dear Kolya, be so good as to convey the enclosed and sealed
> note to Aglaya Ivanovna. Be well.
>
> Lovingly yours, Pr. L. Myshkin.

"All the same, it's ridiculous to confide in such a pipsqueak,"
Aglaya said touchily, handing Kolya's note back, and she scornfully
walked past him.

Now that Kolya could not bear: he had asked Ganya, purposely
for that occasion, without explaining the reason why, to let him
wear his still quite new green scarf. He was bitterly offended.

II

IT WAS THE first days of June, and the weather in Petersburg
had been unusually fine for a whole week. The Epanchins had
their own wealthy dacha in Pavlovsk.[6] Lizaveta Prokofyevna suddenly roused herself and went into action: before not quite two
days of bustling were over, they moved.

A day or two after the Epanchins moved to the country, Prince
Lev Nikolaevich Myshkin arrived from Moscow on the morning
train. No one met him at the station; but as he was getting off
the train, the prince suddenly thought he caught the gaze of two
strange, burning eyes in the crowd surrounding the arriving people.
When he looked more attentively, he could no longer see them.
Of course, he had only imagined it; but it left an unpleasant impression. Besides, the prince was sad and pensive to begin with and
seemed preoccupied with something.

The cabby brought him to a hotel not far from Liteinaya Street.
It was a wretched little hotel. The prince took two small rooms,
dark and poorly furnished, washed, dressed, asked for nothing, and
left hastily, as if afraid of wasting time or of not finding someone
at home.

If anyone who had known him six months ago, when he first
came to Petersburg, had looked at him now, he might have

concluded that his appearance had changed greatly for the better. But that was hardly so. There was merely a complete change in his clothes: they were all different, made in Moscow, and by a good tailor; but there was a flaw in them as well: they were much too fashionably made (as always with conscientious but not very talented tailors), and moreover for a man not the least bit interested in fashion, so that, taking a close look at the prince, someone much given to laughter might have found good reason to smile. But people laugh at all sorts of things.

The prince took a cab and went to Peski. On one of the Rozhdestvensky streets he soon located a rather small wooden house. To his surprise, this house turned out to be attractive, clean, very well kept, with a front garden in which flowers were growing. The windows facing the street were open and from them came the sound of shrill, ceaseless talking, almost shouting, as if someone was reading aloud or even delivering a speech; the voice was interrupted now and then by the laughter of several resounding voices. The prince entered the yard, went up the front steps, and asked for Mr. Lebedev.

"Mister's in there," the cook replied, opening the door, her sleeves rolled up to the elbows, jabbing her finger towards the "drawing room."

In this drawing room, the walls of which were covered with blue wallpaper, and which was decorated neatly and with some pretense—that is, with a round table and a sofa, a bronze clock under a glass bell, a narrow mirror between the two windows, and a very old crystal chandelier, not big, suspended from the ceiling on a bronze chain—in the middle of the room stood Mr. Lebedev himself, his back turned to the entering prince, in a waistcoat but with nothing over it, summer-fashion, beating himself on the breast and delivering a bitter harangue on some subject. The listeners were: a boy of about fifteen with a rather merry and far from stupid face and with a book in his hand, a young girl of about twenty dressed in mourning and with a nursing baby in her arms, a thirteen-year-old girl, also in mourning, who was laughing loudly and opening her mouth terribly widely as she did so, and, finally, an extremely strange listener, a fellow of about twenty, lying on the sofa, rather handsome, dark, with long, thick hair, big, dark eyes, and a small pretense to side-whiskers and a little beard. This listener, it seemed, often interrupted and argued with the haranguing Lebedev; that was probably what made the rest of the audience laugh.

"Lukyan Timofeich, hey, Lukyan Timofeich! No, really! Look here! . . . Well, drat you all!"

And the cook left, waving her arms and getting so angry that she even became all red.

Lebedev turned around and, seeing the prince, stood for a time as if thunderstruck, then rushed to him with an obsequious smile, but froze again on the way, nevertheless having uttered:

"Il-il-illustrious Prince!"

But suddenly, as if still unable to recover his countenance, he turned around and, for no reason at all, first fell upon the girl in mourning with the baby in her arms, so that she even recoiled a little from the unexpectedness of it, then immediately abandoned her and fell upon the thirteen-year-old girl, who hovered in the doorway to the other room and went on smiling with the remnants of her recent laughter. She could not bear his shouting and immediately darted off to the kitchen; Lebedev even stamped his feet behind her, for greater intimidation, but, meeting the prince's eyes, staring in bewilderment, said by way of explanation:

"For . . . respectfulness, heh, heh, heh!"

"There's no need for all this . . ." the prince tried to begin.

"At once, at once, at once . . . like lightning!"

And Lebedev quickly vanished from the room. The prince looked in surprise at the young girl, at the boy, at the one lying on the sofa; they were all laughing. The prince laughed, too.

"He went to put on his tailcoat," said the boy.

"This is all so vexing," the prince began, "and I'd have thought . . . tell me, is he . . ."

"Drunk, you think?" cried the voice from the sofa. "Stone sober! Maybe three or four glasses, well, or make it five, but that's just for discipline."

The prince was about to address the voice from the sofa, but the young girl began to speak and, with a most candid look on her pretty face, said:

"He never drinks much in the mornings; if you've come on business, talk to him now. It's the right time. When he comes home in the evening, he's drunk; and now he mostly weeps at night and reads aloud to us from the Holy Scriptures, because our mother died five weeks ago."

"He ran away because he probably had a hard time answering you," the young man laughed from the sofa. "I'll bet he's about to dupe you and is thinking it over right now."

"Just five weeks! Just five weeks!" Lebedev picked up, coming back in wearing his tailcoat, blinking his eyes and pulling a handkerchief from his pocket to wipe his tears. "Orphans!"

"Why have you come out all in holes?" said the young girl. "You've got a brand-new frock coat lying there behind the door, didn't you see it?"

"Quiet, you fidget!" Lebedev shouted at her. "Ah, you!" he began to stamp his feet at her. But this time she only laughed.

"Don't try to frighten me, I'm not Tanya, I won't run away. But you may wake up Lyubochka, and she'll get into a fit . . . what's all this shouting!"

"No, no, no! Bite your tongue . . ." Lebedev suddenly became terribly frightened and, rushing to the baby asleep in his daughter's arms, with a frightened look made a cross over it several times. "Lord save us, Lord protect us! This is my own nursing baby, my daughter Lyubov," he turned to the prince, "born in the most lawful wedlock of the newly departed Elena, my wife, who died in childbed. And this wee thing is my daughter Vera, in mourning . . . And this, this, oh, this . . ."

"Why do you stop short?" cried the young man. "Go on, don't be embarrassed."

"Your Highness!" Lebedev suddenly exclaimed in a sort of transport, "have you been following the murder of the Zhemarin family⁷ in the newspapers?"

"I have," the prince said in some surprise.

"Well, this is the true murderer of the Zhemarin family, the man himself!"

"What do you mean?" said the prince.

"That is, allegorically speaking, the future second murderer of the future second Zhemarin family, if one turns up. He's headed for that . . ."

Everybody laughed. It occurred to the prince that Lebedev might indeed be squirming and clowning only because, anticipating his questions, he did not know how to answer them and was gaining time.

"He's a rebel! A conspirator!" Lebedev shouted, as if no longer able to control himself. "Well, and can I, do I have the right to regard such a slanderer, such a harlot, one might say, and monster, as my own nephew, the only son of my late sister Anisya?"

"Oh, stop it, you drunkard! Would you believe, Prince, he's now decided to become a lawyer, to plead in the courts; he waxes eloquent and talks in high-flown style with his children at home. Five days ago he spoke before the justices of the peace. And who do you think he defended? Not the old woman who implored, who begged him, because she'd been fleeced by a scoundrel of a moneylender who took five hundred roubles from her, everything she had, but the moneylender himself, some Zeidler or other, a Yid, because he promised him fifty roubles for it . . ."

"Fifty roubles if I win and only five if I lose," Lebedev suddenly explained in a completely different voice than before, as if he had never been shouting.

"Well, it was a washout, of course, the old rules have been changed, they only laughed at him there. But he remained terribly pleased with himself. Remember, he said, impartial gentlemen of the court, that an old man of sorrows, a cripple, who lives by honest labor, is being deprived of his last crust of bread. Remember the wise words of the lawgiver: 'Let mercy reign in the courts.'[8] And believe me: every morning he repeats this speech for us here, exactly as he said it there; this is the fifth day; he was reciting it just before you came, he likes it so much. He drools over himself. And he's getting ready to defend somebody else. You're Prince Myshkin, I believe? Kolya told me about you. He says he's never met anyone in the world more intelligent than you . . ."

"And there is no one! No one! No one more intelligent in the world!" Lebedev picked up at once.

"Well, I suppose this one's just babbling. The one loves you, and the other fawns on you; but I have no intention of flattering you, let that be known to you. You must have some sense, so decide between him and me. Well, do you want the prince to decide between us?" he said to his uncle. "I'm even glad you've turned up, Prince."

"Let him!" Lebedev cried resolutely, looking around involuntarily at his audience, which had again begun to advance upon him.

"What's going on with you here?" the prince said, making a wry face.

He really had a headache, and besides, he was becoming more and more convinced that Lebedev was duping him and was glad that the business could be put off.

"Here's how things stand. I am his nephew, he wasn't lying about that, though everything he says is a lie. I haven't finished my studies, but I want to finish them, and I'll get my way because I have character. And meanwhile, in order to exist, I'm taking a job with the railways that pays twenty-five roubles. I'll admit, besides, that he has already helped me two or three times. I had twenty roubles and lost them gambling. Would you believe it, Prince, I was so mean, so low, that I gambled them away!"

"To a blackguard, a blackguard, who shouldn't have been paid!" cried Lebedev.

"Yes, to a blackguard, but who still had to be paid," the young man went on. "And that he's a blackguard, I, too, will testify, not only because he gave you a beating. He's a rejected officer, Prince, a retired lieutenant from Rogozhin's former band, who teaches boxing. They're all wandering about now, since Rogozhin scattered them. But the worst thing is that I knew he was a blackguard, a scoundrel, and a petty thief, and I still sat down to play with him, and that, as I bet my last rouble (we were playing cribbage), I thought to myself: I'll lose, go to Uncle Lukyan, bow to him—he won't refuse. That was meanness, that was real meanness! That was conscious baseness!"

"Yes, there you have conscious baseness!" repeated Lebedev.

"Well, don't triumph, wait a moment," the touchy nephew cried, "don't be so glad. I came to see him, Prince, and admitted everything; I acted nobly, I didn't spare myself; I denounced myself before him as much as I could, everybody here is a witness. To take this job with the railways, I absolutely must outfit myself at least somehow, because I'm all in rags. Here, look at my boots! Otherwise I can't show up for work, and if I don't show up at the appointed time, somebody else will take the job, and I'll be left hanging again, and who knows when I'll find another job? Now I'm asking him for only fifteen roubles, and I promise that I'll never ask again, and on top of that I'll repay the whole debt to the last kopeck during the first three months. I'll keep my word. I can live on bread and kvass for months at a time, because I have a strong character. For three months I'll get seventy-five roubles. With the previous debt, I'll owe him only thirty-five roubles, so I'll have enough to pay him. Well, he can ask as much interest as he likes, devil take it! Doesn't he know me? Ask him, Prince: when he helped me out before, did I pay him back or not? Why doesn't he want to now? He's angry that I paid that lieutenant; there's no other reason! That's how this man is—doesn't eat himself and won't let others!"

"And he won't go away," Lebedev cried, "he lies here and won't go away!"

"That's what I told you. I won't go away till you give it to me.

You're smiling at something, Prince? Apparently you think I'm in the wrong?"

"I'm not smiling, but in my opinion you actually are somewhat in the wrong," the prince answered reluctantly.

"No, just say outright that I'm totally wrong, don't dodge! What is this 'somewhat'?"

"If you wish, you're totally wrong."

"If I wish! Ridiculous! Can you possibly think I don't know that it's ticklish to act this way, that the money's his, the will is his, and it comes out as violence on my part? But you, Prince . . . you don't know life. If you don't teach them, they'll be of no use. They have to be taught. My conscience is clear; in all conscience, I won't cause him any loss, I'll pay him back with interest. He's already received moral satisfaction as well: he has seen my humiliation. What more does he want? What good is he, if he can't be useful? For pity's sake, what does he do himself? Ask him what he does to others and how he dupes people. How did he pay for this house? I'll bet my life that he has already duped you and has already made plans for how to dupe you further! You're smiling. You don't believe me?"

"It seems to me that all this is quite unconnected with your affair," observed the prince.

"I've been lying here for three days, and the things I've seen!" the young man went on shouting without listening. "Imagine, he suspects this angel, this young girl, now an orphan, my cousin, his own daughter; every night he searches for her sweethearts! He comes here on the sly and also searches for something under my sofa. He's gone crazy from suspiciousness; he sees thieves in every corner. All night he keeps popping out of bed to see whether the windows are well latched, to check the doors, to peek into the stove, as much as seven times a night. He defends swindlers in court, and he gets up three times in the night to pray, here in the living room, on his knees, pounding his head on the floor for half an hour, and who doesn't he pray for, what doesn't he pray for, the drunken mumbler! He prayed for the repose of the soul of the countess Du Barry,[9] I heard it with my own ears; Kolya also heard it: he's gone quite crazy!"

"You see, you hear, how he disgraces me, Prince!" Lebedev cried out, turning red and really getting furious. "And he doesn't know that I, drunkard and profligate, robber and evil-doer, may only be standing on this one thing, that when this scoffer was still an infant, my destitute, widowed sister Anisya's son, I, as destitute as she was, swaddled him, washed him in a tub, sat up with them for whole nights without sleeping, when both of them were sick, stole firewood from the caretaker downstairs, sang him songs, snapped my fingers, hungry belly that I was, and so I nursed him, and see how he laughs at me now! What business is it of yours if I did cross my forehead once for the repose of the soul of the countess Du Barry? Because three days ago, Prince, I read her biography for the first time in an encyclopedia. And do you know what she was, this Du Barry? Tell me, do you know or not?"

"So, what, are you the only one who knows?" the young man muttered mockingly but reluctantly.

"She was a countess who, having risen from a life of shame, ran things in the queen's place, and a great empress wrote her a letter with her own hand, addressing her as *ma cousine*. A cardinal, a papal nuncio, at the levay dew rwah (do you know what the levay dew rwah was?),[10] volunteered personally to put silk stockings on her bare legs, and considered it an honor—such an exalted and holy person! Do you know that? I can see by your face that you don't! Well, how did she die? Answer, if you know!"

"Get out! What a pest."

"The way she died was that, after such honors, this former ruling lady was dragged guiltless to the guillotine by the executioner Samson, for the amusement of the Parisian fishwives, and she was so frightened that she didn't understand what was happening to her. She saw that he was bending her neck down under the knife and kicking her from behind—with the rest all laughing—and she began to cry out: '*Encore un moment, monsieur le bourreau, encore un moment!*' Which means: 'Wait one more little minute, mister boorow, just one!' And maybe the Lord will forgive her for that little minute, because it's impossible to imagine a human soul in worse mizair than that. Do you know what the word mizair means? Well, this is that same mizair. When I read about this countess's cry of one little moment, it was as if my heart was in pincers. And what do you care, worm, if I decided on going to bed at night to remember her, a great sinner, in my prayers? Maybe I remembered her precisely because, as long as this world has stood, probably nobody has ever crossed his forehead for her, or even thought of it. And so, she'll feel good in the other world that another sinner like her has been found, who has prayed for her at least once on earth. What are you laughing at? You don't believe, you atheist. But how do you know? And you also lied, if you did eavesdrop on me; I didn't pray only for the countess Du Barry; what I prayed was: 'Give rest, O Lord, to the soul of the great sinner, the countess Du Barry, and all those like her'—and that's a very different thing; for there are many such great women sinners and examples of the change of fortune, who suffered, and who now find no peace there, and groan, and wait; and I also prayed then for you and those like you, of your kind, impudent offenders, since you decided to eavesdrop on my prayers . . ."

"Well, all right, enough, pray for whoever you like, devil take you, quit shouting!" the nephew interrupted vexedly. "He's very well read, Prince, didn't you know?" he added with a sort of awkward grin. "He's reading all sorts of books and memoirs these days."

"All the same your uncle . . . is not a heartless man," the prince observed reluctantly. He was beginning to find this young man quite repulsive.

"You'll spoil him on us, praising him like that! See, he puts his hand to his heart and purses his lips, relishing it no end. Maybe he's not heartless, but he's a rogue, that's the trouble; what's more, he's drunk, he's all unhinged, like anybody who's been drinking for several years, and everything in him creaks. Granted he loves the children, he respected my deceased aunt . . . He even loves me, by God, and has left me something in his will . . ."

"N-nothing is what you'll get!" Lebedev cried out bitterly.

"Listen, Lebedev," the prince said firmly, turning away from the young man, "I know from experience that you can be businesslike when you want to be . . . I have very little time now, and if you . . . Excuse me, I've forgotten your name."

"Ti-Ti-Timofei."

"And?"

"Lukyanovich."

Everybody in the room burst out laughing.

"A lie!" cried the nephew. "That, too, is a lie! His name isn't Timofei Lukyanovich at all, Prince, it's Lukyan Timofeevich! Tell us, now, why did you lie? Isn't it all the same, Lukyan or Timofei, and what does the prince care? He only lies out of habit, I assure you!"

"Can it be true?" the prince asked impatiently.

"Actually, I'm Lukyan Timofeevich," Lebedev confirmed abashedly, humbly looking down and again putting his hand to his heart.

"Ah, my God, but why did you do it?"

"For self-belittlement," whispered Lebedev, hanging his head more and more humbly.

"Eh, who needs your self-belittlement! If only I knew where to find Kolya now!" said the prince, and he turned to leave.

"I can tell you where Kolya is," the young man volunteered again.

"No, no, no!" Lebedev roused himself, all in a flutter.

"Kolya spent the night here, but in the morning he went to look for his general, whom you, Prince, redeemed from prison, God knows why. The general had promised yesterday to come here and spend the night, but he didn't. Most likely he spent the night in the Scales Hotel, very near here. Which means that Kolya is either there or in Pavlovsk with the Epanchins. He had some money, he wanted to go yesterday. So he's either in the Scales or in Pavlovsk."

"In Pavlovsk, in Pavlovsk! . . . And we'll go this way, this way, to the garden, and . . . have a little coffee . . ."

And Lebedev pulled the prince by the arm. They left the room, walked across the courtyard, and went through the gate. Here there actually was a very small and very sweet little garden, in which, thanks to the fine weather, the trees were already covered with leaves. Lebedev sat the prince down on a green wooden bench, at a green table fixed in the ground, and placed himself opposite him. A minute later coffee actually arrived. The prince did not refuse. Lebedev went on glancing obsequiously and greedily into his eyes.

"I didn't know you had such a homestead," said the prince, with the look of a man who is thinking of something else.

"Or-orphans," Lebedev began, cringing, but stopped: the prince looked ahead of him distractedly and had quite certainly forgotten his question. Another minute passed; Lebedev kept glancing and waiting.

"Well, so?" said the prince, as if coming to his senses. "Ah, yes! You yourself know what our business is, Lebedev: I've come in response to your letter. Speak."

Lebedev became embarrassed, tried to say something, but only stammered: nothing came out. The prince waited and smiled sadly.

"I think I understand you very well, Lukyan Timofeevich: you probably weren't expecting me. You thought I wouldn't emerge from my backwoods at your first indication, and you wrote to clear your own conscience. But I up and came. Well, leave off, don't deceive me. Leave off serving two masters. Rogozhin has been here for three weeks now, I know everything. Did you manage to sell her to him like the other time, or not? Tell me the truth."

"The monster found out himself, himself."

"Don't abuse him. Of course, he treated you badly . . ."

"He beat me, he beat me!" Lebedev chimed in with terrible fervor. "And he chased me with a dog through Moscow, chased me down the street with a borzoi bitch. A horrible bitch."

"You take me for a little boy, Lebedev. Tell me, did she seriously abandon him this time, in Moscow?"

"Seriously, seriously, again right at the foot of the altar. The man was already counting the minutes, and she dashed off here to Petersburg and straight to me: 'Save me, protect me, Lukyan, and don't tell the prince . . .' She's afraid of you, Prince, even more than of him, and that's—most wise!"

And Lebedev slyly put his finger to his forehead.

"But now you've brought them together again?"

"Illustrious Prince, how . . . how could I prevent it?"

"Well, enough, I'll find everything out myself. Only tell me, where is she now? At his place?"

"Oh, no! Never! She's still on her own. I'm free, she says, and, you know, Prince, she stands firm on it, she says, I'm still completely free! She's still on the Petersburg side, at my sister-in-law's, as I wrote to you."

"And she's there now?"

"Yes, unless she's in Pavlovsk, what with the fine weather, at Darya Alexeevna's dacha. I'm completely free, she says; just yesterday she kept boasting to Nikolai Ardalionovich about her freedom. A bad sign, sir!"

And Lebedev grinned.

"Does Kolya see much of her?"

"Light-minded, and incomprehensible, and not secretive."

"Were you there long ago?"

"Every day, every day."

"Meaning yesterday?"

"N-no, three days ago, sir."

"Too bad you're slightly drunk, Lebedev! Otherwise I'd ask you something."

"No, no, no, stone sober!"

Lebedev was all agog.

"Tell me, how was she when you left?"

"S-searching . . ."

"Searching?"

"As if she was searching all over for something, as if she'd lost something. Even the thought of the forthcoming marriage is loath-some to her, and she takes offense at it. Of *him* she thinks as much as of an orange peel, not more, or else more, but with fear and horror, she even forbids all mention of him, and they see each other only by necessity . . . and he feels it all too well! But there's no avoiding it, sir! . . . She's restless, sarcastic, double-tongued, explosive . . ."

"Double-tongued and explosive?"

"Explosive—because she all but seized me by the hair last time for one of my conversations. I was reprimanding her with the Apocalypse."[11]

"How's that?" asked the prince, thinking he had not heard right.

"I was reading the Apocalypse. A lady with a restless imagina-tion, heh, heh! And, besides, I've come to the conclusion that she's much inclined towards serious topics, even unrelated ones. She likes them, likes them, and even takes it as a sign of special respect for her. Yes, sir. And I'm strong on interpreting the Apocalypse and have been doing it for fifteen years. She agreed with me that we live in the time of the third horse, the black one, and the rider with a balance in his hand, because in our time everything is in balances and contracts, and people are all only seeking their rights: 'A measure of wheat for a penny, and three measures of barley for a penny . . .' And with all that they want to preserve a free spirit, and a pure heart, and a healthy body, and all of God's gifts. But they can't do it with rights alone, and there will follow a pale horse and him whose name is Death, and after him Hell[12] . . . We get together and interpret it and—she's strongly affected."

"You believe that yourself?" asked the prince, giving Lebedev a strange look.

"Believe it and interpret it. For I'm poor and naked, and an atom in the whirl of people. Who will honor Lebedev? They all sharpen their wit on him, and accompany him by all but kicks. But here, in this interpreting, I'm the equal of a courtier. The mind! And a courtier trembled once . . . in his chair, feeling it with his mind. His excellency, Nil Alexeevich, two years ago, before Easter, heard about me—when I still worked in their department—and had Pyotr Zakharych summon me specially from my duty to his office, and asked me, when we were alone: 'Is it true that you're a professor of the Antichrist?' And I didn't hide it: 'I am,' I said, and I explained it, and presented it, and didn't soften the fear, but mentally increased it as I unrolled the allegorical scroll and quoted the numbers. And he was smiling, but at the numbers and likenesses he began to tremble, and asked me to close the book, and to leave, and awarded me a bonus for Easter, and on St. Thomas's[13] he gave up his soul to God."

"Come now, Lebedev!"

"It's a fact. He fell out of his carriage after dinner . . . struck his temple on the hitching post and passed away right there, like a baby, like a little baby. He was seventy-three years old according to his papers; a red-faced, gray-haired little fellow, all sprayed with perfume, and he used to smile, to smile all the time, just like a baby. Pyotr Zakharych remembered then: 'You foretold it,' he said."

The prince began to get up. Lebedev was surprised and even puzzled that the prince was already getting up.

"You've grown awfully indifferent, sir, heh, heh!" he ventured to observe obsequiously.

"I really feel unwell—my head is heavy after the journey," the prince replied, frowning.

"You could do with a bit of dacha life, sir," Lebedev hinted timidly.

The prince stood thinking.

"And I myself, after a three-day wait, will be going to my dacha with the whole household, so as to look after the newborn nestling and meanwhile fix up the little house here. And that's also in Pavlovsk."

"You're also going to Pavlovsk?" the prince asked suddenly. "How is it everyone here goes to Pavlovsk? And you say you have a dacha there?"

"Not everyone goes to Pavlovsk. Ivan Petrovich Ptitsyn is letting me have one of the dachas he came by cheaply. It's nice, and sublime, and green, and cheap, and bon ton, and musical, and that's why we all go to Pavlovsk. I, incidentally, will be in a little wing, while the house itself . . ."

"You've rented it out?"

"N-n-no. Not . . . not quite, sir."

"Rent it to me," the prince suddenly suggested.

It seems that this was just what Lebedev had been driving at. The idea had flashed through his mind three minutes earlier. And yet he no longer needed a tenant; he already had a candidate who had informed him that he might take the dacha. Lebedev knew positively, however, that there was no "might" and that he would certainly take it. Yet the thought had suddenly flashed through his mind, a very fruitful one by his reckoning, of renting the dacha to the prince, under the pretext that the other tenant had not expressed himself definitively. "A whole collision and a whole new turn of affairs" suddenly presented itself to his imagination. He received the prince's suggestion almost with rapture, so that he even waved his hands at the direct question of the price.

"Well, as you wish. I'll ask. You won't come out the loser."

They were both leaving the garden.

"I could . . . I could . . . if you like, I could tell you something quite interesting, most esteemed Prince, concerning the same matter," Lebedev muttered, joyfully twining himself about at the prince's side.

The prince stopped.

"Darya Alexeevna also has a little dacha in Pavlovsk, sir."

"Well?"

"And a certain person is friends with her and apparently intends to visit her often in Pavlovsk. With a purpose."

"Well?"

"Aglaya Ivanovna . . ."

"Ah, enough, Lebedev!" the prince interrupted with some unpleasant feeling, as if he had been touched on his sore spot. "It's all . . . not like that. Better tell me, when are you moving? The sooner the better for me, because I'm staying in a hotel . . ."

While talking, they left the garden and, without going inside, crossed the courtyard and reached the gate.

"It would be best," Lebedev finally decided, "if you moved here straight from the hotel today, and the day after tomorrow we can all go to Pavlovsk together."

"I'll have to see," the prince said pensively and went out of the gate.

Lebedev followed him with his eyes. He was struck by the prince's sudden absentmindedness. He had even forgotten to say "good-bye" as he left, had not even nodded his head, which was incompatible with what Lebedev knew of the prince's courtesy and attentiveness.

III

IT WAS GETTING towards noon. The prince knew that of all the Epanchins the only one he might find in town now was the general, because of his official duties, and that, too, was unlikely. It occurred to him that the general would perhaps just take him and drive straight to Pavlovsk, and he wanted very much to make one visit before that. At the risk of coming late to the Epanchins' and delaying his trip to Pavlovsk till tomorrow, the prince decided to go and look for the house he had wanted so much to call at.

This visit, however, was risky for him in a certain sense. He debated and hesitated. He knew that the house was on Gorokhovaya Street, near Sadovaya, and decided to go there, hoping that before he reached the place he would finally manage to make up his mind.

As he neared the intersection of Gorokhovaya and Sadovaya, he himself was surprised at his extraordinary agitation; he had never expected that his heart could pound so painfully. One house, probably because of its peculiar physiognomy, began to attract his attention from far away, and the prince later recalled saying to himself: "That's probably the very house." He approached with extraordinary curiosity to verify his guess; he felt that for some reason it would be particularly unpleasant if he had guessed right. The house was big, grim, three-storied, without any architecture, of a dirty green color. Some, though very few, houses of this sort, built at the end of the last century, have survived precisely on these Petersburg streets (where everything changes so quickly) almost without change. They are sturdily built, with thick walls and extremely few windows; the ground-floor windows sometimes have grilles. Most often there is a moneychanger's shop downstairs. The castrate[14] who sits in the shop rents an apartment upstairs. Both outside and inside, everything is somehow inhospitable and dry, everything seems to hide and conceal itself, and why it should seem so simply from the physiognomy of the house—would be hard to explain. Architectural combinations of lines, of course, have their own secret. These houses are inhabited almost exclusively by commercial folk. Going up to the gates and looking at the inscription, the prince read: "House of the Hereditary Honorary Citizen Rogozhin."

No longer hesitant, he opened the glass door, which slammed noisily behind him, and started up the front stairway to the second floor. The stairway was dark, made of stone, crudely constructed, and its walls were painted red. He knew that Rogozhin with his mother and brother occupied the entire second floor of this dreary house. The servant who opened the door for the prince led him without announcing him and led him a long way; they passed through one reception hall with *faux-marbre* walls, an oak parquet floor, and furniture from the twenties, crude and heavy, passed through some tiny rooms, turning and zigzagging, going up two or three steps and then down the same number, and finally knocked at some door. The door was opened by Parfyon Semyonych himself; seeing the prince, he went pale and froze on the spot, so that for some time he looked like a stone idol, staring with fixed and frightened eyes and twisting his mouth into a sort of smile perplexed in the highest degree—as if he found something impossible and almost miraculous in the prince's visit. The prince, though he had expected something of the sort, was even surprised.

"Parfyon, perhaps I've come at the wrong time. I'll go, then," he finally said in embarrassment.

"The right time! The right time!" Parfyon finally recollected himself. "Please come in."

They addressed each other as familiars. In Moscow they had often happened to spend long hours together, and there had even been several moments during their meetings that had left an all too memorable imprint on both their hearts. Now it was over three months since they had seen each other.

The paleness and, as it were, the quick, fleeting spasm still had not left Rogozhin's face. Though he had invited his guest in, his extraordinary embarrassment persisted. As he was showing the prince to a chair and seating him at the table, the prince chanced to turn to him and stopped under the impression of his extremely strange and heavy gaze. It was as if something pierced the prince and as if at the same time he remembered something—recent, heavy, gloomy. Not sitting down and standing motionless, he looked for some time straight into Rogozhin's eyes; they seemed to flash more intensely in the first moment. Finally Rogozhin smiled, but with some embarrassment and as if at a loss.

"Why are you staring like that?" he muttered. "Sit down!"

The prince sat down.

"Parfyon," he said, "tell me straight out, did you know I would come to Petersburg today, or not?"

"That you would come, I did think, and as you see I wasn't mistaken," the man said, smiling caustically, "but how should I know you'd come today?"

The harsh abruptness and strange irritation of the question contained in the answer struck the prince still more.

"But even if you had known I'd come *today*, why get so irritated?" the prince said softly in embarrassment.

"But why do you ask?"

"This morning, as I was getting off the train, I saw a pair of eyes looking at me exactly the way you were just looking at me from behind."

"Aha! Whose eyes were they?" Rogozhin muttered suspiciously. It seemed to the prince that he gave a start.

"I don't know, in the crowd—it even seems to me that I imagined it; I've somehow begun to imagine things all the time. You know, brother Parfyon, I feel almost the way I did five years ago, when I was still having my fits."

"So, maybe you did imagine it, I don't know . . ." Parfyon went on muttering.

The affectionate smile on his face did not suit it at that moment, as if something had been broken in this smile and, try as he might, Parfyon was unable to glue it back together.

"So you're going abroad again, are you?" he asked and suddenly added: "And do you remember us on the train, in the autumn, coming from Pskov, me here, and you . . . in a cloak, remember, and those gaiters?"

And Rogozhin suddenly laughed, this time with a sort of overt malice and as if delighted that he had managed to express it at least in some way.

"You've settled here for good?" the prince asked, looking around the study.

"Yes, I'm at home here. Where else should I be?"

"We haven't seen each other for a long time. I've heard such things about you, it's as if it were not you."

"People say all kinds of things," Rogozhin observed drily.

"You've scattered your whole company, though; you sit here in the parental house, doing no mischief. So, that's good. Is it your house or all the family's?"

"The house is my mother's. She lives there down the corridor."

"And where does your brother live?"

"Brother Semyon Semyonych is in the wing."

"Does he have a family?"

"He's a widower. Why do you ask?"

The prince looked at him and did not answer; he suddenly became pensive and seemed not to hear the question. Rogozhin did not insist and waited. Silence fell.

"I recognized your house just now from a hundred paces away, as I was approaching," said the prince.

"Why so?"

"I have no idea. Your house has the physiognomy of your whole family and of your whole Rogozhin life, but ask me why I think that—and I can't explain it. Nonsense, of course. I'm even afraid of how much it disturbs me. It never occurred to me before that this would be the sort of house you lived in, but when I saw it, I thought at once: 'Yes, that's exactly the kind of house he had to have!'"

"See!" Rogozhin smiled vaguely, not quite understanding the prince's unclear thought. "This house was built by my grandfather," he observed. "Castrates used to live here, the Khludiakovs, they rent from us even now."

"So gloomy. You sit in such gloom," said the prince, looking around the study.

It was a big room, high, darkish, cluttered with all sorts of furniture—mostly big desks, bureaus, bookcases in which ledgers and papers were kept. A wide red morocco couch apparently served Rogozhin as a bed. On the table at which Rogozhin had seated him, the prince noticed two or three books; one of them, Solovyov's *History*,[15] was open and had a bookmark in it. On the walls, in dull gilt frames, hung several oil paintings, dark, sooty, on which it was hard to make anything out. One full-length portrait drew the prince's attention: it depicted a man of about fifty, in a frock coat of German cut but with long skirts, with two medals on his neck, a very sparse and short, grayish beard, a wrinkled and yellow face, and a suspicious, secretive, and somewhat doleful gaze.

"That wouldn't be your father?" asked the prince.

"The man himself," Rogozhin replied with an unpleasant smile, as if readying himself for some immediate, unceremonious joke about his deceased parent.

"He wasn't an Old Believer, was he?"[16]

"No, he went to church, but it's true he used to say the old belief was more correct. He also had great respect for the castrates. This was his study. Why did you ask about the old belief?"

"Will you celebrate the wedding here?"

"Y-yes, here," replied Rogozhin, almost starting at the sudden question.

"Soon?"

"You know yourself it doesn't depend on me!"

"Parfyon, I'm not your enemy and have no intention of hindering you in anything. I repeat it to you now just as I told it to you once before, in a moment almost like this. When your wedding was under way in Moscow, I didn't hinder you, you know that. The first time it was *she* who came rushing to me, almost from the foot of the altar, begging me to 'save' her from you. I'm repeating her own words. Then she ran away from me, too, and you found her again and led her to the altar, and now they say she ran away from you again and came here. Is that true? Lebedev informed me and that's why I came. And that you've made it up again here, I learned for the first time only yesterday on the train, from one of your former friends, Zalyozhev, if you want to know. I had a purpose in coming here: I wanted finally to persuade *her* to go abroad, to restore her health; she's very upset in body and in soul, in her head especially, and, in my opinion, she has great need to be cared for. I didn't want to go abroad with her myself, but I had a view to arranging it without myself. I'm telling you the real truth. If it's completely true that things have been made up again between you, I won't even allow her a glimpse of me, and I'll never come to see you either. You know I'm not deceiving you, because I've always been candid with you. I've never concealed my thoughts about it from you, and I've always said that marrying you means inevitable ruin for *her*. It also means ruin for you . . . perhaps even more than for her. If you parted again, I would be very glad; but I have no intention of intruding or interfering with you. So be at peace and don't suspect me. And you know for yourself whether I was ever your *real* rival, even when she ran away from you to me. You're laughing now—I know at what. Yes, we lived separately there, and in different towns, and you know it all *for certain*. I explained to you before that I love *her* 'not with love, but with pity.' I think I defined it precisely. You told me then that you understood these words of mine; is it true? did you understand? See how hatefully you look at me! I've come to bring you peace, because you, too, are dear to me. I love you very much, Parfyon. And now I'll go and never come again. Farewell."

The prince stood up.

"Stay with me a little," Parfyon said quietly, without getting up from his place and leaning his head on his right hand, "I haven't seen you for a long time."

The prince sat down. They both fell silent again.

"When you're not in front of me, I immediately feel spite for you, Lev Nikolaevich. In these three months that I haven't seen you, I've felt spiteful towards you every minute, by God. So that I could have up and poisoned you with something! That's how it is. Now you haven't sat with me a quarter of an hour, and all my spite is gone, and I love you again like before. Stay with me a little . . ."

"When I'm with you, you trust me, and when I'm gone, you immediately stop trusting me and suspect me again. You're like your father!" the prince said with a friendly smile, trying to conceal his emotion.

"I trust your voice when I'm with you. I know we'll never be equals, you and me . . ."

"Why did you add that? And now you're irritated again," said the prince, marveling at Rogozhin.

"But here, brother, nobody's asking our opinion," the other replied, "it got decided without us. And we love differently, too, I mean there's difference in everything," he went on quietly, after a pause. "You say you love her with pity. I've got no such pity for her in me. And she hates me more than anything. I dream about her every night now: that she's laughing at me with another man. So it is, brother. She's going to marry me, and yet she forgets even to think about me, as if she's changing a shoe. Believe it or not, I haven't seen her for five days, because I don't dare go to her. She'll ask, 'To what do I owe the honor?' She's disgraced me enough . . ."

"Disgraced you? How so?"

"As if he doesn't know! She ran away with you 'from the foot of the altar,' you just said it yourself."

"But you don't believe that she . . ."

"Didn't she disgrace me in Moscow, with that officer, that Zemtiuzhnikov? I know for sure she did, and that's after she set the date for the wedding herself."

"It can't be!" cried the prince.

"I know for sure," Rogozhin said with conviction. "What, she's not like that, or something? There's no point, brother, in saying she's not like that. It's pure nonsense. With you she wouldn't be like that, and might be horrified at such a thing herself, but with me that's just what she's like. So it is. She looks at me like the worst scum. The thing with Keller, that officer, the one who boxes, I know for sure she made it up just to laugh at me . . . But you don't know yet what she pulled on me in Moscow! And the money, the money I spent . . ."

"But . . . how can you marry her now! . . . How will it be afterwards?" the prince asked in horror.

Rogozhin gave the prince a heavy and terrible look and made no reply.

"For five days now I haven't gone to her," he went on, after a moment's silence. "I keep being afraid she'll drive me away. 'I'm still my own mistress,' she says, 'if I like, I'll drive you away for good and go abroad' (it was she who told me she'd go abroad," he observed as if in parenthesis and looked somehow peculiarly into the prince's eyes); "sometimes, it's true, she's just scaring me, she keeps laughing at me for some reason. But at other times she really scowls, pouts, doesn't say a word; and that's what I'm afraid of. The other day I thought: I shouldn't come empty-handed—but I just made her laugh and then she even got angry. She gave her maid Katka such a shawl of mine that, even if she lived in luxury before, she maybe never saw the like. And I can't make a peep about the time of the wedding. What kind of bridegroom am I, if I'm afraid even to come for a visit? So I sit here, and when I can't stand it any longer, I go on the sly and slink past her house or hide around the corner. The other day I stood watch by her gates almost till daylight—I imagined something then. And she must have spied me through the window: 'What would you do to me,' she says, 'if you saw me deceive you?' I couldn't stand it and said, 'You know what.'"

"What does she know?"

"How should I know!" Rogozhin laughed spitefully. "In Moscow then I couldn't catch her with anybody, though I tried a long time. I confronted her once and said: 'You promised to marry me, you're entering an honest family, and do you know what you are now? Here's what you are!'"

"You said it to her?"

"Yes."

"Well?"

"'I might not even take you as my lackey now,' she says, 'much less be your wife.' 'And I,' I say, 'am not leaving like that, once and for all.' 'And I,' she says, 'will now call Keller and tell him to throw you out the gate.' I fell on her and beat her black and blue."

"It can't be!" cried the prince.

"I tell you: it happened," Rogozhin confirmed quietly, but with flashing eyes. "For exactly a day and a half I didn't sleep, didn't eat, didn't drink, didn't leave her room, stood on my knees before her:

'I'll die,' I said, 'but I won't leave until you forgive me, and if you order me taken away, I'll drown myself; because what will I be now without you?' She was like a crazy woman all that day, she wept, she wanted to stab me with a knife, she abused me. She called Zalyozhev, Keller, Zemtiuzhnikov, and everybody, pointed at me, disgraced me. 'Gentlemen, let's all go to the theater tonight, let him stay here, since he doesn't want to leave, I'm not tied to him. And you, Parfyon Semyonovich, will be served tea here without me, you must have gotten hungry today.' She came back from the theater alone: 'They're little cowards and scoundrels,' she says, 'they're afraid of you, and they try to frighten me: he won't leave you like that, he may put a knife in you. But I'm going to my bedroom and I won't lock the door: that's how afraid of you I am! So that you know it and see it! Did you have tea?' 'No,' I say, 'and I won't.' 'You had the honor of being offered, but this doesn't suit you at all.' And she did what she said, she didn't lock her bedroom. In the morning she came out—laughing. 'Have you gone crazy, or what?' she says. 'You'll starve to death like this.' 'Forgive me,' I say. 'I don't want to forgive you, and I won't marry you, you've been told. Did you really spend the whole night sitting in that chair, you didn't sleep?' 'No,' I say, 'I didn't sleep.' 'Such a clever one! And you won't have tea and won't eat dinner again?' 'I told you I won't—forgive me!' 'This really doesn't suit you,' she says, 'if only you knew, it's like a saddle on a cow. You're not trying to frighten me, are you? A lot I care if you go hungry; I'm not afraid!' She got angry, but not for long; she began nagging me again. And I marveled at her then, that she felt no spite towards me. Because she does remember evil, with others she remembers evil a long time! Then it occurred to me that she considered me so low that she couldn't even be very angry with me. And that's the truth. 'Do you know,' she says, 'what the pope of Rome is?' 'I've heard of him,' I say. 'Parfyon Semyonych,' she says, 'you never studied world history.' 'I never studied anything,' I say. 'Here, then,' she says, 'I'll give you something to read: there was this one pope who got angry with some emperor, and this emperor spent three days without eating or drinking, barefoot, on his knees, in front of his palace, until the pope forgave him; what do you think this emperor thought to himself for those three days, standing on his knees, and what kind of vows did he make? . . . Wait,' she says, 'I'll read it to you myself!' She jumped up, brought a book: 'It's poetry,' she says, and begins reading verses to me about this emperor swearing to take revenge on this pope during those three days.[17] 'Can it be,' she says, 'that you don't like it, Parfyon Semyonych?' 'That's all true,' I say, 'what you read.' 'Aha, you yourself say it's true, that means you, too, may be making vows that "if she marries me, then I'll remember everything she's done, then I'll have fun at her expense!"' 'I don't know,' I say, 'maybe that's what I'm thinking.' 'How is it you don't know?' 'I just don't,' I say, 'that's not what I'm thinking about now.' 'And what are you thinking about now?' 'About how you get up from your place, go past me, and I look at you and watch you; your dress rustles, and my heart sinks, and if you leave the room, I remember every little word you've said, and in what voice, and what it was; and this whole night I wasn't thinking about anything, but I kept listening to how you breathed in your sleep, and how you stirred a couple of times . . .' 'And perhaps,' she laughed, 'you don't think about or remember how you beat me?' 'And maybe I do,' I say, 'I don't know.' 'But what if I don't forgive you and don't marry you?' 'I told you, I'll drown myself.' 'Perhaps you'll still kill me before that . . .' She said it and fell to thinking. Then she got angry and left. An hour later she comes out to me so gloomy. 'I'll marry you, Parfyon Semyonovich,' she says, 'and not because I'm afraid of you, but because I'll perish all the same. And which way is better, eh? Sit down,' she says, 'dinner will be served now. And if I marry you,' she added, 'I'll be your faithful wife, don't doubt it and don't worry.' She was silent a minute, then said: 'You're not a lackey after all. Before I used to think you were as complete a lackey as they come.' Then she set a date for the wedding, and a week later she ran away from me here to Lebedev. When I arrived, she said: 'I don't reject you altogether; I only want to wait a little more, as long as I like, because I'm still my own mistress. You wait, too, if you want.' That's how we are now . . . What do you think of all that, Lev Nikolaevich?"

"What do you think yourself?" the prince asked back, looking sadly at Rogozhin.

"As if I think!" escaped him. He was going to add something, but kept silent in inconsolable anguish.

The prince stood up and was again about to leave.

"All the same I won't hinder you," he said quietly, almost pensively, as if responding to some inner, hidden thought of his own.

"You know what I'll tell you?" Rogozhin suddenly became animated and his eyes flashed. "How can you give her up to me like that? I don't understand. Have you stopped loving her altogether? Before you were in anguish anyway; I could see that. So why have you come galloping here headlong? Out of pity?" (And his face twisted in spiteful mockery.) "Heh, heh!"

"Do you think I'm deceiving you?" asked the prince.

"No, I believe you, only I don't understand any of it. The surest thing of all is that your pity is maybe still worse than my love!"

Something spiteful lit up in his face, wanting to speak itself out at once.

"Well, your love is indistinguishable from spite," smiled the prince, "and when it passes, there may be still worse trouble. This I tell you, brother Parfyon . . ."

"That I'll put a knife in her?"

The prince gave a start.

"You'll hate her very much for this present love, for all this torment that you're suffering now. For me the strangest thing is how she could again decide to marry you. When I heard it yesterday—I could scarcely believe it, and it pained me so. She has already renounced you twice and run away from the altar, which means she has a foreboding! . . . What does she want with you now? Can it be your money? That's nonsense. And you must have spent quite a bit of it by now. Can it be only to have a husband? She could find someone besides you. Anyone would be better than you, because you may put a knife in her, and maybe she knows that only too well now. Because you love her so much? True, that could be . . . I've heard there are women who seek precisely that kind of love . . . only . . ."

The prince paused and pondered.

"Why did you smile again at my father's portrait?" asked Rogozhin, who was observing very closely every change, every fleeting expression of his face.

"Why did I smile? It occurred to me that, if it hadn't been for this calamity, if this love hadn't befallen you, you might have become exactly like your father, and in a very short time at that. Lodged silently alone in this house with your obedient and uncomplaining wife, speaking rarely and sternly, trusting no one, and having no need at all for that, but only making money silently and sullenly. At most you'd occasionally praise some old books or get interested in the two-fingered sign of the cross,[18] and that probably only in old age . . ."

"Go on, jeer. And she said exactly the same thing not long ago, when she was looking at that portrait! Funny how the two of you agree in everything now . . ."

"So she's already been at your place?" the prince asked with curiosity.

"She has. She looked at the portrait for a long time, asked questions about the deceased. 'You'd be exactly like that,' she smiled at me in the end. 'You have strong passions, Parfyon Semyonovich, such passions as would have sent you flying to Siberia, to hard labor, if you weren't also intelligent, because you are very intelligent,' she said (that's what she said, can you believe it? First time I heard such a thing from her!). 'You'd soon drop all this mischief you do now. And since you're a completely uneducated man, you'd start saving money, and you'd sit like your father in this house with his castrates; perhaps you'd adopt their beliefs in the end, and you'd love your money so much that you'd save up not two but ten million, and you'd starve to death on your moneybags, because you're passionate in everything, you carry everything to the point of passion.' That's just how she talked, in almost exactly those words. She'd never spoken with me like that before! Because she always talks about trifles with me, or makes fun of me; and this time, too, she began laughingly, but then turned so grim; she went around looking the whole house over, and seemed to be frightened by something. 'I'll change it all,' I say, 'and do it up, or maybe I'll buy another house for the wedding.' 'No, no,' she says, 'don't change anything here, we'll live in it as it is. When I'm your wife,' she says, 'I want to live near your mother.' I took her to see my mother—she was respectful to her, like her own daughter. Even before, already two years ago, my mother didn't seem quite right in the head (she's sick), but since my father's death she's become like a total infant, doesn't talk, doesn't walk, just sits there and bows to whoever she sees; seems like if you didn't feed her, she wouldn't realize it for three days. I took my mother's right hand, put her fingers together: 'Bless us, mother,' I say, 'this woman is going to marry me.' Then she kissed my mother's hand with feeling: 'Your mother,' she says, 'must have borne a lot of grief.' She saw this book on the table: 'Ah, so you've started reading *Russian History*?' (And she herself told me once in Moscow: 'You ought to edify yourself at least somehow, at least read Solovyov's *Russian History*, you don't know anything at all.') 'That's good,' she said, 'that's what you ought to do, start reading. I'll make a little list for you of which books you should read first; want me to, or not?' And never, never before did she talk to me like that, so that she even surprised me; for the first time I breathed like a living person."

"I'm very glad of it, Parfyon," the prince said with sincere feeling, "very glad. Who knows, maybe God will make things right for you together."

"That will never be!" Rogozhin cried hotly.

"Listen, Parfyon, if you love her so much, how can you not want to deserve her respect? And if you do want to, how can you have no hope? I just said it was a strange riddle for me why she's marrying you. But though I can't answer it, all the same I don't doubt that there's certainly a sufficient, rational reason for it. She's convinced of your love; but she's surely convinced that there are virtues in you as well. It cannot be otherwise! What you just said confirms it. You say yourself that she found it possible to speak to you in a language quite different from her former treatment and way of speaking. You're suspicious and jealous, and so you've exaggerated everything bad you've noticed. Of course, she doesn't think as badly of you as you say. Otherwise it would mean that she was consciously throwing herself into the water or onto the knife by marrying you. Is that possible? Who consciously throws himself into the water or onto the knife?"

Parfyon heard out the prince's ardent words with a bitter smile. His conviction, it seems, was already firmly established.

"How heavily you're looking at me now, Parfyon!" escaped the prince with a heavy feeling.

"Into the water or onto the knife!" the other said at last. "Heh! But that's why she's marrying me, because she probably expects to get the knife from me! But can it be, Prince, that you still haven't grasped what the whole thing is about?"

"I don't understand you."

"Well, maybe he really doesn't understand, heh, heh! They do say you're a bit . . . *like that*! She loves somebody else—understand? Just the way I love her now, she now loves somebody else. And do you know who that somebody else is? It's *you*! What, didn't you know?"

"Me!"

"You. She fell in love with you then, ever since that time, that birthday party. Only she thinks it's impossible for her to marry you, because she'd supposedly disgrace you and ruin your whole life. 'I'm you-know-what,' she says. To this day she maintains it herself. She says it all right in my face. She's afraid to ruin and disgrace you, but me she can marry, meaning it doesn't matter—that's how she considers me, note that as well!"

"But why, then, did she run away from you to me, and . . . from me . . ."

"And from you to me! Heh! All sorts of things suddenly come into her head! She's all like in a fever now. One day she shouts to me: 'I'll marry you like drowning myself. Be quick with the wedding!' She hurries herself, fixes the date, and when the time is near—she gets frightened, or has other ideas—God knows, but you've seen her: she cries, laughs, thrashes around feverishly. What's so strange that she ran away from you, too? She ran away from you then, because she suddenly realized how much she loves you. It was beyond her to be with you. You just said I sought her out then in Moscow; that's not so—she came running to me herself: 'Fix the day,' she says, 'I'm ready! Pour the champagne! We'll go to the gypsies!' she shouts! . . . If it wasn't for me, she'd have drowned herself long ago; it's right what I'm saying. The reason she doesn't do it is maybe because I'm even scarier than the water. So she wants to marry me out of spite . . . If she does it, believe me, she'll be doing it *out of spite*."

"But how can you . . . how can you! . . ." the prince cried and did not finish. He looked at Rogozhin with horror.

"Why don't you finish?" the other added with a grin. "But if you like, I'll tell you how you're reasoning at this very moment: 'So how can she be with him now? How can she be allowed to do it?' I know what you think . . ."

"I didn't come for that, Parfyon, I'm telling you, that's not what I had in mind . . ."

"Maybe it wasn't for that and that wasn't on your mind, only now it's certainly become that, heh, heh! Well, enough! Why are you all overturned like that? You mean you really didn't know? You amaze me!"

"This is all jealousy, Parfyon, it's all illness, you exaggerate it beyond all measure . . ." the prince murmured in great agitation. "What's the matter?"

"Let it alone," Parfyon said and quickly snatched from the prince's hand the little knife he had picked up from the table, next to the book, and put it back where it had been.

"It's as if I knew, when I was coming to Petersburg, as if I had a foreboding . . ." the prince went on. "I didn't want to come here!

I wanted to forget everything here, to tear it out of my heart! Well, good-bye . . . But what's the matter?"

As he was talking, the prince had again absentmindedly picked up the same knife from the table, and again Rogozhin had taken it from him and dropped it on the table. It was a knife of a rather simple form, with a staghorn handle, not a folding one, with a blade six inches long and of a corresponding width.

Seeing that the prince paid particular attention to the fact that this knife had twice been snatched away from him, Rogozhin seized it in angry vexation, put it in the book, and flung the book onto the other table.

"Do you cut the pages with it?" asked the prince, but somehow absentmindedly, still as if under the pressure of a deep pensiveness.

"Yes, the pages . . ."

"Isn't it a garden knife?"

"Yes, it is. Can't you cut pages with a garden knife?"

"But it's . . . brand-new."

"Well, what if it is new? So now I can't buy a new knife?" Rogozhin, who was getting more and more vexed with every word, finally cried out in a sort of frenzy.

The prince gave a start and gazed intently at Rogozhin.

"Look at us!" he suddenly laughed, recovering himself completely. "Forgive me, brother, when my head's as heavy as it is now, and this illness . . . I've become quite absentminded and ridiculous. This is not at all what I wanted to ask about . . . I don't remember what it was. Good-bye . . ."

"Not that way," said Rogozhin.

"I forget!"

"This way, this way, come on, I'll show you."

IV

THEY WENT THROUGH the same rooms the prince had already passed through; Rogozhin walked a little ahead, the prince followed. They came to a big reception room. Here there were several paintings on the walls, all portraits of bishops or landscapes in which nothing could be made out. Over the door to the next room hung a painting rather strange in form, around six feet wide and no more than ten inches high. It portrayed the Savior just taken down from the cross. The prince glanced fleetingly at it, as if recalling something, not stopping, however, wanting to go on through the door. He felt very oppressed and wanted to be out of this house quickly. But Rogozhin suddenly stopped in front of the painting.

"All these paintings here," he said, "my deceased father bought at auctions for a rouble or two. He liked that. One man who's a connoisseur looked at them all: trash, he said, but that one—the painting over the door, also bought for two roubles—he said, isn't trash. In my father's time somebody showed up offering three hundred and fifty roubles for it, and Savelyev, Ivan Dmitrich, a merchant, a great amateur, went up to four hundred, and last week he offered my brother Semyon Semyonych as much as five hundred. I kept it for myself."

"Yes, it's . . . it's a copy from Hans Holbein," said the prince, having managed to take a look at the painting, "and, though I'm no great expert, it seems to be an excellent copy. I saw the painting abroad and cannot forget it.[19] But . . . what's the matter . . ."

Rogozhin suddenly abandoned the painting and went further on his way. Of course, absentmindedness and the special, strangely irritated mood that had appeared so unexpectedly in Rogozhin might have explained this abruptness; but even so the prince thought it somehow odd that a conversation not initiated by him should be so suddenly broken off, and that Rogozhin did not even answer him.

"But I've long wanted to ask you something, Lev Nikolaich: do you believe in God or not?" Rogozhin suddenly began speaking again, after going several steps.

"How strangely you ask and . . . stare!" the prince observed involuntarily.

"But I like looking at that painting," Rogozhin muttered after a silence, as if again forgetting his question.

"At that painting!" the prince suddenly cried out, under the impression of an unexpected thought. "At that painting! A man could even lose his faith from that painting!"

"Lose it he does," Rogozhin suddenly agreed unexpectedly. They had already reached the front door.

"What?" the prince suddenly stopped. "How can you! I was almost joking, and you're so serious! And why did you ask me whether I believe in God?"

"Never mind, I just did. I wanted to ask you before. Many people don't believe nowadays. And is it true (because you've lived abroad) what one drunk man told me, that in our Russia, people don't believe in God even more than in other countries? 'It's easier for us than for them,' he said, 'because we've gone further than they have . . .'"

Rogozhin smiled sarcastically; having uttered his question, he suddenly opened the door and, keeping hold of the handle, waited for the prince to go out. The prince was surprised, but went out. Rogozhin followed him out to the landing and closed the door behind him. The two men stood facing each other, looking as if they had forgotten where they had come to and what they were to do next.

"Good-bye, then," said the prince, holding out his hand.

"Good-bye," said Rogozhin, shaking the extended hand firmly but quite mechanically.

The prince went down one step and turned.

"But with regard to belief," he began, smiling (evidently unwilling to leave Rogozhin like that), and also becoming animated under the impression of an unexpected memory, "with regard to belief, I had four different encounters in two days last week. One morning I was traveling on a new railway line and spent four hours talking on the train with a certain S., having only just made his acquaintance. I had heard a good deal about him before and, among other things, that he was an atheist. He's really a very learned man, and I was glad to be talking with a true scholar. Moreover, he's a man of rare courtesy, and he talked with me as if I were perfectly equal to him in knowledge and ideas. He doesn't believe in God. Only one thing struck me: it was as if that was not at all what he was talking about all the while, and it struck me precisely because before, too, however many unbelievers I've met, however many books I've read on the subject, it has always seemed to me that they were talking or writing books that were not at all about that, though it looked as if it was about that. I said this to him right then, but it must be I didn't speak clearly, or didn't know how to express it, because he didn't understand anything . . . In the evening I stopped to spend the night in a provincial hotel where a murder had taken place the night before, so that everyone was talking about it when I arrived. Two peasants, getting on in years, and not drunk, friends who had known each other a long time, had had tea and were both about to go to bed in the same little room. But, during the last two days, one of them had spied the silver watch that the other wore on a yellow bead string, which he had evidently never noticed before. The man was not a thief, he was even honest, and not all that poor as peasant life goes. But he liked the watch so much and was so tempted by it that he finally couldn't stand it: he pulled out a knife and, while his friend was looking the other way, went up to him cautiously from behind, took aim, raised his eyes to heaven, crossed himself and, after praying bitterly to himself: 'Lord, forgive me for Christ's sake!'—killed his friend with one blow, like a sheep, and took his watch."[20]

Rogozhin rocked with laughter. He guffawed as if he was in some sort of fit. It was even strange to look at this laughter coming right after such a gloomy mood.

"Now that I like! No, that's the best yet!" he cried out spasmodically, nearly breathless. "The one doesn't believe in God at all, and the other believes so much that he even stabs people with a prayer . . . No, that, brother Prince, couldn't have been made up! Ha, ha, ha! No, that's the best yet! . . ."

"The next morning I went out for a stroll about town," the prince went on, as soon as Rogozhin paused, though laughter still twitched spasmodically and fitfully on his lips, "and I saw a drunken soldier staggering along the wooden sidewalk, all in tatters. He comes up to me: 'Buy a silver cross, master. I'm asking only twenty kopecks. It's silver!' I see a cross in his hand—he must have just taken it off—on a worn light blue ribbon, only it's a real tin one, you could see it at first glance, big, eight-pointed, of the full Byzantine design. I took out twenty kopecks, gave them to him, and put the cross on at once—and I could see by his face how pleased he was to have duped the foolish gentleman, and he went at once to drink up his cross, there's no doubt of that. Just then, brother, I was under the strongest impression of all that had flooded over me in Russia; before I understood nothing of it, as if I'd grown up a dumb brute, and I had somehow fantastic memories of it during those five years I spent abroad. So I went along and thought: no, I'll wait before condemning this Christ-seller. God knows what's locked away in these drunken and weak hearts. An hour later, going back to my hotel, I ran into a peasant woman with a nursing baby. She was a young woman, and the baby was about six weeks old. And the baby smiled at her, as far as she'd noticed, for the first time since it was born. I saw her suddenly cross herself very, very piously. 'What is it, young woman?' I say. (I was asking questions all the time then.) 'It's just that a mother rejoices,' she says, 'when she notices her baby's first smile, the same as God rejoices each time he looks down from heaven and sees a sinner standing before him and praying with all his heart.' The woman said that to me, in almost those words, and it was such a deep, such a subtle and truly religious thought, a thought that all at once expressed the whole essence of Christianity, that is, the whole idea of God as our own father, and that God rejoices over man as a father over his own child—the main thought of Christ! A simple peasant woman! True, she's a mother . . . and, who knows, maybe this woman was that soldier's wife. Listen, Parfyon, you asked me earlier, here is my answer: the essence of religious feeling doesn't fit in with any reasoning, with any crimes and trespasses, or with any atheisms; there's something else here that's not that, and it will eternally be not that; there's something in it that atheisms will eternally glance off, and they will eternally be talking *not about that*. But the main thing is that one can observe it sooner and more clearly in a Russian heart, and that is my conclusion! That is one of the first convictions I've formed about our Russia. There are things to be done, Parfyon! There are things to be done in our Russian world, believe me! Remember, there was a time in Moscow when we used to get together and talk . . . And I didn't want to come back here at all now! And this is not at all, not at all how I thought of meeting you! . . . Well, no matter! . . . Farewell, goodbye! God be with you!"

He turned and went down the stairs.

"Lev Nikolaevich!" Parfyon cried from above, when the prince had reached the first landing. "That cross you bought from the soldier, are you wearing it?"

"Yes."

And the prince stopped again.

"Show me."

Again a new oddity! The prince thought a little, went back up, and showed him the cross without taking it from his neck.

"Give it to me," said Rogozhin.

"Why? Or do you . . ."

The prince seemed unwilling to part with this cross.

"I'll wear it, and you can wear mine, I'll give it to you."

"You want to exchange crosses? Very well, Parfyon, if so, I'm glad; we'll be brothers!"[21]

The prince took off his tin cross, Parfyon his gold one, and they exchanged them. Parfyon was silent. With painful astonishment the prince noticed that the former mistrust, the former bitter and almost derisive smile still did not seem to leave the face of his adopted brother—at least it showed very strongly at moments. Finally Rogozhin silently took the prince's hand and stood for a while, as if undecided about something; in the end he suddenly drew the prince after him, saying in a barely audible voice: "Come on." They crossed the first-floor landing and rang at the door facing the one they had just come out of. It was promptly opened. An old woman, all bent over and dressed in black, a kerchief on her head, bowed silently and deeply to Rogozhin. He quickly asked her something and, not waiting for an answer, led the prince further through the rooms. Again there were dark rooms, of some extraordinary, cold cleanness, coldly and severely furnished with old furniture in clean white covers. Without announcing himself, Rogozhin led the prince into a small room that looked like a drawing room, divided by a gleaming mahogany partition with doors at either end, behind which there was probably a bedroom. In the corner of the drawing room, near the stove, in an armchair, sat a little old woman, who did not really look so very old, even had a quite healthy, pleasant, and round face, but was already completely gray-haired and (one could tell at first sight) had fallen into complete senility. She was wearing a black woolen dress, a big black kerchief around her neck, and a clean white cap with black ribbons. Her feet rested on a footstool. Next to her was another clean little old woman, a bit older, also in mourning and also in a white cap, apparently some companion, who was silently knitting a stocking. The two looked as if they were always silent. The first old woman, seeing Rogozhin and the prince, smiled at them and inclined her head affectionately several times as a sign of pleasure.

"Mama," said Rogozhin, kissing her hand, "this is my great friend, Prince Lev Nikolaevich Myshkin; he and I have exchanged crosses; he was like a brother to me in Moscow for a time, and did a lot for me. Bless him, mama, as you would your own son. Wait, old girl, like this, let me put your hand the right way . . ."

But before Parfyon had time to do anything, the old woman raised her right hand, put three fingers together, and piously crossed the prince three times. Then once more she nodded her head gently and tenderly.

"Well, let's go, Lev Nikolaevich," said Parfyon, "I only brought you for that . . ."

When they came back out to the stairs, he added:

"See, she doesn't understand anything people say, and she didn't understand any of my words, yet she blessed you. That means she wanted to herself . . . Well, good-bye, it's time for us both."

And he opened his door.

"But let me at least embrace you as we part, you strange man!" cried the prince, looking at him with tender reproach and trying to embrace him. But Parfyon no sooner raised his arms than he lowered them again at once. He could not resolve to do it; he turned away so as not to look at the prince. He did not want to embrace him.

"Never fear! Maybe I did take your cross, but I won't kill you for your watch!" he muttered unintelligibly, suddenly laughing somehow strangely. But suddenly his whole face was transformed: he turned terribly pale, his lips quivered, his eyes lit up. He raised his arms, embraced the prince tightly, and said breathlessly:

"Take her, then, if it's fate! She's yours! I give her up to you! . . . Remember Rogozhin!"

And, leaving the prince, not even looking at him, he hastily went to his rooms and slammed the door behind him.

V

IT WAS LATE, almost half-past two, and the prince did not find Epanchin at home. Having left his card, he decided to go to the Scales Hotel and ask there for Kolya; if he was not there, he would leave him a note. At the Scales he was told that Nikolai Ardalionovich "had left in the morning, sir, but on his way out had alerted them that, if someone should ask for him, they should tell him that he might be back at three o'clock, sir. And if he was not there by half-past three, it would mean that he had taken the train to Pavlovsk, to Mrs. Epanchin's dacha, sir, and would be having dinner there." The prince sat down to wait and meanwhile ordered dinner for himself.

Kolya did not come back either by half-past three or even by four o'clock. The prince went out and walked mechanically wherever his eyes took him. At the beginning of summer in Petersburg there occasionally occur lovely days—bright, hot, still. As if on purpose, this day was one of those rare days. For some time the prince strolled about aimlessly. He was little acquainted with the city. He stopped occasionally at street corners in front of some houses, on the squares, on the bridges; once he stopped at a pastry shop to rest. Occasionally he would start peering at passersby with great curiosity; but most often he did not notice either the passersby or precisely where he was going. He was tormentingly tense and uneasy, and at the same time felt an extraordinary need for solitude. He wanted to be alone and to give himself over to all this suffering tension completely passively, without looking for the least way out. He was loath to resolve the questions that overflowed his soul and heart. "What, then, am I to blame for it all?" he murmured to himself, almost unaware of his words.

By six o'clock he found himself on the platform of the Tsarskoe Selo railway. Solitude quickly became unbearable to him; a new impulse ardently seized his heart, and for a moment a bright light lit up the darkness in which his soul anguished. He took a ticket for Pavlovsk and was in an impatient hurry to leave; but something was certainly pursuing him, and this was a reality and not a fantasy, as he had perhaps been inclined to think. He was about to get on the train when he suddenly flung the just-purchased ticket to the floor and left the station again, confused and pensive. A short time later, in the street, it was as if he suddenly remembered, suddenly realized, something very strange, something that had long been bothering him. He was suddenly forced to catch himself consciously doing something that had been going on for a long time, but which he had not noticed till that minute: several hours ago, even in the Scales, and perhaps even before the Scales, he had begun now and then suddenly searching for something around him. And he would forget it, even for a long time, half an hour, and then suddenly turn again uneasily and search for something.

But he had only just noted to himself this morbid and till then quite unconscious movement, which had come over him so long ago, when there suddenly flashed before him another recollection that interested him extremely: he recalled that at the moment when he noticed that he kept searching around for something, he was standing on the sidewalk outside a shopwindow and looking with great curiosity at the goods displayed in the window. He now wanted to make absolutely sure: had he really been standing in front of that shopwindow just now, perhaps only five minutes ago, had he not imagined it or confused something? Did that shop and those goods really exist? For indeed he felt himself in an especially morbid mood that day, almost as he had felt formerly at the onset of the fits of his former illness. He knew that during this time before a fit he used to be extraordinarily absentminded and often even confused objects and persons, unless he looked at them with especially strained attention. But there was also a special reason why he wanted very much to make sure that he had been standing in front of the shop: among the things displayed in the shopwindow there had been one that he had looked at and that he had even evaluated at sixty kopecks, he remembered that despite all his absentmindedness and anxiety. Consequently, if that shop existed and that thing was actually displayed among the goods for sale, it meant he had in fact stopped for that thing. Which meant that the thing had held such strong interest for him that it had attracted his attention even at the very time when he had left the railway station and had been so painfully confused. He walked along, looking to the right almost in anguish, his heart pounding with uneasy impatience. But here was the shop, he had found it at last! He had been five hundred paces away from it when he decided to go back. And here was that object worth sixty kopecks. "Of course, sixty kopecks, it's not worth more!" he repeated now and laughed. But he laughed hysterically; he felt very oppressed. He clearly recalled now that precisely here, standing in front of this window, he had suddenly turned, as he had earlier, when he had caught Rogozhin's eyes fixed on him. Having made sure that he was not mistaken (which, incidentally, he had been quite sure of even before checking), he abandoned the shop and quickly walked away from it. All this he absolutely had to think over quickly; it was now clear that he had not imagined anything at the station either, and that something absolutely real had happened to him, which was absolutely connected with all his earlier uneasiness. But some invincible inner loathing again got the upper hand: he did not want to think anything over, he did not think anything over; he fell to thinking about something quite different.

He fell to thinking, among other things, about his epileptic condition, that there was a stage in it just before the fit itself (if the fit occurred while he was awake), when suddenly, amidst the sadness, the darkness of soul, the pressure, his brain would momentarily catch fire, as it were, and all his life's forces would be strained at once in an extraordinary impulse. The sense of life, of self-awareness, increased nearly tenfold in these moments, which flashed by like lightning. His mind, his heart were lit up with an extraordinary light; all his agitation, all his doubts, all his worries were as if placated at once, resolved in a sort of sublime tranquillity, filled with serene, harmonious joy, and hope, filled with reason and

ultimate cause. But these moments, these glimpses were still only
a presentiment of that ultimate second (never more than a second)
from which the fit itself began. That second was, of course, unbearable. Reflecting on that moment afterwards, in a healthy state, he
had often said to himself that all those flashes and glimpses of a
higher self-sense and self-awareness, and therefore of the "highest
being," were nothing but an illness, a violation of the normal state,
and if so, then this was not the highest being at all but, on the
contrary, should be counted as the very lowest. And yet he finally
arrived at an extremely paradoxical conclusion: "So what if it is an
illness?" he finally decided. "Who cares that it's an abnormal strain,
if the result itself, if the moment of the sensation, remembered and
examined in a healthy state, turns out to be the highest degree of
harmony, beauty, gives a hitherto unheard-of and unknown feeling
of fullness, measure, reconciliation, and an ecstatic, prayerful mer-
ging with the highest synthesis of life?" These vague expressions
seemed quite comprehensible to him, though still too weak. That
it was indeed "beauty and prayer," that it was indeed "the highest
synthesis of life," he could not doubt, nor could he admit of any
doubts. Was he dreaming some sort of abnormal and nonexistent
visions at that moment, as from hashish, opium, or wine, which
humiliate the reason and distort the soul? He could reason about
it sensibly once his morbid state was over. Those moments were
precisely only an extraordinary intensification of self-awareness—
if there was a need to express this condition in a single word—
self-awareness and at the same time a self-sense immediate in the
highest degree. If in that second, that is, in the very last conscious
moment before the fit, he had happened to succeed in saying clearly
and consciously to himself: "Yes, for this moment one could give
one's whole life!"—then surely this moment in itself was worth a
whole life.[22] However, he did not insist on the dialectical part of
his reasoning: dullness, darkness of soul, idiocy stood before him
as the clear consequence of these "highest moments." Naturally,
he was not about to argue in earnest. His reasoning, that is, his
evaluation of this moment, undoubtedly contained an error, but all
the same he was somewhat perplexed by the actuality of the sensation. What, in fact, was he to do with this actuality? Because it
had happened, he had succeeded in saying to himself in that very
second, that this second, in its boundless happiness, which he
fully experienced, might perhaps be worth his whole life. "At that
moment," as he had once said to Rogozhin in Moscow, when

they got together there, "at that moment I was somehow able to understand the extraordinary phrase that *time shall be no more*.[23] Probably," he had added, smiling, "it's the same second in which the jug of water overturned by the epileptic Muhammad did not have time to spill, while he had time during the same second to survey all the dwellings of Allah."[24] Yes, in Moscow he and Rogozhin had often gotten together and talked not only about that. "Rogozhin just said I was like a brother to him then; he said it today for the first time," the prince thought to himself.

He thought about that, sitting on a bench under a tree in the Summer Garden. It was around seven o'clock. The garden was deserted; something dark veiled the setting sun for a moment. It was sultry; it was like the distant foreboding of a thunderstorm. There was a sort of lure in his contemplative state right then. His memories and reason clung to every external object, and he liked that: he kept wanting to forget something present, essential, but with the first glance around him he at once recognized his dark thought again, the thought he had wanted so much to be rid of. He remembered talking earlier with a waiter in the hotel restaurant, over dinner, about an extremely strange recent murder, which had caused much noise and talk. But as soon as he remembered it, something peculiar suddenly happened to him again.

An extraordinary, irrepressible desire, almost a temptation, suddenly gripped his whole will. He got up from the bench and walked out of the garden straight to the Petersburg side. Earlier, on the Neva embankment, he had asked some passerby to point out to him the Petersburg side across the river. It had been pointed out to him, but he had not gone there then. And in any case there was no point in going today; he knew that. He had long known the address; he could easily find the house of Lebedev's relation; but he knew almost certainly that he would not find her at home. "She must have gone to Pavlovsk; otherwise Kolya would have left something at the Scales, as we arranged." And so, if he set off now, it was not, of course, in order to see her. A different, dark, tormenting curiosity tempted him. A new, sudden idea had come into his head . . .

But for him it was all too sufficient that he had set off and knew where he was going: a moment later he was walking along again, almost without noticing the way. It at once became terribly disgusting and almost impossible for him to think further about his "sudden idea." With tormentingly strained attention, he peered into everything his eyes lighted upon, he looked at the sky, at the Neva. He addressed a little child he met. It may have been that his epileptic state was intensifying more and more. The thunderstorm, it seemed, was actually approaching, though slowly. Distant thunder had already begun. It was becoming very sultry . . .

For some reason, just as one sometimes recalls an importunate musical tune, tiresome to the point of silliness, he now kept recalling Lebedev's nephew, whom he had seen earlier. The strange thing was that he kept coming to his mind as the murderer Lebedev had mentioned when introducing the nephew to him. Yes, he had read about that murderer very recently. He had read and heard a great deal about such things since his arrival in Russia; he followed them persistently. And earlier he had even become much too interested in his conversation with the waiter about that murder of the Zhemarins. The waiter had agreed with him, he remembered that. He remembered the waiter, too. He was by no means a stupid fellow, grave and cautious, but "anyhow, God knows what he is. It's hard to figure out new people in a new land." He was beginning, however, to believe passionately in the Russian soul. Oh, he had endured so much, so much that was quite new to him in those six months, and unlooked-for, and unheard-of, and unexpected! But another man's soul is murky, and the Russian soul is murky; it is so for many. Here he had long been getting together with Rogozhin, close together, together in a "brotherly" way—but did he know Rogozhin? And anyhow, what chaos, what turmoil, what ugliness there sometimes is in all that! But even so, what a nasty and all-satisfied little pimple that nephew of Lebedev's is! But, anyhow, what am I saying? (the prince went on in his reverie). Was it he who killed those six beings, those six people? I seem to be mixing things up . . . how strange it is! My head is spinning . . . But what a sympathetic, what a sweet face Lebedev's elder daughter has, the one who stood there with the baby, what an innocent, what an almost childlike expression, and what almost childlike laughter! Strange that he had almost forgotten that face and remembered it only now. Lebedev, who stamps his feet at them, probably adores them all. But what is surest of all, like two times two, is that Lebedev also adores his nephew!

But anyhow, what was he doing making such a final judgment of them—he who had come only that day, what was he doing passing such verdicts? Lebedev himself had set him a problem today: had he expected such a Lebedev? Had he known such a

Lebedev before? Lebedev and Du Barry—oh, Lord! Anyhow, if Rogozhin kills, at least he won't kill in such a disorderly way. There won't be this chaos. A tool made to order from a sketch and six people laid out in complete delirium![25] Does Rogozhin have a tool made from a sketch . . . does he have . . . but . . . has it been decided that Rogozhin will kill?! The prince gave a sudden start. "Isn't it a crime, isn't it mean on my part to make such a supposition with such cynical frankness?" he cried out, and a flush of shame all at once flooded his face. He was amazed, he stood as if rooted to the road. He remembered all at once the Pavlovsk station earlier, and the Nikolaevsk station earlier, and his direct question to Rogozhin about the *eyes*, and Rogozhin's cross that he was now wearing, and the blessing of his mother, to whom Rogozhin himself had brought him, and that last convulsive embrace, Rogozhin's last renunciation earlier on the stairs—and after all that to catch himself constantly searching for something around him, and that shopwindow, and that object . . . what meanness! And after all that he was now going with a "special goal," with a specific "sudden idea"! Despair and suffering seized his whole soul. The prince immediately wanted to go back to his hotel; he even turned around and set off; but a minute later he stopped, pondered, and went back the way he had been going.

Yes, and now he was on the Petersburg side, he was near the house; it was not with the former goal that he was going there now, not with any "special idea"! And how could it be! Yes, his illness was coming back, that was unquestionable; the fit might certainly come on him today. It was from the fit that all this darkness came, from the fit that the "idea" came as well! Now the darkness was dispersed, the demon was driven away, doubts did not exist, there was joy in his heart! And—it was so long since he had seen *her*, he had to see her, and . . . yes, he wished he could meet Rogozhin now, he would take him by the hand, and they would walk together . . . His heart was pure; was he any rival of Rogozhin? Tomorrow he would go himself and tell Rogozhin he had seen her; had he not flown here, as Rogozhin put it earlier, only in order to see her? Maybe he would find her at home, it was not certain that she was in Pavlovsk!

Yes, all this had to be clearly set down now, so that they could all clearly read in each other, so that there would be none of these dark and passionate renunciations, like Rogozhin's renunciation earlier, and let it all come about freely and . . . brightly. Is Rogozhin not capable of brightness? He says he loves her in a different way, that there is no compassion in him, "no such pity." True, he added later that "your pity is maybe still worse than my love"—but he was slandering himself. Hm, Rogozhin over a book—isn't that already "pity," the beginning of "pity"? Isn't the very presence of this book a proof that he is fully conscious of his relations with *her*? And his story today? No, that's deeper than mere passion. Does her face inspire mere passion? And is that face even capable of inspiring passion now? It inspires suffering, it seizes the whole soul, it . . . and a burning, tormenting memory suddenly passed through the prince's heart.

Yes, tormenting. He remembered how he had been tormented recently, when for the first time he began to notice signs of insanity in her. What he experienced then was nearly despair. And how could he abandon her, when she then ran away from him to Rogozhin? He ought to have run after her himself, and not waited for news. But . . . can it be that Rogozhin still hasn't noticed any insanity in her? . . . Hm . . . Rogozhin sees other reasons for everything, passionate reasons! And what insane jealousy! What did he mean to say by his suggestion today? (The prince suddenly blushed and something shook, as it were, in his heart.)

Anyhow, why recall it? There was insanity on both sides here. And for him, the prince, to love this woman passionately—was almost unthinkable, would almost be cruelty, inhumanity. Yes, yes! No, Rogozhin was slandering himself; he has an immense heart, which is capable of passion and compassion. When he learns the whole truth and when he becomes convinced of what a pathetic creature this deranged, half-witted woman is—won't he then forgive her all the past, all his suffering? Won't he become her servant, her brother, friend, providence? Compassion will give meaning and understanding to Rogozhin himself. Compassion is the chief and perhaps the only law of being for all mankind. Oh, how unpardonably and dishonorably guilty he was before Rogozhin! No, it's not that "the Russian soul is murky," but the murkiness was in his own soul, if he could imagine such a horror. For a few warm and heartfelt words in Moscow, Rogozhin called him brother, while he . . . But this is illness and delirium! It will all be resolved! . . . How gloomily Rogozhin said today that he was "losing his faith"! The man must be suffering greatly. He says he "likes looking at that painting"; he doesn't like it, it means he feels a need. Rogozhin is not only a passionate soul; he's a fighter after all: he wants to recover his lost faith by force. He needs it now to the point of torment . . . Yes! to believe in something! to believe in somebody! But still, how strange that Holbein painting is . . . Ah, this is the street! And this should be the house, yes, it is, No. 16, "house of Mrs. Filissov, collegiate secretary's widow." Here! The prince rang and asked for Nastasya Filippovna.

The woman of the house herself told him that Nastasya Filippovna had left for Darya Alexeevna's place in Pavlovsk that morning "and it may even happen, sir, that the lady will stay there for several days." Mrs. Filissov was a small, sharp-eyed, and sharp-faced woman of about forty, with a sly and intent gaze. To her question as to his name—a question to which she seemed intentionally to give a tinge of mysteriousness—the prince at first did not want to reply; but he came back at once and insisted that his name be given to Nastasya Filippovna. Mrs. Filissov received this insistence with increased attention and with an extraordinarily secretive air, which was evidently intended to indicate that "you needn't worry, I've understood, sir." The prince's name obviously impressed her greatly. The prince looked at her distractedly, turned, and went back to his hotel. But he left looking not at all the same as when he had rung at Mrs. Filissov's door. Again, and as if in one instant, an extraordinary change came over him: again he walked along pale, weak, suffering, agitated; his knees trembled, and a vague, lost smile wandered over his blue lips: his "sudden idea" had suddenly been confirmed and justified, and—again he believed in his demon!

But had it been confirmed? Had it been justified? Why this trembling again, this cold sweat, this gloom and inner cold? Was it because he had just seen those *eyes* again? But had he not left the Summer Garden with the sole purpose of seeing them? That was what his "sudden idea" consisted in. He insistently wanted to see "today's eyes," so as to be ultimately certain that he would meet them *there* without fail, near that house. That had been his convulsive desire, and why, then, was he so crushed and astounded now, when he really saw them? As if he had not expected it! Yes, they were *those same* eyes (and there was no longer any doubt that they were the *same*!) that had flashed at him that morning, in the crowd, as he was getting off the train at the Nikolaevsk station; the same eyes (perfectly the same!) whose flashing gaze he had caught later that day behind his back, as he was sitting in a chair at Rogozhin's. Rogozhin had denied it; he had asked with a twisted, icy smile: "Whose eyes were they?" And a short time ago, at the Tsarskoe Selo station, when he was getting on the train to go to Aglaya and suddenly saw those eyes again, now for the third time that day—the prince had wanted terribly to go up to Rogozhin and tell *him* "whose eyes they were"! But he had run out of the station and recovered himself only in front of the cutler's shop at the moment when he was standing and evaluating at sixty kopecks the cost of a certain object with a staghorn handle. A strange and terrible demon had fastened on to him definitively, and would no longer let him go. This demon had whispered to him in the Summer Garden, as he sat oblivious under a linden tree, that if Rogozhin had needed so much to keep watch on him ever since morning and catch him at every step, then, learning that he was not going to Pavlovsk (which, of course, was fatal news for Rogozhin), Rogozhin would unfailingly go *there*, to that house on the Petersburg side, and would unfailingly keep watch there for him, the prince, who had given him his word of honor that morning that he "would not see her" and that "he had not come to Petersburg for that." And then the prince rushes convulsively to that house, and what if he actually does meet Rogozhin there? He saw only an unhappy man whose inner state was dark but quite comprehensible. This unhappy man was not even hiding now. Yes, earlier for some reason Rogozhin had denied it and lied, but at the station he had stood almost without hiding. It was even sooner he, the prince, who was hiding, than Rogozhin. And now, at the house, he stood on the other side of the street, some fifty steps away, at an angle, on the opposite sidewalk, his arms crossed, and waited. This time he was in full view and it seemed that he deliberately wanted to be in view. He stood like an accuser and a judge, and not like . . . And not like who?

And why had he, the prince, not gone up to him now, but turned away from him as if noticing nothing, though their eyes had met? (Yes, their eyes had met! and they had looked at each other.) Hadn't he wanted to take him by the hand and go *there* with him? Hadn't he wanted to go to him tomorrow and tell him that he had called on her? Hadn't he renounced his demon as he went there, halfway there, when joy had suddenly filled his soul? Or was there in fact something in Rogozhin, that is, in *today's* whole image of the man, in the totality of his words, movements, actions, glances, something that might justify the prince's terrible foreboding and the disturbing whisperings of his demon? Something visible in itself, but difficult to analyze and speak about, impossible to justify by sufficient reasons, but which nevertheless produced, despite all this difficulty and impossibility, a perfectly whole and irrefutable impression, which involuntarily turned into the fullest conviction? . . .

Conviction—of what? (Oh, how tormented the prince was by the monstrosity, the "humiliation" of this conviction, of "this base foreboding," and how he blamed himself!) "Say then, if you dare, of what?" he said ceaselessly to himself, in reproach and defiance. "Formulate, dare to express your whole thought, clearly, precisely, without hesitation! Oh, I am dishonorable!" he repeated with indignation and with a red face. "With what eyes am I to look at this man now all my life! Oh, what a day! Oh, God, what a nightmare!"

There was a moment, at the end of this long and tormenting way from the Petersburg side, when an irrepressible desire suddenly took hold of the prince—to go right then to Rogozhin's, to wait for him, to embrace him with shame, with tears, to tell him everything and be done with it all at once. But he was already standing by his hotel . . . How he had disliked this hotel earlier—the corridors, the whole building, his room—disliked them at first sight; several times that day he had remembered with a sort of special revulsion that he would have to go back there . . . "How is it that, like an ailing woman, I believe in every foreboding today!" he thought with irritable mockery, stopping at the gate. A new, unbearable surge of shame, almost despair, riveted him to the spot, at the very entrance to the gateway. He stopped for a moment. This sometimes happens with people: unbearable, unexpected memories, especially in connection with shame, ordinarily stop one on the spot for a moment. "Yes, I'm a man without heart and a coward!" he repeated gloomily, and impulsively started walking, but . . . stopped again . . .

In this gateway, which was dark to begin with, it was at that moment very dark: the storm cloud came over, swallowing up the evening light, and just as the prince was nearing the house, the cloud suddenly opened and poured down rain. And at the moment when he set off impulsively, after a momentary pause, he was right at the opening of the gateway, right at the entrance to it from the street. And suddenly, in the depths of the gateway, in the semidarkness, just by the door to the stairs, he saw a man. This man seemed to be waiting for something, but flashed quickly and vanished. The prince could not make the man out clearly and, of course, could not tell for certain who he was. Besides, so many people might pass through there. It was a hotel, and there was a constant walking and running up and down the corridors. But he suddenly felt the fullest and most irrefutable conviction that he had recognized the man and that the man was most certainly Rogozhin. A moment later the prince rushed after him into the stairway. His heart stood still. "Now everything will be resolved!" he said to himself with great conviction.

The stairs which the prince ran up from under the gateway led to the corridors of the first and second floors, on which the hotel rooms were located. This stairway, as in all houses built long ago, was of stone, dark, narrow, and winding around a thick stone pillar. On the first landing, this pillar turned out to have a depression in it, like a niche, no more than one pace wide and a half-pace deep. There was, however, room enough for a man. Having run up to the landing, the prince, despite the darkness, made out at once that a man was for some reason hiding there, in that niche. The prince suddenly wanted to walk past and not look to the right. He had already gone one step, but could not help himself and turned.

Today's two eyes, *the same ones*, suddenly met his gaze. The man hiding in the niche also had time to take one step out of it. For a second the two stood face to face, almost touching. Suddenly the prince seized him by the shoulders and turned back to the stairs, closer to the light: he wanted to see the face more clearly.

Rogozhin's eyes flashed and a furious smile distorted his face. His right hand rose, and something gleamed in it; the prince did not even think of stopping him. He remembered only that he seemed to have cried out:

"Parfyon, I don't believe it! . . ."

Then suddenly it was as if something opened up before him: an extraordinary *inner* light illumined his soul. This moment lasted perhaps half a second; but he nevertheless remembered clearly and consciously the beginning, the very first sound of his terrible scream, which burst from his breast of itself and which no force would have enabled him to stop. Then his consciousness instantly went out, and there was total darkness.

He had had a fit of epilepsy, which had left him very long ago. It is known that these fits, *falling fits* properly speaking, come instantaneously. In these moments the face, especially the eyes, suddenly become extremely distorted. Convulsions and spasms seize the whole body and all the features of the face. A dreadful, unimaginable scream, unlike anything, bursts from the breast; everything human suddenly disappears, as it were, in this scream, and it is quite impossible, or at least very difficult, for the observer to imagine and allow that this is the man himself screaming. It may even seem as if someone else were screaming from inside the man. At least many people have explained their impression that way, and there are many whom the sight of a man in a falling fit fills with a decided and unbearable terror, which even has something mystical in it. It must be supposed that this impression of unexpected terror, in conjunction with all the other dreadful impressions of that moment, suddenly made Rogozhin freeze on the spot and thereby saved the prince from the inevitable blow of the knife that was already coming down on him. Then, before he had time to realize that this was a fit, and seeing the prince recoil from him and suddenly fall backwards, right down the stairs, striking the back of his head hard against the stone step, Rogozhin rushed headlong down the stairs, skirted the fallen man, and, nearly beside himself, ran out of the hotel.

With convulsions, thrashing, and spasms, the sick man's body went down the steps, no more than fifteen in number, to the foot of the stairway. Very soon, in no more than five minutes, the fallen man was noticed, and a crowd gathered. A whole pool of blood by his head caused perplexity: had the man hurt himself, or "had there been foul play?" Soon, however, some of them recognized it as the falling sickness; one of the hotel servants identified the prince as a new guest. The commotion was finally resolved quite happily, owing to a happy circumstance.

Kolya Ivolgin, who had promised to be at the Scales by four o'clock and had gone to Pavlovsk instead, had declined to "dine" with Mrs. Epanchin, owing to a certain unexpected consideration, and had returned to Petersburg and hastened to the Scales, where he arrived at around seven o'clock in the evening. Learning from the message left for him that the prince was in town, he rushed to him at the address given in the message. Informed at the hotel that the prince had gone out, he went downstairs to the buffet room and began to wait, drinking tea and listening to the barrel organ. Happening to hear that someone had had a fit, he ran to the place, following a correct premonition, and recognized the prince. All necessary measures were taken at once. The prince was transported to his room; though he came to his senses, it took him a rather long time to fully recover consciousness. The doctor called in to examine his injured head gave him a lotion and announced that the bruises were not dangerous in the least. When, an hour later, the prince began to understand his surroundings well enough, Kolya brought him in a carriage from the hotel to Lebedev's. Lebedev received the sick man with extraordinary warmth and many bows. For his sake he also hastened the move to the dacha: three days later they were all in Pavlovsk.

VI

LEBEDEV'S DACHA was not large, but it was comfortable and even beautiful. The part meant to be rented out had been specially decorated. On the terrace,[26] a rather spacious one, between the street entrance and the rooms inside, stood several bitter orange, lemon, and jasmine trees in big green wooden tubs, which amounted, by Lebedev's reckoning, to a most enchanting look. He had acquired some of these trees along with the dacha, and he was so charmed by the effect they produced on the terrace that he decided, when the chance came, to complete the set by purchasing more of the same trees in tubs at an auction. When all the trees were finally transported to the dacha and put in place, Lebedev several times that day ran down the steps of the terrace to the street and admired his domain from there, each time mentally increasing the sum he proposed to ask from his future tenant. Weakened, anguished, and physically shattered, the prince liked the dacha very much. Incidentally, on the day of the move to Pavlovsk, that is, on the third day after his fit, the prince already had the outward look of an almost healthy man, though he felt that he had still not recovered inwardly. He was glad of everyone he saw around him during those three days, glad of Kolya, who hardly ever left his side, glad of Lebedev's whole family (minus the nephew, who had disappeared somewhere), glad of Lebedev himself; he was even pleased to receive General Ivolgin, who had visited him still in the city. On the day of the move, which took place in the evening, quite a few guests gathered around him on the terrace: first came Ganya, whom the prince barely recognized— he had changed so much and grown so thin in all that time. Then Varya and Ptitsyn appeared, who also had a dacha in Pavlovsk. As for General Ivolgin, he was at Lebedev's almost uninterruptedly, and had probably even moved along with him. Lebedev tried to keep him away from the prince and near himself; he treated him in a comradely way; evidently they had long been acquainted. The prince noticed that during those three days they sometimes got into long conversations with each other, often shouted and argued, it seemed, even about learned subjects, which evidently gave Lebedev pleasure. One might even have thought that he needed the general. Yet with regard to the prince, he took the same precautions with his own family as with the general, once they had moved to the dacha: he allowed no one to go near the prince, under the pretext of not disturbing him, stamped his feet, ran in pursuit of his daughters, not excepting Vera and the baby, at the first suspicion that they had gone out to the terrace where the prince was, despite all the prince's requests not to chase anyone away.

"First, there won't be any respectfulness if I spoil them like that; and second, it's even improper for them . . ." he finally explained, to the prince's direct question.

"But why?" the prince exhorted him. "You really torment me by all this watching and guarding. I'm bored being alone, I've told you several times, and you weary me still more with all this ceaseless arm-waving and tiptoeing about."

The prince was hinting at the fact that Lebedev, though he chased everyone in the house away from him, under the guise of preserving the peace necessary for the sick man, kept going into the prince's room himself almost every moment during all those three days, and each time would first open the door, put his head in, look around the room as if making sure that he was there, that he had not escaped, and only then, on tiptoe, with slow and stealthy steps, would approach his armchair, so that on occasion he unintentionally frightened his tenant. He ceaselessly inquired whether he needed anything, and when the prince finally began asking to be left alone, Lebedev would turn obediently and silently, make his way on tiptoe back to the door, waving his arms all the while, as if to let him know that it was just so, that he would not say a word, and that here he was going out, and he would not come back, and yet, in ten minutes or at the most a quarter of an hour, he would come back. Kolya, who had free access to the prince, thereby provoked the deepest distress and even wounded indignation in Lebedev. Kolya noticed that Lebedev spent as much as half an hour by the door, eavesdropping on what he and the prince were talking about, of which he naturally informed the prince.

"It's as if you've appropriated me, the way you keep me under lock and key," the prince protested. "At least at the dacha, I want it to be otherwise, and rest assured that I will receive whomever I like and go wherever I like."

"Without the slightest doubt," Lebedev waved his arms.

The prince looked him up and down intently.

"And tell me, Lukyan Timofeevich, that little cupboard of yours, which you had hanging over the head of your bed, did you bring it here?"

"No, I didn't."

"Can you have left it there?"

"It was impossible to take it without tearing it from the wall . . . It's firmly, firmly attached."

"Perhaps there's one like it here?"

"Even better, even better, that's why I bought this dacha."

"Ahh. And who was it you wouldn't let see me? An hour ago?"

"That . . . that was the general, sir. I actually did prevent him, and he's not fitting for you. I deeply respect the man, Prince; he . . . he's a great man, sir; you don't believe me? Well, you'll see, but all the same . . . it would be better, illustrious Prince, if you didn't receive him."

"But why so, may I ask? And why are you standing on tiptoe now, Lebedev, and always approaching me as if you're about to whisper some secret in my ear?"

"I'm mean, mean, I feel it," Lebedev answered unexpectedly, beating his breast with feeling. "But won't the general be too hospitable for you, sir?"

"Be too hospitable?"

"Hospitable, sir. First of all, he's already planning to live in my house; that's all right, sir, but he's enthusiastic, wants straight off to be like family. We've tried several times to figure out our relation, it turns out we're in-laws. You also turn out to be his nephew twice removed on his wife's side, he explained it to me yesterday. If you're his nephew, it means, illustrious Prince, that you and I are related. Never mind that, sir, it's a small weakness, but then he assured me that every day of his life, from when he became a lieutenant through the eleventh of June last year, he had never had less than two hundred persons sitting at his table. It finally went so far that they never got up, so that they had dinner, and supper, and tea fifteen hours a day for thirty years, without the slightest break, with barely time to change the tablecloth. One gets up and leaves, another comes, and on feast days and imperial birthdays the number of guests rose to three hundred. And on the millennium of Russia,[27] he counted seven hundred people. It's awful, sir; such stories—it's a very bad sign, sir; to receive such hospitable people is even frightening, and I thought: won't such a man be too hospitable for you and me?"

"But you seem to be on very good terms with him."

"In a brotherly way, and I take it as a joke; let us be in-laws: the more's the honor for me. Even through two hundred persons and the millennium of Russia, I can discern a very remarkable man in him. I'm speaking sincerely, sir. You mentioned secrets just now, Prince—that is, that I supposedly approach you as though I want to tell you a secret—and, as if on purpose, there is a secret: a certain person has sent a message that she wishes very much to have a secret meeting with you."

"Why secret? On no account. I'll visit her myself, maybe today."

"On no account, no, on no account," Lebedev waved, "and she's not afraid of what you think. Incidentally: the monster comes regularly every day to inquire after your health, do you know that?"

"You call him monster a bit too often, it makes me very suspicious."

"You cannot have any suspicions, not any," Lebedev hastened to defer. "I only wanted to explain that the certain person is not afraid of him, but of something quite different, quite different."

"But of what? Tell me quickly," the prince pressed him impatiently, looking at Lebedev's mysterious grimacing.

"That's the secret."

And Lebedev grinned.

"Whose secret?"

"Yours. You yourself forbade me, illustrious Prince, to speak in your presence . . ." Lebedev murmured and, delighted to have brought his listener's curiosity to the point of morbid impatience, he suddenly concluded: "She's afraid of Aglaya Ivanovna."

The prince winced and was silent for a moment.

"By God, Lebedev, I'll leave your dacha," he said suddenly. "Where are Gavrila Ardalionovich and the Ptitsyns? With you? You've lured them to you as well."

"They're coming, sir, they're coming. And even the general is coming after them. I'll open all the doors and call all my daughters, everybody, now, right now," Lebedev whispered fearfully, waving his arms and dashing from one door to the other.

At that moment Kolya appeared on the terrace, coming in from the street, and announced that visitors, Lizaveta Prokofyevna and her three daughters, were following him.

"Am I or am I not to admit the Ptitsyns and Gavrila Ardaliono-vich? Am I or am I not to admit the general?" Lebedev jumped, struck by the news.

"But why not? All of them, anyone who likes! I assure you, Lebedev, that you've misunderstood something about my relations from the very beginning; you're in some sort of ceaseless error. I don't have the slightest reason to sneak or hide from anyone," the prince laughed.

Looking at him, Lebedev felt it his duty to laugh, too. Despite his extreme agitation, Lebedev evidently was also extremely pleased.

The news reported by Kolya was correct; he had arrived only a few steps ahead of the Epanchins in order to announce them, and thus visitors suddenly appeared on both sides, the Epanchins from the terrace, and the Ptitsyns, Ganya, and General Ivolgin from inside.

The Epanchins had learned of the prince's illness and of his being in Pavlovsk only just then, from Kolya, until when Mrs. Epanchin had been in painful perplexity. Two days ago the general had conveyed the prince's visiting card to his family; this card had awakened an absolute certainty in Lizaveta Prokofyevna that the prince himself would immediately follow the card to Pavlovsk in order to see them. In vain had the girls assured her that a man who had not written for half a year might not be in such a hurry, and that he might have much to do in Petersburg without them— who knew about his affairs? These observations decidedly angered Mrs. Epanchin, and she was ready to bet that the prince would come the very next day at least, though "that will already be much too late." The next day she waited the whole morning; waited till dinner, till evening, and, when it was quite dark, Lizaveta Prokofyevna became angry at everything and quarreled with every-one, naturally without mentioning the prince as the motive of the quarrel. Nor was any word of him mentioned for the whole third day. When Aglaya inadvertently let slip over dinner that *maman* was angry because the prince had not come, to which the general observed at once that "he was not to blame for that"—Lizaveta Prokofyevna got up and wrathfully left the table. Finally, towards evening, Kolya appeared with all the news and descriptions of all the prince's adventures he knew about. As a result, Lizaveta

Prokofyevna was triumphant, but Kolya caught it badly anyway: "He usually spends whole days flitting about here and there's no getting rid of him, but now he might at least have let us know, if it didn't occur to him to come by." Kolya was about to get angry at the phrase "no getting rid of him," but he put it off to another time, and if the phrase itself had not been so offensive, he might have forgiven it altogether: so pleased he was by Lizaveta Prokofyevna's worry and anxiety at the news of the prince's illness. She insisted for some time on the need to send a messenger at once to Petersburg, to get hold of some eminent medical celebrity and rush him here on the first train. But the daughters talked her out of it; they did not want to lag behind their mama, however, when she instantly made ready to go and visit the sick man.

"He's on his deathbed," Lizaveta Prokofyevna said, bustling about, "and we are not going to stand on any ceremony! Is he a friend of our house or not?"

"Still, you should look before you leap," Aglaya observed.

"Don't go, then, it will even be better: Evgeny Pavlych will come and there will be no one to receive him."

After these words Aglaya naturally set out at once after them all, as she had intended to do in any event. Prince Shch., who was sitting with Adelaida, at her request immediately agreed to accompany the ladies. Still earlier, at the beginning of his acquaintance with the Epanchins, he had been extremely interested when he heard about the prince from them. It turned out that he was acquainted with him, that they had become acquainted not long ago and had lived together for a couple of weeks in the same little town. That was about three months ago. Prince Shch. had even told them a good deal about the prince and generally spoke of him with great sympathy, so that now it was with genuine pleasure that he went to visit his old acquaintance. General Ivan Fyodorovich was not at home at the time. Evgeny Pavlovich also had not arrived yet.

Lebedev's dacha was no more than three hundred paces from the Epanchins'. Lizaveta Prokofyevna's first unpleasant impression at the prince's was to find him surrounded by a whole company of guests, not to mention that she decidedly hated two or three persons in that company; the second was her surprise at the sight of the completely healthy-looking, smartly dressed, and laughing young man coming to meet them, instead of a dying man on his deathbed, as she had expected to find him. She even stopped in perplexity, to the extreme delight of Kolya, who, of course, could have explained perfectly well, before she set off from her dacha, that precisely no one was dying, nor was there any deathbed, but who had not done so, slyly anticipating Mrs. Epanchin's future comic wrath when, as he reckoned, she was bound to get angry at finding the prince, her sincere friend, in good health. Kolya was even so indelicate as to utter his surmise aloud, to definitively annoy Lizaveta Prokofyevna, whom he needled constantly and sometimes very maliciously, despite the friendship that bound them.

"Wait, my gentle sir, don't be in such a hurry, don't spoil your triumph!" Lizaveta Prokofyevna replied, settling into the armchair that the prince offered her.

Lebedev, Ptitsyn, and General Ivolgin rushed to offer chairs to the girls. The general offered Aglaya a chair. Lebedev also offered a chair to Prince Shch., even the curve of his back managing to show an extraordinary deference. Varya and the girls exchanged greetings, as usual, with rapture and whispering.

"It's true, Prince, that I thought to find you all but bedridden, so greatly did I exaggerate in my worry, and—I wouldn't lie for anything—I felt terribly vexed just now at your happy face, but, by God, it was only for a moment, till I had time to reflect. When I reflect, I always act and speak more intelligently; you do, too, I suppose. But to speak truly, I might be less glad of my own son's recovery, if I had one, than I am of yours; and if you don't believe me about that, the shame is yours, not mine. And this malicious brat allows himself even worse jokes with me. He seems to be your protégé; so I'm warning you that one fine day, believe me, I shall renounce the further satisfaction of enjoying the honor of his acquaintance."

"What fault is it of mine?" Kolya shouted. "However much I insisted that the prince was almost well now, you'd have refused to believe it, because it was far more interesting to imagine him on his deathbed."

"Will you be staying with us long?" Lizaveta Prokofyevna turned to the prince.

"The whole summer, and perhaps longer."

"And you're alone? Not married?"

"No, not married," the prince smiled at the naïvety of the barb sent his way.

"You've no reason to smile; it does happen. I was referring to the dacha. Why didn't you come to stay with us? We have a whole wing empty; however, as you wish. Do you rent it from him? This one?" she added in a half-whisper, nodding towards Lebedev. "Why is he grimacing all the time?"

Just then Vera came outside to the terrace, with the baby in her arms as usual. Lebedev, who had been cringing by the chairs, decidedly unable to figure out what to do with himself but terribly reluctant to leave, suddenly fell upon Vera, waved his arms at her to chase her from the terrace, and, forgetting himself, even stamped his feet at her.

"Is he crazy?" Mrs. Epanchin suddenly added.

"No, he . . ."

"Drunk, maybe? It's not pretty company you keep," she snapped, taking in the remaining guests at a glance. "What a sweet girl, though! Who is she?"

"That's Vera Lukyanovna, the daughter of this Lebedev."

"Ah! . . . Very sweet. I want to make her acquaintance."

But Lebedev, who had heard Lizaveta Prokofyevna's praises, was already dragging his daughter closer in order to introduce her.

"Orphans, orphans!" he dissolved, approaching. "And this baby in her arms is an orphan, her sister, my daughter Lyubov, born in most lawful wedlock of the newly departed Elena, my wife, who died six weeks ago in childbed, as it pleased the Lord . . . yes, sir . . . in place of a mother, though she's only a sister and no more than a sister . . . no more, no more . . ."

"And you, my dear, are no more than a fool, forgive me. Well, enough, I suppose you realize that yourself," Lizaveta Prokofyevna suddenly snapped in extreme indignation.

"The veritable truth!" Lebedev bowed most respectfully and deeply.

"Listen, Mr. Lebedev, is it true what they say of you, that you interpret the Apocalypse?" asked Aglaya.

"The veritable truth . . . fifteen years now."

"I've heard of you. They wrote about you in the newspapers, I believe?"

"No, that was about another interpreter, another one, ma'am, but that one died, and I remained instead of him," said Lebedev, beside himself with joy.

"Do me a favor, explain it to me one of these days, since we're neighbors. I understand nothing in the Apocalypse."

"I can't help warning you, Aglaya Ivanovna, that it's all mere charlatanism on his part, believe me," General Ivolgin, who had been waiting as if on pins and needles and wished with all his might to somehow start a conversation, suddenly put in quickly. He sat down beside Aglaya Ivanovna. "Of course, dacha life has its rights," he went on, "and its pleasures, and the method of such an extraordinary *intrus** for interpreting the Apocalypse is an undertaking like any other, and even a remarkably intelligent undertaking, but I . . . It seems you are looking at me in astonishment? General Ivolgin, I have the honor of introducing myself. I used to carry you in my arms, Aglaya Ivanovna."

"Delighted. I know Varvara Ardalionovna and Nina Alexandrovna," Aglaya murmured, trying as hard as she could to keep from bursting out laughing.

Lizaveta Prokofyevna flared up. Something that had long been accumulating in her soul suddenly demanded to be let out. She could not stand General Ivolgin, with whom she had once been acquainted, but very long ago.

"You're lying, my dear, as usual, you never carried her in your arms," she snapped at him indignantly.

"You've forgotten, *maman*, he really did, in Tver," Aglaya suddenly confirmed. "We lived in Tver then. I was six years old, I remember. He made me a bow and arrow, and taught me how to shoot, and I killed a pigeon. Remember, you and I killed a pigeon together?"

"And he brought me a cardboard helmet and a wooden sword then, and I remember it!" Adelaida cried out.

"I remember it, too," Alexandra confirmed. "You all quarreled then over the wounded pigeon and were made to stand in the corner; Adelaida stood like this in the helmet and with the sword."

The general, in announcing to Aglaya that he had carried her in his arms, had said it *just so*, only in order to start a conversation, and solely because he almost always started a conversation with young people in that way, if he found it necessary to make their acquaintance. But this time it so happened, as if by design, that he had told the truth and, as if by design, had forgotten that truth himself. So that now, when Aglaya suddenly confirmed that the two of them had shot a pigeon together, his memory suddenly lit up, and he remembered it all himself, to the last detail, as an old person often remembers something from the distant past. It is hard

*Intruder, outsider, or impostor.

to say what in this memory could have had such a strong effect on the poor and, as usual, slightly tipsy general; but he was suddenly extraordinarily moved.

"I remember, I remember it all!" he cried. "I was a staff-captain then. You were such a tiny, pretty little girl. Nina Alexandrovna . . . Ganya . . . I was received . . . in your house. Ivan Fyodorovich . . ."

"And see what you've come to now!" Mrs. Epanchin picked up. "Which means that all the same you haven't drunk up your noble feelings, since it affects you so! But you've worn out your wife. Instead of looking after your children, you've been sitting in debtors' prison. Leave us, my dear, go somewhere, stand in a corner behind a door and have a good cry, remembering your former innocence, and perhaps God will forgive you. Go, go, I'm telling you seriously. There's nothing better for mending your ways than recalling the past in repentance."

But there was no need to repeat that she was speaking seriously: the general, like all constantly tippling people, was very sentimental, and, like all tippling people who have sunk too low, he could not easily bear memories from the happy past. He got up and humbly walked to the door, so that Lizaveta Prokofyevna felt sorry for him at once.

"Ardalion Alexandrych, my dear!" she called out behind him. "Wait a minute! We're all sinners; when you're feeling less remorse of conscience, come and see me, we'll sit and talk about old times. I myself may well be fifty times more of a sinner than you are; well, good-bye now, go, there's no point in your . . ." She was suddenly afraid that he might come back.

"Don't follow him for now," the prince stopped Kolya, who had made as if to run after his father. "Or else he'll get vexed after a moment, and the whole moment will be spoiled."

"That's true, let him be; go in half an hour," Lizaveta Prokofyevna decided.

"That's what it means to tell the truth for once in your life— it moved him to tears!" Lebedev ventured to paste in.

"Well, and you must be a fine one, too, my dear, if what I've heard is true," Lizaveta Prokofyevna pulled him up short at once.

The mutual position of all the guests gathered at the prince's gradually defined itself. The prince, naturally, was able to appreciate and did appreciate the full extent of the concern shown for him by Mrs. Epanchin and her daughters and, of course, told them frankly that he himself, before their visit, had intended to call on them today without fail, despite his illness and the late hour. Lizaveta Prokofyevna, glancing at his guests, replied that this wish could be realized even now. Ptitsyn, a courteous and extremely accommodating young man, very soon got up and withdrew to Lebedev's wing, hoping very much to take Lebedev himself along with him. The latter promised to follow him soon; meanwhile Varya fell to talking with the girls and stayed. She and Ganya were very glad of the general's departure; Ganya himself also soon followed Ptitsyn out. During the few minutes he had spent on the terrace with the Epanchins, he had behaved modestly, with dignity, and had not been taken aback in the least by the determined glances of Lizaveta Prokofyevna, who had twice looked him up and down. Actually, those who had known him before might have thought him quite changed. That pleased Aglaya very much.

"Was it Gavrila Ardalionovich who just left?" she suddenly asked, as she sometimes liked to do, loudly, sharply, interrupting other people's conversation with her question, and not addressing anyone personally.

"Yes, it was," replied the prince.

"I barely recognized him. He's quite changed and . . . greatly for the better."

"I'm very glad for him," said the prince.

"He was very ill," Varya added with joyful sympathy.

"How is he changed for the better?" Lizaveta Prokofyevna asked in irascible perplexity and all but frightened. "Where do you get that? There's nothing better. What precisely seems better to you?"

"There's nothing better than 'the poor knight'!" proclaimed Kolya, who had been standing all the while by Lizaveta Prokofyevna's chair.

"I think the same myself," Prince Shch. said and laughed.

"I'm of exactly the same opinion," Adelaida proclaimed solemnly.

"What 'poor knight'?" Mrs. Epanchin asked, looking around in perplexity and vexation at all the speakers, but, seeing that Aglaya had blushed, she added testily: "Some sort of nonsense! What is this 'poor knight'?"

"As if it's the first time this brat, your favorite, has twisted other people's words!" Aglaya replied with haughty indignation.

In each of Aglaya's wrathful outbursts (and she was often wrathful), almost each time, despite all her ostensible seriousness and implacability, there showed so much that was still childish, impatiently schoolgirlish and poorly concealed, that it was sometimes quite impossible to look at her without laughing, to the great vexation of Aglaya, incidentally, who could not understand why they laughed and "how could they, how dared they laugh." Now, too, the sisters laughed, as did Prince Shch., and even Prince Lev Nikolaevich himself smiled, and for some reason also blushed. Kolya laughed loudly and triumphantly. Aglaya turned seriously angry and became twice as pretty. Her embarrassment, and her vexation with herself for this embarrassment, were extremely becoming to her.

"As if he hasn't twisted enough words of yours," she added.

"I base myself on your own exclamation!" Kolya cried. "A month ago you were looking through *Don Quixote* and exclaimed those words, that there is nothing better than the 'poor knight.' I don't know who you were talking about then—Don Quixote, Evgeny Pavlych, or some other person—but only that you were speaking about someone, and the conversation went on for a long time . . ."

"I see, dear boy, that you allow yourself too much with your guesses," Lizaveta Prokofyevna stopped him with vexation.

"Am I the only one?" Kolya would not keep still. "Everybody was talking then, and they still do; just now Prince Shch. and Adelaida Ivanovna, and everybody said they were for the 'poor knight,' which means that this 'poor knight' exists and is completely real, and in my opinion, if it weren't for Adelaida Ivanovna, we'd all have known long ago who the 'poor knight' is."

"What did I do wrong?" Adelaida laughed.

"You didn't want to draw his portrait—that's what! Aglaya Ivanovna asked you then to draw a portrait of the 'poor knight' and even told you the whole subject for a painting she had thought up, don't you remember the subject? You didn't want to . . ."

"How could I paint it, and whom? The subject says about this 'poor knight':

> From his face the visor
> He ne'er raised for anyone.

What sort of face could it be, then? What should I paint—a visor? An anonymity?"

"I don't understand anything, what's this about a visor?" Mrs. Epanchin was growing vexed and beginning to have a very good idea of who was meant by the name (probably agreed upon long ago) of the "poor knight." But she exploded particularly when Prince Lev Nikolaevich also became embarrassed and finally as abashed as a ten-year-old boy. "Will there be no end to this fool-ishness? Are you going to explain this 'poor knight' to me or not? Is there some terrible secret in it that I can't even go near?"

But they all just went on laughing.

"Quite simply, there's a strange Russian poem," Prince Shch. finally mixed in, obviously wishing to hush things up quickly and change the subject, "about a 'poor knight,' a fragment with no beginning or end.[28] Once, about a month ago, we were all laughing together after dinner and, as usual, suggesting a subject for Adelaida Ivanovna's future painting. You know that our common family task has long consisted in finding subjects for Adelaida Ivanovna's paintings. It was then that we hit upon the 'poor knight,' I don't remember who first . . ."

"Aglaya Ivanovna!" cried Kolya.

"That may be, I agree, only I don't remember," Prince Shch. went on. "Some laughed at this subject, others declared that noth-ing could be loftier, but in order to portray the 'poor knight' there had in any case to be a face. We began going through the faces of all our acquaintances, but none was suitable, and the matter ended there; that's all; I don't understand why Nikolai Ardalionovich suddenly thought of bringing it all up again. What was funny once, and appropriate, is quite uninteresting now."

"Because there's some new sort of foolishness implied in it, sarcastic and offensive," Lizaveta Prokofyevna snapped.

"There isn't any foolishness, only the deepest respect," Aglaya suddenly declared quite unexpectedly in a grave and serious voice, having managed to recover completely and overcome her former embarrassment. Moreover, by certain tokens it could be supposed, looking at her, that she herself was now glad that the joke had gone further and further, and that this turnabout had occurred in her precisely at the moment when the prince's embarrassment, which was increasing more and more and reaching an extreme degree, had become all too noticeable.

"First they laugh dementedly, and then suddenly the deepest respect appears! Raving people! Why respect? Tell me right now, why does this deepest respect of yours appear so suddenly out of the blue?"

"The deepest respect because," Aglaya went on as seriously and gravely, in answer to her mother's almost spiteful question, "because this poem directly portrays a man capable of having an ideal and, second, once he has the ideal, of believing in it and, believing in it, of blindly devoting his whole life to it. That doesn't always happen in our time. In the poem it's not said specifically what made up the ideal of the 'poor knight,' but it's clear that it was some bright image, 'an image of pure beauty,'[29] and instead of a scarf the enamored knight even wore a rosary around his neck. True, there's also some sort of dark, unexpressed motto, the letters A.N.B., that he traced on his shield . . ."

"A.N.D.," Kolya corrected.[30]

"But I say A.N.B., and that's how I want to say it," Aglaya interrupted with vexation. "Be that as it may, it's clear that it made no difference to this 'poor knight' who his lady was or what she might do. It was enough for him that he had chosen her and believed in her 'pure beauty,' and only then did he bow down to her forever; and the merit of it is that she might have turned out later to be a thief, but still he had to believe in her and wield the sword for her pure beauty. It seems the poet wanted to combine in one extraordinary image the whole immense conception of the medieval chivalrous platonic love of some pure and lofty knight; naturally, it's all an ideal. But in the 'poor knight' that feeling reached the ultimate degree—asceticism. It must be admitted that to be capable of such feeling means a lot and that such feelings leave a deep and, on the one hand, a very praiseworthy mark, not to mention Don Quixote. The 'poor knight' is that same Don Quixote, only a serious and not a comic one. At first I didn't understand and laughed, but now I love the 'poor knight' and, above all, respect his deeds."

So Aglaya concluded, and, looking at her, it was hard to tell whether she was speaking seriously or laughing.

"Well, he's some sort of fool, he and his deeds!" Mrs. Epanchin decided. "And you, dear girl, blathered out a whole lecture; in my opinion, it's even quite unsuitable on your part. Inadmissible, in any case. What is this poem? Recite it, you surely know it! I absolutely want to know this poem. All my life I never could stand poetry, as if I had a presentiment. For God's sake, Prince, be patient, it's clear that you and I must be patient together," she turned to Prince Lev Nikolaevich. She was very vexed.

Prince Lev Nikolaevich wanted to say something but, in his continuing embarrassment, was unable to get a word out. Only Aglaya, who had allowed herself so much in her "lecture," was not abashed in the least, she even seemed glad. She stood up at once, still as serious and grave as before, looking as though she had prepared for it earlier and was only waiting to be asked, stepped into the middle of the terrace, and stood facing the prince, who went on sitting in his armchair. They all looked at her with a certain surprise, and nearly all of them—Prince Shch., her sisters, her mother—looked with an unpleasant feeling at this new prank she had prepared, which in any case had gone a bit too far. But it was evident that Aglaya precisely liked all this affectation with which she began the ceremony of reciting the poem. Lizaveta Prokofyevna nearly chased her back to her seat, but just at the moment when Aglaya began to declaim the well-known ballad, two new guests, talking loudly, came from the street onto the terrace. They were General Ivan Fyodorovich Epanchin and after him a young man. There was a slight stir.

VII

THE YOUNG MAN who accompanied the general was about twenty-eight years old, tall, trim, with a handsome and intelligent face, and a bright gaze in his big, dark eyes, filled with wit and mockery. Aglaya did not even turn to look at him and went on reciting the poem, as she affectedly went on looking at the prince alone and addressing him alone. It was clear to the prince that she was doing all this with some special calculation. But the new guests at least improved his awkward position somewhat. Seeing them, he rose slightly, courteously nodded his head to the general from afar, gave a sign not to interrupt the recital, and himself managed to retreat behind the armchair, where, resting his left elbow on the back, he went on listening to the ballad, now, so to speak, in a more comfortable and less "ridiculous" position than sitting in the chair. Lizaveta Prokofyevna, for her part, waved twice with an imperious gesture to the entering men to make them stop. The prince, incidentally, was greatly interested in his new guest who accompanied the general; he guessed clearly that he was Evgeny Pavlovich Radomsky, of whom he had heard so much and had thought more than once. He was thrown off only by his civilian dress; he had heard that Evgeny Pavlovich was a military man. A mocking smile wandered over the lips of the new guest all through the recital of the poem, as if he, too, had already heard something about the "poor knight."

"Maybe it was he who came up with it," the prince thought to himself.

But it was quite different with Aglaya. All the initial affectation and pomposity with which she had stepped out to recite, she covered over with such seriousness and such penetration into the spirit and meaning of the poetic work, she uttered each word of the poem with such meaning, enunciated them with such lofty simplicity, that by the end of the recital she had not only attracted general attention but, by conveying the lofty spirit of the ballad, had as if partially justified the overly affected gravity with which she had so solemnly come out to the middle of the terrace. Now this gravity could be seen only as a boundless and perhaps even naïve respect for that which she had taken it upon herself to convey. Her eyes shone, and a slight, barely perceptible tremor of inspiration and rapture passed twice over her beautiful face. She recited:

> Once there lived a poor knight,
> A silent, simple man,
> Pale and grim his visage,
> Bold and straight his heart.
>
> He had a single vision
> Beyond the grasp of mind,
> It left a deep impression
> Engraved upon his heart.
>
> From then on, soul afire,
> No woman would he see,
> Nor speak a word to any
> Until his dying day.
>
> About his neck a rosary
> Instead of a scarf he bound,
> And from his face the visor
> He ne'er raised for anyone.
>
> Filled with pure love ever,
> True to his sweet dream,
> A. M. D. in his own blood
> He traced upon his shield.
>
> In Palestinian deserts,
> As over the steep cliffs,

Paladins rushed to battle
Shouting their ladies' names,

Lumen coeli, sancta Rosa!
He cried out, wild with zeal,
And at his threat like thunder
Many a Muslim fell.

Back in his distant castle,
He lived a strict recluse,
Ever silent, melancholy,
Like one gone mad he died.

Recalling this whole moment afterwards, the prince, in extreme confusion, suffered for a long time over one question he was unable to resolve: how was it possible to unite such true, beautiful feeling with such obvious, spiteful mockery? That it was mockery he did not doubt; he clearly understood that and had reasons for it: during the recital Aglaya had allowed herself to change the letters A.M.D. to N.F.B. That it was not a mistake or a mishearing on his part he could not doubt (it was proved afterwards). In any case, Aglaya's escapade—certainly a joke, though much too sharp and light-minded—was intentional. Everyone had already been talking about (and "laughing at") the "poor knight" a month ago. And yet, for all the prince could remember, it came out that Aglaya had pronounced those letters not only without any air of joking or any sort of smile, or even any emphasis on the letters meant to reveal their hidden meaning, but, on the contrary, with such unfaltering seriousness, such innocent and naïve simplicity, that one might have thought those letters were in the ballad and it was printed that way in the book. It was as if something painful and unpleasant stung the prince. Of course, Lizaveta Prokofyevna did not understand or notice either the change of letters or the hint. General Ivan Fyodorovich understood only that poetry was being declaimed. Of the other listeners, many did understand and were surprised both at the boldness of the escapade and at its intention, but they kept silent and tried not to let anything show. But Evgeny Pavlovich (the prince was even ready to bet on it) not only understood but even tried to show that he understood: he smiled much too mockingly.

"What a delight!" Mrs. Epanchin exclaimed in genuine rapture, as soon as the recitation was over. "Whose poem is it?"

"Pushkin's, *maman*, don't disgrace us, it's shameful!" exclaimed Adelaida.

"I'll turn into a still worse fool here with you!" Lizaveta Prokofyevna retorted bitterly. "Disgraceful! The moment we get home, give me this poem of Pushkin's at once!"

"But I don't think we have any Pushkin."

"A couple of tattered volumes," Adelaida put in, "they've been lying about since time immemorial."

"Send someone at once to buy a copy in town, Fyodor or Alexei, on the first train—better Alexei. Aglaya, come here! Kiss me, you recite beautifully, but—if it was sincere," she added, almost in a whisper, "then I feel sorry for you; if you read it to mock him, I don't approve of your feelings, so in any case it would have been better for you not to recite it at all. Understand? Go, little miss, I'll talk more with you, but we've overstayed here."

Meanwhile the prince was greeting General Ivan Fyodorovich, and the general was introducing him to Evgeny Pavlovich Radomsky.

"I picked him up on the way, he'd just gotten off the train; he learned that I was coming here and that all of ours were here . . ."

"I learned that you, too, were here," Evgeny Pavlovich interrupted, "and since I've intended for a long time and without fail to seek not only your acquaintance but also your friendship, I did not want to lose any time. You're unwell? I've just learned . . ."

"I'm quite well and very glad to know you, I've heard a lot about you and have even spoken of you with Prince Shch.," replied Lev Nikolaevich, holding out his hand.

Mutual courtesies were exchanged, the two men shook hands and looked intently into each other's eyes. An instant later the conversation became general. The prince noticed (he now noticed everything quickly and greedily, perhaps even what was not there at all) that Evgeny Pavlovich's civilian dress produced a general and extraordinarily strong impression, so much so that all other impressions were forgotten for a time and wiped away. One might have thought that this change of costume meant something particularly important. Adelaida and Alexandra questioned Evgeny Pavlovich in perplexity. Prince Shch., his relation, did so even with great uneasiness; the general spoke almost with agitation. Aglaya alone curiously but quite calmly glanced at Evgeny Pavlovich for a moment, as if wishing merely to compare whether military or civilian dress was more becoming to him, but a moment later she turned away and no longer looked at him. Lizaveta Prokofyevna also did not wish to ask anything, though she, too, was somewhat uneasy. To the prince it seemed that Evgeny Pavlovich might not be in her good graces.

"Surprising! Amazing!" Ivan Fyodorovich kept saying in answer to all the questions. "I refused to believe it when I met him today in Petersburg. And why so suddenly, that's the puzzle. He himself shouted first thing that there's no need to go breaking chairs."[31]

From the ensuing conversation it turned out that Evgeny Pavlovich had already announced his resignation a long time ago; but he had spoken so unseriously each time that it had been impossible to believe him. Besides, he even spoke about serious things with such a jocular air that it was quite impossible to make him out, especially if he himself did not want to be made out.

"It's only a short-term resignation, for a few months, a year at the most," Radomsky laughed.

"But there's no need, at least insofar as I'm acquainted with your affairs," the general went on hotly.

"And what about visiting my estates? You advised me to yourself; and besides, I want to go abroad . . ."

However, they soon changed the subject; but all the same, the much too peculiar and still-continuing uneasiness, in the observant prince's opinion, went beyond the limits, and there must have been something peculiar in it.

"So the 'poor knight' is on the scene again?" Evgeny Pavlovich asked, going up to Aglaya.

To the prince's amazement, she gave him a perplexed and questioning look, as if wishing to let him know that there could be no talk of the "poor knight" between them and that she did not even understand the question.

"But it's too late, it's too late to send to town for Pushkin now, too late!" Kolya argued with Lizaveta Prokofyevna, spending his last strength. "I've told you three thousand times, it's too late."

"Yes, actually, it's too late to send to town now," Evgeny Pavlovich turned up here as well, hastening away from Aglaya. "I think the shops are closed in Petersburg, it's past eight," he confirmed, taking out his watch.

"We've gone so long without thinking of it, we can wait till tomorrow," Adelaida put in.

"And it's also improper," Kolya added, "for high-society people to be too interested in literature. Ask Evgeny Pavlovich. Yellow charabancs with red wheels are much more proper."

"You're talking out of a book again, Kolya," observed Adelaida.

"But he never talks otherwise than out of books," Evgeny Pavlovich picked up. "He expresses himself with whole sentences from critical reviews. I've long had the pleasure of knowing Nikolai Ardalionovich's conversation, but this time he's not talking out of a book. Nikolai Ardalionovich is clearly hinting at my yellow charabanc with red wheels. Only I've already traded it, you're too late."

The prince listened to what Radomsky was saying . . . It seemed to him that he bore himself handsomely, modestly, cheerfully, and he especially liked the way he talked with such perfect equality and friendliness to Kolya, who kept provoking him.

"What's that?" Lizaveta Prokofyevna turned to Vera, Lebedev's daughter, who stood before her holding several books of a large format, beautifully bound and nearly new.

"Pushkin," said Vera. "Our Pushkin. Papa told me to offer it to you."

"How so? How is it possible?" Lizaveta Prokofyevna was surprised.

"Not as a gift, not as a gift! I wouldn't dare!" Lebedev popped out from behind his daughter's shoulder. "For what it cost, ma'am. It's our family Pushkin, Annenkov's edition,[32] which is even impossible to find now—for what it cost, ma'am. I offer it to you with reverence, wishing to sell it and thereby satisfy the noble impatience of Your Excellency's most noble literary feelings."

"Ah, you're selling it, then I thank you. No fear of you not getting your own back. Only please do stop clowning, my dear. I've heard about you, they say you're very well read, we must have a talk some day; will you bring them home for me yourself?"

"With reverence and . . . deference!" Lebedev, extraordinarily pleased, went on clowning, snatching the books from his daughter.

"Well, just don't lose them on me, bring them without deference if you like, but only on one condition," she added, looking him over intently. "I'll let you come as far as the threshold, but I have no intention of receiving you today. Your daughter Vera you may send right now, though, I like her very much."

"Why don't you tell him about those men?" Vera asked her father impatiently. "They'll come in by themselves if you don't: they're already making noise. Lev Nikolaevich," she turned to the prince, who had already picked up his hat, "some people came to see you quite a while ago now, four men, they're waiting in our part and they're angry, but papa won't let them see you."

"What sort of visitors?" asked the prince.

"On business, they say, only they're the kind that, if you don't let them in now, they'll stop you on your way. Better to let them in now, Lev Nikolaevich, and get them off your neck. Gavrila Ardalionovich and Ptitsyn are trying to talk sense into them, but they won't listen."

"Pavlishchev's son! Pavlishchev's son! Not worth it, not worth it!" Lebedev waved his arms. "It's not worth listening to them, sir; and it's not proper for you, illustrious Prince, to trouble yourself for them. That's right, sir. They're not worth it . . ."

"Pavlishchev's son! My God!" cried the prince in extreme embarrassment. "I know . . . but I . . . I entrusted that affair to Gavrila Ardalionovich. Gavrila Ardalionovich just told me . . ."

But Gavrila Ardalionovich had already come out to the terrace; Ptitsyn followed him. In the nearest room noise could be heard, and the loud voice of General Ivolgin, as if he were trying to outshout several other voices. Kolya ran at once to where the noise was.

"That's very interesting," Evgeny Pavlovich observed aloud.

"So he knows about it!" thought the prince.

"What Pavlishchev's son? And . . . how can there be any Pavlishchev's son?" General Ivan Fyodorovich asked in perplexity, looking around curiously at all the faces and noticing with astonishment that this new story was unknown to him alone.

Indeed, the excitement and expectation were universal. The prince was deeply astonished that an affair so completely personal to himself could manage to interest everyone there so strongly.

"It would be very good if you ended this affair at once and *yourself*," said Aglaya, going up to the prince with some sort of special seriousness, "and let us all be your witnesses. They want to besmirch you, Prince, you must triumphantly vindicate yourself, and I'm terribly glad for you beforehand."

"I also want this vile claim to be ended finally," Mrs. Epanchin cried. "Give it to them good, Prince, don't spare them! I've had my ears stuffed with this affair, and there's a lot of bad blood in me on account of you. Besides, it will be curious to have a look. Call them out, and we'll sit here. Aglaya's idea was a good one. Have you heard anything about this, Prince?" she turned to Prince Shch.

"Of course I have, in your own house. But I'd especially like to have a look at these young men," Prince Shch. replied.

"These are those nihilists,[33] aren't they?"

"No, ma'am, they're not really nihilists," Lebedev, who was also all but trembling with excitement, stepped forward. "They're different, ma'am, they're special, my nephew says they've gone further than the nihilists. You mustn't think to embarrass them with your witnessing, Your Excellency; they won't be embarrassed. Nihilists are still sometimes knowledgeable people, even learned ones, but these have gone further, ma'am, because first of all they're practical. This is essentially a sort of consequence of nihilism, though not in a direct way, but by hearsay and indirectly, and they don't announce themselves in some sort of little newspaper article, but directly in practice, ma'am; it's no longer a matter, for instance, of the meaninglessness of some Pushkin or other, or, for instance, the necessity of dividing Russia up into parts; no, ma'am, it's now considered a man's right, if he wants something very much, not to stop at any obstacle, even if he has to do in eight persons to that end. But all the same, Prince, I wouldn't advise you . . ."

But the prince was already going to open the door for his visitors.

"You slander them, Lebedev," he said, smiling. "Your nephew has upset you very much. Don't believe him, Lizaveta Prokofyevna. I assure you that the Gorskys and Danilovs[34] are merely accidents, and these men are merely . . . mistaken . . . Only I wouldn't like it to be here, in front of everybody. Excuse me, Lizaveta Prokofyevna, they'll come in, I'll show them to you and then take them away. Come in, gentlemen!"

He was sooner troubled by another thought that tormented him. He wondered whether this whole affair now had not been arranged earlier, precisely for that time and hour, precisely with these witnesses, perhaps in anticipation of his disgrace and not his triumph. But he was much too saddened by his "monstrous and wicked suspiciousness." He would die, he thought, if anyone should learn that he had such thoughts in his mind, and at the moment when his new visitors came in, he was sincerely prepared to consider himself, among all those around him, the lowest of the low in the moral sense.

Five people came in, four of them new visitors and the fifth General Ivolgin, coming behind them, all flushed, in agitation and a most violent fit of eloquence. "That one's certainly on my side!" the prince thought with a smile. Kolya slipped in with everyone else: he was talking heatedly with Ippolit, who was one of the visitors. Ippolit listened and grinned.

The prince seated his visitors. They were all such young, even such underage people, that one could marvel both at the occasion and at the whole ceremony that proceeded from it. Ivan Fyodoro-vich Epanchin, for instance, who neither knew nor understood anything in this "new affair," even waxed indignant seeing such youth, and probably would have protested in some way, had he not been stopped by what for him was the strange ardor of his spouse for the prince's private interests. He stayed, however, partly out of curiosity, partly out of the goodness of his heart, even hoping to be of help and in any case to be on hand with his authority; but the entering General Ivolgin's bow to him from afar made him indignant again; he frowned and resolved to remain stubbornly silent.

Of the four young visitors, however, one was about thirty years old, the retired "lieutenant from Rogozhin's band, a boxer, who himself used to give fifteen roubles to petitioners." It could be guessed that he had accompanied the others out of bravado, in the capacity of a good friend and, if need be, for support. Among the rest, the first place and the first role was filled by the one to whom the name of "Pavlishchev's son" was attributed, though he introduced himself as Antip Burdovsky. This was a young man, poorly and shabbily dressed, in a frock coat with sleeves so greasy they gleamed like a mirror, in a greasy waistcoat buttoned to the top, in a shirt that had disappeared somewhere, in an impossibly greasy black silk scarf twisted into a plait, his hands unwashed, his face all covered with blackheads, fair-haired, and, if one may put it so, with an innocently impudent gaze. He was of medium height, thin, about twenty-two years old. Not the least irony, not the least reflection showed in his face; on the contrary, there was a full, dull intoxication with his own rights and, at the same time, something that amounted to a strange and permanent need to be and feel constantly offended. He spoke with agitation, hurriedly and falter-ingly, as if not quite enunciating the words, as if he had a speech defect or was a foreigner, though he was, incidentally, of totally Russian origin.

He was accompanied, first, by Lebedev's nephew, already known to the reader, and, second, by Ippolit. Ippolit was a very young man, about seventeen, or perhaps eighteen, with an intelligent but constantly irritated expression on his face, on which illness had left its terrible marks. He was thin as a skeleton, pale yellow, his eyes glittered, and two red spots burned on his cheeks. He coughed incessantly; his every word, almost every breath, was accompanied by wheezing. A rather advanced stage of consumption was evident. It seemed that he had no more than two or three weeks left to live. He was very tired, and sank into a chair before anyone else. The rest made some show of ceremony on entering and were all but abashed, though they looked grave and were obviously afraid of somehow losing their dignity, which was strangely out of harmony with their reputation as negators of all useless social trivialities, prejudices, and almost everything in the world except their own interests.

"Antip Burdovsky," proclaimed "Pavlishchev's son," hurriedly and falteringly.

"Vladimir Doktorenko," Lebedev's nephew introduced himself clearly, distinctly, and as if even boasting that he was Doktorenko.

"Keller," the retired lieutenant muttered.

"Ippolit Terentyev," the last one shrieked in an unexpectedly shrill voice. They all finally sat down in a row on chairs opposite the prince; having introduced themselves, they all immediately frowned and, to encourage themselves, shifted their hats from one hand to the other; they all got ready to speak, and they all nevertheless remained silent, waiting for something with a defiant air, in which could be read: "No, brother, you're not going to hoodwink me!" One could feel that as soon as any one of them began by simply uttering a single first word, they would all immediately start talking at the same time, rivaling and interrupting each other.

VIII

"Gentlemen, I wasn't expecting any of you," began the prince. "I myself was sick till today, and as for your business" (he turned to Antip Burdovsky), "I entrusted Gavrila Ardaliono-vich Ivolgin with it a month ago, of which I then informed you. However, I am not avoiding a personal discussion, only, you must agree, at such an hour . . . I suggest that you come with me to another room, if it won't take long . . . My friends are here now, and believe me . . ."

"Friends . . . as many as you like, but nevertheless, allow us," Lebedev's nephew suddenly interrupted in a rather admonitory tone, though all the same without raising his voice very much, "allow us to declare to you that you might treat us more respectfully and not make us wait for two hours in your lackeys' quarters."

"And, of course . . . and I . . . and that's prince-like! And that . . . you, it means you're a general! And I'm not your lackey! And I, I . . ." Antip Burdovsky suddenly began muttering in extraordinary excitement, with trembling lips, with an offended trembling in his voice, with spit spraying from his mouth, as if he had all burst or exploded, but then hurrying so much that after a dozen words it was no longer possible to understand him.

"That was prince-like!" Ippolit cried out in a shrill, cracked voice.

"It if happened to me," the boxer growled, "that is, if it had a direct relation to me, as a noble person, then if I was in Burdovsky's place, I'd . . . I . . ."

"By God, gentlemen, I learned only a moment ago that you were here," the prince repeated.

"We're not afraid of your friends, Prince, whoever they may be, because we're within our rights," Lebedev's nephew declared again.

"What right did you have, however, if I may ask," Ippolit shrieked again, now becoming extremely excited, "to present Burdovsky's affair for the judgment of your friends? Maybe we don't want the judgment of your friends. It's only too clear what the judgment of your friends may mean! . . ."

"But, Mr. Burdovsky, if you finally do not wish to speak here," the prince, extremely astonished at such a beginning, finally managed to put in, "then I say to you, let us go to another room, and, I repeat, I heard about you all only this minute . . ."

"But you have no right, you have no right, you have no right! . . . your friends . . . There! . . ." Burdovsky began babbling again, looking around wildly and warily, and growing the more excited the greater his mistrust and shyness. "You have no right!" And, having uttered that, he stopped abruptly, as if breaking off, and, wordlessly goggling his nearsighted, extremely protuberant eyes with their thick red veins, he stared questioningly at the prince, leaning forward with his whole body. This time the prince was so astonished that he himself fell silent and also looked at him, goggling his eyes and saying not a word.

"Lev Nikolaevich!" Lizaveta Prokofyevna suddenly called out, "read this now, this very moment, it is directly concerned with your affair."

She hastily handed him a weekly newspaper of the humoristic sort and pointed her finger at an article. While the visitors were still coming in, Lebedev had jumped over to the side of Lizaveta Prokofyevna, whose favor he was currying, and, without saying a word, had taken the newspaper from his side pocket and put it right under her eyes, pointing to a marked-off column. What Lizaveta Prokofyevna had managed to read had astounded and excited her terribly.

"Wouldn't it be better, however, not to read it aloud?" the prince babbled, very embarrassed. "I'll read it by myself . . . later . . ."

"Then you'd better read it, read it right now, aloud! aloud!" Lizaveta Prokofyevna turned to Kolya, snatching the newspaper, which the prince had barely managed to touch, out of his hands. "Read it aloud so that everybody can hear."

Lizaveta Prokofyevna was a hotheaded and passionate lady, so that suddenly and at once, without thinking long, she would sometimes raise all anchors and set out for the open sea without checking the weather. Ivan Fyodorovich stirred anxiously. But meanwhile everyone involuntarily paused at first and waited in perplexity. Kolya unfolded the newspaper and began reading aloud from the place that Lebedev, who had jumped over to him, pointed out:

"*Proletarians and Scions, an Episode from Daily and Everyday Robberies! P r o g r e s s !   R e f o r m !   J u s t i c e !*

"Strange things happen in our so-called Holy Russia, in our age of reforms and corporate initiative, an age of nationality and hundreds of millions exported abroad every year, an age of the encouragement of industry and the paralysis of working hands! etc., etc., it cannot all be enumerated, gentlemen, and so straight to business. A strange incident occurred with one of the scions of our former landowning gentry (*de profundis!*),[35] the sort of scion, incidentally, whose grandfathers already lost everything definitively at roulette, whose fathers were forced to serve as junkers and lieutenants and usually died under investigation for some innocent error to do with state funds, and whose children, like the hero of our account, either grow up idiots or even get caught in criminal dealings, for which, however, the jury acquits them with a view to their admonition and correction; or, finally, they end by pulling off one of those anecdotes which astonish the public and disgrace our already sufficiently disgraced time. About six months ago our scion, shod foreign-style in gaiters and shivering in his unlined little overcoat, returned during the winter to Russia from Switzerland, where he was being treated for idiocy (sic!). It must be admitted that he was fortunately lucky, so that, to say nothing of his interesting illness, for which he was being treated in Switzerland (can one really be treated for idiocy, who could imagine it?!!), he might prove in himself the truthfulness of the Russian saying: a certain category of people is lucky! Consider for yourselves: left a nursing infant after the death of his father, said to have been a lieutenant who died under investigation for the unexpected disappearance of all the company funds during a card game, or perhaps for administering an overdose of birching to a subordinate (remember the old days, gentlemen!), our baron was taken out of charity to be brought up by a certain very rich Russian landowner. This Russian landowner—let's call him P.—in the former golden age the owner of four thousand bonded souls (bonded souls! do you understand this expression, gentlemen? I don't. I must consult a dictionary: 'The memory is fresh, but it's hard to believe'[36]), was apparently one of those Russian lie-a-beds and parasites who spend their idle lives abroad, at spas in the summer, and in the Parisian Château des Fleurs in the winter, where they left boundless sums in their time. One may state positively that at least a third of the quitrent from all former bonded estates went to the owner of the Parisian Château des Fleurs (there was a lucky man!). Be that as it may, the carefree P. raised the orphaned young gentleman in a princely way, hired tutors for him, and governesses (pretty ones, no doubt), whom, incidentally, he brought from Paris himself. But this last scion of a noble family was an idiot. The Château des Fleurs governesses were no help, and till the age of twenty our boy never learned to speak any language, not excluding Russian. This last fact, incidentally, is forgivable. In the end, the fantasy came into P.'s Russian serf-owning head that the idiot could be taught reason in Switzerland—a logical fantasy, incidentally: as a parasite and proprietor, he would naturally imagine that even reason could be bought in the market for money, all the more so in Switzerland. Five years passed under treatment in Switzerland with some well-known professor, and the money spent was in the thousands: the idiot, naturally, did not become intelligent, but they say in any case he began to resemble a human being—only just, no doubt. Suddenly P. up and dies. There's no will, naturally; his affairs are, as usual, in disorder; there's a heap of greedy heirs, who don't care a straw about the last scion of any family being treated for family idiocy in Switzerland out of charity. The scion, though an idiot, tried all the same to cheat his professor, and they say he went on being treated gratis for two years, concealing the death of his benefactor from him. But the professor was quite a charlatan himself; at last, fearing the insolvency and, worse still, the appetite of his twenty-five-year-old parasite, he shod him in his old gaiters, gave him a bedraggled overcoat, and charitably sent him, third-class, *nach Russland**—off his hands and out of Switzerland. It would seem luck had turned its back on our hero. Not a whit, sir: fortune, who starves whole provinces to death, showers all her gifts at once on the little aristocrat, like Krylov's 'Stormcloud'[37] that passed over the parched field and drenched the ocean. At almost the same moment as his arrival in Petersburg from Switzerland, a relation of his mother (who, naturally, was of merchant stock), a childless old bachelor, a merchant, bearded and an Old Believer, dies, leaving an inheritance of several million, indisputable, round, in ready cash—and (oh, if only it were you and me, dear reader!) it all goes to our scion, it all goes to our baron, who was treated for idiocy in Switzerland! Well, now they started playing a different tune. Around our baron in gaiters, who was chasing after a certain kept woman and beauty, a whole crowd of friends and intimates gathered, some relations even turned up, and most of all whole crowds of noble maidens, hungering and thirsting after lawful wedlock, and what could be better: an aristocrat, a millionaire, and an idiot—all qualities at once, you wouldn't find such a husband with a lamp in broad daylight, not even made to order! . . ."

"This . . . this I do not understand!" cried Ivan Fyodorovich in the highest degree of indignation.

"Stop it, Kolya!" the prince cried in a pleading voice. Exclamations came from all sides.

"Read it! Read it despite all!" snapped Lizaveta Prokofyevna, obviously making an extreme effort to control herself. "Prince! if the reading is stopped, we shall quarrel."

There was nothing to be done. Kolya, all worked up, red-faced, in agitation, went on reading in an agitated voice:

"But while our fresh-baked millionaire was soaring, so to speak, in the empyrean, a completely extraneous circumstance occurred. One fine morning a visitor comes to him with a calm and stern face,

*To Russia.

with courteous but dignified and just speech, dressed modestly and nobly, with an obvious progressive tinge to his thinking, and explains in a few words the reason for his visit: he is a well-known lawyer; a certain young man has entrusted him with a case; he has come on his behalf. This young man was no more nor less than the son of the late P., though he bore a different name. The lascivious P., having seduced in his youth a poor, honest girl, a household serf but with European education (in part this was, naturally, a matter of baronial rights under the former serfdom), and having noticed the unavoidable but immediate consequences of his liaison, hastened to give her in marriage to a certain man, something of a dealer and even a functionary, of noble character, who had long been in love with this girl. At first he assisted the newlyweds; but soon the husband's noble character denied him the acceptance of this assistance. Time passed and P. gradually forgot the girl and the son he had had by her, and then, as we know, he died without leaving any instructions. Meanwhile his son, born in lawful wedlock, but raised under a different name and fully adopted by the noble character of his mother's husband, who had nevertheless died in the course of time, was left with no support but himself and with an ailing, suffering, crippled mother in one of our remote provinces; he himself earned money in the capital by daily noble labor, giving lessons to merchants' children, thus supporting himself through high school and then as an auditor at useful lectures, having a further purpose in mind. But how much can one earn from a Russian merchant for ten-kopeck lessons, and that with an ailing, crippled mother besides, whose death, finally, in her remote province, hardly made things any easier for him? Now a question: how should our scion have reasoned in all fairness? You think, of course, dear reader, that he spoke thus to himself: 'All my life I have enjoyed all sorts of gifts from P.; tens of thousands were spent on my upbringing, on governesses, and on my treatment for idiocy in Switzerland; and here I am now with millions, while the noble character of P.'s son, in no way guilty in the trespass of his frivolous and forgetful father, is perishing giving lessons. Everything that went to me should rightfully have gone to him. Those enormous sums spent on me were essentially not mine. It was merely a blind error of fortune; they were owing to P.'s son. He should have gotten them, not I—creature of a fantastic whim of the frivolous and forgetful P. If I were fully noble, delicate, and just, I ought to give his son half of my inheritance; but since I am first of all a calculating man and understand only too well that it is not a legal matter, I will not give him half of my millions. But all the same it would be much too base and shameless (and ill calculated as well, the scion forgot that) on my part, if I did not now return to his son those tens of thousands that P. spent on my idiocy. Here it's not only a matter of conscience and justice! For what would have happened to me if P. had not taken charge of my upbringing, but had concerned himself with his son instead of me?'

"But no, gentlemen! Our scions do not reason that way. No matter how the lawyer presented the young man, saying that he had undertaken to solicit for him solely out of friendship and almost against his will, almost by force, no matter how he pictured for him the duties of honor, nobility, justice, and even simple calculation, the Swiss ward remained inflexible, and what then? All that would be nothing, but here is what was indeed unforgivable and inexcusable by any interesting illness: this millionaire, barely out of his professor's gaiters, could not even grasp that it was not charity or assistance that the young man's noble character, killing himself with lessons, asked of him, but his right and his due, though not juridically so, and he was not even asking, but his friends were merely soliciting for him. With a majestic air, intoxicated by the opportunity offered him to crush people with impunity by his millions, our scion takes out a fifty-rouble note and sends it to the noble young man in the guise of insolent charity. You do not believe it, gentlemen? You are indignant, you are insulted, a cry of resentment bursts from you; and yet he did do it! Naturally, the money was returned to him at once, was, so to speak, thrown in his face. What are we left with to resolve this case! The case is not a juridical one, all that is left is publicity! We convey this anecdote to the public, vouching for its veracity. They say one of our best-known humorists produced a delightful epigram on this occasion, worthy of a place not only in provincial but also in metropolitan articles on our morals:

> "Little Lyova five years long
> In Schneider's overcoat did play,
> And the usual dance and song
> Filled his every day.
>
> Comes home in gaiters, foreign-fashion,
> A million on his plate does find,
> So now he prays to God in Russian
> And robs all student-kind."[38]

When Kolya finished, he quickly handed the newspaper to the prince and, without saying a word, rushed to a corner, huddled tightly into it, and covered his face with his hands. He was unbearably ashamed, and his child's impressionability, which had not yet had time to become accustomed to filth, was upset even beyond measure. It seemed to him that something extraordinary had happened, which had destroyed everything all at once, and that he himself had almost been the cause of it by the mere fact of this reading aloud.

But it seemed they all felt something similar.

The girls felt very awkward and ashamed. Lizaveta Prokofyevna held back her extreme wrath and also, perhaps, bitterly regretted having interfered in the affair; she was now silent. What occurred with the prince was what often happens with very shy people on such occasions: he was so abashed by what others had done, he felt so ashamed for his visitors, that he was afraid at first even to look at them. Ptitsyn, Varya, Ganya, even Lebedev—they all seemed to have a somewhat embarrassed look. The strangest thing was that Ippolit and "Pavlishchev's son" were also as if amazed at something; Lebedev's nephew was also visibly displeased. Only the boxer sat perfectly calm, twirling his moustaches, with an air of importance and his eyes slightly lowered, not from embarrassment, but, on the contrary, it seemed, as if out of noble modesty and all-too-obvious triumph. Everything indicated that he liked the article very much.

"This is the devil knows what," Ivan Fyodorovich grumbled in a half-whisper, "as if fifty lackeys got together to write it and wrote it."

"But al-low me to ask, my dear sir, how can you insult people with such suggestions?" Ippolit declared and trembled all over.

"That, that, that . . . for a noble man . . . you yourself must agree, General, if he's a noble man, that is insulting!" grumbled the boxer, also suddenly rousing himself, twirling his moustache and twitching his shoulders and body.

"First of all, I am not 'my dear sir' to you, and second, I have no intention of giving you any explanation," Ivan Fyodorovich, terribly worked up, answered sharply, rose from his place and, without saying a word, went to the door of the terrace and stood on the top step, his back to the public, in the greatest indignation at Lizaveta Prokofyevna, who even now did not think of budging from her place.

"Gentlemen, gentlemen, let me speak, finally, gentlemen," the prince exclaimed in anguish and agitation. "And do me a favor, let's talk so that we can understand each other. I don't mind the article, gentlemen, let it be; only the thing is, gentlemen, that it's all untrue, what's written in the article: I say that because you know it yourselves; it's even shameful. So that I'm decidedly amazed if it was any one of you who wrote it."

"I knew nothing about this article till this very moment," Ippolit declared. "I don't approve of this article."

"I did know the article had been written, but . . . I also would have advised against publishing it, because it's too early," Lebedev's nephew added.

"I knew, but I have the right . . . I . . ." muttered "Pavlishchev's son."

"What! You made it all up by yourself?" asked the prince, looking at Burdovsky with curiosity. "It's not possible!"

"It is possible, however, not to acknowledge your right to ask such questions," Lebedev's nephew stepped in.

"I was only surprised that Mr. Burdovsky had managed to . . . but . . . I mean to say that, since you've already made this affair public, why were you so offended earlier when I began speaking with my friends about this same affair?"

"Finally!" Lizaveta Prokofyevna muttered in indignation.

"And you've even forgotten, if you please, Prince," Lebedev, unable to contain himself, suddenly slipped between the chairs, almost in a fever, "you've forgotten, if you please, sir, that it's only out of your own good will and the incomparable goodness of your heart that you have received them and are listening to them, and that they have no right to make their demands, especially since you've already entrusted Gavrila Ardalionovich with this affair, and that, too, you did in your exceeding goodness, and that now, illustrious Prince, being amongst your chosen friends, you cannot sacrifice such company for these gentlemen and could show all these gentlemen, so to speak, off the premises this very moment, sir, so that I, in the quality of landlord, even with extreme pleasure . . ."

"Quite right!" General Ivolgin suddenly thundered from the depths of the room.

"Enough, Lebedev, enough, enough . . ." the prince began, but a whole burst of indignation drowned out his words.

"No, excuse us, Prince, excuse us, but now it is not enough!"

Lebedev's nephew nearly outshouted them all. "Now this affair must be stated clearly and firmly, because it's obviously misunderstood. Juridical pettifoggery got mixed into it, and on the basis of this pettifoggery we are threatened with being chucked off the premises! But is it possible, Prince, that you consider us fools to such a degree that we ourselves do not understand to what degree our affair is not a juridical one, and that if we consider it juridically, we cannot demand even a single rouble from you according to the law? But we precisely do understand that, if there is no juridical right here, there is on the other hand a human, natural one; the right of common sense and the voice of conscience, and even if our right is not written in any rotten human code, still, a noble and honest man, that is to say, a man of common sense, must remain a noble and honest man even on points that are not written down in codes. That is why we came in here, not fearing that we would be thrown off the premises (as you just threatened) for the mere reason that we *do not ask* but *demand*, and as for the impropriety of a visit at this late hour (though we did not come at a late hour, it was you who made us wait in the lackeys' quarters), that is why, I say, we came, not fearing anything, because we supposed you were precisely a man of common sense, that is, of honor and conscience. Yes, it's true, we did not come humbly, not like your spongers and fawners, but with our heads high, like free people, and by no means asking, but freely and proudly demanding (do you hear, not asking, but demanding, mark that!). Directly and with dignity, we put before you a question: do you acknowledge yourself as in the right or in the wrong in the Burdovsky affair? Do you acknowledge that Pavlishchev was your benefactor and perhaps even saved you from death? If you do (which is obvious), then do you intend, or do you find it right in all conscience, having obtained millions in your turn, to reward Pavlishchev's needy son, even though he bears the name of Burdovsky? Yes or no? If *yes*, that is, in other words, if there is in you that which you, in your language, call honor and conscience, and which we designate more precisely with the name of common sense, satisfy us and that will be the end of it. Satisfy us without any requests or gratitudes on our part, do not expect them from us, because you are not doing it for us, but for the sake of justice. But if you do not want to satisfy us, that is, if your reply is *no*, we will leave at once, and the affair ceases; but we tell you to your face, in front of all your witnesses, that you are a man of coarse mind and low development; that you dare not and henceforth have no right to call yourself a man of honor and conscience, that you want to buy that right too cheaply. I have finished. I have stated the question. Chase us off the premises now, if you dare. You can do it, you have the power. But remember that all the same we demand, and do not ask. Demand, and do not ask!"

Lebedev's nephew, who had become very excited, stopped.

"Demand, demand, demand, and do not ask! . . ." Burdovsky babbled and turned red as a lobster.

After Lebedev's nephew's words there followed a certain general stir and a murmur even arose, though the whole company had clearly avoided mixing into the affair, with the sole exception of Lebedev, who was as if in a fever. (Strange thing: Lebedev, who was obviously on the prince's side, now seemed to feel a certain satisfaction of family pride after his nephew's speech; at least he looked around at all the public with a certain special air of satisfaction.)

"In my opinion," the prince began rather quietly, "in my opinion, Mr. Doktorenko, half of all you have just said is completely right, and I even agree that it is the greater half, and I would be in complete agreement with you, if you hadn't left something out in your words. Precisely what you left out, I'm not able and am not in a position to say exactly, but something is certainly missing that keeps your words from being wholly fair. But better let us turn to business, gentlemen. Tell me, why did you publish this article? Every word of it is slander; therefore, in my opinion, you have done something base."

"Excuse me! . . ."

"My dear sir! . . ."

"That . . . that . . . that . . ." came at once from the agitated visitors' side.

"Concerning the article," Ippolit picked up shrilly, "concerning this article, I've already told you that I and the others disapprove of it! It was he who wrote it" (he pointed to the boxer, who was sitting next to him), "wrote it indecently, I agree, wrote it illiterately and in the style in which retired officers like him write. He is stupid and, on top of that, a speculator, I agree, I tell him that right to his face every day, but all the same he was half in his rights: publicity is everyone's lawful right, and therefore also Burdovsky's. Let him answer for his own absurdities. As for the fact that I protested earlier on behalf of all concerning the presence of your friends, I consider it necessary, my dear sirs, to explain to you that I protested solely in order to claim our right, but that, in fact, we even welcome witnesses, and earlier, before we came in here, the four of us agreed on that. Whoever your witnesses may be, even if they're your friends, but since they cannot disagree with Burdovsky's right (because it's obvious, mathematical), it's even better if these witnesses are your friends; the truth will be manifested still more obviously."

"That's true, we agreed on that," Lebedev's nephew confirmed.

"Then why was there such noise and shouting earlier from the very first word, if you wanted it that way!" the prince was astonished.

"And concerning the article, Prince," the boxer put in, terribly anxious to stick in something of his own and feeling pleasantly lively (one might suspect that the presence of the ladies had a visible and strong effect on him), "concerning the article, I confess that I am indeed the author, though my ailing friend, whom I am accustomed to forgive because of his weakness, has just criticized it. But I did write it and published it in my good friend's magazine, as correspondence. Only the verses are actually not mine, and actually came from the pen of a famous humorist. The only one I read it to was Burdovsky, and not all of it at that, and I at once got his agreement to publish it, though you must agree that I could have published it even without his agreement. Publicity is a universal right, noble and beneficial. I hope that you yourself, Prince, are progressive enough not to deny that . . ."

"I won't deny anything, but you must agree that in your article . . ."

"Sharp, you want to say? But it's a question, so to speak, of the benefit of society, you must agree, and, finally, was it possible to miss such a provocative occasion? So much the worse for the guilty ones, but the benefit of society comes before all else. As for certain imprecisions, hyperboles, so to speak, you must also agree that the initiative is important before all else, the goal and intention before all else; what's important is the beneficent example, and after that we can analyze particular cases, and, finally, it's a question of style, a question, so to speak, of a humoristic task, and, finally—everybody writes like that, you must agree! Ha, ha!"

"But you're on a completely false track! I assure you, gentlemen," the prince cried, "you published your article on the assumption that I would never agree to satisfy Mr. Burdovsky, and so you wanted to frighten me for that and be revenged somehow. But how do you know: maybe I've decided to satisfy Mr. Burdovsky. I tell you directly now, in front of everyone, that I will satisfy . . ."

"Here at last is an intelligent and noble word from an intelligent and most noble man!" the boxer proclaimed.

"Lord!" escaped from Lizaveta Prokofyevna.

"This is unbearable!" muttered the general.

"Allow me, gentlemen, allow me, I will explain the matter," the prince entreated. "About five weeks ago, Mr. Burdovsky, your agent and solicitor, Chebarov, came to see me in Z——. You describe him very flatteringly in your article, Mr. Keller," the prince, laughing suddenly, turned to the boxer, "but I didn't like him at all. I only understood from the first that this Chebarov was the chief thing and that it may have been he who prompted you to start all this, Mr. Burdovsky, taking advantage of your simplicity, if I may speak frankly."

"You have no right . . . I . . . not simple . . . that . . ." Burdovsky babbled in agitation.

"You have no right to make such assumptions," Lebedev's nephew intervened didactically.

"That is highly insulting!" shrieked Ippolit. "It's an insulting, false, and inappropriate assumption!"

"Sorry, gentlemen, sorry," the prince hastily apologized, "please forgive me; it's because I thought it would be better for us to be completely sincere with each other; but let it be as you will. I told Chebarov that, as I was not in Petersburg, I would immediately entrust a friend of mine with the conduct of this affair, and you, Mr. Burdovsky, will be informed of that. I'll tell you directly, gentlemen, that this seemed to me a most crooked affair, precisely because of Chebarov . . . Ah, don't be offended, gentlemen! For God's sake, don't be offended!" the prince cried fearfully, again seeing expressions of offended confusion in Burdovsky, of agitation and protest in his friends. "It cannot concern you personally if I say that I considered this a crooked affair! I didn't know any of you personally then, and didn't know your last names; I judged only by Chebarov. I'm speaking in general, because . . . if you only knew how terribly people have deceived me since I got my inheritance!"

"You're terribly naïve, Prince," Lebedev's nephew observed mockingly.

"And with all that—a prince and a millionaire! With your maybe indeed kind and somewhat simple heart, you are, of course, still unable to avoid the general law," Ippolit proclaimed.

"That may be, that very well may be, gentlemen," the prince hurried, "though I don't understand what general law you're talking about; but I'll continue, only don't get offended for nothing; I swear I haven't the slightest wish to offend you. And what in fact is this, gentlemen: it's impossible to say a single sincere word, or you get offended at once! But, first of all, I was terribly struck that 'Pavlishchev's son' existed, and existed in such terrible conditions as Chebarov explained to me. Pavlishchev was my benefactor and my father's friend. (Ah, what made you write such an untruth about my father in your article, Mr. Keller? There was no embezzlement of company funds, nor any offending of subordinates—I'm positively sure of that, and how could you raise your hand to write such slander?) And what you wrote about Pavlishchev is absolutely unbearable: you call that noblest of men lascivious and frivolous, so boldly, so positively, as if you were indeed telling the truth, and yet he was the most chaste man in the world! He was even a remarkable scholar; he corresponded with many respected men of science and contributed a great deal of money to science. As for his heart, his good deeds, oh, of course, you have correctly written that I was almost an idiot at that time and could understand nothing (though I did speak Russian and could understand it), but I can well appreciate all that I now remember . . ."

"Excuse me," shrieked Ippolit, "but isn't this a bit too sentimental? We're not children. You wanted to get straight to business, it's past nine, remember that."

"If you please, if you please, gentlemen," the prince agreed at once. "After my initial distrust, I decided that I might be mistaken and that Pavlishchev might actually have a son. But I was terribly struck that this son should so easily, that is, I mean to say, so publicly reveal the secret of his birth and, above all, disgrace his mother. Because Chebarov had already frightened me with publicity then . . ."

"How stupid!" Lebedev's nephew cried.

"You have no right . . . you have no right!" cried Burdovsky.

"A son isn't answerable for his father's depraved conduct, and the mother is not to blame," Ippolit shrieked vehemently.

"The sooner, it seems, she should be spared . . ." the prince said timidly.

"You're not only naïve, Prince, but maybe even more far gone," Lebedev's nephew grinned spitefully.

"And what right did you have! . . ." Ippolit shrieked in a most unnatural voice.

"None, none at all!" the prince hastily interrupted. "You're right about that, I admit, but it was involuntary, and I said to myself at once just then that my personal feelings shouldn't have any influence on the affair, because if I acknowledge it as my duty to satisfy Mr. Burdovsky's demands in the name of my feelings for Pavlishchev, then I must satisfy them in any case, that is, regardless of whether or not I respect Mr. Burdovsky. I began to speak of it, gentlemen, only because it did seem unnatural to me that a son should reveal his mother's secret so publicly . . . In short, that was mainly why I was convinced that Chebarov must be a blackguard and must have prompted Mr. Burdovsky, by deceit, to such crookedness."

"But this is insupportable!" came from the visitors' side, some of whom even jumped up from their seats.

"Gentlemen! That is why I decided that the unfortunate Mr. Burdovsky must be a simple, defenseless man, a man easily swayed by crooks, and thus I had all the more reason to help him as 'Pavlishchev's son'—first, by opposing Mr. Chebarov, second, by my devotion and friendship, in order to guide him, and, third, by arranging to pay him ten thousand roubles, which, as I calculate, is all that Pavlishchev could have spent on me in cash . . ."

"What! Only ten thousand!" cried Ippolit.

"Well, Prince, you're not very strong in arithmetic, or else you're very strong, though you pretend to be a simpleton!" Lebedev's nephew cried out.

"I don't agree to ten thousand," said Burdovsky.

"Antip! Agree!" the boxer, leaning over the back of Ippolit's chair, said in a quick and distinct whisper. "Agree, and then later we'll see!"

"Listen he-e-ere, Mr. Myshkin," shrieked Ippolit, "understand that we're not fools, not vulgar fools, as your guests all probably think we are, and these ladies, who are smirking at us with such indignation, and especially this high-society gentleman" (he pointed to Evgeny Pavlovich), "whom I naturally do not have the honor of knowing, but of whom I seem to have heard a thing or two . . ."

"Excuse me, excuse me, gentlemen, but again you haven't understood me!" the prince addressed them in agitation. "First of all,

Mr. Keller, in your article you give an extremely inexact notion of my fortune: I didn't get any millions; I have only an eighth or a tenth part of what you suppose. Second, no one ever spent any tens of thousands on me in Switzerland: Schneider was paid six hundred roubles a year, and that only for the first three years; and Pavlishchev never went to Paris for pretty governesses—that again is slander. I think far less than ten thousand was spent on me in all, but I decided on ten thousand and, you must agree, in repaying a debt, I simply couldn't offer Mr. Burdovsky more, even if I was terribly fond of him, I couldn't do it simply from a feeling of delicacy, precisely because I was paying him back a debt and not sending him charity. I don't see how you can fail to understand that, gentlemen! But I wanted to make up for it all later by my friendship, my active participation in the fate of the unfortunate Mr. Burdovsky, who had obviously been deceived, because without deceit he himself could not have agreed to such baseness as, for instance, today's public statement about his mother in Mr. Keller's article . . . But why, finally, are you again getting so beside yourselves, gentlemen! We finally won't understand each other at all! Because it turned out my way! I'm now convinced by my own eyes that my guess was correct," the excited prince went on persuading, trying to calm the agitation and not noticing that he was only increasing it.

"How? Convinced of what?" they accosted him almost ferociously.

"But, good heavens, first of all, I myself have had time to take a very good look at Mr. Burdovsky, and I can now see for myself how he is . . . He's an innocent man, but whom everybody is deceiving! A defenseless man . . . and therefore I must spare him. And, second, Gavrila Ardalionovich, whom I entrusted with this affair and from whom I had not heard any news for a long time, because I was on the road and then sick for three days in Petersburg, now suddenly, just an hour ago, at our first meeting, informs me that he has gotten to the bottom of Chebarov's intentions, that he has proofs, and that Chebarov is precisely what I supposed him to be. I know, gentlemen, that many people consider me an idiot, and Chebarov, going by my reputation for giving money away easily, thought it would be very easy to deceive me, counting precisely on my feelings for Pavlishchev. But the main thing is—no, hear me out, gentlemen, hear me out!—the main thing is that now it suddenly turns out that Mr. Burdovsky isn't Pavlishchev's son at all! Gavrila Ardalionovich just told me so, and he assures me that he has obtained positive proofs. Well, how does that strike you? It's impossible to believe it, after all that's gone on already! Positive proofs—you hear! I still don't believe it, I don't believe it myself, I assure you; I'm still doubtful, because Gavrila Ardalionovich hasn't had time yet to tell me all the details, but that Chebarov is a blackguard there is not longer any doubt! He has duped the unfortunate Mr. Burdovsky and all of you, gentlemen, who came nobly to support your friend (for he obviously needs support, I do understand that!), he has duped you all, and involved you in a crooked affair, because it's all essentially knavery and crookedness!"

"What's crooked about it! . . . How is he not 'Pavlishchev's son'? . . . How is it possible! . . ." exclamations rang out. Burdovsky's whole company was in inexpressible confusion.

"But naturally it's crooked! You see, if Mr. Burdovsky now turns out not to be 'Pavlishchev's son,' then in that case Mr. Burdovsky's demand turns out to be downright crooked (that is, of course, if he knew the truth!), but the thing is that he was deceived, that's why I insist that he be vindicated; that's why I say that he deserves to be pitied in his simplicity, and cannot be left without support; otherwise he, too, will come out as a crook in this affair. And I myself am convinced that he doesn't understand a thing! I, too, was in such a condition before I left for Switzerland; I, too, babbled incoherent words—you want to express yourself and can't . . . I understand it; I can sympathize very much, because I'm almost like that myself, I'm permitted to speak! And, finally, I still—despite the fact that 'Pavlishchev's son' is no more and it all turns out to be a mystification—I still haven't changed my decision and am ready to hand over the ten thousand in memory of Pavlishchev. I wanted to use this ten thousand to start a school in memory of Pavlishchev even before Mr. Burdovsky appeared, but now it won't make any difference whether it's a school or Mr. Burdovsky, because if Mr. Burdovsky is not 'Pavlishchev's son,' he's almost like 'Pavlishchev's son,' because he has been so wickedly deceived: he sincerely considered himself the son of Pavlishchev! Now listen to Gavrila Ardalionovich, gentlemen, let's be done with it—don't be angry, don't worry, sit down! Gavrila Ardalionovich will explain it all now, and, I confess, I'm extremely anxious to learn all the details myself. He says he even went to Pskov to see your mother, Mr. Burdovsky, who didn't die at all, as you were forced to write in the article . . . Sit down, gentlemen, sit down!"

The prince sat down and managed to get the Burdovsky company, who had all jumped up from their places, to sit down again. For the last ten or twenty minutes he had been speaking vehemently, loudly, in an impatient patter, carried away, trying to talk above them all, to outshout them, and, of course, later he would bitterly regret some of the phrases and surmises that had escaped him. If he had not been so excited and all but beside himself, he would never have permitted himself to speak some of his guesses and needless sincerities aloud so baldly and hastily. But as soon as he sat down, one burning regret painfully pierced his heart. Besides the fact that he had "insulted" Burdovsky by so publicly supposing him to have the same illness for which he himself had been treated in Switzerland—besides that, the offer of the ten thousand instead of the school had, in his opinion, been made crudely and carelessly, as if it were charity, and precisely in that it had been spoken aloud in front of other people. "I should have waited and offered it tomorrow when we were alone," the prince thought at once, "and now it's unlikely that I can put it right! Yes, I'm an idiot, a real idiot!" he decided to himself in a fit of shame and extreme distress.

Meanwhile Gavrila Ardalionovich, who till then had kept himself apart and remained stubbornly silent, came forward at the prince's invitation, stood beside him, and began calmly and clearly to give an account of the affair entrusted to him by the prince. All talk instantly stopped. Everyone listened with extreme curiosity, especially Burdovsky's whole company.

IX

"You will not, of course, deny," Gavrila Ardalionovich began, directly addressing Burdovsky, who was listening to him as hard as he could, his astonished eyes popping out, and was obviously in great confusion, "you will not, and will not wish, of course, to deny seriously that you were born exactly two years after your esteemed mother entered into lawful wedlock with the collegiate secretary Mr. Burdovsky, your father. The date of your birth is only too easy to prove factually, so that the distortion of this fact in Mr. Keller's article, so offensive to you and to your mother, can be explained only by the playful personal fantasy of Mr. Keller, who hoped thereby to strengthen the obviousness of your right and thereby contribute to your interests. Mr. Keller says that he read the article to you prior to publication, though not all of it . . . no doubt he stopped before reading you this part . . ."

"I didn't, actually," the boxer interrupted, "but I was informed of all the facts by competent persons, and I . . ."

"I beg your pardon, Mr. Keller," Gavrila Ardalionovich stopped him, "allow me to speak. I assure you, we will get to your article in its turn, and then you can offer your explanation, but now let us proceed in order. Quite by chance, with the help of my sister, Varvara Ardalionovna Ptitsyn, I obtained from her close friend, Vera Alexeevna Zubkov, a landowner and a widow, a letter from the late Nikolai Andreevich Pavlishchev, written to her from abroad twenty-four years ago. Having approached Vera Alexeevna, I was directed by her to retired Colonel Timofei Fyodorovich Vyazovkin, a distant relation, and, in his time, a great friend of Mr. Pavlishchev. From him I managed to obtain two more of Nikolai Andreevich's letters, also written from abroad. These three letters, the dates and facts mentioned in them, prove mathematically, with no possibility of refutation or even doubt, that Nikolai Andreevich went abroad (where he spent the next three years) exactly a year and a half before you were born, Mr. Burdovsky. Your mother, as you know, never left Russia . . . I will not read these letters at the present time. It is late now; I am, in any case, only stating the fact. But if you wish to make an appointment with me, Mr. Burdovsky, say, for tomorrow morning, and bring your own witnesses (as many as you like) and experts in the identification of handwriting, I have no doubt that you will not fail to be convinced of the obvious truth of the fact of which I have informed you. And if so, then, naturally, this whole affair collapses and ceases of itself."

Again a general stir and profound agitation ensued. Burdovsky himself suddenly got up from his chair.

"If so, then I was deceived, deceived, not by Chebarov, but long, long ago. I don't want any experts, I don't want any appointments, I believe you, I renounce . . . no need for the ten thousand . . . good-bye . . ."

He took his peaked cap and pushed a chair aside in order to leave.

"If you can, Mr. Burdovsky," Gavrila Ardalionovich said softly and sweetly, "please stay for another five minutes or so. Several more extremely important facts have been discovered in this affair, quite curious ones, especially for you in any case. In my opinion, you ought without fail to become acquainted with them, and for you yourself, perhaps, it will be more pleasant if the affair is completely cleared up . . ."

Burdovsky sat down silently, bowing his head a little, as if in deep thought. After him, Lebedev's nephew, who had also gotten up to go with him, sat down again; though he had not lost his head or his pluck, he was obviously greatly puzzled. Ippolit was downcast, sad, and seemed very surprised. Just then, however, he began to cough so hard that he even got bloodstains on his handkerchief. The boxer was all but frightened.

"Eh, Antip!" he cried bitterly. "Didn't I tell you then . . . two days ago . . . that maybe in fact you're not Pavlishchev's son?"

Suppressed laughter was heard, two or three laughed louder than the others.

"The fact of which you have just informed us, Mr. Keller," Gavrila Ardalionovich picked up, "is a very precious one. Nevertheless I have the full right, on the basis of very precise data, to maintain that Mr. Burdovsky, though he was, of course, only too well aware of the date of his birth, was completely unaware of the circumstances of Pavlishchev's residence abroad, where Mr. Pavlishchev spent the greater part of his life, never returning to Russia for more than short periods. Besides that, the very fact of his departure at that time is so unremarkable in itself that even those who knew Pavlishchev intimately would hardly remember it after more than twenty years, to say nothing of Mr. Burdovsky, who was not even born yet. Of course, to obtain information now turned out to be not impossible; but I must confess that the information I received came to me quite by chance, and might very well not have come; so that for Mr. Burdovsky, and even for Chebarov, this information would indeed have been almost impossible to obtain, even if they had taken it into their heads to obtain it. But they might not have taken it into their heads . . ."

"If you please, Mr. Ivolgin," Ippolit suddenly interrupted him irritably, "why all this galimatias (forgive me)? The affair has been explained, we agree to believe the main fact, why drag out this painful and offensive rigmarole any longer? Maybe you want to boast about the deftness of your research, to show us and the prince what a good investigator and sleuth you are? Or do you mean to try to excuse and vindicate Burdovsky by the fact that he got mixed up in this affair out of ignorance? But that is impudent, my dear sir! Burdovsky has no need of your vindications and excuses, let that be known to you! He's offended, it's painful for him as it is, he's in an awkward position, you ought to have guessed, to have understood that . . ."

"Enough, Mr. Terentyev, enough," Gavrila Ardalionovich managed to interrupt him. "Calm down, don't get irritated; you seem to be very ill? I sympathize with you. In that case, if you wish, I'm done, that is, I am forced to convey only briefly those facts which, in my conviction, it would not be superfluous to know in all their fullness," he added, noticing a general movement that looked like impatience. "I merely wish to tell you, with evidence, for the information of all those interested in the affair, that your mother, Mr. Burdovsky, enjoyed the affection and care of Pavlishchev solely because she was the sister of a house-serf girl with whom Mr. Pavlishchev had been in love in his early youth, so much so that he would certainly have married her if she had not died unexpectedly. I have proofs that this family fact, absolutely precise and true, is very little known, even quite forgotten. Furthermore, I could explain how your mother, as a ten-year-old child, was taken by Mr. Pavlishchev to be brought up like a relation, that a significant dowry was set aside for her, and that all these cares generated extremely alarmed rumors among Pavlishchev's numerous relations: they even thought he might marry his ward, but in the end she married by inclination (and I can prove that in the most precise fashion) a land surveyor, Mr. Burdovsky, when she was nineteen. Here I have gathered several very precise facts proving that your father, Mr. Burdovsky, a totally impractical man, having received fifteen thousand as your mother's dowry, abandoned his job, got into commercial ventures, was cheated, lost his capital, could not bear his grief, began to drink, which caused his illness, and finally died prematurely, in the eighth year of his marriage to your mother. Then, according to your mother's own testimony, she was left destitute and would have perished altogether without the constant and magnanimous assistance of Pavlishchev, who gave her up to six hundred roubles a year as support. Then there are countless testimonies that he was extremely fond of you as a child. According to these testimonies, and again with your mother's confirmation, it appears that he loved you mainly because as a child you had a speech defect and the look of a cripple, a pathetic, miserable child (and Pavlishchev, as I have deduced from precise evidence, had all his life a certain tender inclination towards everything oppressed and wronged by nature, especially in children—a fact, in my conviction, of extreme importance for our affair). Finally, I can boast of the

most precise findings about the main fact of how this great attachment to you on the part of Pavlishchev (through whose efforts you
entered high school and studied under special supervision) in the
end gradually produced among Pavlishchev's relations and household the notion that you were his son and that your father was
merely a deceived husband. But the main thing is that this notion
hardened into a precise and general conviction only in the last years
of Pavlishchev's life, when everyone had fears about the will and
all the original facts were forgotten and inquiries were impossible.
Undoubtedly this notion reached you, Mr. Burdovsky, and took
complete possession of you. Your mother, whose acquaintance I
had the honor of making personally, knew all about these rumors,
but does not know to this day (I, too, concealed it from her) that
you, her son, were also under the spell of this rumor. I found your
much-esteemed mother in Pskov, Mr. Burdovsky, beset by illnesses
and in the most extreme poverty, which she fell into after Pavlishchev's death. She told me with tears of gratitude that she was
alive in the world only through you and your support; she expects
much from you in the future and fervently believes in your future
success . . ."

"This is finally unbearable!" Lebedev's nephew suddenly
declared loudly and impatiently. "Why this whole novel?"

"Disgustingly indecent!" Ippolit stirred violently. But Burdovsky
noticed nothing and did not even budge.

"Why? How so?" Gavrila Ardalionovich said in sly astonishment, venomously preparing to set forth his conclusion. "First, Mr.
Burdovsky can now be fully certain that Mr. Pavlishchev loved him
out of magnanimity and not as a son. It was necessary that Mr.
Burdovsky learn at least this one fact, since he confirmed and
approved of Mr. Keller after the reading of the article. I say this,
Mr. Burdovsky, because I consider you a noble man. Second, it
turns out that there was no thievery or crookedness here even on
Chebarov's part; this is an important point even for me, because
just now the prince, being overexcited, mentioned that I was
supposedly of the same opinion about the thievery and crookedness
in this unfortunate affair. Here, on the contrary, there was full
conviction on all sides, and though Chebarov may be a great crook,
in this affair he comes out as no more than a pettifogger, a scrivener,
a speculator. He hoped to make big money as a lawyer, and his
calculation was not only subtle and masterful, but also most certain:
he based it on the ease with which the prince gives money away

and on his gratefully respectful feeling for the late Pavlishchev; he based it, finally (which is most important), on certain chivalrous views the prince holds concerning the duties of honor and conscience. As far as Mr. Burdovsky himself is concerned, it may even be said that, owing to certain convictions of his, he was so set up by Chebarov and the company around him that he started the affair almost not out of self-interest at all, but almost in the service of truth, progress, and mankind. Now that these facts have been made known, it must be clear to everyone that Mr. Burdovsky is a pure man, despite all appearances, and now the prince can, the sooner and all the more willingly than before, offer him both his friendly assistance and the active help which he mentioned earlier, speaking about schools and Pavlishchev."

"Stop, Gavrila Ardalionovich, stop!" the prince cried in genuine alarm, but it was too late.

"I've said, I've already said three times," Burdovsky cried irritably, "that I don't want any money! I won't accept . . . what for . . . I don't want . . . away!"

And he nearly rushed off the terrace. But Lebedev's nephew seized him by the arm and whispered something to him. The man quickly came back and, taking a large unsealed envelope from his pocket, threw it down on a little table near the prince.

"Here's the money! . . . You shouldn't have dared . . . you shouldn't have! . . . Money! . . ."

"The two hundred and fifty roubles that you dared to send him as charity through Chebarov," Doktorenko explained.

"The article said fifty!" cried Kolya.

"I'm to blame!" said the prince, going up to Burdovsky. "I'm very much to blame before you, Burdovsky, but, believe me, I didn't send it as charity. I'm to blame now . . . I was to blame earlier." (The prince was very upset, he looked tired and weak, and his words were incoherent.) "I said that about crookedness . . . but it wasn't about you, I was mistaken. I said that you . . . are like me— a sick man. But you're not like me, you . . . give lessons, you support your mother. I said you had disgraced your mother, but you love her; she says so herself . . . I didn't know . . . Gavrila Ardalionovich didn't finish telling me . . . I'm to blame. I dared to offer you ten thousand, but I'm to blame, I ought to have done it differently, and now . . . it's impossible, because you despise me . . ."

"This is a madhouse!" Lizaveta Prokofyevna cried out.

"Of course, a house full of madmen!" Aglaya lost patience and spoke sharply, but her words were drowned in the general noise; everyone was talking loudly, everyone was arguing, some disputing, some laughing. Ivan Fyodorovich Epanchin was in the utmost degree of indignation, and, with an air of offended dignity, was waiting for Lizaveta Prokofyevna. Lebedev's nephew put in a last little word:

"Yes, Prince, you must be given credit, you're so good at exploiting your . . . hm, sickness (to put it decently); you managed to offer your friendship and money in such a clever form that it is now quite impossible for a noble man to accept them. It's either all too innocent, or all too clever . . . you, however, know which."

"If you please, gentlemen," cried Gavrila Ardalionovich, who had meanwhile opened the envelope with the money, "there are not two hundred and fifty roubles here, but only a hundred. I say it, Prince, so that there will be no misunderstandings."

"Let it be, let it be," the prince waved his arms at Gavrila Ardalionovich.

"No, don't 'let it be'!" Lebedev's nephew immediately latched on to it. "Your 'let it be' is insulting to us, Prince. We're not hiding, we declare openly: yes, there's only a hundred roubles here, and not the whole two hundred and fifty, but isn't it all the same . . ."

"N-no, it's not all the same," Gavrila Ardalionovich managed to put in, with a look of naïve perplexity.

"Don't interrupt me, we're not such fools as you think, mister lawyer," Lebedev's nephew exclaimed with spiteful vexation. "Of course, a hundred roubles aren't two hundred and fifty, and it's not all the same, but what's important is the principle; it's the initiative that's important and the fact of the missing hundred and fifty roubles is merely a detail. What's important is that Burdovsky does not accept charity from you, Your Highness, that he throws it in your face, and in this sense a hundred is the same as two hundred and fifty. Burdovsky did not accept the ten thousand, you saw that; he wouldn't have brought the hundred roubles if he were dishonest! Those hundred and fifty roubles were Chebarov's expenses for traveling to see the prince. Sooner laugh at our clumsiness and our inexperience in handling the affair; you've already done all you could to make us look ridiculous; but do not dare to say we're dishonest. All of us together will pay the prince back these hundred and fifty roubles, my dear sir; we will pay it back even if it's rouble by rouble, and we will pay it back with interest. Burdovsky is poor, Burdovsky has no millions, and Chebarov presented the bill after his trip. We hoped to win . . . Who would have acted differently in his place?"

"What do you mean who?" exclaimed Prince Shch.

"I'll go out of my mind here!" cried Lizaveta Prokofyevna.

"This reminds me," laughed Evgeny Pavlovich, who had long been standing and watching, "of a famous defense made recently by a lawyer, who, presenting poverty as an excuse for his client, who had murdered six people at one go in order to rob them, suddenly concluded along these lines: 'It is natural,' he says, 'that my client, out of poverty, should have taken it into his head to commit this murder of six people, and who in his place would not have taken it into his head?' Something along those lines, only very amusing."

"Enough!" Lizaveta Prokofyevna suddenly announced, almost trembling with wrath. "It's time to break off this galimatias! . . ."

She was in the most terrible agitation; she threw her head back menacingly and, with haughty, burning, and impatient defiance, passed her flashing gaze over the whole company, scarcely distinguishing at that moment her friends from her enemies. This was the point of a long-suppressed but finally unleashed wrath, when the main impulse is immediate battle, the immediate need to fall upon someone as soon as possible. Those who knew Lizaveta Prokofyevna sensed at once that something peculiar was happening with her. Ivan Fyodorovich said the next day to Prince Shch. that "it happens with her, but even with her it rarely happens to such a degree as yesterday, perhaps once in three years, but never more often! never more often!" he added in clarification.

"Enough, Ivan Fyodorovich! Let me be!" exclaimed Lizaveta Prokofyevna. "Why do you offer me your arm now? You weren't able to take me away earlier; you're a husband, you're the head of the family; you should have led me out by the ear, fool that I am, if I didn't obey you and leave. You should have done it at least for your daughters' sake! But now we'll find our way without you, this is shame enough for a whole year . . . .Wait, I still want to thank the prince! . . . Thank you, Prince, for the treat! Here I sat, listening to our young people . . . How base, how base! It's chaos, outrage, you don't even dream of such things! Are there many like them? . . . Silence, Aglaya! Silence, Alexandra! It's none of your business! . . . Don't fuss around me, Evgeny Pavlych, I'm tired of you! . . . So you, my dearest, are asking their forgiveness," she picked up again, turning to the prince. "'I'm sorry,' you say, 'that

I dared to offer you capital' . . . and what are you laughing at, you little fanfaron!" she suddenly fell upon Lebedev's nephew. "'We refuse the capital,' he says, 'we demand, and do not ask!' As if he doesn't know that tomorrow this idiot will again drag himself to them offering his friendship and capital! Will you go? Will you go or not?"

"I will," said the prince in a quiet and humble voice.

"You've heard it! And that is what you were counting on," she turned to Doktorenko again. "The money's as good as in your pocket, that's why you're playing the fanfaron, blowing smoke in our eyes . . . No, my dear, find yourself some other fools, I can see through you . . . I see your whole game!"

"Lizaveta Prokofyevna!" exclaimed the prince.

"Let's go home, Lizaveta Prokofyevna, it's high time, and we'll take the prince with us," Prince Shch., smiling, said as calmly as he could.

The girls stood to one side, almost frightened, and the general was frightened in earnest; the whole company was astonished. Some, those who stood a little further away, smiled slyly and exchanged whispers; Lebedev's face displayed the utmost degree of rapture.

"You can find outrage and chaos everywhere, ma'am," Lebedev's nephew said, though significantly puzzled.

"But not like that! Not like yours just now, dear boys, not like that!" Lizaveta Prokofyevna picked up gleefully, as if in hysterics. "Oh, do let me be," she shouted at those who were persuading her, "no, since even you yourself, Evgeny Pavlych, told us just now that even the defense lawyer himself said in court that there was nothing more natural than doing in six people out of poverty, then the last times have really come. I've never yet heard of such a thing. Now it's all clear to me! Wouldn't this tongue-tied one here put a knife in somebody?" (She pointed to Burdovsky, who was looking at her in extreme perplexity.) "I bet he would! Your money, your ten thousand, perhaps he won't take, perhaps in good conscience he won't, but he'll come in the night and put a knife in you, and take it from the strongbox. Take it in good conscience! He doesn't find it dishonest! It's 'a noble impulse of despair,' it's 'negation,' or devil knows what it is . . . Pah! Everything's inside out, everybody's topsy-turvy. A girl grows up at home, suddenly in the middle of the street she jumps into a droshky: 'Mummy dear, the other day I got married to somebody-or-other Karlych or Ivanych, good-bye!"[39] Is that a good way to behave, in your opinion? Is it natural, is it worthy of respect? The woman question? This boy here" (she pointed to Kolya), "even he insisted the other day that that is what the 'woman question' means. The mother may be a fool, but still you must treat her humanly! . . . And you, walking in earlier with your heads thrown back? 'Out of the way: we're coming. Give us all the rights, and don't you dare make a peep before us. Show us all respect, even such as doesn't exist, and we'll treat you worse than the lowest lackey!' They seek truth, they insist on their rights, yet they themselves slander him up and down like heathens in their article. 'We demand, and do not ask, and you'll get no gratitude from us, because you do it for the satisfaction of your own conscience!' Nice morality! But if there'll be no gratitude from you, then the prince can also say in answer to you that he feels no gratitude towards Pavlishchev, because Pavlishchev did good for the satisfaction of his own conscience. And this gratitude towards Pavlishchev was the only thing you were counting on: he didn't borrow money from you, he doesn't owe you anything, what were you counting on if not gratitude? How, then, can you renounce it yourselves? Madmen! You acknowledge that society is savage and inhuman because it disgraces a seduced girl. But if you acknowledge that society is inhuman, it means you acknowledge that this girl has been hurt by this society. But if she's been hurt, why, then, do you yourselves bring her out in front of that same society in your newspapers and demand that it not hurt her? Mad! Vainglorious! They don't believe in God, they don't believe in Christ! You're so eaten up by vanity and pride that you'll end by eating each other, that I foretell to you. Isn't this havoc, isn't it chaos, isn't it an outrage? And after that this disgraceful creature goes asking their forgiveness! Are there many like you? What are you grinning at: that I've disgraced myself with you? Well, so I'm disgraced, there's no help for it now! . . . And take that grin off your face, you stinker!" (she suddenly fell on Ippolit). "He can barely breathe, yet he corrupts others. You've corrupted this boy for me" (she pointed to Kolya again). "He raves about you only, you teach him atheism, you don't believe in God, but you could do with a good whipping, my dear sir! Ah, I spit on you all! . . . So you'll go to them, Prince Lev Nikolaevich, you'll go to them tomorrow?" she asked the prince again, almost breathless.

"I will."

"Then I don't want to know you!" She quickly turned to leave, but suddenly turned back again. "And you'll go to this atheist?" she pointed to Ippolit. "Why are you grinning at me!" she exclaimed somehow unnaturally and suddenly rushed at Ippolit, unable to bear his sarcastic grin.

"Lizaveta Prokofyevna! Lizaveta Prokofyevna! Lizaveta Prokofyevna!" came from all sides at once.

"*Maman*, it's shameful!" Aglaya cried loudly.

"Don't worry, Aglaya Ivanovna," Ippolit replied calmly. Lizaveta Prokofyevna, who had run up to him, seized him and for some unknown reason held him tightly by the arm; she stood before him, her furious gaze as if riveted to him. "Don't worry, your *maman* will realize that one cannot fall upon a dying man . . . I'm prepared to explain why I laughed . . . I'd be very glad to be permitted . . ."

Here he suddenly began coughing terribly and for a whole minute could not calm the cough.

"He's dying, and he goes on orating!" exclaimed Lizaveta Prokofyevna, letting go of his arm and watching almost with horror as he wiped the blood from his lips. "What are you talking for! You should simply go to bed . . ."

"So it will be," Ippolit replied quietly, hoarsely, and almost in a whisper. "As soon as I go home tonight, I'll lie down at once . . . in two weeks I'll be dead, I know that . . . Last week B———n[40] told me himself . . . So, with your permission, I would like to say a couple of words to you in farewell."

"Are you out of your mind, or what? Nonsense! You must be treated, this is no time for talking! Go, go, lie down! . . ." Lizaveta Prokofyevna cried in fright.

"If I lie down, then I won't get up till I die," Ippolit smiled. "Yesterday I wanted to lie down like that and not get up till I die, but I decided to postpone it for two days, while I can still use my legs . . . in order to come here with them today . . . only I'm very tired . . ."

"Sit down, sit down, don't stand there! Here's a chair for you," Lizaveta Prokofyevna roused herself and moved a chair for him.

"Thank you," Ippolit continued quietly, "and you sit down opposite me, and we'll talk . . . we'll certainly talk, Lizaveta Prokofyevna, I insist on it now . . ." He smiled at her again. "Think of it, today I'm outside and with people for the last time, and in two weeks I'll probably be under the ground. So this will be a sort of farewell both to people and to nature. Though I'm not very sentimental, you can imagine how glad I am that it all happened here in Pavlovsk: at least you can look at a tree in leaf."

"What's this talk now," Lizaveta Prokofyevna was becoming more and more frightened, "you're all feverish. You were just shrieking and squealing, and now you're out of breath, suffocating!"

"I'll rest presently. Why do you want to deny me my last wish? . . . You know . . . I've long been dreaming of somehow getting to know you, Lizaveta Prokofyevna; I've heard a lot about you . . . from Kolya; he's almost the only one who hasn't abandoned me . . . You're an original woman, an eccentric woman, now I've seen it myself . . . you know, I even loved you a little."

"Lord, and I was really about to hit him."

"It was Aglaya Ivanovna who held you back. I'm not mistaken? This is your daughter Aglaya Ivanovna? She's so pretty that I guessed it was her at first sight earlier, though I'd never seen her before. Grant me at least to look at a beautiful girl for the last time in my life," Ippolit smiled a sort of awkward, crooked smile. "The prince is here, and your husband, and the whole company. Why would you deny me my last wish?"

"A chair!" cried Lizaveta Prokofyevna, but she seized one herself and sat down facing Ippolit. "Kolya," she ordered, "go with him at once, take him home, and tomorrow I myself will be sure to . . ."

"If you'll permit me, I'd like to ask the prince for a cup of tea . . . I'm very tired. You know, Lizaveta Prokofyevna, it seems you wanted to take the prince home with you for tea; stay here instead, we can spend some time together, and the prince will surely give us all tea. Excuse me for giving orders like that . . . But I know you, you're kind, so is the prince . . . we're all so kind it's comical . . ."

The prince got into a flutter, Lebedev rushed headlong out of the room, and Vera ran after him.

"That's true, too," Mrs. Epanchin decided abruptly. "Talk, then, only more softly, and don't get carried away. You've made me all pitiful . . . Prince! You're not worthy of my having tea with you, but so be it, I'm staying, though I ask nobody's forgiveness! Nobody's! Nonsense! . . . Forgive me, though, if I scolded you, Prince— though only if you want to. Though I'm not keeping anybody," she suddenly turned to her husband and daughters with a look of extraordinary wrath, as if it were they who were terribly guilty before her for something, "I can find my way home by myself . . ."

But they did not let her finish. They all came and eagerly gathered around her. The prince at once began begging everyone to stay for tea and apologized for not having thought of it till then. Even the general was so amiable as to mutter something reassuring and amiably ask Lizaveta Prokofyevna whether it was not, after all, too cool for her on the terrace. He even all but asked Ippolit how long he had been studying at the university, but he did not ask. Evgeny Pavlovich and Prince Shch. suddenly became extremely amiable and merry; the faces of Adelaida and Alexandra, through their continuing astonishment, even expressed pleasure; in short, everyone was obviously glad that Lizaveta Prokofyevna's crisis was over. Only Aglaya was sullen and silently sat down a little way off. The rest of the company also stayed; no one wanted to leave, not even General Ivolgin, to whom Lebedev, however, whispered something in passing, probably something not entirely pleasant, because the general at once effaced himself somewhere in a corner. The prince also went and invited Burdovsky and his company, not leaving anyone out. They muttered with a strained air that they would wait for Ippolit, and withdrew at once to the furthest corner of the terrace, where they all sat down side by side again. Lebedev had probably had tea prepared for himself long ago, because it appeared at once. The clock struck eleven.

X

IPPOLIT MOISTENED HIS lips with the cup of tea Vera Lebedev served him, set the cup down on the table, and suddenly, as if abashed, looked around almost in embarrassment.

"Look, Lizaveta Prokofyevna, these cups," he was hurrying somehow strangely, "these china cups, and fine china by the look of it, Lebedev always keeps locked up in a glass case; he never serves them . . . the usual thing, they came with his wife's dowry . . . the usual thing with them . . . and now he's served them, in your honor, naturally, he's so glad . . ."

He wanted to add something more, but found no words.

"He got embarrassed, just as I expected," Evgeny Pavlovich suddenly whispered in the prince's ear. "That's dangerous, eh? The surest sign that now, out of spite, he'll pull off something so eccentric that even Lizaveta Prokofyevna may not be able to sit it out."

The prince looked at him questioningly.

"You're not afraid of eccentricity?" Evgeny Pavlovich added. "I'm not either, I even wish for it; in fact, all I want is that our dear

Lizaveta Prokofyevna be punished, and that without fail, today, right now; I don't want to leave without that. You seem to be feverish?"

"Later, don't interfere. Yes, I'm unwell," the prince replied distractedly and even impatiently. He had heard his name, Ippolit was speaking about him.

"You don't believe it?" Ippolit laughed hysterically. "That's as it should be, but the prince will believe it from the first and won't be the least surprised."

"Do you hear, Prince?" Lizaveta Prokofyevna turned to him. "Do you hear?"

There was laughter all around. Lebedev fussily thrust himself forward and squirmed right in front of Lizaveta Prokofyevna.

"He says that this clown here, your landlord . . . corrected the article for that gentleman, the one that was just read about you."

The prince looked at Lebedev in surprise.

"Why are you silent?" Lizaveta Prokofyevna even stamped her foot.

"Well," the prince murmured, continuing to scrutinize Lebedev, "I can already see that he did."

"Is it true?" Lizaveta Prokofyevna quickly turned to Lebedev.

"The real truth, Your Excellency!" Lebedev replied firmly and unshakeably, placing his hand on his heart.

"It's as if he's boasting!" she all but jumped in her chair.

"I'm mean, mean!" Lebedev murmured, beginning to beat his breast and bowing his head lower and lower.

"What do I care if you're mean! He thinks he can say 'I'm mean' and wriggle out of it. Aren't you ashamed, Prince, to keep company with such wretched little people, I say it again? I'll never forgive you!"

"The prince will forgive me!" Lebedev said with conviction and affection.

"Solely out of nobility," Keller, suddenly jumping over to them, began loudly and resoundingly, addressing Lizaveta Prokofyevna directly, "solely out of nobility, ma'am, and so as not to give away a compromised friend, did I conceal the fact of the correcting earlier, though he suggested chucking us down the stairs, as you heard yourself. So as to reestablish the truth, I confess that I actually did turn to him, for six roubles, though not at all for the style, but, essentially, as a competent person, to find out the facts, which for the most part were unknown to me. About his gaiters, about his appetite at the Swiss professor's, about the fifty roubles instead of two hundred and fifty, in short, that whole grouping, all belongs to him, for six roubles, but the style wasn't corrected."

"I must observe," Lebedev interrupted him with feverish impatience and in a sort of creeping voice, while the laughter spread more and more, "that I corrected only the first half of the article, but since we disagreed in the middle and quarreled over an idea, I left the second half of the article uncorrected, sir, so all that's illiterate there (and it is illiterate!) can't be ascribed to me, sir . . ."

"See what he's fussing about!" cried Lizaveta Prokofyevna.

"If I may ask," Evgeny Pavlovich turned to Keller, "when was the article corrected?"

"Yesterday morning," Keller reported, "we had a meeting, promising on our word of honor to keep the secret on both sides."

"That was when he was crawling before you and assuring you of his devotion! Ah, wretched little people! I don't need your Pushkin, and your daughter needn't come to see me!"

Lizaveta Prokofyevna was about to get up, but suddenly turned irritably to the laughing Ippolit:

"What is it, my dear, have you decided to make me a laughing-stock here?"

"God save us," Ippolit smiled crookedly, "but I'm struck most of all by your extreme eccentricity, Lizaveta Prokofyevna; I confess, I deliberately slipped that in about Lebedev, I knew how it would affect you, affect you alone, because the prince really will forgive him and probably already has . . . maybe has even already found an excuse in his mind—is it so, Prince, am I right?"

He was breathless, his strange excitement was growing with every word.

"Well? . . ." Lizaveta Prokofyevna said wrathfully, surprised at his tone. "Well?"

"About you I've already heard a lot, in that same vein . . . with great gladness . . . have learned to have the highest respect for you," Ippolit went on.

He was saying one thing, but as if he wanted to say something quite different with the same words. He spoke with a shade of mockery and at the same time was disproportionately agitated, looked around suspiciously, was evidently confused and at a loss for every word, all of which, together with his consumptive look and strange, glittering, and as if frenzied gaze, involuntarily continued to draw people's attention to him.

"I'd be quite surprised, however, not knowing society (I admit it), that you not only remained in the company of our people tonight, which is quite unsuitable for you, but that you also kept these . . . girls here to listen to a scandalous affair, though they've already read it all in novels. However, I may not know . . . because I get confused, but, in any case, who except you would have stayed . . . at the request of a boy (yes, a boy, again I admit it) to spend an evening with him and take . . . part in everything and . . . so as . . . to be ashamed the next day . . . (I agree, however, that I'm not putting it right), I praise all that highly and deeply respect it, though by the mere look of his excellency your husband one can see how unpleasant it all is for him . . . Hee, hee!" he tittered, quite confused, and suddenly went into such a fit of coughing that for some two minutes he was unable to go on.

"He even choked!" Lizaveta Prokofyevna said coldly and sharply, studying him with stern curiosity. "Well, dear boy, enough of you. It's time to go!"

"And allow me, my dear sir, for my part, to point out to you," Ivan Fyodorovich, having lost all patience, suddenly said vexedly, "that my wife is here visiting Prince Lev Nikolaevich, our mutual friend and neighbor, and that in any case it is not for you, young man, to judge Lizaveta Prokofyevna's actions, nor to refer aloud and in my teeth to what is written on my face. No, sir. And if my wife stayed here," he went on, growing more and more vexed with every word, "it was sooner out of amazement, sir, and an understandable contemporary curiosity to see some strange young people. And I myself stayed, as I stop sometimes in the street when I see something that can be looked upon as . . . as . . . as . . ."

"As a rarity," prompted Evgeny Pavlovich.

"Excellent and right," rejoiced his excellency, who had become a bit muddled in his comparison, "precisely as a rarity. But in any case, for me what is most amazing and even chagrining, if it may be put that way grammatically, is that you, young man, were not even able to understand that Lizaveta Prokofyevna stayed with you now because you are ill—if you are indeed dying—out of compassion, so to speak, on account of your pathetic words, sir, and that no sort of mud can cling to her name, qualities, and importance . . . Lizaveta Prokofyevna!" the flushed general concluded, "if you want to go, let us take leave of our good prince . . ."

"Thank you for the lesson, General," Ippolit interrupted gravely and unexpectedly, looking at him pensively.

"Let's go, *maman*, how long must this continue!" Aglaya said impatiently and wrathfully, getting up from her chair.

"Two more minutes, my dear Ivan Fyodorovich, if you permit," Lizaveta Prokofyevna turned to her husband with dignity, "it seems to me that he's all feverish and simply raving; I'm convinced by his eyes; he cannot be left like this. Lev Nikolaevich! May he spend the night here, so that they won't have to drag him to Petersburg tonight? *Cher prince*, are you bored?" she suddenly turned to Prince Shch. for some reason. "Come here, Alexandra, your hair needs putting right, my dear."

She put right her hair, which did not need putting right, and kissed her; that was all she had called her for.

"I considered you capable of development . . ." Ippolit spoke again, coming out of his pensiveness. "Yes! this is what I wanted to say." He was glad, as if he had suddenly remembered: "Burdovsky here sincerely wants to protect his mother, isn't that so? And it turns out that he disgraces her. The prince here wants to help Burdovsky, offers him, with purity of heart, his tender friendship and his capital, and is maybe the only one among you all who does not feel loathing for him, and here they stand facing each other like real enemies . . . Ha, ha, ha! You all hate Burdovsky, because in your opinion his attitude towards his mother is not beautiful and graceful—right? right? right? And you're all terribly fond of the beauty and gracefulness of forms, you stand on that alone, isn't it so? (I've long suspected it was on that alone!) Well, know, then, that maybe not one of you has loved his mother as Burdovsky has! You, Prince, I know, sent money to Burdovsky's mother on the quiet, through Ganechka, and I'll bet—hee, hee, hee!" (he giggled hysterically), "I'll bet that Burdovsky himself will now accuse you of indelicacy of form and disrespect for his mother, by God, he will, ha, ha, ha!"

Here he again lost his breath and began to cough.

"Well, is that all? Is that all now, have you said it all? Well, go to bed now, you have a fever," Lizaveta Prokofyevna interrupted impatiently, not taking her worried eyes off him. "Ah, Lord! He's still talking!"

"It seems you're laughing? Why must you keep laughing at me? I've noticed that you keep laughing at me," he suddenly turned anxiously and irritably to Evgeny Pavlovich; the latter was indeed laughing.

"I merely want to ask you, Mr. . . . Ippolit . . . sorry, I've forgotten your last name."

"Mr. Terentyev," said the prince.

"Yes, Terentyev, thank you, Prince, it was mentioned earlier, but it slipped my mind . . . I wanted to ask you, Mr. Terentyev, is it true what I've heard, that you are of the opinion that you need only talk to the people through the window for a quarter of an hour, and they will at once agree with you in everything and follow you at once?"

"I may very well have said it . . ." Ippolit replied, as if trying to recall something. "Certainly I said it!" he suddenly added, becoming animated again and looking firmly at Evgeny Pavlovich. "And what of it?"

"Precisely nothing; merely for my own information, to add it all up."

Evgeny Pavlovich fell silent, but Ippolit went on looking at him in impatient expectation.

"Well, are you finished, or what?" Lizaveta Prokofyevna turned to Evgeny Pavlovich. "Finish quickly, dear boy, it's time he went to bed. Or don't you know how?" (She was terribly vexed.)

"I wouldn't mind adding," Evgeny Pavlovich went on with a smile, "that everything I've heard from your comrades, Mr. Terentyev, and everything you've just explained, and with such unquestionable talent, boils down, in my opinion, to the theory of the triumph of rights, before all, and beyond all, and even to the exclusion of all else, and perhaps even before analyzing what makes up these rights. Perhaps I'm mistaken?"

"Of course you're mistaken, and I don't even understand you . . . go on."

There was also a murmur in the corner. Lebedev's nephew muttered something in a half-whisper.

"There's not much more," Evgeny Pavlovich went on. "I merely wanted to observe that from this case it's possible to jump over directly to the right of force, that is, to the right of the singular fist and personal wanting, as, incidentally, has happened very often in this world. Proudhon stopped at the right of force.[41] In the American war, many of the most progressive liberals declared themselves on the side of the plantation owners, in this sense, that Negroes are Negroes, inferior to the white race, and consequently the right of force belongs to the whites . . ."

"Well?"

"So you don't deny the right of force?"

"Go on."

"You're consistent, then. I only wanted to observe that from the right of force to the right of tigers and crocodiles and even to Danilov and Gorsky is not a long step."

"I don't know; go on."

Ippolit was barely listening to Evgeny Pavlovich, and even if he said "well" and "go on" to him, it seemed to be more from an old, adopted habit of conversation, and not out of attention and curiosity.

"There's nothing more . . . that's all."

"Incidentally, I'm not angry with you," Ippolit suddenly concluded quite unexpectedly and, hardly with full consciousness, held out his hand, even with a smile. Evgeny Pavlovich was surprised at first, but touched the hand held out to him with a most serious air, as though receiving forgiveness.

"I cannot help adding," he said in the same ambiguously respectful tone, "my gratitude to you for the attention with which you have allowed me to speak, because it has been my oft-repeated observation that our liberal has never yet been able to allow anyone to have his own convictions and not reply at once to his opponent with abuse or even worse . . ."

"That is perfectly right," General Ivan Fyodorovich observed and, putting his hands behind his back, with a most bored air retreated to the door of the terrace, where he proceeded to yawn with vexation.

"Well, enough for you, dear boy," Lizaveta Prokofyevna suddenly announced to Evgeny Pavlovich, "I'm tired of you . . ."

"It's time," Ippolit suddenly stood up with a preoccupied and all but frightened look, gazing around in perplexity, "I've kept you; I wanted to tell you . . . I thought that everyone . . . for the last time . . . it was a fantasy . . ."

One could see that he would become animated in bursts, suddenly coming out of what was almost real delirium for a few moments, and with full consciousness would suddenly remember and speak, mostly in fragments, perhaps thought up and memorized much earlier, in the long, boring hours of illness, in bed, alone, sleepless.

"So, farewell!" he suddenly said sharply. "Do you think it's easy for me to say farewell to you? Ha, ha!" he smiled vexedly at his own *awkward* question and suddenly, as if angry that he kept failing to say what he wanted, declared loudly and irritably: "Your Excellency! I have the honor of inviting you to my funeral, if you will vouchsafe me such an honor, and . . . all of you, ladies and gentlemen, along with the general! . . ."

He laughed again; but this was now the laughter of a madman. Lizaveta Prokofyevna fearfully moved towards him and grasped his arm. He gazed at her intently, with the same laughter, though it no longer went on but seemed to have stopped and frozen on his face.

"Do you know that I came here in order to see trees? Those . . ." (he pointed to the trees in the park), "that's not funny, eh? There's nothing funny in it, is there?" he asked Lizaveta Prokofyevna seriously, and suddenly fell to thinking; then, after a moment, he raised his head and began curiously searching through the crowd with his eyes. He was looking for Evgeny Pavlovich, who was standing very near, to the right, in the same spot as before, but he had already forgotten and searched all around. "Ah, you haven't left!" he finally found him. "You laughed at me earlier, that I wanted to talk through the window for a quarter of an hour . . . But do you know that I'm not eighteen years old: I've spent so long lying on that pillow, and spent so long looking out of that window, and thought so much . . . about everybody . . . that . . . A dead man has no age, you know. I thought of that last week, when I woke up in the night . . . But do you know what you're most afraid of? You're most afraid of our sincerity, though you despise us! I thought of that at the same time, at night, on my pillow . . . Do you think I meant to laugh at you earlier, Lizaveta Prokofyevna? No, I wasn't laughing at you, I only meant to praise you . . . Kolya told me that the prince called you a child . . . that's good . . . So, what was I . . . there was something else I wanted . . ."

He covered his face with his hands and fell to thinking.

"It was this: as you were taking your leave earlier, I suddenly thought: here are these people, and they'll never be there anymore, never! And no trees either—there'll just be the brick wall, red brick, of Meyer's house . . . across from my window . . . well, go and tell them about all that . . . try telling them; here's a beautiful girl . . . but you're dead, introduce yourself as a dead man, tell her 'a dead man can say everything' . . . and that Princess Marya Alexeevna won't scold you,[42] ha, ha! . . . You're not laughing?" he looked around mistrustfully. "And you know, a lot of thoughts occurred to me on that pillow . . . you know, I became convinced that nature is very much given to mockery . . . You said earlier that I was an atheist, but you know, this nature . . . Why are you laughing again? You're terribly cruel!" he suddenly said with rueful indignation, looking them all over. "I haven't corrupted Kolya," he ended in a completely different tone, serious and assured, as if also suddenly remembering.

"Nobody, nobody here is laughing at you, calm down!" Lizaveta Prokofyevna was almost suffering. "Tomorrow a new doctor will come; the other one was wrong; and sit down, you can hardly stand on your feet! You're delirious . . . Ah, what's to be done with him now!" she bustled about, sitting him in an armchair. A small tear glistened on her cheek.

Ippolit stopped almost dumbstruck, raised his hand, reached out timidly, and touched that little tear. He smiled a sort of childlike smile.

"I . . . you . . ." he began joyfully, "you don't know how I . . . he always spoke of you with such rapture, him, Kolya . . . I love his rapture. I haven't corrupted him! I have only him to leave . . . I wanted to have them all, all of them—but there was no one, no one . . . I wanted to be an activist, I had the right . . . Oh, there was so much I wanted! Now I don't want anything, I don't want to want anything, I gave myself my word on it, that I would no longer want anything; let them, let them seek the truth without me! Yes, nature is given to mockery! Why does she," he suddenly continued ardently, "why does she create the best beings only so as to mock them afterwards? Didn't she make it so that the single being on earth who has been acknowledged as perfect[43] . . . didn't she make it so that, having shown him to people, she destined him to say things that have caused so much blood to be shed, that if it had been shed all at once, people would probably have drowned in it! Oh, it's good that I'm dying! I, too, might utter some terrible lie, nature would arrange it that way! . . . I haven't corrupted anybody . . . I wanted to live for the happiness of all people, for the discovery and proclaiming of the truth! . . . I looked through my window at Meyer's wall and thought I could talk for only a quarter of an hour and everybody, everybody would be convinced, and for once in my life I got together . . . with you, if not with the people! And what came of it? Nothing! It turned out that you despise me! Therefore I'm not needed, therefore I'm a fool, therefore it's time to go! Without managing to leave any memory! Not a sound, not a trace, not a single deed, not spreading any conviction! . . . Don't laugh at the stupid man! Forget! Forget everything . . . please forget, don't be so cruel! Do you know, if this consumption hadn't turned up, I'd have killed myself . . ."

It seemed he wanted to say more, but he did not finish, dropped into his chair, covered his face with his hands, and wept like a little child.

"Well, what would you have me do with him now?" Lizaveta Prokofyevna exclaimed, jumped over to him, seized his head, and pressed it tightly to her bosom. He was sobbing convulsively. "There, there, there! Don't cry! There, there, enough, you're a good boy, God will forgive you in your ignorance; there, enough, be brave . . . And besides, you'll be ashamed . . ."

"At home," Ippolit said, trying to raise his head, "at home I have a brother and sisters, children, little, poor, innocent . . . *She* will corrupt them! You—you're a saint, you're . . . a child yourself—save them! Tear them away from that . . . she . . . shame . . . Oh, help them, help them, God will reward you for it a hundredfold, for God's sake, for Christ's sake! . . ."

"Speak finally, Ivan Fyodorovich, what's to be done now!" Lizaveta Prokofyevna cried irritably. "Kindly break your majestic silence! If you don't decide anything, be it known to you that I myself will stay and spend the night here; you've tyrannized me enough under your autocracy!"

Lizaveta Prokofyevna asked with enthusiasm and wrath, and expected an immediate answer. But in such cases, those present, even if there are many of them, most often respond with silence, with passive curiosity, unwilling to take anything on themselves, and express their thoughts long afterwards. Among those present this time there were some who were prepared to sit even till morning without saying a word, for instance, Varvara Ardalionovna, who sat a little apart all evening, silent and listening all the while with extreme curiosity, and who may have had her own reasons for doing so.

"My opinion, dear," the general spoke out, "is that what's needed here is, so to speak, sooner a sick-nurse than our agitation, and probably a reliable, sober person for the night. In any case, we must ask the prince and . . . immediately give him rest. And tomorrow we can concern ourselves again."

"It's now twelve o'clock, and we're leaving. Does he come with us or stay with you?" Doktorenko addressed the prince irritably and angrily.

"If you want, you may also stay with him," said the prince, "there will be room enough."

"Your Excellency," Mr. Keller unexpectedly and rapturously

jumped over to the general, "if there's need of a satisfactory person for the night, I'm prepared to make the sacrifice for a friend . . . he's such a soul! I've long considered him a great man, Your Excellency! I, of course, have neglected my education, but when he criticizes, it's pearls, pearls pouring out, Your Excellency! . . ."

The general turned away in despair.

"I'll be very glad if he stays, of course, it's hard for him to go," the prince said in reply to Lizaveta Prokofyevna's irritable questions.

"Are you asleep, or what? If you don't want to, dear boy, I'll have him transported to my place! Lord, he can barely stand up himself! Are you sick, or what?"

Earlier, not finding the prince on his deathbed, Lizaveta Prokofyevna had indeed greatly exaggerated the satisfactoriness of his state of health, judging it by appearances, but the recent illness, the painful memories that accompanied it, the fatigue of the eventful evening, the incident with "Pavlishchev's son," the present incident with Ippolit—all this irritated the prince's morbid impressionability indeed almost to a feverish state. But, besides that, in his eyes there was now some other worry, even fear; he looked at Ippolit warily, as if expecting something more from him.

Suddenly Ippolit stood up, terribly pale and with a look of dreadful, despairing shame on his distorted face. It was expressed mainly in the glance that he shot hatefully and timorously at the gathering, and in the lost, crooked, and creeping grin on his twitching lips. He lowered his eyes at once and trudged, swaying and still smiling in the same way, towards Burdovsky and Doktorenko, who stood by the terrace door: he was leaving with them.

"Well, that's what I was afraid of!" exclaimed the prince. "It had to be so!"

Ippolit quickly turned to him with the most furious spite, and every little line of his face seemed to quiver and speak.

"Ah, you were afraid of that! 'It had to be so,' in your opinion? Know, then, that if I hate anyone here," he screamed, wheezing, shrieking, spraying from his mouth, "and I hate all of you, all of you!—but you, you Jesuitical, treacly little soul, idiot, millionaire-benefactor, I hate you more than anyone or anything in the world! I understood you and hated you long ago, when I'd only heard about you, I hated you with all the hatred of my soul . . . It was you who set it all up! It was you who drove me into a fit! You've driven a dying man to shame, you, you, you are to blame for my mean faintheartedness! I'd kill you, if I stayed alive! I don't need your benefactions, I won't accept anything from anybody, do you hear, from anybody! I was delirious, and don't you dare to triumph! . . . I curse you all now and forever!"

By then he was completely out of breath.

"Ashamed of his tears!" Lebedev whispered to Lizaveta Prokofyevna. "'It had to be so!' That's the prince for you! Read right through him . . ."

But Lizaveta Prokofyevna did not deign to look at him. She stood proud, erect, her head thrown back, and scrutinized "these wretched little people" with scornful curiosity. When Ippolit finished, the general heaved his shoulders; she looked him up and down wrathfully, as if demanding an account of his movement, and at once turned to the prince.

"Thank you, Prince, eccentric friend of our house, for the pleasant evening you have provided for us all. Your heart must surely be glad of your success in hitching us to your foolery . . . Enough, dear friend of our house, thank you for at least allowing us finally to have a look at you! . . ."

She indignantly began straightening her mantilla, waiting until "they" left. At that moment a hired droshky, which Doktorenko had sent Lebedev's son, a high-school student, to fetch a quarter of an hour ago, drove up for "them." Right after his wife, the general put in his own little word:

"Indeed, Prince, I never expected . . . after everything, after all our friendly connections . . . and, finally, Lizaveta Prokofyevna . . ."

"But how, how can this be!" exclaimed Adelaida, and she quickly went up to the prince and gave him her hand.

The prince, looking like a lost man, smiled at her. Suddenly a hot, quick whisper seemed to scald his ear.

"If you don't drop these loathsome people at once, I'll hate you alone all my life, all my life!" whispered Aglaya; she was as if in a frenzy, but she turned away before the prince had time to look at her. However, there was nothing and no one for him to drop: they had meanwhile managed to put the sick Ippolit into the cab, and it drove off.

"Well, is this going to go on long, Ivan Fyodorovich? What do you think? How long am I to suffer from these wicked boys?"

"I, my dear . . . naturally, I'm prepared . . . and the prince . . ."

Ivan Fyodorovich nevertheless held out his hand to the prince, but had no time for a handshake and rushed after Lizaveta

Prokofyevna, who was noisily and wrathfully going down the steps from the terrace. Adelaida, her fiancé, and Alexandra took leave of the prince sincerely and affectionately. Evgeny Pavlovich was also among them, and he alone was merry.

"It turned out as I thought! Only it's too bad that you, too, suffered, poor man," he whispered with the sweetest smile.

Aglaya left without saying good-bye.

But the adventures of that evening were not over yet. Lizaveta Prokofyevna was to endure one more quite unexpected meeting.

Before she had time to go down the steps to the road (which skirted the park), a splendid equipage, a carriage drawn by two white horses, raced past the prince's dacha. Two magnificent ladies were sitting in the carriage. But before it had gone ten paces past, the carriage stopped abruptly; one of the ladies quickly turned, as if she had suddenly seen some needed acquaintance.

"Evgeny Pavlych! Is that you, dear?" a ringing, beautiful voice suddenly cried, which made the prince, and perhaps someone else, give a start. "Well, I'm so glad I've finally found you! I sent a messenger to you in town—two messengers! I've been looking for you all day!"

Evgeny Pavlovich stood on the steps as if thunderstruck. Lizaveta Prokofyevna also stopped in her tracks, but not in horror or petrified like Evgeny Pavlovich: she looked at the brazen woman with the same pride and cold contempt as at the "wretched little people" five minutes earlier, and at once shifted her intent gaze to Evgeny Pavlovich.

"News!" the ringing voice went on. "Don't worry about Kupfer's promissory notes; Rogozhin bought them up at thirty, I persuaded him. You can be at peace for at least another three months. And we'll probably come to terms with Biskup and all that riffraff in a friendly way! Well, so there, it means everything's all right! Cheer up. See you tomorrow!"

The carriage started off and soon vanished.

"She's crazy!" Evgeny Pavlovich cried at last, turning red with indignation and looking around in perplexity. "I have no idea what she's talking about! What promissory notes? Who is she?"

Lizaveta Prokofyevna went on looking at him for another two seconds; finally, she turned quickly and sharply to go to her own dacha, and the rest followed her. Exactly a minute later Evgeny Pavlovich went back to the prince's terrace in extreme agitation.

"Prince, you truly don't know what this means?"

"I don't know anything," replied the prince, who was under extreme and morbid strain himself.

"No?"

"No."

"I don't either," Evgeny Pavlovich suddenly laughed. "By God, I've had nothing to do with these promissory notes, believe my word of honor! . . . What's the matter, are you feeling faint?"

"Oh, no, no, I assure you . . ."

XI

ONLY THREE DAYS later were the Epanchins fully propitiated. Though the prince blamed himself for many things, as usual, and sincerely expected to be punished, all the same he had at first a full inner conviction that Lizaveta Prokofyevna could not seriously be angry with him, but was more angry with herself. Thus it was that such a long period of enmity brought him by the third day to the gloomiest impasse. Other circumstances also brought him there, but one among them was predominant. For all three days it had been growing progressively in the prince's suspiciousness (and lately the prince had been blaming himself for the two extremes: his uncommonly "senseless and importunate" gullibility and at the same time his "dark and mean" suspiciousness). In short, by the end of the third day the adventure with the eccentric lady who had talked to Evgeny Pavlovich from her carriage had taken on terrifying and mysterious proportions in his mind. The essence of the mystery, apart from the other aspects of the matter, consisted for the prince in one grievous question: was it precisely he who was to blame for this new "monstrosity," or only . . . But he never finished who else. As for the letters N.F.B., that was, in his view, nothing but an innocent prank, even a most childish prank, so that it was shameful to reflect on it at all and in one respect even almost dishonest.

However, on the very first day after the outrageous "evening," of the disorder of which he had been so chiefly the "cause," the prince had the pleasure, in the morning, of receiving Prince Shch. and Adelaida: "they came, *chiefly*, to inquire after his health," came together, during a stroll. Adelaida had just noticed a tree in the park, a wonderful old tree, branchy, with long, crooked boughs, all in young green, with a hole and a split in it; she had decided that she had, she simply had to paint it! So that she talked of almost nothing else for the entire half hour of her visit. Prince Shch. was amiable and nice, as usual, asked the prince about former times, recalled the circumstances of their first acquaintance, so that almost nothing was said about the day before. Finally Adelaida could not stand it and, smiling, confessed that they had come incognito; with that, however, the confessions ended, though this incognito made one think that the parents, that is, mainly Lizaveta Prokofyevna, were somehow especially ill-disposed. But Adelaida and Prince Shch. did not utter a single word either about her, or about Aglaya, or even about Ivan Fyodorovich during their visit. They left for a walk again, but did not invite the prince to join them. Of an invitation to call on them there was not so much as a hint; in that regard Adelaida even let slip a very characteristic little phrase: speaking of one of her watercolors, she suddenly wanted very much to show it to him. "How shall we do it the sooner? Wait! I'll either send it to you today with Kolya, if he comes, or bring it over myself tomorrow, when the prince and I go for a walk again," she finally concluded her perplexity, happy to have succeeded in resolving the problem so adroitly and conveniently for everyone.

Finally, on the point of taking his leave, Prince Shch. seemed suddenly to remember:

"Ah, yes," he asked, "might you at least know, dear Lev Nikolaevich, who that person was who shouted to Evgeny Pavlych from her carriage yesterday?"

"It was Nastasya Filippovna," said the prince, "haven't you learned yet that it was she? But I don't know who was with her."

"I know, I've heard!" Prince Shch. picked up. "But what did the shout mean? I confess, it's such a riddle . . . for me and others."

Prince Shch. spoke with extraordinary and obvious amazement.

"She spoke about some promissory notes of Evgeny Pavlych's," the prince replied very simply, "which came to Rogozhin from some moneylender, at her request, and for which Rogozhin will allow Evgeny Pavlych to wait."

"I heard, I heard, my dear Prince, but that simply cannot be! Evgeny Pavlych could not have any promissory notes here. With his fortune . . . True, there were occasions before, owing to his flightiness, and I even used to help him out . . . But with his fortune, to give promissory notes to a moneylender and then worry about them is impossible. And he can't be on such friendly and familiar terms with Nastasya Filippovna—that's the chief puzzle. He swears he doesn't understand anything, and I fully believe him. But the thing is, dear Prince, that I wanted to ask you: do you know anything? That is, has any rumor reached you by some miracle?"

"No, I don't know anything, and I assure you that I took no part in it."

"Ah, Prince, what's become of you! I simply wouldn't know you today. How could I suppose that you took part in such an affair? . . . Well, you're upset today."

He embraced and kissed him.

"That is, took part in what 'such' an affair? I don't see any 'such' an affair."

"Undoubtedly this person wished somehow to hinder Evgeny Pavlych in something, endowing him, in the eyes of witnesses, with qualities he does not and could not have," Prince Shch. replied rather drily.

Prince Lev Nikolaevich was embarrassed, but nevertheless went on looking intently and inquiringly at the prince: but the latter fell silent.

"And not simply promissory notes? Not literally as it happened yesterday?" the prince finally murmured in some impatience.

"But I'm telling you, judge for yourself, what can there be in common between Evgeny Pavlych and . . . her, and with Rogozhin on top of it? I repeat to you, his fortune is enormous, that I know perfectly well; there's another fortune expected from his uncle. Nastasya Filippovna simply . . ."

Prince Shch. suddenly fell silent, evidently because he did not want to go on telling the prince about Nastasya Filippovna.

"It means, in any case, that he's acquainted with her?" Prince Lev Nikolaevich suddenly asked, after a moment's silence.

"It seems so—a flighty fellow! However, if so, it was very long ago, still before, that is, two or three years ago. He used to know Totsky, too. But now there could be nothing of the sort, and they could never be on familiar terms! You know yourself that she hasn't been here; she hasn't been anywhere here. Many people don't know that she's appeared again. I noticed her carriage only three days ago, no more."

"A magnificent carriage!" said Adelaida.

"Yes, the carriage is magnificent."

They both went away, however, in the most friendly, the

most, one might say, brotherly disposition towards Prince Lev Nikolaevich.

But for our hero this visit contained in itself something even capital. We may assume that he himself had suspected a great deal since the previous night (and perhaps even earlier), but till their visit he had not dared to think his apprehensions fully borne out. Now, though, it was becoming clear: Prince Shch. had, of course, interpreted the event wrongly, but still he had wandered around the truth, he had understood that this was an *intrigue*. ("Incidentally, he may understand it quite correctly in himself," thought the prince, "only he doesn't want to say it and therefore deliberately interprets it wrongly.") The clearest thing of all was that people were now visiting him (namely, Prince Shch.) in hopes of some explanation; and if so, then they thought he was a direct participant in the intrigue. Besides that, if it was all indeed so important, then it meant that *she* had some terrible goal, but what was this goal? Terrible! "And how can *she* be stopped? It's absolutely impossible to stop *her* if she's sure of her goal!" That the prince already knew from experience. "A madwoman. A madwoman."

But there were far, far too many other insoluble circumstances that had come together that morning, all at the same time, and all demanding immediate resolution, so that the prince felt very sad. He was slightly distracted by Vera Lebedev, who came with Lyubochka and, laughing, spent a long time telling him something. She was followed by her sister, the one who kept opening her mouth wide, then by the high-school boy, Lebedev's son, who assured him that the "star Wormwood" in the Apocalypse, which fell to earth on the fountains of water,[44] was, in his father's interpretation, the railway network spread across Europe. The prince did not believe that Lebedev interpreted it that way, and they decided to check it with him at the first opportunity. From Vera Lebedev the prince learned that Keller had migrated over to them the day before and, by all tokens, would not be leaving for a long time, because he had found the company of and made friends with General Ivolgin; however, he declared that he was staying with them solely in order to complete his education. The prince was beginning to like Lebedev's children more and more every day. Kolya was away the whole day: he left for Petersburg very early. (Lebedev also left at daybreak on some little business of his own.) But the prince was waiting impatiently for a visit from Gavrila Ardalionovich, who was bound to call on him that same day.

He arrived past six in the evening, just after dinner. With the first glance at him, it occurred to the prince that this gentleman at least must unmistakably know all the innermost secrets—and how could he not, having such helpers as Varvara Ardalionovna and her husband? But the prince's relations with Ganya were somehow special. The prince, for instance, had entrusted him with the handling of the Burdovsky affair and had asked him especially to do it; but, despite this trust and some things that had gone before, there always remained between them certain points on which it was as if they had mutually decided to say nothing. It sometimes seemed to the prince that Ganya, for his part, might be wishing for the fullest and friendliest sincerity; now, for instance, as soon as he came in, it immediately seemed to the prince that Ganya was convinced in the highest degree that the time had come to break the ice between them on all points. (Gavrila Ardalionovich was in a hurry, however; his sister was waiting for him at Lebedev's; the two were hastening about some business.)

But if Ganya was indeed expecting a whole series of impatient questions, inadvertent communications, friendly outpourings, then, of course, he was very much mistaken. For all the twenty minutes of his visit, the prince was even very pensive, almost absentminded. The expected questions or, better to say, the one main question that Ganya expected, could not be asked. Then Ganya, too, decided to speak with great restraint. He spent all twenty minutes talking without pause, laughing, indulging in the most light, charming, and rapid babble, but never touching on the main thing.

Ganya told him, incidentally, that Nastasya Filippovna had been there in Pavlovsk for only four days and was already attracting general attention. She was living somewhere, in some Matrosskaya Street, in a gawky little house, with Darya Alexeevna, but her carriage was just about the best in Pavlovsk. Around her a whole crowd of old and young suitors had already gathered; her carriage was sometimes accompanied by men on horseback. Nastasya Filippovna, as before, was very discriminating, admitting only choice people to her company. But all the same a whole troop had formed around her, to stand for her in case of need. One previously engaged man from among the summer people had already quarreled with his fiancée over her; one little old general had almost cursed his son. She often took with her on her rides a lovely girl, just turned sixteen, a distant relation of Darya Alexeevna's; the girl was a good singer—so that in the evenings their little house attracted attention. Nastasya Filippovna, however, behaved extremely properly, dressed not magnificently but with extraordinary taste, and all the ladies envied "her taste, her beauty, and her carriage."

"Yesterday's eccentric incident," Ganya allowed, "was, of course, premeditated and, of course, should not count. To find any sort of fault with her, one would have to hunt for it on purpose or else use slander, which, however, would not be slow in coming," Ganya concluded, expecting that here the prince would not fail to ask: "Why did he call yesterday's incident a premeditated incident? And why would it not be slow in coming?" But the prince did not ask.

About Evgeny Pavlovich, Ganya again expatiated on his own, without being specially asked, which was very strange, because he inserted him into the conversation with no real pretext. In Gavrila Ardalionovich's view, Evgeny Pavlovich had not known Nastasya Filippovna, and now also knew her only a little, and that because he had been introduced to her some four days ago during a promenade, and it was unlikely that he had been to her house even once along with the others. As for the promissory notes, that was also possible (Ganya even knew it for certain); Evgeny Pavlovich's fortune was big, of course, but "certain affairs to do with the estate were indeed in a certain disorder." On this curious matter Ganya suddenly broke off. About Nastasya Filippovna's escapade yesterday he did not say a single word, beyond what he had said earlier in passing. Varvara Ardalionovna finally came to fetch Ganya, stayed for a moment, announced (also unasked) that Evgeny Pavlovich would be in Petersburg today and maybe tomorrow, that her husband (Ivan Petrovich Ptitsyn) was also in Petersburg, and almost on Evgeny Pavlovich's business as well, because something had actually happened there. As she was leaving, she added that Lizaveta Prokofyevna was in an infernal mood today, but the strangest thing was that Aglaya had quarreled with the whole family, not only with her father and mother but even with both sisters, and "that it was not nice at all." Having imparted as if in passing this last bit of news (extremely meaningful for the prince), the brother and sister left. Ganechka also did not mention a word about the affair of "Pavlishchev's son," perhaps out of false modesty, perhaps "sparing the prince's feelings," but all the same the prince thanked him again for having diligently concluded the affair.

The prince was very glad to be left alone at last; he went down from the terrace, crossed the road, and entered the park; he wanted to think over and decide about a certain step. Yet this "step" was not one of those that can be thought over, but one of those that precisely cannot be thought over, but simply resolved upon: he suddenly wanted terribly to leave all this here and go back where he came from, to some far-off, forsaken place, to go at once and even without saying good-bye to anyone. He had the feeling that if he remained here just a few more days, he would certainly be drawn into this world irretrievably, and this world would henceforth be his lot. But he did not even reason for ten minutes and decided at once that to flee was "impossible," that it would be almost pusillanimous, that such tasks stood before him that he now did not even have any right not to resolve them, or at least not to give all his strength to their resolution. In such thoughts he returned home after barely a quarter of an hour's walk. He was utterly unhappy at that moment.

Lebedev was still not at home, so that towards nightfall Keller managed to barge in on the prince, not drunk, but full of outpourings and confessions. He declared straight out that he had come to tell the prince his whole life's story and that he had stayed in Pavlovsk just for that. There was not the slightest possibility of turning him out: he would not have gone for anything. Keller was prepared to talk very long and very incoherently, but suddenly at almost the first word he jumped ahead to the conclusion and declared that he had lost "any ghost of morality" ("solely out of disbelief in the Almighty"), so much so that he even stole. "If you can imagine that!"

"Listen, Keller, in your place I'd rather not confess it without some special need," the prince began, "and anyhow, maybe you're slandering yourself on purpose?"

"To you, solely to you alone, and solely so as to help my own development! Not to anybody else; I'll die and carry my secret off under the shroud! But, Prince, if you only knew, if you only knew how difficult it is to get money in our age! Where is a man to get it, allow me to ask after that? One answer: bring gold and diamonds, and we'll give you money for them—that is, precisely what I haven't got, can you imagine that? I finally got angry and just stood there. 'And for emeralds?' I say. 'For emeralds, too,' he says. 'Well, that's splendid,' I say, put on my hat, and walk out; devil take you, scoundrels! By God!"

"But did you really have emeralds?"

"What kind of emeralds could I have! Oh, Prince, your view of life is still so bright and innocent, and even, one might say, pastoral!"

The prince finally began to feel not so much sorry as a bit ashamed. The thought even flashed in him: "Wouldn't it be possible to make something of this man under someone's good influence?" His own influence, for certain reasons, he considered quite unsuitable—not out of self-belittlement, but owing to a certain special view of things. They gradually warmed to the conversation, so much so that they did not want to part. Keller confessed with extraordinary readiness to having done such things that it was impossible to imagine how one could tell about them. Starting out each time, he would positively insist that he was repentant and inwardly "filled with tears," and yet he would tell of his action as if he were proud of it, and at the same time occasionally in such a funny way that he and the prince would end up laughing like crazy.

"Above all, there is some childlike trustfulness and extraordinary honesty in you," the prince said at last. "You know, that by itself already redeems you greatly."

"I'm noble, noble, chivalrously noble!" Keller agreed with feeling. "But you know, Prince, it's all only in dreams and, so to speak, for bravado, and in reality nothing ever comes of it! Why is that? I can't understand it."

"Don't despair. Now it can be said affirmatively that you have told me all your inmost truths; at least it seems to me that it's now impossible to add anything more to what you've already said, isn't it?"

"Impossible?!" Keller exclaimed somehow ruefully. "Oh, Prince, you still have such a, so to speak, Swiss understanding of man."

"Could you possibly add to it?" the prince uttered in timid astonishment. "So what did you expect from me, Keller, tell me please, and why did you come with your confession?"

"From you? What did I expect? First, your simple-heartedness alone is pleasant to look at; it's pleasant to sit and talk with you; I know that I at least have a virtuous man before me, and second . . . second . . ."

He faltered.

"Perhaps you wanted to borrow some money?" the prince prompted him very seriously and simply, even as if somewhat timidly.

Keller jumped; he glanced quickly, with the same surprise, straight into the prince's eyes and banged his fist hard on the table.

"Well, see how you throw a man into a final flummox! For pity's sake, Prince: first such simple-heartedness, such innocence as even the golden age never heard of, then suddenly at the same time you pierce a man through like an arrow with this deepest psychology of observation. But excuse me, Prince, this calls for an explanation, because I . . . I'm simply confounded! Naturally, in the final end my aim was to borrow money, but you asked me about money as if you don't find anything reprehensible in it, as if that's how it should be?"

"Yes . . . from you that's how it should be."

"And you're not indignant?"

"But . . . at what?"

"Listen, Prince, I stayed here last night, first, out of particular respect for the French archbishop Bourdaloue[45] (we kept the corks popping at Lebedev's till three in the morning), but second, and chiefly (I'll cross myself with all crosses that I'm telling the real truth!), I stayed because I wanted, so to speak, by imparting to you my full, heartfelt confession, to contribute thereby to my own development; with that thought I fell asleep past three, bathed in tears. Now, if you'll believe the noblest of persons: at the very moment that I was falling asleep, sincerely filled with internal and, so to speak, external tears (because in the end I did weep, I remember that!), an infernal thought came to me: 'And finally, after the confession, why don't I borrow some money from him?' Thus I prepared my confession, so to speak, as a sort of 'finesherbes with tears,' to soften my path with these tears, so that you'd get mellow and count me out a hundred and fifty roubles. Isn't that mean, in your opinion?"

"It's probably also not true, and the one simply coincided with the other. The two thoughts coincided, it happens very often. With me, constantly. I don't think it's nice, however, and, you know, Keller, I reproach myself most of all for it. It's as if you had told me about myself just now. I've even happened to think sometimes," the prince went on very seriously, being genuinely and deeply interested, "that all people are like that, so that I even began to approve of myself, because it's very hard to resist these *double* thoughts; I've experienced it. God knows how they come and get conceived. But here you've called it outright meanness! Now I'll begin to fear these thoughts again. In any case, I'm not your judge. But all the same, in my opinion, that can't be called outright meanness, don't you think? You used cunning in order to wheedle

money out of me by means of tears, but you swear yourself that
your confession had another, noble purpose, not only money. As
for the money, you need it to go carousing, right? After such a
confession, that is, naturally, pusillanimous. But how, also, is one
to give up carousing in a single moment? It's impossible. What
then is to be done? Best of all is to leave it to your own conscience,
don't you think?"

The prince looked at Keller with extreme curiosity. The question
of double thoughts had evidently occupied him for a long time.

"Well, why they call you an idiot after that, I don't understand!"
exclaimed Keller.

The prince blushed slightly.

"The preacher Bourdaloue wouldn't have spared a man, but you
spared a man and reasoned about me in a human way! To punish
myself and show that I'm touched, I don't want a hundred and
fifty roubles, give me just twenty-five roubles, and enough! That's
all I need for at least two weeks. I won't come for money before
two weeks from now. I wanted to give Agashka a treat, but she
doesn't deserve it. Oh, dear Prince, God bless you!"

Lebedev came in at last, having only just returned, and, noticing
the twenty-five-rouble note in Keller's hand, he winced. But Keller,
finding himself in possession of the money, hurried off and effaced
himself immediately. Lebedev at once began talking him down.

"You're unfair, he was actually sincerely repentant," the prince
observed at last.

"What good is his repentance! Exactly like me yesterday: 'mean,
mean,' but it's all just words, sir!"

"So with you it was just words? And I thought . . ."

"Well, to you, to you alone I'll tell the truth, because you can
see through a man: words, deeds, lies, truth—they're all there
together in me and completely sincere. The truth and deeds in me
are made up of sincere repentance, believe it or not, I'll swear to
it, but the words and lies are made up of an infernal (and ever-
present) notion, of somehow snaring a man here, too, of somehow
profiting even from tears of repentance! By God, it's so! I wouldn't
have told any other man—he'd laugh or spit; but you, Prince, you
reason in a human way."

"There, now, that's exactly what he just said to me," cried the
prince, "and it's as if you're both boasting! You even surprise me,
only he's more sincere than you are, with you it's turned into a
decided profession. Well, enough, don't wince, Lebedev, and don't

put your hands to your heart. Haven't you got something to tell me? You never come for nothing . . ."

Lebedev began grimacing and squirming.

"I've been waiting for you all day so as to ask you a single question; at least once in your life tell me the truth straight off: did you participate to any extent in that carriage yesterday or not?"

Lebedev again began grimacing, tittering, rubbing his hands, and finally went into a sneezing fit, but still could not bring himself to say anything.

"I see you did."

"But indirectly, only indirectly! It's the real truth I'm telling! I participated only by sending a timely message to a certain person, that such-and-such a company had gathered at my place and that certain persons were present."

"I know you sent your son *there*, he told me himself earlier, but what sort of intrigue is this!" the prince exclaimed in impatience.

"It's not my intrigue, not mine," Lebedev waved his hands, "others, others are in it, and it's sooner, so to speak, a fantasy than an intrigue."

"What is it about, explain to me, for Christ's sake? Don't you see that it concerns me directly? Evgeny Pavlych was blackened here."

"Prince! Illustrious Prince!" Lebedev squirmed again. "You don't let me speak the whole truth; I've already tried to tell you the truth; more than once; you wouldn't let me go on . . ."

The prince paused and pondered.

"Well, all right, speak the truth," he said heavily, obviously after a great struggle.

"Aglaya Ivanovna . . ." Lebedev began at once.

"Shut up, shut up!" the prince shouted furiously, turning all red with indignation and perhaps with shame. "It can't be, it's all nonsense! You thought it all up yourself, or some madmen like you. I never want to hear any more of it from you!"

Late at night, past ten o'clock, Kolya arrived with a whole bagful of news. His news was of a double sort: from Petersburg and from Pavlovsk. He quickly told the main Petersburg news (mostly about Ippolit and yesterday's story), in order to return to it later, and hastened on to the Pavlovsk news. Three hours ago he came back from Petersburg and, without stopping at the prince's, went straight to the Epanchins'. "Terrible goings-on there!" Naturally, the carriage was in the foreground, but something else had certainly happened there, something unknown to him and the prince. "I naturally didn't spy and didn't want to ask questions; however, they received me well, better than I expected, but not a word about you, Prince!" The chiefest and most interesting thing was that Aglaya had quarreled with her family over Ganya. What the details of the matter were, he did not know, only it was over Ganya (imagine that!), and they had quarreled terribly, so it was something important. The general arrived late, arrived scowling, arrived with Evgeny Pavlovich, who was received excellently, and Evgeny Pavlovich himself was surprisingly merry and nice. The most capital news was that Lizaveta Prokofyevna, without any noise, sent for Varvara Ardalionovna, who was sitting with the girls, and threw her out of the house once and for all, in the most courteous way, incidentally—"I heard it from Varya herself." But when Varya left Lizaveta Prokofyevna and said good-bye to the girls, they did not even know that she had been denied the house once and for all and that she was saying good-bye to them for the last time.

"But Varvara Ardalionovna was here at seven o'clock," said the astonished prince.

"And she was thrown out before eight or at eight. I'm very sorry for Varya, sorry for Ganya . . . no doubt it's their eternal intrigues, they can't do without them. And I've never been able to find out what they're planning, and don't want to know. But I assure you, my dear, my kind Prince, that Ganya has a heart. He's a lost man in many respects, of course, but in many respects there are qualities in him that are worth seeking out, and I'll never forgive myself for not understanding him before . . . I don't know if I should go on now, after the story with Varya. True, I took a completely independent and separate stand from the very beginning, but all the same I must think it over."

"You needn't feel too sorry for your brother," the prince observed to him. "If things have come to that, it means that Gavrila Ardalionovich is dangerous in Lizaveta Prokofyevna's eyes, and that means that certain of his hopes are being affirmed."

"How, what hopes?" Kolya cried out in amazement. "You don't think Aglaya . . . it can't be!"

The prince said nothing.

"You're a terrible skeptic, Prince," Kolya added after a couple of minutes. "I've noticed that since a certain time you've become an extreme skeptic; you're beginning not to believe anything and to suppose everything . . . have I used the word 'skeptic' correctly in this case?"

"I think so, though, anyhow, I don't know for certain myself."

"But I myself am renouncing the word 'skeptic,' and have found a new explanation," Kolya suddenly cried. "You're not a skeptic, you're jealous! You're infernally jealous of Ganya over a certain proud girl!"

Having said this, Kolya jumped up and burst into such laughter as he may never have laughed before. Seeing the prince turn all red, Kolya laughed even harder: he was terribly pleased with the thought that the prince was jealous over Aglaya, but he fell silent at once when he noticed that the prince was sincerely upset. After that they spent another hour or hour and a half in serious and preoccupied conversation.

The next day the prince spent the whole morning in Petersburg on a certain urgent matter. Returning to Pavlovsk past four in the afternoon, he met Ivan Fyodorovich at the railway station. The latter quickly seized him by the arm, looked around as if in fright, and drew the prince with him to the first-class car, so that they could ride together. He was burning with the desire to discuss something important.

"First of all, my dear Prince, don't be angry with me, and if there was anything on my part—forget it. I'd have called on you yesterday, but I didn't know how Lizaveta Prokofyevna would . . . At home . . . it's simply hell, a riddling sphinx has settled in with us, and I go about understanding nothing. As for you, I think you're the least to blame, though, of course, much of it came about through you. You see, Prince, to be a philanthropist is nice, but not very. You've probably tasted the fruits of it by now. I, of course, love kindness, and I respect Lizaveta Prokofyevna, but . . ."

The general went on for a long time in this vein, but his words were surprisingly incoherent. It was obvious that he had been shaken and greatly confused by something he found incomprehensible in the extreme.

"For me there's no doubt that you have nothing to do with it," he finally spoke more clearly, "but don't visit us for a while, I ask you as a friend, wait till the wind changes. As regards Evgeny Pavlych," he cried with extraordinary vehemence, "it's all senseless slander, a slander of slanders! It's calumny, there's some intrigue, a wish to destroy everything and make us quarrel. You see, Prince, I'm saying it in your ear: not a word has been said yet between us and Evgeny Pavlych, understand? We're not bound by anything—but that word may be spoken, and even soon, perhaps even very soon! So this was done to harm that! But why, what for—I don't understand! An astonishing woman, an eccentric woman, I'm so afraid of her I can hardly sleep. And what a carriage, white horses, that's chic, that's precisely what the French call chic! Who from? By God, I sinned, I thought the other day it was Evgeny Pavlych. But it turns out that it can't be, and if it can't be, then why does she want to upset things? That's the puzzle! In order to keep Evgeny Pavlych for herself? But I repeat to you, cross my heart, that he's not acquainted with her, and those promissory notes are a fiction! And what impudence to shout 'dear' to him across the street! Sheer conspiracy! It's clear that we must reject it with contempt and double our respect for Evgeny Pavlych. That is what I told Lizaveta Prokofyevna. Now I'll tell you my most intimate thought: I'm stubbornly convinced that she's doing it to take personal revenge on me, remember, for former things, though I was never in any way guilty before her. I blush at the very recollection. Now she has reappeared again, and I thought she had vanished completely. Where's this Rogozhin sitting, pray tell? I thought *she* had long been Mrs. Rogozhin . . ."

In short, the man was greatly bewildered. During the whole nearly hour-long trip he talked alone, asked questions, answered them himself, pressed the prince's hand, and convinced him of at least this one thing, that he had never thought of suspecting him of anything. For the prince that was important. He ended by telling about Evgeny Pavlych's uncle, the head of some office in Petersburg—"a prominent fellow, seventy years old, a *viveur*, a gastronome, and generally a whimsical old codger . . . Ha, ha! I know he heard about Nastasya Filippovna and even sought after her. I called on him yesterday, he didn't receive me, was unwell, but he's rich, rich and important, and . . . God grant him a long life, but all the same Evgeny Pavlych will get everything . . . Yes, yes . . . but even so I'm afraid! I don't know why, but I'm afraid . . . As if something's hovering in the air, trouble flitting about like a bat, and I'm afraid, afraid! . . ."

And finally, only after three days, as we have already written above, came the formal reconciliation of the Epanchins with Prince Lev Nikolaevich.

XII

IT WAS SEVEN O'CLOCK in the evening; the prince was about to go to the park. Suddenly Lizaveta Prokofyevna came to him on the terrace alone.

"*First*, don't you dare think," she began, "that I've come to ask your forgiveness. Nonsense! You're to blame all around."

The prince was silent.

"Are you to blame or not?"

"As much as you are. However, neither I, nor you, neither of us is to blame for anything deliberate. Two days ago I thought I was to blame, but now I've decided that it's not so."

"So that's how you are! Well, all right; listen then and sit down, because I have no intention of standing."

They both sat down.

"*Second*: not a word about those spiteful brats! I'll sit and talk with you for ten minutes; I've come to you with an inquiry (and you thought for God knows what?), and if you utter so much as a single word about those impudent brats, I'll get up and leave, and break with you altogether."

"Very well," replied the prince.

"Kindly allow me to ask you: about two and a half months ago, around Eastertime, did you send Aglaya a letter?"

"Y-yes."

"With what purpose? What was in the letter? Show me the letter!"

Lizaveta Prokofyevna's eyes were burning, she was almost shaking with impatience.

"I don't have the letter," the prince was terribly surprised and grew timid. "If it still exists, Aglaya Ivanovna has it."

"Don't dodge! What did you write about?"

"I'm not dodging, and I'm not afraid of anything. I see no reason why I shouldn't write . . ."

"Quiet! You can talk later. What was in the letter? Why are you blushing?"

The prince reflected.

"I don't know what you're thinking, Lizaveta Prokofyevna. I can only see that you dislike this letter very much. You must agree that I could refuse to answer such a question; but in order to show you that I have no fear of this letter, and do not regret having written it, and am by no means blushing at it" (the prince blushed nearly twice as much as before), "I'll recite the letter for you, because I believe I know it by heart."

Having said this, the prince recited the letter almost word for word as it was written.

"Sheer galimatias! What might this nonsense mean, in your opinion?" Lizaveta Prokofyevna said sharply, listening to the letter with extraordinary attention.

"I don't quite know myself; I know that my feeling was sincere. I had moments of full life there and the greatest hopes."

"What hopes?"

"It's hard to explain, but they were not the hopes you may be thinking of now . . . well, they were hopes for the future and joy that *there* I might not be a stranger, a foreigner. I suddenly liked my native land very much. One sunny morning I took up a pen and wrote a letter to her; why to her—I don't know. Sometimes one wants to have a friend nearby; I, too, evidently wanted to have a friend . . ." the prince added after a pause.

"Are you in love, or what?"

"N-no. I . . . I wrote as to a sister; I signed it as a brother."

"Hm. On purpose. I understand."

"I find it very painful to answer these questions for you, Lizaveta Prokofyevna."

"I know it's painful, but it's none of my affair that you find it painful. Listen, tell me the truth as before God: are you lying to me or not?"

"I'm not lying."

"It's true what you say, that you're not in love?"

"Perfectly true, it seems."

"Ah, you and your 'it seems'! Did that brat deliver it?"

"I asked Nikolai Ardalionovich . . ."

"The brat! The brat!" Lizaveta Prokofyevna interrupted with passion. "I don't know any Nikolai Ardalionovich! The brat!"

"Nikolai Ardalionovich . . ."

"The brat, I tell you!"

"No, not the brat, but Nikolai Ardalionovich," the prince finally answered, firmly though rather quietly.

"Well, all right, my dear, all right! I shall add that to your account."

For a moment she mastered her excitement and rested.

"And what is this 'poor knight'?"

"I have no idea; I wasn't there; it must be some kind of joke."

"Nice to find out all of a sudden! Only is it possible that she could become interested in you? She herself called you a 'little freak' and an 'idiot.'"

"You might have not told me that," the prince observed reproachfully, almost in a whisper.

"Don't be angry. She's a despotic, crazy, spoiled girl—if she falls in love, she'll certainly abuse the man out loud and scoff in his face; I was just the same. Only please don't be triumphant, dear boy, she's not yours; I won't believe it, and it will never be! I tell you so that you can take measures now. Listen, swear to me you're not married to *that one*."

"Lizaveta Prokofyevna, how can you, for pity's sake?" the prince almost jumped up in amazement.

"But you almost married her?"

"I almost did," the prince whispered and hung his head.

"So you're in love with *her*, is that it? You've come for *her* now? For *that one*?"

"I haven't come to get married," replied the prince.

"Is there anything you hold sacred in this world?"

"There is."

"Swear to me that you haven't come to marry *that one*."

"I swear by whatever you like!"

"I believe you. Kiss me. At last I can breathe freely; but know this: Aglaya doesn't love you, take measures, and she won't be your wife as long as I live! Do you hear?"

"I hear."

The prince was blushing so much that he could not even look directly at Lizaveta Prokofyevna.

"Tie a string round your finger, then. I've been waiting for you as for Providence (you weren't worth it!), I drenched my pillow with tears at night—not over you, dear boy, don't worry, I have another grief of my own, eternal and ever the same. But here is why I waited for you so impatiently: I still believe that God himself sent you to me as a friend and a true brother. I have no one around me, except old Princess Belokonsky, and she, too, has flown away, and besides she's grown stupid as a sheep in her old age. Now answer me simply *yes* or *no*: do you know why *she* shouted from her carriage two days ago?"

"On my word of honor, I had no part in it and know nothing!"

"Enough, I believe you. Now I also have different thoughts about it, but still yesterday, in the morning, I blamed Evgeny Pavlych for everything. Yesterday morning and the whole day before. Now, of course, I can't help agreeing with them: it's obvious that he was being laughed at like a fool for some reason, with some purpose, to some end (that in itself is suspicious! and also unseemly!)—but Aglaya won't be his wife, I can tell you that! Maybe he's a good man, but that's how it will be. I hesitated before, but now I've decided for certain: 'First put me in a coffin and bury me in the earth, then marry off my daughter,' that's what I spelled out to Ivan Fyodorovich today. You see that I trust you, don't you?"

"I see and I understand."

Lizaveta Prokofyevna gazed piercingly at the prince; it may be that she wanted very much to know what impression the news about Evgeny Pavlych had made on him.

"Do you know anything about Gavrila Ivolgin?"

"That is . . . I know a lot."

"Do you or do you not know that he is in touch with Aglaya?"

"I had no idea," the prince was surprised and even gave a start. "So you say Gavrila Ardalionovich is in touch with Aglaya Ivanovna? It can't be!"

"Very recently. His sister spent all winter gnawing a path for him, working like a rat."

"I don't believe it," the prince repeated firmly after some reflection and agitation. "If it was so, I would certainly have known."

"No fear he'd come himself and confess it in tears on your breast! Ah, you simpleton, simpleton! Everybody deceives you like . . . like . . . Aren't you ashamed to trust him? Do you really not see that he's duped you all around?"

"I know very well that he occasionally deceives me," the prince said reluctantly in a low voice, "and he knows that I know it . . ." he added and did not finish.

"To know and to trust him! Just what you need! However, with you that's as it should be. And what am I surprised at? Lord! Has there ever been another man like this? Pah! And do you know that this Ganka or this Varka has put her in touch with Nastasya Filippovna?"

"Whom?!" exclaimed the prince.

"Aglaya."

"I don't believe it! It can't be! With what purpose?"

He jumped up from the chair.

"I don't believe it either, though there's evidence. She's a willful girl, a fantastic girl, a crazy girl! A wicked, wicked, wicked girl! For a thousand years I'll go on insisting that she's wicked! They're all that way now, even that wet hen Alexandra, but this one has already gotten completely out of hand. But I also don't believe it! Maybe because I don't want to believe it," she added as if to herself. "Why didn't you come?" she suddenly turned to the prince again. "Why didn't you come for all these three days?" she impatiently cried to him a second time.

The prince was beginning to give his reasons, but she interrupted him again.

"Everyone considers you a fool and deceives you! You went to town yesterday; I'll bet you got on your knees and begged that scoundrel to accept the ten thousand!"

"Not at all, I never thought of it. I didn't even see him, and, besides, he's not a scoundrel. I received a letter from him."

"Show me the letter!"

The prince took a note from his briefcase and handed it to Lizaveta Prokofyevna. The note read:

My dear sir,

I, of course, do not have the least right in people's eyes to have any self-love. In people's opinion, I am too insignificant for that. But that is in people's eyes, not in yours. I am only too convinced that you, my dear sir, are perhaps better than the others. I disagree with Doktorenko and part ways with him in this conviction. I will never take a single kopeck from you, but you have helped my mother, and for that I owe you gratitude, even though it comes from weakness. In any case, I look upon you differently and consider it necessary to let you know. And with that I assume there can be no further contacts between us.

Antip Burdovsky.

P.S. The rest of the two hundred roubles will be faithfully paid back to you in time.

"What a muddle!" Lizaveta Prokofyevna concluded, tossing the note back. "Not worth reading. What are you grinning at?"

"You must agree that you enjoyed reading it."

"What! This vanity-eaten galimatias! But don't you see they've all lost their minds from pride and vanity?"

"Yes, but all the same he apologized, he's broken with

Doktorenko, and the vainer he is, the dearer the cost to his vanity. Oh, what a little child you are, Lizaveta Prokofyevna!"

"Are you intent on getting a slap in the face from me finally, or what?"

"No, not at all. It's because you're glad of the note, but you conceal it. Why are you ashamed of your feelings? You're like that in everything."

"Don't you dare set foot in my house now," Lizaveta Prokofyevna jumped up, turning pale with wrath, "from now on I don't want to hear a peep from you ever again!"

"But in three days you'll come yourself and invite me . . . Well, aren't you ashamed? These are your best feelings, why be ashamed of them? You only torment yourself."

"I'll die before I ever invite you! I'll forget your name! I have forgotten it!"

She rushed for the door.

"I've already been forbidden to visit you anyway!" the prince called after her.

"Wha-a-at? Who has forbidden you?"

She instantly turned around, as if pricked by a needle. The prince hesitated before answering; he felt he had made an accidental but serious slip.

"Who forbade you?" Lizaveta Prokofyevna cried furiously.

"Aglaya Ivanovna did . . ."

"When? Well, spe-e-eak!!!"

"This morning she sent to tell me that I must never dare come to see you."

Lizaveta Prokofyevna stood like a post, but she was thinking it through.

"What did she send? Whom did she send? Through that brat? Verbally?" she suddenly exclaimed again.

"I received a note," said the prince.

"Where? Give it to me! At once!"

The prince thought for a moment, but nevertheless took from his waistcoat pocket a careless scrap of paper on which was written:

Prince Lev Nikolaevich!

If, after all that has happened, you intend to surprise me by visiting our dacha, then you may be assured that you will not find me among the delighted.

Aglaya Epanchin.

Lizaveta Prokofyevna thought for a moment; then she suddenly rushed to the prince, seized him by the arm, and dragged him with her.

"Now! Go! On purpose, now, this minute!" she cried out in a fit of extraordinary excitement and impatience.

"But you're subjecting me to . . ."

"To what? Innocent simpleton! As if he's not even a man! Well, now I'll see it all for myself, with my own eyes . . ."

"Let me at least take my hat . . ."

"Here's your wretched little hat, let's go! He couldn't even choose the fashion tastefully! . . . She did it . . . She did it after today's . . . it's delirium," Lizaveta Prokofyevna was muttering, dragging the prince with her and not letting go of his arm even for a moment. "Earlier today I defended you, I said aloud that you were a fool, because you didn't come . . . otherwise she wouldn't have written such a witless note! An improper note! Improper for a noble, educated, intelligent, intelligent girl! . . . Hm," she went on, "of course, she herself was vexed that you didn't come, only she didn't reckon that she ought not to write like that to an idiot, because he'd take it literally, which is what happened. What are you doing eavesdropping?" she cried, catching herself in a slip. "She needs a buffoon like you, it's long since she's seen one, that's why she wants you! And I'm glad, glad that she's now going to sharpen her teeth on you! You deserve it. And she knows how, oh, she does know how! . . ."

PART THREE

I

THEY CONSTANTLY complain that in our country there are no practical people; that of political people, for example, there are many; of generals there are also many; of various managers, however many you need, you can at once find any sort you like—but of practical people there are none. At least everybody complains that there are none. They say that on certain railway lines there are even no decent attendants; to set up a more or less passable administration for some steamship company is, they say, quite impossible. In one place you hear that on some newly opened line the trains collided or fell off a bridge; in another they write that a train nearly spent the winter in a snowy field: people went on a few hours' journey and got stuck for five days in the snow. In another they tell about many tons of goods rotting in one place for two or three months, waiting to be transported, and in yet another they claim (though this is even hard to believe) that an administrator, that is, some supervisor, when pestered by some merchant's agent about transporting his goods, instead of transporting the goods, administered one to the agent's teeth, and proceeded to explain his administrative act as the result of "hot temper." It seems there are so many offices in the government service that it is frightening to think of it; everybody has served, everybody is serving, everybody intends to serve—given such material, you wonder, how can they not make up some sort of decent administration for a steamship company?

To this an extremely simple reply is sometimes given—so simple that it is even hard to believe such an explanation. True, they say, in our country everybody has served or is serving, and for two hundred years now this has been going on in the best German fashion, from forefathers to great-grandchildren—but it is the serving people who are the most impractical, and it has gone so far that abstractness and lack of practical knowledge were regarded even among civil servants themselves, still recently, as almost the greatest virtues and recommendations. However, we are wrong to have begun talking about civil servants; in fact, we wanted to talk about practical people. Here there is no doubt that timidity and a total lack of personal initiative have always been regarded among us as the chiefest and best sign of the practical man—and are so regarded even now. But why blame only ourselves—if this opinion can be considered an accusation? Lack of originality, everywhere, all over the world, from time immemorial, has always been considered the foremost quality and the best recommendation of the active, efficient and practical man, and at least ninety-nine out of a hundred people (at least that) have always held to that notion, and only perhaps one out of a hundred people has constantly looked and still looks at it differently.

Inventors and geniuses, at the beginning of their careers (and very often at the end as well), have almost always been regarded in society as no more than fools—that is a most routine observation, well known to everyone. If, for instance, in the course of decades everyone dragged his money to the Lombard and piled up billions there at four percent, then, naturally, when the Lombards ceased to exist and everyone was left to his own initiative, the greater part of those millions ought certainly to have perished in stock-market fever and in the hands of swindlers—decency and decorum even demanded it. Precisely decorum; if decorous timidity and a decent lack of originality have constituted among us up to now, according to a generally accepted conviction, the inalienable quality of the sensible and respectable man, it would be all too unrespectable and even indecent to change quite so suddenly. What mother, for instance, tenderly loving her child, would not become frightened and sick with fear if her son or daughter went slightly off the rails: "No, better let him be happy and live in prosperity without originality," every mother thinks as she rocks her baby to sleep. And our nannies, rocking babies to sleep, from time immemorial have cooed and crooned: "You shall go all dressed in gold, you shall be a general bold!" And so, even among our nannies, the rank of general was considered the limit of Russian happiness and, therefore, was the most popular national ideal of beautiful, peaceful felicity. And, indeed, who among us, having done a mediocre job on his exams and served for thirty-five years, could not finally make a general of himself and squirrel away a certain sum with a Lombard? Thus the Russian man, almost without any effort, finally attained the title of a sensible and practical man. In essence, the only one among us who cannot make a general of himself is the original—in other words, the troublesome—man. Perhaps there is some misunderstanding here, but, generally speaking, that seems to be so, and our society has been fully just in defining its ideal of the practical man. Nevertheless, we have still said much that is superfluous; we wanted, in fact, to say a few clarifying words about our acquaintances the Epanchins. These people, or at least the more reasoning members of the family, constantly suffered from one nearly general family quality, the direct opposite of those virtues we have discussed above. Without fully understanding the fact (because it is very difficult to understand), they occasionally suspected all the same that in their family somehow nothing went the way it did with everyone else. With everyone else things went smoothly, with them unevenly; everyone else rolled along the rails—they constantly went off the rails. Everyone else became constantly and decorously timid, but they did not. True, Lizaveta Prokofyevna could even become too frightened, but all the same this was not that decorous social timidity they longed for. However, perhaps only Lizaveta Prokofyevna was worried: the girls were still young—though very perspicacious and ironic folk—and the general, though he could perspicate (not without effort, however), in difficult cases only said "Hm!" and in the end placed all his hopes in Lizaveta Prokofyevna. Therefore the responsibility lay with her. And it was not, for instance, that the family was distinguished by some initiative of their own, or went off the rails by a conscious inclination for originality, which would have been quite improper. Oh, no! There was, in reality, nothing of the sort, that is, no consciously set goal, but all the same it came out in the end that the Epanchin family, though very respectable, was still not quite the way all respectable families in general ought to be. Recently Lizaveta Prokofyevna had begun to find only herself and her "unfortunate" character to blame for everything—which added to her suffering. She constantly scolded herself with being a "foolish, indecent eccentric" and suffered from insecurity, was continually at a loss, could not find her way out of some most ordinary concurrence of things, and constantly exaggerated her trouble.

We already mentioned at the beginning of our story that the Epanchins enjoyed universal and genuine respect. Even General Ivan Fyodorovich himself, a man of obscure origin, was received everywhere indisputably and with respect. And this respect he deserved, first, as a wealthy man and "not one of the least" and, second, as a fully respectable man, though none too bright. But a certain dullness of mind, it seems, is almost a necessary quality, if not of every active man, at least of every serious maker of money. Finally, the general had respectable manners, was modest, could keep his mouth shut and at the same time not let anyone step on his foot—and not only because of his generalship, but also as an honest and noble man. Most important of all, he was a man with powerful connections. As for Lizaveta Prokofyevna, she, as has been explained above, was of good family, though with us origin is not so highly regarded if it does not come with the necessary connections. But it turned out in the end that she also had connections; she was respected and, in the end, loved by such persons that, after them, naturally, everyone had to respect and receive her. There is no doubt that her family sufferings were groundless, had negligible cause, and were ridiculously exaggerated; but if you have a wart on your nose or forehead, it seems to you that all anyone in the world does and has ever done is to look at your wart, laugh at it, and denounce you for it, though for all that you may have discovered America. Nor is there any doubt that in society Lizaveta Prokofyevna was indeed considered an "eccentric"; but for all that she was indisputably respected; yet Lizaveta Prokofyevna began in the end not to believe that she was respected—that was her whole trouble. Looking at her daughters, she was tormented by the suspicion that she was continually hindering their careers in some way, that her character was ridiculous, indecent, and unbearable—for which, naturally, she continually accused her daughters and Ivan Fyodorovich, and spent whole days quarreling with them and at the same time loving them to distraction and almost to the point of passion.

Most of all she was tormented by the suspicion that her daughters were becoming the same sort of "eccentrics" as she, and that no such girls existed in the world, or ought to exist. "They're growing up into nihilists, that's what!" she constantly repeated to herself. Over the last year and especially most recently this sad thought had grown stronger and stronger in her. "First of all, why don't they get married?" she constantly asked herself. "So as to torment their mother—in that they see the whole purpose of their life, and that is so, of course, because there are all these new ideas, this whole cursed woman question! Didn't Aglaya decide half a year ago to cut off her magnificent hair? (Lord, even I never had such hair in my day!) She already had the scissors in her hand, I had to go on my knees and beg her! . . . Well, I suppose she did it out of wickedness, to torment her mother, because she's a wicked, willful, spoiled girl, but above all wicked, wicked, wicked! But didn't this fat Alexandra also follow her to cut off that mop of hers, and not out of wickedness, not out of caprice, but sincerely, like a fool, because Aglaya convinced her that she'd sleep more peacefully and her head wouldn't ache? And they've had so many suitors—it's five years now—so many, so many! And really, there were some good, even some excellent people among them! What are they waiting for? Why don't they get married? Only so as to vex their mother—there's no other reason! None! None!"

Finally, the sun also rose for her maternal heart; at least one daughter, at least Adelaida, would finally be settled. "That's at least one off my back," Lizaveta Prokofyevna used to say, when she had to express herself aloud (to herself she expressed it much more tenderly). And how nicely, how decently the whole thing got done; even in society it was spoken of respectfully. A known man, a prince, with a fortune, a nice man, and on top of that one pleasing to her heart: what, it seemed, could be better? But she had feared less for Adelaida than for her other daughters even before, though the girl's artistic inclinations sometimes greatly troubled Lizaveta Prokofyevna's ceaselessly doubting heart. "But, then, she's of cheerful character and has much good sense to go with it—which means that the girl won't be lost," she used to comfort herself in the end. She feared most of all for Aglaya. Incidentally, with regard to the eldest, Alexandra, Lizaveta Prokofyevna did not know whether to fear for her or not. Sometimes it seemed to her that "the girl was completely lost"; twenty-five years old—meaning she would be left an old maid. And "with such beauty! . . ." Lizaveta Prokofyevna even wept for her at night, while Alexandra Ivanovna spent those same nights sleeping the most peaceful sleep. "But what is she—a nihilist, or simply a fool?" That she was not a fool—of that, incidentally, Lizaveta Prokofyevna had no doubt: she had extreme respect for Alexandra Ivanovna's opinions and liked to consult her. But that she was a "wet hen"—of that there was no doubt: "So placid, there's no shaking her up!" However, "wet hens aren't placid either—pah! They've got me totally confused!" Lizaveta Prokofyevna had some inexplicable commiserating sympathy with Alexandra Ivanovna, more even than with Aglaya, who was her idol. But her acrimonious outbursts (in which her maternal care and sympathy chiefly expressed itself), her taunts, such names as "wet hen," only made Alexandra laugh. It would reach the point where the most trifling things would anger Lizaveta Prokofyevna terribly and put her beside herself. Alexandra Ivanovna liked, for instance, to sleep long hours and usually had many dreams; but her dreams were always distinguished by a sort of extraordinary emptiness and innocence—suitable for a seven-year-old child; and so even this innocence of her dreams began for some reason to annoy her mother. Once Alexandra Ivanovna saw nine hens in a dream, and this caused a formal quarrel between her and her mother—why?— it is difficult to explain. Once, and only once, she managed to have a dream about something that seemed original—she dreamed of a monk, alone, in some dark room, which she was afraid to enter. The dream was at once conveyed triumphantly to Lizaveta Proko- fyevna by her two laughing sisters; but the mother again became angry and called all three of them fools. "Hm! She's placid as a fool, and really a perfect 'wet hen,' there's no shaking her up, yet she's sad, there are times when she looks so sad. What, what is she grieving about?" Sometimes she put this question to Ivan Fyodorovich, hysterically, as was usual with her, threateningly, expecting an immediate answer. Ivan Fyodorovich would hem, frown, shrug his shoulders, and, spreading his arms, finally decide:

"She needs a husband!"

"Only God grant he's not one like you, Ivan Fyodorych," Liza- veta Prokofyevna would finally explode like a bomb, "not like you in his opinions and verdicts, Ivan Fyodorych; not such a boorish boor as you, Ivan Fyodorych . . ."

Ivan Fyodorovich would immediately run for his life, and Liza- veta Prokofyevna, after her *explosion*, would calm down. Naturally, towards evening that same day she would inevitably become extra- ordinarily attentive, quiet, affectionate, and respectful towards Ivan Fyodorovich, towards her "boorish boor" Ivan Fyodorovich, her kind, dear, and adored Ivan Fyodorovich, because all her life she had loved and had even been in love with her Ivan Fyodorovich, which Ivan Fyodorovich himself knew excellently well and for which he infinitely respected his Lizaveta Prokofyevna.

But her chief and constant torment was Aglaya.

"Exactly, exactly like me, my portrait in all respects," Lizaveta Prokofyevna said to herself, "a willful, nasty little demon! Nihilistic, eccentric, crazy, wicked, wicked, wicked! Oh, Lord, how unhappy she's going to be!"

But, as we have already said, the risen sun softened and brightened everything for a moment. There was nearly a month in Lizaveta Prokofyevna's life when she rested completely from all her worries. On the occasion of Adelaida's impending wedding there was also talk in society about Aglaya, while Aglaya everywhere bore herself so beautifully, so equably, so intelligently, so victoriously, a little proudly, but that was so becoming to her! She was so affectionate, so affable to her mother for the whole month! ("True, this Evgeny Pavlovich must still be very closely scrutinized, plumbed to the depths, and besides, Aglaya doesn't seem to favor him much more than the others!") All the same she had suddenly become such a nice girl—and how pretty she is, God, how pretty she is, and getting better day by day! And then . . .

And then that nasty little prince, that worthless little idiot, appeared and everything immediately got stirred up, everything in the house turned upside down!

What had happened, though?

For other people, probably, nothing would have happened. But this was what made Lizaveta Prokofyevna different, that in a combination and confusion of the most ordinary things, she always managed, through her ever-present worry, to discern something that inspired in her, sometimes to the point of morbidity, a most insecure, most inexplicable, and therefore most oppressive, fear. How must it have been for her now, when suddenly, through that whole muddle of ridiculous and groundless worries, there actually came a glimpse of something that indeed seemed important, something that indeed seemed worthy of alarms, doubts, and suspicions.

"And how dared they, how dared they write me that cursed anonymous letter about that *creature* being in touch with Aglaya?" Lizaveta Prokofyevna thought all the way, as she dragged the prince with her, and at home, when she sat him at the round table where the whole family was gathered. "How dared they even think of it? But I'd die of shame if I believed the smallest drop of it or showed the letter to Aglaya! Such mockery of us, the Epanchins! And all, all through Ivan Fyodorych, all through you, Ivan Fyodorych! Ah, why didn't we move to Elagin: I told them we should move to Elagin! Maybe it was Varka who wrote the letter, I know, or maybe . . . it's all, all Ivan Fyodorych's fault! That *creature* pulled that stunt on him in memory of their former connections, to show him what a fool he is, just as she laughed at him before, the foolish man, and led him by the nose when he brought her those pearls . . . And in the end we're mixed up in it all the same, your daughters are, Ivan Fyodorych, girls, young ladies, young ladies of the best society, marriageable; they were right there, stood there, heard everything, and also got mixed up in the story with the nasty boys, be glad that they were there as well and listening! I won't forgive him, I won't forgive that wretched princeling, I'll never forgive him! And why has Aglaya been in hysterics for three days, why has she nearly quarreled with her sisters, even Alexandra, whose hands she always used to kiss like her mother's—she respected her so much? Why has she been setting everyone riddles for three days? What has Gavrila Ivolgin got to do with it? Why did she take to praising Gavrila Ivolgin yesterday and today and then burst into tears? Why does that anonymous letter mention that cursed 'poor knight,' when she never even showed the prince's letter to her sisters? And why . . . what, what made me go running to him like a singed cat and drag him here myself? Lord, I've lost my mind, what have I done now! To talk with a young man about my daughter's secrets, and what's more . . . what's more, about secrets that all but concern him! Lord, it's a good thing at least that he's an idiot and . . . and . . . a friend of the house! Only, can it be that Aglaya got tempted by such a little freak? Lord, what drivel I'm spouting! Pah! We're originals . . . they should put us all under glass and show us to people, me first, ten kopecks for admission. I won't forgive you that, Ivan Fyodorych, I'll never forgive you! And why doesn't she give him a dressing-down now? She promised to give him a dressing-down and yet she doesn't do it! There, there, she's looking at him all eyes, says nothing, doesn't go away, stays, and it was she who told him not to come . . . He sits there all pale. And that cursed, cursed babbler Evgeny Pavlych keeps up the whole conversation by himself! Look at him talking away, not letting anybody put a word in. I'd have learned everything, if only I could have turned it the right way . . ."

The prince indeed sat, all but pale, at the round table and, it seemed, was at one and the same time extremely frightened and, for moments, in an incomprehensible, exhilarating ecstasy. Oh, how afraid he was to look in that direction, into that corner from which two familiar dark eyes gazed intently at him, and at the same time how seized with happiness he was to be sitting among them again, to hear the familiar voice—after what she had written to him. "Lord, what will she say now!" He himself had not yet uttered a single word and listened tensely to the "talking-away" Evgeny Pavlovich, who was rarely in such a pleased and excited state of mind as now, that evening. The prince listened to him and for a long time hardly understood a single word. Except for Ivan

Fyodorovich, who had not yet come from Petersburg, everyone was gathered. Prince Shch. was also there. It seemed they were going to go and listen to music a little later, before tea. The present conversation had evidently started before the prince's arrival. Soon Kolya, appearing from somewhere, slipped on to the terrace. "So he's received here as before," the prince thought to himself.

The Epanchins' dacha was a luxurious place, in the style of a Swiss chalet, gracefully adorned on all sides with flowers and leaves. It was surrounded on all sides by a small but beautiful flower garden. Everyone was sitting on the terrace as at the prince's; only the terrace was somewhat more spacious and decorated more smartly.

The theme of the conversation they were having seemed not to everyone's liking; the conversation, as could be guessed, had begun as the result of an impatient argument, and, of course, everyone would have liked to change the subject, but Evgeny Pavlovich seemed to persist all the more and regardless of the impression; the prince's arrival aroused him still more, as it were. Lizaveta Prokofyevna scowled, though she did not understand it all. Aglaya, who was sitting apart from everyone, almost in the corner, would not leave, listened, and remained stubbornly silent.

"Excuse me," Evgeny Pavlovich protested hotly, "but I am not saying anything against liberalism. Liberalism is not a sin; it is a necessary part of the whole, which without it would fall apart or atrophy; liberalism has the same right to exist as the most well-mannered conservatism; what I am attacking is Russian liberalism, and I repeat again that I attack it essentially because a Russian liberal is not a *Russian* liberal, but is a *non-Russian* liberal. Give me a Russian liberal and I'll kiss him at once right in front of you."

"Provided he wants to kiss you," said Alexandra Ivanovna, who was extraordinarily excited. Her cheeks even reddened more than usual.

"Just look," Lizaveta Prokofyevna thought to herself, "she sleeps and eats and there's no shaking her up, and then suddenly once a year she goes and starts talking so that you can only spread your arms in wonder."

The prince fleetingly noted that Alexandra Ivanovna seemed very displeased because Evgeny Pavlovich was talking too cheerfully, talking about a serious subject and as if excitedly, and at the same time as if he were joking.

"I was maintaining a moment ago, just before your arrival,

Prince," Evgeny Pavlovich went on, "that up to now our liberals have come from only two strata, the former landowners (abolished) and the seminarians.[1] And as the two estates have finally turned into absolute castes, into something absolutely cut off from the nation, and the more so the further it goes, from generation to generation, it means that all they have done and are doing is absolutely not national . . ."

"How's that? You mean all that's been done—it's all not Russian?" Prince Shch. objected.

"Not national; though it's in Russian, it's not national; our liberals aren't national, our conservatives aren't national, none of them . . . And you may be sure that our nation will recognize nothing of what's been done by landowners and seminarians, either now or later . . ."

"That's a good one! How can you maintain such a paradox, if it's serious? I cannot allow such outbursts concerning Russian landowners, you're a Russian landowner yourself," Prince Shch. objected heatedly.

"But I'm not speaking of the Russian landowner in the sense in which you're taking it. It's a respectable estate, if only for the fact that I myself belong to it; especially now, when it has ceased to exist . . ."

"Can it be that there was nothing national in literature either?" Alexandra Ivanovna interrupted.

"I'm not an expert in literature, but Russian literature, in my opinion, is all non-Russian, except perhaps for Lomonosov, Pushkin, and Gogol."[2]

"First, that's not so little, and second, one of them is from the people and the other two are landowners," laughed Adelaida.

"Quite right, but don't be triumphant. Since up to now only those three of all Russian writers have each managed to say something that is actually *his*, his own, not borrowed from anyone, those same three thereby immediately became national. Whoever of the Russian people says, writes, or does something of his own, *his own*, inalienable and unborrowed, inevitably becomes national, even if he speaks Russian poorly. For me that is an axiom. But it wasn't literature that we started talking about, we were talking about socialists, and the conversation started from them. Well, so I maintain that we don't have a single Russian socialist; we don't have and never had any, because all our socialists also come from the landowners or the seminarians. All our inveterate, much-advertised socialists, here as well as abroad, are nothing more than liberals who come from landowners from the time of serfdom. Why do you laugh? Give me their books, give me their tracts, their memoirs, and I undertake, without being a literary critic, to write a most persuasive literary critique, in which I shall make it clear as day that every page of their books, pamphlets, and memoirs has been written first of all by a former Russian landowner. Their spite, indignation, and wit are a landowner's (even pre-Famusovian![3]); their rapture, their tears—real, perhaps even genuine tears, but— they're a landowner's! A landowner's or a seminarian's . . . Again you laugh, and you're laughing, too, Prince? You also disagree?"

Indeed, they were all laughing, and the prince smiled, too.

"I can't say so directly yet whether I agree or disagree," the prince said, suddenly ceasing to smile and giving a start, like a caught schoolboy, "but I can assure you that I'm listening to you with extreme pleasure . . ."

He was all but breathless as he said this, and a cold sweat even broke out on his forehead. These were the first words he had uttered since he sat down. He was about to try looking around, but did not dare; Evgeny Pavlovich caught his movement and smiled.

"I'll tell you one fact, ladies and gentlemen," he went on in the same tone, that is, with extraordinary enthusiasm and warmth and at the same time almost laughing, perhaps at his own words, "a fact, the observation and even the discovery of which I have the honor of ascribing to myself, and even to myself alone; at least it has not been spoken of or written about anywhere. This fact expresses the whole essence of Russian liberalism of the sort I'm talking about. First of all, what is liberalism, generally speaking, if not an attack (whether reasonable or mistaken is another question) on the existing order of things? Isn't that so? Well, so my fact consists in this, that Russian liberalism is not an attack on the existing order of things, but is an attack on the very essence of our things, on the things themselves and not merely on their order, not on Russian order, but on Russia itself. My liberal has reached the point where he denies Russia itself, that is, he hates and beats his own mother. Every unfortunate and unsuccessful Russian fact evokes laughter in him and all but delight. He hates Russian customs, Russian history, everything. If there's any vindication for him, it is perhaps only that he doesn't understand what he's doing and takes his hatred of Russia for the most fruitful liberalism (oh, among us you will often meet a liberal whom all the rest applaud and who perhaps is in essence the most absurd, the most obtuse and dangerous conservative, without knowing it himself!). Some of our liberals, still not long ago, took this hatred of Russia for all but a genuine love of the fatherland and boasted of seeing better than others what it should consist of; but by now they've become more candid, and have even begun to be ashamed of the words 'love of the fatherland,' have even banished and removed the very notion as harmful and worthless. That is a true fact, I'll stand behind it and . . . some day the truth had to be spoken out fully, simply, and candidly; but at the same time it is a fact such as has never been or occurred anywhere, in all the ages, among any people, and therefore it is an accidental fact and may go away, I agree. There could be no such liberal anywhere as would hate his own fatherland. How, then, can all this be explained in our country? In the same way as before—that the Russian liberal is so far not a Russian liberal; there's no other way, in my opinion."

"I take all you've said as a joke, Evgeny Pavlych," Prince Shch. objected seriously.

"I haven't seen all the liberals and will not venture to judge," said Alexandra Ivanovna, "but I have listened to your thought with indignation: you've taken a particular case and made it a general rule, and that means slander."

"A particular case? Ahh! The word has been spoken," Evgeny Pavlovich picked up. "What do you think, Prince, is it a particular case or not?"

"I also must say that I've seen little of and have spent little time . . . with liberals," said the prince, "but it seems to me that you may be somewhat right and that the Russian liberalism you spoke of is indeed partly inclined to hate Russia itself and not only its order of things. Of course, that's only in part . . . of course, it wouldn't be fair to say of all . . ."

He faltered and did not finish. Despite all his agitation, he was extremely interested in the conversation. There was a special feature in the prince, consisting of the extraordinary naïvety of the attention with which he always listened to something that interested him, and of the replies he gave when he was addressed with questions about it. His face and even the attitude of his body somehow reflected this naïvety, this faith, suspecting neither mockery nor humor. But although Evgeny Pavlovich had long been addressing him not otherwise than with a certain peculiar smile, now, at the prince's response, he looked at him somehow very seriously, as if he had never expected such a response from him.

"So . . . that's strange, though, on your part," he said, "and you really have answered me seriously, Prince?"

"Why, weren't you asking seriously?" the other retorted in surprise.

Everyone laughed.

"Trust him," said Adelaida, "Evgeny Pavlych always makes fools of everyone! If you only knew what stories he tells sometimes in the most serious way!"

"In my opinion, this is a painful conversation, and should never have been started at all," Alexandra observed sharply. "We wanted to go for a walk . . ."

"Let's go, it's a lovely evening!" cried Evgeny Pavlovich. "But, to prove to you that this time I was speaking quite seriously, and, above all, to prove it to the prince (I'm extremely interested in you, Prince, and I swear to you that I'm not at all such an empty man as I must certainly seem—though, in fact, I am an empty man!), and . . . if you will permit me, ladies and gentlemen, I will ask the prince one last question, out of personal curiosity, and we'll end there. This question occurred to me, as if on purpose, two hours ago (you see, Prince, I also sometimes think about serious things); I've answered it, but let's see what the prince says. Mention has just been made of a 'particular case.' This has become a very portentous little phrase among us, one hears it often. Recently everyone was talking and writing about that terrible murder of six people by that . . . young man, and of a strange speech by his defense attorney, in which he said that, given the destitute condition of the criminal, it *naturally* had to occur to him to kill those six people. That's not literal, but the meaning, I think, was that or something approaching it. In my personal opinion, the defense attorney, in voicing such a strange thought, was fully convinced that what he was saying was the most liberal, the most humane and progressive thing that could possibly be said in our time. Well, what would you say: is this perversion of notions and convictions, this possibility of such a warped and extraordinary view of things, a particular case or a general one?"

Everyone burst out laughing.

"A particular one, naturally, a particular one," laughed Alexandra and Adelaida.

"And allow me to remind you again, Evgeny Pavlych," added Prince Shch., "that by now your joke has worn too thin."

"What do you think, Prince?" Evgeny Pavlovich did not listen, having caught the curious and grave gaze of Prince Lev Nikolaevich upon him. "How does it seem to you: is this a particular case or a general one? I confess, it was for you that I thought up this question."

"No, not particular," the prince said quietly but firmly.

"For pity's sake, Lev Nikolaevich," Prince Shch. cried with some vexation, "don't you see that he's trying to trap you; he's decidedly laughing, and it's precisely you that he intends to sharpen his teeth on."

"I thought Evgeny Pavlych was speaking seriously," the prince blushed and lowered his eyes.

"My dear Prince," Prince Shch. went on, "remember what you and I talked about once, about three months ago; we precisely talked about the fact that, in our newly opened young courts,[4] one can already point to so many remarkable and talented defense attorneys! And how many decisions remarkable in the highest degree have been handed down by the juries? How glad you were, and how glad I was then of your gladness . . . we said we could be proud . . . And this clumsy defense, this strange argument, is, of course, an accident, one in a thousand."

Prince Lev Nikolaevich pondered a little, but with the most convinced air, though speaking softly and even as if timidly, replied:

"I only wanted to say that the distortion of ideas and notions (as Evgeny Pavlych put it) occurs very often, and is unfortunately much more of a general than a particular case. And to the point that, if this distortion were not such a general case, there might not be such impossible crimes as these . . ."

"Impossible crimes? But I assure you that exactly the same crimes, and perhaps still more terrible ones, existed before, and have always existed, not only here but everywhere, and, in my opinion, will occur for a very long time to come. The difference is that before we had less publicity, while now we've begun to speak aloud and even to write about them, which is why it seems as if these criminals have appeared only now. That's your mistake, an extremely naïve mistake, Prince, I assure you," Prince Shch. smiled mockingly.

"I myself know that there were very many crimes before, and just as terrible; I was in some prisons not long ago and managed to become acquainted with certain criminals and accused men. There are even more horrible criminals than this one, who have killed ten people and do not repent at all. But at the same time I noticed this: the most inveterate and unrepentant murderer still knows that he is a *criminal*, that is, in all conscience he considers that he has done wrong, though without any repentance. And every one of them is the same; but those whom Evgeny Pavlych has begun speaking about do not even want to consider themselves criminals and think to themselves that they had the right and . . . even did a good thing, or almost. That, in my opinion, is what makes the terrible difference. And note that they're all young people, that is, precisely of an age when they can most easily and defenselessly fall under the influence of perverse ideas."

Prince Shch. was no longer laughing and listened to the prince with perplexity. Alexandra Ivanovna, who had long been wanting to make some remark, kept silent, as if some special thought stopped her. But Evgeny Pavlovich looked at the prince in decided astonishment and this time without any smile.

"Why are you so astonished at him, my dear sir?" Lizaveta Prokofyevna stepped in unexpectedly. "What, is he stupider than you or something, can't he reason as well as you?"

"No, ma'am, it's not that," said Evgeny Pavlovich, "but how is it, Prince (forgive the question), if that's the way you see and observe it, then how is it (again, forgive me) that in that strange affair . . . the other day . . . with Burdovsky, I believe . . . how is it that you didn't notice the same perversion of ideas and moral convictions? Exactly the same! It seemed to me then that you didn't notice it at all."

"But the thing is, my dear," Lizaveta Prokofyevna was very excited, "that we noticed everything, we sit here and boast before him, and yet he received a letter today from one of them, the main one, with the blackheads, remember, Alexandra? He apologizes in his letter, though in his own manner, and says he has dropped that friend of his, the one who egged him on then—remember, Alexandra?—and that he now believes more in the prince. Well, and we haven't received such a letter yet, though we know well enough how to turn up our noses at him."

"And Ippolit also just moved to our dacha!" cried Kolya.

"What? He's already here?" the prince became alarmed.

"You had only just left with Lizaveta Prokofyevna when he came. I brought him!"

"Well, I'll bet," Lizaveta Prokofyevna suddenly boiled over, completely forgetting that she had just praised the prince, "I'll bet he went to his attic yesterday and begged his forgiveness on his knees, so that the spiteful little stinker would deign to come here. Did you go yesterday? You admitted it yourself earlier. Is it so or not? Did you get on your knees or not?"

"That's quite wrong," cried Kolya, "and it was quite the contrary: Ippolit seized the prince's hand yesterday and kissed it twice, I saw it myself, and that was the end of all the explanations, except that the prince simply said it would be better for him at the dacha, and he instantly agreed to come as soon as he felt better."

"You shouldn't, Kolya . . ." the prince murmured, getting up and taking his hat, "why are you telling them about that, I . . ."

"Where now?" Lizaveta Prokofyevna stopped him.

"Don't worry, Prince," the inflamed Kolya went on, "don't go and don't trouble him, he's fallen asleep after the trip; he's very glad; and you know, Prince, in my opinion it will be much better if you don't meet today, even put it off till tomorrow, otherwise he'll get embarrassed again. This morning he said it was a whole six months since he'd felt so well and so strong; he even coughs three times less."

The prince noticed that Aglaya suddenly left her place and came over to the table. He did not dare to look at her, but he felt with his whole being that she was looking at him at that moment, and perhaps looking menacingly, that there was certainly indignation in her dark eyes and her face was flushed.

"But it seems to me, Nikolai Ardalionovich, that you shouldn't have brought him here, if it's that same consumptive boy who wept the other time and invited us to his funeral," Evgeny Pavlovich observed. "He spoke so eloquently then about the wall of the neighboring house that he's bound to feel sad without it, you may be sure."

"What he says is true: he'll quarrel and fight with you and then leave, that's what I say!"

And Lizaveta Prokofyevna moved her sewing basket towards her with dignity, forgetting that they were all getting up to go for a walk.

"I remember him boasting a great deal about that wall," Evgeny Pavlovich picked up again. "Without that wall he won't be able to die eloquently, and he wants very much to die eloquently."

"What of it?" murmured the prince. "If you don't want to forgive him, he'll die without it . . . He moved now for the sake of the trees."

"Oh, for my part I forgive him everything; you can tell him that."

"That's not how it should be understood," the prince replied quietly and as if reluctantly, continuing to look at one spot on the floor and not raising his eyes. "It should be that you, too, agree to accept his forgiveness."

"What is it to me? How am I guilty before him?"

"If you don't understand, then . . . but, no, you do understand. He wanted then . . . to bless you all and to receive your blessing, that's all."

"My dear Prince," Prince Shch. hastened to pick up somehow warily, exchanging glances with some of those present, "paradise on earth is not easily achieved; but all the same you are counting on paradise in a way; paradise is a difficult thing, Prince, much more difficult than it seems to your wonderful heart. We'd better stop, otherwise we may all get embarrassed again, and then . . ."

"Let's go and listen to the music," Lizaveta Prokofyevna said sharply, getting up angrily from her seat.

They all stood up after her.

II

THE PRINCE SUDDENLY went over to Evgeny Pavlovich.

"Evgeny Pavlych," he said with a strange ardor, seizing him by the arm, "you may be sure that I consider you the noblest and best of men, in spite of everything; you may be sure of that . . ."

Evgeny Pavlovich even stepped back in surprise. For a moment he tried to suppress an unbearable fit of laughter; but, on looking closer, he noticed that the prince was as if not himself, or at least in some sort of peculiar state.

"I'll bet," he cried, "that you were going to say something quite different, Prince, and maybe not to me at all . . . But what's the matter? Do you feel bad?"

"That may be, that may well be, and it was a very subtle observation that I may have wanted to approach someone else!"

Having said this, he smiled somehow strangely and even ridiculously, but suddenly, as if becoming excited, he exclaimed:

"Don't remind me of what I did three days ago! I've been feeling very ashamed these three days . . . I know I'm to blame . . ."

"But . . . but what did you do that was so terrible?"

"I can see that you are perhaps more ashamed for me than

anyone else, Evgeny Pavlovich; you're blushing, that's the sign of a beautiful heart. I'll leave presently, you may be sure."

"What's the matter with him? Is this how his fits begin?" Lizaveta Prokofyevna turned fearfully to Kolya.

"Never mind, Lizaveta Prokofyevna, I'm not having a fit; I'll leave right now. I know I've been . . . mistreated by nature. I've been ill for twenty-four years, from birth to the age of twenty-four. Take it from me now as from a sick man. I'll leave right now, right now, you may be sure. I'm not blushing—because it would be strange to blush at that, isn't it so?—but I'm superfluous in society . . . I don't say it out of vanity . . . I was thinking it over during these three days and decided that I should inform you candidly and nobly at the first opportunity. There are certain ideas, there are lofty ideas, which I ought not to start talking about, because I'll certainly make everyone laugh; Prince Shch. has just reminded me of that very thing . . . My gestures are inappropriate, I have no sense of measure; my words are wrong, they don't correspond to my thoughts, and that is humiliating for the thoughts. And therefore I have no right . . . then, too, I'm insecure, I . . . I'm convinced that I cannot be offended in this house, that I am loved more than I'm worth, but I know (I know for certain) that after twenty years of illness there must surely be some trace left, so that it's impossible not to laugh at me . . . sometimes . . . is that so?"

He looked around as if waiting for a response and a decision. Everyone stood in painful perplexity from this unexpected, morbid, and, as it seemed, in any case groundless outburst. But this outburst gave occasion to a strange episode.

"Why do you say that here?" Aglaya suddenly cried. "Why do you say it to *them*? To them! To them!"

She seemed to be in the ultimate degree of indignation: her eyes flashed fire. The prince stood dumb and speechless before her and suddenly turned pale.

"There's no one here who is worth such words!" Aglaya burst out. "No one, no one here is worth your little finger, or your intelligence, or your heart! You're more honest than all of them, nobler than all of them, better than all of them, kinder than all of them, more intelligent than all of them! There are people here who aren't worthy of bending down to pick up the handkerchief you've just dropped . . . Why do you humiliate yourself and place yourself lower than everyone else? Why have you twisted everything in yourself, why is there no pride in you?"

"Lord, who'd have thought it?" Lizaveta Prokofyevna clasped her hands.

"The poor knight! Hurrah!" Kolya shouted in delight.

"Quiet! . . . How do they dare offend me here in your house!" Aglaya suddenly fell upon Lizaveta Prokofyevna, now in that hysterical state in which one disregards all limits and overcomes all obstacles. "Why do they all torment me, every last one of them! Why do they all badger me on account of you, Prince? I won't marry you for anything! Know that, never and not for anything! Can one marry such a ridiculous man as you? Look at yourself in the mirror now, see how you're standing there! . . . Why, why do they tease me, saying that I should marry you? You must know it! You're also in conspiracy with them!"

"No one ever teased her!" Adelaida murmured in fright.

"It never entered anyone's mind, no one ever said a word about it!" cried Alexandra Ivanovna.

"Who teased her? When? Who could have told her that? Is she raving?" Lizaveta Prokofyevna, trembling with wrath, turned to them all.

"You all said it, all of you, all these three days! I'll never, never marry him!"

Having shouted that, Aglaya dissolved in bitter tears, covered her face with a handkerchief, and collapsed into a chair.

"But he hasn't asked you yet . . ."

"I haven't asked you, Aglaya Ivanovna," suddenly escaped from the prince.

"Wha-a-at?" Lizaveta Prokofyevna suddenly drew out in astonishment, indignation, and horror. "What's tha-a-at?"

She refused to believe her ears.

"I meant to say . . . I meant to say," the prince was trembling, "I only meant to explain to Aglaya Ivanovna . . . to have the honor of explaining to her that I never had any intention . . . to have the honor of asking for her hand . . . even once . . . I'm not to blame for any of it, by God, I'm not, Aglaya Ivanovna! I never meant to, it never entered my mind and never will, you'll see for yourself: you may be sure! Some wicked man has slandered me before you! You may rest assured!"

Saying this, he approached Aglaya. She took away the handkerchief with which she had covered her face, quickly glanced at him and his whole frightened figure, realized what he had just said, and suddenly burst out laughing right in his face—such merry,

irrepressible laughter, such funny and mocking laughter, that
Adelaida was the first to succumb, especially when she also looked
at the prince, rushed to her sister, embraced her, and laughed the
same irrepressible, merry schoolgirl's laughter as Aglaya. Looking
at them, the prince suddenly began to smile, too, and to repeat
with a joyful and happy expression:

"Well, thank God, thank God!"

At this point Alexandra also could not help herself and laughed
wholeheartedly. It seemed there would be no end to this laughter
of the three of them.

"Ah, crazy girls!" Lizaveta Prokofyevna muttered. "First they
frighten you, then . . ."

But Prince Shch., too, was laughing now, Evgeny Pavlovich was
laughing, Kolya was guffawing nonstop, and, looking at them all,
the prince also guffawed.

"Let's go for a walk, let's go for a walk!" cried Adelaida. "All of
us together, and certainly the prince with us. There's no need for
you to leave, you dear man! What a dear man he is, Aglaya! Isn't
it so, mama? Besides, I must certainly, certainly kiss him and
embrace him for . . . for what he just said to Aglaya. *Maman*, dear,
will you allow me to kiss him? Aglaya, allow me to kiss *your* prince!"
cried the mischievous girl, and she indeed ran over to the prince
and kissed him on the forehead. He seized her hands, squeezed
them so hard that Adelaida nearly cried out, looked at her with
infinite joy, and suddenly brought her hand quickly to his lips and
kissed it three times.

"Let's go, then!" Aglaya called. "Prince, you'll escort me. Can
he, *maman*? A suitor who has rejected me? You have rejected me
forever, haven't you, Prince? No, you don't offer a lady your arm
like that, don't you know how to take a lady's arm? Like this, come
on, we'll go ahead of them all; do you want to go ahead of them,
tête-à-tête?"

She talked nonstop, still with bursts of laughter.

"Thank God! Thank God!" Lizaveta Prokofyevna kept
repeating, not knowing herself what she was glad about.

"Extremely strange people!" thought Prince Shch., maybe for
the hundredth time since he had become close with them, but . . .
he liked these strange people. As for the prince, maybe he did not
like him so much; Prince Shch. was a bit glum and as if preoccupied
as they all went out for a walk.

Evgeny Pavlovich seemed to be in the merriest spirits; he made

Alexandra and Adelaida laugh all the way to the vauxhall, and they laughed somehow especially readily at his jokes, so much so that he began to have a sneaking suspicion that they might not be listening to him at all. At this thought, suddenly and without explaining the reason, he burst at last into extremely and absolutely sincere laughter (such was his character!). The sisters, though they were in a most festive mood, glanced constantly at Aglaya and the prince, who were walking ahead of them; it was clear that their little sister had set them a great riddle. Prince Shch. kept trying to strike up a conversation with Lizaveta Prokofyevna about unrelated things, perhaps in order to distract her, but she found him terribly tiresome. Her thoughts seemed quite scattered, she gave inappropriate answers and sometimes did not answer at all. But Aglaya Ivanovna's riddles were not yet ended for that evening. The last one fell to the prince's lot. When they had gone about a hundred steps from the dacha, Aglaya said in a rapid half whisper to her stubbornly silent escort:

"Look to the right."

The prince looked.

"Look closer. Do you see the bench in the park, where those three big trees are . . . the green bench?"

The prince answered that he did.

"Do you like the setting? Sometimes I come early, at seven o'clock, when everyone is still asleep, to sit there by myself."

The prince murmured that it was a wonderful setting.

"And now go away from me, I don't want to walk arm in arm with you anymore. Or better, let's walk arm in arm, but don't say a word to me. I want to think alone to myself . . ."

The warning was in any case unnecessary: the prince would certainly not have uttered a single word all the way even without orders. His heart began to pound terribly when he heard about the bench. After a moment he thought better of it and, in shame, drove away his absurd notion.

As is known and as everyone at least affirms, the public that gathers at the Pavlovsk vauxhall on weekdays is "more select" than on Sundays and holidays, when "all sorts of people" arrive from the city. The dresses are not festive but elegant. The custom is to get together and listen to music. The orchestra, which may indeed be one of our best garden orchestras, plays new things. The decency and decorum are extreme, in spite of a certain generally familial and even intimate air. The acquaintances, all of them dacha people, get together to look each other over. Many do it with genuine pleasure and come only for that; but there are also those who come just for the music. Scandals are extraordinarily rare, though, incidentally, they do occur even on weekdays. But, then, there's no doing without them.

This time the evening was lovely, and there was a good-sized audience. All the places near the orchestra were taken. Our company sat down in chairs a little to one side, close to the far left-hand door of the vauxhall. The crowd and the music revived Lizaveta Prokofyevna somewhat and distracted the young ladies; they managed to exchange glances with some of their acquaintances and to nod their heads amiably to others from afar; managed to look over the dresses, to notice some oddities, discuss them, and smile mockingly. Evgeny Pavlovich also bowed rather often. People already paid attention to Aglaya and the prince, who were still together. Soon some young men of their acquaintance came over to the mama and the young ladies; two or three stayed to talk; they were all friends of Evgeny Pavlovich. Among them was one young and very handsome officer, very gay, very talkative; he hastened to strike up a conversation with Aglaya and tried as hard as he could to attract her attention. Aglaya was very gracious with him and laughed easily. Evgeny Pavlovich asked the prince's permission to introduce him to this friend; the prince barely understood what they wanted to do with him, but the introductions were made, the two men bowed and shook hands with each other. Evgeny Pavlovich's friend asked a question, but the prince seemed not to answer it, or muttered something to himself so strangely that the officer gave him a very intent look, then glanced at Evgeny Pavlovich, realized at once why he had thought up this acquaintance, smiled faintly, and turned again to Aglaya. Evgeny Pavlovich alone noticed that Aglaya unexpectedly blushed at that.

The prince did not even notice that other people were talking and paying court to Aglaya; he even all but forgot at moments that he was sitting next to her. Sometimes he wanted to go away somewhere, to disappear from there completely, and he would even have liked some dark, deserted place, only so that he could be alone with his thoughts and no one would know where he was. Or at least to be in his own home, on the terrace, but so that nobody else was there, neither Lebedev nor his children; to throw himself on his sofa, bury his face in his pillow, and lie there like that for a day, a night, another day. At moments he imagined the mountains, and precisely one familiar spot in the mountains that he always liked to remember and where he had liked to walk when he still lived there, and to look down from there on the village, on the white thread of the waterfall barely glittering below, on the white clouds, on the abandoned old castle. Oh, how he wanted to be there now and to think about one thing—oh! all his life only about that—it would be enough for a thousand years! And let them, let them forget all about him here. Oh, it was even necessary, even better, that they not know him at all, and that this whole vision be nothing but a dream. And wasn't it all the same whether it was a dream or a reality? Sometimes he would suddenly begin studying Aglaya and for five minutes could not tear his gaze from her face; but his gaze was all too strange: it seemed he was looking at her as if at an object a mile away, or as if at her portrait and not at herself.

"Why are you looking at me like that, Prince?" she said suddenly, interrupting her merry conversation and laughter with those around her. "I'm afraid of you; I keep thinking you want to reach your hand out and touch my face with your finger, in order to feel it. Isn't it true, Evgeny Pavlych, that he looks like that?"

The prince listened, seeming to be surprised that he was being addressed, realized it, though he may not quite have understood, did not reply, but, seeing that she and all the others were laughing, suddenly extended his mouth and began to laugh himself. The laughter increased around him; the officer, who must have been a man who laughed easily, simply burst with laughter. Aglaya suddenly whispered wrathfully to herself:

"Idiot!"

"Lord! Can she really . . . such a . . . is she going completely crazy?" Lizaveta Prokofyevna rasped to herself.

"It's a joke. It's the same kind of joke as with the 'poor knight,'" Alexandra whispered firmly in her ear, "and nothing more! She's poking fun at him again, in her own way. Only the joke has gone too far; it must be stopped, *maman!* Earlier she was clowning like an actress, frightening us for the fun of it . . ."

"It's a good thing she landed on such an idiot," Lizaveta Prokofyevna whispered to her. Her daughter's observation made her feel better all the same.

The prince, however, heard that he had been called an idiot, and gave a start, but not because he had been called an idiot. The "idiot" he forgot at once. But in the crowd, not far from where he was sitting, somewhere to the side—he would not have been able to show in what precise place and in what spot—a face flashed, a pale face with dark, curly hair, with a familiar, a very familiar, smile and gaze—flashed and disappeared. It might well have been that he only imagined it; of the whole apparition he was left with the impression of the crooked smile, the eyes, and the pale green, foppish tie that the gentleman who flashed was wearing. Whether this gentleman disappeared in the crowd or slipped into the vauxhall, the prince also could not have determined.

But a moment later he suddenly began looking quickly and uneasily around him; this first apparition might be the herald and forerunner of a second. That was surely the case. Could he have forgotten the possibility of a meeting when they set out for the vauxhall? True, as he walked to the vauxhall, he seemed not at all aware that he was going there—he was in such a state. If he had been or could have been more attentive, he might have noticed a quarter of an hour ago that Aglaya, every so often and also as if uneasily, glanced furtively about, as though looking for something around her. Now, when his uneasiness had become quite noticeable, Aglaya's agitation and uneasiness also grew, and each time he looked behind him, she almost at once looked around as well. The resolution of their anxiety soon followed.

From the same side door to the vauxhall near which the prince and all the Epanchin company had placed themselves, a whole crowd, at least ten people, suddenly emerged. At the head of the crowd were three women; two of them were remarkably good-looking, and there was nothing strange in so many admirers following after them. But both the admirers and the women—all this was something peculiar, something quite unlike the rest of the public gathered for the music. Nearly everyone noticed them at once, but the greater part tried to pretend that they had not seen them at all, and perhaps only some of the young people smiled at them, commenting to each other in low voices. Not to see them at all was impossible; they made themselves conspicuous, talked loudly, laughed. One might suppose that many of them were drunk, though by the look of it some were smartly and elegantly dressed; but alongside them there were rather strange-looking people, in strange clothes, with strangely inflamed faces; there were several military men among them; not all of them were young; some were dressed comfortably in loose and elegantly made clothes, with signet rings and cuff links, in magnificent, pitch-black wigs and side-whiskers, and with a particularly noble, though somewhat squeamish, expression on their faces—the sort of people, however, who are avoided like the plague in society. Among our suburban societies, of course, there are some that are distinguished by an extraordinary decorum and enjoy a particularly good reputation; but even the most cautious person cannot protect himself at every moment against a brick falling from a neighboring house. This brick was now preparing to fall upon the decorous public that had gathered for the music.

To pass from the vauxhall to the green where the orchestra was playing, one had to go down three steps. The crowd stopped just at these steps; they did not venture to go down, but one of the women stepped forward; only two of her retinue dared to follow her. One was a rather modest-looking middle-aged man, of decent appearance in all respects, but having the air of a confirmed old bachelor, that is, one of those who never know anybody and whom nobody knows. The other one not to lag behind his lady was a complete ragamuffin of the most ambiguous appearance. No one else followed the eccentric lady; but, going down, she did not even turn to look back, as if it decidedly made no difference to her whether she was followed or not. She laughed and talked as loudly as before; she was dressed extremely tastefully and expensively, but somewhat more magnificently than she ought to have been. She went past the orchestra to the other side of the green, near the road, where somebody's carriage was waiting for someone.

The prince had not seen *her* for more than three months. All those days since his arrival in Petersburg, he had been preparing to call on her; but perhaps a secret foreboding had held him back. At least he could in no way anticipate what impression awaited him on meeting her, but sometimes he fearfully tried to imagine it. One thing was clear to him—that the meeting would be painful. Several times during those six months he had recalled the first sensation that the face of this woman had produced in him, when he had only seen it in a portrait; but even in the impression of the portrait, he recalled, there was a great deal of pain. That month in the provinces, when he had seen her almost every day, had had a terrible effect on him, so much so that the prince drove away even the memory of that still-recent time. For him there was something tormenting in the very face of this woman; the prince, talking with Rogozhin, had translated this feeling as one of infinite pity, and that was true: this face, ever since the portrait, had evoked in his heart all the suffering of pity; the impression of compassion and even of suffering for this being never left his heart and had not left it now. Oh, no, it was even stronger. Yet the prince remained dissatisfied with what he had said to Rogozhin; and only now, at this moment of her unexpected appearance, did he understand, perhaps through immediate sensation, what had been lacking in his words to Rogozhin. Words had been lacking expressive of horror—yes, horror! Now, at this moment, he felt it fully; he was sure, he was fully convinced, for his own special reasons, that this woman was mad. If a man, loving a woman more than anything in the world, or anticipating the possibility of such a love, were suddenly to see her on a chain, behind iron bars, under a warden's stick—the impression would be somewhat similar to what the prince was feeling now.

"What's the matter?" Aglaya whispered quickly, glancing at him and naïvely tugging at his arm.

He turned his head to her, looked at her, looked into her dark eyes, whose flashing was incomprehensible to him at that moment, tried to smile at her, but suddenly, as if instantly forgetting her, again turned his eyes to the right and again began to watch his extraordinary apparition. At that moment Nastasya Filippovna was just walking past the young ladies' chairs. Evgeny Pavlovich went on telling Alexandra Ivanovna something that must have been very funny and interesting, speaking quickly and animatedly. The prince remembered Aglaya suddenly saying in a half-whisper: "What a . . ."

The phrase was uncertain and unfinished; she instantly checked herself and did not add anything more, but that was already enough. Nastasya Filippovna, who was walking along as if not noticing anyone in particular, suddenly turned in their direction, and seemed only now to recognize Evgeny Pavlovich.

"Hah! Here he is!" she exclaimed, suddenly stopping. "First there's no finding him with any messengers, then, as if on purpose, he sits here where you'd never imagine . . . And I thought you were there, darling . . . at your uncle's!"

Evgeny Pavlovich flushed, looked furiously at Nastasya Filippovna, but quickly turned away again.

"What?! Don't you know? He doesn't know yet, imagine! He shot himself! Your uncle shot himself this morning! They told me earlier, at two o'clock; half the city knows by now; they say three hundred and fifty thousand in government funds are missing, others say five hundred thousand. And here I was counting on him leaving you an inheritance; he blew it all. A most depraved old fellow he was . . . Well, good-bye, *bonne chance*!* So you really won't go? That's why you resigned in good time, smart boy! Oh, nonsense, you knew, you knew beforehand; maybe even yesterday . . ."

Though there was certainly some purpose in this impudent pestering, this advertising of an acquaintance and an intimacy that did not exist, and there could now be no doubt of it—Evgeny Pavlovich had thought first to get rid of her somehow or other, and did his best to ignore the offender. But Nastasya Filippovna's words struck him like a thunderbolt; hearing of his uncle's death, he went pale as a sheet and turned to the bearer of the news. At that moment Lizaveta Prokofyevna quickly got up from her seat, got everyone up with her, and all but rushed out. Only Prince Lev Nikolaevich stayed where he was for a second, as if undecided, and Evgeny Pavlovich went on standing there, not having come to his senses. But the Epanchins had not managed to go twenty steps before a frightful scandal broke out.

The officer, a great friend of Evgeny Pavlovich's, who had been talking with Aglaya, was indignant in the highest degree.

"Here you simply need a whip, there's no other way with this creature!" he said almost aloud. (It seems he had been Evgeny Pavlovich's confidant even before.)

Nastasya Filippovna instantly turned to him. Her eyes flashed; she rushed to a young man completely unknown to her who was standing two steps away and holding a thin, braided riding crop, tore it out of his hand, and struck her offender across the face as hard as she could. All this occurred in a second . . . The officer, forgetting himself, rushed at her; Nastasya Filippovna's retinue was no longer around her; the decent middle-aged gentleman had already managed to efface himself completely, and the tipsy gentleman stood to one side and guffawed with all his might. In a minute, of course, the police would arrive, but for that minute things would have gone badly for Nastasya Filippovna if unexpected help had not come in time: the prince, who had also stopped two paces away, managed to seize the officer by the arms from behind. Pulling his arm free, the officer shoved him hard in the chest; the prince was sent flying about three paces and fell on a chair. But by then

*Good luck.

two more defenders had turned up for Nastasya Filippovna. Before the attacking officer stood the boxer, author of the article already familiar to the reader and an active member of Rogozhin's former band.

"Keller! Retired lieutenant," he introduced himself with swagger. "If you'd like to fight hand to hand, Captain, I'm at your service, to replace the weaker sex; I've gone through the whole of English boxing. Don't push, Captain; I sympathize with the *bloody* offense, but I cannot allow for the right of fists with a woman before the eyes of the public. But if, as befits a no-o-oble person, you'd prefer it in a different manner, then—naturally, you must understand me, Captain . . ."

But the captain had already recovered himself and was no longer listening to him. At that moment Rogozhin emerged from the crowd, quickly took Nastasya Filippovna by the arm, and led her away with him. For his part, Rogozhin seemed terribly shaken, was pale and trembling. As he led Nastasya Filippovna away, he still had time to laugh maliciously in the officer's face and say, with the look of a triumphant shopkeeper:

"Nyah! Take that! Your mug's all bloody! Nyah!"

Having recovered and realizing perfectly well whom he was dealing with, the officer politely (though covering his face with a handkerchief) addressed the prince, who had gotten up from the chair:

"Prince Myshkin, whose acquaintance I had the pleasure of making?"

"She's crazy! Mad! I assure you!" the prince replied in a trembling voice, reaching his trembling hands out to him for some reason.

"I, of course, cannot boast of being so well informed; but I do need to know your name."

He bowed his head and walked off. The police arrived exactly five seconds after the last of the participants had gone. However, the scandal had lasted no more than two minutes. Some of the public got up from their chairs and left, others merely changed places; a third group was very glad of the scandal; a fourth began intensely talking and questioning. In short, the matter ended as usual. The orchestra started playing again. The prince followed after the Epanchins. If it had occurred to him or he had managed to look to the left, as he sat on the chair after being shoved away, he would have seen Aglaya, who had stopped some twenty paces from him to watch the scandalous scene and did not heed the calls of her mother and sisters, who had already moved further off. Prince Shch., running up to her, finally persuaded her to leave quickly. Lizaveta Prokofyevna remembered that Aglaya rejoined them in such agitation that she could hardly have heard their calls. But exactly two minutes later, just as they entered the park, Aglaya said in her usual indifferent and capricious voice:

"I wanted to see how the comedy would end."

III

THE INCIDENT AT the vauxhall struck both mother and daughters almost with terror. Alarmed and agitated, Lizaveta Prokofyevna literally all but ran with her daughters the whole way home from the vauxhall. In her view and understanding, all too much had occurred and been revealed in this incident, so that in her head, despite all the disorder and fear, resolute thoughts were already germinating. But everyone else also understood that something special had happened and that, perhaps fortunately, some extraordinary mystery was beginning to be revealed. Despite the earlier assurances of Prince Shch., Evgeny Pavlovich had now been "brought into the open," exposed, uncovered, and "formally revealed as having connections with that creature." So thought Lizaveta Prokofyevna and even her two elder daughters. The profit of this conclusion was that still more riddles accumulated. The girls, though inwardly somewhat indignant at their mother's exaggerated alarm and so obvious flight, did not dare to trouble her with questions in the first moments of the turmoil. Besides that, for some reason it seemed to them that their little sister, Aglaya Ivanovna, might know more about this affair than the three of them, including the mother. Prince Shch. was also dark as night and also very pensive. Lizaveta Prokofyevna did not say a word to him all the way, but he seemed not to notice it. Adelaida tried to ask him who this uncle was who had just been spoken of and what had happened in Petersburg. But he mumbled in reply to her, with a very sour face, something very vague about some inquiries and that it was all, of course, an absurdity. "There's no doubt of that!" Adelaida replied and did not ask him anything more. Aglaya was somehow extraordinarily calm and only observed, on the way, that they were running much too quickly. Once she turned and saw the prince, who was trying to catch up with them. Noticing his efforts, she smiled mockingly and did not turn to look at him anymore.

Finally, almost at their dacha, they met Ivan Fyodorovich walking towards them; he had just come from Petersburg. At once, with the first word, he inquired about Evgeny Pavlovich. But his spouse walked past him menacingly, without answering and without even glancing at him. By the looks of his daughters and Prince Shch., he immediately guessed that there was a storm in the house. But even without that, his own face reflected some extraordinary anxiety. He at once took Prince Shch. by the arm, stopped him at the entrance, and exchanged a few words with him almost in a whisper. By the alarmed look of the two men as they went up onto the terrace afterwards and went to Lizaveta Prokofyevna's side, one might have thought they had both heard some extraordinary news. Gradually they all gathered in Lizaveta Prokofyevna's drawing room upstairs, and only the prince was left on the terrace. He was sitting in the corner as if waiting for something, though he did not know why himself; it did not even occur to him to leave, seeing the turmoil in the house; it seemed he had forgotten the whole universe and was prepared to sit it out for two years in a row, wherever he might be sitting. From time to time echoes of anxious conversation came to his ears. He himself would have been unable to say how long he had been sitting there. It was getting late and quite dark. Suddenly Aglaya came out on the terrace; she looked calm, though somewhat pale. Seeing the prince, whom she "obviously wasn't expecting" to meet there, sitting on a chair in the corner, Aglaya smiled as if in perplexity.

"What are you doing here?" she went over to him.

The prince murmured something in embarrassment and jumped up from his chair; but Aglaya at once sat down next to him, and he sat down again. She looked him over, suddenly but attentively, then looked out the window, as if without any thought, then again at him. "Maybe she wants to laugh," it occurred to the prince, "but no, she'd just laugh then."

"Maybe you'd like some tea. I'll tell them," she said after some silence.

"N-no . . . I don't know . . ."

"Well, how can you not know that! Ah, yes, listen: if someone challenged you to a duel, what would you do? I meant to ask you earlier."

"But . . . who . . . no one is going to challenge me to a duel."

"Well, but if someone did? Would you be very afraid?"

"I think I'd be very . . . afraid."

"Seriously? So you're a coward?"

"N-no, maybe not. A coward is someone who is afraid and runs away; but someone who is afraid but doesn't run away is not a coward yet," the prince smiled after pondering a little.

"And you wouldn't run away?"

"Maybe I wouldn't," he finally laughed at Aglaya's questions.

"I'm a woman, but I wouldn't run away for anything," she observed, almost touchily. "And, anyhow, you're clowning and making fun of me in your usual way, to make yourself more interesting. Tell me: don't they usually shoot from twelve paces? Sometimes even from ten? Doesn't that mean you're sure to be killed or wounded?"

"People must rarely be hit at duels."

"Rarely? Pushkin was killed."[5]

"That may have been accidental."

"Not accidental at all. They fought to kill and he was killed."

"The bullet struck so low that d'Anthès must have been aiming somewhere higher, at his chest or head; no one aims to hit a man where he did, so the bullet most likely hit Pushkin accidentally, from a bad shot. Competent people have told me so."

"But I was told by a soldier I once talked with that, according to regulations, when they open ranks, they're ordered to aim on purpose at the half-man; that's how they say it: 'at the half-man.' That means not at the chest, not at the head, but they're ordered to aim on purpose at the half-man. Later I asked an officer, and he said that was exactly right."

"It's right because they shoot from a great distance."

"And do you know how to shoot?"

"I've never done it."

"Do you at least know how to load a pistol?"

"No, I don't. That is, I understand how it's done, but I've never loaded one myself."

"Well, that means you don't know how, because it takes practice! Listen now and learn well: first, buy good gunpowder, not damp (they say it mustn't be damp, but very dry), the fine sort, you can ask about it, but not the kind used for cannons. They say you have to mold the bullet yourself. Do you have pistols?"

"No, and I don't need any," the prince suddenly laughed.

"Ah, what nonsense! You must certainly buy one, a good one,

French or English, they say they're the best. Then take some powder, a thimbleful or maybe two thimblefuls, and pour it in. Better put in more. Ram it down with felt (they say it absolutely must be felt for some reason), you can get that somewhere, from some mattress, or doors are sometimes upholstered with felt. Then, when you've stuffed the felt in, you put in the bullet—do you hear, the bullet after, and the felt before, otherwise it won't fire. Why are you laughing? I want you to shoot several times a day and learn to hit the mark without fail. Will you do it?"

The prince laughed; Aglaya stamped her foot in vexation. Her serious air, in such a conversation, surprised the prince a little. He partly felt that he had to find out about something, to ask about something—in any case about something more serious than how to load a pistol. But everything flew out of his mind, except for the one fact that she was sitting before him, and he was looking at her, and what she talked about at that moment made scarcely any difference to him.

Finally Ivan Fyodorovich himself came down to the terrace from upstairs; he was headed somewhere with a frowning, preoccupied, and determined look.

"Ah, Lev Nikolaich, it's you . . . Where to now?" he asked, though Lev Nikolaevich had not thought of moving from his place. "Come along, I'll tell you a little something."

"Good-bye," said Aglaya, and she gave the prince her hand.

It was already rather dark on the terrace; the prince could not make out her face quite clearly at that moment. A minute later, as he and the general were leaving the dacha, he suddenly turned terribly red and clenched his right hand tightly.

It turned out that Ivan Fyodorovich was going the same way he was; despite the late hour, Ivan Fyodorovich was hurrying to speak with someone about something. But meanwhile he suddenly began talking with the prince, quickly, anxiously, rather incoherently, often mentioning Lizaveta Prokofyevna. If the prince could have been more attentive at that moment, he might have guessed that Ivan Fyodorovich wanted among other things to find out something from him as well, or, better, to ask him directly and openly about something, but never managed to touch on the chiefest point. To his shame, the prince was so distracted that at the very beginning he did not even hear anything, and when the general stopped in front of him with some burning question, he was forced to confess that he understood nothing.

The general shrugged his shoulders.

"You've all become some sort of strange people, in all respects," he started talking again. "I tell you, I utterly fail to understand Lizaveta Prokofyevna's ideas and anxieties. She's in hysterics, she weeps and says we've been covered with shame and disgrace. By whom? How? With whom? When and why? I confess I'm to blame (I admit it), greatly to blame, but the importunities of this . . . troublesome woman (and ill-behaved besides) can finally be restricted by the police, and even tonight I intend to see a certain person and give warning. Everything can be arranged quietly, meekly, affectionately even, through connections and without any scandal. I also agree that the future is fraught with events and much is unexplained; there's some intrigue involved; but if they don't know anything here, they can't explain anything there either; if I haven't heard, you haven't heard, this one hasn't heard, that one hasn't heard, then who, finally, has heard, I ask you? What can explain it, in your opinion, except that the affair is half a mirage, doesn't exist, like moonlight, for instance . . . or other phantoms."

"*She* is a madwoman," the prince murmured, suddenly remembering, with pain, all that had happened earlier.

"That's the word, if you mean her. Somewhat the same idea used to visit me, and then I'd sleep peacefully. But now I see that others think more correctly, and I don't believe it's madness. She's a cantankerous woman, granted, but with that also a subtle one, anything but crazy. Today's escapade to do with Kapiton Alexeich proves it only too well. It's a crooked business on her part, Jesuitical at the very least, for her own purposes."

"What Kapiton Alexeich?"

"Ah, my God, Lev Nikolaich, you're not listening at all. I began by telling you about Kapiton Alexeich; I'm so struck that even now I'm trembling from head to foot. That's why I came late from the city today. Kapiton Alexeich Radomsky, Evgeny Pavlych's uncle . . ."

"What!" cried the prince.

"Shot himself this morning at dawn, at seven o'clock. A venerable man, seventy years old, an Epicurean—and it's just as she said about the government funds, a mighty sum!"

"How did she . . ."

"Find out, you mean? Ha, ha! As soon as she appeared here, a whole staff formed around her. You know what sort of persons visit her now and seek the 'honor of her acquaintance.' Naturally, she could have heard something earlier from her visitors, because the whole of Petersburg knows already and half, if not the whole, of Pavlovsk. But what a subtle observation she made about the uniform, as I've been told, that is, about Evgeny Pavlych managing to resign from the army in good time! What an infernal allusion! No, that doesn't suggest insanity. I, of course, refuse to believe that Evgeny Pavlych could have known about the catastrophe beforehand, that is, on such-and-such a day, at seven o'clock, and so on. But he might have anticipated it all. And here I am, here we all are, including Prince Shch., counting on the old man leaving him an inheritance! Terrible! Terrible! Understand, however, that I'm not accusing Evgeny Pavlych of anything, and I hasten to make that clear to you, but all the same it's suspicious. Prince Shch. is extremely struck. It's all fallen out so strangely."

"But what is suspicious in Evgeny Pavlych's behavior?"

"Nothing! He behaved in the noblest fashion. I wasn't hinting at anything. His own fortune, I think, is intact. Lizaveta Prokofyevna, naturally, won't hear anything . . . But the main thing is all these family catastrophes, or, better, all these squabbles, one doesn't even know what to call them . . . You, truly speaking, are a friend of the house, Lev Nikolaich, and imagine, it now turns out—though, by the way, not precisely—that Evgeny Pavlych supposedly proposed to Aglaya more than a month ago and supposedly received a formal rejection from her."

"That can't be!" the prince cried hotly.

"Perhaps you know something? You see, my dearest," the general roused himself in surprise, stopping as if rooted to the spot, "maybe I spilled it out to you needlessly and improperly, but it's because you're . . . you're . . . one might say, that sort of man. Maybe you know something particular?"

"I know nothing . . . about Evgeny Pavlych," the prince murmured.

"Neither do I! They . . . they decidedly want to dig a hole in the ground and bury me, brother, and they refuse to understand that it's hard on a man and that I won't survive it. There was such a terrible scene just now! I'm telling you like my own son. The main thing is that Aglaya seems to be laughing at her mother. That she apparently rejected Evgeny Pavlych about a month ago, and that they had a rather formal talk, her sisters told us, as a guess . . . a firm guess, however. But she's such a willful and fantastic being, it's impossible to describe! All those magnanimities, all those brilliant qualities of heart and mind—all that, perhaps, is there in her, but along with such caprices and mockeries—in short, a demoniacal character, and with fantasies on top of it. She just laughed in her mother's face, at her sisters, at Prince Shch.; to say nothing of me, it's rare that she doesn't laugh at me, but what am I, you know, I love her, love it even that she laughs at me—and the little demon seems to love me especially for that, that is, more than the others, it seems. I'll bet she's already laughed at you for something. I just found the two of you talking, after the storm upstairs; she was sitting with you as if nothing had happened."

The prince turned terribly red and clenched his right hand, but said nothing.

"My dear, kind Lev Nikolaich!" the general suddenly said with feeling and warmth, "I . . . and even Lizaveta Prokofyevna herself (who, incidentally, began railing at you again, and at me along with you and on account of you, only I don't understand what for), we love you all the same, sincerely love you and respect you, even in spite of everything, that is, all appearances. But you must agree, dear friend, you yourself must agree, what a riddle it is suddenly, and how vexing to hear, when suddenly this cold-blooded little demon (because she stood before her mother with an air of the profoundest contempt for all our questions, and mostly for mine, because, devil take me, I got foolish, I decided to show my severity, since I'm the head of the family—well, and got foolish), this cold-blooded little demon suddenly up and announced with a grin that this 'madwoman' (that was how she put it, and I find it strange that she used the same word as you: 'Couldn't you have figured it out by now?' she says), that this madwoman 'has taken it into her head to marry me off at all costs to Prince Lev Nikolaich, and that's why she's trying to drive Evgeny Pavlych out of our house . . .' That's all she said; she gave no further explanation, just laughed loudly, while we stood there gaping, slammed the door, and was gone. Then they told me about the incident today between her and you . . . and . . . and . . . listen, my dear Prince, you're a very reasonable man, not about to take offense, I've noticed that in you, but . . . don't be angry: by God, she's making fun of you. She does it like a child, so don't be angry with her, but it's decidedly so. Don't think anything—she simply makes fools of you and us, out of idleness. Well, good-bye! You do know our feelings? Our sincere feelings for you? They haven't changed, never, not in anything . . . but . . . I go that way now, good-bye! I've rarely sat so

poorly in my plate (or how does it go?) than I'm sitting now[6] . . .
Dacha life!"

Left alone at the intersection, the prince looked around, quickly
crossed the road, went up to the lighted window of a dacha,
unfolded a small piece of paper he had been clenching tightly in
his right hand during the whole conversation with Ivan Fyodorovich, and read, catching a faint beam of light:

> Tomorrow at seven o'clock in the morning I will be on the
> green bench in the park, waiting for you. I have decided to talk
> with you about an extremely important matter that concerns you
> directly.
>
> P.S. I hope you won't show this note to anyone. Though I'm
> ashamed to write such instructions to you, I consider that you
> deserve it, and so I've written it—blushing with shame at your
> ridiculous character.
>
> P.P.S. It is that same green bench I showed you today. Shame
> on you! I was forced to add that as well.

The note had been written hastily and folded anyhow, most
likely just before Aglaya came out to the terrace. In inexpressible
agitation, resembling fear, the prince again clenched the paper
tightly in his hand and quickly jumped away from the window,
from the light, like a frightened thief; but in making this movement
he suddenly ran smack into a gentleman who turned up right at
his shoulder.

"I've been watching you, Prince," said the gentleman.

"Is that you, Keller?" the prince cried in surprise.

"I've been looking for you, Prince. I waited by the Epanchins'
dacha—naturally, I couldn't go in. I followed you as you walked
with the general. I'm at your service, Prince, you may dispose of
Keller. Ready to sacrifice myself and even to die, if necessary."

"But . . . what for?"

"Well, there's sure to be a challenge. This Lieutenant Molovtsov,
I know him, that is, not personally . . . he won't suffer an insult.
Our sort, that is, me and Rogozhin, he's naturally inclined to
consider riffraff, and maybe deservedly—so you turn out to be the
only one answerable. You'll have to pay the piper, Prince. He's
made inquiries about you, I've heard, and a friend of his is sure to
call on you tomorrow, or maybe he's waiting for you now. If you
grant me the honor of choosing me as a second, I'm ready to accept
the red cap for you;[7] that's why I was waiting for you, Prince."

"So you're also talking about a duel!" the prince suddenly burst out laughing, to the great astonishment of Keller. He laughed his head off. Keller, who had indeed been on pins and needles, waiting until he had the satisfaction of offering himself as a second, was almost offended, seeing how merrily the prince laughed.

"Nevertheless, Prince, you seized him by the arms. For a noble person, it's hard to suffer that in public."

"And he shoved me in the chest!" the prince exclaimed, laughing. "We have nothing to fight about! I'll apologize to him and that's that. But if it's a fight, it's a fight. Let him shoot; I even want it. Ha, ha! I know how to load a pistol now! Do you know how to load a pistol, Keller? First you have to buy powder, gunpowder, not damp and not the coarse kind used for cannons; and then you start by putting in some powder, you get felt from a door somewhere, and only then drop in the bullet, not the bullet before the powder, because it won't fire. Do you hear, Keller: because it won't fire. Ha, ha! Isn't that a splendid reason, friend Keller? Ah, Keller, you know, I'm going to embrace you and kiss you now. Ha, ha, ha! How was it that you so suddenly turned up in front of him today? Call on me sometime soon and we'll have champagne. We'll all get drunk! Do you know that I have twelve bottles of champagne in Lebedev's cellar? Lebedev offered it to me as a 'bargain' two days ago, the day after I moved to his place, so I bought it all! I'll get the whole company together! And you, are you going to sleep this night?"

"Like every other, Prince."

"Well, sweet dreams then! Ha, ha!"

The prince crossed the road and disappeared into the park, leaving the somewhat puzzled Keller pondering. He had never seen the prince in such a strange mood, and could not have imagined it till then.

"A fever, maybe, because he's a nervous man, and all this has affected him, but he certainly won't turn coward. His kind doesn't turn coward, by God!" Keller thought to himself. "Hm, champagne! Interesting news, by the way. Twelve bottles, sir, a tidy dozen; that's a decent stock. I'll bet Lebedev took it in pledge from somebody. Hm . . . he's a sweet enough fellow, though, this prince; I really like that sort; there's no time to waste, though, and . . . if there's champagne, then this is the moment . . ."

That the prince was as if in a fever was certainly correct.

For a long time he wandered through the dark park and finally "found himself" pacing along a certain alley. His consciousness retained the memory that he had already walked along that alley, from the bench to a certain old tree, tall and conspicuous, about a hundred steps, some thirty or forty times up and down. He would have been quite unable to remember what he had thought about during that whole hour, at least, in the park, even if he had wanted to. He caught himself, however, in a certain thought, which made him suddenly rock with laughter; though there was nothing to laugh at, he still wanted to laugh. He imagined that the supposition of a duel might not have been born in Keller's head alone, and that, therefore, the story about loading a pistol might not have been accidental . . . "Hah!" he stopped suddenly, as another idea dawned on him, "she came down to the terrace tonight when I was sitting in the corner, and was terribly surprised to find me there, and—laughed so . . . talked about tea; but at that time she already had this note in her hand, which means she must have known I was sitting on the terrace, so why was she surprised? Ha, ha, ha!"

He snatched the note from his pocket and kissed it, but at once stopped and pondered.

"How strange! How strange!" he said after a moment, even with a sort of sadness: he always felt sad at moments of great joy, he did not know why himself. He looked around intently and was surprised that he had come there. He was very tired, went over to the bench and sat down. It was extremely quiet all around. The music in the vauxhall was over. There was probably no one in the park now; it was certainly at least half-past eleven. The night was quiet, warm, bright—a Petersburg night at the beginning of the month of June—but in the thick, shady park, in the alley where he was, it was almost completely dark.

If anyone had told him at that moment that he had fallen in love, that he was passionately in love, he would have rejected the idea with astonishment and perhaps even with indignation. And if anyone had added that Aglaya's note was a love letter, setting up a lovers' tryst, he would have burned with shame for that man and might have challenged him to a duel. All this was perfectly sincere, and he never once doubted it or allowed for the slightest "second" thought about the possibility of this girl loving him or even the possibility of him loving this girl. The possibility of loving him, "a man like him," he would have considered a monstrous thing. He vaguely thought that it was simply a prank on her part, if there indeed was anything to it; but he was somehow all too indifferent to the prank itself and found it all too much in the order of things; he himself was concerned and preoccupied with something completely different. He fully believed the words that had escaped the agitated general earlier, that she was laughing at everyone and especially at him, the prince. He had not felt insulted by it in the least; in his opinion, it had to be so. The main thing for him was that tomorrow he would see her again, early in the morning, would sit beside her on the green bench, listen to how a pistol is loaded, and look at her. He needed nothing more. The question of what it was that she intended to tell him, and what the important matter was that concerned him directly, also flashed once or twice in his head. Besides, he had never doubted even for a minute the actual existence of this "important matter" for which he had been summoned, but he almost did not think of this important matter now, to the point that he even did not feel the slightest urge to think about it.

The crunch of quiet steps on the sand of the alley made him raise his head. A man, whose face it was difficult to make out in the darkness, came up to the bench and sat down beside him. The prince quickly moved close to him, almost touching him, and made out the pale face of Rogozhin.

"I just knew you'd be wandering about here somewhere, I didn't have to look long," Rogozhin muttered through his teeth.

It was the first time they had come together since their meeting in the corridor of the inn. Struck by Rogozhin's sudden appearance, the prince was unable to collect his thoughts for some time, and a painful sensation rose again in his heart. Rogozhin evidently understood the impression he had made; but though at first he kept getting confused, spoke as if with the air of a sort of studied casualness, it soon seemed to the prince that there was nothing studied in him and not even any particular embarrassment; if there was any awkwardness in his gestures and conversation, it was only on the outside; in his soul this man could not change.

"How . . . did you find me here?" asked the prince, in order to say something.

"I heard from Keller (I went by your place) that 'he went to the park.' Well, I thought, so there it is."

"There what is?" the prince anxiously picked up the escaped remark.

Rogozhin grinned, but gave no explanation.

"I got your letter, Lev Nikolaich; you don't need all that . . . what do you care! . . . And now I'm coming to you from *her*: she told me to be sure and invite you; she needs very much to tell you something. She asks you to come tonight."

"I'll come tomorrow. Right now I'm going home; will you . . . come with me?"

"Why? I've told you everything. Good-bye."

"You won't come?" the prince asked softly.

"You're a queer one, Lev Nikolaich, you really amaze me." Rogozhin grinned sarcastically.

"Why? What makes you so spiteful towards me now?" the prince picked up sadly and ardently. "You know now that everything you were thinking was not true. I did think, however, that your spite towards me had still not gone away, and do you know why? Because you raised your hand against me, that's why your spite won't go away. I tell you that I remember only the Parfyon Rogozhin with whom I exchanged crosses that day as a brother; I wrote that to you in my letter yesterday, so that you'd forget to think about all that delirium and not start talking with me about it. Why are you backing away from me? Why are you hiding your hand from me? I tell you, I consider all that happened then as nothing but delirium: all that you went through that day I now know as well as I know my own self. What you were imagining did not and could not exist. Why, then, should our spite exist?"

"What spite could you have!" Rogozhin laughed again in response to the prince's ardent, unexpected speech. He was indeed standing back from him, two steps to the side, and hiding his hands.

"It's not a right thing for me to come to you at all now, Lev Nikolaich," he added in conclusion, slowly and sententiously.

"Do you really hate me so much?"

"I don't like you, Lev Nikolaich, so why should I come to you? Eh, Prince, you're just like some child, you want a toy, you've got to have it right now, but you don't understand what it's about. Everything you're saying now is just like what you wrote in your letter, and do you think I don't believe you? I believe every word of yours, and I know you've never deceived me and never will in the future; but I still don't like you. You write that you've forgotten everything and only remember your brother Rogozhin that you exchanged crosses with, and not the Rogozhin who raised a knife against you that time. But how should you know my feelings?"

(Rogozhin grinned again.) "Maybe I never once repented of it afterwards, and you've gone and sent me your brotherly forgiveness. Maybe that evening I was already thinking about something completely different, and . . ."

"Forgot all about it!" the prince picked up. "What else! And I'll bet you went straight to the train that time, and here in Pavlovsk to the music, and watched and searched for her in the crowd just as you did today. Some surprise! But if you hadn't been in such a state then that you could only think of one particular thing, maybe you wouldn't have raised a knife at me. I had a presentiment that morning, as I looked at you; do you know how you were then? When we were exchanging crosses, this thought began to stir in me. Why did you take me to see the old woman then? Did you want to restrain your hand that way? But it can't be that you thought of it, you just sensed it, as I did . . . We sensed it word for word then. If you hadn't raised your hand against me (which God warded off), how would I come out before you now? Since I suspected you of it anyway, our sin is the same, word for word! (And don't make a wry face! Well, and what are you laughing for?) 'I've never repented!' But even if you wanted to, maybe you wouldn't be able to repent, because on top of it all you don't like me. And if I were as innocent as an angel before you, you still wouldn't be able to stand me, as long as you think it's not you but me that she loves. That's jealousy for you. Only I was thinking about it this week, Parfyon, and I'll tell you: do you know that she may now love you most of all, and so much, even, that the more she torments you, the more she loves you? She won't tell you that, but you must be able to see it. Why in the end is she going to marry you all the same? Someday she'll tell you herself. There are women who even want to be loved in that way, and that's precisely her character! And your character and your love had to strike her! Do you know that a woman is capable of torturing a man with her cruelties and mockeries, and will not feel remorse even once, because she thinks to herself each time she looks at you: 'Now I'll torture him to death, but later I'll make up for it with my love . . .'"

Rogozhin, having listened to the prince, burst out laughing.

"And have you happened upon such a woman yourself, Prince? I've heard a little something about you, if it's true!"

"What, what could you have heard?" the prince suddenly shook and stopped in extreme embarrassment.

Rogozhin went on laughing. He had listened to the prince not without curiosity and perhaps not without pleasure; the prince's joyful and ardent enthusiasm greatly struck and encouraged him.

"I've not only heard it, but I see now that it's true," he added. "Well, when did you ever talk the way you do now? That kind of talk doesn't seem to come from you at all. If I hadn't heard as much about you, I wouldn't have come here; and to the park, at midnight, besides."

"I don't understand you at all, Parfyon Semyonych."

"She explained to me about you long ago, and now today I saw it myself, the way you were sitting at the music with the other one. She swore to me by God, yesterday and today, that you're in love like a tomcat with Aglaya Epanchin. It makes no difference to me, Prince, and it's none of my business: even if you don't love her anymore, she still loves you. You know, she absolutely wants you to marry that girl, she gave me her word on it, heh, heh! She says to me: 'Without that I won't marry you, they go to church, and we go to church.' What it's all about, I can't understand and never could: either she loves you no end, or . . . but if she loves you, why does she want you to marry another woman? She says: 'I want to see him happy'—so that means she loves you."

"I told you and wrote to you that she's . . . not in her right mind," said the prince, having listened to Rogozhin with suffering.

"Lord knows! You may be mistaken about that . . . anyhow, today she set the date for me, when I brought her home from the music: in three weeks, and maybe sooner, she says, we'll certainly get married; she swore to me, took down an icon, kissed it. So, Prince, now it's up to you, heh, heh!"

"That's all raving! What you're saying about me will never, never happen! I'll come to you tomorrow . . ."

"What kind of madwoman is she?" observed Rogozhin. "How is it she's in her right mind for everybody else, and for you alone she's crazy? How is it she writes letters there? If she's a madwoman, it would have been noticed there from her letters."

"What letters?" the prince asked in alarm.

"She writes there, to *that one*, and she reads them. Don't you know? Well, then you will; she's sure to show you herself."

"That's impossible to believe!" cried the prince.

"Eh, Lev Nikolaich, it must be you haven't gone very far down that path yet, as far as I can see, you're just at the beginning. Wait a while: you'll hire your own police, you'll keep watch yourself day and night, and know every step they make there, if only . . ."

"Drop it and never speak of it again!" cried the prince. "Listen, Parfyon, I was walking here just now before you came and suddenly began to laugh, I didn't know what about, but the reason was that I remembered that tomorrow, as if on purpose, is my birthday. It's nearly midnight now. Let's go and meet the day! I have some wine, we'll drink wine, you must wish me something I myself don't know how to wish for now, and it's precisely you who must wish it, and I'll wish you your fullest happiness. Or else give me back my cross! You didn't send it back to me the next day! You're wearing it? Wearing it even now?"

"I am," said Rogozhin.

"Come on, then. I don't want to meet my new life without you, because my new life has begun! Don't you know, Parfyon, that my new life begins today?"

"Now I myself see and know that it's begun; and I'll report it to *her*. You're not yourself at all, Lev Nikolaich!"

IV

As he approached his dacha with Rogozhin, the prince noticed with extreme astonishment that a noisy and numerous society had gathered on his brightly lit terrace. The merry company was laughing, shouting; it seemed they were even arguing loudly; one would have suspected at first glance that they were having quite a joyful time of it. And indeed, going up onto the terrace, he saw that they were all drinking, and drinking champagne, and it seemed they had been at it for quite a while, so that many of the revelers had managed to become quite pleasantly animated. The guests were all acquaintances of the prince, but it was strange that they had all gathered at once, as if they had been invited, though the prince had not invited anyone, and he himself had only just chanced to remember about his birthday.

"You must have told somebody you'd stand them to champagne, so they came running," Rogozhin muttered, following the prince up onto the terrace. "That point we know; just whistle to them . . ." he added almost with spite, remembering, of course, his recent past.

They all met the prince with shouts and good wishes, and surrounded him. Some were very noisy, others much quieter, but they all hastened to congratulate him, having heard about his birthday, and each one waited his turn. The prince found the presence of some persons curious, Burdovsky's, for instance; but the most astonishing thing was that amidst this company Evgeny Pavlovich suddenly turned up. The prince could hardly believe his eyes and was almost frightened when he saw him.

Meanwhile Lebedev, flushed and nearly ecstatic, ran up to him with explanations; he was rather well *loaded*. From his babble it turned out that they had all gathered quite naturally and even accidentally. First of all, towards evening, Ippolit had come and, feeling much better, had wanted to wait for the prince on the terrace. He had settled himself on the sofa; then Lebedev had come down to see him, and then his whole family, that is, his daughters and General Ivolgin. Burdovsky had come with Ippolit as his escort. Ganya and Ptitsyn, it seemed, had dropped in not long ago, while passing by (their appearance coincided with the incident in the vauxhall); then Keller had turned up, told them about the birthday, and asked for champagne. Evgeny Pavlovich had come only about half an hour ago. Kolya had also insisted with all his might on champagne and that a celebration be arranged. Lebedev readily served the wine.

"But my own, my own!" he babbled to the prince. "At my own expense, to glorify and celebrate, and there'll be food, a little snack, my daughter will see to that; but if you only knew, Prince, what a theme we've got going. Remember in *Hamlet*: 'To be or not to be'? A modern theme, sir, modern! Questions and answers . . . And Mr. Terentyev is in the highest degree . . . unwilling to sleep! He had just a sip of champagne, a sip, nothing harmful . . . Come closer, Prince, and decide! Everybody's been waiting for you, everybody's only been waiting for your happy wit . . ."

The prince noticed the sweet, tender eyes of Vera Lebedev, who was also hurriedly making her way to him through the crowd. He reached past them all and gave her his hand first; she blushed with pleasure and wished him "a happy life *starting this very day*." Then she rushed off to the kitchen; she was preparing the snack there; but before the prince's arrival—the moment she could tear herself away from her work—she would come to the terrace and listen as hard as she could to the heated arguments constantly going on among the tipsy guests about things that were most abstract and strange to her. Her younger sister, the one who opened her mouth, fell asleep on a trunk in the next room, but the boy, Lebedev's son, stood beside Kolya and Ippolit, and the very look on his animated face showed that he was prepared to stand there in the same spot, relishing and listening, for another ten hours on end.

"I've been especially waiting for you, and I'm terribly glad you've come so happy," Ippolit said, when the prince went over to shake hands with him immediately after Vera.

"And how do you know that I'm 'so happy'?"

"By the look on your face. Greet the gentlemen, and then quickly come to sit with us. I've been waiting especially for you," he added, significantly stressing the fact that he had been waiting. To the prince's remark that it might be bad for him to stay up so late, he replied that he was surprised at his wanting to die three days ago and that he had never felt better than that evening.

Burdovsky jumped up and murmured that he had come "just so . . . ," that he was with Ippolit "as an escort," and that he was also glad; that he had "written nonsense" in his letter, and that now he was "simply glad . . ." He did not finish, pressed the prince's hand firmly, and sat down on a chair.

After everyone else, the prince went over to Evgeny Pavlovich. The latter immediately took him by the arm.

"I have only a couple of words to say to you," he whispered in a low voice, "and about an extremely important circumstance. Let's step aside for a moment."

"A couple of words," another voice whispered into the prince's other ear, and another hand took him by the arm from the other side. The prince was surprised to see a terribly disheveled, flushed, winking and laughing face, in which he instantly recognized Ferdyshchenko, who had appeared from God knows where.

"Remember Ferdyshchenko?" the man asked.

"Where did you come from?" cried the prince.

"He repents!" cried Keller, running up. "He was hiding, he didn't want to come out to you, he was hiding there in the corner, he repents, Prince, he feels guilty."

"But of what, of what?"

"It was I who met him, Prince, I met him just now and brought him along; he's a rare one among my friends; but he repents."

"I'm very glad, gentlemen. Go and sit there with everyone, I'll be back presently." The prince finally got rid of them and hurried to Evgeny Pavlovich.

"It's amusing here," Evgeny Pavlovich observed, "and it was with pleasure that I waited half an hour for you. The thing is, my most gentle Lev Nikolaevich, that I've settled everything with

Kurmyshev and have come to put you at ease; there's nothing to worry about, he took the matter very, very reasonably, the more so because, in my opinion, it was sooner his fault."

"What Kurmyshev?"

"The one you seized by the arms today . . . He was so infuriated that he wanted to send someone to you tomorrow for explanations."

"Come, come, what nonsense!"

"Naturally it's nonsense and would probably have ended in non-sense; but these people . . ."

"Perhaps you've come for something else, Evgeny Pavlovich?"

"Oh, naturally there's something else," the man laughed. "Tomorrow at daybreak, my dear Prince, I'm going to Petersburg on this unfortunate business (I mean, about my uncle). Imagine to yourself: it's all true and everybody already knows it except me. I was so struck that I haven't had time to go *there* (to the Epanchins'); I won't see them tomorrow either, because I'll be in Petersburg, you understand? I may not be back for three days—in short, my affairs are in poor shape. Though the matter is not of infinite importance, I reasoned that I ought to have a most candid talk with you about certain things, and without losing time, that is, before my departure. I'll sit here now and wait, if you tell me to, till the company disperses; besides, I have nothing else to do with myself: I'm so agitated that I won't be able to sleep. Finally, though it's shameless and improper to pursue a person so directly, I'll tell you directly: I've come to seek your friendship, my dear Prince. You are a most incomparable man, that is, you don't lie at every step, and maybe not at all, and there's one matter in which I need a friend and an advisor, because I now decidedly find myself among the unfortunate . . ."

He laughed again.

"The trouble is," the prince reflected for a moment, "that you want to wait till they disperse, but God knows when that will be. Wouldn't it be better to go down to the park now? They'll wait, really; I'll apologize."

"No, no, I have my reasons for not arousing the suspicion that we are having an urgent conversation with some purpose; there are people here who are very interested in our relations—don't you know that, Prince? And it will be much better if they see that they are the most friendly relations, and not merely urgent ones—you understand? They'll leave in a couple of hours; I'll take about twenty minutes of your time—maybe half an hour . . ."

"You're most welcome, please stay. I'm very glad even without explanations; and thank you very much for your kind words about our friendly relations. You must forgive me for being absentminded tonight; you know, I simply cannot be attentive at the moment."

"I see, I see," Evgeny Pavlovich murmured with a slight smile. He laughed very easily that evening.

"What do you see?" the prince roused himself up.

"And don't you suspect, dear Prince," Evgeny Pavlovich went on smiling, without answering the direct question, "don't you suspect that I've simply come to hoodwink you and, incidentally, to worm something out of you, eh?"

"There's no doubt at all that you've come to worm something out of me," the prince finally laughed, too, "and it may even be that you've decided to deceive me a bit. But so what? I'm not afraid of you; what's more, it somehow makes no difference to me now, can you believe that? And . . . and . . . and since I'm convinced before all that you are still an excellent person, we may indeed end by becoming friends. I like you very much, Evgeny Pavlych; in my opinion, you're . . . a very, very decent man!"

"Well, in any case it's very nice dealing with you, even in whatever it may be," Evgeny Pavlovich concluded. "Come, I'll drink a glass to your health; I'm terribly pleased to have joined you here. Ah!" he suddenly stopped, "has this gentleman Ippolit come to live with you?"

"Yes."

"He's not going to die at once, I suppose?"

"Why?"

"No, nothing; I spent half an hour with him here . . ."

All this time Ippolit was waiting for the prince and constantly glancing at him and Evgeny Pavlovich, while they stood aside talking. He became feverishly animated as they approached the table. He was restless and agitated; sweat broke out on his forehead. His eyes, along with a sort of roving, continual restlessness, also showed a certain vague impatience; his gaze moved aimlessly from object to object, from person to person. Though up to then he had taken great part in the general noisy conversation, his animation was only feverish; he paid no attention to the conversation itself; his arguments were incoherent, ironic, and carelessly paradoxical; he did not finish and dropped something he himself had begun saying a moment earlier with feverish ardor. The prince learned with surprise and regret that he had been allowed, unhindered, to drink two full glasses of champagne that evening, and that the glass he had started on, which stood before him, was already the third. But he learned it only later; at the present moment he was not very observant.

"You know, I'm terribly glad that precisely today is your birthday!" cried Ippolit.

"Why?"

"You'll see. Sit down quickly. First of all, because all these . . . your people have gathered. I reckoned there would be people; for the first time in my life my reckoning came out right! Too bad I didn't know about your birthday, or I'd have come with a present . . . Ha, ha! Maybe I did come with a present! Is it long before daylight?"

"It's less than two hours till dawn," Ptitsyn said, looking at his watch.

"Who needs the dawn, if you can read outside as it is?" someone observed.

"It's because I need to see the rim of the sun. Can one drink the sun's health, Prince, what do you think?"

Ippolit asked abruptly, addressing everyone without ceremony, as if he were in command, but he seemed not to notice it himself.

"Perhaps so; only you ought to calm down, eh, Ippolit?"

"You're always talking about sleep; you're my nanny, Prince! As soon as the sun appears and 'resounds' in the sky (who said that in a poem: 'the sun resounded in the sky'?[8] It's meaningless, but good!)—we'll go to bed. Lebedev! Is the sun the wellspring of life? What are the 'wellsprings of life' in the Apocalypse? Have you heard of 'the star Wormwood,'[9] Prince?"

"I've heard that Lebedev thinks this 'star Wormwood' is the network of railways spread over Europe."

"No, excuse me, sir, that's not it, sir!" Lebedev cried, jumping up and waving his arms, as if wishing to stop the general laughter that was beginning. "Excuse me, sir! With these gentlemen . . . all these gentlemen," he suddenly turned to the prince, "in certain points, it's like this, sir . . ." and he unceremoniously rapped the table twice, which increased the laughter still more.

Lebedev, though in his usual "evening" state, was much too agitated and irritated this time by the preceding long "learned" argument, and on such occasions his attitude towards his opponents was one of boundless and highly candid contempt.

"That's not it, sir! Half an hour ago, Prince, we made an

agreement not to interrupt; not to laugh while someone is talking; to allow him to say everything freely, and then let the atheists object if they want to; we made the general our chairman, so we did, sir! Or else what, sir? Or else anybody can get thrown off, even with the highest idea, sir, even with the deepest idea . . ."

"Well, speak, speak: nobody's throwing you off!" voices rang out.

"Speak, but not through your hat."

"What is this 'star Wormwood'?" somebody asked.

"I have no idea!" General Ivolgin answered, taking his recently appointed place as chairman with an air of importance.

"I have a remarkable fondness for all these arguments and irritations, Prince—learned ones, naturally," murmured Keller, meanwhile stirring on his chair in decided rapture and impatience, "learned and political ones," he turned suddenly and unexpectedly to Evgeny Pavlovich, who was sitting almost next to him. "You know, I'm terribly fond of reading about the English Parliaments in the newspapers, that is, not in the sense of what they discuss (I'm no politician, you know), but of the way they discuss things together, and behave, so to speak, like politicians: 'the noble viscount sitting opposite me,' 'the noble earl, who shares my thinking,' 'my noble opponent, who has astonished Europe with his proposal,' that is, all those little expressions, all that parliamentarianism of a free nation—that's what our sort finds attractive! I'm captivated, Prince. I've always been an artist in the depths of my soul, I swear to you, Evgeny Pavlych."

"So then," Ganya was seething in another corner, "it turns out, in your opinion, that the railways are cursed, that they're the bane of mankind, a plague that has fallen upon the earth to muddy the 'wellsprings of life'?"[10]

Gavrila Ardalionovich was in a particularly agitated mood that evening, a merry, almost triumphant mood, as it seemed to the prince. He was, of course, joking with Lebedev, egging him on, but soon he became excited himself.

"Not the railways, no, sir!" Lebedev protested, beside himself and at the same time enjoying himself tremendously. "By themselves the railways won't muddy the wellsprings of life, but the thing as a whole is cursed, sir, all this mood of our last few centuries, as a general whole, scientific and practical, is maybe indeed cursed, sir."

"Certainly cursed or only maybe? It's important in this case," inquired Evgeny Pavlovich.

"Cursed, cursed, certainly cursed!" Lebedev confirmed with passion.

"Don't rush, Lebedev, you're much kinder in the mornings," Ptitsyn observed, smiling.

"But more candid in the evenings! More heartfelt and more candid in the evenings!" Lebedev turned to him heatedly. "More simple-hearted and more definite, more honest and more honorable, and though I expose myself to you in this way, I spit on it, sir. I challenge you all now, all you atheists: how are you going to save the world, and what is the normal path you've found for it—you men of science, industry, associations, salaries, and the rest? What is it? Credit? What is credit? What will credit lead you to?"

"Aren't you a curious one!" observed Evgeny Pavlovich.

"My opinion is that whoever isn't interested in such questions is a high-society *chenapan*,* sir!"

"At least it will lead to general solidarity and the balance of interests," observed Ptitsyn.

"And that's all, that's all! Without recognizing any moral foundations except the satisfaction of personal egoism and material necessity? Universal peace, universal happiness—from necessity! May I venture to ask if I understand you correctly, my dear sir?"

"But the universal necessity to live, eat, and drink, and the full, finally scientific, conviction that you will never satisfy that necessity without universal association and solidarity of interests is, it seems, a strong enough thought to serve as a foothold and a 'wellspring of life' for the future ages of mankind," observed the now seriously excited Ganya.

"The necessity to eat and drink, that is, the mere sense of self-preservation . . ."

"But isn't the sense of self-preservation enough? The sense of self-preservation is the normal law of mankind . . ."

"Who told you that?" Evgeny Pavlovich cried suddenly. "A law it is, true, but no more normal than the law of destruction, and perhaps also of self-destruction. Can self-preservation be the only normal law of mankind?"

"Aha!" cried Ippolit, turning quickly to Evgeny Pavlovich and looking him over with wild curiosity; but seeing that the man was laughing, he laughed himself, nudged Kolya, who was standing

*Rascal or good-for-nothing.

beside him, and again asked him what time it was, even pulling Kolya's silver watch towards him and greedily looking at the dial. Then, as if forgetting everything, he stretched out on the sofa, put his hands behind his head, and began staring at the ceiling; half a minute later he was sitting at the table again, straight-backed and listening attentively to the babble of the thoroughly excited Lebedev.

"A perfidious and derisive thought, a goading thought," Lebedev eagerly picked up Evgeny Pavlovich's paradox, "a thought uttered with the purpose of inciting the adversaries to fight—but a correct thought! Because, worldly scoffer and cavalier that you are (though not without ability!), you don't know yourself to what degree your thought is a profound and correct thought! Yes, sir. The law of self-destruction and the law of self-preservation are equally strong in mankind! The devil rules equally over mankind until a limit in time still unknown to us. You laugh? You don't believe in the devil? Disbelief in the devil is a French notion, a frivolous notion. Do you know who the devil is? Do you know what his name is? And without even knowing his name, you laugh at his form, following Voltaire's example,[11] at his hoofs, his tail, and his horns, which you yourselves have invented; for the unclean spirit is a great and terrible spirit, and not with the hoofs and horns you have invented for him. But he's not the point now! . . ."

"How do you know he's not the point now?" Ippolit suddenly cried, and guffawed as if in a fit.

"A clever and suggestive thought!" Lebedev praised. "But, again, that's not the point, but the question is whether the 'wellsprings of life' have not weakened with the increase . . ."

"Of railroads?" cried Kolya.

"Not of railway communications, my young but passionate adolescent, but of that whole tendency, of which railways may serve as an image, so to speak, an artistic expression. Hurrying, clanging, banging, and speeding, they say, for the happiness of mankind! 'It's getting much too noisy and industrial in mankind, there is too little spiritual peace,' complains a secluded thinker. 'Yes, but the banging of carts delivering bread for hungry mankind may be better than spiritual peace,' triumphantly replies another, a widely traveled thinker, and walks off vaingloriously. I, the vile Lebedev, do not believe in the carts that deliver bread to mankind! For carts that deliver bread to all mankind, without any moral foundations for their action, may quite cold-bloodedly exclude a considerable part of mankind from enjoying what they deliver, as has already happened . . ."

"So carts may quite cold-bloodedly exclude?" someone picked up.

"As has already happened," Lebedev repeated, not deigning to notice the question. "There has already been Malthus, the friend of mankind.[12] But a friend of mankind with shaky moral foundations is a cannibal of mankind, to say nothing of his vainglory; insult the vainglory of one of these numberless friends of mankind, and he is ready at once to set fire to the four corners of the world out of petty vengeance—the same, however, as any one of us, to speak fairly, as myself, the vilest of all, for I might be the first to bring wood and then run away. But again, that's not the point!"

"Then what is it, finally?"

"How tiresome!"

"The point is in the following anecdote from olden times, for it's necessary that I tell you this anecdote from olden times. In our day, in our fatherland, which I hope you love as much as I do, gentlemen, because for my part I'm even ready to spill all my blood . . ."

"Go on! Go on!"

"In our fatherland, as well as in Europe, mankind is visited by universal, ubiquitous, and terrible famines, by possible reckonings and as far as I can remember, not more often now than once in a quarter century, in other words, once every twenty-five years. I won't argue about the precise number, but comparatively quite rarely."

"Comparatively to what?"

"To the twelfth century and its neighboring centuries on either side. For at that time, as writers write and maintain, universal famines visited mankind once every two or three years at least, so that in such a state of affairs man even resorted to anthropophagy, though he kept it a secret. One of these parasites, approaching old age, announced on his own and without being forced, that in the course of a long and meager life he had personally killed and eaten in deepest secrecy sixty monks and several lay babies—about six, not more, that is, remarkably few compared with the quantity of clergy he had eaten. Of lay adults, as it turned out, he had never touched any with that purpose."

"That cannot be!" cried the chairman himself, the general, in an all but offended voice. "I often discuss and argue with him, always about similar thoughts, gentlemen; but most often he produces such absurdities that one's ears fall off, not a groatsworth of plausibility!"

"General! Remember the siege of Kars, and you, gentlemen, should know that my anecdote is the naked truth. For my own part, I will observe that almost every actuality, though it has its immutable laws, is almost always incredible and implausible. And the more actual it is, the more implausible it sometimes seems."

"But how can one eat sixty monks?" they laughed all around.

"Though he didn't eat them all at once, which is obvious, but maybe over the course of fifteen or twenty years, which is quite understandable and natural . . ."

"And natural?"

"And natural!" Lebedev snapped at them with pedantic persistence. "And besides all that, a Catholic monk is prying and curious by his very nature, and it's quite easy to lure him into a forest or some other secluded place and deal with him in the above-mentioned way—but all the same I don't deny that the quantity of persons eaten comes out as extraordinary, even to the point of intemperance."

"Maybe it's true, gentlemen," the prince suddenly observed.

Up to then he had listened silently to the arguers and had not entered the conversation; he had often laughed heartily following the general outbursts of laughter. It was obvious that he was terribly glad that it was so merry, so noisy; even that they were drinking so much. Perhaps he would not have said a word the whole evening, but suddenly he somehow decided to speak. He spoke with extreme seriousness, so that everyone suddenly turned to him with curiosity.

"Essentially, gentlemen, what I want to say is that there were such frequent famines back then. I've heard about it, too, though I have a poor knowledge of history. But it seems it must have been so. When I found myself in the Swiss mountains, I was terribly astonished by the ruins of the ancient knightly castles, built on the sides of the mountains, on steep cliffs, and at least half a mile straight up (meaning several miles by little paths). We know what a castle is: it's a whole mountain of stones. Terrible, impossible labor! And, of course, they were built by all those poor people, the vassals. Besides that, they had to pay all sorts of taxes and support the clergy. How could they feed themselves and work the land? There were few of them then, they must have been terribly starved, and there may have been literally nothing to eat. I even used to think sometimes: how is it that these people did not cease altogether then and that nothing happened to them, how could they hold out and endure? Lebedev is undoubtedly right that there were cannibals, and perhaps a great many of them; only what I don't know is why precisely he mixed monks into it and what does he mean to say by that?"

"Probably that in the twelfth century only monks could be eaten, because only monks were fat," observed Gavrila Ardalionovich.

"A most splendid and correct thought!" cried Lebedev. "For he never even touched a layman. Not a single layman to sixty head of clergy, and this is a horrible thought, a historical thought, a statistical thought, finally, and it is from such facts that the knowing man constructs history; for it is asserted with numerical exactitude that the clergy lived at least sixty times more happily and freely than the rest of mankind at that time. And were, perhaps, at least sixty times fatter than the rest of mankind . . ."

"An exaggeration, an exaggeration, Lebedev!" they guffawed all around.

"I agree that it's a historical thought, but what are you getting at?" the prince went on asking. (He spoke with such seriousness and such an absence of any joking or mockery of Lebedev, whom everyone laughed at, that his tone, amidst the general tone of the whole company, involuntarily became comical; a little more and they would have started making fun of him as well, but he did not notice it.)

"Don't you see he's crazy, Prince?" Evgeny Pavlovich leaned towards him. "I was told here earlier that he went crazy over being a lawyer and making speeches, and that he wants to pass an examination. I'm expecting an excellent parody."

"I'm getting at a tremendous conclusion," Lebedev meanwhile thundered. "But first of all let us analyze the psychological and juridical condition of the criminal. We see that the criminal, or, so to speak, my client, despite all the impossibility of finding other eatables, shows more than once, in the course of his peculiar career, a desire to repent, and avoids clergymen. We see it clearly from the facts: it is mentioned that he did, after all, eat five or six babies—a comparatively insignificant number, but portentous in another respect. It is obvious that, suffering from terrible remorse (for my client is a religious and conscientious man, as I shall prove), and in order to diminish his sin as far as possible, six times, by way of experiment, he changed monastic food for lay food. That it was by way of experiment is, again, unquestionable; for if it was only for gastronomic variety, the number six would be too insignificant: why only six and not thirty? (I'm considering a fifty-fifty proportion.) But if it was only an experiment, only out of despair before the fear of blaspheming and insulting the Church, then the number six becomes all too comprehensible; for six experiments, to satisfy the remorse of conscience, are quite sufficient, because the experiments could not have been successful. And, first of all, in my opinion, a baby is too small, that is, not of large size, so that for a given period of time he would need three or five times the number of lay babies as of clergymen, so that the sin, while diminishing on the one hand, would in the final end be increased on the other, if not in quality, then in quantity. In reasoning this way, gentlemen, I am, of course, descending into the heart of the twelfth-century criminal. For my own part, as a nineteenth-century man, I might have reasoned differently, of which I inform you, so there's no need to go grinning at me, gentlemen, and for you, General, it is quite unsuitable. Second, a baby, in my personal opinion, is not nourishing, is perhaps even too sweet and cloying, so that, while not satisfying the need, it leaves one with nothing but remorse of conscience. Now for the conclusion, the finale, gentlemen, the finale which contains the answer to one of the greatest questions of that time and ours! The criminal ends by going and denouncing himself to the clergy, and surrenders to the hands of the authorities. One may ask, what tortures did he face, considering the time, what wheels, fires, and flames? Who prompted him to go and denounce himself? Why not simply stop at the number sixty, keeping your secret till your last breath? Why not simply give up monks and live in penitence as a recluse? Why, finally, not become a monk himself? Now here is the answer! It means there was something stronger than fire and flame and even than a twenty-year habit! It means there was a thought stronger than all calamities, crop failures, torture, plague, leprosy, and all that hell, which mankind would have been unable to endure without that thought which binds men together, guides their hearts, and makes fruitful the wellsprings of the life of thought! Show me something resembling such a force in our age of crime and railways . . . that is, I should have said: our age of steam and railways, but I say: in our age of crime and railways, because I'm drunk, but just! Show me a thought binding present-day mankind together that is half as strong as in those centuries. And dare to say, finally, that the wellsprings of life have not weakened, have not turned muddy under this 'star,' under this network that ensnares people. And don't try to frighten me with your prosperity, your wealth, the rarity of famines, and the speed of communication! There is greater wealth, but less force; the binding idea is gone; everything has turned soft, everything is overstewed, everyone is overstewed! We're all, all, all overstewed! . . . But enough, that's not the point now; the point is, shouldn't we give orders, my highly esteemed Prince, about the little snack prepared for our guests?"

Lebedev, who had almost driven some of his listeners to real indignation (the bottles, it should be noted, did not cease to be uncorked all the while), immediately won over all his opponents by unexpectedly concluding his speech with a little snack. He himself called such a conclusion a "clever, advocatory rounding off of the case." Merry laughter arose again, the guests became animated; they all got up from the table to stretch and stroll about the terrace. Only Keller remained displeased with Lebedev's speech and was in extreme agitation.

"The man attacks enlightenment, preaches rabid twelfth-century fanaticism, clowns, and even without any innocence of heart: how did he pay for this house, may I ask?" he said aloud, stopping all and sundry.

"I've seen a real interpreter of the Apocalypse," the general said in another corner to other listeners, among them Ptitsyn, whom he seized by a button, "the late Grigory Semyonovich Burmistrov: he burned through your heart, so to speak. First, he put on his spectacles, opened a big old book bound in black leather, well, and a gray beard along with it, two medals for his donations. He'd begin sternly and severely, generals bowed down to him, and ladies swooned—well, and this one ends with a snack. I've never seen the like!"

Ptitsyn listened to the general, smiled, and seemed about to take his hat, but could not quite make up his mind or else kept forgetting his intention. Ganya, before the moment when they all got up from the table, had suddenly stopped drinking and pushed his glass away; something dark had passed over his face. When they got up from the table, he went over to Rogozhin and sat down next to him. One might have thought they were on the most friendly terms. Rogozhin, who at first also made as if to leave quietly several times, now sat motionless, his head bowed, and also seemed to have forgotten that he wanted to leave. He did not drink a single drop of wine all evening and was very pensive; only from time to time he raised his eyes and looked them all over. Now one might have thought he was waiting there for something extremely important for him and was resolved not to leave till the time came.

The prince drank only two or three glasses and was merely merry. Getting up from the table, he met Evgeny Pavlovich's gaze, remembered about their forthcoming talk, and smiled affably. Evgeny Pavlovich nodded to him and suddenly pointed to Ippolit, whom he was observing intently at that moment. Ippolit was asleep, stretched out on the sofa.

"Tell me, Prince, why has this boy foisted himself on you?" he said suddenly, with such obvious vexation and even spite that the prince was surprised. "I'll bet he's got something wicked in mind!"

"I've noticed," said the prince, "or at least it seems to me, that he interests you very much today, Evgeny Pavlych. Is it true?"

"And add that in my circumstances I have a lot to think about, so that I'm surprised myself that I've been unable to tear myself away from that repulsive physiognomy all evening!"

"He has a handsome face . . ."

"There, there, look!" cried Evgeny Pavlovich, pulling the prince's arm. "There! . . ."

The prince again looked Evgeny Pavlovich over with surprise.

V

IPPOLIT, WHO TOWARDS the end of Lebedev's dissertation had suddenly fallen asleep on the sofa, now suddenly woke up, as if someone had nudged him in the side, gave a start, sat up, looked around, and turned pale; he looked around even in a sort of fright; but horror almost showed in his face when he recalled and understood everything.

"What, they're going home? Is it over? Is it all over? Has the sun risen?" he asked in alarm, seizing the prince's hand. "What time is it? For God's sake, what time? I've overslept. Did I sleep long?" he added with an almost desperate look, as if he had slept through something on which at least his whole destiny depended.

"You slept for seven or eight minutes," Evgeny Pavlovich replied.

Ippolit looked at him greedily and pondered for a few moments.

"Ah . . . that's all! So, I . . ."

And he drew his breath deeply and greedily, as if throwing off an immense burden. He finally realized that nothing was "over," that it was not dawn yet, that the guests had gotten up from the table only to have a snack, and that the only thing that was over was Lebedev's babble. He smiled, and a consumptive flush in the form of two bright spots played on his cheeks.

"So you've been counting the minutes while I slept, Evgeny Pavlych," he picked up mockingly. "You haven't torn yourself away from me all evening, I saw . . . Ah! Rogozhin! I just saw him in a dream," he whispered to the prince, frowning and nodding towards Rogozhin, who was sitting by the table. "Ah, yes," he again skipped on suddenly, "where is the orator, where is Lebedev? So Lebedev's finished? What was he talking about? Is it true, Prince, that you once said 'beauty' would save the world? Gentlemen," he cried loudly to them all, "the prince insists that beauty will save the world! And I insist that he has such playful thoughts because he's in love now. Gentlemen, the prince is in love; as soon as he came in today, I was convinced of it. Don't blush, Prince, or I'll feel sorry for you. What beauty will save the world? Kolya told me what you said . . . Are you a zealous Christian? Kolya says you call yourself a Christian."

The prince studied him attentively and did not answer.

"You don't answer me? Maybe you think I love you very much?" Ippolit suddenly added, as if breaking off.

"No, I don't think so. I know you don't love me."

"What? Even after yesterday? Wasn't I sincere with you yesterday?"

"Yesterday, too, I knew you didn't love me."

"Because I envy you, envy you, is that it? You've always thought so and you think so now, but . . . but why am I telling you that? I want more champagne; pour me some, Keller."

"You shouldn't drink more, Ippolit, I won't let you . . ."

And the prince moved the glass away from him.

"In fact . . ." he agreed at once, as if pondering, "they might say . . . ah, what the devil do I care what they say! Isn't it true, isn't it true? Let them talk afterwards, right, Prince? As if it's any of our business what happens *afterwards*! . . . Anyhow, I'm still not quite awake. I had a terrible dream. I've just remembered it . . . I don't wish you such dreams, Prince, though maybe I actually don't love you. Anyhow, if you don't love someone, why wish him ill, isn't it true? See how I keep asking, asking all the time! Give me your hand; I'll press it firmly, like this . . . You do still give me your hand, though? Does that mean you know I'm sincere? . . . Maybe I won't drink anymore. What time is it? Never mind, though, I know what time it is. The hour has come! It's just the right time. What, they've put out the food in the corner? So this table is free? Excellent! Gentlemen, I . . . however, these gentlemen are not all listening . . . I intend to read an article, Prince; food is, of course, more interesting, but . . ."

And suddenly, quite unexpectedly, he pulled from his upper side pocket a big, official-sized envelope, sealed with a big red seal. He placed it on the table in front of him.

This unexpectedness had an effect on the company, which was unprepared for it, or, better, was *prepared*, but not for that. Evgeny Pavlovich even jumped in his chair; Ganya quickly moved to the table; Rogozhin did the same, but with a sort of gruff vexation, as if he knew what it was about. Lebedev, who happened to be near by, came closer with his curious little eyes and gazed at the envelope, trying to guess what it was about.

"What have you got there?" the prince asked uneasily.

"With the first little rim of the sun, I'll lie down, Prince, I told you that; on my word of honor: you'll see!" cried Ippolit. "But . . . but . . . can you possibly think I'm not capable of opening this envelope?" he added, passing his gaze over them all with a sort of defiance, and as if addressing them all indiscriminately. The prince noticed that he was trembling all over.

"None of us thinks that," the prince answered for everyone, "and why do you think that anyone has such an idea, and what . . . what has given you this strange idea of reading? What is it you've got there, Ippolit?"

"What is it? Has something happened to him again?" they asked all around. Everyone came closer, some still eating; the envelope with the red seal attracted them all like a magnet.

"I wrote it myself yesterday, right after I gave you my word that I'd come and live with you, Prince. I spent all day yesterday writing it, then last night, and finished it this morning. Last night, towards morning, I had a dream . . ."

"Wouldn't it be better tomorrow?" the prince interrupted timidly.

"Tomorrow 'there will be no more time!'"[13] Ippolit chuckled hysterically. "Don't worry, however, I can read it through in forty minutes . . . well, in an hour . . . And you can see how interested everyone is; everyone came over; everyone is looking at my seal; if I hadn't sealed the article in an envelope, there would have been no effect! Ha, ha! That's what mysteriousness means! Shall I open it, gentlemen, or not?" he cried, laughing his strange laugh and flashing his eyes. "A mystery! A mystery! And do you remember, Prince, who it was who announced that 'there will be no more time'? A huge and powerful angel in the Apocalypse announces it."

"Better not read it!" Evgeny Pavlovich suddenly exclaimed, but with an air of uneasiness so unexpected in him that many found it strange.

"Don't read it!" the prince, too, cried, putting his hand on the envelope.

"What's this about reading? Right now we're eating," somebody observed.

"An article? For a magazine, or what?" inquired another.

"Maybe it's boring?" added a third.

"What have you got?" inquired the rest. But the prince's frightened gesture seemed to frighten Ippolit himself.

"So . . . I shouldn't read it?" he whispered somehow fearfully to the prince, with a crooked smile on his blue lips. "I shouldn't read it?" he murmured, passing his gaze over all the public, all the eyes and faces, and as if again snatching at everything with his former, almost aggressive expansiveness. "Are you . . . afraid?" he turned to the prince again.

"Of what?" the latter asked, changing countenance more and more.

"Does anybody have a twenty-kopeck piece?" Ippolit suddenly jumped up from his chair as if he had been pulled from it. "A coin of any kind?"

"Here!" Lebedev offered at once; the thought flashed in him that the sick Ippolit had gone crazy.

"Vera Lukyanovna!" Ippolit hastily invited, "take it and toss it on the table: heads or tails? Heads I read!"

Vera looked fearfully at the coin, at Ippolit, then at her father, and, somehow awkwardly, her head thrown back, as if convinced that she herself should not look at the coin, tossed it on the table. It came up heads.

"I read!" whispered Ippolit, as if crushed by the decision of fate; he could not have turned more pale if a death sentence had been read to him. "But anyhow," he suddenly gave a start after pausing half a minute, "what is it? Have I just cast the die?" and with the same aggressive frankness he looked at everyone around him. "But this is an astonishing psychological feature!" he suddenly cried, turning to the prince in genuine amazement. "This . . . this is an inconceivable feature, Prince!" he confirmed, growing animated and as if coming to his senses. "Write this down, Prince, remember it, I believe you collect materials about capital punishment . . . so I was told, ha, ha! Oh, God, what senseless absurdity!" He sat down on the sofa, leaned both elbows on the table, and clutched his head with his hands. "It's even shameful! . . . The devil I care if it's shameful," he raised his head almost at once. "Gentlemen! Gentlemen, I am opening the envelope," he announced with a sort of unexpected resolve, "I . . . however, I'm not forcing you to listen! . . ."

His hands trembling with excitement, he opened the envelope, took out several sheets of paper covered with small writing, placed them in front of him, and began smoothing them out.

"But what is it? What have you got there? What are you going to read?" some muttered gloomily; others kept silent. But they all sat down and watched curiously. Perhaps they indeed expected something extraordinary. Vera gripped her father's chair and all but wept from fear; Kolya was almost as frightened. Lebedev, who had already settled down, suddenly got up, seized the candles, and moved them closer to Ippolit, so that there would be enough light to read by.

"Gentlemen, you . . . you'll presently see what it is," Ippolit added for some reason and suddenly began his reading: "'A Necessary Explanation'! Epigraph: *Après moi le déluge** . . . Pah, devil take it!" he cried as if burned. "Could I have seriously set down such a stupid epigraph? . . . Listen, gentlemen! . . . I assure you that in the final end this may all be the most terrible trifles! It's just some of my thoughts . . . If you think it's . . . something mysterious or . . . forbidden . . . in short . . ."

"Read without any prefaces," Ganya interrupted.

"He's dodging!" somebody added.

"Too much talk," put in Rogozhin, who had been silent the whole time.

Ippolit suddenly looked at him, and when their eyes met, Rogozhin grinned bitterly and sarcastically, and slowly pronounced some strange words:

"That's not how the thing should be handled, man, that's not . . ."

---

*After me the great flood.

What Rogozhin meant to say, no one, of course, understood, but his words made a rather strange impression on them all; it was as if they had all brushed up against a common thought. But the impression these words made on Ippolit was terrible; he trembled so much that the prince reached out to support him, and he would probably have cried out, if his voice had not suddenly failed him. For a whole minute he was unable to utter a word and, breathing heavily, stared at Rogozhin. At last, breathlessly and with great effort he spoke:

"So that . . . that was you . . . you?"

"What? What about me?" Rogozhin answered in perplexity, but Ippolit, flushed, and suddenly seized almost by rage, cried sharply and loudly:

"*You* were in my room last week, at night, past one o'clock, the same day I went to see you in the morning! *You!* Admit it was you!"

"Last week, at night? You must have gone clean out of your mind, man."

The "man" was silent again for a minute, putting his forefinger to his forehead and as if thinking hard; but in his pale smile, still twisted with fear, there suddenly flashed something cunning, as it were, and even triumphant.

"It was you!" he repeated at last, almost in a whisper, but with extraordinary conviction. "*You* came to my room and sat silently on my chair, by the window, for a whole hour; more; from one till past two in the morning; then you got up and left after two . . . It was you, you! Why you frightened me, why you came to torment me—I don't understand, but it was you!"

And in his eyes there suddenly flashed a boundless hatred, in spite of his frightened trembling, which had still not subsided.

"You'll find out all about it presently, gentlemen, I . . . I . . . listen . . ."

Again, and in terrible haste, he seized his pages; they had spilled and scattered, he tried to gather them up; they trembled in his trembling hands; for a long time he could not settle down.

The reading finally began. At first, for about five minutes, the author of the unexpected *article* was still breathless and read disjointedly and unevenly; but then his voice grew firm and began to express fully the meaning of what he read. Only occasionally a very strong cough interrupted him; by the middle of the article his voice became very hoarse; the extraordinary animation that came over him more and more as he read, in the end reached the highest pitch, as did its painful impression on his listeners. Here is the whole of this "article."

My Necessary Explanation

Après moi le déluge!

Yesterday morning the prince came to see me; incidentally, he talked me into moving to his dacha. I knew he would certainly insist on that, and I was sure he would blurt right out to me that it would be "easier for me to die among people and trees," as he puts it. But this time he did not say *to die*, but said "it would be easier to live," which, however, makes almost no difference for me in my situation. I asked him what he meant by his incessant "trees," and why he was foisting these "trees" on me—and was surprised to learn from him that I myself supposedly said the other evening that I had come to Pavlovsk to look at the trees for the last time. When I observed to him that it made no difference whether I died under the trees or looking out the window at my bricks, and that there was no point in making a fuss over two weeks, he agreed at once; but greenery and clean air, in his opinion, are bound to produce some physical change in me, and my agitation and *my dreams* will change and perhaps become lighter. I again observed to him laughingly that he spoke like a materialist. He replied with his smile that he had always been a materialist. Since he never lies, these words must mean something. His smile is nice; I've looked at him more attentively now. I do not know whether I love him or not now; I have no time to bother with that now. My five-month hatred of him, it should be noted, has begun to abate in this last month. Who knows, maybe I went to Pavlovsk mainly to see him. But . . . why did I leave my room then? A man condemned to death should not leave his corner; and if I had not taken a final decision now, but had decided, on the contrary, to wait till the last hour, then, of course, I would not have left my room for anything and would not have accepted the suggestion of moving out "to die" in his place in Pavlovsk.

I must hurry and finish all this "explanation" by tomorrow without fail. Which means I will not have time to reread and correct it; I will reread it tomorrow when I read it to the prince and the two or three witnesses I intend to find there. Since there will not be a single lying word in it, but only the whole truth, ultimate and solemn, I am curious beforehand what sort of impression it will make on me at that hour and that moment when I start to reread it. However, I need not have written the words "ultimate and solemn truth"; there is no need to lie for the sake of two weeks anyway, because it is not worth living for two weeks; that is the best proof that I will write nothing but the truth. (NB. Do not forget the thought: am I not mad at this moment, that is, at moments? I have been told positively that people in the last stages of consumption sometimes lose their minds temporarily. Check this tomorrow during the reading by the impression made on the listeners. This question must be resolved with the utmost precision; otherwise it is impossible to set about anything.)

It seems to me that I have just written something terribly stupid, but I have no time to correct it, as I said; besides, I give myself my word purposely not to correct a single line in this manuscript, even if I notice that I am contradicting myself every five lines. I precisely want to determine tomorrow during the reading whether the logical course of my thought is correct; whether I notice my own mistakes, and thus whether everything I have thought through during these six months in this room is true or mere raving.

If, just two months ago, I had had to leave my room, as I am doing now, and say good-bye to Meyer's wall, I'm sure I would have felt sad. But now I do not feel anything, and yet tomorrow I am leaving both my room and the wall *forever*! Thus my conviction that for the sake of two weeks it is not worth regretting anything or giving oneself up to any sort of emotions, has overcome my nature and can now command all my feelings. But is that true? Is it true that my nature is now utterly defeated? If I were to be tortured now, I would surely start shouting, and would not say that it is not worth shouting and feeling pain because I have only two weeks left to live.

But is it true that I have only two weeks left to live, and no more? I lied that time in Pavlovsk: B—n never told me anything and never saw me; but about a week ago the student Oxigenov was brought to me; in his convictions he is a materialist, an atheist, and a nihilist, which is precisely why I invited him; I needed somebody who would finally tell me the naked truth, without mawkishness or ceremony. That is what he did, and not only readily and without ceremony, but even with obvious pleasure (which, in my opinion, was unnecessary). He blurted right out to me that I had about a month left; maybe a little more, if the conditions are good; but I may even die much sooner. In his opinion, I may die unexpectedly, even, for instance, tomorrow: such facts have occurred, and only two days ago a young lady, a consumptive and in a state resembling mine, in Kolomna, was about to go to the market for provisions, but suddenly felt ill, lay down on the sofa, sighed, and died. Oxigenov told me all this, even flaunting his unfeelingness and carelessness somewhat, as if thereby doing me honor, that is, showing that he took me to be just such an all-denying higher being as himself, for whom dying, naturally, amounts to nothing. In the end, all the same, the fact is determined: a month and no more! I am perfectly convinced that he is not mistaken about it.

It surprised me very much how the prince guessed the other day that I have "bad dreams"; he said literally that in Pavlovsk "my agitation and *dreams*" would change. And why dreams? He is either a doctor or indeed of an extraordinary intelligence and able to guess a great many things. (But that he is ultimately an "idiot" there can be no doubt at all.) As if on purpose, just before he came I had a nice little dream (of a kind, however, that I now have by the hundred). I fell asleep—an hour before he came, I think—and saw myself in a room (but not mine). The room was bigger and higher than mine, better furnished, bright; a wardrobe, a chest of drawers, a sofa, and my bed, big and wide and covered with a green silk quilt. But in this room I noticed a terrible animal, a sort of monster. It resembled a scorpion, but it was not a scorpion, it was more vile and much more terrible, and precisely, it seemed, in that there are no such creatures in nature and that it had come to me *on purpose*, and that very fact presumably contained some sort of mystery. I made it out very well: it was brown and had a shell, a creeping reptile, about seven inches long, about two fingers thick at the head, gradually tapering towards the tail, so that the very tip of the tail was no more than one-fifth of an inch thick. About two inches from the head, a pair of legs came out of the body, at a forty-five-degree angle, one on each side, about three and a half inches long, so that the whole animal, if seen from above, looked like a trident. I could not make out the head very well, but I saw two feelers, not long, like two strong needles, also brown. Two identical feelers at the tip of the tail and at the tip of each foot, making eight feelers in all. The animal ran about the room very quickly, supported on its legs and tail, and when it ran, its body and legs wriggled like little snakes, with extraordinary rapidity, despite its shell, and this was very repulsive to look at. I was terribly afraid it would sting me; I had been told it was venomous, but I was most tormented by who could have sent it to my room, what did they want to do to me, and what was the secret of it? It hid under the chest of drawers, under the wardrobe, crawled into the corners. I sat on a chair with my legs tucked under me. It quickly ran diagonally across the room and disappeared somewhere near my chair. I looked around in fear, but as I was sitting with my legs tucked under me, I hoped it would not crawl up the chair. Suddenly I heard a sort of crackling rustle behind me, almost by my head. I turned and saw that the reptile was crawling up the wall and was already level with my head and even touching my hair with its tail, which was turning and twisting with extreme rapidity. I jumped up, and the animal disappeared. I was afraid to lie down in bed, lest it crawl under the pillow. My mother and an acquaintance of hers came into the room. They tried to catch the reptile, but were calmer than I, and not even afraid. But they understood nothing. Suddenly the reptile crawled out again; this time it crawled very quietly, and as if with some particular intention, twisting slowly, which was still more repulsive, again diagonally across the room, towards the door. Here my mother opened the door and called Norma, our dog—an enormous Newfoundland, black and shaggy; she died some five years ago. She rushed into the room and stopped over the reptile as if rooted to the spot. The reptile also stopped, but was still twisting and flicking the tips of its legs and tail against the floor. Animals cannot feel mystical fear, if I am not mistaken; but at that moment it seemed to me that in Norma's fear there was something as if very extraordinary, as if almost mystical, which meant that she also sensed, as I did, that there was something fatal and some sort of mystery in the beast. She slowly backed away from the reptile, which was quietly and cautiously crawling towards her; it seemed that it wanted to rush at her suddenly and sting her. But, despite all her fear, Norma's gaze was terribly angry, though she was trembling all over. Suddenly she slowly bared her terrible teeth, opened her entire red maw, took aim, readied herself, resolved, and suddenly seized the reptile with her teeth. The reptile must have made a strong movement to escape, because Norma caught it once more, this time in the air, and twice got her whole mouth around it, still in the air, as if gulping it down. The shell cracked in her teeth; the animal's tail and legs stuck out of her mouth, moving with terrible rapidity. Suddenly Norma squealed pitifully: the reptile had managed after all to sting her on the tongue. Squealing and howling with pain, she opened her mouth, and I saw that the bitten reptile was still stirring as it lay across her mouth, its half-crushed body oozing a large quantity of white juice onto her tongue, resembling the juice of a crushed black cockroach . . . Here I woke up, and the prince came in.

"Gentlemen," said Ippolit, suddenly tearing himself away from his reading and even almost shamefacedly, "I didn't reread it, but it seems I indeed wrote a lot that's superfluous. This dream . . ."

"Is that," Ganya hastened to put in.

"There's too much of the personal, I agree, that is, about me myself . . ."

As he said this, Ippolit looked weary and faint and wiped the sweat from his brow with a handkerchief.

"Yes, sir, you're much too interested in yourself," hissed Lebedev.

"Again, gentlemen, I'm not forcing anyone: whoever doesn't want to listen can leave."

"Throws us . . . out of somebody else's house," Rogozhin growled barely audibly.

"And what if we all suddenly get up and leave?" Ferdyshchenko, who until then, incidentally, had not dared to speak aloud, said unexpectedly.

Ippolit suddenly dropped his eyes and clutched his manuscript; but in that same second he raised his head again and, his eyes flashing, with two red spots on his cheeks, said, looking point-blank at Ferdyshchenko:

"You don't love me at all!"

There was laughter; however, the majority did not laugh. Ippolit blushed terribly.

"Ippolit," said the prince, "close your manuscript and give it to me, and go to bed here in my room. We can talk before we sleep and tomorrow; but on condition that you never open these pages again. Do you want that?"

"Is this possible?" Ippolit looked at him in decided astonishment. "Gentlemen!" he cried, again growing feverishly animated, "a stupid episode, in which I was unable to behave myself. There will be no further interruptions of the reading. Whoever wants to listen, can listen . . ."

He hurriedly gulped some water from a glass, hurriedly leaned his elbow on the table, in order to shield himself from others' eyes, and stubbornly went on with his reading. The shame, however, soon left him . . .

The idea (he went on reading) that it was not worth living for a few weeks began to take possession of me in a real sense about a month ago, I think, when I still had four weeks left to live, but it overcame me completely only three days ago, when I returned from that evening in Pavlovsk. The first moment of my being fully, directly pervaded by this thought occurred on the prince's terrace, precisely at the moment when I had decided to make a last test of life, wanted to see people and trees (I said so myself), became excited, insisted on Burdovsky's—"my neighbor's"—rights, and dreamed that they would all suddenly splay their arms wide and take me into their embrace, and ask my forgiveness for something, and I theirs; in short, I ended up as a giftless fool. And it was during those hours that "the ultimate conviction" flared up in me. I am astonished now at how I could have lived for a whole six months without this "conviction"! I knew positively that I had consumption and it was incurable; I did not deceive myself and understood the matter clearly. But the more clearly I understood it, the more convulsively I wanted to live; I clung to life and wanted to live whatever the cost. I agree that I could have become angry then at the dark and blank fate which had decreed that I be squashed like a fly, and, of course, without knowing why; but why did I not end just with anger? Why did I actually *begin* to live, knowing that it was no longer possible for me to begin; why did I try, knowing that there was no longer anything to try? And meanwhile I could not even read through a book and gave up reading; why read, why learn for six months? This thought made me drop a book more than once.

Yes, that wall of Meyer's can tell a lot! I have written a lot on it! There is not a spot on that dirty wall that I have not learned by heart. That cursed wall! But all the same it is dearer to me than all of Pavlovsk's trees, that is, it should be dearer, if it were not all the same to me now.

I recall now with what greedy interest I began to follow *their* life; there was no such interest before. Sometimes, when I was so ill that I could not leave the room, I waited for Kolya with impatience and abuse. I went so much into all the little details, was so interested in every sort of rumor, that it seemed I turned into a gossip. I could not understand, for instance, how it was that these people, having so much life, were not able to become rich (however, I don't understand it now either). I knew one poor fellow of whom I was told later that he starved to death, and, I remember, that

made me furious: if it had been possible to revive the poor fellow,
I think I would have executed him. Sometimes I felt better for
whole weeks and was able to go out in the street; but the street
finally began to produce such bitterness in me that I would spend
whole days inside on purpose, though I could have gone out like
everybody else. I could not bear those scurrying, bustling, eternally
worried, gloomy, and anxious people who shuttled around me on
the sidewalks. Why their eternal sorrow, their eternal anxiety and
bustle; their eternal gloomy spite (for they are spiteful, spiteful,
spiteful)? Whose fault is it that they are unhappy and do not know
how to live, though they have sixty years of life ahead of them?
Why did Zarnitsyn allow himself to die, having sixty years ahead
of him? And each of them displays his tatters, his hardworking
hands, gets angry and cries: "We work like oxen, we toil, we are
hungry as dogs, and poor! The others do not work, do not toil, yet
they are rich!" (The eternal refrain!) Alongside them some luckless
runt "of the gentlefolk" runs and bustles about from morning till
night—Ivan Fomich Surikov, he lives over us, in our house—
eternally with holes in his elbows, with torn-off buttons, running
errands for various people, delivering messages, and that from
morning till night. Go and start a conversation with him: "Poor,
destitute, and wretched, the wife died, there was no money for
medicine, and in the winter the baby froze to death; the older
daughter has become a kept woman . . ." he's eternally whimpering,
eternally complaining! Oh, never, never have I felt any pity for
these fools, not now, not before—I say it with pride! Why isn't he
a Rothschild himself? Whose fault is it that he has no millions, as
Rothschild has, that he has no mountain of gold imperials and
napoleondors,[14] a mountain as high as the ice mountains for sliding
during carnival week with all its booths! If he's alive, everything is
in his power! Whose fault is it that he doesn't understand that?

Oh, now it's all one to me, now I have no time to be angry, but
then, then, I repeat, I literally chewed my pillow at night and tore
my blanket with rage. Oh, how I dreamed then, how I wished,
how I purposely wished, that I, eighteen years old, barely clothed,
barely covered, could suddenly be thrown out in the street and left
completely alone, with no lodgings, no work, no crust of bread, no
relations, not a single acquaintance in the enormous city, hungry,
beaten (so much the better!), but healthy, and then I'd show
them . . .

Show them what?

Oh, can you possibly suppose that I do not know how I have humiliated myself as it is with my "Explanation"! Well, who is not going to consider me a runt who knows nothing of life, forgetting that I am no longer eighteen years old; forgetting that to live as I have lived for these six months means to live till you're gray-haired! But let them laugh and say that it is all tall tales. I did really tell myself tall tales. I filled whole nights with them; I remember them all now.

But do I really have to tell them again now—now, when the time for tall tales is past for me as well? And to whom! For I delighted in them then, when I saw clearly that I was forbidden even to study Greek grammar, as I once conceived of doing: "I won't get as far as the syntax before I die"—I thought at the first page and threw the book under the table. It is still lying there; I forbade Matryona to pick it up.

Let him into whose hands my "Explanation" falls and who has enough patience to read it, consider me a crazy person or even a schoolboy, or most likely of all, a man condemned to death, to whom it naturally seemed that all people except himself value their life too little, are accustomed to spending it too cheaply, too lazily, use it much too shamelessly, and are therefore unworthy of it one and all! And what then? I declare that my reader will be mistaken, and that my conviction is completely independent of my death sentence. Ask them, only ask them one and all, what they understand by happiness? Oh, you may be sure that Columbus was happy not when he had discovered America, but when he was discovering it; you may be sure that the highest moment of his happiness was, perhaps, exactly three days before the discovery of the New World, when the mutinous crew in their despair almost turned the ship back to Europe, right around! The New World is not the point here, it can just as well perish. Columbus died having seen very little of it and in fact not knowing what he had discovered. The point is in life, in life alone—in discovering it, constantly and eternally, and not at all in the discovery itself! But why talk! I suspect that everything I am saying now sounds so much like the most common phrases that I will probably be taken for a student in the lowest grade presenting his essay on "the sunrise," or they will say that I may have wanted to speak something out, but despite all my wishes I was unable to . . . "develop." But, nevertheless, I will add that in any ingenious or new human thought, or even simply in any serious human thought born in someone's head, there always remains something which it is quite impossible to convey to other people, though you may fill whole volumes with writing and spend thirty-five years trying to explain your thought; there always remains something that absolutely refuses to leave your skull and will stay with you forever; you will die with it, not having conveyed to anyone what is perhaps most important in your idea. But if I also fail now to convey all that has been tormenting me for these six months, people will at least understand that, having reached my present "ultimate conviction," I may have paid too dearly for it; it is this that I have considered it necessary, for my own purposes, to set forth in my "Explanation."

However, I continue.

VI

I DO NOT WANT to lie: reality kept catching me on its hook for these six months, and I sometimes got so carried away that I forgot about my sentence or, better, did not want to think about it and even started doing things. Incidentally, about my situation then. When I became very ill about eight months ago, I broke off all my former relations and dropped all my former comrades. As I had always been a rather sullen man, my comrades easily forgot me; of course, they would have forgotten me even without this circumstance. My situation at home, that is, "in the family," was also solitary. Some five months before, I had locked myself in once and for all and separated myself completely from the family rooms. I was always obeyed, and no one dared to enter my room except at a certain hour to tidy up and bring me my dinner. My mother trembled before my orders and did not even dare to whimper in my presence, when I occasionally decided to let her in. She constantly beat the children on my account, for fear they would make noise and bother me; I often complained about their shouting; I can imagine how they must love me now! I think I also tormented "faithful Kolya," as I called him, quite a bit. Lately he has tormented me as well: all that is quite natural, people are created to torment each other. But I noticed that he put up with my irritability as if he had promised himself beforehand to spare the sick man. Naturally, that irritated me; but it seems he had decided to imitate the prince in his "Christian humility," which was slightly ridiculous. He is a young and ardent boy and, of course, imitates everybody; but it sometimes seems to me that it is time he lived by his own reason. I love him very much. I also tormented Surikov, who lived over us and ran around from morning till night on other people's errands; I was constantly proving to him that he himself was to blame for his poverty, so that he finally got frightened and stopped coming to see me. He is a very humble man, the humblest of beings (NB. They say that humility is an awesome force; I must ask the prince about that, it's his expression); but when, in the month of March, I went up to his place, to see how, in his words, they had "frozen" the baby, and unintentionally smiled over his infant's body, because I again began explaining to Surikov that "he himself was to blame," the runt's lips suddenly trembled and, seizing me by the shoulder with one hand, he showed me the door with the other, and softly, that is, almost in a whisper, said to me: "Go, sir!" I went out, and I liked it very much, liked it right then, even at the very moment when he was leading me out; but for a long time afterwards, in my memory, his words made the painful impression of a sort of strange, contemptuous pity for him, which I did not want to feel at all. Even at the moment of such an insult (I do feel that I insulted him, though I had no intention of doing so), even at such a moment the man could not get angry! His lips quivered then not at all out of anger, I will swear to that: he seized me by the arm and uttered his splendid "Go, sir!" decidedly without being angry. There was dignity, even a great deal of it, even quite unsuited to him (so that, in truth, it was quite comical), but there was no anger. Maybe he simply began suddenly to despise me. Two or three times after that, when I met him on the stairs, he suddenly started taking his hat off to me, something he never did before, but he no longer stopped as before, but ran past me in embarrassment. If he despised me, he did it in his own way: he "*humbly* despised" me. But maybe he took his hat off simply out of fear of me, as his creditor's son, because he was constantly in debt to my mother and was never able to get out of it. And that is even the most likely thing of all. I wanted to have a talk with him, and I know for certain that in ten minutes he would have started asking my forgiveness; but I reasoned that it was better not to touch him.

At that same time, that is, around the time when Surikov "froze" his baby, around the middle of March, I felt much better for some reason, and that lasted for about two weeks. I started going out, most often at twilight. I loved the March twilight, when it turned frosty and the gaslights were lit; I sometimes walked far. Once, in Shestilavochnaya Street, someone of the "gentlefolk" sort overtook me in the dark; I did not make him out very well; he was carrying something wrapped in paper and was dressed in a short and ugly coat—too light for the season. When he came to a streetlight, some ten steps ahead of me, I noticed that something fell out of his pocket. I hastened to pick it up—just in time, because someone in a long kaftan had already rushed for it, but, seeing the object in my hands, did not argue, took a fleeting glance at my hands, and slipped past. The object was a big morocco wallet of old-fashioned design and tightly stuffed; but for some reason I guessed at first glance that there was anything you like in it, except money. The passerby who had lost it was already some forty steps ahead of me and soon dropped from sight in the crowd. I ran and started shouting to him; but as I could only shout "Hey!" he did not turn around. Suddenly he darted to the left into the gateway of some house. When I ran into this gateway, where it was very dark, there was no one there. The house was enormously big, one of those huge things entrepreneurs build to make into little apartments; some of these buildings have as many as a hundred apartments in them. When I ran through the gateway, I thought I saw a man walking in the far right-hand corner of the enormous courtyard, though I could barely make out anything in the darkness. I ran to that corner and saw the entrance to a stairway; the stairway was narrow, extremely dirty, and quite unlighted; but I could hear a man running up the stairs above me, and I raced after him, hoping that while the door was being opened for him, I could catch up with him. And so it happened. The flights were very short, and there was no end of them, so that I was terribly out of breath; a door opened and closed again on the fifth floor, I guessed that from three flights down. Before I ran up, caught my breath on the landing, and found the doorbell, several minutes passed. The door was finally opened for me by a woman who was lighting a samovar in a tiny kitchen; she listened silently to my questions, understood nothing, of course, and silently opened for me the door to the next room, also small, terribly low, with vile necessary furniture and a huge, wide bed under a canopy, on which lay "Terentyich" (as the woman called to him), drunk, as it seemed to me. On the table stood an iron night-light with a candle burning down in it and a nearly empty bottle. Terentyich grunted something to me lying down and waved towards the next door, while the woman left, so that nothing remained for me but to open that door. I did so and went into the next room.

This room was still smaller and narrower than the previous one, so that I did not even know where to turn in it; a narrow single bed in the corner took up terribly much space; the rest of the furniture consisted of three simple chairs heaped with all sorts of rags and a very simple wooden kitchen table in front of an old oilcloth sofa, so that it was almost impossible to pass between the table and the bed. The same iron night-light with a tallow candle as in the other room burned on the table, and on the bed squealed a tiny baby, maybe only three weeks old, judging by its cry; it was being "changed," that is, put into a clean diaper, by a sick and pale woman, young-seeming, in extreme négligé, and perhaps just beginning to get up after her confinement; but the baby would not be quiet and cried in anticipation of the lean breast. On the sofa another child slept, a three-year-old girl, covered, it seemed, with a tailcoat. By the table stood a gentleman in a very shabby frock coat (he had already taken his coat off and it was lying on the bed), unwrapping the blue paper in which about two pounds of wheat bread and two small sausages were wrapped. On the table, besides that, there was a teapot with tea and some scattered pieces of black bread. An unlocked suitcase showed from under the bed, and two bundles with some rags stuck out.

In short, there was terrible disorder. It seemed to me, at first glance, that both of them—the gentleman and the lady—were decent people, but reduced by poverty to that humiliating state in which disorder finally overcomes every attempt to struggle with it and even reduces people to the bitter necessity of finding in this disorder, as it increases daily, some bitter and, as it were, vengeful sense of pleasure.

When I came in, this gentleman, who had come in just before me and was unwrapping his provisions, was talking rapidly and heatedly with his wife; she, though she had not yet finished swaddling the baby, had already begun to whimper; the news must have been bad, as usual. The face of this gentleman, who was about twenty-eight by the look of it, swarthy and dry, framed in black side-whiskers, with his chin shaved till it gleamed, struck me as rather respectable and even agreeable; it was sullen, with a sullen gaze, but with some morbid tinge of a pride that was all too easily irritated. When I came in, a strange scene took place.

There are people who take extreme pleasure in their irritable touchiness, and especially when it reaches (which always happens very quickly) the ultimate limit in them; in that instant it even seems they would rather be offended than not offended. Afterwards these irritable people always suffer terrible remorse, if they are intelligent, naturally, and able to realize that they had become ten times angrier than they should have. For some time this gentleman looked at me in amazement, and his wife in fright, as if it were dreadfully outlandish that anyone should come into their room; but suddenly he fell upon me almost in a rage; I had not yet managed to mumble even a couple of words, but he, especially seeing that I was decently dressed, must have considered himself dreadfully offended that I dared to look so unceremoniously into his corner and see all his hideous situation, which he was so ashamed of himself. Of course, he was glad of the chance to vent his anger for all his misfortunes at least on someone. There was a moment when I even thought he would start fighting; he grew pale, like a woman in hysterics, and frightened his wife terribly.

"How dare you come in like that? Out!" he shouted, trembling and even barely articulating the words. But suddenly he saw his wallet in my hand.

"It seems you dropped it," I said as calmly and drily as I could. (Anyhow, that was the only proper way.)

The man stood before me totally frightened and for some time was as if unable to understand anything; then he quickly clutched his side pocket, opened his mouth in horror, and struck himself on the forehead with his hand.

"God! Where did you find it? How on earth?"

I explained in the briefest terms and as drily as I could how I had picked up the wallet, how I had run and called out to him, and how, finally, by guessing and almost groping my way, I had run after him up the stairs.

"Oh, God!" he cried, turning to his wife. "All our documents are in it, all my last instruments, everything . . . oh, my dear sir, do you know what you have done for me? I'd have perished!"

I had taken hold of the door handle meanwhile, so as to leave without replying; but I was out of breath myself and suddenly my agitation broke out in such a violent fit of coughing that I could barely stay on my feet. I saw how the gentleman rushed in all directions to find an empty chair for me, finally seized all the rags on one chair, threw them on the floor, and hurriedly offered me the chair and carefully sat me down on it. But my coughing went on and did not let up for about three more minutes. When I recovered, he was sitting next to me on another chair, from which he had probably also thrown the rags on the floor, and was studying me intently.

"You seem to be . . . suffering?" he said in the tone in which doctors usually speak when they approach a patient. "I myself am a . . . medical man" (he did not say "doctor"), and having said that, he pointed to the room with his hand for some reason, as if protesting against his present situation. "I see that you . . ."

"I have consumption," I said as curtly as possible and stood up. He also jumped up at once.

"Maybe you exaggerate and . . . if measures are taken . . ."

He was very bewildered and still as if unable to come to his senses; the wallet stuck out of his left hand.

"Oh, don't worry," I interrupted again, taking hold of the door handle, "last week B—n examined me" (again I put B—n into it) "and my case is decided. Excuse me . . ."

I was again about to open the door and leave my embarrassed, grateful, and crushed-with-shame doctor, but just then the cursed cough seized me again. Here my doctor insisted that I again sit down to rest; he turned to his wife, and she, without leaving her place, spoke a few friendly words of gratitude. She became very embarrassed as she did so, and color even played over her dry, pale yellow cheeks. I stayed, but with a look which showed every second that I was terribly afraid of being in their way (as was proper). Remorse finally tormented my doctor, I could see that.

"If I . . ." he began, constantly breaking off and jumping to another subject, "I'm so grateful to you, and so guilty before you . . . I . . . you see . . ." and again he pointed to the room, "at the present moment my situation . . ."

"Oh," I said, "there's nothing to see; it's a well-known thing; you must have lost your job, and you've come to explain things and look for another job?"

"How . . . did you know?" he asked in surprise.

"It's obvious at first glance," I said with unintentional mockery. "Many people come here from the provinces with hopes, go running around, and live like this."

He suddenly began speaking heatedly, his lips trembling; he complained, talked, and, I confess, got me carried away; I sat there for almost an hour. He told me his story, a very ordinary one, by the way. He had been a provincial doctor, had occupied a government post, but then some intrigues had started, which his wife was even mixed up in. He had shown his pride, his hot temper; a change had occurred in the provincial government to the advantage of his enemies; there had been sabotage, complaints; he had lost his job and on his last means had come to Petersburg for an explanation; in Petersburg, to be sure, they did not listen to him for a long time, then they heard him out, then responded with a refusal, then lured him with promises, then responded with severity, then told him to write something in explanation, then refused to accept what he had written, told him to petition—in short, it was already the fifth month that he had been running around, everything had been eaten up, his wife's last clothes had been pawned, and now the baby had been born and, and . . . "today came the final negative response to my petition, and I have almost no food, nothing, my wife has given birth. I . . . I . . ."

He jumped up from his chair and turned away. His wife wept in the corner, the baby began squealing again. I took out my notebook and started writing in it. When I finished and got up, he was standing before me and looking at me with timorous curiosity.

"I've written down your name," I said to him, "well, and all the rest: the place of work, the name of your governor, the days, the months. I have a friend from my school days, Bakhmutov, and his uncle, Pyotr Matveevich Bakhmutov, an actual state councillor,[15] who serves as the director . . ."

"Pyotr Matveevich Bakhmutov!" my medical man cried out, all but trembling. "But it's on him that almost everything depends!"

Indeed, in my medical man's story and in its denouement, to which I inadvertently contributed, everything came together and got settled as if it had been prepared that way on purpose, decidedly as in a novel. I told these poor people that they should try not to place any hopes in me, that I myself was a poor high-school student (I exaggerated the humiliation on purpose; I finished my studies long ago and am not a student), and that they need not know my name, but that I would go at once to Vassilievsky Island, to see my friend Bakhmutov, and as I knew for certain that his uncle, an actual state councillor, a bachelor, and with no children, decidedly adored his nephew and loved him to the point of passion, seeing in him the last bearer of his name, "maybe my friend will be able to do something for you—and for me, of course—through his uncle . . ."

"If only I could be allowed to explain things to his excellency!

If only I could be vouchsafed the honor of explaining it verbally!" he exclaimed, trembling as if in fever and with flashing eyes. He did say *vouchsafed*. Having repeated once more that the thing would probably be a flop and turn out to be all nonsense, I added that if I did not come to see them the next morning, it would mean that the matter was ended and they had nothing to expect. They saw me off, bowing, they were nearly out of their minds. I will never forget the expressions on their faces. I hired a cab and headed at once for Vassilievsky Island.

In school, over the course of several years, I was constantly at enmity with this Bakhmutov. Among us he was considered an aristocrat, or at least I called him one: he was excellently dressed, drove around in his own carriage, did not show off in the least, was always a wonderful comrade, was always remarkably cheerful and sometimes even very witty, though none too long on intelligence, despite the fact that he was always first in the class; while I was never first in anything. All our classmates liked him, except for me alone. He approached me several times during those several years; but each time I sullenly and irritably turned my back on him. Now I had not seen him for about a year; he was at the university. When, towards nine o'clock, I entered his room (with great ceremony: I was announced), he met me at first with surprise, even quite ungraciously, but he cheered up at once and, looking at me, suddenly burst into laughter.

"But why did you take it into your head to call on me, Terentyev?" he cried with his usual sweet casualness, sometimes bold but never offensive, which I so loved in him and for which I so hated him. "But what's wrong," he cried in fear, "you're quite ill!"

Coughing tormented me again, I fell into a chair and was barely able to catch my breath.

"Don't worry, I have consumption," I said. "I've come to you with a request."

He sat down in surprise, and I at once told him the doctor's whole story and explained that he himself, having great influence on his uncle, might be able to do something.

"I will, I certainly will, I'll assault my uncle tomorrow; and I'm even glad, and you told it all so well . . . But still, Terentyev, why did you take it into your head to turn to me?"

"So much of it depends on your uncle, and besides, Bakhmutov, you and I were always enemies, and since you are a noble man, I thought you would not refuse an enemy," I added with irony.

"Like Napoleon turning to England!"[16] he cried, bursting into laughter. "I'll do it, I'll do it! I'll even go right now if I can!" he hastened to add, seeing that I was getting up seriously and sternly from my chair.

And in fact the matter, quite unexpectedly, got settled for us in the best possible way. A month and a half later our medical man obtained a new post, in another province, was given travel money and even financial assistance. I suspect that Bakhmutov, who began calling on them frequently (while I, because of that, purposely stopped seeing them and received the doctor, who kept running by, almost drily)—Bakhmutov, I suspect, even persuaded the doctor to accept a loan from him. I saw Bakhmutov a couple of times during those six weeks, we met for a third time when we saw the doctor off. Bakhmutov arranged a farewell party at his own house, in the form of a dinner with champagne, at which the doctor's wife was also present; she left very soon, however, to go to the baby. It was at the beginning of May, the evening was bright, the enormous ball of the sun was sinking into the bay. Bakhmutov saw me home; we crossed the Nikolaevsky Bridge; we were both a bit drunk. Bakhmutov spoke of his delight that the matter had ended so well, thanked me for something, explained how pleasant it was for him now, after this good deed, insisted that all the credit was mine, and that what many now taught and preached about the meaninglessness of individual good deeds was wrong. I also wanted terribly to talk.

"Whoever infringes upon individual 'charity,'" I began, "infringes upon man's nature and scorns his personal dignity. But the organizing of 'social charity' and the question of personal freedom are two different questions and are not mutually exclusive. Individual goodness will always abide, because it is a personal need, a living need for the direct influence of one person on another. In Moscow there lived an old man, a 'general,' that is, an actual state councillor, with a German name; all his life he dragged himself around to jails and prisoners; every group of exiles to Siberia knew beforehand that 'the little old general' would visit them on Sparrow Hills. He did it all seriously and piously in the highest degree; he arrived, walked along the rows of exiles, who surrounded him, stopped before each one, asked each one about his needs, hardly ever admonished anyone, called them all 'dear hearts.' He gave them money, sent them necessary things—leg wrappings, foot-cloths, pieces of linen, sometimes brought pious tracts and gave them to all who were literate, fully convinced that they would read them on the way, and that the literate ones would read to the illiterate. He rarely asked about their crimes, though he would listen when a prisoner began talking. He placed all the criminals on an equal footing, he made no distinctions. He talked with them as with brothers, but in the end they themselves came to regard him as a father. If he noticed some woman exile with a baby in her arms, he would go up to her, caress the child, snap his fingers to make the child laugh. He did this for many years, till his own death; it reached the point where he was known over the whole of Russia and the whole of Siberia, that is, to all the criminals. I was told by someone who had been in Siberia that he himself had witnessed how the most hardened criminals remembered the general, and yet, when he visited them, he would rarely give them more than twenty kopecks each. True, they did not remember him all that warmly or in any very serious way. Some one of those 'unfortunates,' who had killed some twelve souls, who had stabbed six children solely for his own pleasure (they say there were such men), suddenly, out of the blue, at some point, and maybe only once in all of twenty years, would suddenly sigh and say: 'And what's with the little old general now, can he still be alive?' He might even smile as he said it—and that was all. But how do you know what seed had been sown forever in his soul by this 'little old general' whom he had not forgotten in twenty years? How do you know, Bakhmutov, what meaning this communion of one person with another will have in the destiny of the person communed with? . . . Here the whole of life stands before us and a countless number of ramifications that are hidden from us. The best chess player, the sharpest of them, can calculate only a few moves ahead; one French player, who could calculate ten moves ahead, was written about as a wonder. And how many moves are there, and how much is unknown to us? In sowing your seed, in sowing your 'charity,' your good deed in whatever form it takes, you give away part of your person and receive into yourself part of another's; you mutually commune in each other; a little more attention, and you will be rewarded with knowledge, with the most unexpected discoveries. You will be bound, finally, to look at your work as a science; it will take in the whole of your life and maybe fill the whole of it. On the other hand, all your thoughts, all the seeds you have sown, which you may already have forgotten, will take on flesh and grow; what was received from you will be passed on to someone else. And how do you know what share you will have in the future outcome of human destiny? And if the knowledge and the whole life of this work finally raises you so high that you are able to plant a tremendous seed, to bequeath a tremendous thought to mankind, then . . ." And so on, I talked a lot then.

"And to think that it is you to whom life has been denied!" Bakhmutov cried with burning reproach against someone.

At that moment we were standing on the bridge, leaning on the handrail, and looking at the Neva.

"And do you know what's just come into my head?" I said, bending still further over the handrail.

"Not to throw yourself into the river?" cried Bakhmutov, almost in fright. Perhaps he had read my thought in my face.

"No, for the time being it's just the following reflection: here I'm left now with two or three months to live, maybe four; but, for instance, when I have only two months left, and I want terribly to do a good deed that would require work, running around and petitioning, something like our doctor's affair, I would in that case have to renounce the deed for lack of sufficient time and look for another 'good deed,' a smaller one, which would be within my *means* (if I should happen to have the urge to do good deeds). You must agree, it's an amusing thought."

Poor Bakhmutov was very alarmed about me; he went with me as far as my home and was so delicate that he never once tried to comfort me and was silent nearly all the way. Taking leave of me, he warmly pressed my hand and asked permission to visit me. I answered him that if he came to me as a "comforter" (because even if he was silent, he would still be coming as a comforter, I explained that to him), then it meant that each time he would be reminding me still more of death. He shrugged his shoulders, but he agreed with me; we parted rather politely, something I had not even expected.

But that evening and that night the first seed of my "ultimate conviction" was sown. I greedily seized upon this *new* thought, greedily analyzed it in all its windings, in all its aspects (I did not sleep all night), and the more I delved into it, the more I received it into myself, the more frightened I was. A dreadful fear came over me finally and did not leave me during the days that followed. Sometimes, thinking about this constant fear of mine, I would quickly freeze from a new terror: from this fear I was able to conclude that my "ultimate conviction" had lodged itself all too seriously in me and was bound to reach its resolution. But I lacked resolve for that resolution. Three weeks later it was all over, and the resolve came, but owing to a very strange circumstance.

Here in my explanation I am noting down all these numbers and dates. For me, of course, it will make no difference, but *now* (and maybe only at this moment) I want those who will judge my act to be able to see clearly from what logical chain of conclusions my "ultimate conviction" came. I just wrote above that the final resolution, which I lacked for the accomplishing of my "ultimate conviction," came about in me, it seems, not at all as a logical conclusion, but from some strange jolt, a certain strange circumstance, perhaps quite unconnected with the course of events. About ten days ago Rogozhin came to see me on business of his own, which I need not discuss here. I had never seen Rogozhin before, but I had heard a lot about him. I gave him all the information he needed, and he quickly left, and as he had come only for information, the business between us should have ended there. But he interested me greatly, and I spent that whole day under the influence of strange thoughts, so that I decided to call on him myself the next day, to return the visit. Rogozhin was obviously not glad to see me, and even hinted "delicately" that there was no point in our continuing the acquaintance; but all the same I spent a very curious hour, as he probably did, too. There was this contrast between us, which could not fail to tell in both of us, especially me: I was a man whose days were already numbered, while he was living the fullest immediate life, in the present moment, with no care for "ultimate" conclusions, numbers, or anything at all that was not concerned with what . . . with what . . . well, say, with what he's gone crazy over; may Mr. Rogozhin forgive me this expression of, shall we say, a bad writer, who is unable to express his thought. Despite all his ungraciousness, it seemed to me that he was a man of intelligence and could understand a great deal, though he had little interest in extraneous things. I gave him no hint of my "ultimate conviction," but for some reason it seemed to me that he guessed it as he listened to me. He said nothing, he is terribly taciturn. I hinted to him, as I was leaving, that in spite of all the differences between us and all the contrasts—*les extrémités se touchent*[*17] (I explained it to him in Russian), so that he himself might not be so far from my "ultimate conviction" as it seemed.

*Extremes meet.

To this he responded with a very sullen and sour grimace, stood up, fetched my cap for me himself, pretending that I was leaving on my own, and quite simply led me out of his gloomy house on the pretext of politely seeing me off. His house struck me; it resembles a graveyard, but he seems to like it, which, however, is understandable: such a full, immediate life as he lives is too full in itself to need any setting.

This visit to Rogozhin was very exhausting for me. Besides, I had been feeling unwell since morning; by evening I was very weak and lay in bed, and at times felt very feverish and even momentarily delirious. Kolya stayed with me till eleven o'clock. However, I remember everything that he said and that we talked about. But when my eyes closed at moments, I kept picturing Ivan Fomich, who had supposedly received millions in cash. He did not know where to put it, racked his brains over it, trembled from fear that it might be stolen from him, and finally seemed to decide to bury it in the ground. I finally advised him, instead of burying such a heap of gold in the ground for nothing, to cast it into a little gold coffin for the "frozen" child, and to dig the child up for that purpose. Surikov took this mockery of mine with tears of gratitude and at once set about realizing the plan. It seems I spat and left him there. Kolya assured me, when I had completely come to my senses, that I had not been asleep at all, but had been talking with him the whole time about Surikov. At moments I was in great anguish and confusion, so that Kolya left in alarm. When I got up to lock the door after him, I suddenly remembered the picture I had seen that day at Rogozhin's, in one of the gloomiest rooms of his house, above the door. He himself had shown it to me in passing; I think I stood before it for about five minutes. There was nothing good about it in the artistic respect; but it produced a strange uneasiness in me.

This picture portrays Christ just taken down from the cross. It seems to me that painters are usually in the habit of portraying Christ, both on the cross and taken down from the cross, as still having a shade of extraordinary beauty in his face; they seek to preserve this beauty for him even in his most horrible suffering. But in Rogozhin's picture there is not a word about beauty; this is in the fullest sense the corpse of a man who had endured infinite suffering before the cross, wounds, torture, beating by the guards, beating by the people as he carried the cross and fell down under it, and had finally suffered on the cross for six hours (at least according to my calculation). True, it is the face of a man who has *only just* been taken down from the cross, that is, retaining in itself a great deal of life, of warmth; nothing has had time to become rigid yet, so that the dead man's face even shows suffering as if he were feeling it now (the artist has caught that very well); but the face has not been spared in the least; it is nature alone, and truly as the dead body of any man must be after such torments. I know that in the first centuries the Christian Church already established that Christ suffered not in appearance but in reality, and that on the cross his body, therefore, was fully and completely subject to the laws of nature. In the picture this face is horribly hurt by blows, swollen, with horrible, swollen, and bloody bruises, the eyelids are open, the eyes crossed; the large, open whites have a sort of deathly, glassy shine. But, strangely, when you look at the corpse of this tortured man, a particular and curious question arises: if all his disciples, his chief future apostles, if the women who followed him and stood by the cross, if all those who believed in him and worshipped him had seen a corpse like that (and it was bound to be exactly like that), how could they believe, looking at such a corpse, that this sufferer would resurrect? Here the notion involuntarily occurs to you that if death is so terrible and the laws of nature are so powerful, how can they be overcome? How overcome them, if they were not even defeated now, by the one who defeated nature while he lived, whom nature obeyed, who exclaimed: "*Talitha cumi*" and the girl arose, "Lazarus, come forth" and the dead man came out?[18] Nature appears to the viewer of this painting in the shape of some enormous, implacable, and dumb beast, or, to put it more correctly, much more correctly, strange though it is—in the shape of some huge machine of the most modern construction, which has senselessly seized, crushed, and swallowed up, blankly and unfeelingly, a great and priceless being—such a being as by himself was worth the whole of nature and all its laws, the whole earth, which was perhaps created solely for the appearance of this being alone! The painting seems precisely to express this notion of a dark, insolent, and senselessly eternal power, to which everything is subjected, and it is conveyed to you involuntarily. The people who surrounded the dead man, none of whom is in the painting, must have felt horrible anguish and confusion on that evening, which at once smashed all their hopes and almost their beliefs. They must have gone off in terrible fear, though each carried within himself a tremendous thought that could never be torn out of him.

And if this same teacher could have seen his own image on the eve of the execution, would he have gone to the cross and died as he did? That question also comes to you involuntarily as you look at the painting.

All this came to me in fragments, perhaps indeed through delirium, sometimes even in images, for a whole hour and a half after Kolya left. Can something that has no image come as an image? But it was as if it seemed to me at moments that I could see that infinite power, that blank, dark, and dumb being, in some strange and impossible form. I remember it seemed as if someone holding a candle led me by the hand and showed me some huge and repulsive tarantula and started assuring me that this was that dark, blank, and all-powerful being, and laughed at my indignation. In my room a little lamp is always lighted before the icon at night— the light is dim and negligible, but nevertheless you can see everything, and close to the lamp you can even read. I think it was already going on one o'clock; I was completely awake and lay with open eyes; suddenly the door of my room opened, and Rogozhin came in.

He came in, closed the door, silently looked at me, and quietly went to the corner, to the table that stands almost under the icon lamp. I was very surprised and watched in expectation; Rogozhin leaned his elbow on the little table and started looking at me silently. Two or three minutes passed that way, and I remember that his silence greatly offended and vexed me. Why did he not want to speak? The fact that he had come so late seemed strange to me, of course, yet I remember that I was not so greatly astonished by that in itself. Even the opposite: though I had not spoken my thought out clearly to him in the morning, I know he had understood it; and that thought was of such kind that, apropos of it, of course, one might come for another talk, even though it was very late. And so I thought he had come for that. In the morning we had parted somewhat hostilely, and I even remember him glancing at me very mockingly a couple of times. That mockery, which I could now read in his glance, was what offended me. That it actually was Rogozhin himself, and not a vision, not delirium, I at first did not doubt in the least. I did not even think of it.

Meanwhile he went on sitting and looking at me with the same smile. I turned over spitefully on my bed, also leaned my elbow on the pillow, and decided to be silent on purpose, even if we sat like that the whole time. For some reason I absolutely wanted him to begin first. I think about twenty minutes passed that way. Suddenly a thought occurred to me: what if it is not Rogozhin, but only a vision?

Neither during my illness nor before it have I ever once seen a single apparition; but it always seemed to me, when I was still a boy, and even now, that is, recently, that if I should see an apparition just once, I would die right on the spot, even though I do not believe in apparitions. But as soon as it occurred to me that it was not Rogozhin, but only an apparition, I remember that I wasn't frightened in the least. Not only that, but it even made me angry. Another strange thing was that the answer to the question whether it was an apparition or Rogozhin himself somehow did not interest or trouble me as much as it would seem it should have; it seems to me that I was thinking about something else then. For some reason I was much more interested in why Rogozhin, who had been wearing a dressing gown and slippers earlier, was now in a tailcoat, a white waistcoat, and a white tie. The thought also flashed: if this is an apparition, and I am not afraid of it, why not get up, go over to it, and make sure myself? It may be, however, that I didn't dare and was afraid. But I just had time to think I was afraid, when suddenly it was as if ice passed all over my body; I felt cold in my back, and my knees trembled. At that very moment, as if he had guessed that I was afraid, Rogozhin drew back the arm he had been leaning on, straightened up, and began to extend his mouth, as if getting ready to laugh; he looked at me point-blank. I was so infuriated that I decidedly wanted to fall upon him, but as I had sworn that I would not begin speaking first, I stayed in bed, the more so as I was not sure whether it was Rogozhin himself or not.

I do not remember for certain how long this went on; nor do I remember for certain whether I had moments of oblivion or not. Only, in the end Rogozhin got up, looked me over as slowly and attentively as before, when he came in, but stopped grinning and quietly, almost on tiptoe, went to the door, opened it, closed it, and was gone. I did not get out of bed; I don't remember how long I lay there thinking with open eyes; God knows what I was thinking about; I also don't remember how I became oblivious. The next morning I woke up when they knocked at my door, past nine o'clock. I had arranged it so that if I myself did not open the door by nine o'clock and call for tea to be served, Matryona herself should knock for me. When I opened the door to her, the thought immediately occurred to me: how could he have come in if the door was locked? I made inquiries and became convinced that the real Rogozhin could not have come in, because all our doors are locked for the night.

This particular case, which I have described in such detail, was the reason why I became completely "resolved." Which means that what contributed to my definitive resolve was not logic, not logical conviction, but revulsion. It is impossible to remain in a life that assumes such strange, offensive forms. This apparition humiliated me. I am unable to submit to a dark power that assumes the shape of a tarantula. And it was only at twilight, when I finally sensed in myself the definitive moment of full resolution, that I felt better. That was only the first moment; for the second moment I went to Pavlovsk, but that has already been sufficiently explained.

VII

I HAD A SMALL pocket pistol, I acquired it when I was still a child, at that ridiculous age when one suddenly begins to like stories about duels, about highway robberies, about how I, too, would be challenged to a duel, and how nobly I would stand facing the pistol. A month ago I examined it and prepared it. I found two bullets in the box with it, and enough powder in the powder horn for three shots. It is a trashy pistol, doesn't shoot straight, and is accurate only up to fifteen paces; but, of course, it would shove your skull sideways if you put it right to your temple.

I decided to die in Pavlovsk, at sunrise, and to do it in the park, so as not to trouble anyone in the dacha. My "Explanation" will sufficiently explain the whole matter to the police. Fanciers of psychology and those who feel the need can deduce whatever they like from it. However, I would not want this manuscript to be made public. I ask the prince to keep one copy for himself and to convey the other copy to Aglaya Ivanovna Epanchin. Such is my will. I bequeath my skeleton to the Medical Academy for the benefit of science.

I recognize no judges over me and know that I am now beyond all judicial power. Not long ago I was amused by a certain supposition: what if I should suddenly take it into my head now to kill whomever I like, even a dozen people at once, or to do something most terrible, that is simply considered the most terrible thing in the world, what a quandary the court would find itself in before me, with my two- or three-week term and with torture and the rack abolished! I would die comfortably in their hospital, in warmth, and with an attentive doctor, and perhaps be much more comfortable and warm than in my own house. I don't understand why the same thought doesn't occur to people in the same situation as mine, if only as a joke? However, maybe it does occur to them; there are lots of merry people to be found among us, too.

But if I do not recognize any judgment over me, I know all the same that I will be judged, once I have become a deaf and speechless defendant. I do not want to go without leaving a word of reply—a free word, not a forced one—not to justify myself—oh, no! I have nothing to ask forgiveness for from anyone—but just because I myself want it so.

First of all, there is a strange thought here: who, in the name of what right, in the name of what motive, would now take it into his head to dispute my right to these two or three weeks of my term? What court has any business here? Who precisely needs that I should not only be sentenced, but should graciously keep to the term of my sentence? Can it really be that anyone needs that? For the sake of morality? If, in the bloom of health and strength, I were to make an attempt on my life, which "could be useful to my neighbor," and so on, then I could understand that morality might reproach me, out of old habit, for having dealt with my life arbitrarily, or whatever. But now, now, when the term of the sentence has been read out to me? What sort of morality needs, on top of your life, also your last gasp, with which you give up the last atom of life, listening to the consolations of the prince, who is bound to go as far in his Christian reasoning as the happy thought that, essentially, it's even better that you're dying. (Christians like him always get to that idea: it's their favorite hobbyhorse.) And what do they want to do with their ridiculous "Pavlovsk trees"? Sweeten the last hours of my life? Don't they understand that the more oblivious I become, the more I give myself up to that last phantom of life and love with which they want to screen my Meyer's wall from me, with all that is written on it so frankly and simple-heartedly, the more unhappy they will make me? What do I need your nature for, your Pavlovsk park, your sunrises and sunsets, your blue sky, and your all-contented faces, when this whole banquet, which has no end, began by counting me alone as superfluous? What do I care about all this beauty, when every minute, every second, I must and am forced to know that even this tiny fly that is now buzzing near me in a ray of sunlight, even it participates in this banquet and chorus, knows its place, loves it, and is happy, while I alone am a castaway, and only in my pusillanimity did not want to understand it till now! Oh, don't I know how the prince and all of them would like to drive me to the point where, instead of all these "perfidious and spiteful" speeches, I would sing, out of good behavior and for the triumph of morality, the famous and classical strophe of Millevoye:[19]

> *O, puissent voir votre beauté sacrée*
> *Tant d'amis sourds à mes adieux!*
> *Qu'ils meurent pleins de jours, que leur mort soit pleurée,*
> *Qu'un ami leur ferme les yeux!**

But believe me, believe me, simple-hearted people, in this well-behaved strophe, in this academic blessing of the world in French verse, there is lodged so much hidden bile, so much implacable spite indulging itself in rhymes, that even the poet himself, perhaps, was duped and took this spite for tears of tenderness, and died with that—may he rest in peace! Know that there is a limit to disgrace in the consciousness of one's own nonentity and weakness, beyond which man cannot go and at which he begins to take a tremendous pleasure in the disgrace itself . . . Well, of course, humility is a tremendous force in this sense, I admit that—though not in the sense in which religion takes humility for a force.

Religion! I do admit eternal life and perhaps have always admitted it. Let consciousness be lit up by the will of a higher power, let it look at the world and say: "I am!" and let the higher power suddenly decree its annihilation, because for some reason—or even without explaining for what reason—that is needed: let it be so, I admit all that, but again comes the eternal question: why is my humility needed here? Isn't it possible simply to eat me, without demanding that I praise that which has eaten me? Can it be that someone there will indeed be offended that I don't want to wait for two weeks? I don't believe it; and it would be much more likely to suppose that my insignificant life, the life of an atom, was simply needed for the fulfillment of some universal harmony as a whole,

*O, may they behold your sacred beauty / So many friends deaf to my farewells! / May they die full of days, may their death be wept, / May a friend close their eyes!

for some plus and minus, for some sort of contrast, and so on and so forth, just as daily sacrifice requires the lives of a multitude of beings, without whose death the rest of the world could not stand (though it must be noted that this is not a very magnanimous thought in itself). But so be it! I agree that it was quite impossible to arrange the world otherwise, that is, without the ceaseless devouring of each other; I even agree to admit that I understand nothing of this arrangement; but on the other hand, I know this for certain: if I have once been given the consciousness that "I am," what business is it of mine that the world has been arranged with mistakes and that otherwise it cannot stand? Who is going to judge me after that, and for what? Say what you will, all this is impossible and unjust.

And meanwhile, even in spite of all my desire, I could never imagine to myself that there is no future life and no providence. Most likely there is all that, but we don't understand anything about the future life and its laws. But if it is so difficult and even completely impossible to understand it, can it be that I will have to answer for being unable to comprehend the unknowable? True, they say, and the prince, of course, along with them, that it is here that obedience is necessary, that one must obey without reasoning, out of sheer good behavior, and that I am bound to be rewarded for my meekness in the other world. We abase providence too much by ascribing our own notions to it, being vexed that we can't understand it. But, again, if it's impossible to understand it, then, I repeat, it is hard to have to answer for something it is not given to man to understand. And if so, how are they going to judge me for being unable to understand the true will and laws of providence? No, we'd better leave religion alone.

But enough. When I get to these lines, the sun will probably already be risen and "resounding in the sky," and a tremendous, incalculable force will pour out on all that is under the sun. So be it! I will die looking straight into the wellspring of force and life, and I will not want this life! If it had been in my power not to be born, I probably would not have accepted existence on such derisive conditions. But I still have the power to die, though I'm giving back what's already numbered. No great power, no great rebellion either.

A last explanation: I am by no means dying because I cannot endure these three weeks; oh, I would have strength enough, and if I wanted to, I could be sufficiently comforted by the very consciousness of the offense done to me; but I am not a French poet and do not want such comforting. Finally, there is the temptation: nature has so greatly limited my activity by her three-week sentence that suicide may be the only thing I still have time to begin and end of my own will. So, maybe I want to use my last opportunity of *doing* something? A protest is sometimes no small matter . . .

The "Explanation" was over; Ippolit finally stopped . . .

There is in extreme cases that degree of ultimate cynical frankness, when a nervous man, irritated and beside himself, no longer fears anything and is ready for any scandal, even glad of it; he throws himself at people, having at the same time an unclear but firm goal of certainly leaping from a belfry a minute later and thus resolving at once all misunderstandings, in case they turn up along the way. An imminent exhaustion of physical strength is usually an indication of this state. The extreme, almost unnatural tension that had so far sustained Ippolit had reached that ultimate degree. In himself this eighteen-year-old boy, exhausted by illness, seemed as weak as a trembling leaf torn from a tree; but he no sooner looked around at his listeners—for the first time during the last hour—than the same haughty, almost contemptuous and offensive revulsion showed at once in his eyes and smile. He hurried with his defiance. But his listeners were also totally indignant. They were all getting up from the table with noise and vexation. Fatigue, wine, and tension had heightened the disorderliness and, as it were, the filth of the impressions, if it may be so expressed.

Suddenly Ippolit jumped quickly from his chair, as if torn from his place.

"The sun has risen!" he cried, seeing the glowing treetops and pointing them out to the prince like a miracle. "It's risen!"[20]

"And did you think it wouldn't, or what?" observed Ferdyshchenko.

"Another whole day of torrid heat," Ganya muttered with careless vexation, hat in hand, stretching and yawning. "Well, there may be a month of drought like this! . . . Are we going or not, Ptitsyn?"

Ippolit listened with an astonishment that reached the point of stupefaction; suddenly he turned terribly pale and began to shake all over.

"You're very clumsily affecting your indifference in order to insult me," he addressed Ganya, looking at him point-blank. "You're a scoundrel!"

"Well, devil knows, a man shouldn't unbutton himself like that!" shouted Ferdyshchenko. "What phenomenal weakness!"

"Simply a fool," said Ganya.

Ippolit restrained himself somewhat.

"I understand, gentlemen," he began, trembling and faltering at each word as before, "that I may deserve your personal vengeance and . . . I'm sorry that I wore you out with this raving" (he pointed to the manuscript), "though I'm sorry I didn't wear you out completely . . ." (he smiled stupidly). "Did I wear you out, Evgeny Pavlych?" he suddenly jumped over to him with the question. "Did I wear you out, or not? Speak!"

"It was a bit drawn out, but anyhow . . ."

"Say it all! Don't lie for at least once in your life!" Ippolit commanded, trembling.

"Oh, it decidedly makes no difference to me! Do me a favor, I beg you, leave me in peace," Evgeny Pavlovich squeamishly turned away.

"Good night, Prince," Ptitsyn went over to the prince.

"But he's going to shoot himself now, don't you see? Look at him!" cried Vera, and she rushed to Ippolit in extreme fright and even seized his hands. "He said he'd shoot himself at sunrise, don't you see?"

"He won't shoot himself!" several voices muttered gloatingly, Ganya's among them.

"Watch out, gentlemen!" Kolya cried, also seizing Ippolit by the hand. "Just look at him! Prince! Prince, don't you see?"

Vera, Kolya, Keller, and Burdovsky crowded around Ippolit; all four seized him with their hands.

"He has the right, the right! . . ." muttered Burdovsky, who nevertheless looked quite lost.

"Excuse me, Prince, what are your orders?" Lebedev went up to the prince, drunk and spiteful to the point of impudence.

"What orders?"

"No, sir; excuse me, sir; I'm the host, sir, though I do not wish to show a lack of respect for you. Let's grant that you, too, are the host, but I don't want any of that in my own house . . . So there, sir."

"He won't shoot himself; it's a boyish prank," General Ivolgin cried unexpectedly with indignation and aplomb.

"Bravo, General!" Ferdyshchenko picked up.

"I know he won't shoot himself, General, my much-esteemed General, but all the same . . . for I'm the host."

"Listen, Mr. Terentyev," Ptitsyn said suddenly, having taken leave of the prince and holding his hand out to Ippolit, "in your notebook I believe you mention your skeleton and bequeath it to the Academy? It's your skeleton, your very own, that is, your own bones, that you're bequeathing?"

"Yes, my own bones . . ."

"Aha. Because there might be a mistake: they say there already was such a case."

"Why do you tease him?" the prince cried suddenly.

"You've driven him to tears," added Ferdyshchenko.

But Ippolit was not crying at all. He tried to move from his place, but the four people standing around him suddenly all seized him by the arms. There was laughter.

"That's what he was getting at, that people should hold him by the arms; that's why he read his notebook," observed Rogozhin. "Good-bye, Prince. We've sat enough; my bones ache."

"If you actually intended to shoot yourself, Terentyev," laughed Evgeny Pavlovich, "then if I were in your place, after such compliments, I would deliberately not shoot myself, so as to tease them."

"They want terribly to see how I shoot myself!" Ippolit reared up at him.

He spoke as if he were attacking him.

"They're vexed that they won't see it."

"So you, too, think they won't see it?"

"I'm not egging you on; on the contrary, I think it's quite possible that you will shoot yourself. Above all, don't get angry . . ." Evgeny Pavlovich drawled, drawing the words out patronizingly.

"Only now do I see that I made a terrible mistake in reading them this notebook!" said Ippolit, looking at Evgeny Pavlovich with such an unexpectedly trusting air as if he were asking friendly advice from a friend.

"The situation is ridiculous, but . . . really, I don't know what to advise you," Evgeny Pavlovich replied, smiling.

Ippolit sternly looked at him point-blank, not tearing his eyes away, and said nothing. One might have thought he was totally oblivious at moments.

"No, excuse me, sir, look at the way he does it, sir," said Lebedev.

" 'I'll shoot myself,' he says, 'in the park, so as not to trouble anybody'! So he thinks he won't trouble anybody if he goes three steps down into the garden."

"Gentlemen . . ." the prince began.

"No, sir, excuse me, sir, my much-esteemed Prince," Lebedev latched on furiously, "since you yourself are pleased to see that this is not a joke and since at least half of your guests are of the same opinion and are sure that now, after the words that have been spoken here, he certainly must shoot himself out of honor, then I, being the host, announce in front of witnesses that I am asking you to be of assistance!"

"What needs to be done, Lebedev? I'm ready to assist you."

"Here's what: first of all, he should immediately hand over his pistol, which he boasted about to us, with all the accessories. If he hands it over, then I agree to allow him to spend this one night in this house, in view of his ill condition, and, of course, under supervision on my part. But tomorrow let him go without fail wherever he likes—forgive me, Prince! If he doesn't hand over his weapon, then I at once, immediately, seize him by one arm, the general by the other, and also at once send somebody to notify the police, and then the matter passes over to the police for consideration, sir. Mr. Ferdyshchenko will go, sir, being an acquaintance."

Noise broke out; Lebedev was excited and already overstepping the limits; Ferdyshchenko was preparing to go to the police; Ganya furiously insisted that no one was going to shoot himself. Evgeny Pavlovich was silent.

"Prince, have you ever leaped from a belfry?" Ippolit suddenly whispered to him.

"N-no . . ." the prince answered naïvely.

"Do you really think I didn't foresee all this hatred?" Ippolit whispered again, flashing his eyes, and looking at the prince as if he indeed expected an answer from him. "Enough!" he cried suddenly to the whole public. "I'm to blame . . . most of all! Lebedev, here's the key" (he took out his wallet and from it a steel ring with three or four little keys on it), "this one, the next to last . . . Kolya will show you . . . Kolya! Where's Kolya?" he cried, looking at Kolya and not seeing him, "yes . . . he'll show you; he and I packed my bag yesterday. Take him, Kolya; in the prince's study, under the table . . . my bag . . . with this key, at the bottom, in the little box . . . my pistol and the powder horn. He packed it himself yesterday, Mr. Lebedev, he'll show you; so long as you give me back the pistol early tomorrow, when I go to Petersburg. Do you hear? I'm doing it for the prince, not for you."

"Well, that's better!" Lebedev snatched the key and, smiling venomously, ran to the other room.

Kolya stopped, was about to say something, but Lebedev pulled him after him.

Ippolit was looking at the laughing guests. The prince noticed that his teeth were chattering as if in a most violent chill.

"What scoundrels they all are!" Ippolit again whispered frenziedly to the prince. When he spoke to the prince, he kept leaning towards him and whispering.

"Let them be; you're very weak . . ."

"One moment, one moment . . . I'll go in a moment."

He suddenly embraced the prince.

"Maybe you find me crazy?" He looked at him, laughing strangely.

"No, but you . . ."

"One moment, one moment, be quiet; don't say anything; stand there . . . I want to look in your eyes . . . Stand like that, let me look. Let me say good-bye to Man."

He stood and looked at the prince motionlessly and silently for about ten seconds, very pale, his temples moist with sweat, and somehow clutching at the prince strangely with his hand, as if afraid to let him go.

"Ippolit, Ippolit, what's the matter?" cried the prince.

"One moment . . . enough . . . I'll lie down. I'll drink one gulp to the sun's health . . . I want to, I want to, let me be!"

He quickly snatched a glass from the table, tore from the spot, and an instant later was on the steps of the terrace. The prince was about to run after him, but it so happened that, as if on purpose, at that same moment Evgeny Pavlovich held out his hand to say good-bye. A second passed, and suddenly a general cry arose on the terrace. Then came a moment of extreme disarray.

Here is what happened:

Having gone right to the steps of the terrace, Ippolit stopped, holding the glass in his left hand, his right hand thrust into the right side pocket of his coat. Keller insisted later that Ippolit had kept that hand in his right pocket before as well, while he was talking with the prince and clutching at his shoulder and collar with his left hand, and this right hand in the pocket, Keller insisted, had supposedly aroused a first suspicion in him. Be that as it may, a certain uneasiness made him also run after Ippolit. But he, too, was late. He saw only how something suddenly flashed in Ippolit's right hand, and in that same second the small pocket pistol was pressed to his temple. Keller rushed to seize his hand, but in that same second Ippolit pulled the trigger. The sharp, dry click of the trigger rang out, but no shot followed. As Keller put his arms around Ippolit, the latter collapsed as if unconscious, perhaps indeed imagining that he was killed. The pistol was already in Keller's hand. Ippolit was picked up, a chair was brought, he was seated, and everyone crowded around, everyone shouted, everyone asked questions. Everyone had heard the click of the trigger and now saw the man alive, not even scratched. Ippolit himself sat, not understanding what was happening, and looked at everyone around him with senseless eyes. Lebedev and Kolya came running at that moment.

"A misfire?" some asked.

"Maybe it's not loaded?" others tried to guess.

"It is loaded!" Keller announced, examining the pistol, "but . . ."

"A misfire, then?"

"There wasn't any cap," Keller declared.

It is hard to describe the pitiful scene that followed. The initial and general alarm quickly gave way to laughter; some even guffawed, finding a malicious pleasure in it. Ippolit sobbed as if in hysterics, wrung his hands, rushed to everyone, even to Ferdyshchenko, seized him with both hands, and swore to him that he had forgotten, "had forgotten quite by chance and not on purpose" to put a cap in, that "the caps are all here in his waistcoat pocket, about ten of them" (he showed them to everyone around him), that he had not put one in earlier for fear it might accidentally go off in his pocket, that he had reckoned he would always have time to put one in when necessary, and had suddenly forgotten. He rushed to the prince, to Evgeny Pavlovich, he implored Keller to give him the pistol, so that he could prove it to them all right then, that "his honor, honor" . . . that he was now "dishonored forever! . . ."

In the end he really fell unconscious. They carried him to the prince's study, and Lebedev, completely sobered, immediately sent for the doctor and stayed at the sick boy's bedside, along with his daughter, his son, Burdovsky, and the general. When the unconscious Ippolit was taken out, Keller stepped to the middle of the room and announced for everyone to hear, distinctly and emphasizing each word, in decided inspiration:

"Gentlemen, if any of you doubts once more, aloud, in my presence, whether the cap was forgotten on purpose, and begins to maintain that the unfortunate young man was only putting on a show—that person will have to deal with me."

No one answered him. The guests finally left in a crowd and hurriedly. Ptitsyn, Ganya, and Rogozhin went off together.

The prince was very surprised that Evgeny Pavlovich had changed his mind and was leaving without having a talk with him.

"Didn't you want to talk to me once everyone was gone?" he asked him.

"So I did," said Evgeny Pavlovich, suddenly sitting down on a chair and sitting the prince down next to him, "but for the time being I've changed my mind. I'll confess to you that I'm somewhat perplexed, and you are, too. My thoughts are confused; besides, the matter I wanted to talk over with you is all too important for me, and for you, too. You see, Prince, I would like at least once in my life to do a completely honest deed, that is, completely without second thoughts, but I think that right now, at this moment, I'm not quite capable of a completely honest deed, and perhaps you're not either . . . so . . . and . . . well, we'll talk later. Perhaps the matter will gain in clarity, both for me and for you, if we wait those three days which I shall now be spending in Petersburg."

Here he got up from his chair again, which made it strange that he had sat down at all. It also seemed to the prince that Evgeny Pavlovich was displeased and irritated and looked about hostilely, and his gaze was not at all what it had been yesterday.

"By the way, are you going to the sufferer now?"

"Yes . . . I'm afraid," said the prince.

"Don't be afraid; he'll probably live another six weeks and may even recover here. But the best thing would be to send him away tomorrow."

"Maybe I really forced his hand by . . . not saying anything; maybe he thought that I, too, doubted that he would shoot himself? What do you think, Evgeny Pavlych?"

"No, no. It's too kind of you to be still worried. I've heard of it, but I've never seen in real life how a man can purposely shoot himself in order to be praised, or out of spite at not being praised. Above all, this sincerity of weakness is not to be believed! But you should still send him away tomorrow."

"You think he'll shoot himself again?"

"No, he won't shoot himself now. But you should beware of these homegrown Lacenaires[21] of ours! I repeat to you that crime is all too common a resort for such giftless, impatient, and greedy nonentities."

"Is he a Lacenaire?"

"The essence is the same, though the line may be different. You'll see whether this gentleman isn't capable of doing in a dozen souls merely for a 'joke,' just as he read earlier in his 'Explanation.' Now those words won't let me sleep."

"Perhaps you're worrying too much."

"You're amazing, Prince. Don't you believe he's capable *now* of killing a dozen souls?"

"I'm afraid to answer you; it's all very strange, but . . ."

"Well, as you wish, as you wish!" Evgeny Pavlovich concluded irritably. "Besides, you're such a brave man; only don't get yourself included in that dozen."

"Most likely he won't kill anybody," said the prince, looking pensively at Evgeny Pavlovich.

The man laughed maliciously.

"Good-bye, it's time to go! And did you notice that he bequeathed a copy of his 'Confession' to Aglaya Ivanovna?"

"Yes, I did and . . . I'm thinking about it."

"Do so, in case of those dozen souls," Evgeny Pavlovich laughed again and left.

An hour later, already past three o'clock, the prince went down into the park. He had tried to fall asleep at home, but could not, because of the violent beating of his heart. At home, however, everything was settled and peaceful, as far as possible; the sick boy had fallen asleep, and the doctor had come and had declared that there was no special danger. Lebedev, Kolya, and Burdovsky lay down in the sick boy's room to take turns watching over him; there was therefore nothing to fear.

But the prince's uneasiness was growing minute by minute. He wandered through the park, absentmindedly looking around, and stopped in surprise when he came to the green in front of the vauxhall and saw a row of empty benches and music stands for the orchestra. The place struck him and for some reason seemed terribly ugly. He turned back and straight down the path he had taken to the vauxhall the day before with the Epanchins, which brought him to the green bench appointed to him for the meeting, sat down on it, and suddenly laughed out loud, which at once made him terribly indignant. His anguish continued; he would have liked to go away somewhere . . . He did not know where. Above him in the tree a little bird was singing, and he started searching for it with his eyes among the leaves; suddenly the bird flew away from the tree, and at that moment for some reason he recalled the "little fly" in a "hot ray of sunlight," of which Ippolit had written that even this fly "knows its place and participates in the general chorus, and he alone was a castaway." This phrase had struck him earlier, and he remembered it now. A long-forgotten memory stirred in him and suddenly became clear all at once.

It was in Switzerland, during the first year of his treatment, even during the first months. He was still quite like an idiot then, could not even speak properly, and sometimes did not understand what was required of him. Once he went into the mountains on a clear, sunny day, and wandered about for a long time with a tormenting thought that refused to take shape. Before him was the shining sky, below him the lake, around him the horizon, bright and infinite, as if it went on forever. For a long time he looked and suffered. He remembered now how he had stretched out his arms to that bright, infinite blue and wept. What had tormented him was that he was a total stranger to it all. What was this banquet, what was this great everlasting feast, to which he had long been drawn, always, ever since childhood, and which he could never join? Every morning the same bright sun rises; every morning there is a rainbow over the waterfall; every evening the highest snowcapped mountain, there, far away, at the edge of the sky, burns with a crimson flame; every "little fly that buzzes near him in a hot ray of sunlight participates in this whole chorus: knows its place, loves it, and is happy"; every little blade of grass grows and is happy! And everything has its path, and everything knows its path, goes with a song and comes back with a song; only he knows nothing, understands nothing, neither people nor sounds, a stranger to everything and a castaway. Oh, of course, he could not speak then with these words and give voice to his question; he suffered blankly and mutely; but now it seemed to him that he had said it all then, all those same words, and that Ippolit had taken the words about the "little fly" from him, from his own words and tears of that time. He was sure of it, and for some reason his heart throbbed at this thought . . .

He dozed off on the bench, but his anxiousness continued in his sleep. Before falling asleep, he remembered that Ippolit would kill a dozen people, and he smiled at the absurdity of the suggestion. Around him there was a beautiful, serene silence, with only the rustling of leaves, which seemed to make it still more silent and solitary. He had a great many dreams, and all of them anxious, so that he kept shuddering. Finally a woman came to him; he knew her, knew her to the point of suffering; he could have named her and pointed to her any time, but—strangely— she now seemed to have a different face from the one he had always known, and he was painfully reluctant to recognize her as that woman. There was so much repentance and horror in this face that it seemed she was a terrible criminal who had just committed a horrible crime. A tear trembled on her pale cheek; she beckoned to him with her hand and put her finger to her lips, as if cautioning him to follow her more quietly. His heart stood still; not for anything, not for anything did he want to recognize her as a criminal; yet he felt that something horrible was just about to happen, for the whole of his life. It seemed she wanted to show him something, not far away, there in the park. He got up to follow her, and suddenly someone's bright, fresh laughter rang out close by; someone's hand was suddenly in his hand; he grasped this hand, pressed it hard, and woke up. Before him, laughing loudly, stood Aglaya.

VIII

S HE WAS LAUGHING, but she was also indignant.
    "Asleep! You were asleep!" she cried with scornful surprise.
    "It's you!" murmured the prince, not quite recovered yet and recognizing her with surprise. "Ah, yes! Our meeting . . . I was sleeping here."
    "So I saw."
    "Did no one else wake me up except you? Was there no one here except you? I thought there was . . . another woman here . . ."
    "There was another woman here?!"
    He finally recovered himself completely.
    "It was only a dream," he said pensively, "strange, such a dream at such a moment . . . Sit down."
    He took her by the hand and sat her on the bench; he sat down beside her and fell to thinking. Aglaya did not begin a conversation,

but only studied her interlocutor intently. He also kept glancing at her, but at times it was as if he did not see her before him at all. She was beginning to blush.

"Ah, yes!" the prince gave a start. "Ippolit shot himself!"

"When? At your place?" she said, but with no great surprise. "Yesterday evening, I believe, he was still alive? How could you fall asleep here after all that?" she cried with unexpected animation.

"But he didn't die, the pistol didn't fire."

At Aglaya's insistence the prince had to retell right then, and even in great detail, the whole story of the past night. She kept hurrying him as he told it, yet she herself interrupted him continually with questions, almost all of them beside the point. Among other things, she listened with great curiosity to what Evgeny Pavlovich had said, and several times even asked the prince to repeat it.

"Well, enough, we must hurry," she concluded, having heard it all, "we can only stay here for an hour, till eight o'clock, because at eight o'clock I must be at home without fail, so they won't know I've been sitting here, and I've come on business; I have a lot to tell you. Only you've got me all thrown off now. About Ippolit, I think his pistol was bound not to fire, it's more suited to him. But are you sure he really wanted to shoot himself and there was no deception in it?"

"No deception at all."

"That's more likely, too. So he wrote that you should bring me his confession? Why didn't you bring it?"

"But he didn't die. I'll ask him."

"Bring it without fail, and there's no need to ask. He'll probably be very pleased, because it may be that his purpose in shooting himself was so that I should read his confession afterwards. Please, Lev Nikolaich, I beg you not to laugh at my words, because it may very well be so."

"I'm not laughing, because I'm sure myself that in part it may very well be so."

"You're sure? Do you really think so, too?" Aglaya suddenly became terribly surprised.

She questioned him quickly, spoke rapidly, but seemed to get confused at times and often did not finish; she kept hurrying to warn him about something; generally she was extraordinarily anxious, and though she looked at him very bravely and with a sort of defiance, she was perhaps also a little frightened. She was wearing a most ordinary and simple dress, which was very becoming to her. She often started, blushed, and sat on the edge of the bench. She was very surprised when the prince agreed that Ippolit shot himself so that she should read his confession.

"Of course," the prince explained, "he wanted not only you but the rest of us also to praise him . . ."

"How do you mean, praise him?"

"I mean it's . . . how shall I tell you? It's very hard to say. Only he surely wanted everyone to stand around him and tell him that they love and respect him very much, and start begging him to remain alive. It may well be that he had you in mind most of all, since he mentioned you at such a moment . . . though he may not have known himself that he had you in mind."

"That I don't understand at all: had me in mind, but didn't know he had me in mind. Though I think I do understand: do you know that I myself, even when I was still a thirteen-year-old girl, thought at least thirty times of poisoning myself, and of writing all about it in a letter to my parents, and I also thought of how I would lie in the coffin, and they would all weep over me and accuse themselves for being so cruel to me . . . Why are you smiling again?" she added quickly, frowning. "And what do you think to yourself when you dream alone? Maybe you imagine you're a field marshal and have crushed Napoleon?"

"Well, on my word of honor, that's just what I do think about, especially as I'm falling asleep," laughed the prince, "only it's not Napoleon I crush but the Austrians."

"I have no wish to joke with you, Lev Nikolaich. I will go to see Ippolit myself; I ask you to warn him. And on your side I find all this very bad, because it's very rude to look at and judge a man's soul the way you're judging Ippolit. You have no tenderness, only truth, that makes it unfair."

The prince reflected.

"I think you're being unfair to me," he said. "I don't find anything bad in his thinking that way, because everyone is inclined to think that way; besides, maybe he didn't think at all, but merely wanted . . . he wanted to meet people for the last time, to deserve their respect and love; those are very good feelings, only somehow nothing turned out right; it's his sickness, and something else as well! Anyhow, with some people everything always turns out right, and with others it's like nothing in the world . . ."

"You probably added that about yourself," Aglaya observed.

"Yes, about myself," replied the prince, not noticing any malice in the question.

"Only, all the same, I should never have fallen asleep in your place; it means that wherever you snuggle up, you fall asleep at once; that's not very nice on your part."

"But I didn't sleep all night, then I walked and walked, got to the music . . ."

"What music?"

"Where they played yesterday, and then I came here, sat down, thought and thought, and fell asleep."

"Ah, so that's how it was? That changes everything in your favor . . . And why did you go to the music?"

"I don't know, I just . . ."

"All right, all right, later; you keep interrupting me, and what do I care if you went to the music? Who was that woman you dreamed about?"

"It was . . . about . . . you saw her . . ."

"I understand, I understand very well. You're very much . . . How did you dream of her, what did she look like? However, I don't want to know anything," she suddenly snapped in vexation, "don't interrupt me . . ."

She waited a while, as if gathering her courage or trying to drive her vexation away.

"Here's the whole matter I invited you for: I want to propose that you be my friend. Why do you suddenly stare at me like that?" she added almost with wrath.

The prince was indeed peering at her intently at that moment, noticing that she had again begun to blush terribly. On such occasions, the more she blushed, the more she seemed to be angry with herself for it, as showed clearly in her flashing eyes; usually she would transfer her wrath a moment later to the one she was talking with, whether or not it was his fault, and begin to quarrel with him. Knowing and feeling her wildness and shyness, she usually entered little into conversation and was more taciturn than the other sisters, sometimes even much too taciturn. When, especially on such ticklish occasions, she absolutely had to speak, she would begin the conversation with an extraordinary haughtiness and as if with a sort of defiance. She always felt beforehand when she was beginning or about to begin to blush.

"Perhaps you don't want to accept my proposal?" she glanced haughtily at the prince.

"Oh, no, I do, only it's quite unnecessary . . . that is, I never thought there was any need to propose such a thing," the prince was abashed.

"And what did you think? Why would I have invited you here? What do you have in mind? However, maybe you consider me a little fool, as they all do at home?"

"I didn't know they considered you a fool. I . . . I don't."

"You don't? Very intelligent on your part. The way you put it is especially intelligent."

"In my opinion, you may even be very intelligent at times," the prince went on. "Earlier you suddenly said something very intelligent. You said of my doubt about Ippolit: 'There's only truth in it, and that makes it unfair.' I'll remember that and think about it."

Aglaya suddenly flushed with pleasure. All these changes took place in her extremely openly and with extraordinary swiftness. The prince also rejoiced and even laughed with joy, looking at her.

"Now listen," she began again, "I've been waiting for you a long time, in order to tell you all this, I've been waiting ever since you wrote me that letter from there, and even earlier . . . You already heard half of it from me yesterday: I consider you a most honest and truthful man, the most honest and truthful of all, and if they say your mind . . . that is, that you're sometimes sick in your mind, it isn't right; I've decided and argued about it, because though you are in fact sick in your mind (you won't, of course, be angry at that, I'm speaking from a higher point), the main mind in you is better than in any of them, such as they would never even dream of, because there are two minds: the main one and the non-main one. Well? Isn't that so?"

"Maybe so," the prince barely uttered; his heart trembled and pounded terribly.

"I just knew you'd understand," she went on gravely. "Prince Shch. and Evgeny Pavlych don't understand anything about these two minds, neither does Alexandra, but imagine: *maman* did."

"You're very much like Lizaveta Prokofyevna."

"How's that? Can it be?" Aglaya was surprised.

"By God, it's so."

"I thank you," she said after some thought. "I'm very glad that I'm like *maman*. So you respect her very much?" she added, quite unaware of the naïvety of the question.

"Very, very much, and I'm glad you've understood it so directly."

"I'm glad, too, because I've noticed that people sometimes . . . laugh at her. But now hear the main thing: I've thought for a long time, and I've finally chosen you. I don't want them to laugh at me at home; I don't want them to consider me a little fool; I don't want them to tease me . . . I understood it all at once and flatly refused Evgeny Pavlych, because I don't want them to be constantly marrying me off! I want . . . I want . . .well, I want to run away from home, and I've chosen you to help me."

"To run away from home!" the prince cried.

"Yes, yes, yes, to run away from home!" she cried suddenly, blazing up with extraordinary wrath. "I don't, I don't want them to be eternally making me blush there. I don't want to blush either before them, or before Prince Shch., or before Evgeny Pavlych, or before anybody, and so I've chosen you. I want to talk about everything with you, everything, even the main thing, whenever I like; and you, for your part, must hide nothing from me. I want to talk about everything with at least one person as I would with myself. They suddenly started saying that I was waiting for you and that I loved you. That was before you arrived, and I didn't show them your letter; but now they all say it. I want to be brave and not afraid of anything. I don't want to go to their balls, I want to be useful. I wanted to leave long ago. They've kept me bottled up for twenty years, and they all want to get me married. When I was fourteen I already thought of running away, though I was a fool. Now I have it all worked out and was waiting for you, to ask you all about life abroad. I've never seen a single gothic cathedral, I want to be in Rome, I want to examine all the learned collections, I want to study in Paris; all this past year I've been preparing and studying, and I've read a great many books; I've read all the forbidden books. Alexandra and Adelaida have read all the books; they're allowed but I'm forbidden, they supervise me. I don't want to quarrel with my sisters, but I announced to my father and mother long ago that I want to change my social position completely. I've decided to occupy myself with education, and I'm counting on you, because you said you loved children. Can we occupy ourselves with education together, if not now, then in the future? We'll be useful together; I don't want to be a general's daughter . . . Tell me, are you a very learned man?"

"Oh, not at all."

"That's a pity, and I thought . . . what made me think that? You'll guide me all the same, because I've chosen you."

"This is absurd, Aglaya Ivanovna."

"I want it, I want to run away from home!" she cried, and again her eyes flashed. "If you don't agree, then I'll marry Gavrila Ardalionovich. I don't want to be considered a loathsome woman at home and be accused of God knows what."

"Are you out of your mind?" the prince nearly jumped up from his place. "What do they accuse you of? Who accuses you?"

"At home, everybody, my mother, my sisters, my father, Prince Shch., even your loathsome Kolya! If they don't say it outright, they think it. I told them all so to their faces, my mother and my father. *Maman* was ill for the whole day; and the next day Alexandra and papa told me I didn't understand what I was babbling myself and what kind of words I'd spoken. At which point I just snapped at them that I already understood everything, all the words, that I was not a little girl, that I had read two novels by Paul de Kock[22] on purpose two years ago in order to learn about everything. When she heard that, *maman* nearly fainted."

A strange thought suddenly flashed in the prince's head. He looked intently at Aglaya and smiled.

It was even hard for him to believe that this was the same haughty girl sitting before him who had once so proudly and arrogantly read Gavrila Ardalionovich's letter to him. He could not understand how such an arrogant, stern beauty could turn out to be such a child, who even *now* might actually not understand *all the words*.

"Have you always lived at home, Aglaya Ivanovna?" he asked. "I mean to say, you haven't gone anywhere, to any kind of school, never studied at an institute?"

"I've never gone anywhere; I've always sat at home, bottled up, and I'll get married right out of the bottle. Why are you smiling again? I notice that you, too, seem to be laughing at me and to be on their side," she added, with a menacing frown. "Don't make me angry, I don't know what's the matter with me as it is . . . I'm sure you've come here completely convinced that I'm in love with you and was inviting you to a tryst," she snapped irritably.

"I actually was afraid of that yesterday," the prince blurted out simple-heartedly (he was very embarrassed), "but today I'm sure that you . . ."

"What!" Aglaya cried, and her lower lip suddenly trembled. "You were afraid that I . . . you dared to think that I . . . Lord! Maybe you suspected that I invited you here in order to lure you into my nets, and then they would find us here and force you to marry me . . ."

"Aglaya Ivanovna! Aren't you ashamed? How could such a dirty thought be born in your pure, innocent heart? I'll bet you yourself don't believe a word you've said and . . . you don't know what you're saying!"

Aglaya sat stubbornly looking down, as if she herself was frightened at what she had said.

"I'm not ashamed at all," she murmured. "How do you know my heart is innocent? How did you dare to send me a love letter then?"

"A love letter? My letter—a love letter? That letter was most respectful, that letter poured from my heart at the most painful moment of my life! I remembered about you then as of some sort of light [23] . . . I . . ."

"Well, all right, all right," she suddenly interrupted, no longer in the same tone at all, but in complete repentance and almost in alarm; she even bent towards him, still trying not to look straight at him, and made as if to touch his shoulder, to ask him more convincingly not to be angry, "all right," she added, terribly shame-faced, "I feel that I used a very stupid expression. I did it just like that . . . to test you. Take it as if I hadn't said it. And if I offended you, forgive me. Please don't look straight at me, turn your head. You said it was a very dirty thought: I said it on purpose to needle you. Sometimes I myself am afraid of what I want to say, and then suddenly I say it. You said just now that you wrote that letter at the most painful moment of your life . . . I know what moment it was," she said softly, again looking at the ground.

"Oh, if only you could know everything!"

"I do know everything!" she cried with new agitation. "You lived in the same rooms for a whole month then with that loathsome woman you ran away with . . ."

She did not blush now but turned pale as she said it, and she suddenly got up from her place, as if forgetting herself, but, recollecting herself, she at once sat down; her lower lip went on trembling for a long time. The silence went on for about a minute. The prince was terribly struck by the suddenness of her outburst and did not know what to ascribe it to.

"I don't love you at all," she suddenly snapped out.

The prince did not reply; again there was a minute of silence.

"I love Gavrila Ardalionovich . . ." she said in a quick patter, but barely audibly and bowing her head still more.

"That's not true," said the prince, almost in a whisper.

"You mean I'm lying? It is true; I gave him my promise, two days ago, on this same bench."

The prince was alarmed and thought for a moment.

"That's not true," he said resolutely, "you've made it all up."

"How wonderfully polite. Know that he has mended his ways; he loves me more than life itself. He burned his hand in front of me just to prove that he loves me more than life itself."

"Burned his hand?"

"Yes, his hand. Believe it or don't—it's all the same to me."

The prince fell silent again. There was no joking in Aglaya's words; she was angry.

"What, did he bring a candle here with him, if it happened here? Otherwise I can't imagine . . ."

"Yes . . . a candle. What's so incredible?"

"Whole or in a candlestick?"

"Well, yes . . . no . . . half a candle . . . a candle end . . . a whole candle—it's all the same, leave me alone! . . . And he brought matches, if you like. He lit the candle and held his finger over the flame for a whole half hour; can't that be?"

"I saw him yesterday; there was nothing wrong with his fingers."

Aglaya suddenly burst out laughing, just like a child.

"You know why I lied to you just now?" she suddenly turned to the prince with the most childlike trustfulness and with laughter still trembling on her lips. "Because when you lie, if you skillfully put in something not quite usual, something eccentric, well, you know, something that happens quite rarely or even never, the lie becomes much more believable. I've noticed that. Only with me it came out badly, because I wasn't able to . . ."

Suddenly she frowned again, as if recollecting herself.

"If," she turned to the prince, looking at him gravely and even sadly, "if I read to you that time about the 'poor knight,' it was because I wanted . . . to praise you for one thing, but at the same time I wanted to stigmatize you for your behavior and to show you that I know everything . . ."

"You're very unfair to me . . . and to that unfortunate woman, of whom you just spoke so terribly, Aglaya."

"Because I know everything, everything, that's why I spoke like that! I know that, six months ago, you offered her your hand in front of everybody. Don't interrupt, you can see I'm speaking without commentaries. After that she ran away with Rogozhin; then you lived with her in some village or town, and she left you for someone else." (Aglaya blushed terribly.) "Then she went back to Rogozhin, who loves her like . . . like a madman. Then you, who are also a very intelligent man, came galloping after her here, as soon as you learned she was back in Petersburg. Yesterday evening you rushed to her defense, and just now you saw her in a dream . . . You see, I know everything; isn't it for her, for her, that you came here?"

"Yes, for her," the prince replied softly, bowing his head sadly and pensively, and not suspecting with what flashing eyes Aglaya glanced at him, "for her, just to find out . . . I don't believe she can be happy with Rogozhin, though . . . in short, I don't know what I could do for her here and how I could help, but I came."

He gave a start and looked at Aglaya; she was listening to him with hatred.

"If you came without knowing why, you must love her very much," she said at last.

"No," replied the prince, "no, I don't love her. Oh, if you knew with what horror I remember the time I spent with her!"

A shudder even went through his body at these words.

"Tell me everything," said Aglaya.

"There's nothing in it that you shouldn't hear. Why it is precisely you that I wanted to tell it to, and you alone—I don't know; maybe because I indeed loved you very much. This unfortunate woman is deeply convinced that she is the most fallen, the most depraved being in all the world. Oh, don't disgrace her, don't cast a stone.[24] She has tormented herself all too much with the awareness of her undeserved disgrace! And what is she guilty of, oh my God! Oh, in her frenzy she cries constantly that she does not acknowledge her guilt, that she is the victim of people, the victim of a debaucher and a villain; but whatever she tells you, know that she is the first not to believe it herself and that, on the contrary, she believes with all her conscience that she herself . . . is the guilty one. When I tried to dispel this darkness, her suffering reached such a degree that my heart will never be healed as long as I remember that terrible time. It's as if my heart was pierced through forever. She ran away from me, and do you know why? Precisely to prove to me alone that she is base. But the most terrible thing here is that she herself may not have known that she wanted to prove it to me alone, but ran away because inwardly she felt she absolutely had to do something disgraceful, in order to tell herself then and there: 'So now you've committed some new disgrace, that means you're a base creature!' Oh, perhaps you won't understand this, Aglaya! You know, there may be some terrible, unnatural pleasure for her in this constant awareness of disgrace, a sort of revenge on someone. Sometimes I managed to bring her to a point where she seemed to see light around her; but she would become indignant at once and go so far as to reproach me bitterly for putting myself far above her (when it never entered my mind), and she finally told me straight out, in response to my proposal of marriage, that she asked no one for supercilious compassion, or for help, or to be 'raised up to his level.' You saw her yesterday; do you really think she's happy with that company, that it's her kind of society? You don't know how developed she is and what she can understand! She even surprised me sometimes!"

"And did you also preach her such . . . sermons?"

"Oh, no," the prince went on pensively, not noticing the tone of the question, "I was silent most of the time. I often wanted to speak, but I really didn't know what to say. You know, on certain occasions it's better not to speak at all. Oh, I loved her; oh, I loved her very much . . . but then . . . then . . . then she guessed everything."

"What did she guess?"

"That I only pitied her and . . . no longer loved her."

"How do you know, maybe she really fell in love with that . . . landowner she went off with?"

"No, I know everything; she only laughed at him."

"And did she ever laugh at you?"

"N-no. She laughed out of spite; oh, she reproached me terribly then, in anger—and suffered herself! But . . . then . . . oh, don't remind me, don't remind me of it!"

He covered his face with his hands.

"And do you know that she writes me letters almost every day?"

"So it's true!" the prince cried in anxiety. "I heard it, but I still didn't want to believe it."

"Who did you hear it from?" Aglaya roused herself fearfully.

"Rogozhin told me yesterday, only not quite clearly."

"Yesterday? Yesterday morning? When yesterday? Before the music or after?"

"After, in the evening, past eleven o'clock."

"Ahh, well, if it's Rogozhin . . . And do you know what she writes to me in those letters?"

"Nothing would surprise me; she's insane."

"Here are the letters" (Aglaya took from her pocket three letters in three envelopes and threw them down in front of the prince). "For a whole week now she's been imploring, persuading, luring me into marrying you. She . . . ah, yes, she's intelligent, though she's insane, and you say rightly that she's much more intelligent than I am . . . she writes to me that she's in love with me, that every day she looks for a chance of seeing me at least from afar. She writes that you love me, that she knows it, that she noticed it long ago, and that you spoke with her about me there. She wants to see you happy; she's sure that only I can make you happy . . . She writes so wildly . . . strangely . . . I haven't shown anyone these letters, I was waiting for you. Do you know what it means? Can you guess anything?"

"It's madness; it's proof that she's insane," said the prince, and his lips trembled.

"You're not crying, are you?"

"No, Aglaya, no, I'm not crying," the prince looked at her.

"What am I to do about it? What do you advise me? I cannot keep receiving these letters!"

"Oh, let her be, I implore you!" the prince cried. "What can you do in this darkness; I'll make every effort so that she doesn't write to you anymore."

"If so, then you're a man with no heart!" cried Aglaya. "Can't you see that it's not me she's in love with, but you, you alone that she loves! Can it be that you've managed to notice everything in her, but didn't notice that? Do you know what these letters mean? It's jealousy; it's more than jealousy! She . . . do you think she'll really marry Rogozhin, as she writes here in these letters? She'll kill herself the very day after we get married!"

The prince gave a start; his heart sank. But he looked at Aglaya in surprise: it was strange for him to admit that this child had long been a woman.

"God knows, Aglaya, I'd give my life to bring back her peace and make her happy, but . . . I can't love her now, and she knows it!"

"Sacrifice yourself, then, it suits you so well! You're such a great benefactor. And don't call me 'Aglaya' . . . Earlier, too, you called me simply 'Aglaya' . . . You must resurrect her, it's your duty, you must go away with her again to pacify and soothe her heart. Anyway, you do love her!"

"I can't sacrifice myself like that, though I did want to once and . . . maybe still want to. But I know *for certain* that she'll perish with me, and that's why I'm leaving her. I was to see her tonight at seven o'clock; maybe I won't go now. In her pride she'll never forgive me my love—and we'll both perish! It's unnatural, but everything here is unnatural. You say she loves me, but is this love? Can there be such a love, after what I've already endured? No, there's something else here, but not love!"

"How pale you've grown!" Aglaya suddenly became alarmed.

"Never mind; I didn't sleep enough; I feel weak, I . . . we actually did talk about you then, Aglaya."

"So it's true? You really *could talk with her about me* and . . . and how could you love me, if you'd seen me only once?"

"I don't know how. In my darkness then I dreamed . . . perhaps I thought I'd seen a new dawn. I don't know how it was that you were the first one I thought of. I wrote you the truth then, that I didn't know. It was all only a dream, from the horror of that time . . . I began to study then; I wouldn't have come back here for three years . . ."

"So you came for her sake?"

And something trembled in Aglaya's voice.

"Yes, for her sake."

Two minutes of gloomy silence passed on both sides. Aglaya got up from her place.

"If you say," she began in an unsteady voice, "if you yourself believe that this . . . your woman . . . is insane, then I have nothing to do with her insane fantasies . . . I ask you, Lev Nikolaevich, to take these three letters and throw them at her from me! And if she dares," Aglaya suddenly cried, "if she dares once more to send me even a single line, tell her that I will complain to my father, and she will be taken to the madhouse . . ."

The prince jumped up and stared in alarm at Aglaya's sudden rage; and all at once it was as if a mist fell before him . . .

"You can't feel that way . . . it's not true!" he murmured.

"It is true! True!" Aglaya cried, almost forgetting herself.

"What is true? How is it true?" a frightened voice was heard close by.

Before them stood Lizaveta Prokofyevna.

"It's true that I'm going to marry Gavrila Ardalionovich! That I love Gavril Ardalionovich and am eloping from the house with him tomorrow!" Aglaya fell upon her. "Do you hear? Is your curiosity satisfied? Are you pleased?"

And she ran home.

"No, my dear man, you're not leaving now," Lizaveta Prokofyevna stopped the prince. "Do me a service, kindly come home and explain yourself to me . . . This is such a torment, and I didn't sleep all night as it is . . ."

The prince followed after her.

IX

ON ENTERING HER HOUSE, Lizaveta Prokofyevna stopped in the very first room; she could not go any further and lowered herself onto the couch, quite strengthless, forgetting even to invite the prince to sit down. It was a rather large room, with a round table in the middle, a fireplace, a multitude of flowers on what-nots by the windows, and with another glass door to the garden in the far wall. Adelaida and Alexandra came in at once, looking at the prince and their mother questioningly and with perplexity.

The girls usually got up at around nine o'clock in the country; only Aglaya, during the last two or three days, had taken to getting up a little earlier and going for a stroll in the garden, but all the same not at seven o'clock, but at eight or even a bit later. Lizaveta Prokofyevna, who indeed had not slept all night because of her various worries, got up at around eight o'clock, on purpose to meet Aglaya in the garden, supposing that she was already up; but she did not find her either in the garden or in her bedroom. At this point she became definitively alarmed and awakened her daughters. They learned from the maid that Aglaya Ivanovna had gone out to the park before seven. The girls smiled at this new fantasy of their fantastic little sister's and observed to their mama that if she went looking for her in the park, Aglaya might get angry, and that she was probably now sitting with a book on the green bench, which she had already spoken of three days ago and over which she had almost quarreled with Prince Shch., because he did not find anything special in the location of this bench. Coming upon the meeting and hearing her daughter's strange words, Lizaveta Prokofyevna was terribly frightened, for many reasons; but, now that she had brought the prince home with her, she felt cowardly at having begun the business: "Why shouldn't Aglaya have met and conversed with the prince in the park, even, finally, if it was a previously arranged meeting?"

"Don't imagine, my dear Prince," she finally pulled herself together, "that I've dragged you here today for an interrogation . . .

After yesterday evening, dear heart, I might not have wanted to meet you for a long time . . ."

She faltered slightly.

"But all the same you'd like very much to know how Aglaya Ivanovna and I met today?" the prince finished quite calmly.

"Well, and what if I would!" Lizaveta Prokofyevna flared up at once. "I'm not afraid of speaking directly. Because I'm not offending anyone and have never wished to offend . . ."

"Good heavens, even without any offense you naturally want to know; you're her mother. Aglaya Ivanovna and I met today by the green bench at exactly seven o'clock in the morning following her invitation yesterday. In her note yesterday evening, she informed me that she had to see me and speak to me about an important matter. We met and spent a whole hour discussing things of concern to Aglaya Ivanovna alone, and that is all."

"Of course it is all, my dear man, and without any doubt it is all," Lizaveta Prokofyevna pronounced with dignity.

"Splendid, Prince!" said Aglaya, suddenly coming into the room. "I thank you with all my heart for considering me unable to stoop to lying. Is that enough for you, *maman*, or do you intend to inquire further?"

"You know that up to now I have never had occasion to blush before you . . . though you might have been glad if I had," Lizaveta Prokofyevna replied didactically. "Good-bye, Prince; forgive me for having troubled you. And I hope you remain assured of my unfailing respect for you."

The prince bowed at once to both sides and silently went out. Alexandra and Adelaida smiled and whispered something to each other. Lizaveta Ivanovna gave them a stern look.

"It's only because the prince bowed so wonderfully, *maman*," Adelaida laughed. "Sometimes he's a perfect sack, but now suddenly he's like . . . like Evgeny Pavlych."

"Delicacy and dignity are taught by one's own heart, not by a dancing master," Lizaveta Prokofyevna concluded sententiously and went to her rooms upstairs without even glancing at Aglaya.

When the prince returned home, at around nine o'clock, he found Vera Lukyanovna and the maid on the terrace. They were tidying and sweeping up together after yesterday's disorder.

"Thank God we finished before you came!" Vera said joyfully.

"Good morning. My head is spinning a little; I slept poorly; I'd like to sleep."

"Here on the terrace like yesterday? Very well. I'll tell everyone not to wake you up. Papa has gone somewhere."

The maid went out; Vera followed her, but then came back and worriedly went over to the prince.

"Prince, have pity on this . . . unfortunate boy; don't send him away today."

"I wouldn't do that for anything; it will be as he likes."

"He won't do anything now, and . . . don't be severe with him."

"Oh, no, why would I?"

"And . . . don't laugh at him; that's the most important thing."

"Oh, certainly not!"

"It's stupid of me to say that to a man like you," Vera blushed. "And though you're tired," she laughed, half turning to leave, "you have such nice eyes at this moment . . . happy eyes."

"Happy, really?" the prince asked with animation and laughed joyfully.

But Vera, simple-hearted and unceremonious as a young boy, suddenly became embarrassed, blushed all the more, and, still laughing, hastily left the room.

"Such a . . . nice girl . . ." the prince thought and forgot about her at once. He went to the corner of the terrace, where there was a couch with a little table in front of it, sat down, covered his face with his hands, and went on sitting for some ten minutes; suddenly he thrust his hand hastily and anxiously into his side pocket and took out the three letters.

But the door opened again and Kolya came in. The prince seemed glad that he had to put the letters back into his pocket and postpone the moment.

"Well, quite an event!" said Kolya, sitting on the couch and going straight to the subject, like all his fellows. "How do you look at Ippolit now? Without respect?"

"Why should . . . but I'm tired, Kolya . . . Besides, it's too sad to start about that again . . . How is he, though?"

"Asleep, and he'll go on sleeping for another couple of hours. I understand; you didn't sleep at home, you walked in the park . . . agitation, of course . . . what else!"

"How do you know that I walked in the park and didn't sleep at home?"

"Vera just said so. She insisted that I not come in; I couldn't help it, for a moment. I've spent these two hours watching at his bedside; now it's Kostya Lebedev's turn. Burdovsky left. Lie down, then, Prince. Good . . . well, good day! Only, you know, I'm really struck!"

"Of course . . . all this . . ."

"No, Prince, no; I'm struck by the confession. Above all by the place where he speaks about providence and the future life. There's a gi-gan-tic thought there!"

The prince gazed affectionately at Kolya, who had certainly come only to talk the sooner about the gigantic thought.

"But the main thing, the main thing is not in the thought alone, but in the whole situation! If it had been written by Voltaire, Rousseau, Proudhon,[25] I'd read it, make note of it, but I wouldn't be struck to such a degree. But a man who knows for certain that he has ten minutes left, and who speaks like that—oh, that's proud! That's the highest independence of personal dignity, that means a direct challenge . . . No, it's gigantic strength of spirit! And after that to maintain that he didn't put the cap in on purpose—it's mean, unnatural! And, you know, he deceived us yesterday, he tricked us: I never packed his bag with him and never saw the pistol; he packed everything himself, and then he suddenly got me confused. Vera says you're letting him stay here; I swear there won't be any danger, especially since we never leave him for an instant."

"And who of you was there during the night?"

"Kostya Lebedev, Burdovsky, and I; Keller stayed for a while and then went to sleep at Lebedev's, because we had no bed. Ferdyshchenko also slept at Lebedev's; he left at seven. The general is always at Lebedev's; he also left just now . . . Lebedev may come to see you presently; he's been looking for you, I don't know why, he asked twice. Shall I let him in or not, since you're going to bed? I'm also going to sleep. Ah, yes, there's something I might tell you; the general surprised me earlier: Burdovsky woke me up after six for my turn on duty, even almost at six; I stepped out for a minute and suddenly met the general, still so drunk that he didn't recognize me; stood in front of me like a post; the moment he came to his senses, he simply fell on me: 'How's the sick boy?' he says. 'I was on my way to find out about the sick boy . . .' I reported to him, well—this and that. 'That's all fine,' he says, 'but I was on my way, mainly, which is why I got up, to warn you; I have reasons to think that not everything can be said in front of Mr. Ferdyshchenko, and . . . one must restrain oneself.' Can you understand that, Prince?"

"Really? However . . . it's all the same to us."

"Yes, undoubtedly it's all the same, we're not Masons![26] So that I even wondered why the general was coming at night on purpose to wake me up for that."

"Ferdyshchenko left, you say?"

"At seven. He stopped to see me on his way; I was on duty! He said he was going to spend the rest of the night at Vilkin's—there's this drunk named Vilkin! Well, I'm going! And here is Lukyan Timofeich . . . The prince wants to sleep, Lukyan Timofeich; about-face!"

"Just for one minute, my much-esteemed Prince, on a certain matter which is significant in my eyes," the entering Lebedev said in a half-whisper, stiffly and in a sort of heartfelt tone, and bowed gravely. He had just returned and had not even had time to stop at his own quarters, so that he still had his hat in his hand. His face was preoccupied and had a special, extraordinary tinge of personal dignity. The prince invited him to sit down.

"You asked for me twice? Perhaps you're still worried about yesterday's . . ."

"About that boy yesterday, you mean, Prince? Oh, no, sir; yesterday my thoughts were in disarray . . . but today I no longer intend to countercarrate your intentions in any way."

"Counter . . . what did you say?"

"I said countercarrate; it's a French word,[27] like many other words that have entered the Russian language; but I don't especially insist on it."

"What is it with you today, Lebedev, you're so grave and decorous, and enunciate so distinctly," the prince smiled.

"Nikolai Ardalionovich!" Lebedev addressed Kolya in an all but affectionate voice, "having to inform the prince of a matter essentially of concern . . ."

"Ah, yes, naturally, naturally, it's none of my business! Goodbye, Prince!" Kolya left at once.

"I like the child for his quick wits," Lebedev said, looking at his back, "a nimble boy, though an importunate one. It is a great misfortune that I have experienced, my much-esteemed Prince, yesterday evening or today at dawn . . . I hesitate to specify the exact time."

"What is it?"

"The disappearance of four hundred roubles from my side pocket, my much-esteemed Prince; I've been marked!" Lebedev added with a sour smile.

"You lost four hundred roubles? That's a pity."

"And especially if one is a poor man who lives nobly by his own labor."

"Of course, of course. How did it happen?"

"On account of wine, sir. I am turning to you as to providence, my much-esteemed Prince. I received the sum of four hundred roubles in silver from a debtor yesterday at five o'clock in the afternoon and came here by train. I had the wallet in my pocket. Having changed from my uniform[28] into a frock coat, I transferred the money to the frock coat, with a view to keeping it with me, counting on handing it over that same evening on a certain request . . . as I was expecting an agent."

"By the way, Lukyan Timofeich, is it true that you put a notice in the newspaper that you lend money for gold and silver objects?"

"Through an agent; my name wasn't mentioned, nor was my address. Having insignificant capital and in view of my growing family, you must agree that an honest percentage . . ."

"Well, yes, yes; I merely wanted to know; excuse me for interrupting."

"The agent did not come. Meanwhile the unfortunate young man was brought; I was already under the influence, after dinner; those guests came, we had . . . tea, and . . . I waxed merry, to my undoing. And when, at a late hour, this Keller came and announced your celebration and your orders about the champagne, I, my dear and much-esteemed Prince, having a heart (which you have probably noticed by now, for I deserve it), having a heart which is, I do not say sensitive, but grateful, and I am proud of it—I, for the greater solemnity of the impending meeting and in expectation of personally offering my congratulations, decided to go and exchange my old rags for my uniform, which I had taken off on my return, and so I did, as you probably noticed, Prince, seeing me in my uniform all evening. In changing my clothes, I forgot the wallet in my frock coat . . . Verily, when God wishes to punish a man, he first deprives him of reason.[29] And it was only today, at half-past seven, on awakening, that I jumped up like a half-wit and snatched my frock coat first thing—only an empty pocket! Not a trace of the wallet."

"Ah, that's unpleasant!"

"Precisely unpleasant; and you with your genuine tact have just found the suitable expression," Lebedev added, not without insidiousness.

"How is it, though . . ." the prince pondered, beginning to worry, "no, this is serious."

"Precisely serious—you've sought out yet another word, Prince, to signify . . ."

"Oh, enough, Lukyan Timofeich, what was there to seek out? The words aren't important . . . Do you suppose that, in a drunken state, you might have dropped it out of your pocket?"

"I might have. Everything is possible in a drunken state, as you have so sincerely expressed it, my much-esteemed Prince! But I beg you to consider, sir: if I dropped the wallet out of my pocket while changing my frock coat, the dropped object should be lying there on the floor. Where is that object, sir?"

"You didn't stuff it into a desk drawer somewhere?"

"I've looked all over, rummaged everywhere, the more so as I never hid it anywhere or opened any drawer, which I remember distinctly."

"Did you look in the little cupboard?"

"First thing, sir, and even several times today . . . And how could I have put it into the little cupboard, my truly-esteemed Prince?"

"I confess, Lebedev, this worries me. So someone found it on the floor?"

"Or stole it from the pocket! Two alternatives, sir."

"This worries me very much, because who precisely . . . That's the question!"

"Without any doubt, that is the main question; you find words and thoughts and define the situation with astonishing precision, illustrious Prince."

"Ah, Lukyan Timofeich, stop your mockery, there's . . ."

"Mockery!" cried Lebedev, clasping his hands.

"Well, well, all right, I'm not angry, there's something else here . . . I'm afraid for people. Whom do you suspect?"

"A most difficult and . . . most complicated question! I cannot suspect my maid: she was sitting in her kitchen. Nor my own children . . ."

"Hardly!"

"That means it was someone among the guests, sir."

"But is that possible?"

"It is totally and in the highest degree impossible, but it must certainly be so. I agree, however, to allow, and am even convinced, that if there was a theft, it was carried out not in the evening, when we were all together, but at night or even towards morning, by someone who stayed overnight."

"Ah, my God!"

"Burdovsky and Nikolai Ardalionovich I naturally exclude; they never entered my quarters, sir."

"Hardly, and even if they had! Who spent the night with you?"

"Counting me, there were four who spent the night, in two adjacent rooms: me, the general, Keller, and Mr. Ferdyshchenko. Which means it's one of us four, sir!"

"Three, that is; but who?"

"I included myself for the sake of fairness and order; but you must agree, Prince, that I couldn't rob myself, though such things have happened in the world . . ."

"Ah, Lebedev, this is so tedious!" the prince cried impatiently. "To business, why drag it out! . . ."

"So three remain, sir, and first of all Mr. Keller, an unstable man, a drunk man, and on certain occasions a liberal, that is, with regard to the pocket, sir; in everything else his inclinations are, so to speak, more old chivalric than liberal. He slept here at first, in the sick boy's room, and it was only at night that he moved over to us, on the pretext that it was hard to sleep on the bare floor."

"Do you suspect him?"

"I did, sir. When I jumped up like a half-wit past seven in the morning and slapped myself on the forehead, I at once woke up the general, who was sleeping the sleep of the innocent. After considering the strange disappearance of Ferdyshchenko, which in itself aroused our suspicion, we both decided at once to search Keller, who was lying there like . . . like . . . almost like a doornail, sir. We searched him thoroughly: not a centime in his pockets, and not even a single pocket without holes in it. A blue, checked cotton handkerchief, sir, in indecent condition. Then a love note from some serving girl, with demands for money and threats, and the scraps of the feuilleton already familiar to you, sir. The general decided he was innocent. To obtain full information, we woke him up; we had a hard time jostling him; he was barely able to understand what it was all about; a gaping mouth, a drunken look, an absurd and innocent, even stupid, expression—it wasn't he, sir!"

"Well, I'm so glad!" the prince sighed joyfully. "I was so afraid for him!"

"Afraid? Does that mean you have reasons to be?" Lebedev narrowed his eyes.

"Oh, no, I just said it," the prince checked himself. "It was stupid of me to say I was afraid. Kindly don't tell anyone, Lebedev . . ."

"Prince, Prince! Your words are in my heart . . . deep in my heart! A grave, sir! . . ." Lebedev said rapturously, pressing his hat to his heart.

"All right, all right! . . . So it's Ferdyshchenko? That is, I mean to say, you suspect Ferdyshchenko?"

"Who else?" Lebedev said quietly, looking intently at the prince.

"Well, yes, naturally . . . who else . . . that is, once again, what evidence is there?"

"There is evidence, sir. First of all, his disappearance at seven o'clock or even before seven o'clock in the morning."

"I know, Kolya told me he came and said he was going to spend the rest of the night at . . . I forget whose place, some friend's."

"Vilkin, sir. So Nikolai Ardalionovich told you already?"

"He didn't say anything about the theft."

"He doesn't know, for I have so far kept the matter a secret. And so, he goes to Vilkin; you might think, what's so puzzling about a drunk man going to see another drunk man just like himself, even though it's the wee hours of the morning and without any reason at all, sir? But it's here that the trail begins: on his way out, he leaves the address . . . Now follow the question, Prince: why did he leave the address? . . . Why does he purposely go to Nikolai Ardalionovich, making a detour, sir, and tell him, 'I'm going to spend the rest of the night at Vilkin's'? And who is interested in his leaving and going precisely to Vilkin's? Why announce it? No, there's a subtlety here, a thievish subtlety! It means: 'Look here, I'm not concealing my tracks, what kind of thief am I after that? Would a thief announce where he's going?' An excessive concern about diverting suspicion and, so to speak, wiping away his tracks in the sand . . . Do you understand me, my much-esteemed Prince?"

"I understand, I understand very well, but is that enough?"

"A second piece of evidence, sir: the trail turned out to be false, and the address he gave was inexact. An hour later, that is, at eight o'clock, I was already knocking on Vilkin's door; he lives here, on Fifth Street, sir, I'm even acquainted with him. There wasn't any Ferdyshchenko there. Though I did get out of the maid—she's completely deaf, sir—that an hour earlier someone had actually knocked, and even rather hard, so that he broke the bell. But the maid didn't open the door, not wishing to waken Mr. Vilkin, and maybe not wanting to get out of bed herself. It happens, sir."

"And that is all your evidence? It's not much."

"But, Prince, who else should I suspect, just think?" Lebedev concluded sweetly, and something sly showed in his smile.

"Why don't you look around the rooms once more and in all the drawers!" the prince said worriedly, after some thought.

"I did, sir!" Lebedev sighed still more sweetly.

"Hm! . . . and why, why did you have to change that frock coat!" the prince exclaimed, pounding the table in vexation.

"A question from an old comedy, sir. But, my most good-natured Prince! You take my misfortune too much to heart! I don't deserve it. That is, by myself I don't deserve it; but you also suffer for the criminal . . . for the worthless Mr. Ferdyshchenko?"

"Well, yes, yes, you've really got me worried," the prince interrupted him absentmindedly and with displeasure. "And so, what do you intend to do . . . if you're so sure it's Ferdyshchenko?"

"Prince, much-esteemed Prince, who else is there, sir?" Lebedev squirmed with ever-increasing sweetness. "The unavailability of anyone else to point to and the, so to speak, perfect impossibility of suspecting anyone besides Mr. Ferdyshchenko, is, so to speak, more evidence against Mr. Ferdyshchenko, a third piece! For, again, who else is there? Can I really suspect Mr. Burdovsky, heh, heh, heh?"

"Ah, no, what nonsense!"

"Or the general, finally, heh, heh, heh?"

"What a wild idea!" the prince said almost crossly, turning impatiently on his seat.

"Wild it is! Heh, heh, heh! And the man did make me laugh, the general, I mean, sir! He and I set out this morning hot on the trail to Vilkin, sir . . . and I must point out to you that the general was even more struck than I was when I woke him up first thing after the disappearance, so that he even changed countenance, turned red, then pale, and in the end suddenly arrived at such bitter and noble indignation that I even never expected such a degree, sir. A most noble man! He lies incessantly, out of weakness, but he's a man of the loftiest feelings, and with that a man of little understanding, inspiring complete trust by his innocence. I've already told you, my much-esteemed Prince, that I not only have a soft spot for him, but even love him, sir. He suddenly stops in the middle of the street, opens his frock coat, offers his chest: 'Search me,' he says, 'you searched Keller, why don't you search me? Justice demands it!' he says. The man's arms and legs are trembling, he's even turning pale, he has a menacing look. I laughed and said: 'Listen, General,' I said, 'if somebody else said it about you, I'd take my head off with my own hands, put it on a big platter, and offer it myself to all who doubt: "Here," I'd say, "see this head, so with this same head of mine I vouch for him, and not only with the head, but I'd even go through fire." That's how ready I am to vouch for you!' At this point he threw himself into my arms, right in the middle of the street, sir, became tearful, trembled and pressed me to his heart so tightly I could hardly clear my throat: 'You,' he says, 'are the only friend I have left in my misfortunes!' A sentimental man, sir! Well, naturally, on our way he told me an appropriate story about how, in his youth, he had once been suspected of having stolen five hundred thousand roubles, but that the very next day he had thrown himself into the flames of a burning house and saved the count who suspected him and Nina Alexandrovna, who was a young girl then. The count embraced him, and thus his marriage to Nina Alexandrovna came about, and the very next day the box with the lost money was found in the ruins of the burned-down house; it was made of iron, after an English design, with a secret lock, and had somehow fallen through the floor, so that no one noticed, and it was found only owing to the fire. A complete lie, sir. But when he spoke of Nina Alexandrovna, he even started sniveling. A most noble person, Nina Alexandrovna, though she's cross with me."

"You're not acquainted?"

"Nearly not, sir, but I wish with my whole soul that I were, if only so as to vindicate myself before her. Nina Alexandrovna has a grudge against me for supposedly corrupting her husband with drink. But I not only don't corrupt him, but sooner curb him; it may be that I keep him away from more pernicious company. What's more, he's my friend, sir, and, I confess to you, I'm not ever going to leave him, sir, that is, even like this, sir: where he goes, I go, because you can't get anywhere with him except through sentimentality. He doesn't even visit his captain's widow at all now, though secretly he pines for her and even occasionally groans over her, especially each morning, when he gets up and puts his boots on—why precisely then I don't know. He has no money, sir, that's the trouble, and it's quite impossible to go to her without money. Has he asked you for money, my most-esteemed Prince?"

"No, he hasn't."

"He's ashamed. He was going to: he even confessed to me that he intended to trouble you, but he's ashamed, sir, since you gave him a loan just recently, and he supposed, besides, that you wouldn't give him anything. He poured it all out to me as a friend."

"And you don't give him money?"

"Prince! Much-esteemed Prince! Not only money, but for this man even, so to speak, my life . . . no, however, I don't want to exaggerate, not my life, but if, so to speak, it's a fever, or some abscess, or even a cough—then, by God, I'd be ready to endure it, if there's a very big need; for I consider him a great but lost man! There, sir; and not only money, sir!"

"So you give him money?"

"N-no, I've never given him money, sir, and he knows himself that I won't, but it's solely with a view to restraining and reforming him. Now he wants to tag after me to Petersburg; you see, I'm going to Petersburg, sir, hot on Ferdyshchenko's trail, because I know for certain that he's already there, sir. My general is just seething, sir; but I suspect he'll slip away from me in Petersburg in order to visit the captain's widow. I confess, I'll even let him go on purpose, since we've already arranged to go in different directions immediately upon arrival, the better to catch Mr. Ferdyshchenko. So I'll let him go and then suddenly, out of the blue, I'll find him with the captain's widow—essentially in order to shame him as a family man and a man generally speaking."

"Only don't make noise, Lebedev, for God's sake don't make noise," the prince said in a low voice, greatly worried.

"Oh, no, sir, essentially just so as to shame him and see what kind of face he makes—for one can learn a lot by the face, my much-esteemed Prince, and especially with such a man! Ah, Prince! Great as my own trouble is, even now I cannot help thinking about him and about the reforming of his morals. I have a special request to make of you, my much-esteemed Prince, I even confess that this is essentially why I have come, sir: you are already acquainted with the house and have even lived with them, sir; what if you, my most good-hearted Prince, should decide to assist me in this, essentially just for the sake of the general and his happiness . . ."

Lebedev even pressed his hands together as if in supplication.

"What is it? How can I assist? I assure you that I would like very much to understand you fully, Lebedev."

"It is solely in that assurance that I have come to you! It may be possible to work through Nina Alexandrovna; by observing and, so to speak, keeping a constant watch on his excellency, in the bosom of his own family. I, unfortunately, am not acquainted, sir . . . then, too, Nikolai Ardalionovich, who adores you, so to speak, from the bosom of his young soul, could perhaps be of help here . . ."

"N-no . . . Nina Alexandrovna in this business . . . God forbid! Not Kolya either . . . However, maybe I still haven't understood you, Lebedev."

"But there's nothing at all to understand here!" Lebedev even jumped in his chair. "Sensitivity and tenderness alone, alone— that's all the medicine our sick man needs. Will you allow me, Prince, to consider him a sick man?"

"It even shows your delicacy and intelligence."

"I shall explain it to you, for the sake of clarity, with an example taken from practice. See what kind of man he is, sir: here he now has a certain weakness for this captain's widow, whom he cannot go to without money and at whose place I intend to catch him today, for the sake of his own happiness, sir; but suppose it wasn't only the captain's widow, but he was even to commit a real crime— well, some very dishonest act (though he's totally incapable of that)—then, too, I say only noble tenderness, so to speak, will get anywhere with him, for he is a most sensitive man, sir! Believe me, he won't last five days, he'll let it out himself, start weeping, and confess everything—especially if we act skillfully and nobly, through your and his family's supervision of all his, so to speak, traits and steps . . . Oh, my most good-hearted Prince!" Lebedev jumped up even in some sort of inspiration, "I am not affirming that it was certainly he . . . I am ready, so to speak, to shed all my blood for him right now, though you must agree that intemperance, and drunkenness, and the captain's widow, and all of it taken together, could drive him to anything."

"I am, of course, always ready to assist in such a purpose," the prince said, standing up, "only, I confess to you, Lebedev, I'm terribly worried; tell me, do you still . . . in short, you yourself say that you suspect Mr. Ferdyshchenko."

"And who else? Who else, my most sincere Prince?" Lebedev again pressed his hands together sweetly, and with a sweet smile.

The prince frowned and got up from his place.

"You see, Lukyan Timofeich, it would be a terrible thing to be mistaken. This Ferdyshchenko . . . I have no wish to speak ill of him . . . but this Ferdyshchenko . . . that is, who knows, maybe he's the one! . . . I mean to say that he may be more capable of it than . . . than the other man."

Lebedev was all eyes and ears.

"You see," the prince was becoming confused and frowned more and more as he paced up and down the room, trying not to raise his eyes to Lebedev, "I've been given to understand . . . I've been told about Mr. Ferdyshchenko, that he is supposedly, besides everything else, a man in whose presence one must restrain oneself and not say anything . . . superfluous—understand? By which I mean that perhaps he actually is more capable than the other man . . . so as to make no mistake—that's the main thing, understand?"

"And who told you that about Mr. Ferdyshchenko?" Lebedev simply heaved himself up.

"It's just a whisper; anyhow, I don't believe it myself . . . it's terribly vexing that I've been forced to tell you about it, I assure you, I don't believe it myself . . . it's some sort of nonsense . . . Pah, what a stupid thing for me to do!"

"You see, Prince," Lebedev was even shaking all over, "it's important, it's all too important now, that is, not concerning Mr. Ferdyshchenko, but concerning how this information came to you." As he said this, Lebedev was running up and down after the prince, trying to get in step with him. "Look here, Prince, I'll now inform you: when the general and I were going to this Vilkin's, after he told me about the fire, and seething, naturally, with wrath, he suddenly began hinting the same thing to me about Mr. Ferdyshchenko, but it was so without rhyme or reason that I involuntarily asked him certain questions, as a result of which I became fully convinced that this information was nothing but his excellency's inspiration . . . Essentially, so to speak, from good-heartedness alone. For he lies solely because he cannot control his feelings. Now kindly see, sir: if he was lying, and I'm sure of that, how could you have heard of it, too? Understand, Prince, that it was a momentary inspiration of his—who, then, informed you of it? It's important, sir, it's . . . it's very important, sir, and . . . so to speak . . ."

"Kolya just told it to me, and he was told earlier by his father, whom he met sometime at six o'clock or after, in the front hall, when he stepped out for something."

And the prince recounted everything in detail.

"Well, sir, that's what we call a trail, sir," Lebedev laughed inaudibly, rubbing his hands. "It's just as I thought, sir! It means that his excellency purposely interrupted his sleep of the innocent before six o'clock in order to go and wake up his beloved son and inform him of the extreme danger of being neighborly with Mr. Ferdyshchenko! What a dangerous man Mr. Ferdyshchenko must be in that case, and how great is his excellency's parental concern, heh, heh, heh! . . ."

"Listen, Lebedev," the prince was definitively confused, "listen, act quietly! Don't make noise! I beg you, Lebedev, I beseech you . . . In that case I swear I'll assist you, but so that nobody knows, so that nobody knows!"

"I assure you, my most good-hearted, most sincere, and most noble Prince," Lebedev cried in decided inspiration, "I assure you that all this will die in my most noble heart. With quiet steps, together, sir! With quiet steps, together! I'd even shed all my blood . . . Most illustrious Prince, I am mean in soul and spirit, but ask any scoundrel even, not only a mean man: who is it better to deal with, a scoundrel like himself, or a most noble man like you, my most sincere Prince? He will reply that it is with a most noble man, and in that is the triumph of virtue! Good-bye, my much-esteemed Prince! With quiet steps . . . quiet steps . . . and together, sir."

X

THE PRINCE FINALLY understood why he went cold every time he touched those three letters and why he had put off the moment of reading them all the way till evening. When, that morning, he had fallen into a heavy sleep on his couch, still without resolving to open any one of those three envelopes, he again had a heavy dream, and again that same "criminal woman" came to him. She again looked at him with tears glistening on her long lashes, again called him to follow her, and again he woke up, as earlier, painfully trying to remember her face. He wanted to go to *her* at once, but could not; at last, almost in despair, he opened the letters and began to read.

These letters also resembled a dream. Sometimes you dream strange dreams, impossible and unnatural; you wake up and remember them clearly, and are surprised at a strange fact: you remember first of all that reason did not abandon you during the whole course of your dream; you even remember that you acted extremely cleverly and logically for that whole long, long time when you were surrounded by murderers, when they were being clever with you, concealed their intentions, treated you in a friendly way, though they already had their weapons ready and were only waiting for some sort of sign; you remember how cleverly you finally deceived them, hid from them; then you realize that they know your whole deception by heart and merely do not show you that they know where you are hiding; but you are clever and deceive them again—all that you remember clearly. But why at the same time could your reason be reconciled with such obvious absurdities and impossibilities, with which, among other things, your dream was filled? Before your eyes, one of your murderers turned into a woman, and from a woman into a clever, nasty little dwarf—and all that you allowed at once, as an accomplished fact, almost without the least perplexity, and precisely at the moment when, on the other hand, your reason was strained to the utmost, displaying extraordinary force, cleverness, keenness, logic? Why, also, on awakening from your dream and entering fully into reality, do you feel almost every time, and occasionally with an extraordinary force of impression, that along with the dream you are leaving behind something you have failed to fathom? You smile at the absurdity of your dream and feel at the same time that the tissue of those absurdities contains some thought, but a thought that is real, something that belongs to your true life, something that exists and has always existed in your heart; it is as if your dream has told you something new, prophetic, awaited; your impression is strong, it is joyful or tormenting, but what it is and what has been told you—all that you can neither comprehend nor recall.

It was almost the same after these letters. But even without opening them, the prince felt that the very fact of their existence and possibility was already like a nightmare. How did *she* dare write to *her*, he asked, wandering alone in the evening (sometimes not even remembering himself where he was walking). How could she write *about that*, and how could such an insane dream have been born in her head? But that dream had already been realized, and what was most astonishing for him was that, while he was reading these letters, he almost believed himself in the possibility and even the justification of that dream. Yes, of course, it was a dream, a nightmare, and an insanity; but there was also something in it that was tormentingly actual and painfully just, which justified the dream, the nightmare, and the insanity. For several hours in a row he was as if delirious with what he had read, continually recalled fragments, lingered over them, reflected on them. Sometimes he even wanted to tell himself that he had sensed and foreseen it all before; it even seemed to him as if he had read it all long, long ago and that everything he had yearned for since then, everything he had suffered over and been afraid of—all of it was contained in these letters read long ago.

"When you open this letter" (so the first one began), "you will first of all look at the signature. The signature will tell you everything and explain everything, so that I need not justify myself before you or explain anything to you. If I were even slightly your equal, you might be offended at such boldness; but who am I and who are you? We are two such opposites, and I am so far out of rank with you, that I could not offend you in any way, even if I wanted to."

Further on in another place she wrote:

"Do not consider my words the morbid rapture of a morbid mind, but for me you are—perfection! I have seen you, I see you every day. I do not judge you; it is not by reason that I have come to consider you perfection; I simply believe it. But there is also a sin in me before you: I love you. Perfection cannot be loved, perfection can only be looked at as perfection, isn't that so? And yet I am in love with you. Love equates people, but don't worry, I have never equated myself with you even in my innermost thoughts. I have written: 'don't worry'; but how could you worry? . . . If it were possible, I would kiss the prints of your feet. Oh, I am not trying to make us equals . . . Look at the signature, quickly look at the signature!"

"I notice, however" (she wrote in another letter), "that I am uniting him with you, and have not yet asked whether you love him. He loved you after seeing you only once. He remembered you as 'light'; those were his own words, I heard them from him. But even without words I understood that you were his light. I lived by him for a whole month, and here I understood that you love him as well; you and he are one for me."

"How is it" (she also wrote) "that I walked past you yesterday, and you seemed to blush? It cannot be, I must have imagined it. Even if they bring you to the filthiest den and show you naked vice, you should not blush; you cannot possibly be indignant over an offense. You may hate all those who are mean and base, but not for your own sake, but for others, for those who are offended. No one can offend you. You know, it seems to me that you should even love me. You are the same for me as for him: a bright spirit; an angel cannot hate, and cannot not love. Can one love everyone, all people, all one's neighbors? I have often asked myself that question. Of course not, and it is even unnatural. In an abstract love for mankind, one almost always loves oneself. It is impossible for us, but you are another matter: how could there be anyone you do not love, when you cannot compare yourself with anyone and when you are above any offense, above any personal indignation? You alone can love without egoism, you alone can love not for yourself but for the one you love. Oh, how bitter it would be for me to learn that you feel shame or wrath because of me! That would be the ruin of you: you would at once become equal to me . . .

"Yesterday, after meeting you, I came home and thought up a painting. Artists all paint Christ according to the Gospel stories; I would paint him differently: I would portray him alone—the disciples did sometimes leave him alone. I would leave only a small child with him. The child would be playing beside him, perhaps telling him something in his child's language. Christ had been listening to him, but now he has become pensive; his hand has inadvertently, forgetfully, remained on the child's blond head. He gazes into the distance, at the horizon; a thought as great as the whole world reposes in his eyes; his face is sad. The child has fallen silent, leaning his elbow on his knees, and, his cheek resting on his hand, has raised his little head and pensively, as children sometimes become pensive, gazes intently at him. The sun is setting . . . That is my painting! You are innocent, and all your perfection is in your innocence. Oh, remember only that! What do you care about my passion for you? You are mine now, I shall be near you all my life . . . I shall die soon."

Finally, in the very last letter there was:

"For God's sake, do not think anything about me; do not think, also, that I humiliate myself by writing to you like this or that I am one of those who take pleasure in humiliating themselves, even though it is only out of pride. No, I have my own consolations; but it is hard for me to explain that to you. It would be hard for me to say it clearly even to myself, though it torments me. But I know that I cannot humiliate myself even in a fit of pride. Nor am I capable of self-humiliation out of purity of heart. And that means I do not humiliate myself at all.

"Why do I want to unite the two of you: for your sake or for my own? For my own, naturally, then everything will be resolved for me, I told myself that long ago . . . I have heard that your sister Adelaida once said of my portrait that one could overturn the world with such beauty. But I have renounced the world; do you find it funny to hear that from me, meeting me in lace and diamonds, with drunkards and scoundrels? Pay no attention to that, I almost do not exist now and I know it; God knows what lives in me in place of me. I read that every day in two terrible eyes that constantly look at me, even when they are not before me. Those eyes are *silent* now (they are always silent), but I know their secret. His house is gloomy, dreary, and there is a secret in it. I am sure that hidden in a drawer he has a razor, wound in silk, like the one that Moscow murderer had; that one also lived in the same house with his mother and also tied silk around his razor in order to cut a certain throat. All the while I was in their house, it seemed to me that somewhere, under the floorboards, maybe even hidden by his father, there was a dead man wrapped in oilcloth, like the one in Moscow, and surrounded in the same way by bottles of Zhdanov liquid,[30] I could even show you the corner. He is always silent; but I know he loves me so much that by now he cannot help hating me. Your wedding and my wedding will come together: that is how he and I have decided it. I have no secrets from him. I could kill him out of fear . . . But he will kill me first . . . he laughed just now and says I'm raving. He knows I'm writing to you."

And there was much, much more of the same sort of raving in these letters. One of them, the second, was on two sheets of stationery, of large format, in small handwriting.

The prince finally left the somber park, in which he had wandered for a long time, as he had the day before. The bright, transparent night seemed brighter than usual to him. "Can it be so early?" he thought. (He had forgotten to take his watch.) Music reached him from somewhere far away. "In the vauxhall, it must be," he thought again, "of course, they didn't go there today." Realizing that, he saw that he was standing right by their dacha; he simply knew he would have to end up there, finally, and with a sinking heart he went onto the terrace. No one met him, the terrace was deserted. He waited a while and then opened the door to the drawing room. "They never close this door," flashed in him, but the drawing room, too, was deserted; it was almost totally dark. He stood perplexed in the middle of the room. Suddenly the door opened and Alexandra Ivanovna came in carrying a candle. Seeing the prince, she was surprised and stopped in front of him as if questioningly. It was obvious that she was only passing through the room, from one door to the other, not thinking at all of finding anyone there.

"How did you end up here?" she said at last.

"I . . . came by . . ."

"*Maman* isn't feeling well, and neither is Aglaya. Adelaida's going to bed, and so am I. We spent the whole evening sitting at home alone. Papa and the prince are in Petersburg."

"I've come . . . I've come to you . . . now . . ."

"Do you know what time it is?"

"N-no . . ."

"Half-past twelve. We always go to bed at one."

"Ah, I thought it was . . . half-past nine."

"Never mind!" she laughed. "But why didn't you come earlier? Maybe we were expecting you."

"I . . . thought . . ." he babbled, going out.

"Good-bye! Tomorrow I'll make everybody laugh."

He went down the road that skirted the park to his dacha. His heart was pounding, his thoughts were confused, and everything around him seemed like a dream. And suddenly, just as earlier, both times when he was awakened by the same vision, so the same vision again appeared before him. The same woman came out of the park and stood before him, as if she had been waiting for him there. He shuddered and stopped; she seized his hand and pressed it hard. "No, this is not a vision!"

And so she finally stood before him face to face, for the first time since their parting; she was saying something to him, but he looked at her silently; his heart overflowed and was wrung with pain. Oh, never afterwards could he forget this meeting with her, and he always remembered it with the same pain. She went down on her knees before him right there in the street, as if beside herself; he stepped back in fear, but she tried to catch his hand in order to kiss it, and, just as earlier in his dream, tears glistened now on her long lashes.

"Get up, get up!" he said in a frightened whisper, trying to raise her. "Get up quickly!"

"Are you happy? Are you?" she kept asking. "Tell me just one word, are you happy now? Today, right now? With her? What did she say?"

She would not get up, she did not listen to him; she asked hurriedly and was in a hurry to speak, as though she were being pursued.

"I'm leaving tomorrow, as you told me to. I won't . . . I'm seeing you for the last time, the last! Now it really is the last time!"

"Calm yourself, get up!" he said in despair.

She peered at him greedily, clutching his hands.

"Farewell!" she said at last, stood up, and quickly walked away from him, almost ran. The prince saw that Rogozhin was suddenly beside her, took her arm, and led her away.

"Wait, Prince," cried Rogozhin, "in five minutes I'll come back for a bit."

In five minutes he indeed came back; the prince was waiting for him in the same place.

"I put her in the carriage," he said. "It's been waiting there on the corner since ten o'clock. She just knew you'd spend the whole evening with the other one. I told her exactly what you wrote me today. She won't write to the other one anymore; she promised; and she'll leave here tomorrow, as you wished. She wanted to see you one last time, even though you refused; we waited here in this place for you to go back—over there, on that bench."

"She brought you along herself?"

"And what of it?" Rogozhin grinned. "I saw what I knew. You read her letters, eh?"

"But can you really have read them?" asked the prince, astounded by the thought.

"What else; she showed me each letter herself. Remember about the razor? Heh, heh!"

"She's insane!" cried the prince, wringing his hands.

"Who knows, maybe she's not," Rogozhin said softly, as if to himself.

The prince did not answer.

"Well, good-bye," said Rogozhin, "I'm leaving tomorrow, too; don't think ill of me! And how come, brother," he added, turning quickly, "how come you didn't say anything in answer to her? 'Are you happy or not?'"

"No, no, no!" the prince exclaimed with boundless sorrow.

"As if you'd say 'yes!'" Rogozhin laughed spitefully and walked off without looking back.

PART FOUR

I

ABOUT A WEEK went by after the two persons of our story met on the green bench. One bright morning, around half-past ten, Varvara Ardalionovna Ptitsyn, having gone out to visit some of her acquaintances, returned home in great and rueful pensiveness.

There are people of whom it is difficult to say anything that would present them at once and fully, in their most typical and characteristic aspect; these are those people who are usually called "ordinary" people, the "majority," and who indeed make up the vast majority in any society. Writers in their novels and stories for the most part try to take social types and present them graphically and artistically—types which in their full state are met with extremely rarely in reality and which are nonetheless almost more real than reality itself. Podkolesin[1] in his typical aspect may well be an exaggeration, but he is by no means an impossibility. What a host of intelligent people, having learned about Podkolesin from Gogol, at once began to find that dozens and hundreds of their good acquaintances and friends were terribly like Podkolesin. They knew before Gogol that these friends were like Podkolesin, they simply did not know yet precisely what their name was. In reality it is terribly rare that bridegrooms jump out of windows before their weddings, because, to say nothing else, it is even inconvenient; nonetheless, how many bridegrooms, even worthy and intelligent people, in the depths of their conscience, have been ready before marriage to acknowledge themselves as Podkolesins. Nor does every husband cry at each step: "*Tu l'as voulu, Georges Dandin!*"[*][2] But, God, how many millions and billions of times have the husbands of the whole world repeated this heartfelt cry after their honeymoon, and, who knows, maybe even the day after the wedding.

And so, without going into more serious explanations, we shall say only that in reality the typicality of persons is watered down, as it were, and all these Georges Dandins and Podkolesins really

*You asked for it, Georges Dandin!

exist, scurry and run around in front of us daily, but as if in a somewhat diluted state. Having mentioned, finally, for the sake of the complete truth, that the full Georges Dandin, as Molière created him, may also be met with in reality, though rarely, we shall therewith end our discourse, which is beginning to resemble a critical article in some journal. Nonetheless, a question remains before us all the same: what is a novelist to do with ordinary, completely "usual" people, and how can he present them to the reader so as to make them at least somewhat interesting? To bypass them altogether in a story is quite impossible, because ordinary people are constantly and for the most part the necessary links in the chain of everyday events; in bypassing them we would thus violate plausibility. To fill novels with nothing but types or even simply, for the sake of interest, with strange and nonexistent people, would be implausible—and perhaps uninteresting as well. In our opinion, the writer should try to seek out interesting and instructive nuances even among ordinary people. And when, for instance, the very essence of certain ordinary people consists precisely in their permanent and unchanging ordinariness, or, better still, when, despite all the extreme efforts of these people to get out of the rut of the usual and the routine, they end up all the same by remaining unchangingly and eternally in one and the same routine, then such people even acquire a kind of typicality—as that ordinariness which refuses to remain what it is and wants at all costs to become original and independent, but has not the slightest means of achieving independence.

To this category of "usual" or "ordinary" people belong certain persons of our story, who till now (I admit it) have been little explained to the reader. Such, namely, are Varvara Ardalionovna Ptitsyn, her husband, Mr. Ptitsyn, and Gavrila Ardalionovich, her brother.

Indeed, there is nothing more vexing, for instance, than to be rich, of respectable family, of decent appearance, of rather good education, not stupid, even kind, and at the same time to have no talent, no particularity, no oddity even, not a single idea of one's own, to be decidedly "like everybody else." There is wealth, but not a Rothschild's; an honorable family, but which has never distinguished itself in any way; a decent appearance, but very little expression; a proper education, but without knowing what to apply it to; there is intelligence, but with no *ideas of one's own*; there is a heart, but with no magnanimity, etc., etc., in all respects. There are a great many such people in the world and even far more than it seems; they are divided, as all people are, into two main categories: one limited, the other "much cleverer." The first are happier. For the limited "usual" man, for instance, there is nothing easier than to imagine himself an unusual and original man and to revel in it without any hesitation. As soon as some of our young ladies cut their hair, put on blue spectacles, and called themselves nihilists, they became convinced at once that, having put on the spectacles, they immediately began to have their own "convictions." As soon as a man feels in his heart just a drop of some sort of generally human and kindly feeling for something or other, he immediately becomes convinced that no one else feels as he does, that he is in the forefront of general development. As soon as a man takes some thought or other at its word or reads a little page of something without beginning or end, he believes at once that these are "his own thoughts" and were conceived in his own brain. The impudence of naïvety, if one may put it so, goes so far in such cases as to be astonishing; all this is incredible, but one meets with it constantly. This impudence of naïvety, this stupid man's unquestioningness of himself and his talent, is excellently portrayed by Gogol in the astonishing type of Lieutenant Pirogov.[3] Pirogov never even doubts that he is a genius, even higher than any genius; he is so far from doubting it that he never even asks himself about it; anyhow, questions do not exist for him. The great writer was finally forced to give him a whipping, for the satisfaction of his reader's offended moral sense, but, seeing that the great man merely shook himself and, to fortify himself after his ordeal, ate a puff pastry, he spread his arms in amazement and thus left his readers. I have always regretted that Gogol bestowed such low rank on the great Pirogov, because Pirogov is so given to self-satisfaction that there would be nothing easier for him than to imagine himself, while his epaulettes grow thicker and more braided as the years pass and "according to his rank," as being, for instance, a great commander; not even to imagine it, but simply to have no doubt of it: he has been made a general, why not a commander? And how many of them later cause a terrible fiasco on the battlefield? And how many Pirogovs have there been among our writers, scholars, propagandists? I say "have there been," but, of course, there still are . . .

One character figuring in our story, Gavrila Ardalionovich Ivolgin, belonged to the other category; he belonged to the category of people who are "much cleverer," though he was all infected, from head to foot, with the desire to be original. But this category, as we have already noted above, is much more unhappy than the first. The thing is that a *clever* "usual" man, even if he imagines himself momentarily (or perhaps throughout his life) to be a man of genius and originality, nevertheless preserves in his heart a little worm of doubt, which drives him so far that the clever man sometimes ends up in complete despair; if he submits, then he is already completely poisoned by vanity turned in upon itself. However, we have in any case chosen an extreme instance: in the great majority of this *clever* category of people, things generally do not go so tragically; the liver gives out more or less towards the end of his days, and that's all. But still, before reconciling and submitting, these people sometimes spend an extremely long time acting up, from their youth till the age of submission, and all out of a desire to be original. One even comes upon strange cases: some honest man, out of a desire to be original, is even ready to commit a base deed; it can even happen that one of these unhappy persons is not only honest but even kind, the providence of his family, who by his labor supports and provides not only for his own but even for others—and what then? All his life he is unable to be at peace! For him, the thought that he has fulfilled his human obligations so well brings neither peace nor comfort; on the contrary, that is even what irritates him: "This," he says, "is what I've blown my whole life for, this is what has bound me hand and foot, this is what has kept me from discovering gunpowder! If it hadn't been for that, I'd certainly have discovered either gunpowder or America—I don't know what for sure, but I'd certainly have discovered it!" What is most characteristic in these gentlemen is that all their lives they are indeed unable to find out for sure what precisely they need so much to discover and what precisely they have been preparing all their lives to discover: gunpowder or America? But of suffering, of longing for discovery, they truly have enough of a share in them for a Columbus or a Galileo.

Gavrila Ardalionovich was starting out precisely in that line; but he was only starting out. He still had a long time ahead for acting up. A profound and continual awareness of his talentlessness and at the same time an insuperable desire to be convinced that he was an independent man, painfully wounded his heart, even almost from the age of adolescence. He was a young man with envious and impulsive desires and, it seemed, had even been born with frayed nerves. He mistook the impulsiveness of his desires for their strength. With his passionate desire to distinguish himself, he was sometimes ready for a most reckless leap; but when it came to the point of making the reckless leap, our hero always proved too clever to venture upon it. This was killing him. He might even have ventured, on occasion, upon an extremely base deed, so long as he achieved at least something of what he dreamed; but, as if on purpose, when it reached the limit, he always proved too honest for an extremely base deed. (On a small base deed, however, he was always ready to agree.) He looked upon the poverty and decline of his own family with loathing and hatred. He even treated his mother haughtily and contemptuously, though he understood very well that his mother's character and reputation had so far constituted the main support of his own career. Having entered Epanchin's service, he immediately said to himself: "If I am to be mean, then I shall be mean to the end, so long as I win out"—and—he was almost never mean to the end. And why did he imagine that he would absolutely have to be mean? He had simply been frightened of Aglaya then, but he had not dropped the affair, but dragged it on just in case, though he never seriously believed that she would stoop to him. Then, during his story with Nastasya Filippovna, he had suddenly imagined to himself that the achievement of *everything* lay in money. "If it's meanness, it's meanness," he had repeated to himself every day then with self-satisfaction, but also with a certain fear; "if it's meanness, it's also getting to the top," he encouraged himself constantly, "a routine man would turn timid in this case, but we won't turn timid!" Having lost Aglaya and been crushed by circumstances, he had lost heart completely and had actually brought the prince the money thrown to him then by a crazy woman, to whom it had also been brought by a crazy man. Afterwards he regretted this returning of the money a thousand times, though he constantly gloried in it. He had actually wept for three days, while the prince remained in Petersburg, but during those three days he had also come to hate the prince for looking upon him much too compassionately, whereas the fact that he had returned so much money was something "not everyone would bring himself to do." But the noble self-recognition that all his anguish was only a constantly pinched vanity made him suffer terribly. Only a long time afterwards did he see clearly and become convinced of how seriously his affair with such an innocent and strange being as Aglaya might have turned out. Remorse gnawed at him; he abandoned his work and sank into anguish and dejection. He lived in Ptitsyn's house and at his expense, with his father and mother, and despised Ptitsyn openly, though at the same time he listened to his advice and was almost always sensible enough to ask for it. Gavrila Ardalionovich was angry, for instance, at the fact that Ptitsyn did not aim to become a Rothschild and had not set himself that goal. "If you're a usurer, go through with it, squeeze people dry, coin money out of them, become a character, become the king of the Jews!"[4] Ptitsyn was modest and quiet; he only smiled, but once he even found it necessary to have a serious talk with Ganya and even did it with a certain dignity. He proved to Ganya that he was not doing anything dishonest and that he should not go calling him a Jew; that if money had so much value, it was not his fault; that he acted truthfully and honestly, and that in reality he was only an agent in "these" affairs, and, finally, that thanks to his accuracy in business he was already known from quite a good standpoint to some most excellent people, and that his business was expanding. "Rothschild I won't be, and why should I," he added, laughing, "but I'll have a house on Liteinaya, maybe even two, and that will be the end of it." "And, who knows, maybe three!" he thought to himself, but never said it aloud and kept his dream hidden. Nature loves and coddles such people: she will certainly reward Ptitsyn not with three but with four houses, and that precisely because he has known since childhood that he would never be a Rothschild. But beyond four houses nature will not go for anything, and with Ptitsyn matters will end there.

Gavrila Ardalionovich's little sister was an entirely different person. She also had strong desires, but more persistent than impulsive. There was a good deal of reasonableness in her, when things reached the final limit, but it did not abandon her before the limit either. True, she was also one of the "usual" people, who dream of originality, but she very quickly managed to realize that she did not have a drop of any particular originality, and she did not grieve over it all that much—who knows, maybe from a peculiar sort of pride. She had made her first practical step with extreme resoluteness by marrying Mr. Ptitsyn; but in marrying him she did not say to herself: "If I'm to be mean, I'll be mean, so long as I reach my goal"—something Gavrila Ardalionovich would not have failed to say on such an occasion (and even almost did say in her presence, when approving of her decision as an older brother).

Quite the contrary even: Varvara Ardalionovna got married after solidly convincing herself that her future husband was a modest, agreeable man, almost educated, who would never commit any great meanness. Varvara Ardalionovna did not look into small meannesses, as too trifling; and where are there not such trifles? No one's looking for ideals! Besides, she knew that by marrying, she was providing a corner for her mother, her father, her brothers. Seeing her brother in misfortune, she wanted to help him, in spite of all previous family misunderstandings. Ptitsyn sometimes urged Ganya—in a friendly way, naturally—to find a job. "You despise generals and generalship," he sometimes said to him jokingly, "but look, all of 'them' will end up as generals in their turn; if you live long enough, you'll see it." "What made them decide that I despise generals and generalship?" Ganya thought to himself sarcastically. To help her brother, Varvara Ardalionovna decided to widen the circle of her activities; she wormed her way in with the Epanchins, childhood memories contributing much to that end: both she and her brother had played with the Epanchin girls in childhood. We shall note here that if, in her visits to the Epanchins, Varvara Ardalionovna had been pursuing some extraordinary dream, she might at once have left the category of people in which she had confined herself; but she was not pursuing a dream; there was even a rather well-founded calculation here on her part: it was founded on the character of this family. Aglaya's character she studied tirelessly. She had set herself the task of turning the two of them, her brother and Aglaya, to each other again. It may be that she actually achieved something; it may be that she fell into error, in counting too much on her brother, for instance, and expecting something from him that he could never and in no way give. In any case, she acted rather skillfully at the Epanchins': for weeks at a time she made no mention of her brother, was always extremely truthful and candid, bore herself simply but with dignity. As for the depths of her conscience, she was not afraid of looking there and did not reproach herself for anything at all. It was this that gave her strength. There was only one thing that she sometimes noticed in herself—that she, too, was perhaps angry, that in her, too, there was a great deal of self-love and even all but pinched vanity; she noticed it especially at certain moments, almost every time she left the Epanchins'.

And now she was returning from them and, as we have already said, in rueful pensiveness. Something bitterly mocking could also be glimpsed in this ruefulness. Ptitsyn lived in Pavlovsk in an unattractive but roomy wooden house that stood on a dusty street and which would soon come into his full possession, so that he in turn was already beginning to sell it to someone. Going up to the porch, Varvara Ardalionovna heard an extremely loud noise upstairs and could make out the voices of her brother and father shouting. Going into the drawing room and seeing Ganya, who was running up and down the room, pale with fury and almost tearing his hair out, she winced and, with a weary air, lowered herself onto the sofa without taking off her hat. Knowing very well that if she kept silent for another minute and did not ask her brother why he was running like that, he would unfailingly become angry, Varya hastened, finally, to say, in the guise of a question:

"Same as ever?"

"As ever, hah!" exclaimed Ganya. "As ever! No, the devil knows what's going on here now, and not as ever! The old man's getting rabid . . . mother's howling . . . By God, Varya, say what you will, I'll throw him out of the house or . . . or leave myself," he added, probably recalling that he really could not throw people out of a house that was not his.

"You must be tolerant," Varya murmured.

"Tolerant of what? Of whom?" Ganya flared up. "Of his abominations? No, say what you will, it's impossible like this! Impossible, impossible, impossible! And such a manner: he's to blame and yet he swaggers even more! 'If it won't fit through the gate, knock the fence down! . . .' Why are you sitting there like that? You don't look yourself!"

"I look as I look," Varya answered with displeasure.

Ganya studied her more intently.

"You've been there?" he asked suddenly.

"Yes."

"Wait, they're shouting again! What a shame, and at such a time!"

"Why such a time? It's no special time."

Ganya looked still more intently at his sister.

"Did you find out anything?" he asked.

"Nothing unexpected, at least. I found out that it's all true. My husband was more right than either of us; he predicted it from the very beginning, and so it's turned out. Where is he?"

"Not at home. What's turned out?"

"The prince is formally her fiancé, the matter's settled. The older girls told me. Aglaya has agreed; they've even stopped hiding it. (It was all so mysterious there till now.) Adelaida's wedding will be postponed again, so as to celebrate both weddings together, on the same day—how poetic! Like verse! Why don't you go and write some verses for the nuptials instead of running up and down the room for nothing? Tonight they'll be having old Belokonsky; she arrived just in time; there will be guests. He'll be introduced to Belokonsky, though he's already met her; it seems they're going to announce it publicly. They're only afraid he'll drop and break something as he comes into the room in front of the guests, or just fall down himself; that would be like him."

Ganya listened very attentively, but, to his sister's surprise, this striking news did not seem to make any striking effect on him.

"Well, that was clear," he said after some thought, "so, it's over!" he added with a strange smile, peeking slyly into his sister's face and still pacing up and down the room, but much more slowly now.

"It's good that you can take it philosophically; I'm truly glad," said Varya.

"It's off our backs; off yours, at least."

"I believe I served you sincerely, without arguing and pestering; I never asked you what sort of happiness you wanted to look for with Aglaya."

"But was I . . . looking for happiness with Aglaya?"

"Well, kindly don't go getting into philosophy! Of course you were. It's over, and enough for us—two fools. I must confess to you, I never could look seriously on this affair; I took it up 'just in case,' counting on her funny character, and above all to humor you; there was a ninety percent chance it would be a flop. Even now I don't know myself what you were after."

"Now you and your husband will start urging me to get a job; give me lectures on persistence and willpower, on not scorning small things, and so on—I know it by heart," Ganya laughed loudly.

"There's something new on his mind!" thought Varya.

"So, what—are they glad there, the parents?" Ganya asked suddenly.

"N-no, it seems not. However, you can judge for yourself; Ivan Fyodorovich is pleased; the mother's afraid; before, too, she loathed seeing him as a suitor; you know why."

"That's not what I mean; the suitor is impossible and

unthinkable, that's clear. I'm asking about now, how are things there now? Has she formally accepted him?"

"She hasn't said 'no' yet—that's all, but then it couldn't be otherwise with her. You know how preposterously shy and modest she's been all along: as a child she used to get into the wardrobe and sit there for two or three hours, only so as not to come out to the guests; she's grown into such a big thing, but it's the same now. You know, for some reason I think there's actually something serious in it, even on her part. They say she keeps laughing her head off at the prince, from morning till night, so as not to let anything show, but she must certainly manage to say something to him on the quiet every day, because he looks as though he's walking on air, beaming . . . They say he's terribly funny. I heard it from them. It also seemed to me that they were laughing in my face—the older ones, I mean."

Ganya finally started to scowl; maybe Varya had deliberately gone deeper into the subject in order to penetrate to his real thoughts. But again a shout came from upstairs.

"I'll throw him out!" Ganya simply roared, as if glad to vent his vexation.

"And then he'll go and disgrace us again everywhere, like yesterday."

"How—like yesterday? What do you mean like yesterday? Did he . . ." Ganya suddenly became terribly alarmed.

"Ah, my God, don't you know?" Varya recollected herself.

"How . . . so it's really true that he was there?" Ganya exclaimed, flushing with shame and fury. "My God, you were just there! Did you find anything out? Was the old man there? Was he or wasn't he?"

And Ganya rushed to the door; Varya dashed to him and seized him with both arms.

"What is it? Where are you going?" she said. "If you let him out now, he'll do something worse, he'll go to everybody! . . ."

"What did he do there? What did he say?"

"They weren't able to tell and didn't understand themselves; he just frightened them all. He came to see Ivan Fyodorovich—he wasn't there; he demanded to see Lizaveta Prokofyevna. First he asked her for a job, to enter the service, then he started complaining about me, my husband, and you especially . . . said all kinds of things."

"You couldn't find out?" Ganya was trembling as if in hysterics.

"Oh, come now! He himself barely understood what he was saying, and maybe they didn't tell me all of it."

Ganya clutched his head and ran to the window; Varya sat down by the other window.

"Aglaya's funny," she suddenly observed, "she stops me and says: 'Convey my particular personal respects to your parents; one of these days I shall probably find an occasion to see your father.' And she says it so seriously. It's terribly odd . . ."

"Not mockingly? Not mockingly?"

"Precisely not; that's the odd thing."

"Does she know about the old man or doesn't she, what do you think?"

"It's not known to them in the house, I have no doubt of that; but you've given me an idea: maybe Aglaya does know. She alone knows, because the sisters were also surprised that she sent her greetings to father so seriously. Why on earth precisely to him? If she knows, then it's the prince who told her!"

"It takes no cleverness to find out who told her! A thief! Just what we needed. A thief in our family, 'the head of the family'!"

"Oh, nonsense!" cried Varya, becoming quite angry. "A drunken incident, nothing more. And who came up with it? Lebedev, the prince . . . fine ones they are; palatial minds. I don't care a whit about it."

"The old man's a thief and a drunkard," Ganya went on biliously, "I'm a pauper, my sister's husband is a usurer—Aglaya had something to covet! Pretty, I must say!"

"That sister's husband, the usurer, is your . . ."

"Feeder, is that it? Kindly don't mince words."

"Why are you angry?" Varya recollected herself. "You don't understand anything, just like a schoolboy. Do you think all that could harm you in Aglaya's eyes? You don't know her character; she'd turn her back on the foremost suitor, but she'd be pleased to run to some student in a garret and starve to death—that's her dream! You've never been able to understand how interesting you'd become in her eyes if you could endure our circumstances with firmness and pride. The prince caught her on his hook, first of all, because he never tried to catch her and, second, because in everybody's eyes he's an idiot. This one thing alone, that she'll muddle up the whole family because of him—that's what she likes now. Ah, none of you understands anything!"

"Well, we've yet to see whether we understand or not," Ganya muttered mysteriously, "only all the same I wouldn't want her to find out about the old man. I thought the prince would keep it to himself and not tell. He kept Lebedev from telling, and he didn't want to tell me everything either, when I badgered him . . ."

"So you can see for yourself that everything's known already even without him. But what is it to you now? What is there to hope for? And if there were any hope left, it would only give you a look of suffering in her eyes."

"Well, in the face of a scandal even she would turn coward, despite all her love of novels. Everything up to a certain limit, and everybody up to a certain limit—you're all the same."

"Aglaya would turn coward?" Varya flared up, looking contemptuously at her brother. "You really have a mean little soul, though! None of you is worth anything. She may be funny and eccentric, but she's a thousand times nobler than any of us."

"Well, never mind, never mind, don't be angry," Ganya again muttered smugly.

"I'm only sorry for mother," Varya went on. "I'm afraid this story with father may get to her, oh, I'm afraid!"

"And it surely has," Ganya observed.

Varya got up to go upstairs to Nina Alexandrovna, but stopped and looked intently at her brother.

"Who could have told her?"

"Ippolit, it must be. I suppose he considered it his prime pleasure to report it to mother, as soon as he moved in with us."

"But how does he know, pray tell? The prince and Lebedev decided not to tell anyone, even Kolya doesn't know."

"Ippolit? He found it out himself. You can't imagine what a cunning creature he is; what a gossip he is; what a nose he's got for smelling out everything bad, everything scandalous. Well, believe it or not, but I'm convinced that he's already got Aglaya in his hands! And if he hasn't, he will. Rogozhin has also entered into relations with him. How does the prince not notice it! And how he wants to do me a bad turn now! He considers me his personal enemy, I saw through him long ago, and why, what is it to him, he'll die anyway—I can't understand it! But I'll fool him; I'll do him a bad turn, and not he me, you'll see."

"Why did you lure him here, then, if you hate him so much? And is it worth it to do him a bad turn?"

"It was you who advised me to lure him here."

"I thought he'd be useful; and do you know that he has now

fallen in love with Aglaya himself and has written to her? They questioned me . . . it's just possible that he's written to Lizaveta Prokofyevna, too."

"He's no danger in that sense!" Ganya said with a spiteful laugh. "However, there's probably something else in it. He may very well be in love, because he's a boy! But . . . he wouldn't write anonymous letters to the old lady. He's such a spiteful, worthless, self-satisfied mediocrity! . . . I'm convinced, I know for certain, that he represented me to her as an intriguer, and began with that. I confess that like a fool I let things slip to him at first; I thought he'd take up my interests just to be revenged on the prince; he's such a cunning creature! Oh, now I've seen through him completely. And the theft he heard about from his own mother, the captain's widow. If the old man ventured to do that, it was for her sake. Suddenly, out of the blue, he tells me that 'the general' has promised his mother four hundred roubles, and he does it just like that, out of the blue, without any ceremony. Then I understood everything. And he just peeks into my eyes with some kind of relish; he probably also told mother solely for the pleasure of breaking her heart. And why doesn't he die, pray tell? He promised to die in three weeks, but he's even grown fatter here! He doesn't cough any more; yesterday evening he said himself that he hadn't coughed up blood for two days."

"Throw him out."

"I don't hate him, I despise him," Ganya said proudly. "Well, yes, yes, I do hate him, I do!" he suddenly cried with extraordinary fury. "And I'll say it right to his face, even when he's about to die, on his pillow! If you'd only read his 'Confession'—God, what naïvety of impudence! It's Lieutenant Pirogov, it's Nozdryov[5] in a tragedy, and above all—a little brat! Oh, with what relish I'd have given him a whipping then, precisely to astonish him. He's taking revenge on everybody now, because it didn't come off then . . . But what's that? More noise there? No, what is it, finally? I won't put up with it, finally! Ptitsyn!" he shouted to Ptitsyn, who was coming into the room. "What is this, what are things here coming to, finally? It's . . . it's . . ."

But the noise was quickly approaching, the door was suddenly flung open, and old man Ivolgin, in wrath, purple, shaken, beside himself, also fell upon Ptitsyn. The old man was followed by Nina Alexandrovna, Kolya, and, last of all, Ippolit.

II

IT WAS ALREADY five days since Ippolit had moved to the Ptitsyns' house. It had happened somehow naturally, without any special words or any falling-out between him and the prince; not only had they not quarreled, but it seemed they had even parted friends. Gavrila Ardalionovich, so hostile to Ippolit on that earlier evening, had come to see him himself, though only three days after the event, probably guided by some sudden thought. For some reason Rogozhin also began to visit the sick boy. At first it seemed to the prince that it would even be better for the "poor boy" if he moved out of his house. But at the time of moving, Ippolit kept saying that he was moving to Ptitsyn's, "who had been so kind as to give him a corner," and, as if on purpose, never once said that he was moving to Ganya's, though it was Ganya who had insisted that he be taken into the house. Ganya noticed it then and touchily laid it up in his heart.

He was right when he said to his sister that the sick boy had improved. Indeed, Ippolit felt slightly better than before, which could be noticed from the first glance at him. He came into the room unhurriedly, after everyone else, with a mocking and unkindly smile. Nina Alexandrovna came in very frightened. (She had changed greatly during these six months, had grown thinner; having married off her daughter and moved to live with her, she had almost ceased to interfere externally in her children's affairs.) Kolya was preoccupied and as if perplexed; there was much that he did not understand in "the general's madness," as he put it, not knowing, of course, the main reasons for this new turmoil in the house. But it was clear to him that his father was quarreling so much, everywhere and always, and had suddenly changed so much, that it was as if he were quite a different man than before. It also worried him that in the last three days the old man had even stopped drinking entirely. He knew that he had broken and even quarreled with Lebedev and the prince. Kolya had just come home with a bottle of vodka, which he had purchased with his own money.

"Really, mother," he had assured Nina Alexandrovna while still upstairs, "really, it's better to let him have a drink. He hasn't touched a drop in three days now; from anguish, it means. Really, it's better! I used to bring it to him in debtors' prison . . ."

The general flung the door wide open and stood on the sill as if trembling with indignation.

"My dear sir!" he cried out to Ptitsyn in a thundering voice, "if you have indeed decided to sacrifice a venerable old man, your father, that is, your wife's father at least, honored by his sovereign, to a milksop and an atheist, I shall never set foot in your house again from this very hour. Choose, sir, choose immediately: either me, or this . . . screw! Yes, screw! I said it by accident, but he is a screw! Because he bores into my soul like a screw, and without any respect . . . like a screw!"

"Or a corkscrew?" Ippolit put in.

"No, not a corkscrew, because I'm a general to you, not a bottle. I have medals, medals of honor . . . and you've got a fig. Either him or me! Decide, sir, this minute, this very minute!" he again cried in frenzy to Ptitsyn. Here Kolya moved a chair for him, and he sank onto it almost in exhaustion.

"Really, it would be better for you . . . to go to sleep," the dumbfounded Ptitsyn murmured.

"And what's more, he threatens!" Ganya said in a low voice to his sister.

"To sleep!" cried the general. "I am not drunk, my dear sir, and you offend me. I see," he went on, standing up again, "I see that everything is against me here, everything and everyone. Enough! I am leaving . . . But know, my dear sir, know . . ."

They did not let him finish and sat him down again; they began begging him to calm himself. Ganya, in fury, went to the far corner. Nina Alexandrovna trembled and wept.

"But what have I done to him? What is he complaining about?" cried Ippolit, baring his teeth.

"So you did nothing?" Nina Alexandrovna suddenly observed. "You especially should be ashamed and . . . to torment an old man so inhumanly . . . and that in your position."

"First of all, what is this position of mine, madam! I respect you very much, precisely you, personally, but . . ."

"He's a screw!" the general shouted. "He bores into my soul and heart! He wants me to believe in atheism! Know, milksop, that you weren't even born yet when I was already showered with honors; and you are merely an envious worm, torn in two, coughing . . . and dying of spite and unbelief . . . And why did Gavrila bring you here? Everybody's against me, from strangers to my own son!"

"Enough, you're starting a tragedy!" cried Ganya. "It would be better if you didn't go disgracing us all over town!"

"How have I disgraced you, milksop! You? I can only bring you honor, and not dishonor!"

He jumped up and they could no longer restrain him; but Gavrila Ardalionovich, too, had obviously broken loose.

"Look who's talking about honor!" he cried spitefully.

"What did you say?" the general thundered, turning pale and taking a step towards him.

"I need only open my mouth in order to . . ." Ganya screamed suddenly and did not finish. The two stood facing each other, shaken beyond measure, especially Ganya.

"Ganya, how can you!" cried Nina Alexandrovna, rushing to stop her son.

"What nonsense all around!" Varya snapped indignantly. "Enough, mother," she seized her.

"I spare you only for mother's sake," Ganya said tragically.

"Speak!" the general bellowed, totally beside himself. "Speak for fear of a father's curse . . . speak!"

"As if I'm afraid of your curse! Whose fault is it if you've been like a crazy man for the past eight days? Eight days, you see, I know it by the dates . . . Watch out, don't drive me to the limit: I'll tell everything . . . Why did you drag yourself to the Epanchins' yesterday? Calling yourself an old man, gray-haired, the father of a family! A fine one!"

"Shut up, Ganka!" cried Kolya. "Shut up, you fool!"

"But I, how have I insulted him?" Ippolit insisted, in what seemed like the same mocking tone. "Why does he call me a screw? Did you hear? He pesters me himself; just now he came and started talking about some Captain Eropegov. I have no wish for your company, General; I avoided you before, you know that. I have nothing to do with Captain Eropegov, don't you agree? I did not move here for the sake of Captain Eropegov. I merely voiced my opinion that this Captain Eropegov may never have existed at all. And he started kicking up dust."

"He undoubtedly never existed!" snapped Ganya.

But the general stood as if stunned and only looked around senselessly. His son's phrase struck him by its extreme frankness. For the first moment he was even at a loss for words. And at last, only when Ippolit burst out laughing at Ganya's reply and shouted: "Well, do you hear, your own son also says there was no Captain Eropegov," did the old man babble, completely confounded:

"Kapiton Eropegov, not Captain . . . Kapiton . . . a retired lieutenant-colonel, Eropegov . . . Kapiton."

"There was no Kapiton either!" Ganya was now thoroughly angry.

"Wh . . . why wasn't there?" mumbled the general, and color rose to his face.

"Well, enough!" Ptitsyn and Varya tried to pacify him.

"Shut up, Ganka!" Kolya cried again.

But the intercession seemed to have brought the general to his senses.

"How wasn't there? Why didn't he exist?" he menacingly turned on his son.

"There just wasn't. There wasn't, that's all, and there simply cannot be! So there. Leave me alone, I tell you."

"And this is my son . . . my own son, whom I . . . oh, God! Eropegov, Eroshka Eropegov never lived!"

"Well, so, now it's Eroshka, now it's Kapitoshka!" Ippolit put in.

"Kapitoshka, sir, Kapitoshka, not Eroshka! Kapiton, Captain Alexeevich, that is, Kapiton . . . a lieutenant-colonel . . . retired . . . married to Marya . . . Marya Petrovna Su . . . Su . . . a friend and comrade . . . Sutugov, even as a junker.[6] For him I shed . . . I shielded him . . . killed. No Kapitoshka Eropegov! Never existed!"

The general was shouting in excitement, but in such a way that one might have thought the point went one way and the shouting another. True, at another time he would have borne something much more offensive than the news about the total non-existence of Kapiton Eropegov, would have shouted a little, started a scandal, lost his temper, but all the same in the end he would have withdrawn to his room upstairs and gone to bed. But now, owing to the extraordinary strangeness of the human heart, it so happened that precisely such an offense as the doubt of Eropegov made the cup run over. The old man turned purple, raised his arms, and shouted:

"Enough! My curse . . . away from this house! Nikolai, bring my bag, I'm going . . . away!"

He went out, hurrying and in extreme wrath. Nina Alexandrovna, Kolya, and Ptitsyn rushed after him.

"Well, what have you done now!" Varya said to her brother. "He may drag himself there again. Ah, what shame, what shame!"

"So don't go stealing!" Ganya cried, all but choking with spite; suddenly his glance met with Ippolit; Ganya almost began to shake. "And you, my dear sir," he cried, "ought to remember that you are not, after all, in your own house and . . . are enjoying hospitality, instead of vexing an old man who has obviously lost his mind . . ."

Ippolit also seemed to wince, but he immediately checked himself.

"I don't quite agree with you that your father has lost his mind," he replied calmly. "It seems to me, on the contrary, that his mind has been working much better lately, by God; don't you believe so? He has become so cautious, suspicious, keeps asking questions, weighs every word . . . He started talking with me about that Kapitoshka with some aim; imagine, he wanted to suggest to me . . ."

"Eh, the devil I care what he wanted to suggest to you! I ask you, sir, not to be clever and try to dodge with me!" Ganya shrieked. "If you also know the real reason why the old man is in such a state (and you've been spying so much in these five days here that you surely do know it), then you ought never to have vexed . . . the unfortunate man and tormented my mother by exaggerating the affair, because the whole affair is nonsense, just a drunken incident, nothing more, not even proved in any way, and I don't care a whit about it . . . But you have to go taunting and spying, because you're . . . you're . . ."

"A screw," Ippolit grinned.

"Because you're trash, you tormented people for half an hour, thinking you'd frighten them that you were going to shoot yourself with your unloaded pistol, with which you bungled it so shamefully, you failed suicide, you . . . walking bile. I showed you hospitality, you've grown fatter, stopped coughing, and you repay me . . ."

"Just a couple of words, if you please, sir; I am staying with Varvara Ardalionovna, not with you; you have not offered me any hospitality, and I even think that you yourself are enjoying the hospitality of Mr. Ptitsyn. Four days ago I asked my mother to find lodgings for me in Pavlovsk and to move here herself, because I actually do feel better here, though I haven't grown fatter and I still cough. Yesterday evening my mother informed me that the apartment is ready, and I hasten to inform you for my part that, after thanking your dear mother and sister, I will move to my own place today, as I already decided to do last evening. Excuse me, I interrupted you; it seems you had much more to say."

"Oh, in that case . . ." Ganya began to tremble.

"But in that case, allow me to sit down," Ippolit added, sitting down most calmly on the chair that the general had been sitting on. "I am ill after all; well, now I'm ready to listen to you, the more so as this is our last conversation and perhaps even our last meeting."

Ganya suddenly felt ashamed.

"Believe me, I shall not lower myself to squaring accounts with you," he said, "and if you . . ."

"You needn't be so supercilious," Ippolit interrupted. "For my part, on the first day I moved here I promised myself not to deny myself the pleasure of speaking my mind to you as we said good-bye, and that in the most frank way. I intend to do so precisely now—after you, naturally."

"And I ask you to leave this room."

"Better speak, you'll regret not saying everything."

"Stop it, Ippolit! All this is terribly shameful. Be so good as to stop!" said Varya.

"Only for a lady," Ippolit laughed, standing up. "If you please, Varvara Ardalionovna, I'm prepared to make it shorter for you, but only shorter, because some explanation between your brother and me has become quite necessary, and not for anything will I go away and leave any perplexity behind."

"You're quite simply a gossip," Ganya cried out, "that's why you won't leave without gossiping."

"There, you see," Ippolit observed coolly, "you've already lost control of yourself. You really will regret not saying everything. Once more I yield the floor to you. I shall wait."

Gavrila Ardalionovich was silent and looked at him contemptuously.

"You don't want to? You intend to stand firm—as you will. For my part, I shall be as brief as possible. Two or three times today I have listened to a reproach about hospitality; that is unfair. In inviting me to stay with you, you wanted to catch me in your nets; you calculated that I wanted to be revenged on the prince. Moreover, you heard that Aglaya Ivanovna had shown concern for me and was reading my 'Confession.' Calculating, for some reason, that I would surrender myself entirely to your interests, you may have hoped to find some support in me. I shall not go into detail! Nor do I demand any acknowledgment or recognition on your part; suffice it that I leave you with your own conscience and that we now understand each other perfectly."

"But you make God knows what out of a most ordinary matter!" cried Varya.

"I told you: 'a gossip and a little brat,'" said Ganya.

"If you please, Varvara Ardalionovna, I shall continue. Of course, I can neither love nor respect the prince, but he is decidedly a kind man, though . . . a ridiculous one. But I have absolutely no reason to hate him; I remained impassive when your brother incited me against the prince; I precisely counted on having a good laugh at the denouement. I knew your brother would let things slip and miss the mark in the highest degree. And so it happened . . . I'm ready to spare him now, but solely out of respect for you, Varvara Ardalionovna. But, having explained to you that it is not so easy to catch me on a hook, I will also explain to you why I wanted so much to make a fool of your brother. Know that I did it out of hatred, I confess it frankly. In dying (because I shall die all the same, even though I've grown fatter, as you assure me), in dying, I have felt that I would go to paradise incomparably more peacefully if I managed to make a fool out of at least one of that numberless sort of people who have hounded me all my life, whom I have hated all my life, and of whom your much-esteemed brother serves as such a vivid representation. I hate you, Gavrila Ardaliono-vich, solely because—this may seem astonishing to you—*solely because* you are the type and embodiment, the personification and apex of the most impudent, the most self-satisfied, the most vulgar and vile ordinariness! You are a puffed-up ordinariness, an unquestioning and Olympianly calm ordinariness; you are the routine of routines! Not the least idea of your own will ever be embodied in your mind or in your heart. But you are infinitely envious; you are firmly convinced that you are the greatest of geniuses, but all the same, doubt visits you occasionally in your darkest moments, and you become angry and envious. Oh, there are still dark spots on your horizon; they will go away when you become definitively stupid, which is not far off; but all the same a long and diverse path lies ahead of you, I do not say a cheerful one, and I'm glad of that. First of all, I predict to you that you will not attain a certain person . . ."

"No, this is unbearable!" Varya cried out. "Will you ever finish, you disgusting little stinker?"

Ganya was pale, trembling, and silent. Ippolit stopped, looked at him intently and with relish, shifted his gaze to Varya, grinned, bowed, and left without adding a single word.

Gavrila Ardalionovich could justly complain of his fate and ill luck. For some time Varya did not dare to address him, did not even glance at him, as he paced by her with big strides; finally, he went to the window and stood with his back to her. Varya was thinking about the proverb: every stick has two ends. There was noise again upstairs.

"Are you leaving?" Ganya suddenly turned, hearing her get up from her seat. "Wait. Look at this."

He went over to her and flung down on the chair before her a small piece of paper folded like a little note.

"Lord!" Varya cried and clasped her hands.

There were exactly seven lines in the note:

Gavrila Ardalionovich! Being convinced that you are kindly disposed towards me, I venture to ask your advice in a matter that is of importance for me. I would like to meet you tomorrow, at exactly seven o'clock in the morning, by the green bench. It is not far from our dacha. Varvara Ardalionovna, who must accompany you *without fail*, knows the place very well.   *A.E.*

"Try figuring her out after that!" Varvara Ardalionovna spread her arms.

Much as Ganya would have liked to swagger at that moment, he simply could not help showing his triumph, especially after such humiliating predictions from Ippolit. A self-satisfied smile shone openly on his face, and Varya herself became all radiant with joy.

"And that on the very day when they're announcing the engagement! Try figuring her out after that!"

"What do you think she's going to talk about tomorrow?" asked Ganya.

"That makes no difference, the main thing is that she wishes to see you for the first time after six months. Listen to me, Ganya: whatever there is to it, however it turns out, know that this is *important*! It's all too important! Don't swagger again, don't miss the mark again, but watch out you don't turn coward either! Could she have failed to grasp why I dragged myself there for half a year? And imagine: she didn't say a word to me today, didn't show a thing. I sneaked in to see them, the old woman didn't know I was sitting with them, otherwise she might have chased me out. I risked that for you, to find out at all costs . . ."

Shouting and noise again came from overhead; several people were going down the stairs.

"Don't allow it now for anything!" Varya cried, frightened and all aflutter. "There mustn't be even the shadow of a scandal! Go and apologize!"

But the father of the family was already in the street. Kolya lugged his bag after him. Nina Alexandrovna stood on the porch and wept; she was about to run after him, but Ptitsyn held her back.

"You'll only egg him on more that way," he said to her. "He has nowhere to go, they'll bring him back in half an hour, I've already discussed it with Kolya; let him play the fool a little."

"What are you showing off for, where are you going!" Ganya shouted out the window. "You've got nowhere to go!"

"Come back, papa!" cried Varya. "The neighbors can hear."

The general stopped, turned around, stretched out his arm, and exclaimed:

"My curse upon this house!"

"And inevitably in a theatrical tone!" Ganya muttered, noisily shutting the window.

The neighbors were indeed listening. Varya rushed from the room.

When Varya was gone, Ganya took the note from the table, kissed it, clucked his tongue, and performed an entrechat.

III

AT ANY OTHER TIME the commotion with the general would have come to nothing. Before, too, there had been occasions of unexpected whimsicality of the same sort with him, though rather seldom, because generally speaking he was a very mild man and of almost kindly inclinations. A hundred times, perhaps, he had taken up the struggle with the disorder that had come over him in recent years. He would suddenly remember that he was the "father of the family," make peace with his wife, weep sincerely. He respected Nina Alexandrovna to the point of adoration for having silently forgiven him so much and loved him even in his clownishness and humiliation. But his magnanimous struggle with disorder usually did not last long; the general was also all too "impulsive" a man, though in his own way; he usually could not bear a repentant and idle life in his family and ended by rebelling;

he would fall into a fit of passion, perhaps reproaching himself for it at the same moment, but unable to control himself: he would quarrel, begin talking floridly and grandiloquently, demand a disproportionate and impossible respect for himself, and in the end disappear from the house, sometimes even for a long time. For the last two years, he had known about the affairs of his family only in general or by hearsay; he had stopped going into more detail, feeling not the slightest call for it.

But this time something unusual manifested itself in the "commotion with the general": everyone seemed to know about something and everyone seemed afraid to speak about something. The general had "formally" appeared in the family, that is, to Nina Alexandrovna, only three days ago, but somehow not humbly and not with repentance, as had always happened in his previous "appearances," but on the contrary—with extraordinary irritability. He was garrulous, agitated, talked heatedly with everyone he met, as if falling upon the person, but it was all about such diverse and unexpected subjects that it was in no way possible to get at what, in essence, he was now so worried about. At moments he was merry, but more often brooding, though he himself did not know about what; he would suddenly begin talking about something— the Epanchins, or the prince and Lebedev—and would suddenly break off and stop talking altogether, and respond to further questions only with a dull smile, though without even noticing that he had been asked something and had merely smiled. He had spent the last night moaning and groaning, and had worn out Nina Alexandrovna, who for some reason kept heating poultices for him all night; towards morning he had suddenly fallen asleep, slept for four hours, and woke up in a most violent and disorderly fit of hypochondria, which had ended in a quarrel with Ippolit and the "curse upon this house." It had also been noticed that during those three days he was constantly having the most violent fits of ambition, and consequently of extraordinary touchiness. But Kolya insisted, reassuring his mother, that it was all the longing for a drink, and perhaps also for Lebedev, with whom the general had become extraordinarily friendly in recent days. But three days ago he had suddenly quarreled with Lebedev and parted from him in a terrible rage; there had even been some sort of scene with the prince. Kolya had asked the prince for an explanation, and had finally begun to suspect that he, too, had something that he was apparently unwilling to tell him. If, as Ganya quite plausibly supposed, there had been some special conversation between Ippolit and Nina Alexandrovna, then it was odd that this wicked gentleman, whom Ganya so directly called a gossip, had denied himself the pleasure of enlightening Kolya in the same way. It may well be that he was not such a wicked "little brat," as Ganya had described him, talking with his sister, but was wicked in some other way; and he had hardly informed Nina Alexandrovna of some observation of his solely in order to "break her heart." Let us not forget that the reasons for human actions are usually incalculably more complex and diverse than we tend to explain them later, and are seldom clearly manifest. Sometimes it is best for the narrator to limit himself to a simple account of events. So we shall do in our further clarification of the present catastrophe with the general; for, in spite of all our efforts, we find ourselves in the decided necessity of giving a bit more attention and space to this secondary character of our story than we had hitherto intended.

The events followed one another in this order:

When Lebedev, after his journey to Petersburg in search of Ferdyshchenko, returned that same day, together with the general, he did not tell the prince anything in particular. If at that time the prince had not been so distracted and taken up with other impressions important for him, he might soon have noticed that for the following two days Lebedev not only did not offer him any explanations but even, on the contrary, seemed to avoid meeting him. Paying attention to that at last, the prince wondered why, during those two days, when he had chanced to meet Lebedev, he remembered him not otherwise than in the most radiant spirits, and almost always together with the general. The two friends never parted for a moment now. Occasionally the prince heard loud and rapid conversation, guffawing, merry argument, coming to him from upstairs; once even, very late in the evening, suddenly and unexpectedly, the sounds of a military-bacchic song reached him, and he immediately recognized the general's hoarse bass. But the resounding song did not come off and suddenly died out. Then, for about an hour more, a very animated and, by all tokens, drunken conversation went on. One could guess that the merrymaking friends upstairs kept embracing, and one of them finally wept. Then suddenly a violent quarrel ensued, which also died out quickly and soon. All this while Kolya was in a somehow especially preoccupied mood. The prince was most often away from home and sometimes came back very late; he was always told that Kolya had been looking for him and asking after him all day long. But when they met, Kolya could not say anything special, except that he was decidedly "displeased" with the general and his present behavior: "They drag themselves around, drink in the local tavern, embrace each other, quarrel in the streets, egg each other on, and simply cannot part." When the prince observed to him that earlier as well it had been the same almost every day, Kolya decidedly did not know what to answer to that and how to explain precisely what caused his present anxiety.

The morning after the bacchic song and quarrel, when the prince was leaving the house at around eleven o'clock, the general suddenly appeared before him, extremely agitated by something, almost shaken.

"I have long been seeking the honor and occasion of meeting you, my much-esteemed Lev Nikolaevich, long, very long," he murmured, pressing the prince's hand extremely hard, almost painfully, "very, very long."

The prince invited him to sit down.

"No, I won't sit down, and moreover I'm keeping you, I will— some other time. It seems I may take this opportunity to congratulate you on . . . the fulfillment . . . of your heart's desires."

"What heart's desires?"

The prince was embarrassed. Like a great many people in his position, he thought that decidedly no one saw anything, guessed anything, understood anything.

"Don't worry, don't worry! I won't upset your most delicate feelings. I have experienced and know myself how it is when a stranger's . . . nose, so to speak . . . according to the saying . . . goes poking where it hasn't been invited. I experience it every morning. I have come on a different matter, Prince, an important one. A very important matter, Prince."

The prince once again invited him to sit down and sat down himself.

"Perhaps for one second . . . I've come for advice. I, of course, live without any practical goals, but, having respect for myself and . . . for efficiency, which is so lacking in the Russian man, generally speaking . . . I wish to put myself, my wife, and my children in a position . . . in short, Prince, I am looking for advice."

The prince warmly praised his intention.

"Well, that's all nonsense," the general quickly interrupted, "moreover, I'm not talking about that, I'm talking about something different, and important. And I shall venture to explain it precisely to you, Lev Nikolaevich, as a man the sincerity of whose reception and the nobility of whose feelings I trust as . . . as . . . You're not surprised at my words, Prince?"

The prince was following his visitor with great attention and curiosity, if not with any particular surprise. The old man was slightly pale, his lips occasionally twitched a little, his hands seemed unable to find a place to rest. He had been sitting for only a few minutes, and had twice managed to get up suddenly from his chair for some reason and suddenly to sit down again, obviously not paying the least attention to his maneuvers. Some books were lying on the table; he took one, went on talking, opened it and peeked at a page, closed it again at once and put it on the table, snatched another book, which he did not open now, but spent the rest of the time holding in his right hand, constantly brandishing it in the air.

"Enough!" he cried suddenly. "I see I've greatly inconvenienced you."

"Why, not in the least, good heavens, you're quite welcome. On the contrary, I've been listening and wish I could guess . . ."

"Prince! I wish to put myself in a respectable position . . . I wish to respect myself and . . . my rights."

"A man with such wishes is deserving of every respect for that alone."

The prince uttered this copybook phrase in the firm conviction that it would have an excellent effect. He somehow instinctively guessed that such a hollow but agreeable phrase, if spoken aptly, might suddenly subdue and pacify the soul of such a man, and especially in such a position as the general's. In any case, such a visitor had to be sent away with his heart eased, and in that lay his task.

The phrase flattered, touched, and greatly pleased: the general suddenly waxed sentimental, instantly changed tone, and lapsed into rapturously lengthy explanations. But no matter how the prince strained, no matter how he listened, he literally could not understand a thing. The general spoke for some ten minutes, heatedly, quickly, as if he had no time to articulate his crowding thoughts; in the end tears even glistened in his eyes, but all the same it was only phrases with no beginning or end, unexpected words and unexpected thoughts, which broke through quickly and unexpectedly and leaped one over the other.

"Enough! You've understood me, and I am at peace," he suddenly concluded, getting up. "A heart such as yours cannot fail to understand a sufferer. Prince, you are as noble as an ideal! What are others compared with you? But you are young, and I give you my blessing. In the final end I have come to ask you to appoint me an hour for a serious conversation, and in this lies my chiefest hope. I seek only friendship and heart, Prince; I never could control the demands of my heart."

"But why not now? I'm prepared to hear out . . ."

"No, Prince, no!" the general interrupted hotly. "Not now! Now is a dream! It is too, too important, too important! This hour of conversation will be the hour of my ultimate destiny. It will be *my* hour, and I would not wish us to be interrupted at such a sacred moment by the first comer, the first impudent fellow, and not seldom such an impudent fellow," he suddenly bent over the prince with a strange, mysterious, and almost frightened whisper, "such an impudent fellow as is not worth the heel . . . of your foot, my beloved Prince! Oh, I don't say of my foot! Make special note that I did not mention my foot; I respect myself enough to be able to say it without beating around the bush; but you alone are able to understand that, by rejecting my own heel in this case, I am showing, perhaps, an extraordinary pride of dignity. Besides you, no one else will understand, and *he* at the head of all the others. *He* doesn't understand anything, Prince; he's totally, totally unable to understand! One must have heart in order to understand!"

In the end the prince was almost frightened and arranged to meet the general the next day at the same hour. The man went away cheerful, extremely comforted, and almost calm. In the evening, past six o'clock, the prince sent to ask Lebedev to come to him for a moment.

Lebedev appeared with extreme haste, "considering it an honor," as he began to say at once on coming in; there seemed to be no shadow of that three-day-long hiding and obvious avoidance of meeting the prince. He sat down on the edge of a chair, with grimaces, with smiles, with laughing and peering little eyes, with a rubbing of hands, and with an air of the most naïve expectation of hearing some sort of capital information, long awaited and guessed by all. The prince winced again; it was becoming clear to him that everyone had suddenly begun to expect something from him, that everyone looked at him as if wishing to congratulate him for something, dropping hints, smiling, and winking. Keller had already stopped by three times for a moment, and also with an obvious wish to congratulate him: he began each time rapturously and vaguely, never finished anything, and quickly effaced himself. (For the last few days he had been drinking especially heavily somewhere and had made a row in some billiard parlor.) Even Kolya, despite his sadness, also once or twice began talking vaguely about something with the prince.

The prince asked Lebedev directly and somewhat irritably what he thought of the general's present state and why he was in such anxiety. In a few words he recounted that day's scene for him.

"Everybody has his anxieties, Prince, and . . . especially in our strange and anxious age, sir; so it is, sir," Lebedev answered with a certain dryness and fell silent, looking hurt, like a man whose expectations have been badly disappointed.

"What philosophy!" smiled the prince.

"Philosophy's needed, sir, very much needed in our age, for practical application, sir, but it's held in disdain, sir, that's what. For my part, my much-esteemed Prince, though I used to be honored by your trustfulness towards me in a certain point, which is known to you, sir, but only to a certain degree, and by no means further than the circumstances that essentially concern that same point . . . I realize it and am not complaining in the least."

"Lebedev, you seem to be angry about something?"

"Not at all, not in the least, my much-esteemed and most radiant Prince, not in the least!" Lebedev cried out ecstatically, putting his hand to his heart. "But, on the contrary, I precisely and immediately comprehended that, neither in worldly position, nor in development of mind and heart, nor in accumulated wealth, nor in my previous behavior, nor yet in learning am I in any way deserving of your honored and lofty trust, which far exceeds my hopes; and that if I may serve you, it is as a slave or a hired servant, not otherwise . . . I am not angry, but sad, sir."

"Lukyan Timofeich, for pity's sake!"

"Not otherwise! And so it is now, so it is in the present case! Meeting you and following you with my heart and thought, I said to myself: I'm unworthy of friendly communications, but in my quality as landlord I may, perhaps, receive orders in due time, by the expected date, so to speak, or at least notification in view of certain forthcoming and expected changes . . ."

As he uttered this, Lebedev simply riveted his sharp little eyes on the prince, who was staring at him in amazement; he was still hoping to satisfy his curiosity.

"I understand decidedly nothing," the prince cried all but wrathfully, "and . . . you are a terrible intriguer!" He suddenly burst into the most genuine laughter.

Lebedev instantly laughed, too, and his brightened eyes showed at once that his hopes had now become clearer and even twice greater.

"And do you know what I shall tell you, Lukyan Timofeich? Only don't be angry with me, but I'm surprised at your naïvety, and not only yours! You expect something from me with such naïvety, precisely now, at this moment, that I'm even abashed and ashamed before you, because I have nothing to satisfy you with; but I swear to you that there is decidedly nothing, if you can imagine that!"

The prince laughed again.

Lebedev assumed a dignified air. It is true that he was sometimes even too naïve and importunate in his curiosity; but at the same time he was a rather cunning and devious man, and on certain occasions even too insidiously taciturn; by constantly rebuffing him, the prince had almost prepared in him an enemy for himself. But the prince rebuffed him not because he despised him, but because the theme of his curiosity was a delicate one. Only a few days ago the prince had looked upon some of his dreams as upon a crime, but Lukyan Timofeich had taken the prince's retorts as personal revulsion and suspicion towards himself, had gone away with a wounded heart, and was jealous not only of Kolya and Keller, but even of his own daughter, Vera Lukyanovna. Even at that very moment, he could have informed the prince of a certain piece of news interesting for him in the highest degree, and may have sincerely wished to, but he fell gloomily silent and did not inform him.

"In what, essentially, can I be of service to you, my much-esteemed Prince, since all the same you have now . . . summoned me?" he said finally, after some silence.

"It was, essentially, about the general," the prince, who had lapsed into a moment's thought, roused himself, "and . . . concerning that theft of yours, which you informed me about . . ."

"Concerning what, sir?"

"Well, so now it's as if you don't understand me! Oh, God, Lukyan Timofeich, what are all these roles of yours! The money, the money, the four hundred roubles you lost then, in your wallet, and came here to tell me about, that morning, before going to Petersburg—do you understand finally?"

"Ah, it's about those four hundred roubles!" Lebedev drew out, as if he had only just realized. "Thank you, Prince, for your genuine concern; it is only too flattering for me, but . . . I found the money, sir, a long time ago."

"Found it! Ah, thank God!"

"A most noble exclamation on your part, for four hundred roubles are a matter of no small importance for a poor man who lives by hard work, with a numerous family of orphans . . ."

"But I didn't mean that! Of course, I'm also glad you found it," the prince quickly corrected his slip, "but . . . how did you find it?"

"Extremely simply, sir. I found it under the chair on which the frock coat was hanging, which obviously means that the wallet slipped out of the pocket onto the floor."

"Under the chair? That can't be, you told me you searched in every corner; how could you have missed it in the most important place?"

"It's a fact that I looked, sir! I remember very, very well that I looked there, sir! I went down on all fours, felt the place with my hands, moved the chair aside, not believing my own eyes: I saw there was nothing there, an empty and smooth space, like the palm of my hand, sir, and I went on feeling all the same. Such faintheartedness always repeats itself with a man when he wants very much to find something . . . in the case of a considerable and sad loss, sir: one sees that there's nothing there, an empty space, and yet one looks fifteen times over."

"Yes, granted; only how can it be, though? . . . I still don't understand," the prince muttered confusedly. "You say it wasn't there before, that you searched in that spot, and suddenly it turned up there?"

"And suddenly it turned up there, sir!"

The prince gave Lebedev a strange look.

"And the general?" he asked suddenly.

"What about the general, sir?" Lebedev again did not understand.

"Ah, my God! I'm asking you, what did the general say when you found the wallet under the chair? Didn't you look for it together before?"

"Together before, sir. But this time, I confess, sir, I said nothing and preferred not to tell him I found the wallet all by myself."

"Wh . . . why so? Is the money all there?"

"I opened the wallet; the money was all there, even to the last rouble, sir."

"You might at least have come and told me," the prince observed pensively.

"I was afraid to disturb you personally, Prince, considering your personal and, perhaps, extraordinary, so to speak, impressions; besides, I myself made it look as if I hadn't found anything. I opened the wallet, examined it, then closed it and put it back under the chair."

"What on earth for?"

"Just so, sir; out of further curiosity, sir," Lebedev suddenly tittered, rubbing his hands.

"So it's lying there now, for the third day?"

"Oh, no, sir; it lay there only one day. You see, I partly wanted the general to find it, too, sir. Because if I finally found it, why shouldn't the general also find an object sticking out from under the chair and, so to speak, striking the eye? I took that chair several times and moved it, so that the wallet wound up in full view, but the general never noticed it at all, and so it went on for the whole day. He's obviously very absentminded now, and hard to make out; he talks, tells stories, laughs, guffaws, then suddenly gets terribly angry with me, I don't know why, sir. As we were finally going out of the room, I purposely left the door open; he hesitated, was about to say something, probably afraid for the wallet with so much money in it, then suddenly became terribly angry and said nothing, sir; before we'd gone two steps down the street, he abandoned me and went the other way. We came together only that evening in the tavern."

"But did you finally take the wallet from under the chair?"

"No, sir; that same night it disappeared from under the chair, sir."

"So where is it now?"

"Here, sir," Lebedev suddenly laughed, rising from the chair to his full height and looking pleasantly at the prince. "It suddenly turned up here, in the skirt of my own frock coat. Here, kindly look for yourself, feel it, sir."

Indeed, it was as if a whole pouch had been formed in the left skirt of the frock coat, right in front, in full view, and by feeling it one could tell at once that it was a leather wallet, which had fallen there through a torn pocket.

"I took it out and looked, it's all there, sir. I put it back and since yesterday morning I've been walking around like that, carrying it in my skirt, it even hits against my legs."

"And you don't notice it?"

"And I don't notice it, heh, heh! And imagine, my much-esteemed Prince—though the subject is unworthy of such special attention from you—my pockets are always in good condition, and now suddenly, in one night, such a hole! I started examining it curiously—as if somebody had cut it with a penknife; it's almost incredible, sir!"

"And . . . the general?"

"He was angry all day yesterday and today; he's terribly displeased, sir; first he's joyful and bacchic even to the point of flattery, then he's sentimental to the point of tears, then he suddenly gets so angry that I even turn coward, by God; I'm not a military man after all, sir. Yesterday we're sitting in the tavern, and, as if by accident, my skirt is exposed to view, a big bump; he looks askance, gets angry. He hasn't looked me straight in the eye for a long time, sir, except when he's very drunk or waxes sentimental; but yesterday a couple of times he gave me such a look that a chill ran down my spine. Anyhow, I intend to find the wallet tomorrow, but before tomorrow I'll spend another little evening having fun with him."

"But why do you torment him so?" cried the prince.

"I'm not tormenting him, Prince, I'm not," Lebedev picked up hotly, "I love him sincerely, sir, and . . . I respect him; and now, believe it or not, sir, he's become even dearer to me; I've come to appreciate him still more, sir!"

Lebedev said it all so seriously and sincerely that the prince even became indignant.

"You love him, yet you torment him so! For pity's sake, by the fact alone that he put what you lost in full view like that, under the table and then in your frock coat, by that alone he shows you directly that he doesn't want to dodge with you, but is simple-heartedly asking your forgiveness. Do you hear: he's asking your forgiveness! That means he's relying on the delicacy of your feelings; which means he trusts in your friendship for him. And you drive such a . . . a most honest man to such humiliation!"

"A most honest man, Prince, most honest!" Lebedev picked up, his eyes flashing. "And precisely you alone, most noble Prince, are able to speak such a just word! For that I am devoted to you even to the point of adoration, sir, though I am rotten with various vices! It's decided! I shall find the wallet right now, at once, not tomorrow; here, I take it out before your eyes, sir; here it is; and all the money's in it; here, take it, most noble Prince, take it and keep it till tomorrow. Tomorrow or the day after I'll take it, sir; and you know, Prince, it obviously lay somewhere in my garden, under a stone, the first night it was lost, sir; what do you think?"

"Watch out, don't tell him right to his face that you found the wallet. Let him simply see that there's nothing in the skirt anymore, and he'll understand."

"Is that so, sir? Wouldn't it be better to tell him I found it, sir, and pretend that till now I never guessed?"

"N-no," the prince reflected, "n-no, it's too late now; it's more dangerous; really, you'd better not say it! And be gentle with him, but . . . don't let it show too much, and . . . and . . . you know . . ."

"I know, Prince, I know—that is, I know that I probably won't do it; for here one must have a heart like yours. And besides, he's irritable and moody himself, he's started treating me sometimes much too haughtily now; first he whimpers and wants to embrace me, then he suddenly begins to humiliate me and scornfully jeer at me; well, then I'll deliberately stick my skirt out, heh, heh! Good-bye, Prince, for I am obviously keeping you and interfering, so to speak, in your most interesting feelings . . ."

"But, for God's sake, keep it a secret!"

"With quiet steps, sir, with quiet steps!"

But though the matter was ended, the prince was left almost more preoccupied than before. He waited impatiently for tomorrow's meeting with the general.

IV

THE APPOINTED HOUR was twelve, but the prince was quite unexpectedly late. Returning home, he found the general there waiting for him. He noticed at first glance that he was displeased, perhaps precisely at being forced to wait. Apologizing, the prince hastened to sit down, but somehow with a strange timidity, as if his visitor were made of porcelain and he was in constant fear of breaking him. He had never felt timid with the general before, and it had not occurred to him to feel timid. The prince soon discerned that this was now a completely different man than the day before: instead of perturbation and absentmindedness, he showed a sort of extraordinary restraint; one might have concluded that this was a man who was ultimately resolved on something. His composure, however, was more ostensible than real. But in any case the visitor was nobly casual, though with restrained dignity; at first he even treated the prince as if with an air of some condescension—precisely the way certain proud but unjustly offended people are sometimes nobly casual. He spoke gently, though not without a certain ruefulness in his speech.

"Your book, which I borrowed from you the other day," he nodded significantly at the book he had brought with him, which lay on the table. "Many thanks."

"Ah, yes; you read that article, General? How did you like it? Curious, isn't it?" The prince was glad of the possibility of quickly beginning a somewhat extraneous conversation.

"Curious, perhaps, but crude and, of course, absurd. And maybe a lie at every step."

The general spoke with aplomb and even drew the words out slightly.

"Ah, it's such a simple-hearted story; the story of an old soldier, an eyewitness to the French occupation of Moscow; there are charming things in it. Besides, any memoirs by eyewitnesses are precious, whoever the eyewitness may be. Isn't it true?"

"In the editor's place, I wouldn't have published it; as for memoirs by eyewitnesses in general, people sooner believe a crude liar, but an amusing one, than a man of dignity and merit. I know certain memoirs about the year twelve[7] that . . . I've taken a decision, Prince, I am leaving this house—the house of Mr. Lebedev."

The general gave the prince a meaningful look.

"You have your own quarters in Pavlovsk, at . . . at your daughter's . . ." said the prince, not knowing what to say. He remembered that the general had come for advice about a matter of extreme importance on which his destiny depended.

"At my wife's; in other words, my home and that of my daughter."

"Forgive me, I . . ."

"I am leaving Lebedev's house, my dear Prince, because I have broken with that man; I broke with him yesterday evening, with regret that it was not sooner. I demand respect, Prince, and I wish to receive it even from those persons to whom I have, so to speak, given my heart. I often give my heart to people, Prince, and I am almost always deceived. That man was unworthy of my gift."

"There is much disorder in him," the prince observed with restraint, "and certain traits . . . but amidst all that one notices a heart, and a cunning, but sometimes also amusing, mind."

The refinement of the expressions and the deferential tone obviously flattered the general, though he still sometimes glanced around with unexpected mistrust. But the prince's tone was so natural and sincere that it was impossible to doubt it.

"That there are also good qualities in him," the general picked up, "I was the first to proclaim, on the point of granting that individual my friendship. I do not need his home and his hospitality, because I have a family of my own. I do not justify my vices; I am intemperate; I drank with him, and now perhaps I lament it. But it was not for the drinking alone (forgive me, Prince, the crude candor of an irritated man), not for the drinking alone that I became connected with him. I was precisely charmed by his qualities, as you say. But all things have their limits, even qualities; and if he is suddenly bold enough to assure me to my face that in the year twelve, while still a child, he lost his left leg and buried it in the Vagankovsky Cemetery in Moscow, that goes over the line, that reveals disrespect, that shows insolence . . ."

"Maybe it was only a joke for the sake of a merry laugh."

"I understand, sir. An innocent lie for the sake of a merry laugh, even a crude one, is not offensive to the human heart. A man may lie, if you wish, out of friendship alone, to give pleasure to his interlocutor; but if disrespect shows through it, if that disrespect is precisely meant to indicate that the connection is burdensome, then the only thing that remains for a noble man is to turn away and break off the connection, showing the offender his true place."

The general even became red as he spoke.

"But Lebedev couldn't have been in Moscow in the year twelve; he's too young for that; it's ridiculous."

"First, there's that; but let us suppose he could already have been born then; but how can he assure me to my face that the French chasseur aimed his cannon at him and shot his leg off, just for fun; that he picked the leg up and brought it home, and then buried it in the Vagankovsky Cemetery, saying that he put a tombstone over it with an inscription on one side: 'Here lies the leg of Collegiate Secretary Lebedev,' and on the other: 'Rest, dear dust, till the gladsome morning,'[8] and, finally, that every year he has a panikhida[9] served for it (which is a sacrilege), and that he goes to Moscow every year for that. As proof, he invites me to Moscow, in order to show me the grave and even that very French cannon, which was taken captive, in the Kremlin; he insists it's the eleventh from the gate, a French falconet of an old design."

"And what's more he has both legs intact, in plain sight!" laughed the prince. "I assure you, it's an innocent joke; don't be angry."

"But allow me some understanding, too, sir; concerning legs in plain sight—that, let us suppose, is not entirely implausible; he assures me that it is Chernosvitov's leg . . ."[10]

"Ah, yes, they say one can dance with Chernosvitov's leg."

"I'm perfectly aware of that, sir; when Chernosvitov invented his leg, he came first thing to show it to me. But Chernosvitov's leg was invented incomparably later . . . And besides, he insists that even his late wife, during the whole course of their married life, never knew that he, her husband, had a wooden leg. 'If you,' he said, when I pointed all these absurdities out to him, 'if you could be Napoleon's chamber-page in the year twelve, then you can also allow me to bury my leg in the Vagankovsky Cemetery.'"

"And were you really . . ." the prince began and became embarrassed.

The general gave the prince a decidedly haughty and all but mocking look.

"Finish what you were saying, Prince," he drew out especially smoothly, "finish what you were saying. I'm indulgent, you may say everything: admit that you find the very thought ridiculous of seeing before you a man in his present humiliation and . . . uselessness, and hearing at the same time that this man was a personal witness . . . of great events. Is there anything that *he* has managed to . . . gossip to you about?"

"No, I haven't heard anything from Lebedev—if it's Lebedev you're speaking of . . ."

"Hm, I thought the opposite. As a matter of fact, our conversation yesterday began on the occasion of this . . . strange article in the *Archive*.[11] I pointed out its absurdity, and since I myself was a personal witness . . . you're smiling, Prince, you're looking into my face?"

"N-no, I . . ."

"I look young for my age," the general drew the words out, "but I'm slightly older than I actually seem to be. In the year twelve I was ten or eleven. I don't know my own age very well myself. My papers lower it; and I have had the weakness of lowering my age in the course of my life."

"I assure you, General, that I do not find it at all strange that you were in Moscow in the year twelve and . . . of course, you have things to tell . . . as have all who were there. One of our autobiographers[12] begins his book precisely by telling how, in the year twelve, he, a nursing infant, was given bread by the French soldiers in Moscow."

"You see," the general approved condescendingly, "my case is, of course, out of the ordinary, but neither is there anything extraordinary in it. Quite often the truth seems impossible. A chamber-page! It's a strange thing to hear, of course. But the adventures of a ten-year-old child may be explained precisely by his age. It wouldn't have happened to a fifteen-year-old, and that is absolutely so, because if I had been fifteen years old, I wouldn't have run away from our wooden house in Old Basmannaya Street on the day Napoleon entered Moscow, away from my mother, who was too late in leaving Moscow[13] and trembling with fear. If I had been fifteen, I would have turned coward, but, being ten, I feared nothing and pushed my way through the crowd up to the very porch of the palace, just as Napoleon was dismounting from his horse."

"Unquestionably, you have made an excellent observation, that precisely at ten one might not be afraid . . ." the prince yessed him shyly, pained by the thought that he was about to blush.

"Unquestionably, and it all happened so simply and naturally, as things can only happen in reality; if a novelist were to turn to it, he would heap up all sorts of incredible tales."

"Oh, that's quite so!" cried the prince. "I was struck by that same thought, and quite recently. I know about an actual murder over a watch, it's in all the newspapers now. If a writer had invented it, the critics and connoisseurs of popular life would have shouted at once that it was incredible; but reading it in the newspapers as a fact, you feel that it is precisely from such facts that you learn about Russian reality. That is a wonderful observation, General!" the prince concluded warmly, terribly glad that he could evade the color appearing on his face.

"Isn't it true? Isn't it true?" cried the general, his eyes even flashing with pleasure. "A boy, a child, who has no understanding of danger, makes his way through the crowd, to see the splendor, the uniforms, the suite, and, finally, the great man, about whom he has heard so much shouting. Because at that time everyone, for several years in a row, had been shouting about him alone. The world was filled with his name; I had, so to speak, sucked it in with my mother's milk. Napoleon, passing within two steps of me, happened to catch my glance; I was dressed like a young gentleman, in very good clothes. I was the only one dressed like that in the crowd, you'll agree . . ."

"Unquestionably, that must have struck him and proved to him that not everybody had left, that some of the nobility had stayed with their children."

"Precisely, precisely! He wanted to attract the boyars![14] When he cast his eagle's gaze on me, my eyes must have flashed in response to him. '*Voilà un garçon bien éveillé! Qui est ton père?*'* I answered at once, almost breathless with excitement: 'A general who died on the battlefields of his fatherland.' '*Le fils d'un boyard et d'un brave par-dessus le marché! J'aime les boyards. M'aimes-tu, petit?*'† To this quick question I replied as quickly: 'The Russian heart can discern a great man even in the enemy of his fatherland!' That is, as a matter of fact, I don't remember whether I literally expressed myself that way . . . I was a child . . . but that must have been the sense of it! Napoleon was struck, he pondered and said to his suite: 'I like this boy's pride! But if all Russians think as this child does, then . . .' He didn't finish and went into the palace. I at once mingled with his suite and ran after him. In the suite they already stepped back for me and looked on me as a favorite. But all that merely flashed by . . . I remember only that, on going into the first hall, the emperor suddenly stopped before the portrait of the empress Catherine, looked at it thoughtfully for a long time, and finally said: 'That was a great woman!'—and walked on. Two days later everybody already knew me in the palace and in the Kremlin and called me '*le petit boyard.*' I went home only to sleep. At home they nearly lost their minds. Two days after that Napoleon's chamber-page, the Baron de Bazancourt,[15] died from the hardships of the campaign. Napoleon remembered about me; I was taken, brought there without any explanations, the uniform of the deceased, a boy of about twelve, was tried on me, and when they brought me before the emperor in the uniform, and he nodded his head at me, they announced to me that I had been granted a favor and made his majesty's chamber-page. I was glad. I actually felt a

---

*There's a sprightly lad! Who is your father?
†The son of a boyar and of a brave man to boot! I like the boyars. Do you like me, little boy?

warm sympathy for him, and had for a long time . . . well, and besides, you'll agree, there was the splendid uniform, which means a lot for a child . . . I went about in a dark green tailcoat, with long and narrow tails, gold buttons, red piping on the gold-embroidered sleeves, a high, stiff, open collar, embroidered with gold, and embroidered coattails; white, close-fitting chamois breeches, a white silk waistcoat, silk stockings, and buckled shoes . . . or, during the emperor's promenades on horseback, if I was in his suite, high top-boots. Though the situation was not brilliant, and there was already a presentiment of great calamities, etiquette was observed as far as possible, and the more punctually the stronger the presentiment of those calamities."

"Yes, of course . . ." murmured the prince, looking almost lost, "your memoirs would be . . . extremely interesting."

The general, of course, was repeating what he had told Lebedev the day before, and therefore repeating it very smoothly; but here again he mistrustfully glanced sidelong at the prince.

"My memoirs," he spoke with redoubled pride, "to write my memoirs? That doesn't tempt me, Prince! If you wish, my memoirs have already been written, but . . . but they are lying in my desk. Let them, when earth has closed my eyes, let them appear then and, undoubtedly, be translated into other languages, not for their literary merit, no, but for the importance of the tremendous facts of which I was an evident witness, though a child; but all the more so: as a child I penetrated into the very intimate, so to speak, bedroom of 'the great man'! At night I heard the groaning of this 'giant in misfortune,' he could not be ashamed of groaning and weeping before a child, though I already understood that the cause of his suffering was the silence of the emperor Alexander."

"Yes, he did write letters . . . with offers of peace . . ." the prince agreed timidly.

"As a matter of fact, we do not know precisely with what offers he wrote, but he wrote every day, every hour, letter after letter! He was terribly worried. Once, during the night, when we were alone, I rushed to him in tears (oh, yes, I loved him!): 'Ask forgiveness, ask forgiveness of the emperor Alexander!' I cried to him. That is, I ought to have said: 'Make peace with the emperor Alexander,' but, being a child, I naïvely spoke my whole mind. 'Oh, my little one!' he answered—he was pacing up and down the room—'oh, my little one!' It was as if he didn't understand then that I was ten years old, and he even liked talking with me. 'Oh, my little one, I am ready to kiss the feet of the emperor Alexander, but as for the Prussian king, as for the Austrian emperor, oh, they have my eternal hatred, and . . . finally . . . you don't understand anything about politics!' It was as if he suddenly remembered whom he was talking with, and he fell silent, but his eyes shot fire for a long time. Well, if I were to describe all these facts—and I was witness to greater facts—if I were to publish them now, and all these critics, all these literary vanities, all these jealousies, parties, and . . . no, sir, I humbly thank you!"

"Concerning parties, your observation is, of course, correct, and I agree with you," the prince replied quietly, after a short silence. "Quite recently I also read a book by Charras[16] about the Waterloo campaign. The book is obviously a serious one, and the specialists maintain that it is written extremely knowledgeably. But a joy in Napoleon's humiliation shows through on every page, and if it were possible to dispute even any little sign of talent in Napoleon's other campaigns, it seems Charras would be extremely glad of it; and that is not a good thing in such a serious work, because it's a party spirit. Were you kept very busy then by your service to the . . . emperor?"

The general was in raptures. The prince's observation, by its seriousness and simple-heartedness, dispelled the last remnants of his mistrust.

"Charras! Oh, I was indignant myself! I wrote to him at the time, but . . . as a matter of fact, I don't remember now . . . You ask whether my service kept me busy? Oh, no! They called me a chamber-page, but even then I did not regard it as serious. What's more, Napoleon very soon lost all hope of drawing any Russians to him, and, of course, would have forgotten about me as well, having drawn me to him for political reasons, had it not been . . . had it not been for his personal love for me, I say it boldly now. My heart also drew me to him. My service was not a required thing; I had to come to the palace occasionally and . . . accompany the emperor during his promenades on horseback, and that's all. I was a decent horseman. He used to go out for a ride before dinner; in his suite usually there was Davout, myself, the mameluke Rustan. . ."

"Constant,"[17] the prince suddenly came out with for some reason.

"N-no, Constant wasn't there then; he had gone then with a letter . . . to the empress Josephine;[18] but instead of him there were two orderlies, several Polish uhlans . . . well, that was all the suite, except for the generals, naturally, and some marshals, whom Napoleon took along to examine the terrain, the disposition of the army, to discuss . . . Most often it was Davout who accompanied him, I remember it as if it were yesterday: an enormous, corpulent, cool-headed man in spectacles, with a strange gaze. The emperor most often discussed things with him. He valued his thoughts. I remember them holding a special council for several days; Davout used to come in the morning and in the evening, and often they even argued; in the end, it seemed that Napoleon began to agree. The two of them were in the study, I was the third, almost unnoticed by them. Suddenly Napoleon's gaze happens to fall on me, a strange thought flashes in his eyes. 'Child!' he suddenly says to me, 'what do you think: if I embrace Orthodoxy and free your slaves, will the Russians follow me or not?' 'Never!' I cried in indignation. Napoleon was struck. 'In this child's eyes flashing with patriotism,' he said, 'I have read the opinion of the whole Russian people. Enough, Davout! It's all fantasies! Tell me your other plan.' "

"Yes, but that plan was a strong thought as well!" said the prince, obviously interested. "So you ascribe that project to Davout?"

"At least they discussed it together. Of course it was a Napoleonic thought, an eagle's thought, but the other project was also a thought . . . It was that same famous *'conseil du lion,'** as Napoleon himself called this advice of Davout's. It consisted of locking themselves in the Kremlin with the entire army, building a lot of barracks, entrenching themselves behind fortifications, positioning the cannon, killing as many horses as possible and pickling the meat; of procuring or pillaging as much bread as possible and weathering the winter; and of breaking through the Russians in the spring. This plan strongly appealed to Napoleon. We went around the walls of the Kremlin every day, and he pointed out where to demolish, where to build, where there would be a lunette, where a ravelin, where a row of blockhouses—the eye, the speed, the stroke! Everything was finally decided; Davout kept pestering him to make the final decision. Again they were alone, and I was the third. Again Napoleon paced the room, his arms crossed. I couldn't tear my eyes from his face; my heart was pounding. 'I'm off,' said Davout. 'Where to?' asked Napoleon. 'To pickle horses,' said Davout. Napoleon gave a start; destiny was being decided. 'Little one,' he

*Lion's advice.

said to me suddenly, 'what do you think of our intentions?' To be sure, he asked me just so, as a man of the greatest mind occasionally resorts to heads or tails in the last moment. Instead of Napoleon, I turn to Davout and say, as if inspired: 'You'd better go back where you came from, General!' The plan was destroyed. Davout shrugged and whispered on his way out: *'Bah! Il devient superstit-ieux!'* * And the next day the retreat was announced."

"All that is extremely interesting," the prince said terribly quietly, "if that's how it all was . . . that is, I mean to say . . ." he hastened to correct himself.

"Oh, Prince!" cried the general, so intoxicated by his story that he might not have been able to stop now even before the greatest imprudence, "you say: 'It all was!' But there was more, I assure you, there was much more! These are merely facts, small, political facts. But I repeat to you, I was witness to the nightly tears and groans of this great man, and no one saw it except me! Towards the end, true, he no longer wept, there were no tears, only an occasional groan; but his face seemed more and more veiled in gloom. As if eternity were already overshadowing him with its dark wing. Sometimes, at night, we spent whole hours together alone, silent—the mameluke Rustan would be snoring in the next room; the man was a very sound sleeper. 'But he is faithful to me and my dynasty,' Napoleon used to say of him. Once I felt terribly grieved, and he suddenly noticed tears in my eyes; he looked at me with tenderness: 'You pity me!' he cried. 'You, little one, and perhaps yet another child pities me, my son, *le roi de Rome*; †[19] the rest all hate me, all of them, and my brothers will be the first to sell me in my misfortune!' I burst into sobs and rushed to him; here he, too, could not restrain himself; we embraced each other and our tears mingled. 'Write, write a letter to the empress Josephine!' I said through my sobs. Napoleon gave a start, reflected, and said to me: 'You have reminded me of the third heart that loves me; thank you, my friend!' He sat down at once and wrote that letter to Josephine which was sent off with Constant the next morning."

"You did a beautiful thing," said the prince. "Amidst his wicked thoughts you prompted him to a kind feeling."

"Precisely, Prince, and how beautifully you explain it, in con-formity with your own heart!" the general cried rapturously, and,

*Bah! He's becoming superstitious!
†The king of Rome.

strangely enough, real tears glistened in his eyes. "Yes, Prince, that was a great spectacle! And, you know, I nearly followed him to Paris and, of course, would have shared with him 'the torrid prison isle,'[20] but, alas! our fates were separated! We parted ways: he went to the torrid isle, where once at least, in a moment of terrible sorrow, he may have remembered the tears of the poor boy who embraced and forgave him in Moscow; while I was sent to the cadet corps, where I found nothing but drill, the coarseness of my comrades, and . . . Alas! Everything went to wrack and ruin! 'I do not want to part you from your mother and will not take you with me!' he said to me on the day of the retreat, 'but I would like to do something for you.' He was about to mount his horse. 'Write something in my sister's album as a souvenir,' I said timidly, because he was very upset and gloomy. He went back, asked for a pen, took the album. 'How old is your sister?' he asked me, pen in hand. 'Three,' I replied. '*Petite fille alors.*'* And he scribbled in the album:

> '*Ne mentez jamais!*
> *Napoléon, votre ami sincère.*'†

"Such advice and at such a moment, you must agree, Prince!"

"Yes, it is portentous."

"That page, in a gilded frame, under glass, hung in my sister's drawing room all her life, in the most conspicuous place, right up to her death—she died in childbirth. Where it is now, I don't know . . . but . . . ah, my God! It's already two o'clock! I've kept you so long, Prince! It's unforgivable!"

The general got up from his chair.

"Oh, on the contrary!" the prince mumbled. "You've diverted me and . . . finally . . . it's so interesting; I'm so grateful to you!"

"Prince!" said the general, again pressing his hand painfully and looking at him intently, with flashing eyes, as if suddenly recollecting himself and stunned by some unexpected thought, "Prince! You are so kind, so simple-hearted, that I sometimes even feel sorry for you. I look upon you with tenderness; oh, God bless you! May your life begin and blossom . . . in love. Mine is over! Oh, forgive me, forgive me!"

He left quickly, covering his face with his hands. The prince could not doubt the sincerity of his emotion. He also realized that

---

*A little girl, then.
†Never tell a lie. Napoleon, your sincere friend.

the old man had left intoxicated by his success; but all the same he had a presentiment that he was one of that category of liars who, though they lie to the point of sensuality and even self-forgetfulness, at the highest point of their intoxication suspect to themselves all the same that people do not and even cannot believe them. In his present state, the old man might recollect himself, become ashamed beyond measure, suspect the prince of an excessive compassion for him, feel insulted. "Didn't I do worse by driving him to such inspiration?" the prince worried and suddenly could not help himself and laughed terribly, for about ten minutes. He was about to reproach himself for this laughter; but he understood at once that there was nothing to reproach himself for, because he felt a boundless pity for the general.

His presentiment came true. That evening he received a strange note, brief but resolute. The general informed him that he was also parting with him forever, that he respected him and was grateful to him, but that even from him he would not accept "tokens of compassion humiliating to the dignity of a man already unfortunate without that." When the prince heard that the old man had locked himself up at Nina Alexandrovna's, he almost stopped worrying about him. But we have already seen that the general had also caused some sort of trouble at Lizaveta Prokofyevna's. We cannot go into detail here, but will note briefly that the essence of their meeting consisted in the general's frightening Lizaveta Prokofyevna and driving her to indignation with his bitter allusions to Ganya. He had been led out in disgrace. That was why he had spent such a night and such a morning, had become definitively cracked and had rushed out to the street almost in a state of insanity.

Kolya did not fully understand the matter yet and even hoped to win out by severity.

"Well, where are we going to drag ourselves now, General?" he said. "You don't want to go to the prince, you've quarreled with Lebedev, you have no money, and I never have any: so here we are in the street without a shirt to our name."

"It's better than having a shirt and no name," the general murmured. "This pun of mine . . . was received with raptures . . . a company of officers . . . in the year forty-four . . . Eighteen . . . hundred . . . and forty-four, yes! . . . I don't remember . . . Oh, don't remind me, don't remind me! 'Where is my youth, where is my freshness!' So exclaimed . . . Who exclaimed that, Kolya?"

"It's from Gogol, in *Dead Souls*,[21] papa," Kolya replied and gave his father a frightened sidelong glance.

"Dead souls! Oh, yes, dead! When you bury me, write on my tombstone: 'Here lies a dead soul!'

Disgrace pursues me!

Who said that, Kolya?"

"I don't know, papa."

"There was no Eropegov! No Eroshka Eropegov! . . ." he cried out in a frenzy, stopping in the street, "and that is my son, my own son! Eropegov, who for eleven months was like a brother to me, for whom I'd have gone to a duel . . . Prince Vygoretsky, our captain, says to him over a bottle: 'You, Grisha, where did you get your Anna,[22] tell me that?' 'On the battlefields of my fatherland, that's where!' 'Bravo, Grisha!' I shout. Well, that led to a duel, and then he married . . . Marya Petrovna Su . . . Sutugin and was killed on the battlefield . . . The bullet ricocheted off the cross on my chest and hit him right in the forehead. 'I'll never forget!' he cried and fell on the spot. I . . . I served honestly, Kolya; I served nobly, but disgrace—'disgrace pursues me'! You and Nina will come to my little grave . . . 'Poor Nina!' I used to call her that, Kolya, long ago, in the beginning, and she so loved . . . Nina, Nina! What have I done to your life! What can you love me for, patient soul! Your mother is an angelic soul, do you hear, Kolya, an angelic soul!"

"I know that, papa. Papa, dearest, let's go home to mama! She ran after us! Well, why are you standing there? As if you don't understand . . . What are you crying for?"

Kolya himself was crying and kissing his father's hands.

"You're kissing my hands, mine!"

"Yes, yours, yours. What's so surprising? Well, what are you doing howling in the middle of the street—and he calls himself a general, a military man! Well, come on!"

"God bless you, my dear boy, for showing respect to a disgraceful—yes! to a disgraceful old fellow, your father . . . may you also have such a son . . . *le roi de Rome* . . . Oh, 'a curse, a curse upon this house!'"

"But what is really going on here!" Kolya suddenly seethed. "What's the matter? Why don't you want to go back home now? What are you losing your mind for?"

"I'll explain, I'll explain it to you . . . I'll tell you everything;

don't shout, they'll hear you . . . *le roi de Rome* . . . Oh, I'm sick, I'm sad!

Nanny, where's your grave![23]

Who exclaimed that, Kolya?"

"I don't know, I don't know who exclaimed it! Let's go home right now, right now! I'll give Ganka a beating, if I have to . . . where are you going now?"

But the general was pulling him towards the porch of a nearby house.

"Where are you going? That's not our porch!"

The general sat down on the porch and kept pulling Kolya towards him by the hand.

"Bend down, bend down!" he murmured. "I'll tell you everything . . . disgrace . . . bend down . . . your ear, I'll tell it in your ear . . ."

"What's the matter!" Kolya was terribly frightened, but offered his ear anyway.

"*Le roi de Rome* . . ." the general whispered, also as if he were trembling all over.

"What? . . . What have you got to do with *le roi de Rome*? . . . Why?"

"I . . . I . . ." the general whispered again, clutching "his boy's" shoulder tighter and tighter, "I . . . want . . . I'll tell you . . . everything, Marya, Marya . . . Petrovna Su-su-su . . ."

Kolya tore himself free, seized the general by the shoulders, and looked at him like a crazy man. The old man turned purple, his lips became blue, small spasms kept passing over his face. Suddenly he bent over and quietly began to collapse onto Kolya's arm.

"A stroke!" the boy cried out for the whole street to hear, realizing at last what was wrong.

V

To TELL THE TRUTH, Varvara Ardalionovna, in her conversation with her brother, had slightly exaggerated the accuracy of her information about the prince's proposal to Aglaya Epanchin. Perhaps, as a perspicacious woman, she had divined what was to happen in the near future; perhaps, being upset that her dream (which, in truth, she did not believe in herself) had been scattered like smoke, she, as a human being, could not deny herself the pleasure of pouring more venom into her brother's heart by exaggerating the calamity, though, incidentally, she loved him sincerely and compassionately. In any case, she had not been able to get such accurate information from her friends, the Epanchin girls; there had been only hints, words unspoken, omissions, enigmas. And perhaps Aglaya's sisters had also let certain things slip on purpose, in order to find something out from Varvara Ardalionovna; and it might have been, finally, that they were unable to deny themselves the feminine pleasure of teasing a friend slightly, even a childhood one: it could not have been that in so long a time they had not glimpsed at least a small edge of her intentions.

On the other hand, the prince, too, though he was perfectly right in assuring Lebedev that there was nothing he could tell him and that precisely nothing special had happened to him, was also, perhaps, mistaken. In fact, something very strange seemed to have occurred with everyone: nothing had happened, and at the same time it was as if a great deal had happened. It was this last that Varvara Ardalionovna had divined with her sure feminine instinct.

How it happened, however, that everyone at the Epanchins' suddenly came up at once with one and the same notion that something major was occurring with Aglaya and that her fate was being decided—is very difficult to present in an orderly way. But this notion had no sooner flashed in everyone at once, than they all immediately insisted at once that they had perceived the whole thing long ago, and it had all been clearly foreseen; that it had all been clear since the "poor knight," and even before, only then they had not wanted to believe in such an absurdity. So the sisters insisted; and, of course, Lizaveta Prokofyevna had foreseen and known everything before everyone else, and she had long had "an aching heart," but—long or not—the notion of the prince now suddenly went too much against the grain, essentially because it disconcerted her. A question presented itself here that had to be resolved immediately; yet not only was it impossible to resolve it, but poor Lizaveta Prokofyevna could not even pose the question to herself with full clarity, try as she might. It was a difficult matter: "Was the prince good or not? Was the whole thing good or not? If it was not good (which was unquestionable), what precisely was not good about it? And if it was good (which was also possible), then, again, what was good about it?" The father of the family himself, Ivan Fyodorovich, was naturally the first to be surprised, but then suddenly confessed that "by God, he, too, had fancied something of the sort all along; every now and then he suddenly seemed to fancy it!" He fell silent at once under the terrible gaze of his spouse, but he fell silent in the morning, while in the evening, alone with his spouse and forced to speak again, he suddenly and, as it were, with particular pertness, expressed several unexpected thoughts: "Though, essentially, what's wrong? . . ." (Silence.) "Of course, this is all very strange, provided it's true, and he doesn't dispute it, but . . ." (Again silence.) "And on the other hand, if you look at things directly, the prince is a wonderful fellow, by God, and . . . and, and—well, finally, the name, our family name, all this will have the look, so to speak, of an upholding of the family name, which has been lowered in the eyes of society, because, looked at from this point of view, that is, because . . . of course, society; society is society; but still the prince is not without a fortune, even if it's only so much. He also has . . . and . . . and . . . and . . ." (A prolonged silence and a decided misfire.) Having listened to her spouse, Lizaveta Prokofyevna went completely overboard.

In her opinion, everything that had happened was "unpardonable and even criminal nonsense, a fantastic picture, stupid and absurd!" First of all there was the fact that "this wretched princeling is a sick idiot, second of all he's a fool, who neither knows society nor has any place in society: to whom can he be shown, where can he be tucked in? He's some sort of unpardonable democrat, without even the least rank, and . . . and . . . what will old Belokonsky say? And is this, is this the sort of husband we imagined and intended for Aglaya?" The last argument was, naturally, the most important. The mother's heart trembled at the thought, bled and wept, though at the same time something stirred in that heart which suddenly said to her: "And what makes the prince not the sort you want?" Well, it was these objections against her own heart that were most troublesome for Lizaveta Prokofyevna.

Aglaya's sisters for some reason liked the notion of the prince; it did not even seem very strange to them; in short, they might even suddenly turn out to be completely on his side. But they both decided to keep silent. It had been noted once and for all in the family that the more stubborn and persistent Lizaveta Prokofyevna's objections and retorts became, on some general and disputed family point, the more it could serve them all as a sign that she might be about to agree on that point. Alexandra Ivanovna, however, could never be completely silent. Having long since acknowledged her as her advisor, the mother constantly summoned her now and asked for her opinions, and above all her memories—that is: "How had it all happened? Why had no one seen it? Why had there been no talk then? What had this nasty 'poor knight' signified then? Why was it that she, Lizaveta Prokofyevna, was the only one doomed to worry about everyone, to notice and foresee everything, while all the rest were merely—woolgathering?" etc., etc. Alexandra Ivanovna was cautious at first and only observed that she thought her father's idea was quite correct, that in the eyes of society the choice of Prince Myshkin as a husband for one of the Epanchin girls might appear very satisfactory. She gradually became excited and added that the prince was by no means a "little fool" and never had been, and as for his significance—God alone knew what the significance of a respectable man would consist of in our Russia a few years hence: success in the service, as used to be necessary, or something else? To all this the mother immediately rapped out that Alexandra was "a freethinker and that it was all their cursed woman question." Half an hour later she went to the city, and from there to Kamenny Island, in order to catch Princess Belokonsky, who, as if on purpose, happened to be in Petersburg just then, though she would be leaving soon. The princess was Aglaya's godmother.

"Old" Belokonsky listened to all the feverish and desperate confessions of Lizaveta Prokofyevna and was not touched in the least by the tears of the disconcerted mother of the family, but even looked at her mockingly. She was a terrible despot; in friendship, even an old friendship, she could not bear equality, and she decidedly looked upon Lizaveta Prokofyevna as her protégée, just as thirty-five years ago, and she simply could not be reconciled with the sharpness and independence of her character. She noticed, among other things, that "it seemed they had all rushed too far ahead there, as was their habit, and made a mountain out of a molehill; that listen as she might, she was not convinced that anything serious had actually happened; that it might be better to wait until something did; that the prince was, in her opinion, a respectable young man, though sick, strange, and much too insignificant. The worst thing was that he openly kept a woman." Lizaveta Prokofyevna realized very well that Belokonsky was a bit cross about the unsuccess of Evgeny Pavlovich, whom she had recommended. She returned home to Pavlovsk still more irritated than when she had left, and everyone immediately got it from her, above all because they had "lost their minds," because decidedly nobody else did things the way they did them; and "what's the hurry? What has happened? However much I look at it, I can in no way conclude that anything has actually happened! Wait until something does! No matter what Ivan Fyodorovich may have fancied, are we going to make a mountain out of a molehill?" etc., etc.

The result, therefore, was that they needed to calm down, watch cool-headedly, and wait. But, alas, the calm did not hold out for even ten minutes. The first blow to cool-headedness came from the news of what had happened while the mother absented herself to Kamenny Island. (Lizaveta Prokofyevna's trip took place the morning after the prince had come calling past midnight instead of before ten.) The sisters answered their mother's impatient questioning in great detail, and said, first of all, that "precisely nothing, it seemed, had happened while she was away," that the prince came, that Aglaya took a long time, half an hour, before coming out to him, and when she did come out, suggested at once that she and the prince play chess; that the prince did not know the first thing about chess, and Aglaya beat him at once; she became very merry and shamed the prince terribly for his lack of skill, and laughed at him terribly, so that the prince was a pity to see. Then she suggested that they play cards, a game of "fools." But here it turned out quite the opposite: the prince proved to be as good at "fools" as . . . as a professor; he played masterfully; Aglaya cheated, put cards back, stole his own tricks before his very eyes, and all the same he left her each time as the "fool"; five times in a row. Aglaya flew into a rage, even quite forgot herself; she said so many impudent and sarcastic things to the prince that he even stopped laughing, and he turned quite pale when she told him, finally, that "she would not set foot in this room while he was sitting there, and that it was even shameless on his part to call on them, and in the night at that, past midnight, *after all that had happened*." She then slammed the door and left. The prince went out as if from a funeral, despite all their attempts to comfort him. Suddenly, fifteen minutes after the prince left, Aglaya came running down to the terrace from upstairs, and in such a hurry that she did not even wipe her eyes, which were wet with tears. She came running down because Kolya arrived and brought a hedgehog. They all started looking at the hedgehog; to their questions, Kolya explained that the hedgehog was not his, and that he was now walking with his comrade, another schoolboy, Kostya Lebedev, who had stayed outside and was embarrassed to come in because he was carrying an axe; that they had bought both the hedgehog and the axe from a peasant they had met. The peasant was selling the hedgehog and took fifty kopecks for it, and then they persuaded him to sell the axe as well, because it was an opportunity, and also a very good axe. Here Aglaya suddenly began pestering Kolya terribly to sell her the hedgehog at once, turned inside out, even called Kolya "dear." Kolya would not agree for a long time, but finally gave in and called Kostya Lebedev, who indeed came in carrying the axe and feeling very embarrassed. But here it suddenly turned out that the hedgehog did not belong to them at all, but to a third boy, Petrov, who had given them money to buy Schlosser's *History*[24] from some fourth boy, who, being in need of money, was selling it at a bargain price; that they set out to buy Schlosser's *History*, but could not help themselves and bought the hedgehog, and therefore both the hedgehog and the axe belonged to that third boy, to whom they were now taking them in place of Schlosser's *History*. But Aglaya pestered them so much that they finally decided to sell her the hedgehog. As soon as Aglaya got the hedgehog, she put it into a wicker basket with Kolya's help, covered it with a napkin, and started asking Kolya to go at once and, without stopping anywhere, take the hedgehog to the prince on her behalf, with the request that he accept it as "a token of her profoundest respect." Kolya gladly agreed and promised to deliver it, but immediately began to pester her: "What was the meaning of the hedgehog and of such a present?" Aglaya replied that that was none of his business. He replied that he was sure it contained some allegory. Aglaya became angry and snapped at him that he was a little brat and nothing more. Kolya at once retorted that if it were not for his respect for the woman in her, and for his own convictions on top of it, he would immediately prove to her that he knew how to respond to such insults. It ended, however, with Kolya delightedly going all the same to deliver the hedgehog, and Kostya Lebedev running after him; Aglaya could not help herself and, seeing Kolya swinging the basket too hard, shouted behind him from the terrace: "Please, Kolya dearest, don't drop it!"—as if she had not just quarreled with him; Kolya stopped and, also as if he had not just been quarreling, shouted with great readiness: "No, I won't drop it, Aglaya Ivanovna. Be completely assured!" and ran on at breakneck speed. After that Aglaya laughed terribly and ran to her room extremely pleased, and then was very cheerful all day.

This news completely dumbfounded Lizaveta Prokofyevna. One

might wonder, why so? But such, evidently, was the mood she had come to. Her anxiety was aroused to the utmost degree, and above all—the hedgehog; what was the meaning of the hedgehog? Was it prearranged? Did it imply something? Was it some sort of sign? A telegram? What's more, poor Ivan Fyodorovich, who happened to be present at the interrogation, spoiled things completely with his answer. In his opinion, there was no telegram, and the hedgehog was "just a simple hedgehog—and perhaps also meant friendship, the forgetting of offenses, and reconciliation; in short, it was all a prank, but in any case innocent and pardonable."

Let us note parenthetically that he had guessed perfectly right. The prince, having returned home from seeing Aglaya, mocked and driven out by her, had been sitting for half an hour in the darkest despair, when Kolya suddenly arrived with the hedgehog. At once the sky cleared. It was as if the prince rose from the dead; he questioned Kolya, hanging on his every word, repeated his questions ten times, laughed like a child, and kept pressing the hands of the two laughing and bright-eyed boys. So it turned out that Aglaya had forgiven him, and the prince could go to see her again that very evening, and for him that was not only the main thing, but even everything.

"What children we still are, Kolya! and . . . and . . . how good it is that we're children!" he finally exclaimed in ecstasy.

"She's quite simply in love with you, Prince, that's all!" Kolya replied imposingly and with authority.

The prince blushed, but this time he said nothing, and Kolya only guffawed and clapped his hands; a minute later the prince, too, burst out laughing, and then right until evening he kept looking at his watch every five minutes, to see how much time had passed and how much remained till evening.

But her mood got the upper hand: Lizaveta Prokofyevna was finally unable to help herself and succumbed to a hysterical moment. Despite all the objections of her husband and daughters, she immediately sent for Aglaya, in order to put the ultimate question to her and get from her the most clear and ultimate answer. "So as to be done with it all at once, and get it off my shoulders, and never think of it again!" "Otherwise," she announced, "I won't survive till evening!" And only then did they all realize what a muddle things had been brought to. Apart from feigned astonishment, indignation, laughter, and mockery of the prince and all her questioners, they got nothing from Aglaya. Lizaveta Prokofyevna took to her bed and came out only for tea, by which time the prince was expected. She awaited the prince with trepidation, and when he arrived she nearly had hysterics.

And the prince himself came in timidly, all but gropingly, with a strange smile, peeking into all their eyes and as if asking them all a question, because Aglaya again was not in the room, which alarmed him at once. That evening there were no outsiders, only members of the family. Prince Shch. was still in Petersburg on business connected with Evgeny Pavlovich's uncle. "If only he could happen by and say something," Lizaveta Prokofyevna pined for him. Ivan Fyodorovich sat with an extremely preoccupied air; the sisters were serious and, as if on purpose, silent. Lizaveta Prokofyevna did not know how to begin the conversation. In the end she suddenly produced an energetic denunciation of the railways and looked at the prince in decided defiance.

Alas! Aglaya did not come out, and the prince was perishing. Nearly babbling and at a loss, he expressed the opinion that it would be of great utility to repair the railways, but Adelaida suddenly laughed, and the prince was again annihilated. At that very moment Aglaya came in calmly and gravely, gave the prince a ceremonious bow, and solemnly took the most conspicuous place at the round table. She looked questioningly at the prince. Everyone realized that the resolution of all misunderstandings was at hand.

"Did you receive my hedgehog?" she asked firmly and almost crossly.

"I did," the prince replied, blushing and with a sinking heart.

"Then explain immediately what you think about it. It is necessary for my mother's peace and that of the whole family."

"Listen, Aglaya . . ." the general suddenly began to worry.

"This, this is beyond all limits!" Lizaveta Prokofyevna suddenly became frightened of something.

"There aren't any limits here, *maman*," the daughter replied sternly and at once. "Today I sent the prince a hedgehog, and I wish to know his opinion. What is it, Prince?"

"You mean my opinion, Aglaya Ivanovna?"

"Of the hedgehog."

"That is . . . I think, Aglaya Ivanovna, that you want to know how I took . . . the hedgehog . . . or, better to say, how I looked at . . . this sending . . . of the hedgehog, that is . . . in which case, I suppose that . . . in a word . . ."

He ran out of breath and fell silent.

"Well, you haven't said much," Aglaya paused for five seconds. "Very well, I agree to drop the hedgehog; but I'm very glad that I can finally put an end to all the accumulated misunderstandings. Allow me, finally, to learn from you yourself and personally: are you proposing to me or not?"

"Oh, Lord!" escaped Lizaveta Prokofyevna.

The prince gave a start and drew back; Ivan Fyodorovich was dumbstruck; the sisters frowned.

"Don't lie, Prince, tell the truth. On account of you, I'm hounded by strange interrogations; are there any grounds for those interrogations? Well?"

"I haven't proposed to you, Aglaya Ivanovna," said the prince, suddenly becoming animated, "but . . . you know yourself how much I love you and believe in you . . . even now . . ."

"My question was: are you asking for my hand or not?"

"I am," the prince replied, his heart sinking.

A general and strong commotion followed.

"This is all not right, my dear friend," Ivan Fyodorovich said in great agitation, "this . . . this is almost impossible, if it's so, Glasha . . . Forgive me, Prince, forgive me, my dear! . . . Lizaveta Prokofyevna!" he turned to his wife for help. "We must . . . look into it . . ."

"I refuse, I refuse!" Lizaveta Prokofyevna waved her hands.

"Allow me to speak as well, *maman*; I also mean something in such a matter: the great moment of my destiny is being decided" (that is precisely how Aglaya put it), "and I myself want to know, and besides, I'm glad it's in front of everybody . . . Allow me to ask you, Prince, if you do 'nurture such intentions,' precisely how do you propose to ensure my happiness?"

"I don't really know how to answer you, Aglaya Ivanovna; there . . . what is there to say? And . . . is there any need?"

"You seem to be embarrassed and breathless; rest a little and gather fresh strength; drink a glass of water; anyhow, tea will be served presently."

"I love you, Aglaya Ivanovna, I love you very much; I love only you and . . . don't joke, please, I love you very much."

"But, nevertheless, this is an important matter; we're not children, we must look positively . . . Take the trouble now to tell us, what does your fortune amount to?"

"Now, now, now, Aglaya. What are you doing! This is wrong, wrong . . ." Ivan Fyodorovich muttered fearfully.

"A disgrace!" Lizaveta Prokofyevna whispered loudly.

"She's lost her mind!" Alexandra also whispered loudly.

"My fortune . . . meaning money?" the prince was surprised.

"Precisely."

"I . . . I now have one hundred and thirty-five thousand," the prince murmured, turning red.

"That's all?" Aglaya was loudly and frankly surprised, not blushing in the least. "Anyhow, never mind; particularly if one is economical . . . Do you intend to enter the service?"

"I wanted to pass an examination to be a private tutor . . ."

"Very appropriate; of course, it will increase our means. Do you plan to be a kammerjunker?"

"A kammerjunker? I've never imagined it, but . . ."

But here the two sisters, unable to help themselves, burst out laughing. Adelaida had long noticed in Aglaya's twitching features the signs of rapidly approaching and irrepressible laughter, which she had so far been holding back with all her might. Aglaya looked menacingly at the laughing sisters, but could not stand it a second longer and dissolved into the maddest, almost hysterical laughter; in the end she jumped up and ran out of the room.

"I just knew it was only for fun and nothing more!" cried Adelaida. "Right from the beginning, from the hedgehog."

"No, this I will not allow, I will not allow it!" Lizaveta Prokofyevna suddenly boiled over with anger and quickly rushed out in Aglaya's wake. The two sisters at once ran after her. The prince and the father of the family were left in the room.

"This, this . . . could you have imagined anything like it, Lev Nikolaich?" the general cried out sharply, evidently not understanding himself what he wanted to say. "No, speaking seriously, seriously?"

"I see that Aglaya Ivanovna was making fun of me," the prince replied sadly.

"Wait, brother; I'll go, but you wait . . . because . . . you at least explain to me, Lev Nikolaich, you at least: how did all this happen and what does it all mean, so to speak, as a whole? You'll agree, brother, I am her father, I am after all her father, which is why I don't understand a thing; so you at least explain it."

"I love Aglaya Ivanovna; she knows that and . . . has known it, I think, for a long time."

The general heaved his shoulders.

"Strange, strange . . . and you love her very much?"

"Yes, very much."

"Strange, strange, I find it all. That is, it's such a surprise and a blow that . . . You see, my dear, I'm not referring to your fortune (though I did expect that you had a bit more), but . . . for me, my daughter's happiness . . . finally . . . are you able, so to speak, to make that . . . happiness? And . . . and . . . what is it, a joke or the truth on her side? Not on yours, that is, but on her side?"

From behind the door came the voice of Alexandra Ivanovna: they were calling the father.

"Wait, brother, wait! Wait and think it over, and I'll be . . ." he said in haste and almost fearfully rushed off to Alexandra's call.

He found his wife and daughter in each other's arms and flooding each other with their tears. These were tears of happiness, tenderness, and reconciliation. Aglaya kissed her mother's hands, cheeks, lips; the two clung warmly to each other.

"Well, there, look at her, Ivan Fyodorych, she's quite herself now!" said Lizaveta Prokofyevna.

Aglaya turned her happy and tear-bathed little face from her mother's bosom, looked at her father, laughed loudly, jumped over to him, embraced him tightly, and kissed him several times. Then she rushed to her mother again and buried her face completely in her bosom, so that no one could see her, and at once began weeping again. Lizaveta Prokofyevna covered her with the end of her shawl.

"Well, what is it, what is it you're doing to us, cruel girl that you are after that!" she said, but joyfully now, as if she suddenly could breathe more freely.

"Cruel! yes, cruel!" Aglaya suddenly picked up. "Rotten! Spoiled! Tell papa that. Ah, but he's here. Papa, are you here? Listen!" she laughed through her tears.

"My dearest, my idol!" the general, all beaming with happiness, kissed her hand. (Aglaya did not withdraw it.) "So it means that you love this . . . young man? . . ."

"No, no, no! I can't bear . . . your young man, I can't bear him!" Aglaya suddenly boiled over and raised her head. "And if you dare once more, papa . . . I'm saying it to you seriously; do you hear: I'm saying it seriously!"

And she indeed said it seriously: she even turned all red and her eyes shone. Her father broke off and became frightened, but Lizaveta Prokofyevna made a sign to him behind Aglaya's back, and he understood that it meant: "Don't ask questions."

"If that is how you want it, my angel, it's as you will, he's waiting there alone; shouldn't we delicately hint to him that he should leave?"

The general in turn winked at Lizaveta Prokofyevna.

"No, no, that's quite superfluous, especially if it's 'delicate.' Go out to him; I'll come out afterwards, right away. I want to ask forgiveness of this . . . young man, because I've hurt him."

"Very much so," Ivan Fyodorovich confirmed seriously.

"Well, so . . . it will be better if you all stay here and I go alone first, and you follow me right away, that same second; that will be better."

She had already reached the door, but suddenly she came back.

"I'll burst out laughing! I'll die of laughter!" she announced ruefully.

But that same second she turned and ran to the prince.

"Well, what is it? What do you think?" Ivan Fyodorovich said hastily.

"I'm afraid even to say," Lizaveta Prokofyevna replied, also hastily, "but I think it's clear."

"I, too, think it's clear. Clear as day. She loves him."

"Not just loves him, she's in love with him!" Alexandra Ivanovna echoed. "Only I wonder what for?"

"God bless her, if such is her fate!" Lizaveta Prokofyevna piously crossed herself.

"It means it's fate," the general confirmed, "there's no escaping fate!"

And they all went to the drawing room, but there another surprise awaited them.

Aglaya not only did not burst out laughing, as she feared, when she walked up to the prince, but she said to him even almost timidly:

"Forgive a foolish, bad, spoiled girl" (she took his hand), "and be assured that we all have boundless respect for you. And if I dared to make a mockery of your beautiful . . . kind simpleheartedness, then forgive me as you would a child for a prank; forgive me that I insisted on an absurdity which, of course, cannot have the least consequences . . ."

Aglaya uttered these last words with special emphasis.

Father, mother, and sisters all arrived in the drawing room in time to see and hear everything, and they were all struck by the "absurdity which, of course, cannot have the least consequences," and still more by the serious air with which Aglaya spoke of this absurdity. They all exchanged questioning glances; but the prince, it seemed, did not understand these words and was in the highest degree of happiness.

"Why do you speak like that," he murmured, "why do you . . . ask . . . forgiveness . . ."

He was even going to say that he was unworthy of having anyone ask his forgiveness. Who knows, perhaps he did notice the meaning of the words about the "absurdity which cannot have the least consequences," but, as a strange man, he may even have been glad of those words. Unquestionably, for him the height of bliss was the fact alone that he could again visit Aglaya without hindrance, that he would be allowed to talk with her, sit with her, walk with her, and, who knows, perhaps that alone would have contented him for the rest of his life! (It was this contentment, it seems, that Lizaveta Prokofyevna was secretly afraid of; she had divined it; she secretly feared many things that she did not even know how to express.)

It is hard to describe how animated and encouraged the prince became that evening. He was so merry that one became merry just looking at him—so Aglaya's sisters put it afterwards. He talked a great deal, and that had not happened to him since the very morning, six months earlier, when he had first made the acquaintance of the Epanchins; on his return to Petersburg, he had been noticeably and intentionally silent, and very recently, in front of everyone, had let slip to Prince Shch. that he had to restrain himself and keep silent, because he had no right to humiliate a thought by stating it. He was almost the only one who spoke all that evening, telling many stories; he answered questions clearly, gladly, and in detail. However, nothing resembling polite conversation showed in his words. The thoughts were all quite serious, sometimes even quite abstruse. The prince even stated some of his own views, his own private observations, so that it would all even have been ridiculous, if it had not been so "well stated," as all the listeners agreed afterwards. Though the general loved serious topics of conversation, both he and Lizaveta Prokofyevna personally found that there was too much learning, so that by the end of the evening they even began to feel sad. However, in the end the prince went so far as to tell several very funny anecdotes, at which he was the first to laugh, so that the others laughed more at his joyful laughter than at the anecdotes themselves. As for Aglaya, she hardly even spoke all evening; instead, she listened to Lev Nikolaevich, without tearing herself away, and even did not so much listen to him as look at him.

"She just looks at him, can't take her eyes away; hangs on his every little word; snatches at it, snatches at it!" Lizaveta Prokofyevna said later to her husband. "But tell her she loves him, and God save us all!"

"No help for it—it's fate!" the general shrugged his shoulders and for a long time went on repeating this little phrase that had caught his fancy. We shall add that, as a practical man, he also found much in the present state of all these things that displeased him greatly—above all the indefiniteness of the situation; but for the time being he also decided to keep silent and look . . . into Lizaveta Prokofyevna's eyes.

The family's joyful mood did not last long. The very next day Aglaya again quarreled with the prince, and so it went on incessantly, during all the days that followed. She would spend hours at a time making fun of the prince and all but turning him into a buffoon. True, they sometimes spent an hour or two sitting in the garden, in the gazebo, but it was noticed that at those times the prince almost always read the newspapers or some book to Aglaya.

"You know," Aglaya once said to him, interrupting the newspaper, "I've noticed that you are terribly uneducated; you don't know anything properly, if somebody asks you: neither precisely who, nor in what year, nor in what article. You're quite pathetic."

"I told you that I have little learning," the prince replied.

"What do you amount to after that? How can I respect you after that? Keep reading; or, no, stop reading, there's no need to."

And again that same evening there was a glimpse of something very mysterious on her part. Prince Shch. returned. Aglaya was very nice to him, asked many questions about Evgeny Pavlovich. (Prince Lev Nikolaevich had not arrived yet.) Suddenly Prince Shch. somehow permitted himself to allude to "the near and new change in the family," in response to a few words that Lizaveta Prokofyevna let drop about possibly having to postpone Adelaida's wedding again, so as to have both weddings take place together. It was impossible even to imagine how Aglaya flared up at "all these stupid suppositions"; and, among other things, the words escaped her that "she still had no intention of replacing anyone's mistresses."

These words struck everyone, but the parents most of all.

Lizaveta Prokofyevna, in a secret consultation with her husband, insisted on having a decisive talk with the prince concerning Nastasya Filippovna.

Ivan Fyodorovich swore that it was all only an "outburst," which came from Aglaya's "modesty"; that if Prince Shch. had not begun speaking about the wedding, there would have been no such outburst, because Aglaya herself knew, knew for certain, that it was all the slander of unkind people and that Nastasya Filippovna was going to marry Rogozhin; that the prince counted for nothing at all here, not only in any liaison; and even never had counted, if the whole truth were to be told.

But all the same the prince was not embarrassed by anything and went on being blissful. Oh, of course, he, too, sometimes noticed something dark and impatient, as it were, in Aglaya's eyes; but he believed more in something else, and the darkness vanished of itself. Once having believed, he could no longer be shaken by anything. Perhaps he was all too calm; so, at least, it seemed to Ippolit, who once chanced to meet him in the park.

"Well, wasn't it the truth I told you then, that you were in love?" he began, going up to the prince himself and stopping him. The latter gave him his hand and congratulated him on "looking well." The sick boy did seem cheerful, as is often the case with consumptives.

His purpose in going up to the prince was to say something sarcastic about his happy look, but he got thrown off at once and started talking about himself. He began to complain, complained much and long and rather incoherently.

"You wouldn't believe," he concluded, "the degree to which they are all irritable, petty, egoistic, vainglorious, ordinary; would you believe, they took me in only on the condition that I should die as soon as possible, and now everybody's furious that I don't die and, on the contrary, feel better. A comedy! I'll bet you don't believe me!"

The prince did not want to object.

"I sometimes even think of moving back to your place," Ippolit added casually. "So you, however, do not consider them capable of receiving a person with the notion that he should die without fail and as soon as possible?"

"I thought they invited you with something else in mind."

"Aha! No, you're not at all as simple as they recommend you to be! Now's not the time, or I'd reveal to you a thing or two about that Ganechka and his hopes. You're being undermined, Prince, pitilessly undermined, and . . . it's even a pity you're so calm. But alas—you couldn't be otherwise!"

"What a thing to be pitied for!" laughed the prince. "So in your opinion I'd be happier if I worried more?"

"It's better to be unhappy, but to *know*, than to be happy and live . . . as a fool. It seems you don't believe in the least that you have a rival and . . . on that side?"

"Your words about rivalry are slightly cynical, Ippolit; I'm sorry I don't have the right to answer you. As for Gavrila Ardalionovich, you must agree that he can't remain calm after all he has lost, if you know his affairs at least in part. It seems to me that it's better to look at it from that point of view. He still has time to change; he has a long life ahead of him, and life is rich . . . but anyhow . . . anyhow," the prince was suddenly at a loss, "as for the undermining . . . I don't even understand what you're talking about; it's better if we drop this conversation, Ippolit."

"We'll drop it for a time; besides, it's impossible to do without the noble pose on your part. Yes, Prince, you'll have to touch it with your own finger in order to stop believing again, ha, ha![25] And, what do you think, do you despise me very much now?"

"What for? For having suffered and for suffering more than we?"

"No, but for being unworthy of my suffering."

"If someone can suffer more, it means he's worthy of suffering more. Aglaya Ivanovna wanted to see you, when she read your 'Confession,' but . . ."

"She's putting it off . . . it's impossible for her, I understand, I understand . . ." Ippolit interrupted, as if trying to divert the conversation quickly. "By the way, they say you read all that galimatias to her out loud; it was truly written and . . . done in delirium. And I don't understand the extent to which one must be—I won't say cruel (that would be humiliating to me), but childishly vain and vengeful, to reproach me with that 'Confession' and use it against me as a weapon! Don't worry, I'm not saying that with regard to you . . ."

"But I'm sorry that you reject that notebook, Ippolit; it's sincere, and you know that even its ridiculous sides, and it has many" (Ippolit winced deeply), "are redeemed by suffering, because to admit them was also suffering and . . . perhaps took great courage. The thought that moved you certainly had a noble basis, however it may seem. The further it goes, the more clearly I see it, I swear to you. I'm not judging you, I'm saying it in order to speak my whole mind, and I'm sorry I was silent then . . ."

Ippolit flushed. The thought occurred to him that the prince was pretending and trying to catch him; but, peering into his face, he could not help believing in his sincerity; his face brightened.

"And here I have to die all the same!" he said, and nearly added: "such a man as I!" "And imagine how your Ganechka plagues me; he thought up, in the guise of an objection, that of those who listened to my notebook, three or four might die before me! I like that! He thinks it's a consolation, ha, ha! First of all, they haven't died yet; and even if those people all died off, what sort of consolation would it be, you'll agree! He judges by himself; however, he goes further still, he now simply abuses me, saying that a respectable man dies silently in such cases, and that the whole thing was only egoism on my part! I like that! No, but what egoism on his part! What a refinement or, better to say, at the same time what an ox-like crudeness of their egoism, which all the same they are in no way able to notice in themselves! . . . Have you read, Prince, about a certain death, of a certain Stepan Glebov, in the eighteenth century? I read it by chance yesterday . . ."

"What Stepan Glebov?"

"He was impaled under Peter."[26]

"Ah, my God, I do know! He spent fifteen hours on the stake, in the freezing cold, in his fur coat, and died with extreme magnanimity; of course, I read that . . . but what of it?"

"God grants such deaths to some people, but not to us! Maybe you think I'm incapable of dying the way Glebov did?"

"Oh, not at all," the prince was embarrassed, "I only wanted to say that you . . . I mean, that it's not that you wouldn't be like Glebov, but . . . that you . . . that then you'd sooner be like . . ."

"I can guess: Osterman[27] and not Glebov—is that what you want to say?"

"What Osterman?" the prince was surprised.

"Osterman, the diplomat Osterman, from Peter's time," murmured Ippolit, suddenly thrown off a little. A certain perplexity followed.

"Oh, n-n-no! That's not what I wanted to say," the prince drew out after some silence. "It seems to me you could . . . never be an Osterman . . ."

Ippolit frowned.

"However, the reason I maintain that," the prince suddenly

picked up, obviously wishing to correct himself, "is because people back then (I swear to you, it has always struck me) were not at all the same sort of people as we are now, not the same breed as now, in our time,[28] really, like a different species . . . At that time people were somehow of one idea, while now they're more nervous, more developed, sensitive, somehow of two or three ideas at once . . . today's man is broader—and, I swear, that's what keeps him from being such a monolithic man as in those times . . . I . . . I said it solely with that in mind, and not . . ."

"I understand; to make up for the naïvety with which you disagreed with me, you are now foisting your consolations on me, ha, ha! You're a perfect child, Prince! However, I notice that you keep treating me like . . . a porcelain cup . . . Never mind, never mind, I'm not angry. In any case, we've had a very funny conversation; you're a perfect child sometimes, Prince. Know, however, that I might like to be something better than Osterman; it wouldn't be worthwhile to rise from the dead in order to be an Osterman . . . However, I see I must die as soon as possible, otherwise I, too . . . Leave me. Good-bye! Well, all right, tell me yourself, well, how, in your opinion: how will it be best for me to die? So that it will go as well as . . . more virtuously, that is? Well, speak!"

"Pass us by and forgive us our happiness!" the prince said in a low voice.

"Ha, ha, ha! Just as I thought! I certainly expected something of that sort! You, though . . . you, though . . . Well, well! Eloquent people! Good-bye, good-bye!"

VI

VARVARA ARDALIONOVNA had also informed her brother quite correctly about the evening gathering at the Epanchins' dacha, where Belokonsky was expected; guests were expected precisely that evening; but, again, the way she had put it was slightly stronger than it should have been. True, the affair had been organized too hastily and even with a certain quite unnecessary excitement, and that precisely because in this family "everything was done as no one else did it." Everything was explained by the impatience of Lizaveta Prokofyevna, "who did not wish to have any more doubts" and by the ardent throbbings of both parental hearts over the happiness of their beloved daughter. Besides,

Belokonsky was in fact leaving soon; and since her protection indeed meant much in society and since it was hoped that she would look favorably on the prince, the parents reckoned that "society" would receive Aglaya's fiancé straight from the hands of the all-powerful "old woman," and so, if there was something strange in it, under such protection it would appear much less strange. The whole thing was that the parents were simply unable to decide for themselves: "Was there anything strange in this whole affair, and if so, precisely how much? Or was there nothing strange at all?" The friendly and candid opinion of people of authority and competence would precisely be useful at the present moment, when, thanks to Aglaya, nothing had been ultimately resolved yet. In any case, the prince had sooner or later to be introduced into society, of which he had not the slightest idea. In short, the intention was to "show" him. The evening, however, was planned without ceremony; only "friends of the house" were expected, a very small number of them. Besides Princess Belokonsky, a certain lady was expected, the wife of a very important gentleman and a dignitary. Among the young men they counted perhaps only on Evgeny Pavlovich; he was to arrive escorting Belokonsky.

Of the fact that Belokonsky would be there, the prince had heard possibly some three days before the evening; of the party he learned only the day before. Naturally, he noticed the busy look of the members of the family, and even grasped, from certain allusive and preoccupied remarks made to him, that they feared for the impression he might make. But somehow all the Epanchins to a person formed the idea that he, in his simplicity, would never be able to guess that they were so worried for him. Which was why, looking at him, they all felt an inner anguish. However, he in fact ascribed almost no significance to the forthcoming event; he was concerned with something else entirely: with every hour Aglaya was becoming more capricious and gloomy—this was killing him. When he learned that Evgeny Pavlovich was also expected, he was very glad and said he had long been wanting to see him. For some reason no one liked these words; Aglaya left the room in vexation, and only late in the evening, sometime past eleven, when the prince was leaving, did she seize the chance to tell him a few words alone, as she was seeing him off.

"I wish you wouldn't come to see us all day tomorrow, but come in the evening, when these . . . guests have gathered. You know there will be guests?"

She spoke impatiently and with increased sternness; this was the first time she had spoken of this "evening." For her, too, the thought of guests was almost unbearable; everyone noticed it. She might have wanted very much to quarrel with her parents over it, but pride and modesty kept her from speaking. The prince understood at once that she, too, feared for him (and did not want to admit it), and he suddenly felt afraid himself.

"Yes, I've been invited," he replied.

She was obviously embarrassed to go on.

"Is it possible to speak with you about anything serious? At least once in your life?" she suddenly became extremely angry, not knowing why herself and not able to restrain herself.

"It's possible, and I'm listening to you; I'm very glad," the prince murmured.

Aglaya paused again for about a minute and began with obvious repugnance:

"I didn't want to argue about it with them; in certain cases they can't be brought to reason. The rules that *maman* sometimes goes by have always been repugnant to me. I'm not speaking of father, there's nothing to be expected from him. *Maman* is, of course, a noble woman; dare to suggest something mean to her and you'll see . . . Well, but before this . . . trash—she stands in awe! I'm not speaking of this Belokonsky alone: a trashy little hag, and with a trashy character, but she's intelligent and knows how to hold them all in her hand—that, at least, is a good thing about her. Oh, meanness! And it's ridiculous: we've always been people of the middle circle, as middle as can be; why climb into that high-society circle? And my sisters, too: this Prince Shch. has got them all confused. Why are you glad that Evgeny Pavlych will come?"

"Listen, Aglaya," said the prince, "it seems to me you're very afraid for me, that I'll flunk it tomorrow . . . in that company?"

"For you? Afraid?" Aglaya flared up. "Why should I be afraid for you, even if you . . . even if you disgrace yourself completely? What is it to me? And how can you use such words? What does 'flunk' mean? It's a trite, trashy word."

"It's a . . . school word."

"Ah, yes, a school word! A trashy word! You intend, apparently, to speak in such words tomorrow. Go home and pick more words like that from your lexicon: what an effect you'll make! Too bad you seem to know how to make a proper entrance; where did you learn that? Will you be able to take a cup of tea and drink it decently, while everybody's looking at you on purpose?"

"I think I'll be able to."

"That's too bad; otherwise I'd have had a good laugh. At least break the Chinese vase in the drawing room! It's expensive: please break it; it was a gift, mama will lose her mind and cry in front of everybody—it's so precious to her. Make some gesture, the way you always do, hit it and break it. Sit next to it on purpose."

"On the contrary, I'll try to sit as far away as possible: thank you for warning me."

"So you're afraid beforehand that you'll make grand gestures. I bet you'll start discussing some 'topic,' something serious, learned, lofty? That will be . . . proper!"

"I think it would be stupid . . . if it's inappropriate."

"Listen once and for all," Aglaya finally could not stand it, "if you start talking about something like capital punishment or the economic situation in Russia, or that 'beauty will save the world'. . . I'll certainly be glad and laugh very much, but . . . I'm warning you ahead of time: don't let me set eyes on you afterwards! Do you hear? I'm speaking seriously! This time I'm speaking seriously!"

She actually uttered her threat *seriously*, so that something extraordinary could even be heard in her words and glimpsed in her eyes, something that the prince had never noticed before and that certainly bore no resemblance to a joke.

"Well, you've made it so that now I'll be sure to 'start talking' and even . . . maybe . . . break the vase as well. I wasn't afraid of anything before, but now I'm afraid of everything. I'm sure to flunk."

"Then keep quiet. Sit there and keep quiet."

"It won't be possible; I'm sure to start talking from fear and to break the vase from fear. Maybe I'll trip on the smooth floor, or something else like that will happen, because it's happened before; I'll dream about it all night; why did you speak of it!"

Aglaya gave him a dark look.

"You know what: I'd better not come at all tomorrow! I'll report myself sick and be done with it!" he decided at last.

Aglaya stamped her foot and even turned pale with wrath.

"Lord! Have you ever seen the like! He won't come when it's purposely for him and . . . oh, God! What a pleasure to deal with such a . . . senseless man as you!"

"Well, I'll come, I'll come!" the prince hastily interrupted. "And

I give you my word of honor that I'll sit all evening without saying a word. That's what I'll do."

"Splendid. You just said you'd 'report yourself sick.' Where indeed do you get these expressions? What makes you speak with me in such words? Are you teasing me or something?"

"I'm sorry; that's also a school phrase; I'll stop. I realize very well that you're . . . afraid for me . . . (no, don't be angry!), and I'm terribly glad of it. You won't believe how afraid I am now and—how glad I am of your words. But all this fear, I swear to you, it's all pettiness and nonsense. By God, Aglaya! And the joy will remain. I like it terribly that you're such a child, such a good and kind child! Ah, how beautiful you can be, Aglaya!"

Aglaya would of course have become angry, and was just about to, but suddenly some completely unexpected feeling seized her whole soul in an instant.

"And you won't reproach me for these rude words . . . sometime . . . afterwards?" she suddenly asked.

"How can you, how can you! And why have you blushed again? And again you have this dark look! You sometimes have this dark look, Aglaya, which you never had before. I know why . . ."

"Be quiet, be quiet!"

"No, it's better to say it. I've long wanted to say it; I already have, but . . . it wasn't enough, because you didn't believe me. Between us a certain being still stands . . ."

"Quiet, quiet, quiet, quiet!" Aglaya suddenly interrupted, seizing him firmly by the hand and looking at him in all but horror. At that moment someone called her; as if glad of it, she left him and ran off.

The prince was in a fever all night. Strangely, for several nights in a row he had been in a fever. This time, in half-delirium, the thought came to him: what if he should have a fit tomorrow in front of everybody? Had he not had fits in a waking state? The thought petrified him; all night he imagined himself in some odd and unheard-of company, among some strange people. The main thing was that he "started talking"; he knew that he should not be talking, yet he talked all the time, trying to convince them of something. Evgeny Pavlovich and Ippolit were also among the guests and seemed to be on extremely friendly terms.

He woke up past eight o'clock with a headache, with disordered thoughts, with strange impressions. For some reason he wanted terribly to see Rogozhin, to see him and talk a great deal with him—about what he did not know himself; then he became fully resolved to go for some reason to see Ippolit. There was something vague in his heart, so much so that the adventures that befell him that morning made an impression on him which, while extremely strong, was still somehow incomplete. One of those adventures was a visit from Lebedev.

Lebedev appeared quite early, just after nine, and almost completely drunk. Though the prince had not been observant of late, it had somehow struck his eye that, ever since General Ivolgin moved out of his house three days ago, Lebedev had begun to behave very badly. He had suddenly become somehow very dirty and greasy, his necktie was all askew, and the collar of his frock coat was torn. At home he even raged, and it could be heard across the little yard; Vera had come once in tears and told him something about it. Having appeared now, he began speaking very strangely, beating his breast and confessing something.

"I got . . . I got my requital for my treason and my meanness . . . I got a slap in the face!" he finally concluded tragically.

"A slap in the face? From whom? . . . And at such an early hour?"

"Early?" Lebedev smiled sarcastically. "Time means nothing here . . . even for a physical requital . . . but I got a moral . . . a moral slap, not a physical one!"

He suddenly sat down unceremoniously and began telling the story. It was very incoherent; the prince frowned and wanted to leave, but suddenly a few words struck him. He was struck dumb with astonishment . . . Mr. Lebedev had strange things to tell.

To begin with, the matter apparently had to do with some letter; the name of Aglaya Ivanovna was spoken. Then suddenly Lebedev started bitterly accusing the prince himself; it was clear that he had been offended by the prince. First, he said, the prince had honored him with his trust in dealing with a certain "personage" (Nastasya Filippovna); but then had broken with him completely and driven him away in disgrace, and even to such an offensive degree that last time he was supposed to have rudely dismissed his "innocent question about imminent changes in the house." With drunken tears Lebedev confessed that "after that he could no longer endure, the less so as he knew a great deal . . . a very great deal . . . both from Rogozhin and from Nastasya Filippovna, and from Nastasya Filippovna's friend, and from Varvara Ardalionovna . . . herself, sir . . . and from . . . and even from Aglaya Ivanovna herself, if you can imagine, sir, through Vera, sir, through my beloved daughter Vera, my only-begotten[29] . . . yes, sir . . . though not my only-begotten, for I have three. And who informed Lizaveta Prokofyevna by letters, and that in the deepest secret, sir, heh, heh! Who reported to her on all the relations and . . . on the movements of the personage Nastasya Filippovna, heh, heh, heh! Who, who is this anonymous person, may I ask?"

"Can it be you?" cried the prince.

"Precisely," the drunkard replied with dignity, "and it was today at half-past eight, only half an hour, no, already three-quarters of an hour ago, that I notified the noblest of mothers that I had an adventure to tell her of . . . an important one. I sent her a note, by a maid, at the back door, sir. She received it."

"You've just seen Lizaveta Prokofyevna?" the prince asked, scarcely believing his ears.

"I just saw her and got a slap in the face . . . a moral one. She gave me back my letter, even flung it at me, unopened . . . and threw me out on my ear . . . though only morally, not physically . . . though almost physically even, just short of it!"

"What letter did she fling at you unopened?"

"Didn't I . . . heh, heh, heh! So I haven't told you yet! And I thought I had . . . There's this little letter I received, to be passed on, sir . . ."

"From whom? To whom?"

But certain of Lebedev's "explanations" were extremely difficult to make out and even partially understand. The prince nevertheless realized, as far as he could, that the letter had been given to Vera Lebedev early in the morning, through a maid, to be delivered to the address . . . "the same as before . . . the same as before, to a certain personage and from the same person, sir . . . (for one of them I designate by the name of 'person,' sir, and the other only as 'personage,' for humiliation and for distinction; for there is a great difference between the innocent and highly noble daughter of a general and a . . . kept woman, sir), and so, the letter was from a 'person,' sir, beginning with the letter *A* . . ."

"How can it be? To Nastasya Filippovna? Nonsense!" cried the prince.

"It was, it was, sir, and if not to her, then to Rogozhin, sir, it's all the same, to Rogozhin, sir . . . and once there was even one to be passed on to Mr. Terentyev, sir, from the person with the letter *A*," Lebedev winked and smiled.

Since he often jumped from one thing to another and forgot what he had begun to say, the prince kept still so as to let him speak everything out. But all the same it was extremely unclear whether the letters had gone through him or through Vera. If he himself insisted that "to Rogozhin was all the same as to Nastasya Filippovna," it meant that most likely they had not gone through him, if there were any letters at all. And how it happened that the letter now ended up with him, remained decidedly unexplained; most likely of all would be to suppose that he had somehow stolen it from Vera . . . carried it off on the sly and taken it with some sort of intention to Lizaveta Prokofyevna. So the prince finally figured it out and understood it.

"You've lost your mind!" he cried, extremely disconcerted.

"Not entirely, my much-esteemed Prince," Lebedev answered, not without anger. "True, I was going to give it to you, into your own hands, so as to be of service . . . but I chose rather to be of service there and tell the most noble mother about everything . . . just as I had informed her once before in an anonymous letter; and when I wrote a note today, asking beforehand to be received at twenty past eight, I also signed it: 'your secret correspondent'; I was admitted at once, immediately, even with great haste, by the back door . . . to see the most noble mother."

"Well?"

"And you know the rest, sir. She nearly gave me a beating, sir; that is, very nearly, sir, so that one might consider that she all but gave me a beating, sir. And she flung the letter at me. True, she wanted to keep it—I could see that, I noticed it—but she changed her mind and flung it at me: 'If you, such as you are, were entrusted with delivering it, then go and deliver it . . .' She even got offended. If she didn't feel ashamed to say it in front of me, it means she got offended. A hot-tempered lady!"

"And where is the letter now?"

"Still here with me, sir."

And he handed the prince the note from Aglaya to Gavrila Ardalionovich, which the latter triumphantly showed to his sister that same morning, two hours later.

"This letter cannot remain with you."

"For you, for you! I brought it for you, sir," Lebedev picked up hotly. "Now I'm yours again, entirely, from head to heart, your servant, sir, after a fleeting betrayal, sir! Punish my heart, spare my beard, as Thomas Morus[30] said . . . in England and in Great

Britain, sir. *Mea culpa, mea culpa,*[31] so says the Roman papa . . . that is, he's the pope of Rome, but I call him the 'Roman papa.'"

"This letter must be sent at once," the prince bustled, "I'll deliver it."

"But wouldn't it be better, wouldn't it be better, my most well-mannered Prince, wouldn't it be better, sir . . . sort of, sir!"

Lebedev made a strange, ingratiating grimace; he suddenly fidgeted terribly in his chair, as if he had suddenly been pricked by a needle, and, winking slyly, gestured and indicated something with his hands.

"What do you mean?" the prince asked menacingly.

"Open it beforehand, sir!" he whispered ingratiatingly and as if confidentially.

The prince jumped up in such fury that Lebedev was about to run away, but having reached the door, he stopped, waiting to see if he would be pardoned.

"Eh, Lebedev! Is it possible, is it possible to reach such mean disorder as you have?" the prince cried ruefully. Lebedev's features brightened.

"I'm mean, mean!" he approached at once, with tears, beating his breast.

"That's loathsome!"

"Precisely loathsome, sir. That's the word, sir!"

"And what is this way you have . . . of acting so strangely? You're . . . simply a spy! Why did you write an anonymous letter and trouble . . . that most noble and kind woman? Why, finally, does Aglaya Ivanovna have no right to correspond with whomever she likes? Why did you go there today, to make a complaint? What did you hope to gain? What moved you to turn informer?"

"Only pleasant curiosity and . . . an obligingly noble soul, yes, sir!" Lebedev murmured. "But now I'm all yours, all yours again! You can hang me!"

"Did you go to Lizaveta Prokofyevna's the way you are now?" the prince inquired with repugnance.

"No, sir . . . fresher . . . and even more decent, sir; it was after my humiliation that I achieved . . . this look, sir."

"Very well, leave me."

However, this request had to be repeated several times before the visitor finally decided to leave. Having already opened the door,

*It is my fault, it is my fault.

he came back again, tiptoed to the middle of the room, and again began to make signs with his hands, showing how to open a letter; he did not dare to put this advice into words; then he went out, smiling quietly and sweetly.

All this was extremely painful to hear. One chief and extraordinary fact stood out amidst it all: that Aglaya was in great anxiety, in great indecision, in great torment for some reason ("from jealousy," the prince whispered to himself). It was also clear, of course, that unkind people were confusing her, and it was all the more strange that she trusted them so much. Of course, some special plans were ripening in that inexperienced but hot and proud little head, ruinous plans, perhaps . . . and like nothing else. The prince was extremely alarmed and in his confusion did not know what to decide. He absolutely had to prevent something, he could feel it. Once again he looked at the address on the sealed letter: oh, there was no doubt or anxiety for him here, because he trusted her; something else troubled him in this letter: he did not trust Gavrila Ardalionovich. And, nevertheless, he decided to give him the letter himself, personally, and had already left the house in order to do so, but on his way he changed his mind. As if on purpose, almost at Ptitsyn's house, the prince ran into Kolya and charged him with putting the letter into his brother's hands, as if directly from Aglaya Ivanovna herself. Kolya asked no questions and delivered it, so that Ganya never even imagined the letter had gone through so many stations. On returning home, the prince asked to see Vera Lukyanovna, told her as much as was necessary, and calmed her down, because she had been searching for the letter and weeping all the while. She was horrified when she learned that her father had taken the letter. (The prince later learned from her that she had secretly served Rogozhin and Aglaya Ivanovna more than once; it had never occurred to her that it might be something harmful to the prince . . .)

And the prince finally became so upset that when, two hours later, a messenger came running to him from Kolya with news of his father's illness, he could scarely understand at first what it was all about. But this same incident restored him, because it distracted him greatly. He stayed at Nina Alexandrovna's (where, of course, the sick man had been transported) almost till evening. He was of almost no use, but there are people whom, for some reason, it is pleasant to see around one at certain difficult moments. Kolya was terribly struck, wept hysterically, but nevertheless ran errands all the time: ran to fetch a doctor and found three, ran to the pharmacy, to the barber.[32] The general was revived, but he did not come to his senses; as the doctors put it, "in any case the patient is in danger." Varya and Nina Alexandrovna never left the sick man's side; Ganya was confused and shaken, but did not want to go upstairs and was even afraid to see the sick man; he wrung his hands and in an incoherent conversation with the prince managed to say, "just look, such a misfortune, and, as if on purpose, at such a time!" The prince thought he understood precisely what time he was talking about. The prince found that Ippolit was no longer in Ptitsyn's house. Towards evening Lebedev, who had slept uninterruptedly since their morning "talk," came running. He was almost sober now and wept real tears over the sick man, as if over his own brother. He loudly blamed himself, though without explaining what for, and pestered Nina Alexandrovna, assuring her every moment that "he, he himself was the cause, and no one but he . . . solely out of pleasant curiosity . . . and that the 'deceased'" (as he stubbornly called the still-living general for some reason) "was even a man of great genius!" He insisted especially seriously on his genius, as if some extraordinary benefit could be derived from it at that moment. Nina Alexandrovna, seeing his genuine tears, finally said to him, without any reproach and even almost with tenderness: "Well, God be with you, don't weep now, God will forgive you!" Lebedev was so struck by these words and their tone that he would not leave Nina Alexandrovna's side all evening (and in all the following days, till the general's death, he stayed in their house almost from morning till night). Twice in the course of the day a messenger came to Nina Alexandrovna from Lizaveta Prokofyevna to ask after the sick man's health. When, at nine o'clock that evening, the prince appeared in the Epanchins' drawing room, which was already filled with guests, Lizaveta Prokofyevna at once began questioning him about the sick man, with sympathy and in detail, and responded gravely to Belokonsky's question: "Who is this sick man and who is Nina Alexandrovna?" The prince liked that very much. He himself, in talking with Lizaveta Prokofyevna, spoke "beautifully," as Aglaya's sisters explained afterwards: "modestly, softly, without unnecessary words, without gestures, with dignity; he entered beautifully, was excellently dressed," and not only did not "trip on the smooth floor," but obviously even made a pleasant impression on everyone.

For his part, having sat down and looked around, he noticed at once that this whole gathering bore no resemblance to the specters Aglaya had frightened him with yesterday, or to the nightmares he had had during the night. For the first time in his life he saw a small corner of what is known by the terrible name of "society." For a long time now, owing to certain special intentions, considerations, and yearnings of his own, he had desired to penetrate this magic circle of people and was therefore greatly interested in his first impression. This first impression of his was even delightful. It appeared to him somehow at once and suddenly that all these people had, as it were, been born to be together; that there was no "evening" at the Epanchins' that evening and no invited guests, that these were all "our people," and it was as if he himself had long been their devoted and like-minded friend, who had now returned to them after a recent separation. The charm of elegant manners, the simplicity and seeming candor were almost magical. It would never have occurred to him that all this simple-heartedness and nobility, sharp wit and lofty dignity might only be a splendid artistic contrivance. The majority of the guests, despite their imposing appearance, were even rather empty people, who, incidentally, in their self-satisfaction did not know themselves that much of what was good in them was only a contrivance, for which, moreover, they were not to blame, for they had acquired it unconsciously and by inheritance. This the prince did not even want to suspect, under the spell of his lovely first impression. He saw, for instance, that this old man, this important dignitary, who by his age might have been his grandfather, even interrupted his own conversation in order to listen to such a young and inexperienced man as he, and not only listened to him but clearly valued his opinion, was so gentle with him, so sincerely good-natured, and yet they were strangers and were seeing each other for the first time. Perhaps in his ardent susceptibility the prince was most affected by the refinement of this politeness. Perhaps he had been all too disposed beforehand and even won over to a happy impression.

And yet all these people—though they were, of course, "friends of the house" and of each other—were, nevertheless, far from being such friends either of the house or of each other as the prince took them to be when he was introduced to them and made their acquaintance. There were people there who would never for anything have acknowledged the Epanchins as ever so slightly equal to themselves. There were people there who even absolutely detested each other; old Belokonsky had "despised" the wife of the "little old dignitary" all her life, and she in turn was far from liking Lizaveta Prokofyevna. This "dignitary," her husband, who for some reason had been the patron of the Epanchins from their very youth, and presided here as well, was such a tremendous person in Ivan Fyodorovich's eyes that he could feel nothing but awe and fear in his presence, and would even have genuinely despised himself if for one minute he had considered himself equal to him, or him not an Olympian Jupiter. There were people who had not seen each other for several years and felt nothing for each other but indifference, if not repugnance, but who met now as if they had seen each other only the day before in the most friendly and agreeable company. However, the gathering was not numerous. Besides Belokonsky and the "little old dignitary," who was indeed an important person, besides his wife, there was, first, a very important army general, a baron or a count, with a German name—an extremely taciturn man, with a reputation for an astonishing knowledge of government affairs and even almost with a reputation for learning—one of those Olympian administrators who know everything, "except perhaps Russia itself," a man who once every five years makes an utterance "remarkable for its profundity," but such as, anyhow, unfailingly becomes proverbial and is known even in the most exalted circles; one of those superior officials who usually, after extremely (even strangely) prolonged service, die in high rank, at excellent posts, and with great fortunes, though without any great deeds and even with a certain aversion to deeds. This general was Ivan Fyodorovich's immediate superior in the service, whom he, from the fervor of his grateful heart and even from a sort of self-love, also considered his benefactor, while he by no means considered himself Ivan Fyodorovich's benefactor, treated him with perfect equanimity, though he liked to take advantage of his manifold services, and would at once have replaced him with some other official, if certain considerations, even of a not very lofty sort, demanded it. There was also an important elderly gentleman, supposedly even a relation of Lizaveta Prokofyevna's, though that was decidedly incorrect; a man of good rank and title, a rich and well-born man, of sturdy build and very good health, a big talker, and even with the reputation of a malcontent (though, incidentally, in the most permissible sense of the word), even of an acrimonious man (but in him this, too, was agreeable), with the manners of English aristocrats and with English tastes (with regard to bloody roast beef, horse harness, lackeys, etc.). He was great friends with the "dignitary," amused him, and, besides that, Lizaveta Prokofyevna for some reason nurtured the strange thought that this elderly gentleman (a somewhat light-minded man and something of a fancier of the female sex) might suddenly up and decide to make Alexandra's happiness by proposing.

After this highest and most solid stratum of the gathering came the stratum of the younger guests, though also shining with quite gracious qualities. To this stratum, besides Prince Shch. and Evgeny Pavlovich, there also belonged the well-known, charming Prince N., a former seducer and winner of women's hearts all over Europe, now a man of about forty-five, still of handsome appearance, a wonderful storyteller, a man of fortune, though somewhat disordered, who, out of habit, lived mostly abroad. There were, finally, people who seemed even to make up a third special stratum, and who did not in themselves belong to the "coveted circle" of society, but who, like the Epanchins, could sometimes be met for some reason in this "coveted" circle. Owing to a sort of tact which they made into a rule, the Epanchins liked, on the rare occasions when they held social gatherings, to mix high society with people of a lower stratum, with chosen representatives of "people of the middle sort." The Epanchins were even praised for that, and it was said that they understood their place and were people of tact, and the Epanchins were proud of such an opinion about themselves. One representative of this middle sort of people that evening was a colonel of the engineers, a serious man, a rather close friend of Prince Shch., who had introduced him to the Epanchins, a man, however, who was taciturn in society and who wore on the large index finger of his right hand a large and conspicuous signet ring, most likely an award of some kind. There was, finally, even a writer-poet, of German origin, but a Russian poet, and, moreover, a perfectly respectable man, so that he could be introduced without apprehension into good society. He was of fortunate appearance, though slightly repulsive for some reason, about thirty-eight, impeccably dressed, belonged to a German family that was bourgeois in the highest degree, but also respectable in the highest degree; he knew how to make use of various occasions, to win his way to the patronage of highly placed people, and to remain in their good graces. Once he translated from the German some important work by some important German poet, was able to write a verse dedication for his translation, was able to boast of his friendship with a certain famous but dead Russian poet (there is a whole stratum of writers who are extremely fond of appointing themselves in print as friends of great but dead writers), and had been introduced to the Epanchins very recently by the wife of the "little old dignitary." This lady passed for being a patroness of writers and scholars, and had actually obtained pensions for one or two writers, through highly placed persons for whom she had importance. And she did have her own sort of importance. She was a lady of about forty-five (and therefore quite a young wife for such an old man as her husband), a former beauty, who even now, from a mania peculiar to many forty-five-year-old women, liked to dress all too magnificently; she did not have much of a mind, and her knowledge of literature was rather dubious. But patronizing writers was the same sort of mania with her as dressing magnificently. Many writings and translations had been dedicated to her; two or three writers, with her permission, had published their letters to her on extremely important subjects . . . And it was this entire company that the prince took at face value, for pure, unalloyed gold. However, that evening all these people, as if on purpose, were in the happiest spirits and very pleased with themselves. Every last one of them knew that they were doing the Epanchins a great honor by visiting them. But, alas, the prince had no suspicion of such subtleties. He did not suspect, for instance, that the Epanchins, having in mind such an important step as the deciding of their daughter's fate, would not have dared not to show him, Prince Lev Nikolaevich, to the little old dignitary, the acknowledged benefactor of their family. And the little old dignitary, who, for his part, would have borne quite calmly the news of even the most terrible misfortune of the Epanchins, would certainly have been offended if the Epanchins got their daughter engaged without asking his advice and, so to speak, permission. Prince N., that charming, that unquestionably witty and so loftily pure-hearted man, was convinced in the highest degree that he was something like a sun, risen that night over the Epanchins' drawing room. He considered them infinitely beneath him, and it was precisely this simple-hearted and noble thought that produced in him his wonderfully charming casualness and friendliness towards these same Epanchins. He knew very well that he absolutely had to tell some story that evening to charm the company, and he was preparing for it even with a certain inspiration. Prince Lev Nikolaevich, listening to this story later, realized that he had never heard anything like such brilliant humor and such wonderful gaiety and naïvety, which was almost touching on the lips of such a Don Juan as Prince N. And yet, if he had only known how old and worn out this same story was, how everyone knew it by heart and was sick and tired of it in all drawing rooms, and only at the innocent Epanchins' did it appear again as news, as the sudden, sincere, and brilliant recollection of a brilliant and excellent man! Finally, even the little German poeticule, though he behaved himself with extraordinary courtesy and modesty, almost considered that he, too, was doing this house an honor by visiting it. But the prince did not notice the reverse side, did not notice any lining. This disaster Aglaya had not foreseen. She herself was remarkably beautiful that evening. All three girls were dressed up, though not too magnificently, and even had their hair done in some special way. Aglaya sat with Evgeny Pavlovich, talking and joking with him in an extraordinarily friendly way. Evgeny Pavlovich behaved himself somewhat more solidly, as it were, than at other times, also, perhaps, out of respect for the dignitaries. However, he had long been known in society; he was a familiar man there, though a young man. That evening he came to the Epanchins' with crape on his hat, and Belokonsky praised him for this crape: another society nephew, under the circumstances, might not have worn crape after such an uncle. Lizaveta Prokofyevna was also pleased by it, but generally she seemed somehow too preoccupied. The prince noticed that Aglaya looked at him attentively a couple of times and, it seemed, remained pleased with him. Little by little he was becoming terribly happy. His former "fantastic" thoughts and apprehensions (after his conversation with Lebedev) now seemed to him, in sudden but frequent recollections, such an unrealizable, impossible, and even ridiculous dream! (Even without that, his first, though unconscious, desire and longing all that day had been somehow to make it so as not to believe in that dream!) He spoke little and then only to answer questions, and finally became quite silent, sat and listened, but was clearly drowning in delight. Little by little something like inspiration prepared itself in him, ready to blaze up when the chance came . . . He began speaking by chance, also in answer to a question, and apparently without any special intention . . .

VII

WHILE HE GAZED delightedly at Aglaya, who was talking gaily with Prince N. and Evgeny Pavlovich, the elderly gentleman Anglophile, who was entertaining the "dignitary" in another corner, animatedly telling him about something, suddenly spoke the name of Nikolai Andreevich Pavlishchev. The prince quickly turned in their direction and began to listen.

The matter had to do with present-day regulations and some sort of irregularities in the landowners' estates in —— province. There must also have been something funny in the Anglophile's stories, because the little old man finally began to laugh at the acrimonious verve of the storyteller. Speaking smoothly, drawing out his words somehow peevishly, with a tender emphasis on the vowels, the man told why he had been forced, precisely owing to today's regulations, to sell a magnificent estate of his in —— province, and even, not being in great need of money, at half price, and at the same time to keep a ruined estate, money-losing and in litigation, and even to spend more on it. "I fled from them to avoid further litigation over Pavlishchev's land. Another one or two inheritances like that and I'm a ruined man. Though I had about ten thousand acres of excellent land coming to me there!"

"You see . . . Ivan Petrovich is a relation of the late Nikolai Andreevich Pavlishchev . . . you were looking for relations, I believe," Ivan Fyodorovich, who suddenly turned up beside the prince and noticed his extreme attention to the conversation, said to him in a half-whisper. Till then he had been entertaining his superior, the general, but he had long since noticed the exceptional solitude of Lev Nikolaevich and had begun to worry; he wanted to draw him into the conversation to some degree, and thus to show and recommend him for a second time to the "higher persons."

"Lev Nikolaich was Nikolai Andreich Pavlishchev's ward after his parents' death," he put in, having caught Ivan Petrovich's eye.

"De-light-ed," the man remarked, "and I even remember you. Earlier, when Ivan Fyodorych introduced us, I recognized you at once, even your face. You've really changed little externally, though I saw you as a child of about ten or eleven. Something in your features reminded me . . ."

"You saw me as a child?" the prince asked with a sort of extraordinary surprise.

"Oh, a very long time ago," Ivan Petrovich went on, "in Zlatoverkhovo, where you then lived with my cousins. I used to visit Zlatoverkhovo rather often—you don't remember me? Ve-ry possible that you don't . . . You had . . . some sort of illness then, so that I once even wondered about you . . ."

"I don't remember a thing!" the prince confirmed heatedly.

A few more words of explanation, extremely calm on Ivan Petrovich's part and surprisingly excited on the prince's, and it turned out that the two ladies, the old spinsters, relations of the late Pavlishchev, who lived on his estate in Zlatoverkhovo and who were entrusted with the prince's upbringing, were in turn Ivan Petrovich's cousins. Ivan Petrovich, like everyone else, could give almost no explanation of the reasons why Pavlishchev had been so taken up with the little prince, his ward. "I forgot to ask about it then," but all the same it turned out that he had an excellent memory, because he even remembered how strict the elder cousin, Marfa Nikitishna, had been with her little charge, "so that I even quarreled with her once over the system of education, because it was all birching and birching—for a sick child . . . you must agree . . . it's . . ."—and, on the contrary, how affectionate the younger cousin, Natalya Nikitishna, had been with the poor boy . . . "The two of them," he explained further, "now live in —— province (only I don't know if they're still alive), where Pavlishchev left them a quite, quite decent little estate. Marfa Nikitishna, I believe, wanted to enter a convent; though I won't insist on that; maybe I heard it about somebody else . . . yes, I heard it about a doctor's widow the other day . . ."

The prince listened to this with eyes shining with rapture and tenderness. He declared in his turn, with extraordinary ardor, that he would never forgive himself for not finding an opportunity, during those six months of traveling in the provinces, to locate and visit his former guardians. "He had wanted to go every day and kept being distracted by circumstances . . . but now he promised himself . . . without fail . . . even to —— province . . . So you know Natalia Nikitishna? What a beautiful, what a saintly soul! But Marfa Nikitishna, too . . . forgive me, but I believe you're mistaken about Marfa Nikitishna! She was strict, but . . . it was impossible not to lose patience . . . with such an idiot as I was then (hee, hee!). For I was quite an idiot then, you wouldn't believe it (ha, ha!). However . . . however, you saw me then and . . . How is it I don't remember you, pray tell? So you . . . ah, my God, so you're really Nikolai Andreich Pavlishchev's relation?"

"I as-sure you," Ivan Petrovich smiled, looking the prince over.

"Oh, I didn't say that because I . . . doubted . . . and, finally, how could one doubt it (heh, heh!) . . . at least a little? That is, even a little!! (Heh, heh!) But what I mean is that the late Nikolai Andreich Pavlishchev was such an excellent man! A most magnanimous man, really, I assure you!"

It was not that the prince was breathless, but he was, so to speak, "choking from the goodness of his heart," as Adelaida put it the next morning in a conversation with her fiancé, Prince Shch.

"Ah, my God!" laughed Ivan Petrovich, "why can't I be the relation of a mag-na-nimous man?"

"Ah, my God!" cried the prince, embarrassed, hurrying, and becoming more and more enthusiastic. "I've . . . I've said something stupid again, but . . . it had to be so, because I . . . I . . . I . . . though again that's not what I mean! And what am I now, pray tell, in view of such interests . . . of such enormous interests! And in comparison with such a magnanimous man—because, by God, he was a most magnanimous man, isn't it true? Isn't it true?"

The prince was even trembling all over. Why he suddenly became so agitated, why he became so emotionally ecstatic, for absolutely no reason, and, it seemed, out of all proportion with the subject of the conversation—it would be hard to tell. He was simply in that sort of mood and even all but felt at that moment the warmest and sincerest gratitude to someone for something—perhaps even to Ivan Petrovich, if not to all the guests in general. He became much too "happified." Ivan Petrovich finally began to look at him more attentively; the "dignitary," too, studied him very attentively. Belokonsky turned a wrathful gaze on the prince and pressed her lips. Prince N., Evgeny Pavlovich, Prince Shch., the girls—everybody broke off their conversation and listened. Aglaya seemed alarmed, and Lizaveta Prokofyevna was simply scared. They were strange, the daughters and their mama: they themselves thought it would be better for the prince to spend the evening in silence; but as soon as they saw him in a corner, completely alone and perfectly content with his lot, they at once became worried. Alexandra had been about to go over to him and lead him carefully across the whole room to join their company, that is, the company of Prince N., around Belokonsky.

But now that the prince had begun to speak, they became still more worried.

"He was a most excellent man, you're right about that," Ivan Petrovich said imposingly and now without a smile, "yes, yes . . . he was a wonderful man! Wonderful and worthy," he added after a pause. "Worthy, one might even say, of all respect," he added still more imposingly after a third pause, "and . . . and it's even very agreeable that you, for your part, show . . ."

"Was it with this Pavlishchev that some story happened . . . a strange story . . . with the abbot . . . the abbot . . . I forget which abbot, only everybody was talking about it then," the "dignitary" said, as if recollecting.

"With the abbot Gouraud, a Jesuit," Ivan Petrovich reminded him. "Yes, sir, that's our most excellent and worthy people for you! Because after all he was a man of good family, with a fortune, a gentleman-in-waiting, and if he . . . had continued in the service . . . And then suddenly he abandons his service and all in order to embrace Catholicism and become a Jesuit, and that almost openly, with a sort of ecstasy. Really, he died just in time . . . yes, everybody said so then . . ."

The prince was beside himself.

"Pavlishchev . . . Pavlishchev embraced Catholicism? That can't be!" he cried in horror.

"Well, 'that can't be,'" Ivan Petrovich maundered imposingly, "is saying too much, and you will agree yourself, my dear Prince . . . However, you value the deceased man so . . . indeed, the man was very kind, to which I ascribe, for the main part, the success of that trickster Gouraud. But just ask me, ask me, how much hustle and bustle I had afterwards over this affair . . . and precisely with that same Gouraud! Imagine," he suddenly turned to the little old man, "they even wanted to present claims for the inheritance, and I had to resort to the most energetic measures then . . . to bring them to reason . . . because they're masters at it! As-ton-ishing! But, thank God, it happened in Moscow, I went straight to the count, and we . . . brought them to reason . . ."

"You wouldn't believe how you've upset and shocked me!" the prince cried again.

"I'm sorry; but, as a matter of fact, all this, essentially speaking, was trifles and would have ended in trifles, as always; I'm sure of it. Last summer," he again turned to the little old man, "they say Countess K. also joined some Catholic convent abroad; our people somehow can't resist, once they give in to those . . . finaglers . . . especially abroad."

"It all comes, I think, from our . . . fatigue," the little old man mumbled with authority, "well, and the manner they have of preaching . . . elegant, their own . . . and they know how to frighten. In the year thirty-two they frightened me in Vienna, I can assure you; only I didn't give in, I fled from them, ha, ha!"

"I heard, my dear man, that you abandoned your post and fled from Vienna to Paris that time with the beautiful Countess Levitsky, and not from a Jesuit," Belokonsky suddenly put in.

"Well, but it was from a Jesuit, all the same it comes out that it was from a Jesuit!" the little old man picked up, laughing at the pleasant memory. "You seem to be very religious, something rarely to be met with nowadays in a young man," he benignly addressed Prince Lev Nikolaevich, who listened open-mouthed and was still shocked; the little old man obviously wanted to get to know the prince more closely; for some reason he had begun to interest him very much.

"Pavlishchev was a bright mind and a Christian, a true Christian," the prince suddenly said, "how could he submit to . . . an unchristian faith? . . . Catholicism is the same as an unchristian faith!" he added suddenly, his eyes flashing and staring straight ahead, his gaze somehow taking in everyone at once.

"Well, that's too much," the little old man murmured and looked at Ivan Fyodorovich with astonishment.

"How is it that Catholicism is an unchristian religion?" Ivan Petrovich turned on his chair. "What is it, then?"

"An unchristian faith, first of all!" the prince began speaking again, in extreme agitation and much too sharply. "That's first, and second, Roman Catholicism is even worse than atheism itself, that's my opinion! Yes, that's my opinion! Atheism only preaches a zero, but Catholicism goes further: it preaches a distorted Christ, a Christ it has slandered and blasphemed, a counter Christ! It preaches the Antichrist, I swear to you, I assure you! That is my personal and longstanding conviction, and it has tormented me . . . Roman Catholicism believes that without universal state power the Church on earth cannot stand, and it shouts: *Non possumus!**[33] In my opinion, Roman Catholicism is not even a faith, but decidedly the continuation of the Western Roman empire, and everything in

---

*We cannot!

it is subject to that idea, beginning with faith. The pope seized land, an earthly throne, and took up the sword; since then everything has gone on that way, only to the sword they added lies, trickery, deceit, fanaticism, superstition, villainy; they played upon the most holy, truthful, simple-hearted, ardent feelings of the people; they traded everything, everything, for money, for base earthly power. Isn't that the teaching of the Antichrist?! How could atheism not come out of them? Atheism came out of them, out of Roman Catholicism itself! Atheism began, before all else, with them themselves: could they believe in themselves? It grew stronger through repugnance against them; it is a product of their lies and spiritual impotence! Atheism! In Russia so far only exceptional classes of society do not believe, those who have lost their roots, as Evgeny Pavlovich put it so splendidly the other day; while there, in Europe, awful masses of the people themselves are beginning not to believe—formerly from darkness and deceit, but now from fanaticism, from hatred of the Church and of Christianity!"

The prince paused to catch his breath. He was speaking terribly quickly. He was pale and breathless. Everyone exchanged glances; but at last the little old man laughed openly. Prince N. took out his lorgnette and studied the prince, not taking his eyes away. The German poeticule crept out of the corner and moved closer to the table, smiling a sinister smile.

"You greatly ex-ag-ge-rate," Ivan Petrovich drew out with some boredom and even as if embarrassed at something. "In their Church there are also representatives who are worthy of all respect and vir-tu-ous men . . ."

"I never spoke of individual representatives of the Church. I was speaking of Roman Catholicism in its essence, I was speaking of Rome. The Church cannot disappear entirely. I never said that!"

"Agreed, but this is all well known and even—unnecessary and . . . belongs to theology . . ."

"Oh, no, no! Not only to theology, I assure you! It concerns us much more closely than you think. That is our whole mistake, that we're still unable to see that this is not only an exclusively theological matter! For socialism is also a product of Catholicism and the Catholic essence! It, too, like its brother atheism, came from despair, opposing Catholicism in a moral sense, in order to replace the lost moral force of religion with itself, in order to quench the spiritual thirst of thirsting mankind and save it not through Christ, but also through violence! It is also freedom through violence, it is also unity through blood and the sword! 'Do not dare to believe in God, do not dare to have property, do not dare to have personality, *fraternité ou la mort*,* two million heads!'[34] You shall know them by their deeds,[35] it is said! And don't think that it's all so innocent and unthreatening for us; oh, we must respond, and swiftly, swiftly! Our Christ, whom we have preserved and they have never known, must shine forth as a response to the West! Not by being slavishly caught on the Jesuits' hook, but by bringing them our Russian civilization, we must now confront them, and let it not be said among us that their preaching is elegant, as someone just said . . ."

"But excuse me, excuse me," Ivan Petrovich became terribly worried, looking around and even beginning to get frightened, "your thoughts are all, of course, praiseworthy and full of patriotism, but it's all exaggerated in the highest degree and . . . it's even better if we drop it . . ."

"No, it's not exaggerated, but rather understated; precisely understated, because I'm not able to express it, but . . ."

"Ex-cuse me!"

The prince fell silent. He was sitting upright on his chair and looking at Ivan Petrovich with fixed, burning eyes.

"It seems to me that you've been too greatly shocked by the incident with your benefactor," the little old man observed gently and without losing his equanimity. "You're inflamed . . . perhaps from solitude. If you live more with people, and I hope society will welcome you as a remarkable young man, your animation will, of course, subside, and you will see that it's all much simpler . . . and besides, such rare cases . . . come, in my view, partly from our satiety, and partly from . . . boredom . . ."

"Precisely, precisely so," the prince cried, "a splendid thought! Precisely 'from our boredom,' not from satiety, but, on the contrary, from thirst . . . not from satiety, there you're mistaken! Not only from thirst, but even from inflammation, from feverish thirst! And . . . and don't think it's all on such a small scale that one can simply laugh; forgive me, but one must be able to foresee! The Russian people, as soon as they reach the shore, as soon as they believe it's the shore, are so glad of it that they immediately go to the ultimate pillars.[36] Why is that? You marvel at Pavlishchev, you ascribe everything to his madness or to his kindness, but that's not so! And not only we but the whole of Europe marvels, on such occasions, at

*Brotherhood or death.

our Russian passion: if one of us embraces Catholicism, then he's bound to become a Jesuit, and of the most underground sort at that;[37] if he becomes an atheist, he is bound to start demanding the eradication of belief in God by force, which means by the sword! Why is that, why is there such frenzy all at once? You really don't know? Because he has found his fatherland, which he had missed here, and he rejoices; he has found the shore, the land, and he rushes to kiss it! It's not only from vainglory, not only from nasty, vainglorious feelings that Russian atheists and Russian Jesuits proceed, but from spiritual pain, spiritual thirst, from the longing for a lofty cause, a firm shore, a native land, in which we've ceased to believe because we've never known it! It's so easy for a Russian man to become an atheist, easier than for anyone else in the whole world! And our people don't simply become atheists, but they must *believe* in atheism, as in a new faith, without ever noticing that they are believing in a zero. Such is our thirst! 'Whoever has no ground under his feet also has no God.' That is not my phrase. It is the phrase of a merchant, an Old Believer,[38] I met on my travels. True, he didn't put it that way, he said: 'Whoever has renounced his native land, has also renounced his God.' Only think that some of our most educated people got themselves into flagellantism[39] . . . And in that case, incidentally, what makes flagellantism worse than nihilism, Jesuitism, atheism? It may even be a little more profound! But that is how far their anguish went! . . . Open to the thirsting and inflamed companions of Columbus the shores of the New World, open to the Russian man the Russian World, let him find the gold, the treasure, hidden from him in the ground! Show him the future renewal of all mankind and its resurrection, perhaps by Russian thought alone, by the Russian God and Christ, and you'll see what a mighty and righteous, wise and meek giant will rise up before the astonished world, astonished and frightened, because they expect nothing from us but the sword, the sword and violence, because, judging by themselves, they cannot imagine us without barbarism. And that is so to this day, and the more so the further it goes! And . . ."

But here an incident suddenly occurred, and the orator's speech was interrupted in the most unexpected way.

This whole feverish tirade, this whole flow of passionate and agitated words and ecstatic thoughts, as if thronging in some sort of turmoil and leaping over each other, all this foreboded something dangerous, something peculiar in the mood of the young man, who had boiled up so suddenly for no apparent reason. Of those present in the drawing room, all who knew the prince marveled fearfully (and some also with shame) at his outburst, which so disagreed with his usual and even timid restraint, with the rare and particular tact he showed on certain occasions and his instinctive sense of higher propriety. They could not understand where it came from: the news about Pavlishchev could not have been the cause of it. In the ladies' corner they looked at him as at one gone mad, and Belokonsky later confessed that "another moment and she would have run for her life." The "little old men" were nearly at a loss from their initial amazement; the general-superior gazed, displeased and stern, from his chair. The engineer-colonel sat perfectly motionless. The little German even turned pale, but was still smiling his false smile, glancing at the others to see how they would react. However, all this and "the whole scandal" could have been resolved in the most ordinary and natural way, perhaps, even a minute later; Ivan Fyodorovich was extremely surprised but, having collected his thoughts sooner than the others, had already tried several times to stop the prince; failing in that, he was now making his way towards him with firm and resolute purposes. Another moment and, if it had really been necessary, he might have decided to take the prince out amicably, under the pretext of his illness, which might actually have been true and of which Ivan Fyodorovich was very much convinced in himself . . . But things turned out otherwise.

From the very beginning, as soon as the prince entered the drawing room, he sat down as far as possible from the Chinese vase, with which Aglaya had frightened him so. Can one possibly believe that, after Aglaya's words the day before, some sort of indelible conviction settled in him, some sort of astonishing and impossible premonition that the next day he would unfailingly break that vase, however far away he kept from it, however much he avoided the disaster? But it was so. In the course of the evening other strong but bright impressions began to flow into his soul; we have already spoken of that. He forgot his premonition. When he heard about Pavlishchev, and Ivan Fyodorovich brought him and introduced him again to Ivan Petrovich, he moved closer to the table and ended up right in the armchair next to the enormous, beautiful Chinese vase, which stood on a pedestal almost at his elbow, slightly behind him.

With his last words he suddenly got up from his place, carelessly waved his arm, somehow moved his shoulder—and . . . a general cry rang out! The vase rocked, as if undecided at first whether it might not fall on the head of one of the little old men, but suddenly it leaned in the opposite direction, towards the little German, who barely managed to jump aside in terror, and toppled onto the floor. Noise, shouts, precious pieces scattered over the rug, fear, amazement—oh, it is difficult and almost unnecessary to depict how it was for the prince! But we cannot omit mention of one strange sensation that struck him precisely at that very moment and suddenly made itself distinct in the crowd of all the other vague and strange sensations: it was not the shame, not the scandal, not the fear, not the unexpectedness that struck him most of all, but the fulfilled prophecy! Precisely what was so thrilling in this thought he would have been unable to explain to himself; he felt only that he was struck to the heart, and he stood in a fear that was almost mystical. Another moment and everything before him seemed to expand, instead of horror there was light, joy, rapture; his breath was taken away, and . . . but the moment passed. Thank God, it was not that! He caught his breath and looked around.

For a long time he seemed not to understand the turmoil seething around him, that is, he understood it perfectly well and saw everything, but stood as if he were a special person, not taking part in anything, like the invisible man in a fairy tale, who has gotten into a room and is observing people who are strangers but who interest him. He saw the broken pieces being removed, heard rapid talk, saw Aglaya, pale and looking at him strangely, very strangely: there was no hatred in her eyes at all, nor any wrath; she looked at him with frightened but such sympathetic eyes, and at the others with such flashing eyes . . . his heart suddenly ached sweetly. Finally he saw with strange amazement that everyone was sitting down and even laughing, as if nothing had happened! Another moment and the laughter grew louder; they laughed looking at him, at his stunned speechlessness, but they laughed amicably, merrily; many addressed him and spoke so gently, above all Lizaveta Prokofyevna: she was laughing and saying something very, very kind. Suddenly he felt Ivan Fyodorovich giving him a friendly pat on the shoulder; Ivan Petrovich was also laughing; but still better, still more attractive and sympathetic was the little old man; he took the prince by the hand and, pressing it lightly, patting it lightly with the palm of his other hand, was persuading him to recollect himself, as if he were a frightened little boy, which the prince liked terribly much, and finally sat him down next to him.

The prince peered into his face with delight and for some reason was still unable to speak; he was breathless; he liked the old man's face so much.

"What?" he finally murmured. "So you really forgive me? And . . . you, too, Lizaveta Prokofyevna?"

The laughter increased; tears welled up in the prince's eyes; he could not believe it and was enchanted.

"Of course, it was a beautiful vase. I remember it being here for all of fifteen years, yes . . . fifteen . . ." Ivan Petrovich began.

"Well, it's no disaster! A man, too, comes to an end, and this was just a clay pot!" Lizaveta Prokofyevna said loudly. "You're not so frightened, are you, Lev Nikolaich?" she added even with fear. "Enough, dear boy, enough; you really frighten me."

"And you forgive me for *everything*? For *everything* besides the vase?" the prince suddenly began to get up from his place, but the little old man at once pulled him down again by the hand. He did not want to let him go.

"*C'est très curieux, et c'est très sérieux!*"* he whispered across the table to Ivan Petrovich, though quite loudly; the prince may have heard it.

"So I didn't offend any of you? You wouldn't believe how happy that thought makes me; but so it should be! How could I have offended anyone here? I'd offend you again by thinking so."

"Calm yourself, my friend, that is an exaggeration. And you generally have no reason to thank us so much; it's a beautiful feeling, but it's exaggerated."

"I'm not thanking you, I simply . . . admire you, I'm happy looking at you; perhaps I'm speaking foolishly, but I—I need to speak, I need to explain . . . even if only out of respect for myself."

Everything in him was impulsive, vague, and feverish; it may well be that the words he spoke were often not the ones he wanted to say. By his gaze he seemed to be asking: may I speak to you? His gaze fell on Belokonsky.

"Never mind, dear boy, go on, go on, only don't get out of breath," she observed. "You started breathlessly earlier and see what it led to; but don't be afraid to speak: these gentlemen have seen queerer than you, they won't be surprised, and God knows you're not all that clever, you simply broke a vase and frightened us."

Smiling, the prince listened to her.

*It's very curious, and very serious!

"Wasn't it you," he suddenly turned to the little old man, "wasn't it you who saved the student Podkumov and the clerk Shvabrin from being exiled three months ago?"

The little old man even blushed slightly and murmured that he ought to calm down.

"Wasn't it you I heard about," he turned to Ivan Petrovich at once, "who gave free timber to your burned-out peasants in —— province, though they were already emancipated and had caused you trouble?"

"Well, that's an ex-ag-ger-ation," murmured Ivan Petrovich, though assuming a look of pleased dignity; but this time he was perfectly right that it was "an exaggeration": it was merely a false rumor that had reached the prince.

"And you, Princess," he suddenly turned to Belokonsky with a bright smile, "didn't you receive me six months ago in Moscow like your own son, following a letter from Lizaveta Prokofyevna, and give me, as if I were indeed your own son, some advice which I will never forget? Do you remember?"

"Why get so worked up?" Belokonsky responded vexedly. "You're a kind man, but a ridiculous one: someone gives you two cents, and you thank them as if they'd saved your life. You think it's praiseworthy, but it's disgusting."

She was getting quite angry, but suddenly burst out laughing, and this time it was kindly laughter. Lizaveta Prokofyevna's face also lit up; Ivan Fyodorovich brightened, too.

"I told you that Lev Nikolaich is a man . . . a man . . . in short, if only he didn't become breathless, as the princess observed . . ." the general murmured in joyful rapture, repeating Belokonsky's words, which had struck him.

Aglaya alone was somehow sad; but her face still burned, perhaps with indignation.

"He really is very nice," the little old man again murmured to Ivan Petrovich.

"I came here with pain in my heart," the prince went on, with a somehow ever-increasing perturbation, speaking faster and faster, more strangely and animatedly, "I . . . I was afraid of you, afraid of myself as well. Most of all of myself. Returning here to Petersburg, I promised myself to be sure and see our foremost people, the elders, the ancient stock, to whom I myself belong, among whom I am one of the first by birth. For I am now sitting with princes like myself, am I not? I wanted to know you, that was necessary; very, very necessary! I've always heard so much more bad than good about you, about the pettiness and exclusiveness of your interests, about your backwardness, your shallow education, your ridiculous habits—oh, so much has been written and said about you! It was with curiosity that I came here today, with perturbation: I had to see for myself and become personally convinced: is it actually so that this whole upper stratum of the Russian people is good for nothing, has outlived its time, has exhausted its ancient life, and is only capable of dying out, but in a petty, envious struggle with people . . . of the future, hindering them, not noticing that it is dying itself? Before, too, I never fully believed this opinion, because we've never had any higher estate, except perhaps at court, according to the uniform, or . . . by chance, and now it has quite vanished, isn't it so, isn't it so?"

"Well, no, that's not so at all," Ivan Petrovich laughed sarcastically.

"Well, he's yammering away again!" Belokonsky could not help saying.

"*Laissez-le dire*,* he's even trembling all over," the little old man warned again in a half whisper.

The prince was decidedly beside himself.

"And what then? I saw gracious, simple-hearted, intelligent people; I saw an old man who was gentle and heard out a boy like me; I see people capable of understanding and forgiveness, people who are Russian and kind, people almost as kind and cordial as I met there, almost no worse. You can judge how joyfully surprised I was! Oh, allow me to speak this out! I had heard a lot and believed very much myself that in society everything is a manner, everything is a decrepit form, while the essence is exhausted; but I can see for myself now that among us that cannot be; anywhere else, but not among us. Can it be that you are all now Jesuits and swindlers? I heard Prince N. tell a story tonight: wasn't it all artless, inspired humor, wasn't it genuinely good-natured? Can such words come from the lips of a . . . dead man, with a dried-up heart and talent? Could dead people have treated me the way you have treated me? Is this not material . . . for the future, for hopes? Can such people fail to understand and lag behind?"

"Once more I beg you, calm yourself, my dear, we'll come back to it all another time, and it will be my pleasure . . ." the "dignitary" smiled.

*Let him speak.

Ivan Petrovich grunted and shifted in his chair; Ivan Fyodorovich stirred; the general-superior was talking with the dignitary's wife, no longer paying the slightest attention to the prince; but the dignitary's wife kept listening and glancing at him.

"No, you know, it's better that I talk!" the prince went on with a new feverish impulse, addressing the little old man somehow especially trustfully and even confidentially. "Yesterday Aglaya Ivanovna forbade me to talk, and even mentioned the topics I shouldn't talk about; she knows I'm ridiculous at them. I'm going on twenty-seven, but I know I'm like a child. I don't have the right to express my thoughts, I said so long ago; I only spoke candidly in Moscow, with Rogozhin . . . He and I read Pushkin together, we read all of him; he knew nothing, not even Pushkin's name . . . I'm always afraid of compromising the thought and the *main idea* by my ridiculous look. I lack the gesture. My gesture is always the opposite, and that provokes laughter and humiliates the idea. I have no sense of measure either, and that's the main thing; that's even the most main thing . . . I know it's better for me to sit and be silent. When I persist in being silent, I even seem very reasonable, and what's more I can think things over. But now it's better that I speak. I started speaking because you looked at me so wonderfully; you have a wonderful face! Yesterday I gave Aglaya Ivanovna my word that I'd keep silent all evening."

"*Vraiment?*"* smiled the little old man.

"But I have moments when I think that I'm wrong to think that way: sincerity is worth a gesture, isn't it so? Isn't it so?"

"Sometimes."

"I want to explain everything, everything, everything! Oh, yes! Do you think I'm a utopian? An ideologist? Oh, no, by God, my thoughts are all so simple . . . You don't believe it? You smile? You know, I'm sometimes mean, because I lose my faith; today I was walking here and thinking: 'Well, how shall I start speaking to them? What word should I begin with, so that they understand at least something?' I was so afraid, but I was more afraid for you, terribly, terribly afraid! And yet how could I be afraid, wasn't it shameful to be afraid? What of it, if for one advanced person there are such myriads of backward and unkind ones? This is precisely my joy, that I'm now convinced that it's not so at all, and that there is living material! Nor is there any embarrassment in the fact that

*Really?

we're ridiculous, isn't that true? For it's actually so, we are ridiculous, light-minded, with bad habits, we're bored, we don't know how to look, how to understand, we're all like that, all, you, and I, and they! Now, you're not offended when I tell you to your face that you're ridiculous? And if so, aren't you material? You know, in my opinion it's sometimes even good to be ridiculous, if not better: we can the sooner forgive each other, the sooner humble ourselves; we can't understand everything at once, we can't start right out with perfection! To achieve perfection, one must first begin by not understanding many things! And if we understand too quickly, we may not understand well. This I tell you, you, who have already been able to understand . . . and not understand . . . so much. I'm not afraid for you now; surely you're not angry that such a boy is saying such things to you? You're laughing, Ivan Petrovich. You thought I was afraid for *them*, that I was *their* advocate, a democrat, a speaker for equality?" he laughed hysterically (he laughed every other minute in short, ecstatic bursts). "I'm afraid for you, for all of you, for all of us together. For I myself am a prince of ancient stock, and I am sitting with princes. It is to save us all that I speak, to keep our estate from vanishing for nothing, in the darkness, having realized nothing, squabbling over everything and losing everything. Why vanish and yield our place to others, when we can remain the vanguard and the elders? Let us be the vanguard, then we shall be the elders. Let us become servants, in order to be elders."[40]

He kept trying to get up from his chair, but the little old man kept holding him back, looking at him, however, with growing uneasiness.

"Listen! I know that talking is wrong: it's better simply to set an example, better simply to begin . . . I have already begun . . . and—and is it really possible to be unhappy? Oh, what are my grief and my trouble, if I am able to be happy? You know, I don't understand how it's possible to pass by a tree and not be happy to see it. To talk with a man and not be happy that you love him! Oh, I only don't know how to say it . . . but there are so many things at every step that are so beautiful, that even the most confused person finds beautiful. Look at a child, look at God's sunrise, look at the grass growing, look into the eyes that are looking at you and love you . . ."

He had long been standing, speaking. The little old man now looked at him fearfully. Lizaveta Prokofyevna cried: "Oh, my God!"

realizing before anyone else, and clasped her hands. Aglaya quickly rushed to him, had time to receive him into her arms, and with horror, her face distorted by pain, heard the wild shout of the "spirit that convulsed and dashed down"[41] the unfortunate man. The sick man lay on the carpet. Someone managed quickly to put a pillow under his head.

No one had expected this. A quarter of an hour later Prince N., Evgeny Pavlovich, and the little old man tried to revive the party, but in another half an hour everybody had gone. There were many words of sympathy uttered, many laments, a few opinions. Ivan Petrovich, among other things, declared that "the young man is a Slav-o-phile,[42] or something of the sort, but anyhow it's not dangerous." The little old man did not come out with anything. True, afterwards, for the next couple of days, everyone was a bit cross; Ivan Petrovich was even offended, but not greatly. The general-superior was somewhat cold to Ivan Fyodorovich for a while. The "patron" of the family, the dignitary, for his part, also mumbled some admonition to the father of the family, and said flatteringly that he was very, very interested in Aglaya's fate. He was in fact a rather kind man; but among the reasons for his curiosity about the prince, in the course of the evening, had also been the old story between the prince and Nastasya Filippovna; he had heard something about this story and was even very interested; he would even have liked to ask about it.

Belokonsky, on leaving the party, said to Lizaveta Prokofyevna:

"Well, he's both good and bad; and if you want to know my opinion, he's more bad. You can see for yourself what sort of man—a sick man!"

Lizaveta Prokofyevna decided definitively to herself that the fiancé was "impossible," and promised herself during the night that "as long as she lived, the prince was not going to be Aglaya's husband." With that she got up in the morning. But that same day, between noon and one, at lunch, she fell into surprising contradiction with herself.

To one question, though an extremely cautious one, from her sisters, Aglaya suddenly answered coldly but haughtily, as if cutting them off:

"I've never given him any sort of promise, and never in my life considered him my fiancé. He's as much a stranger to me as anyone else."

Lizaveta Prokofyevna suddenly flared up.

"That I did not expect of you," she said bitterly. "As a fiancé he's impossible, I know, and thank God it all worked out this way; but I did not expect such words from you! I thought there would be something else from you. I'd throw out all those people from yesterday and keep him, that's what kind of man he is! . . ."

Here she suddenly stopped, frightened herself at what she had said. But if she had known how unjust she was being at that moment towards her daughter? Everything was already decided in Aglaya's head; she was also waiting for her hour, which was to decide everything, and every hint, every careless touch made a deep wound in her heart.

VIII

FOR THE PRINCE, too, that morning began under the influence of painful forebodings; they might have been explained by his sickly condition, but he was too indefinitely sad, and that was the most tormenting thing for him. True, the facts stood before him, vivid, painful, and biting, but his sadness went beyond anything he recalled and realized; he understood that he could not calm down by himself. The expectation gradually took root in him that something special and definitive was going to happen to him that same day. His fit of the evening before had been a mild one; besides hypochondria, some heaviness in the head and pain in his limbs, he did not feel upset in any other way. His head worked quite distinctly, though his soul was sick. He got up rather late and at once clearly recalled the previous evening; though not quite distinctly, he recalled all the same that about half an hour after the fit he had been brought home. He learned that a messenger had already come from the Epanchins to inquire after his health. Another came at half-past eleven; this pleased him. Vera Lebedev was one of the first who came to visit him and look after him. The moment she saw him, she suddenly burst into tears, but the prince at once calmed her down, and she laughed. He was somehow suddenly struck by the strong compassion this girl felt for him; he seized her hand and kissed it. Vera blushed.

"Ah, don't, don't!" she exclaimed in fear, quickly pulling her hand away.

She soon left in some strange embarrassment. Among other things, she had time to tell him that that morning, at daybreak, her father had gone running to "the deceased," as he called the general, to find out whether or not he had died in the night, and had heard it said that he would probably die soon. Towards noon Lebedev himself came home and called on the prince, but, essentially, "just for a moment, to inquire after his precious health," and so on, and, besides that, to pay a visit to the "little cupboard." He did nothing but "oh" and "ah," and the prince quickly dismissed him, but all the same the man tried to ask questions about yesterday's fit, though it was obvious that he already knew about it in detail. Kolya stopped to see him, also for a moment; this one was indeed in a hurry and in great and dark anxiety. He began by asking the prince, directly and insistently, to explain everything that had been concealed from him, adding that he had already learned almost everything yesterday. He was strongly and deeply shaken.

With all the possible sympathy that he was capable of, the prince recounted the whole affair, restoring the facts with full exactitude, and he struck the poor boy as if with a thunderbolt. He could not utter a word, and wept silently. The prince sensed that this was one of those impressions that remain forever and mark a permanent break in a young man's life. He hastened to tell him his own view of the affair, adding that in his opinion the old man's death had been caused, mainly, by the horror that remained in his heart after his misdeed, and that not everyone was capable of that. Kolya's eyes flashed as he heard the prince out.

"Worthless Ganka, and Varya, and Ptitsyn! I'm not going to quarrel with them, but our paths are different from this moment on! Ah, Prince, since yesterday I've felt so much that's new; it's a lesson for me! I also consider my mother as directly on my hands now; though she's provided for at Varya's, it's all not right . . ."

He jumped up, remembering that he was expected, hurriedly asked about the state of the prince's health and, having heard the answer, suddenly added hastily:

"Is there anything else? I heard yesterday . . . (though I have no right), but if you ever need a faithful servant in anything, he's here before you. It seems neither of us is entirely happy, isn't it so? But . . . I'm not asking, I'm not asking . . ."

He left, and the prince began to ponder still more deeply: everyone was prophesying unhappiness, everyone had already drawn conclusions, everyone looked as if they knew something, and something that he did not know; Lebedev asks questions, Kolya hints outright, and Vera weeps. At last he waved his hand in vexation:

"Cursed, morbid insecurity," he thought. His face brightened when, past one o'clock, he saw the Epanchins coming to call on him "for a moment." They indeed dropped in for a moment. Lizaveta Prokofyevna, getting up from lunch, announced that they were all going for a walk right then and together. The information was given in the form of an order, abruptly, drily, without explanations. They all went out—that is, mama, the girls, and Prince Shch. Lizaveta Prokofyevna went straight in the opposite direction from the one they took every day. They all understood what it meant, and they all kept silent, fearing to annoy the mother, while she, as if to shelter herself from reproaches and objections, walked ahead of them all without looking back. Finally Adelaida observed that there was no need to run like that during a stroll and that there was no keeping up with mother.

"I tell you what," Lizaveta Prokofyevna suddenly turned around, "we're now passing his house. Whatever Aglaya may think and whatever may happen afterwards, he's not a stranger to us, and now on top of it he's unhappy and sick; I at least will stop and see him. Whoever wants to come with me can come, whoever doesn't can walk past; the way is clear."

They all went in, of course. The prince, as was proper, hastened once again to apologize for yesterday's vase and . . . the scandal.

"Well, never mind that," replied Lizaveta Prokofyevna, "we're not sorry for the vase, we're sorry for you. So you yourself now realize that there was a scandal: that's what 'the morning after . . .' means, but never mind that either, because everyone can see now that you're not answerable for anything. Well, good-bye, anyhow; if you're strong enough, go for a walk and then sleep again—that's my advice. And if you think of it, come and see us as formerly; rest assured, once and for all, that whatever happens, whatever may come, you'll still remain a friend of our house: of mine at least. I can at least answer for myself . . ."

They all responded to the challenge and confirmed the mother's feelings. They left, but this simple-hearted haste to say something affectionate and encouraging concealed much that was cruel, of which Lizaveta Prokofyevna was unaware. In the invitation to come "as formerly" and in the words "of mine at least" again something ominous sounded. The prince began to remember Aglaya; true, she had smiled wonderfully at him as she came in and as she left, but she had not said a word, even when they had all expressed their assurances of friendship, though she had looked at him intently a couple of times. Her face had been paler than usual, as if she had slept badly that night. The prince decided that he would certainly go to them that evening "as formerly," and he glanced feverishly at his watch. Vera came in exactly three minutes after the Epanchins left.

"Lev Nikolaevich, Aglaya Ivanovna has just given me a little word for you in secret."

The prince simply trembled.

"A note?"

"No, verbally; she barely had time. She asks you very much not to leave your house all day today, not for a single moment, till seven o'clock in the evening, or even till nine, I didn't quite hear."

"But . . . what for? What does it mean?"

"I don't know anything about that; only she asked me to tell you firmly."

"She said 'firmly'?"

"No, sir, she didn't say it straight out: she barely had time to turn around and tell me, once I ran up to her myself. But firmly or not, I could see by her face that it was an order. She looked at me with such eyes that my heart stopped . . ."

A few more questions and the prince, though he learned nothing further, instead became still more anxious. Left alone, he lay on the sofa and again began to think. "Maybe someone will be there till nine o'clock, and she's afraid for me again, that I might act up again in front of the guests," he thought up finally and again began waiting impatiently for evening and looking at his watch. But the answer to the riddle came long before evening and also in the form of a new visit, an answer in the form of a new, tormenting riddle: exactly half an hour after the Epanchins left, Ippolit came in, so tired and worn out that, on coming in, and without saying a word, he literally collapsed into an armchair, as if unconscious, and instantly broke into an unbearable fit of coughing. In the end he coughed up blood. His eyes glittered and red spots glowed on his cheeks. The prince murmured something to him, but he did not answer and for a long time, without answering, only waved his hand, so as not to be bothered meanwhile. Finally he recovered.

"I'm leaving!" he finally forced himself to say in a hoarse voice.

"If you like, I'll see you off," said the prince, getting up from his place, and he stopped short, remembering the recent ban on leaving the house.

Ippolit laughed.

"I'm not leaving you," he went on with an incessant choking and gurgling. "On the contrary, I've found it necessary to come to you, and on business . . . otherwise I wouldn't bother you. I'm leaving *there*, and this time, it seems, seriously. Kaput! I'm not asking for commiseration, believe me . . . I already lay down today, at ten o'clock, so as not to get up at all till *that* time comes, but I changed my mind and got up once more to come to you . . . which means I had to."

"It's a pity to look at you; you'd have done better to send for me than to trouble yourself."

"Well, enough of that. So you've pitied me, and that's enough for social civility . . . Ah, I forgot: how is your own health?"

"I'm well. Yesterday I was . . . not very . . ."

"I heard, I heard. The Chinese vase got it; a pity I wasn't there! I've come on business. First, today I had the pleasure of seeing Gavrila Ardalionovich meeting with Aglaya Ivanovna by the green bench. I marveled at how stupid a man can look. I observed as much to Aglaya Ivanovna herself, after Gavrila Ardalionovich left . . . It seems you're surprised at nothing, Prince," he added, looking mistrustfully at the prince's calm face. "To be surprised at nothing, they say, is a sign of great intelligence; in my opinion, it might serve equally as a sign of great stupidity . . . However, I'm not alluding to you, forgive me . . . I'm very unlucky with my expressions today."

"I knew yesterday that Gavrila Ardalionovich . . ." the prince broke off, clearly embarrassed, though Ippolit was vexed that he was not surprised.

"You knew! That's news! But anyhow, kindly don't tell me about it . . . And mightn't you have been a witness to today's meeting?"

"You saw I wasn't, since you were there yourself."

"Well, maybe you were sitting behind a bush somewhere. However, I'm glad in any case, for you, naturally, because I was already thinking that Gavrila Ardalionovich was the favorite!"

"I ask you not to speak of it with me in such expressions, Ippolit!"

"The more so as you already know everything."

"You're mistaken. I know almost nothing, and Aglaya Ivanovna surely knows that I know nothing. Even of this meeting I knew exactly nothing . . . You say there was a meeting? Well, all right, let's drop it . . ."

"But how is it, first you know, then you don't know? You say 'all right, let's drop it'? No, don't be so trustful! Especially if you don't know anything. You're trustful because you don't know. And do you know what these two persons, this nice little brother and sister, are calculating? Maybe you do suspect that? . . . All right, all right, I'll drop it . . ." he added, noticing the prince's impatient gesture. "But I've come on my own business and about that I want to . . . explain myself. Devil take it, it's simply impossible to die without explanations; I do an awful lot of explaining. Do you want to listen?"

"Speak, I'm listening."

"But anyhow, I've changed my mind again: I'll begin with Ganechka all the same. If you can imagine it, I, too, had an appointment at the green bench today. However, I don't want to lie: I insisted on the meeting myself, I invited myself and promised to reveal a secret. I don't know, maybe I came too early (it seems I actually did come early), but as soon as I took my place beside Aglaya Ivanovna, lo and behold, Gavrila Ardalionovich and Varvara Ardalionovna showed up, arm in arm, as if out for a stroll. It seems they were both very struck when they saw me; it wasn't what they were expecting, they even became embarrassed. Aglaya Ivanovna blushed and, believe it or not, was even a bit at a loss, either because I was there, or simply seeing Gavrila Ardalionovich, because he's so good-looking, but she just blushed all over and ended the business in a second, very amusingly: she stood up, responded to Gavrila Ardalionovich's bow and to the ingratiating smile of Varvara Ardalionovna, and suddenly snapped: 'I've invited you only in order to express my personal pleasure at your sincere and friendly feelings, and if I ever have need of them, believe me . . .' Here she made her bows, and the two of them left—feeling like fools, or else triumphant, I don't know; Ganechka, of course, felt like a fool; he didn't understand anything and turned red as a lobster (he sometimes has an extraordinary expression!), but Varvara Ardalionovna, I think, realized that they had to clear out quickly, and that this was more than enough from Aglaya Ivanovna, and she dragged her brother away. She's smarter than he is and, I'm sure, feels triumphant now. As for me, I came to talk with Aglaya Ivanovna, in order to arrange her meeting with Nastasya Filippovna."

"With Nastasya Filippovna!" cried the prince.

"Aha! It seems you're losing your cool-headedness and beginning to be surprised? I'm very glad you want to resemble a human being. For that I'm going to amuse you. This is what it means to be of service to young and high-minded ladies: today I got a slap in the face from her!"

"A m-moral one?" the prince asked somehow involuntarily.

"Yes, not a physical one. I don't think anybody's going to raise his hand now against someone like me; even a woman wouldn't hit me now; even Ganechka wouldn't! Though there was a moment yesterday when I thought he was going to leap at me . . . I'll bet I know what you're thinking now. You're thinking: 'Granted he shouldn't be beaten, but he could be smothered with a pillow or a wet rag in his sleep—he even ought to be . . .' It's written all over your face that you're thinking that at this very second."

"I never thought that!" the prince said with repugnance.

"I don't know, last night I dreamed that I was smothered with a wet rag . . . by a certain man . . . well, I'll tell you who: imagine—Rogozhin! What do you think, is it possible to smother a man with a wet rag?"

"I don't know."

"I've heard it is. All right, let's drop it. So, what makes me a gossip? What made her call me a gossip today? And, please note, once she had already heard everything to the last little word and had even asked questions . . . But women are like that! It was for her that I got into relations with Rogozhin, an interesting man; it was in her interest that I arranged a personal meeting for her with Nastasya Filippovna. Was it because I wounded her vanity by hinting that she was glad of Nastasya Filippovna's 'leavings'? But it was in her own interest that I explained it to her all the time, I don't deny it, I wrote two letters in that line, and today a third about our meeting . . . This is what I started with, that it was humiliating on her side . . . And besides, that phrase about 'leavings' isn't mine, in fact, but somebody else's; at least everybody was saying it at Ganechka's; and she herself repeated it. Well, so what makes me a gossip for her? I see, I see: you find it terribly funny now to look at me, and I'll bet you're trying to fit those stupid verses to me:

> And perhaps a parting smile of love will shine
> Upon the sad sunset of my decline.[43]

Ha, ha, ha!" he suddenly dissolved in hysterical laughter and began to cough. "Please note," he croaked through his coughing, "about our Ganechka: he goes talking about 'leavings,' and now look what he wants to make use of!"

The prince said nothing for a long time; he was horrified.

"You mentioned a meeting with Nastasya Filippovna?" he murmured at last.

"Eh, but can you really and truly not know that there will be a meeting today between Aglaya Ivanovna and Nastasya Filippovna, for which Nastasya Filippovna has been summoned purposely from Petersburg, through Rogozhin, at Aglaya Ivanovna's invitation and by my efforts, and is now staying, together with Rogozhin, not very far from you, in her former house, with that lady, Darya Alexeevna . . . a very ambiguous lady, her friend, and it's there, to that ambiguous house, that Aglaya Ivanovna will go today for a friendly conversation with Nastasya Filippovna and for the solving of various problems. They want to do some arithmetic. You didn't know? Word of honor?"

"That's incredible!"

"Well, all right, so it's incredible; anyhow, where could you find out from? Though here a fly flies by and everybody knows: it's that kind of little place! I've warned you, however, and you can be grateful to me. Well, good-bye—see you in the other world, most likely. And here's another thing: even though I acted meanly towards you, because . . . why should I lose what's mine, kindly tell me? For your benefit, or what? I dedicated my 'Confession' to her (you didn't know that?). Yes, and how she accepted it! Heh, heh! But I've never behaved meanly towards her, I'm not guilty of anything before her; it was she who disgraced me and let me down . . . And, incidentally, I'm not guilty of anything before you either; if I did make mention of those 'leavings' and all the rest in the same sense, to make up for it I'm now telling you the day, and the hour, and the address of the meeting, and revealing this whole game to you . . . out of vexation, naturally, and not out of magnanimity. Good-bye, I'm talkative, like a stammerer or a consumptive; watch out, take measures, and quickly, if you're worthy to be called a human being. The meeting is this evening, that's certain."

Ippolit went to the door, but the prince called out to him, and he stopped in the doorway.

"So, Aglaya Ivanovna, in your opinion, will go herself this evening to see Nastasya Filippovna?" the prince asked. Red spots appeared on his cheeks and forehead.

"I don't know exactly, but probably so," Ippolit answered, glancing over his shoulder. "And anyhow it can't be otherwise. Can Nastasya Filippovna go to her? And not to Ganechka's either; he's almost got himself a dead man there. That general's something, eh?"

"It's impossible for that alone!" the prince picked up. "How could she leave, even if she wanted to? You don't know . . . the ways of that house: she can't leave by herself and go to see Nastasya Filippovna; it's nonsense!"

"You see, Prince: nobody jumps out of windows, but if the house is on fire, then the foremost gentleman and the foremost lady might up and jump out of the window. If the need comes along, there's no help for it, our young lady will go to Nastasya Filippovna. Don't they let them go out anywhere, those young ladies?"

"No, that's not what I . . ."

"If it's not that, then she only has to go down the front steps and walk straight off, and then she may not even come back. There are occasions when one may burn one's boats, and one may even not come back: life doesn't consist only of lunches and dinners and Princes Shch. It seems to me that you take Aglaya Ivanovna for some sort of young lady or boarding-school girl; I talked to her about that; it seems she agreed. Expect it at seven or eight . . . If I were you, I'd send somebody to keep watch there, to catch the moment when she goes down the front steps. Well, you could even send Kolya; he'd be very pleased to do some spying, rest assured— for you, that is . . . because everything's relative . . . Ha, ha!"

Ippolit left. The prince had no cause to ask anyone to spy, even if he were capable of it. Aglaya's order to stay at home was now almost explained: perhaps she wanted to take him along. True, it might be that she precisely did not want him to end up there, and that was why she told him to stay home . . . That, too, could be. His head was spinning; the whole room whirled around. He lay down on the sofa and closed his eyes.

One way or the other, the matter was decisive, definitive. No, the prince did not consider Aglaya a young lady or a boarding-school girl; he felt now that he had long been afraid, and precisely of something like this; but why did she need to see her? A chill ran through his whole body; again he was in a fever.

No, he did not consider her a child! Lately, certain of her looks, certain of her words had horrified him. Sometimes it had seemed to him as if she was restraining herself, holding herself back too much, and he remembered that this had frightened him. True, for all those days he had tried not to think of it, had driven the painful thoughts away, but what was hidden in that soul? This question had long tormented him, though he trusted in that soul. And here it all had to be resolved and revealed today. A terrible thought! And again—"that woman!" Why had it always seemed to him that that woman would appear precisely at the very last minute and snap his whole destiny like a rotten thread? He was ready to swear now that it had always seemed so to him, though he was almost semidelirious. If he had tried to forget about *her* lately, it was solely because he was afraid of her. What then: did he love that woman or hate her? That question he had never once asked himself today; here his heart was pure: he knew whom he loved . . . He was afraid, not so much of the meeting of the two women, not of the strangeness, not of the reason for the meeting, which he did not know, not of its outcome, whatever it might be—he was afraid of Nastasya Filippovna herself. He remembered afterwards, a few days later, that almost all the time during those feverish hours he pictured to himself her eyes, her gaze, heard her words—some sort of strange words, though little stayed in his memory after those feverish and anguished hours. He barely remembered, for instance, how Vera brought him dinner and he ate it; he did not remember whether he slept after dinner or not. He knew only that he began to make everything out clearly that evening only from the moment when Aglaya suddenly came to his terrace and he jumped up from the sofa and went to meet her in the middle of the room: it was a quarter past seven. Aglaya was quite alone, dressed simply and as if in haste in a light cloak. Her face was as pale as in the morning, and her eyes flashed with a bright, dry glint; he had never known her to have such an expression of the eyes. She looked him over attentively.

"You're all ready," she observed softly and as if calmly, "you're dressed and have your hat in your hand; that means someone warned you, and I know who: Ippolit?"

"Yes, he told me . . ." the prince murmured, nearly half dead.

"Let's go, then: you know that you absolutely must accompany me. I suppose you're strong enough to go out?"

"Yes, I am, but . . . can this be possible?"

He broke off after a moment and could not utter anything more. This was his only attempt to stop the crazy girl, and after that he followed her like a slave. However clouded his thoughts were, he still understood that she would go *there* even without him, and therefore he had to follow her in any case. He guessed the strength of her resolve; it was not for him to stop this wild impulse. They walked in silence, hardly saying a single word all the way. He only noticed that she knew the way well, and when he wanted to make a detour through a further lane, because the way was more deserted there, and he suggested it to her, she listened as if straining her attention, and answered curtly: "It makes no difference!" When they had almost come right up to Darya Alexeevna's house (a large and old wooden house), a magnificent lady and a young girl were stepping off the porch; laughing and talking loudly, the two got into a splendid carriage that was waiting at the porch and did not glance even once at the approaching people, as if they did not notice them. As soon as the carriage drove off, the door immediately opened again, and the waiting Rogozhin let the prince and Aglaya in and locked the door behind them.

"There's nobody in the whole house now except the four of us," he observed aloud and gave the prince a strange look.

In the very first room, Nastasya Filippovna, too, was waiting for them, also dressed very simply and all in black; she rose to meet them, but did not smile and did not even offer the prince her hand.

Her intent and anxious gaze impatiently turned to Aglaya. The two women sat down at some distance from each other, Aglaya on the sofa in the corner of the room, Nastasya Filippovna by the window. The prince and Rogozhin did not sit down, and were not invited to sit down. With perplexity and as if with pain, the prince again looked at Rogozhin, but the man went on smiling his former smile. The silence continued for another few moments.

A sort of sinister feeling finally passed over Nastasya Filippovna's face; her gaze was becoming stubborn, firm, and almost hateful, not tearing itself from her guest for a single moment. Aglaya was obviously abashed, but not intimidated. Coming in, she had barely glanced at her rival and so far had been sitting all the time with downcast eyes, as if lost in thought. Once or twice, as if by chance, she looked around the room; an obvious repugnance showed itself in her face, as if she feared soiling herself there. She mechanically straightened her clothes and once even changed her place anxiously, moving towards the corner of the sofa. She herself was hardly aware of all her movements; but the unawareness increased the offense still more. At last she looked firmly and directly into Nastasya Filippovna's eyes, and at once clearly read everything that flashed in the incensed gaze of her rival. Woman understood woman. Aglaya shuddered.

"You know, of course, why I asked for this meeting," she spoke finally, but very quietly, and even pausing a couple of times in this short phrase.

"No, I have no idea," Nastasya Filippovna answered drily and curtly.

Aglaya blushed. Perhaps it suddenly seemed terribly strange and incredible to her that she was now sitting with "that woman," in "that woman's" house, and was in need of her reply. At the first sounds of Nastasya Filippovna's voice, it was as if a shudder passed over her body. All this, of course, was very well noted by "that woman."

"You understand everything . . . but you deliberately make it look as if you don't," Aglaya said almost in a whisper, looking sullenly at the ground.

"Why would I do that?" Nastasya Filippovna smiled slightly.

"You want to take advantage of my position . . . that I am in your house," Aglaya went on absurdly and awkwardly.

"You are to blame for that position, not I!" Nastasya Filippovna suddenly flared up. "I didn't invite you, but you me, and so far I don't know why."

Aglaya raised her head arrogantly.

"Hold your tongue; it is not with this weapon of yours that I have come to fight with you . . ."

"Ah! So you've come to 'fight' after all? Imagine, I thought that, anyhow, you were . . . more clever . . ."

They both looked at each other, no longer concealing their spite. One of these women was the same one who had so recently written such letters to the other. And now everything scattered at their first meeting and with their first words. What then? At that moment it seemed that none of the four people in the room found it strange. The prince, who the day before would not have believed it possible even to dream of it, now stood, looked, and listened as if he had long anticipated it all. The most fantastic dream had suddenly turned into the most glaring and sharply outlined reality. One of these women despised the other so much at that moment, and wished so much to say it to her (perhaps she had come only for that, as Rogozhin put it the next day), that, however fantastic the other woman was, with her disordered mind and sick soul, it seemed no preconceived idea could withstand the venomous, purely female despite of her rival. The prince was certain that Nastasya Filippovna would not start talking about the letters on her own; by her flashing glances, he could tell what those letters might cost her now; but he would have given half his life if Aglaya, too, would not start talking about them now.

But Aglaya suddenly seemed to make an effort and at once gained control of herself.

"You misunderstand me," she said. "I haven't come . . . to quarrel with you, though I don't like you. I . . . I've come to you . . . for a human talk. When I summoned you, I had already decided what I was going to speak about, and I will not go back on my decision, though you may misunderstand me completely. That will be the worse for you, not for me. I wanted to reply to what you wrote to me, and to reply in person, because it seemed more convenient to me. Listen, then, to my reply to all your letters: I felt sorry for Prince Lev Nikolaevich for the first time the very day I made his acquaintance and later when I learned about all that had happened at your party. I felt sorry for him because he is such a simple-hearted man and in his simplicity believed that he could be happy . . . with a woman . . . of such character. What I feared for him was just what happened: you could not love him, you tormented him and abandoned him. You could not love him because you are too proud . . . no, not proud, I'm mistaken, but because you are vain . . . and not even that: you are selfish to the point of madness, of which your letters to me also serve as proof. You could not love him, simple as he is, and may even have despised him and laughed at him to yourself; you could love only your own disgrace and the incessant thought that you had been disgraced and offended. If you had had less disgrace or none at all, you would have been unhappier . . ." (It was a pleasure for Aglaya to articulate these words, so hurriedly leaping out, yet long prepared and pondered, already pondered when today's meeting could not even have been pictured in a dream; with a venomous gaze she followed their effect in Nastasya Filippovna's face, distorted with emotion.) "You remember," she went on, "he wrote me a letter then; he says you know about the letter and have even read it? I understood everything from that letter and understood it correctly; he recently confirmed it to me himself, that is, everything I'm telling you now, even word for word. After the letter I began to wait. I guessed that you'd have to come here, because you really can't do without Petersburg: you're still too young and good-looking for the provinces . . . However, those are also not my words," she added, blushing terribly, and from that moment on the color never left her face to the very end of her speech. "When I saw the prince again, I felt terribly pained and offended for him. Don't laugh; if you laugh, you're not worthy of understanding it . . ."

"You can see that I'm not laughing," Nastasya Filippovna said sadly and sternly.

"However, it's all the same to me, laugh as much as you like. When I asked him myself, he told me that he had stopped loving you long ago, that even the memory of you was painful for him, but that he pitied you, and that when he remembered you, his heart felt 'pierced forever.' I must tell you, too, that I have never met a single person in my life who is equal to him in noble simple-heartedness and infinite trustfulness. I guessed after what he said that anyone who wanted to could deceive him, and whoever deceived him he would forgive afterwards, and it was for that that I loved him . . ."

Aglaya stopped for a moment, as if struck, as if not believing herself that she could utter such a word; but at the same moment an almost boundless pride flashed in her eyes; it seemed that it was now all the same for her, even if "that woman" should laugh now at the confession that had escaped her.

"I've told you everything, and, of course, you've now understood what I want from you?"

"Perhaps I have; but say it yourself," Nastasya Filippovna replied quietly.

Wrath lit up in Aglaya's face.

"I wanted to find out from you," she said firmly and distinctly, "by what right do you interfere in his feelings towards me? By what right do you dare write letters to me? By what right do you declare every minute to me and to him that you love him, after you yourself abandoned him and ran away from him in such an offensive and . . . disgraceful way?"

"I have never declared either to him or to you that I love him," Nastasya Filippovna spoke with effort, "and . . . you're right, I ran away from him . . ." she added barely audibly.

"What do you mean you 'never declared either to him or to me'?" cried Aglaya. "And what about your letters? Who asked you to matchmake us and persuade me to marry him? Isn't that a declaration? Why do you force yourself on us? At first I thought you wanted, on the contrary, to make me loathe him by meddling with us, so that I would abandon him, and only later did I guess what it was: you simply imagined that you were doing a lofty deed with all this posturing . . . Well, how could you love him, if you love your vanity so much? Why didn't you simply go away, instead of writing ridiculous letters to me? Why don't you now marry the noble man who loves you so much and has honored you by offering his hand? It's all too clear why: if you marry Rogozhin, what sort of offense will you have left then? You'll even get too much honor! Evgeny Pavlych said of you that you've read too many poems and are 'too well educated for your . . . position'; that you're a bookish woman and a lily-white; add your vanity, and there are all your reasons . . ."

"And you're not a lily-white?"

The matter had arrived too hastily, too nakedly at such an unexpected point, unexpected because Nastasya Filippovna, on her way to Pavlovsk, had still been dreaming of something, though, of course, she anticipated it would sooner be bad than good; as for Aglaya, she was decidedly carried along by the impulse of the moment, as if falling down a hill, and could not resist the terrible pleasure of revenge. For Nastasya Filippovna it was even strange to see Aglaya like this; she looked at her and could not believe her eyes, and was decidedly at a loss for the first moment. Whether she was a woman who had read too many poems, as Evgeny Pavlovich suggested, or was simply a madwoman, as the prince was convinced, in any case this woman—who on occasion had so cynical and brazen a manner—was in reality far more shy, tender, and trustful than one might have thought. True, there was much in her that was bookish, dreamy, self-enclosed, and fantastical, but much, too, that was strong and deep . . . The prince understood that; suffering showed in his face. Aglaya noticed it and trembled with hatred.

"How dare you address me like that?" she said with inexpressible haughtiness, in reply to Nastasya Filippovna's remark.

"You probably misheard me," Nastasya Filippovna was surprised. "How did I address you?"

"If you wanted to be an honest woman, why didn't you drop your seducer Totsky then, simply . . . without theatrics?" Aglaya said suddenly out of the blue.

"What do you know about my position, that you dare to judge me?" Nastasya Filippovna gave a start and turned terribly pale.

"I know that you didn't go to work, but went off with the rich Rogozhin, in order to present yourself as a fallen angel. I'm not surprised that Totsky wanted to shoot himself because of a fallen angel!"

"Stop it!" Nastasya Filippovna said with repugnance and as if through pain. "You understand me as well as . . . Darya Alexeevna's chambermaid, who went to the justice of the peace the other day to make a complaint against her fiancé. She'd have understood better than you . . ."

"She's probably an honest girl and lives by her own labor. Why do you have such contempt for a chambermaid?"

"I don't have contempt for labor, but for you when you speak about labor."

"If you wanted to be an honest woman, you should have gone to work as a washerwoman."

The two women stood up, pale-faced, and looked at each other.

"Aglaya, stop! This is unfair," the prince cried out like a lost man. Rogozhin was no longer smiling, but listened with compressed lips and crossed arms.

"Here, look at her," Nastasya Filippovna said, trembling with spite, "at this young lady! And I took her for an angel! Have you come to see me without your governess, Aglaya Ivanovna? . . . And do you want . . . do you want me to tell you straight out, here and now, without embellishments, why you came? You were scared, that's why."

"Scared of you?" asked Aglaya, beside herself with naïve and impudent amazement that the woman would dare to address her that way.

"Yes, of me! You're afraid of me, since you decided to come and see me. If you're afraid of someone, you don't despise him. And to think that I respected you, even up to this very minute! But do you know why you're afraid of me and what your main purpose is now? You wanted to find out personally whether he loves me more than you or not, because you're terribly jealous . . ."

"He has already told me that he hates you . . ." Aglaya barely murmured.

"Maybe; maybe I'm not worthy of him, only . . . only I think you're lying! He can't hate me, and he couldn't have said that! However, I'm prepared to forgive you . . . considering your position . . . only all the same I did think better of you; I thought you were more intelligent, yes, and even better-looking, by God! . . . Well, so take your treasure . . . here he is, looking at you, unable to collect his wits, take him for yourself, but on one condition: get out right now! This minute! . . ."

She fell into an armchair and dissolved in tears. But suddenly something new began to gleam in her eyes; she looked intently and fixedly at Aglaya and got up from her seat:

"Or if you like, my girl, right now . . . I'll or-der him, do you hear? I'll simply or-der him, and he'll drop you at once and stay with me forever, and marry me, and you'll run home alone! Would you like that, my girl, would you?" she cried like a crazy woman, perhaps almost not believing herself that she could utter such words.

Aglaya rushed to the door in fear, but stopped in the doorway as if rooted there and listened.

"Would you like me to throw Rogozhin out? You thought, my girl, that I was going to up and marry Rogozhin for your good pleasure? Now I'll shout in front of you: 'Go, Rogozhin!' and say to the prince: 'Remember what you promised?' Lord! Why did I humiliate myself so before them? Didn't you assure me yourself, Prince, that you'd follow me whatever happened and never leave me; that you loved me, and forgave me everything, and re . . . resp . . . Yes, you said that, too! And I ran away from you only in order to unbind you, but now I don't want to! Why did she treat me like a loose woman? Ask Rogozhin how loose I am, he'll tell you! Now, when she has disgraced me, and that right in front of you, are you going to turn away from me and go out arm in arm with her? Then may you be cursed for that, because you're the only one I trusted. Go, Rogozhin, I don't need you!" she cried, almost oblivious, struggling to free the words from her breast, her face distorted and her lips parched, obviously not believing one drop of her own bravado, but at the same time wishing to prolong the moment if only for a second and deceive herself. The impulse was so strong that she might have died, or so at least it seemed to the prince. "Here he is, look, my girl!" she finally cried out to Aglaya, pointing at the prince with her hand. "If he doesn't come to me right now, if he doesn't take me and drop you, then you can have him, I give him up, I don't need him! . . ."

Both she and Aglaya stopped as if in expectation, and they both gave him mad looks. But he may not have understood all the force of this challenge, even certainly did not, one may say. He only saw before him the desperate, insane face, because of which, as he had once let slip to Aglaya, "his heart was forever pierced." He could no longer bear it and with entreaty and reproach turned to Aglaya, pointing to Nastasya Filippovna:

"It's not possible! She's . . . so unhappy!"

But that was all he managed to say, going dumb under Aglaya's terrible look. That look expressed so much suffering, and at the same time such boundless hatred, that he clasped his hands, cried out, and rushed to her, but it was already too late! She could not bear even a moment of hesitation in him, covered her face with her hands, cried: "Oh, my God!"—and rushed out of the room, Rogozhin going after her to unlock the street door.

The prince also ran, but arms seized him on the threshold. Nastasya Filippovna's stricken, distorted face looked at him point-blank, and her blue lips moved, saying:

"After her? After her? . . ."

She fell unconscious in his arms. He picked her up, brought her into the room, laid her in an armchair, and stood over her in dull expectation. There was a glass of water on the table; Rogozhin, who had returned, snatched it up and sprinkled her face with water; she opened her eyes and for a moment understood nothing; but suddenly she looked around, gave a start, cried out, and rushed to the prince.

"Mine! Mine!" she cried. "Is the proud young lady gone? Ha, ha, ha!" she laughed hysterically, "ha, ha, ha! I wanted to give him to that young lady! But why? What for? Madwoman! Madwoman! . . . Get out, Rogozhin, ha, ha, ha!"

Rogozhin looked at them intently, did not say a word, took his hat, and left. Ten minutes later the prince was sitting beside Nastasya Filippovna, gazing at her without tearing his eyes away, and stroking her dear head and face with both hands, like a little child. He laughed when she laughed and was ready to weep at her tears. He did not say anything, but listened intently to her fitful, rapturous, and incoherent babbling, hardly understood anything, but smiled quietly, and as soon as it seemed to him that she had begun to be anguished again, or to weep, or reproach, or complain, he would at once begin again to stroke her dear head and tenderly pass his hands over her cheeks, comforting and reassuring her like a child.

IX

TWO WEEKS WENT BY after the events recounted in the last chapter, and the position of the characters in our story changed so much that it is extremely difficult for us to set out on the continuation without special explanations. And yet we feel that we must limit ourselves to the simple statement of facts, as far as possible without special explanations, and for a very simple reason: because we ourselves, in many cases, have difficulty explaining what happened. Such a warning on our part must appear quite strange and unclear to the reader: how recount that of which we have neither a clear understanding nor a personal opinion? Not to put ourselves in a still more false position, we had better try to explain things with an example, and perhaps the benevolent reader will understand precisely what our difficulty is, the more so as this example will not be a digression, but, on the contrary, a direct and immediate continuation of the story.

Two weeks later, that is, at the beginning of July, and over the course of those two weeks, the story of our hero, and especially the last adventure of that story, turned into a strange, rather amusing, almost unbelievable, and at the same time almost graphic anecdote, which gradually spread through all the streets neighboring the dachas of Lebedev, Ptitsyn, Darya Alexeevna, the Epanchins, in short, over almost the whole town and even its environs. Almost all of society—the locals, the summer people, those who came for the music—everyone began telling one and the same story, in a thousand different versions, about a certain prince who, having caused a scandal in an honorable and well-known house, and having rejected the daughter of that house, already his fiancée, had been enticed away by a well-known tart, had broken all his former connections, and, regardless of everything, regardless of threats, regardless of general public indignation, intended to marry the disgraced woman one of those days, right there in Pavlovsk, openly, publicly, with head held high and looking everyone straight in the eye. The anecdote was becoming so embroidered with scandals, so many well-known and important persons were mixed up in it, it was endowed with such a variety of fantastic and mysterious nuances, and, on the other hand, it was presented in such irrefutable and graphic facts, that the general curiosity and gossip were, of course, quite excusable. The most subtle, clever, and at the same time plausible interpretation belonged to several serious gossips, from that stratum of sensible people who, in every society, always hasten first of all to explain an event to others, finding in it a vocation, and often also a consolation. According to their interpretation, a young man, of good family, a prince, almost wealthy, a fool, but a democrat, and gone crazy over modern nihilism, which was discovered by Mr. Turgenev,[44] barely able to speak Russian, had fallen in love with a daughter of General Epanchin, and had succeeded in being received in the house as a fiancé. But, like that French seminarian about whom an anecdote had just been published, who had purposely allowed himself to be ordained a priest, had purposely sought this ordination, had performed all the rites, all the bowing, kissing, vows, etc., in order to proclaim publicly, the next day, in a letter to his bishop, that, not believing in God, he considered it dishonest to deceive folk and be fed by them gratis, and therefore he was laying aside his yesterday's dignity, and would publish his letter in the liberal newspapers—like this atheist, the prince was supposed to have dissembled in his own way. The story went that he had supposedly waited on purpose for a solemn, formal party given by his fiancée's parents, at which he had been introduced to a great many important persons, in order to proclaim his way of thinking aloud and in front of everyone, to denounce the venerable dignitaries, to reject his fiancée publicly and offensively, and, while resisting the servants who were taking him out, to smash a beautiful Chinese vase. To this was added, with a view to characterizing modern morals, that the muddle-headed young man actually loved his fiancée, the general's daughter, but had rejected her solely out of nihilism and for the sake of the imminent scandal, so as not to deny himself the pleasure of marrying a fallen woman before the whole world and thereby proving that in his conviction there were neither fallen nor virtuous women, but only free women; that he did not believe in the social and old distinction, but believed only in the "woman question." That, finally, a fallen woman, in his eyes, was even somewhat higher than an unfallen one. This explanation seemed quite plausible and was accepted by the majority of the summer people, the more so as it was confirmed by everyday facts. True, many things remained unexplained: the story went that the poor girl loved her fiancé—her "seducer" according to some—so much that she came running to him the very next day after he abandoned her and sat there with his mistress; others insisted, on the contrary, that he purposely lured her to his mistress, solely out of nihilism, that is, for the sake of the disgrace and offense. Be that as it may, interest in the event grew daily, the more so as there remained not the slightest doubt that the scandalous wedding would actually take place.

And so, if we were asked to explain—not about the nihilistic nuances of the event, but simply to what extent the appointed wedding satisfied the actual desires of the prince, precisely what those desires consisted in at the present moment, precisely how to define our hero's state of mind at the present moment, etc., etc., in the same vein—we confess, we would have great difficulty in answering. We know only one thing, that the wedding was indeed appointed, and that the prince himself had entrusted Lebedev, Keller, and some acquaintance of Lebedev's, whom he had introduced to the prince for the occasion, to take upon themselves all the cares connected with the matter, both churchly and practical; that money was not to be spared, that Nastasya Filippovna was hurrying and insisting on the wedding; that Keller, at his own fervent request, had been appointed the prince's groomsman,[45] and for Nastasya Filippovna—Burdovsky, who accepted the appointment with rapture, and that the day of the wedding was appointed for the beginning of July. But apart from these very specific circumstances, some other facts are known to us which have decidedly thrown us off, precisely because they contradict the foregoing ones. We strongly suspect, for instance, that, having entrusted Lebedev and the others to take all the cares on themselves, the prince all but forgot that very same day that he had a master of ceremonies, and a groomsman, and a wedding, and that if he so quickly arranged the transfer of his cares to others, it was solely so as not to think about them himself, and even perhaps to forget them as quickly. What was he thinking about, in that case? What did he want to remember, and what was he striving for? There was also no doubt that there had been no forcing of him here (on Nastasya Filippovna's part, for instance); that Nastasya Filippovna indeed wished absolutely for a quick wedding, and that the wedding had been her idea and not the prince's at all; but the prince had consented freely, even somehow distractedly and as if he had been asked some rather ordinary thing. Of such strange facts we have a great many before us, yet they not only do not explain, but, in our opinion, even obscure the interpretation of the affair, however many we may cite; but, anyhow, we shall present one more.

Thus, it is perfectly well known to us that in the course of those two weeks the prince spent whole days and evenings with Nastasya Filippovna; that she took him with her for walks, for concerts; that he went for rides with her every day in the carriage; that he would begin to worry about her if he did not see her for only an hour (which meant that, by all tokens, he sincerely loved her); that he listened to her with a quiet and meek smile, whatever she might talk to him about, for whole hours, saying almost nothing himself. But we also know that during those same days, several times and even many times, he suddenly betook himself to the Epanchins', not concealing it from Nastasya Filippovna, which drove her almost to despair. We know that he was not received at the Epanchins' while they remained in Pavlovsk, that he was constantly denied a meeting with Aglaya Ivanovna; that he would leave without saying a word and the next day go to them again, as though he had completely forgotten the previous day's refusal, and, naturally, receive a new refusal. It is also known to us that an hour after Aglaya Ivanovna ran out of Nastasya Filippovna's house, and perhaps even earlier, the prince was already at the Epanchins', in the certainty, of course, of finding Aglaya there, and that his appearance at the Epanchins' had caused extreme confusion and fear in the house, because Aglaya had not come home yet, and it was only from him that they first heard that she had gone with him to Nastasya Filippovna's. It was said that Lizaveta Prokofyevna, her daughters, and even Prince Shch. had treated the prince extremely harshly, inimically, and right then refused him, in vehement terms, their acquaintance and friendship, especially when Varvara Ardalionovna suddenly came to Lizaveta Prokofyevna and announced that Aglaya Ivanovna had been at her house for an hour, in a terrible state, and seemed not to want to go home. This last news struck Lizaveta Prokofyevna most of all, and it was perfectly correct: having left Nastasya Filippovna's, Aglaya indeed would sooner have died than show herself now to the eyes of her family, and therefore she had rushed to Nina Alexandrovna's. Varvara Ardalionovna, for her part, had at once found it necessary to inform Lizaveta Prokofyevna of all this without the least delay. Mother, daughters, everyone at once rushed to Nina Alexandrovna's, followed by the father of the family, Ivan Fyodorovich himself, who had just returned home; after them trudged Prince Lev Nikolaevich, in spite of the banishment and harsh words; but, on Varvara Ardalionovna's orders, he was not permitted to see Aglaya there either. The end of the matter, however, was that when Aglaya saw her mother and sisters weeping over her and not reproaching her at all, she threw herself into their arms and at once returned home with them. It was said, though the rumors were not quite precise, that Gavrila Ardalionovich was terribly unlucky this time as well; that, seizing the moment when Varvara Ardalionovna had run to Lizaveta Prokofyevna's, he, alone with Aglaya, had decided to try and speak to her about his love; that, listening to him, Aglaya, despite all her anguish and tears, had suddenly burst out laughing and suddenly asked him a strange question: would he, in proof of his love, burn his finger right now in a candle? Gavrila Ardalionovich was, they say, dumbfounded by the suggestion and so much at a loss, showed such extreme perplexity on his face, that Aglaya laughed at him as if in hysterics and ran away from him upstairs to Nina Alexandrovna, where her parents found her. This anecdote reached the prince through Ippolit the next day. Bedridden by then, Ippolit purposely sent for the prince to tell him the story. How this rumor had reached Ippolit we do not know, but when the prince heard about the candle and the finger, he burst into such laughter that he even surprised Ippolit; then he suddenly trembled and dissolved in tears . . . Generally during those days he was in great anxiety and extraordinary confusion, vague and tormenting. Ippolit affirmed directly that the prince had lost his mind; but that could not yet be said affirmatively.

In presenting all these facts and declining to explain them, we by no means wish to justify our hero in our readers' eyes. What's more, we are fully prepared to share the same indignation he aroused in his friends. Even Vera Lebedev was indignant with him for a time; even Kolya was indignant; Keller was even indignant, up to the time when he was chosen as groomsman, to say nothing of Lebedev himself, who even began to intrigue against the prince, also out of indignation, which was even quite genuine. But we shall speak of that later. In general, we sympathize fully and in the highest degree with certain words, quite forceful and even profound in their psychology, which Evgeny Pavlovich said to the prince, directly and without ceremony, in a friendly talk on the sixth or seventh day after the event at Nastasya Filippovna's. We shall note, incidentally, that not only the Epanchins themselves, but everyone directly or indirectly affiliated with the house of the Epanchins, found it necessary to break off all relations with the prince entirely. Prince Shch., for instance, even looked away when he met the prince and did not return his bow. But Evgeny Pavlovich was not afraid of compromising himself by calling on the prince, though he had again begun visiting the Epanchins every day and was received even with an obviously increased cordiality. He went to see the prince exactly the day after all the Epanchins left Pavlovsk. He came in already knowing all the rumors spread among the public and having perhaps even contributed to them himself. The prince was terribly glad to see him and at once spoke about the Epanchins; such a simple-hearted and direct opening completely unbound Evgeny Pavlovich as well, so that without preliminaries he, too, went straight to the point.

The prince did not know yet that the Epanchins had left; he was struck, turned pale; but a moment later he shook his head, embarrassed and pensive, and admitted that "it had to be so"; after which he quickly asked "where did they go?"

Evgeny Pavlovich meanwhile watched him intently, and all of it —that is, the quickness of the questions, their simple-heartedness, the embarrassment, and at the same time some strange frankness, anxiousness, and agitation—all of it surprised him not a little. He, however, told the prince about everything courteously and in detail: there were many things the prince still did not know, and this was his first news from that house. He confirmed that Aglaya had indeed been sick, in a fever, and had hardly slept for three nights; that she was better now and out of all danger, but in a nervous, hysterical condition . . . "It's already a good thing that there is perfect peace in the house! They try not to allude to what happened, even among themselves, not only in front of Aglaya. The parents have discussed between them the possibility of going abroad in the autumn, right after Adelaida's wedding; Aglaya received the first mention of it in silence." He, Evgeny Pavlovich, might also go abroad. Even Prince Shch. might decide to go, for a couple of months, with Adelaida, if his affairs permitted. The general himself would stay. They had now all moved to Kolmino, their estate, about twenty miles from Petersburg, where they had a roomy mansion. Princess Belokonsky had not yet gone to Moscow and, it seemed, was even staying on purpose. Lizaveta Prokofyevna had strongly insisted that it was impossible to remain in Pavlovsk after all that had happened; he, Evgeny Pavlovich, had informed her every day of the rumors going around town. They also had not found it possible to settle in their dacha on Elagin Island.

"Well, yes, and in fact," Evgeny Pavlovich added, "you'll agree yourself, how could they stand it . . . especially knowing all that goes on here every hour, in your house, Prince, and after your daily visits *there*, despite the refusals . . ."

"Yes, yes, yes, you're right, I wanted to see Aglaya Ivanovna . . ." The prince again began shaking his head.

"Ah, my dear Prince," Evgeny Pavlovich exclaimed suddenly, with animation and sadness, "how could you have allowed . . . all that to happen? Of course, of course, it was all so unexpected for you . . . I agree that you were bound to be at a loss and . . . you couldn't have stopped the crazy girl, that was beyond your power! But you ought to have understood how serious and strong the girl's . . . attitude towards you was. She didn't want to share with the other one, and you . . . and you could abandon and break such a treasure!"

"Yes, yes, you're right; yes, I'm to blame," the prince said again in terrible anguish, "and you know: only she, only Aglaya, looked at Nastasya Filippovna that way . . . No one else looked at her that way."

"But that's what makes it so outrageous, that there was nothing serious in it!" cried Evgeny Pavlovich, decidedly carried away. "Forgive me, Prince, but . . . I . . . I've thought about it, Prince; I've thought a lot about it; I know everything that happened before, I know everything that happened half a year ago, everything, and—it was all not serious! It was all only a cerebral infatuation, a picture, a fantasy, smoke, and only the frightened jealousy of a totally inexperienced girl could have taken it for something serious!"

Here Evgeny Pavlovich, now completely without ceremony, gave free rein to all his indignation. Sensibly and clearly and, we repeat, even extremely psychologically, he unfolded before the prince the picture of all the prince's relations with Nastasya Filippovna. Evgeny Pavlovich had always had a gift for speaking; now he even attained to eloquence. "From the very beginning," he pronounced, "you began with a lie; what began with a lie was bound to end with a lie; that is a law of nature. I don't agree and even feel indignant when they—well, whoever—call you an idiot; you're too intelligent to be called that; but you're strange enough not to be like all other people, you'll agree. I've decided that the foundation of all that has happened was composed, first, of your, so to speak, innate inexperience (note that word, Prince: 'innate'), then of your extraordinary simple-heartedness; further, of a phenomenal lack of the sense of measure (which you've admitted several times)—and, finally, of an enormous, flooding mass of cerebral convictions, which you, with all your extraordinary honesty, have taken all along for genuine, natural, and immediate convictions! You yourself will agree, Prince, that your relations with Nastasya Filippovna from the very beginning had something *conventionally democratic* about them (I put it that way for the sake of brevity), the charm, so to speak, of the 'woman question' (to put it still more briefly). I know in exact detail that whole strange, scandalous scene that took place at Nastasya Filippovna's when Rogozhin brought his money. If you like, I'll analyze you for yourself, counting off on my fingers; I'll show you to yourself as in a mirror, so exactly do I know what it was about and why it turned out that way! You, a young man, longed for your native land in Switzerland, you strained towards Russia as towards a promised but unknown land; you read a lot of books about Russia, excellent books, perhaps, but harmful for you; you arrived with the initial fervor of the desire to act, you, so to speak, fell upon action! And so, on that same day they tell you a sad, heart-stirring story about an offended woman, they tell you, that is, a knight, a virgin, about a woman! On that same day you meet the woman; you're enchanted by her beauty, her fantastic, demonic beauty (I do agree that she's a beauty). Add nerves, add your falling sickness, add our nerve-shattering Petersburg thaw; add that whole day in an unknown and almost fantastic city, a day of encounters and scenes, a day of unexpected acquaintances, a day of the most unexpected reality, a day of the three Epanchin beauties, and Aglaya among them; add fatigue, dizziness; add Nastasya Filippovna's drawing room and the tone of that drawing room, and . . . what do you think you could have expected of yourself at that moment?"

"Yes, yes; yes, yes," the prince was shaking his head and beginning to blush, "yes, it was almost so; and, you know, I actually hardly slept all the previous night, on the train, or the night before, and I was very disconcerted . . ."

"Well, of course, that's what I'm driving at," Evgeny Pavlovich went on vehemently. "It's clear that, drunk with rapture, you fell upon the opportunity of publicly proclaiming the magnanimous thought that you, a born prince and a pure man, did not find dishonorable a woman who had been disgraced through no fault of her own, but through the fault of a loathsome high-society debaucher. Oh, Lord, it's so understandable! But that's not the point, my dear Prince, the point is whether there was truth here, whether your feeling was genuine, was it natural, or was it only a cerebral rapture? What do you think: a woman was forgiven in the Temple,[46] the same sort of woman, but was she told that she had done well and was worthy of all honor and respect? Didn't common sense whisper to you, after three months, telling you what it was about? Let her be innocent now—I don't insist, because I have no wish to—but can all her adventures justify such unbearable demonic pride as hers, such insolent, such greedy egoism? Forgive me, Prince, I'm getting carried away, but . . ."

"Yes, that all may be; it may be that you're right . . ." the prince began to murmur again, "she really is very edgy, and you're right, of course, but . . ."

"She deserves compassion? Is that what you want to say, my good Prince? But for the sake of compassion and for the sake of her good pleasure, was it possible to disgrace this other, this lofty and pure girl, to humiliate her before *those* arrogant, before those hateful eyes? How far can compassion go, then? That is an incredible exaggeration! Is it possible, while loving a girl, to humiliate her so before her rival, to abandon her for the other one, right in front of that other one, after making her an honorable proposal yourself . . . and you did make her a proposal, you said it to her in front of her parents and sisters! Are you an honorable man after that, Prince, may I ask? And . . . and didn't you deceive a divine girl, after assuring her that you loved her?"

"Yes, yes, you're right, ah, I feel I'm to blame!" the prince said in inexpressible anguish.

"But is that enough?" Evgeny Pavlovich cried in indignation. "Is it sufficient merely to cry out: 'I'm to blame!' You're to blame, and yet you persist! And where was your heart then, your 'Christian' heart! You saw her face at that moment: tell me, did she suffer less than *that* one, than *your* other one, her rival? How could you see it and allow it? How?"

"But . . . I didn't allow it . . ." murmured the unhappy prince.

"What do you mean you didn't?"

"By God, I didn't allow anything. I still don't understand how it all came about . . . I—I ran after Aglaya Ivanovna then, and Nastasya Filippovna fainted; and since then I haven't been allowed to see Aglaya Ivanovna."

"All the same! You should have run after Aglaya, even though the other one fainted!"

"Yes . . . yes, I should have . . . but she would have died! She would have killed herself, you don't know her, and . . . all the same, I'd have told everything to Aglaya Ivanovna afterwards, and . . . You see, Evgeny Pavlych, I can see that you don't seem to know everything. Tell me, why won't they let me see Aglaya Ivanovna? I'd have explained everything to her. You see: neither of them talked about the right thing, not about the right thing at all, that's why it turned out like this . . . There's no way I can explain it to you; but I might be able to explain it to Aglaya . . . Ah, my God, my God! You speak of her face at the moment she ran out . . . oh, my God, I remember! Let's go, let's go!" he suddenly pulled Evgeny Pavlovich's sleeve, hurriedly jumping up from his seat.

"Where?"

"Let's go to Aglaya Ivanovna, let's go right now! . . ."

"But I told you, she's not in Pavlovsk, and why go?"

"She'll understand, she'll understand!" the prince murmured, pressing his hands together in entreaty. "She'll understand that it's all not *that*, but something completely, completely different!"

"How is it completely different? Aren't you getting married all the same? That means you persist . . . Are you getting married or not?"

"Well, yes . . . I am; yes, I am getting married!"

"Then how is it not that?"

"Oh, no, not that, not that! It makes no difference that I'm getting married, it doesn't matter!"

"It makes no difference and doesn't matter? It's not a trifling thing, is it? You're marrying a woman you love in order to make her happiness, and Aglaya Ivanovna sees and knows it, so how does it make no difference?"

"Happiness? Oh, no! I'm simply getting married; she wants it; and so what if I'm getting married, I . . . Well, it makes no difference! Only she would certainly have died. I see now that this marriage to Rogozhin was madness! I now understand everything I didn't understand before, and you see: when the two of them stood facing each other, I couldn't bear Nastasya Filippovna's face then . . . You don't know, Evgeny Pavlych" (he lowered his voice mysteriously), "I've never spoken to anyone about this, not even Aglaya, but I can't bear Nastasya Filippovna's face . . . You spoke the truth earlier about that evening at Nastasya Filippovna's; but there was one thing you left out, because you don't know it: I was looking at *her face*! That morning, in her portrait, I already couldn't bear it . . . Take Vera, Vera Lebedev, she has completely different eyes; I . . . I'm afraid of her face!" he added with extreme fear.

"Afraid?"

"Yes; she's—mad!" he whispered, turning pale.

"You know that for certain?" Evgeny Pavlovich asked with extreme curiosity.

"Yes, for certain; now it's certain; now, in these days, I've learned it quite certainly!"

"But what are you doing to yourself?" Evgeny Pavlovich cried out in alarm. "It means you're marrying out of some sort of fear? It's impossible to understand anything here . . . Even without loving her, perhaps?"

"Oh, no, I love her with all my soul! She's . . . a child; now she's a child, a complete child! Oh, you don't know anything!"

"And at the same time you assured Aglaya Ivanovna of your love?"

"Oh, yes, yes!"

"How's that? So you want to love them both?"

"Oh, yes, yes!"

"Good heavens, Prince, what are you saying? Come to your senses!"

"Without Aglaya I . . . I absolutely must see her! I . . . I'll soon die in my sleep; I thought last night that I was going to die in my sleep. Oh, if Aglaya knew, knew everything . . . that is, absolutely everything. Because here you have to know everything, that's the first thing! Why can we never know *everything* about another person when it's necessary, when the person is to blame! . . . However, I don't know what I'm saying, I'm confused; you struck me terribly . . . Can she really still have the same face as when she ran out? Oh, yes, I'm to blame! Most likely I'm to blame for everything! I still don't know precisely for what, but I'm to blame . . . There's something in it that I can't explain to you, Evgeny Pavlych, I lack the words, but . . . Aglaya Ivanovna will understand! Oh, I've always believed she would understand."

"No, Prince, she won't understand! Aglaya Ivanovna loved as a woman, as a human being, not as . . . an abstract spirit. You know, my poor Prince: most likely you never loved either of them!"

"I don't know . . . maybe, maybe; you're right about many things, Evgeny Pavlych. You're extremely intelligent, Evgeny Pavlych; ah, my head's beginning to ache again, let's go to her! For God's sake, for God's sake!"

"I tell you, she's not in Pavlovsk, she's in Kolmino."

"Let's go to Kolmino, let's go now!"

"That is im-pos-sible!" Evgeny Pavlovich drew out, getting up.

"Listen, I'll write a letter; take a letter to her!"

"No, Prince, no! Spare me such errands, I cannot!"

They parted. Evgeny Pavlovich left with some strange convictions: and, in his opinion, it came out that the prince was slightly out of his mind. And what was the meaning of this *face* that he was afraid of and that he loved so much! And at the same time he might actually die without Aglaya, so that Aglaya might never know he loved her so much! Ha, ha! And what was this about loving two women? With two different loves of some sort? That's interesting . . . the poor idiot! And what will become of him now?

X

THE PRINCE, HOWEVER, did not die before his wedding, either awake or "in his sleep," as he had predicted to Evgeny Pavlovich. He may indeed have slept poorly and had bad dreams, but in the daytime, with people, he seemed kind and even content, only sometimes very pensive, but that was when he was alone. They were hurrying the wedding; it was to take place about a week after Evgeny Pavlovich's call. Given such haste, even the prince's best friends, if he had any, were bound to be disappointed in their efforts to "save" the unfortunate madcap. There was a rumor that General Ivan Fyodorovich and his wife Lizaveta Prokofyevna were partly responsible for Evgeny Pavlovich's visit. But even if the two of them, in the immeasurable goodness of their hearts, might have wanted to save the pathetic madman from the abyss, they had, of course, to limit themselves to this one feeble attempt; neither their position, nor even, perhaps, the disposition of their hearts (as was natural) could correspond to more serious efforts. We have mentioned that even those around the prince partly rose up against him. Vera Lebedev, however, limited herself only to solitary tears and to staying home more and looking in on the prince less often than before. Kolya was burying his father at that time; the old man died of a second stroke eight days after the first. The prince shared greatly in the family's grief and in the first days spent several hours a day at Nina Alexandrovna's; he attended the burial and the church service. Many noticed that the public in the church met the prince and saw him off with involuntary whispers; the same thing happened in the streets and in the garden: when he walked or drove by, people talked, spoke his name, pointed at him, mentioned Nastasya Filippovna's name. She was looked for at the burial, but she was not at the burial. Neither was the captain's widow, whom Lebedev had managed to stop and cancel in time. The burial service made a strong and painful impression on the prince; he whispered to Lebedev, still in church, in reply to some question, that it was the first time he had attended an Orthodox burial service and only from childhood did he remember one other burial in some village church.

"Yes, sir, it's as if it's not the same man lying there in the coffin, sir, as the one we set up so recently to preside over us, remember, sir?" Lebedev whispered to the prince. "Who are you looking for, sir?"

"Never mind, I just imagined . . ."

"Not Rogozhin?"

"Is he here?"

"In the church, sir."

"That's why it seemed I saw his eyes," the prince murmured in embarrassment. "And what . . . why is he here? Was he invited?"

"Never thought of it, sir. They don't know him at all, sir. There are all sorts of people here, the public, sir. Why are you so amazed? I often meet him now; this past week I met him some four times here in Pavlovsk."

"I haven't seen him once . . . since that time," the prince murmured.

Because Nastasya Filippovna had also never once told him that she had met him "since that time," the prince now concluded that Rogozhin was deliberately keeping out of sight for some reason. That whole day he was in great pensiveness; but Nastasya Filippovna was extraordinarily merry all day and all evening.

Kolya, who had made peace with the prince before his father's death, suggested (since it was an essential and urgent matter) inviting Keller and Burdovsky to be his groomsmen. He guaranteed that Keller would behave properly and might even "be of use," and for Burdovsky it went without saying, he was a quiet and modest man. Nina Alexandrovna and Lebedev pointed out to the prince that if the wedding was already decided on, why have it in Pavlovsk of all places, and during the fashionable summer season, why so publicly? Would it not be better in Petersburg and even at home? It was only too clear to the prince what all these fears were driving at; but he replied briefly and simply that such was the absolute wish of Nastasya Filippovna.

The next day Keller also came to see the prince, having been informed that he was a groomsman. Before coming in, he stopped in the doorway and, as soon as he saw the prince, held up his right hand with the index finger extended and cried out by way of an oath:

"I don't drink!"

Then he went up to the prince, firmly pressed and shook both his hands, and declared that, of course, at first, when he heard, he was against it, which he announced over the billiard table, and for no other reason than that he had intentions for the prince and was waiting every day, with the impatience of a friend, to see him married to none other than the Princess de Rohan;[47] but now he could see for himself that the prince was thinking at least ten times more nobly than all of them "taken together!" For he wanted not brilliance, not riches, and not even honor, but only—truth! The sympathies of exalted persons were all too well known, and the prince was too exalted by his education not to be an exalted person, generally speaking! "But scum and all sorts of riffraff judge differently; in town, in the houses, at gatherings, in dachas, at concerts, in bars, over billiards, there was no other talk, no other cry than about the impending event. I hear they even want to organize a charivari under your windows, and that, so to speak, on the first night! If you need the pistol of an honest man, Prince, I'm ready to exchange a half-dozen noble shots, even before you get up the next morning from your honey bed." He also advised having a fire hose ready in the yard, in anticipation of a big influx of thirsty people at the church door; but Lebedev objected: "They'll smash the house to splinters," he said, "if there's a fire hose."

"This Lebedev is intriguing against you, Prince, by God! They want to put you into government custody, if you can imagine that, with everything, with your free will and your money, that is, with the two things that distinguish each of us from the quadrupeds! I've heard it, indeed I have! It's the real, whole truth!"

The prince remembered that he seemed to have heard something of the kind himself, but, naturally, he had paid no attention to it. This time, too, he only laughed and forgot it again at once. Lebedev actually was bustling about for a time; the man's calculations were always conceived as if by inspiration and, from excessive zeal, grew more complex, branched out, and moved away from their starting point in all directions; that was why he had succeeded so little in life. When afterwards, almost on the day of the wedding, he came to the prince with his repentance (he had an unfailing habit of always coming with his repentance to those he had intrigued against, especially if he had not succeeded), he announced to him that he was born a Talleyrand[48] and in some unknown way had remained a mere Lebedev. Then he laid out his whole game before him, which interested the prince enormously. By his own admission, he began by seeking the protection of exalted persons, in whom he might find support in case of need, and went to General Ivan Fyodorovich. General Ivan Fyodorovich was perplexed, very much wished the "young man" well, but declared that "for all his desire to save him, it was improper for him to act here." Lizaveta Prokofyevna did not want either to see or to hear him; Evgeny Pavlovich and Prince Shch. only waved him away. But he, Lebedev, did not lose heart and consulted a clever lawyer, a venerable old man, his great friend and almost his benefactor; the man concluded that the business was perfectly possible as long as there were competent witnesses to his derangement and total insanity, and with that, above all, the patronage of exalted persons. Lebedev did not despond here either, and once even brought a doctor to see the prince, also a venerable old man, a summer person, with an Anna on his neck,[49] solely in order to reconnoiter the terrain, so to speak, to get acquainted with the prince and, not yet officially but, so to speak, in a friendly way, to inform him of his conclusions. The prince remembered the doctor calling on him; he remembered that the day before Lebedev had been nagging him about his being unwell, and when the prince resolutely rejected medicine, he suddenly showed up with the doctor, under the pretext that the two of them were just coming from Mr. Terentyev, who was very sick, and the doctor had something to tell the prince about the patient. The prince praised Lebedev and received the doctor with extreme cordiality. They at once got to talking about the sick Ippolit; the doctor asked for a more detailed account of the scene of the suicide, and the prince absolutely fascinated him with his story and his explanation of the event. They talked about the Petersburg climate, about the prince's own illness, about Switzerland, about Schneider. The doctor was so interested in the prince's stories and his account of Schneider's system of treatment that he stayed for two hours; he smoked the prince's excellent cigars all the while, and from Lebedev's side a most tasty liqueur appeared, brought by Vera, and the doctor, a married and family man, let himself go into particular compliments before Vera, which aroused profound indignation in her. They parted friends. Having left the prince, the doctor said to Lebedev that if all such people were taken into custody, who then would be the custodians? To the tragic account, on Lebedev's part, of the impending event, the doctor shook his head slyly and insidiously, and finally observed that, not to mention the fact that "men marry all kinds of women," "this seductive individual, at least as far as he had heard, besides her immeasurable beauty, which in itself could attract a man of wealth, also possesses capital from Totsky and from Rogozhin, pearls and diamonds, shawls and furniture, and therefore the impending choice not only does not show any, so to speak, especially eye-striking stupidity on the dear prince's part, but even testifies to the cleverness of a subtle, worldly intelligence and calculation, and therefore contributes to the opposite conclusion, quite favorable to the prince . . ." This thought struck Lebedev as well; he stayed with that, and now, he added to the prince, "now you won't see anything from me but devotion and the shedding of blood; that's what I've come to say."

Ippolit, too, diverted the prince during those last days; he sent for him quite often. They lived nearby, in a small house; the little children, Ippolit's brother and sister, were glad of the dacha, because they could at least go to the garden to escape the sick boy; but the poor captain's widow remained entirely under his will and was wholly his victim; the prince had to separate and arbitrate between them every day, and the sick boy continued to call him his "nanny," at the same time not daring, as it were, not to despise him for his role as conciliator. He bore a big grudge against Kolya for hardly visiting him at all, staying first with his dying father and then with his widowed mother. He finally set up as the target of his mockery the impending marriage of the prince and Nastasya Filippovna, and ended by offending the prince and making him finally lose his temper: the prince stopped visiting him. Two days later the captain's widow came trudging in the morning and tearfully begged the prince please to come, otherwise *that one* would eat her alive. She added that he wanted to reveal a big secret. The prince went. Ippolit wanted to make peace, wept, and after his tears, naturally, became still more spiteful, only he was afraid to show his spite. He was very sick, and everything indicated that he would now die soon. There was no secret, except for certain extreme entreaties, breathless, so to speak, from excitement (perhaps affected), to "beware of Rogozhin." "He's a man who won't give up what's his; he's not like you and me, Prince; if he wants to, he won't flinch at . . ." etc., etc. The prince began to inquire in more detail, wanting to obtain some facts; but there were no facts, except for Ippolit's personal feelings and impressions. To his extreme satisfaction, Ippolit ended by finally frightening the prince terribly. At first the prince did not want to answer certain particular questions of his and only smiled at his advice "to run away, even abroad; there are Russian priests everywhere, you can be married there." But, finally, Ippolit ended with the following thought: "I'm only afraid for Aglaya Ivanovna: Rogozhin knows how much you love her; love for love; you've taken Nastasya Filippovna from him, he'll kill Aglaya Ivanovna; though she's not yours now, all the same it will be hard for you, won't it?" He achieved his goal; the prince went away no longer himself.

These warnings about Rogozhin came on the eve of the wedding. That same evening the prince saw Nastasya Filippovna for the last time before their marriage; but Nastasya Filippovna was unable to calm him down, and recently, on the contrary, had even increased his confusion still more. Before, that is, several days earlier, at her meetings with him, she had made every effort to divert him, and was terribly afraid of his sad look: she had even tried to sing for him; most often she told him all the funny things she could remember. The prince almost always pretended to laugh very much, and sometimes did in fact laugh at the brilliant intelligence and bright feeling with which she sometimes told a story, when she got carried away, and she often got carried away. Seeing the prince laugh, seeing the impression she made on him, she was delighted and felt proud of herself. But now her sadness and pensiveness grew with almost every hour. His opinion of Nastasya Filippovna was settled, otherwise, naturally, everything in her would now have seemed mysterious and incomprehensible. But he sincerely believed that she could still rise. He had said quite correctly to Evgeny Pavlovich that he sincerely and fully loved her, and his love for her indeed consisted in being drawn, as it were, towards some pitiful and sick child whom it was difficult and even impossible to abandon to its own will. He did not explain his feelings for her to anyone and even did not like talking about it, if it was impossible to avoid talking; and when he and Nastasya Filippovna sat together, they never discussed "feelings," as if they had both promised not to. Anyone could take part in their ordinary, cheerful, and animated conversation. Darya Alexeevna said afterwards that she had simply admired and rejoiced looking at them all that while.

But this view he had of the state of Nastasya Filippovna's soul and mind delivered him in part from many other perplexities. This was now a completely different woman from the one he had known some three months earlier. He did not brood, for instance, on why she had run away from marrying him then, with tears, curses, and reproaches, but now insisted herself on a speedy marriage. "It means she's not afraid, as she was then, that marrying her would be his unhappiness," thought the prince. Such quickly reborn self-assurance could not, in his view, be natural to her. Nor, again, could this assurance come only from hatred of Aglaya: Nastasya Filippovna was capable of somewhat deeper feelings. Nor from fear of facing her life with Rogozhin. In short, all these reasons, together with the rest, might have had a share in it; but the clearest thing of all for him was that it was precisely what he had long suspected, and that the poor, sick soul had been unable to endure. All this, though it delivered him, in a way, from perplexities, could not give him either peace or rest all that time. Sometimes he tried not to think about anything; it did seem, in fact, that he looked upon marriage as some sort of unimportant formality; he valued his own fate much too cheaply. With regard to objections, to conversations, such as the one with Evgeny Pavlovich, here he could say decidedly nothing in reply and felt himself totally incompetent, and therefore he avoided all conversations of that sort.

He noticed, however, that Nastasya Filippovna knew and understood only too well what Aglaya meant to him. She did not say anything, but he saw her "face" at those times when she occasionally caught him, in the beginning, on the point of going to the Epanchins'. When the Epanchins left, she really brightened. Unobservant and unsuspecting as the prince was, he had been worried by the thought that Nastasya Filippovna might venture upon some scandal in order to drive Aglaya out of Pavlovsk. The noise and rumble about the wedding in all the dachas was, of course, partly maintained by Nastasya Filippovna in order to annoy her rival. Since it was difficult to meet the Epanchins, Nastasya Filippovna put the prince into the carriage once and gave orders that they be driven right past the windows of their dacha. This was a terrible surprise for the prince: he realized it, as usual, when it was impossible to do anything about it and the carriage was already driving right past the windows. He did not say anything, but was ill for two days afterwards; Nastasya Filippovna did not repeat the experiment again. In the last days before the wedding she began to lapse into deep thought; she always ended by overcoming her sadness and becoming merry again, but somehow more quietly, not so noisily, not so happily merry as before, still so recently. The prince redoubled his attention. He was curious why she never spoke to him about Rogozhin. Only once, some five days before the wedding, Darya Alexeevna suddenly sent for him to come immediately, because Nastasya Filippovna was very unwell. He found her in a state resembling total madness: she was exclaiming, trembling, crying that Rogozhin was hiding in the garden, in their own house, that she had just seen him, that he was going to kill her in the night . . . put a knife in her! She could not calm down the whole day. But that same evening, when the prince stopped at Ippolit's for a moment, the captain's widow, who had just come back from town, where she had gone on some little errands of her own, told them that Rogozhin had called on her that day in her apartment in Petersburg and questioned her about Pavlovsk. When the prince asked precisely when Rogozhin had called, the captain's widow named almost the same hour when Nastasya Filippovna had supposedly seen him that day in her garden. The matter was explained as a simple mirage; Nastasya Filippovna herself went to the captain's widow for more detail and was extremely comforted.

On the eve of the wedding the prince left Nastasya Filippovna in great animation: the next day's finery had arrived from the dressmaker in Petersburg, the wedding dress, the headpiece, etc., etc. The prince had not expected that she would be so excited over the finery; he praised everything himself, and his praise made her still happier. But she let something slip: she had heard that there was indignation in town and that some scapegraces were indeed arranging a charivari, with music and all but with verses written specially for the occasion, and that it was all but approved of by the rest of society. And so now she precisely wanted to hold her head still higher before them, to outshine them all with the taste and wealth of her finery—"let them shout, let them whistle, if they dare!" The mere thought of it made her eyes flash. She had yet another secret thought, but she did not voice it aloud: she dreamed that Aglaya, or at least someone sent by her, would also be in the crowd, incognito, in the church, would look and see, and she was inwardly preparing herself for that. She parted from the prince, all taken up with these thoughts, at about eleven o'clock in the evening; but before it struck midnight, a messenger came running to the prince from Darya Alexeevna saying "come quickly, it's very bad." The prince found his fiancée locked in the bedroom, in tears, in despair, in hysterics; for a long time she refused to listen to anything they said to her through the locked door; at last she opened it, let in only the prince, locked the door after him, and fell on her knees before him. (So, at least, Darya Alexeevna reported afterwards, having managed to spy out a thing or two.)

"What am I doing! What am I doing! What am I doing to you!" she kept exclaiming, convulsively embracing his legs.

The prince stayed for a whole hour with her; we do not know what they talked about. According to Darya Alexeevna, they parted after an hour, reconciled and happy. The prince sent once more that night to inquire, but Nastasya Filippovna was already asleep. In the morning, before she woke up, two more messengers came to Darya Alexeevna's from the prince, and a third was instructed to tell him that "Nastasya Filippovna is now surrounded by a whole swarm of dressmakers and hairdressers from Petersburg, that there was no trace of yesterday's mood, that she was occupied as only such a beauty could be occupied with dressing for her wedding, and that now, precisely at that moment, an extraordinary congress was being held about precisely which of the diamonds to wear and how to wear them." The prince was completely set at ease.

The whole following story about this wedding was told by knowledgeable people in the following way and seems to be correct:

The wedding was set for eight o'clock in the evening; Nastasya Filippovna was ready by seven. From six o'clock on, crowds of idlers gradually began to gather around Lebedev's dacha, but more especially near Darya Alexeevna's house; after seven o'clock the church also began to fill up. Vera Lebedev and Kolya were terribly afraid for the prince; however, they were very busy at home: they were responsible for the reception and refreshments in the prince's rooms. However, almost no real gathering was planned after the wedding; besides the necessary persons present at the church ceremony, Lebedev had invited the Ptitsyns, Ganya, the doctor with an Anna on his neck, and Darya Alexeevna. When the curious prince asked Lebedev why he had decided to invite the doctor, "almost a total stranger," Lebedev answered self-contentedly: "An order on his neck, a respectable man, for appearances, sir"—and made the prince laugh. Keller and Burdovsky, in tailcoats and gloves, looked very proper; only Keller still worried the prince and his own backers slightly by his open propensity for battle and the very hostile look he gave the idlers who were gathering around the house. Finally, at half-past seven, the prince set out for the church in a carriage. We will note, incidentally, that he himself purposely did not want to leave out any of the usual habits and customs; everything was done publicly, obviously, openly, and "as it should be." In the church, having somehow passed through the crowd, to the ceaseless whispers and exclamations of the public, under the guidance of Keller, who cast menacing looks to right and left, the prince hid for a time in the sanctuary, while Keller went to fetch the bride, where he found the crowd at the porch of Darya Alexeevna's house not only two or three times denser than at the prince's, but perhaps even three times more uninhibited. Going up to the porch, he heard such exclamations that he could not restrain himself and was just about to turn to the public with the intention of delivering an appropriate speech, but fortunately he was stopped by Burdovsky and Darya Alexeevna herself, who ran out to the porch; they seized him and took him inside by force. Keller was annoyed and hurried. Nastasya Filippovna stood up, glanced once more in the mirror, observed with a "crooked" smile, as Keller reported later, that she was "pale as a corpse," bowed piously before the icon, and went out to the porch. A buzz of voices greeted her appearance. True, in the first moment there was laughter, applause, almost whistling; but after a moment other voices were heard:

"What a beauty!" someone shouted in the crowd.

"She's not the first and she's not the last!"

"Marriage covers up everything, fools!"

"No, go and find another beauty like that! Hurrah!" the nearest ones shouted.

"A princess! I'd sell my soul for such a princess!" some clerk shouted. " 'A life for one night with me! . . . ' "[50]

Nastasya Filippovna indeed came out white as a sheet; but her large black eyes flashed at the crowd like burning coals; it was this gaze that the crowd could not bear; indignation turned into enthusiastic shouts. The door of the carriage was already open, Keller had already offered the bride his arm, when she suddenly gave a cry and threw herself off the porch straight into the mass of people. All who were accompanying her froze in amazement, the crowd parted before her, and Rogozhin suddenly appeared five or six steps from the porch. It was his gaze that Nastasya Filippovna had caught in the crowd. She rushed to him like a madwoman and seized him by both hands.

"Save me! Take me away! Wherever you like, now!"

Rogozhin almost picked her up in his arms and all but carried her to the carriage. Then, in an instant, he took a hundred-rouble note from his wallet and gave it to the driver.

"To the station, and another hundred roubles if you make the train!"

And he jumped into the carriage after Nastasya Filippovna and closed the door. The driver did not hesitate a moment and whipped up the horses. Afterwards Keller blamed the unexpectedness of it all: "Another second and I'd have found what to do, I wouldn't have let it happen!" he explained as he recounted the adventure. He and Burdovsky jumped into another carriage that happened to be there and set off in pursuit, but he changed his mind on the way, thinking that "it's too late in any case! You can't bring her back by force!"

"And the prince wouldn't want that!" the shaken Burdovsky decided.

Rogozhin and Nastasya Filippovna came galloping up to the station in time. Getting out of the carriage, Rogozhin, as he was about to board the train, managed to stop a girl passing by in an old but decent dark mantilla and with a foulard kerchief thrown over her head.

"How's about fifty roubles for your mantilla!" he suddenly held the money out to the girl. Before she had time to be surprised, before she tried to understand, he had already put the fifty-rouble note into her hand, taken off the mantilla and foulard, and thrown it all over Nastasya Filippovna's shoulders and head. Her much too magnificent finery struck the eye, it would have attracted attention on the train, and only later did the girl understand why her worthless old rag had been bought at such profit for her.

The buzz about the adventure reached the church with extraordinary speed. As Keller was making his way to the prince, a host of people totally unknown to him ran up to ask him questions. There was loud talk, a shaking of heads, even laughter; no one left the church, they all waited to see how the groom would take the news. He blanched, but took the news quietly, saying barely audibly: "I was afraid; but all the same I didn't think it would be that . . ."—and then, after some silence, added: "However . . . in her condition . . . it's completely in the order of things." Such a reaction Keller himself later called "unexampled philosophy." The prince left the church looking calm and brisk; so at least many noticed and reported afterwards. It seemed he wanted very much to get home and be left alone as quickly as possible; but that he was not allowed to do. He was followed into his rooms by some of the invited people, Ptitsyn and Gavrila Ardalionovich among others, and with them the doctor, who also showed no intention of leaving. Besides that, the whole house was literally besieged by the idle public. While still on the terrace, the prince heard Keller and Lebedev get into a fierce argument with some completely unknown but decent-looking people, who wanted at all costs to enter the terrace. The prince went up to the arguers, asked what it was about, and, politely pushing Lebedev and Keller aside, delicately addressed a gray-haired and stocky gentleman, who was standing on the porch steps at the head of several other aspirants, and invited him to do him the honor of favoring him with his visit. The gentleman became embarrassed but nevertheless went in; and after him a second, a third. Out of all the crowd, some seven or eight persons were found who did go in, trying to do it as casually as possible; but no more volunteers turned up, and soon the same crowd began to denounce the parvenus. The visitors were seated, a conversation began, tea was served—and all that extremely decently, modestly, to the slight surprise of the visitors. There were, of course, several attempts to liven up the conversation and lead it to an "appropriate" theme; several immodest questions were asked, several "daring" observations were made. The prince answered everyone so simply and affably, and at the same time with such dignity, such trust in his guests' decency, that the immodest questions faded away of themselves. The conversation gradually began to turn almost serious. One gentleman, seizing on a word, suddenly swore in extreme indignation that he would not sell his estate, whatever happened; that, on the contrary, he would wait and bide his time, and that "enterprises are better than money"; "that, my dear sir, is what my economic system consists in, if you care to know, sir." As he was addressing the prince, the prince warmly praised him, though Lebedev whispered in his ear that this gentleman did not have a penny to his name and had never had any estate. Almost an hour went by, the tea was finished, and after tea the guests finally felt ashamed to stay longer. The doctor and the gray-haired gentleman warmly took leave of the prince; and everyone else also took their leave warmly and noisily. Wishes and opinions were expressed, such as that "there was nothing to grieve about, and perhaps it was all the better this way," etc. True, there were attempts to ask for champagne, but the older guests stopped the younger ones. When they were all gone, Keller leaned over to Lebedev and said: "You and I would start shouting, fighting, disgrace ourselves, get the police involved; and here he's got himself some new friends, and what friends! I know them!" Lebedev, who was already "loaded," sighed and said: "Hidden from the wise and clever, and revealed unto babes,[51] I said that about him before, but now I'll add that God has preserved the babe himself, saved him from the abyss, he and all his saints!"

Finally, at around half-past ten, the prince was left alone; he had a headache; the last to leave was Kolya, who helped him to change his wedding costume for house clothes. They parted warmly. Kolya did not talk about what had happened, but promised to come early the next day. He later testified that the prince had not warned him about anything at this last farewell, which meant that he had concealed his intentions even from him. Soon there was almost no one left in the whole house: Burdovsky went to Ippolit's, Keller and Lebedev also took themselves off somewhere. Only Vera Lebedev remained in the rooms for some time, hastily turning everything from a festive to its ordinary look. As she was leaving, she peeked into the prince's room. He was sitting at the table, both elbows resting on it and his head in his hands. She quietly went up to him and touched his shoulder; the prince looked at her in perplexity, and for almost a minute seemed as if he was trying to remember; but having remembered and realized everything, he suddenly became extremely excited. It all resolved itself, however, in a great and fervent request to Vera, that she knock at his door the next morning at seven o'clock, before the first train. Vera promised; the prince began asking her heatedly not to tell anyone about it; she promised that as well, and finally, when she had already opened the door to leave, the prince stopped her for a third time, took her hands, kissed them, then kissed her on the forehead, and with a certain "extraordinary" look, said: "Till tomorrow!" So at least Vera recounted afterwards. She left fearing greatly for him. In the morning she was heartened a little when she knocked at his door at seven o'clock, as arranged, and announced to him that the train for Petersburg would leave in a quarter of an hour; it seemed to her that he was quite cheerful and even smiling when he opened the door to her. He had almost not undressed for the night, but he had slept. In his opinion, he might come back that same day. It turned out, therefore, that at that moment she was the only one he had found it possible and necessary to inform that he was going to town.

XI

An hour later he was in Petersburg, and after nine o'clock he was ringing at Rogozhin's. He came in by the front entrance and had to wait a long time. At last, the door of old Mrs. Rogozhin's apartment opened, and an elderly, decent-looking maid appeared.

"Parfyon Semyonovich is not at home," she announced from the doorway. "Whom do you want?"

"Parfyon Semyonovich."

"He's not at home, sir."

The maid looked the prince over with wild curiosity.

"At least tell me, did he spend the night at home? And . . . did he come back alone yesterday?"

The maid went on looking, but did not reply.

"Didn't he come here yesterday . . . in the evening . . . with Nastasya Filippovna?"

"And may I ask who you are pleased to be yourself?"

"Prince Lev Nikolaevich Myshkin, we're very well acquainted."

"He's not at home, sir."

The maid dropped her eyes.

"And Nastasya Filippovna?"

"I know nothing about that, sir."

"Wait, wait! When will he be back?"

"We don't know that either, sir."

The door closed.

The prince decided to come back in an hour. Looking into the courtyard, he met the caretaker.

"Is Parfyon Semyonovich at home?"

"He is, sir."

"How is it I was just told he's not at home?"

"Did somebody at his place tell you?"

"No, the maid at his mother's, but when I rang at Parfyon Semyonovich's nobody answered."

"Maybe he went out," the caretaker decided. "He doesn't always say. And sometimes he takes the key with him and the rooms stay locked for three days."

"Are you sure he was at home yesterday?"

"He was. Sometimes he comes in the front entrance, so I don't see him."

"And wasn't Nastasya Filippovna with him yesterday?"

"That I don't know, sir. She doesn't care to come often; seems we'd know if she did."

The prince went out and for some time walked up and down the sidewalk, pondering. The windows of the rooms occupied by Rogozhin were all shut; the windows of the half occupied by his mother were almost all open; it was a hot, clear day; the prince went across the street to the opposite sidewalk and stopped to look once more at the windows; not only were they shut, but in almost all of them the white blinds were drawn.

He stood there for a minute and—strangely—it suddenly seemed to him that the edge of one blind was raised and Rogozhin's face flashed, flashed and disappeared in the same instant. He waited a little longer and decided to go and ring again, but changed his mind and put it off for an hour: "Who knows, maybe I only imagined it . . ."

Above all, he now hurried to the Izmailovsky quarter, where Nastasya Filippovna recently had an apartment. He knew that, having moved out of Pavlovsk three weeks earlier at his request, she had settled in the Izmailovsky quarter with one of her good acquaintances, a teacher's widow, a respectable and family lady, who sublet a good furnished apartment in her house, which was almost her whole subsistence. It was very likely that Nastasya Filippovna had kept the apartment when she went back to Pavlovsk; at least it was quite possible that she had spent the night in this apartment, where Rogozhin would surely have brought her yesterday. The prince took a cab. On the way it occurred to him that he ought to have started there, because it was incredible that she would have gone at night straight to Rogozhin's. Here he also recalled the caretaker's words, that Nastasya Filippovna did not care to come often. If she had never come often anyway, then why on earth would she now be staying at Rogozhin's? Encouraging himself with such consolations, the prince finally arrived at the Izmailovsky quarter more dead than alive.

To his utter astonishment, not only had no one heard of Nastasya Filippovna at the teacher's widow's either yesterday or today, but they ran out to look at him as at some sort of wonder. The whole numerous family of the teacher's widow—all girls with a year's difference, from fifteen down to seven years old—poured out after their mother and surrounded him, their mouths gaping. After them came their skinny yellow aunt in a black kerchief, and, finally, the grandmother of the family appeared, a little old lady in spectacles. The teacher's widow urged him to come in and sit down, which the prince did. He realized at once that they were well informed about who he was, and knew perfectly well that his wedding was to have taken place yesterday, and were dying to ask about both the wedding and the wonder that he was there asking them about the woman who should have been nowhere else but with him in Pavlovsk, but they were too delicate to ask. In a brief outline, he satisfied their curiosity about the wedding. There was amazement, gasps and cries, so that he was forced to tell almost all the rest, in broad outline, of course. Finally, the council of wise and worried ladies decided that they absolutely had to go first of all and knock at Rogozhin's till he opened, and find out everything positively from him. And if he was not at home (which was to be ascertained) or did not want to tell, they would drive to the Semyonovsky quarter, to a certain German lady, Nastasya Filippovna's acquaintance, who lived with her mother: perhaps Nastasya Filippovna, in her agitation and wishing to hide, had spent the night with them. The prince got up completely crushed; they reported afterwards that he "turned terribly pale"; indeed, his legs nearly gave way under him. Finally, through the terrible jabber of voices, he discerned that they were arranging to act in concert with him and were asking for his town address. He turned out to have no address; they advised him to put up somewhere in a hotel. The prince thought and gave the address of his former hotel, the one where he had had a fit some five weeks earlier. Then he went back to Rogozhin's.

This time not only Rogozhin's door but even the one to the old lady's apartment did not open. The prince went for the caretaker and had great difficulty finding him in the courtyard; the caretaker was busy with something and barely answered, even barely looked at him, but all the same declared positively that Parfyon Semyonovich "left very early in the morning, went to Pavlovsk, and wouldn't be home today."

"I'll wait; maybe he'll come towards evening?"

"And he may not be home for a week, who knows about him."

"So he did spend the night here?"

"The night, yes, he spent the night . . ."

All this was suspicious and shady. The caretaker might very well have had time, during that interval, to receive new instructions: earlier he had even been talkative, while now he simply turned his back. But the prince decided to come by once more in about two hours, and even to stand watch by the house, if need be, while now there was still hope for the German woman, and he drove to the Semyonovsky quarter.

But at the German woman's they did not even understand him. From certain fleeting remarks, he was even able to guess that the German beauty had quarreled with Nastasya Filippovna some two weeks ago, so that she had not even heard of her in all those days, and tried as hard as she could to make it clear that she was not interested in hearing anything now, "even if she's married all the princes in the world." The prince hastened to leave. It occurred to him, among other things, that she might have left for Moscow, as she did the other time, and Rogozhin, naturally, would have followed her, or perhaps had gone with her. "At least let me find some trace!" He remembered, however, that he had to stop at the inn, and he hurried to Liteinaya; there he was given a room at once. The floorboy asked if he wanted a bite to eat; he answered absentmindedly that he did, and on second thought was furious with himself, because eating would take an extra half hour, and only later did he realize that nothing prevented him from leaving the food uneaten on the table. A strange sensation came over him in this dim and stifling corridor, a sensation that strove painfully to realize itself in some thought; but he was quite unable to tell what this new importunate thought was. He finally left the inn, no longer himself; his head was spinning, but—anyhow, where to go? He raced to Rogozhin's again.

Rogozhin had not come back; no one opened to his ringing; he rang at old Mrs. Rogozhin's; they opened the door and also announced that Parfyon Semyonovich was not at home and might not be back for some three days. What disturbed the prince was that he was again studied with the same wild curiosity. The caretaker this time was nowhere to be found. He went, as earlier, to the opposite sidewalk, looked at the windows, and paced up and down in the torrid heat for about half an hour or maybe more; this time nothing stirred; the windows did not open, the white blinds were motionless. It finally occurred to him that he had probably only imagined it earlier, that the windows by all tokens were even so dim, so long in need of washing, that it would have been hard to make anything out, even if anyone in fact had looked through the glass. Gladdened by this thought, he again went to the Izmailovsky quarter, to the teacher's widow.

He was expected there. The teacher's widow had already gone

to three or four places and had even stopped at Rogozhin's: not the slightest trace. The prince listened silently, went into the room, sat on the sofa, and began looking at them all as if not understanding what they were telling him. Strange: first he was extremely observant, then suddenly impossibly distracted. The whole family reported later that he had been an "astonishingly" strange man that day, so that "perhaps all the signs were already there." He finally stood up and asked to be shown Nastasya Filippovna's rooms. These were two large, bright, high-ceilinged rooms, quite well furnished, and not cheap. All these ladies reported afterwards that the prince studied every object in the rooms, saw an open book on the table, from a lending library, the French novel *Madame Bovary*,[52] looked at it, earmarked the page on which the book lay open, asked permission to take it with him, and, not listening to the objection that it was a library book, put it into his pocket. He sat down by the open window and, seeing a card table covered with writing in chalk, asked who played. They told him that Nastasya Filippovna had played every night with Rogozhin—fools, preference, millers, whist, hearts—all sorts of games, and that the cards had appeared only very recently, when she moved from Pavlovsk to Petersburg, because Nastasya Filippovna kept complaining that she was bored, that Rogozhin sat silent for whole evenings and could not talk about anything, and she often wept; and suddenly the next evening Rogozhin took cards from his pocket; here Nastasya Filippovna laughed and they began to play. The prince asked where the cards they had played with were. But there were no cards; Rogozhin himself always brought the cards in his pocket, a new deck every day, and then took them away with him.

The ladies advised him to go once more to Rogozhin's and to knock harder once more, not now, but in the evening: "something might turn up." The teacher's widow herself volunteered meanwhile to go to Pavlovsk to see Darya Alexeevna before evening: they might know something there. The prince was invited to come by ten o'clock that evening, in any case, to make plans for the next day. Despite all consolations and reassurances, a perfect despair overwhelmed the prince's soul. In inexpressible anguish, he reached his inn on foot. The dusty, stifling summer Petersburg squeezed him as in a vice; he jostled among stern or drunken people, aimlessly peered into faces, probably walked much more than he had to; it was nearly evening when he entered his hotel room. He decided to rest a little and then go again to Rogozhin's, as he had been advised, sat down on the sofa, rested both elbows on the table, and fell to thinking.

God knows how long he thought and God knows what about. There was much that he feared, and he felt painfully and tormentingly that he was terribly afraid. Vera Lebedev came into his head; then it occurred to him that Lebedev might know something about this matter, and if he did not, he would be able to find out sooner and more easily than he would himself. Then he remembered Ippolit, and that Rogozhin had gone to see Ippolit. Then he remembered Rogozhin himself: recently at the burial, then in the park, then—suddenly here in the corridor, when he had hidden himself in the corner that time and waited for him with a knife. His eyes he now remembered, his eyes looking out of the darkness then. He gave a start: the earlier importunate thought now came to his head.

It was in part that if Rogozhin was in Petersburg, then even if he was hiding for a time, all the same he would end by coming to him, the prince, with good or bad intentions, perhaps, just as then. At least, if Rogozhin had to come for some reason or other, then he had nowhere else to come than here, to this same corridor again. He did not know his address; therefore he would very possibly think that the prince was staying at the same inn; at least he would try looking here . . . if he needed him very much. And, who knows, perhaps he would need him very much?

So he reflected, and for some reason this thought seemed perfectly possible to him. He would not have been able to account for it to himself, if he had begun to go deeper into this thought: "Why, for instance, should Rogozhin suddenly need him so much, and why was it even impossible that they should not finally come together?" But the thought was painful: "If things are well with him, he won't come," the prince went on thinking, "he'll sooner come if things are not well with him; and things are probably not well . . ."

Of course, with such a conviction, he ought to have waited for Rogozhin at home, in his hotel room; but he was as if unable to bear his new thought, jumped up, seized his hat, and ran. It was now almost quite dark in the corridor: "What if he comes out of that corner now and stops me by the stairs?" flashed in him as he approached the familiar spot. But no one came out. He went down under the gateway, walked out to the sidewalk, marveled at the dense crowd of people who came pouring outside at sunset (as always in Petersburg at vacation time), and went in the direction of Gorokhovaya Street. Fifty paces from the inn, at the first intersection, in the crowd, someone suddenly touched his elbow and said in a low voice, just at his ear:

"Lev Nikolaevich, come with me, brother, you've got to."

It was Rogozhin.

Strange: the prince began telling him, suddenly, with joy, babbling and almost not finishing the words, how he had been expecting him just now in the corridor, at the inn.

"I was there," Rogozhin answered unexpectedly, "let's go."

The prince was surprised by the answer, but he was surprised at least two minutes later, when he understood. Having understood the answer, he became frightened and began studying Rogozhin. The man was walking almost half a step ahead, looking straight in front of him and not glancing at anyone he met, giving way to them all with mechanical care.

"Then why didn't you ask for me in my room . . . if you were at the inn?" the prince asked suddenly.

Rogozhin stopped, looked at him, thought, and, as if not understanding the question at all, said:

"So, now, Lev Nikolaevich, you go straight on here, right to the house, you know? And I'll go along the other side. And watch out that we keep together . . ."

Having said this, he crossed the street, stepped onto the opposite sidewalk, looked whether the prince was following, and seeing that he was standing and staring at him, waved his hand in the direction of Gorokhovaya and went on, constantly turning to look at the prince and beckoning to him to follow. He was obviously heartened to see that the prince had understood him and did not cross the street to join him. It occurred to the prince that Rogozhin had to keep an eye out for someone and not miss him on the way, and that that was why he had crossed to the other side. "Only why didn't he tell me who to look for?" They went some five hundred paces that way, and suddenly the prince began to tremble for some reason; Rogozhin still kept looking back, though more rarely; the prince could not help himself and beckoned to him with his hand. The man at once came across the street to him.

"Is Nastasya Filippovna at your house?"

"Yes."

"And was it you who looked at me from behind the curtain earlier?"

"It was . . ."

"Then why did you . . ."

But the prince did not know what to ask further and how to finish the question; besides, his heart was pounding so hard that it was difficult for him even to speak. Rogozhin was also silent and looked at him as before, that is, as if pensively.

"Well, I'm going," he said suddenly, preparing to cross the street again, "and you go, too. Let's stay separated in the street . . . it's better for us that way . . . on different sides . . . you'll see."

When they finally turned from two different sidewalks onto Gorokhovaya and approached Rogozhin's house, the prince's legs again began to give way under him, so that he had difficulty walking. It was nearly ten o'clock in the evening. The windows on the old lady's side were open as before, Rogozhin's were closed, and the drawn white blinds seemed to have become still more noticeable in the twilight. The prince came up to the house from the opposite sidewalk; Rogozhin stepped onto the porch from his sidewalk and waved his hand to him. The prince went up to him on the porch.

"Even the caretaker doesn't know about me now, that I've come back home. I told him earlier that I was going to Pavlovsk, and I said the same thing at my mother's," he whispered with a sly and almost contented smile. "We'll go in and nobody'll hear."

He already had the key in his hand. Going up the stairs, he turned and shook his finger at the prince to step more quietly, quietly opened the door to his rooms, let the prince in, carefully came in after him, locked the door behind him, and put the key in his pocket.

"Let's go," he said in a whisper.

He had begun speaking in a whisper still on the sidewalk in Liteinaya. Despite all his external calm, he was in some deep inner anguish. When they entered the big room, just before his study, he went up to the window and beckoned mysteriously to the prince:

"So when you rang my bell earlier, I guessed straight off that it was you all right; I tiptoed to the door and heard you talking with Pafnutyevna, and I'd already been telling her at dawn: if you, or somebody from you, or anybody else starts knocking at my door, she shouldn't tell about me under any pretext; and especially if you came asking for me yourself, and I told her your name. And then, when you left, it occurred to me: what if he's standing there now and spying on me, or watching from the street? I went up to this same window, raised the curtain a bit, looked, and you were standing there looking straight at me . . . That's how it was."

"And where is . . . Nastasya Filippovna?" the prince brought out breathlessly.

"She's . . . here," Rogozhin said slowly, as if waiting a bit before he answered.

"But where?"

Rogozhin raised his eyes to the prince and looked at him intently:

"Let's go . . ."

He kept speaking in a whisper and without hurrying, slowly and, as before, with some strange pensiveness. Even when he was telling about the curtain, it was as if he wanted to express something different with his story, despite all the expansiveness of the telling.

They went into the study. A certain change had taken place in this room since the prince had been there: a green silk damask curtain was stretched across the whole room, with openings at both ends, separating the study from the alcove in which Rogozhin's bed was set up. The heavy curtain was drawn and the openings were closed. But it was very dark in the room; the Petersburg "white" summer nights were beginning to turn darker, and if it had not been for the full moon, it would have been difficult to see anything in Rogozhin's dark rooms with the blinds drawn. True, it was still possible to make out faces, though not very clearly. Rogozhin's face was very pale, as usual; his eyes looked intently at the prince, with a strong gleam, but somehow motionlessly.

"Why don't you light a candle?" asked the prince.

"No, better not," Rogozhin replied and, taking the prince by the hand, he bent him down onto a chair; he sat down facing him and moved the chair so that his knees almost touched the prince's. Between them, a little to the side, was a small, round table. "Sit down, let's sit a while!" he said, as if persuading him to sit down. They were silent for a minute. "I just knew you'd stay in that same inn," he began, as people sometimes do, approaching the main conversation by starting with extraneous details, not directly related to the matter. "As soon as I stepped into the corridor, I thought: maybe he's sitting and waiting for me now, like me him, this same minute? Did you go to the teacher's widow's?"

"I did," the prince could barely speak for the strong pounding of his heart.

"I thought about that, too. There'll be talk, I thought . . . and then I thought: I'll bring him here to spend the night, so that this night together . . ."

"Rogozhin! Where is Nastasya Filippovna?" the prince suddenly whispered and stood up, trembling in every limb. Rogozhin got up, too.

"There," he whispered, nodding towards the curtain.

"Asleep?" whispered the prince.

Again Rogozhin looked at him intently, as earlier.

"Okay, let's go! . . . Only you . . . Well, let's go!"

He raised the curtain, stopped, and again turned to the prince.

"Come in!" he nodded towards the opening, inviting him to go first. The prince went in.

"It's dark here," he said.

"You can see!" Rogozhin muttered.

"I can barely see . . . the bed."

"Go closer," Rogozhin suggested quietly.

The prince took one step closer, then another, and stopped. He stood and peered for a minute or two; neither man said anything all the while they were there by the bed; the prince's heart was pounding so that it seemed audible in the dead silence of the room. But his eyes were accustomed now, so that he could make out the whole bed; someone was sleeping there, a completely motionless sleep; not the slightest rustle, not the slightest breath could be heard. The sleeper was covered from head to foot with a white sheet, but the limbs were somehow vaguely outlined; one could only see by the raised form that a person lay stretched out there. Scattered in disorder on the bed, at its foot, on the chair next to the bed, even on the floor, were the taken-off clothes, a costly white silk dress, flowers, ribbons. On the little table by the head of the bed, the taken-off and scattered diamonds sparkled. At the foot of the bed some lace lay crumpled in a heap, and against this white lace, peeping from under the sheet, the tip of a bare foot was outlined; it seemed carved from marble and was terribly still. The prince looked and felt that the more he looked, the more dead and quiet the room became. Suddenly an awakened fly buzzed, flew over the bed, and alighted by its head. The prince gave a start.

"Let's get out," Rogozhin touched his arm.

They went out, sat down again in the same chairs, again facing each other. The prince was trembling more and more, and did not take his questioning eyes off Rogozhin's face.

"You're trembling, I notice, Lev Nikolaevich," Rogozhin said at last, "almost like when your disorder comes over you, remember, how it was in Moscow? Or the way it was once before a fit. And I just can't think what I'm going to do with you now . . ."

The prince listened, straining all his powers to understand, and still asking with his eyes.

"It was you?" he finally managed to say, nodding towards the curtain.

"It was . . . me . . ." Rogozhin whispered and looked down.

They were silent for about five minutes.

"Because," Rogozhin suddenly began to go on, as if he had not interrupted his speech, "because if it's your illness, and a fit, and shouting now, somebody may hear it in the street or the courtyard, and they'll figure that people are spending the night in the apartment; they'll start knocking, they'll come in . . . because they all think I'm not home. I didn't light a candle so they wouldn't suspect that in the street or the courtyard. Because when I'm not home, I take the key with me, and nobody comes in for three or four days, even to tidy up, that's how I set it up. Now, so they won't know we're spending the night . . ."

"Wait," said the prince, "I asked the caretaker and the old woman earlier whether Nastasya Filippovna hadn't spent the night. So they already know."

"I know you asked. I told Pafnutyevna that Nastasya Filippovna came yesterday and left for Pavlovsk yesterday, and that she spent ten minutes at my place. They don't know she spent the night—nobody knows. Yesterday we came in very quietly, like you and me today. I thought to myself on the way that she'd refuse to go in quietly—forget it! She talked in a whisper, walked on tiptoe, gathered her dress up all around her so it wouldn't rustle, and held it with her hands, she shook her finger at me on the stairs—all because she was frightened of you. On the train it was like she was completely crazy, all from fear, and she herself wanted to come here to spend the night; I first thought I'd take her to the teacher's widow's—forget it! 'He'll find me there,' she says, 'at dawn, but you can hide me, and tomorrow morning I'll go to Moscow,' and then she wanted to go to Orel somewhere. And as she was getting ready for bed, she kept saying we'd go to Orel . . ."

"Wait, what about now, Parfyon, what do you want now?"

"See, I just have doubts about you trembling all the time. We'll spend the night here together. There's no other bed here than that one, so I decided to take the pillows from the two sofas, and I'll arrange them next to each other there, by the curtain, for you and me, so we're together. Because if they come in, they'll start looking and searching, they'll see her at once and take her out. They'll start questioning me, I'll tell them it was me, and they'll take me away at once. So let her lie here now, next to us, next to me and you . . ."

"Yes, yes!" the prince agreed warmly.

"Meaning not to confess or let them take her out."

"N-not for anything!" the prince decided. "No, no, no!"

"That's how I decided, too, so as not to give her up, man, not for anything, not to anybody! We'll spend the night quietly. Today I left the house only for one hour, in the morning, otherwise I was always by her. And then in the evening I went to get you. I'm also afraid it's stuffy and there'll be a smell. Do you notice the smell or not?"

"Maybe I do, I don't know. By morning there will be."

"I covered her with oilcloth, good American oilcloth, and the sheet's on top of the oilcloth, and I put four uncorked bottles of Zhdanov liquid there, they're standing there now."

"It's like there . . . in Moscow?"

"Because of the smell, brother. But she's lying there so . . . In the morning, when it's light, have a look. What, you can't get up?" Rogozhin asked with timorous surprise, seeing the prince trembling so much that he could not stand up.

"My legs won't work," the prince murmured. "It's from fear, I know it . . . The fear will pass, and I'll get up . . ."

"Wait, I'll make up the bed meanwhile, and then you can lie down . . . and I'll lie down with you . . . and we'll listen . . . because I don't know yet, man . . . I don't know everything yet, man, so I'm telling you ahead of time, so you'll know all about it ahead of time . . ."

Muttering these vague words, Rogozhin began to make up the beds. It was clear that he had perhaps thought of these beds as early as that morning. He himself had spent the past night lying on the sofa. But two people could not lie on the sofa, and he absolutely wanted to make up beds now side by side, and that was why, with great effort, he now dragged pillows of various sizes from both sofas all the way across the room, right up to the opening in the curtain. The bed got made up anyhow; he went over to the prince, took him tenderly and rapturously by the arm, got him to his feet, and led him to the bed; but it turned out that the prince could walk by himself; which meant that "the fear was passing"; and yet he still went on trembling.

"Because, brother," Rogozhin began suddenly, laying the prince down on the left, better, pillows and himself stretching out on the right side, without undressing and thrusting both hands behind his head, "it's hot now, and sure to smell . . . I'm afraid to open the windows; but at my mother's there are pots of flowers, a lot of flowers, and they have such a wonderful smell; I thought I might bring them here, but Pafnutyevna would guess, because she's a curious one."

"She's a curious one," agreed the prince.

"We could buy some bouquets and lay flowers all around her? But I think it'd be a pity, friend, to cover her with flowers!"

"Listen . . ." the prince asked, as if in confusion, as if groping for precisely what he had to ask and forgetting it at once, "listen, tell me: what did you use? A knife? That same one?"

"That same one."

"Wait now! I also want to ask you, Parfyon . . . I have a lot to ask you, about everything . . . but to begin with, you'd better tell me, from the first beginning, so that I know: did you want to kill her before my wedding, before the ceremony, on the church porch, with the knife? Did you want to or not?"

"I don't know if I wanted to or not . . ." Rogozhin replied drily, as if he even marveled somewhat at the question and could not comprehend it.

"You never brought the knife to Pavlovsk with you?"

"I never brought it. I can only tell you this about the knife, Lev Nikolaevich," he added, after a pause. "I took it out of the locked drawer this morning, because the whole thing happened this morning, between three and four. I kept it like a bookmark in a book . . . And . . . and this is still a wonder to me: the knife seemed to go in about three inches . . . or even three and a half . . . just under the left breast . . . but only about half a tablespoon of blood came out on her nightshirt; no more than that . . ."

"That, that, that," the prince suddenly raised himself up in terrible agitation, "that, that I know, that I've read about . . . it's called an internal hemorrhage . . . Sometimes there isn't even a drop. If the blow goes straight to the heart . . ."

"Wait, do you hear?" Rogozhin suddenly interrupted quickly and sat up fearfully on his bed. "Do you hear?"

"No!" the prince said quickly and fearfully, looking at Rogozhin.

"Footsteps! Do you hear? In the big room . . ."

They both began to listen.

"I hear," the prince whispered firmly.

"Footsteps?"

"Footsteps."

"Should we shut the door or not?"

"Shut it . . ."

They shut the door, and both lay down again. There was a long silence.

"Ah, yes!" the prince suddenly whispered in the same agitated and hurried whisper, as if he had caught the thought again and was terribly afraid of losing it again, even jumping up a little on his bed, "yes . . . I wanted . . . those cards! cards . . . They say you played cards with her?"

"I did," Rogozhin said after some silence.

"Where are . . . the cards?"

"They're here . . ." Rogozhin said after a still longer silence, "here . . ."

He pulled a used deck, wrapped in paper, out of his pocket and handed it to the prince. The prince took it, but as if in perplexity. A new, sad, and cheerless feeling weighed on his heart; he suddenly realized that at that moment, and for a long time now, he had not been talking about what he needed to talk about, and had not been doing what he needed to do, and that these cards he was holding in his hands, and which he was so glad to have, would be no help, no help at all now. He stood up and clasped his hands. Rogozhin lay motionless, as if he did not see or hear his movements; but his eyes glittered brightly through the darkness and were completely open and motionless. The prince sat on a chair and began to look at him in fear. About half an hour went by; suddenly Rogozhin cried out loudly and abruptly and began to guffaw, as if forgetting that he had to talk in a whisper:

"That officer, that officer . . . remember how she horsewhipped that officer at the concert, remember, ha, ha, ha! A cadet, too . . . a cadet . . . came running . . ."

The prince jumped up from the chair in new fright. When Rogozhin quieted down (and he did suddenly quiet down), the prince quietly bent over him, sat down beside him, and with a pounding heart, breathing heavily, began to examine him. Rogozhin did not turn his head to him and even seemed to forget about him. The prince watched and waited; time passed, it began to grow light. Now and then Rogozhin sometimes suddenly began to mutter, loudly, abruptly, and incoherently; began to exclaim and laugh; then the prince would reach out his trembling hand to him and quietly touch his head, his hair, stroke it and stroke his cheeks . . . there was nothing more he could do! He was beginning to tremble again himself, and again he suddenly lost the use of his legs. Some completely new feeling wrung his heart with infinite anguish. Meanwhile it had grown quite light; he finally lay down on the pillows, as if quite strengthless now and in despair, and pressed his face to the pale and motionless face of Rogozhin; tears flowed from his eyes onto Rogozhin's cheeks, but perhaps by then he no longer felt his own tears and knew nothing about them . . .

In any case, when, after many hours, the door opened and people came in, they found the murderer totally unconscious and delirious. The prince was sitting motionless on the bed beside him, and each time the sick man had a burst of shouting or raving, he quietly hastened to pass his trembling hand over his hair and cheeks, as if caressing and soothing him. But he no longer understood anything of what they asked him about, and did not recognize the people who came in and surrounded him. And if Schneider himself had come now from Switzerland to have a look at his former pupil and patient, he, too, recalling the state the prince had sometimes been in during the first year of his treatment in Switzerland, would have waved his hand now and said, as he did then: "An idiot!"

XII

Conclusion

THE TEACHER'S WIDOW, having galloped to Pavlovsk, went straight to Darya Alexeevna, who had been upset since the previous day, and, having told her all she knew, frightened her definitively. The two ladies immediately decided to get in touch with Lebedev, who was also worried in his quality as his tenant's friend and in his quality as owner of the apartment. Vera Lebedev told them everything she knew. On Lebedev's advice, they decided that all three of them should go to Petersburg so as to forestall the more quickly "what might very well happen." And so it came about that the next morning, at about eleven o'clock, Rogozhin's apartment was opened in the presence of the police, Lebedev, the ladies, and Rogozhin's brother, Semyon Semyonovich Rogozhin, who was quartered in the wing. What contributed most to the success of the affair was the evidence of the caretaker, who had seen Parfyon Semyonovich and his guest going in from the porch and as if on the quiet. After this evidence they did not hesitate to break down the door, which did not open to their ringing.

Rogozhin survived two months of brain fever and, when he recovered—the investigation and the trial. He gave direct, precise, and perfectly satisfactory evidence about everything, as a result of which the prince was eliminated from the case at the very beginning. Rogozhin was taciturn during his trial. He did not contradict his adroit and eloquent lawyer, who proved clearly and logically that the crime he had committed was the consequence of the brain fever, which had set in long before the crime as a result of the defendant's distress. But he did not add anything of his own in confirmation of this opinion and, as before, clearly and precisely, confirmed and recalled all the minutest circumstances of the event that had taken place. He was sentenced, with allowance for mitigating circumstances, to Siberia, to hard labor, for fifteen years, and heard out his sentence sternly, silently, and "pensively." All his enormous fortune, except for a certain, comparatively speaking, rather small portion spent on the initial carousing, went to his brother, Semyon Semyonovich, to the great pleasure of the latter. Old Mrs. Rogozhin goes on living in this world and seems to recall her favorite son Parfyon occasionally, but not very clearly: God spared her mind and heart all awareness of the horror that had visited her sad house.

Lebedev, Keller, Ganya, Ptitsyn, and many other characters of our story are living as before, have changed little, and we have almost nothing to tell about them. Ippolit died in terrible anxiety and slightly sooner than he expected, two weeks after Nastasya Filippovna's death. Kolya was profoundly struck by what had happened; he became definitively close to his mother. Nina Alexandrovna fears for him, because he is too thoughtful for his years; a good human being will perhaps come out of him. Incidentally, partly through his efforts, the further fate of the prince has been arranged: among all the people he had come to know recently, he had long singled out Evgeny Pavlovich Radomsky; he was the first to go to him and tell him all the details he knew about what had happened and about the prince's present situation. He was not mistaken: Evgeny Pavlovich took the warmest interest in the fate of the unfortunate "idiot," and as a result of his efforts and concern, the prince ended up abroad again, in Schneider's Swiss institution. Evgeny Pavlovich himself, who has gone abroad, intends to stay in Europe for a very long time, and candidly calls himself "a completely superfluous man in Russia," visits his sick friend at Schneider's rather often, at least once every few months; but Schneider frowns and shakes his head more and more; he hints at a total derangement of the mental organs; he does not yet speak positively of incurability, but he allows himself the saddest hints. Evgeny Pavlovich takes it very much to heart, and he does have a heart, as he has already proved by the fact that he receives letters from Kolya and even sometimes answers those letters. But besides that, yet another strange feature of his character has become known; and as it is a good feature, we shall hasten to mark it: after each visit to Schneider's institution, Evgeny Pavlovich, besides writing to Kolya, sends yet another letter to a certain person in Petersburg, with a most detailed and sympathetic account of the state of the prince's illness at the present moment. Apart from the most respectful expressions of devotion, there have begun to appear in these letters (and that more and more often) certain candid accounts of his views, ideas, feelings—in short, something resembling friendly and intimate feelings have begun to appear. This person who is in correspondence (though still rather rarely) with Evgeny Pavlovich, and who has merited his attention and respect to such a degree, is Vera Lebedev. We have been quite unable to find out exactly how such relations could have been established; they were established, of course, on the occasion of the same story with the prince, when Vera Lebedev was so grief-stricken that she even became ill, but under what circumstances the acquaintance and friendship came about, we do not know. We have made reference to these letters mainly for the reason that some of them contain information about the Epanchin family and, above all, about Aglaya Ivanovna Epanchin. Evgeny Pavlovich, in a rather incoherent letter from Paris, told of her that, after a brief and extraordinary attachment to some émigré, a Polish count, she had suddenly married him, against the will of her parents, who, if they did finally give their consent, did so only because the affair threatened to turn into an extraordinary scandal. Then, after an almost six-month silence, Evgeny Pavlovich informed his correspondent, again in a long and detailed letter, that during his last visit to Professor Schneider in Switzerland, he had met all the Epanchins there (except, of course, Ivan

Fyodorovich, who, on account of business, stays in Petersburg) and Prince Shch. The meeting was strange: they all greeted Evgeny Pavlovich with some sort of rapture; Adelaida and Alexandra even decided for some reason that they were grateful to him for his "angelic care of the unfortunate prince." Lizaveta Prokofyevna, seeing the prince in his sick and humiliated condition, wept with all her heart. Apparently everything was forgiven him. Prince Shch. voiced several happy and intelligent truths on the occasion. It seemed to Evgeny Pavlovich that he and Adelaida had not yet become completely close with each other; but the future seemed to promise a completely willing and heartfelt submission of the ardent Adelaida to the intelligence and experience of Prince Shch. Besides, the lessons endured by the family had affected her terribly and, above all, the last incident with Aglaya and the émigré count. Everything that had made the family tremble as they gave Aglaya up to this count, everything had come true within half a year, with the addition of such surprises as they had never even thought of. It turned out that this count was not even a count, and if he was actually an émigré, he had some obscure and ambiguous story. He had captivated Aglaya with the extraordinary nobility of his soul, tormented by sufferings over his fatherland, and had captivated her to such an extent that, even before marrying him, she had become a member of some foreign committee for the restoration of Poland and on top of that had ended up in the Catholic confessional of some famous padre, who had taken possession of her mind to the point of frenzy. The count's colossal fortune, of which he had presented nearly irrefutable information to Lizaveta Prokofyevna and Prince Shch., had turned out to be completely nonexistent. What's more, some six years after the marriage, the count and his friend, the famous confessor, had managed to bring about a complete quarrel between Aglaya and her family, so that they had not seen her for several months already . . . In short, there was a lot to tell, but Lizaveta Prokofyevna, her daughters, and even Prince Shch. had been so struck by all this "terror" that they were even afraid to mention certain things in conversation with Evgeny Pavlovich, though they knew that even without that, he was well acquainted with the story of Aglaya Ivanovna's latest passions. Poor Lizaveta Prokofyevna wanted to be in Russia and, as Evgeny Pavlovich testified, she bitterly and unfairly criticized everything abroad: "They can't bake good bread anywhere, in the winter they freeze like mice in the cellar," she said. "But here at least I've had a good Russian cry over this poor man," she added, pointing with emotion to the prince, who did not recognize her at all. "Enough of these passions, it's time to serve reason. And all this, and all these foreign lands, and all this Europe of yours, it's all one big fantasy, and all of us abroad are one big fantasy . . . remember my words, you'll see for yourself!" she concluded all but wrathfully, parting from Evgeny Pavlovich.

NOTES

For many details in the following notes we are indebted to the commentaries in volume 9 of the Soviet Academy of Sciences edition (Leningrad, 1974).

PART ONE

1. Eydkuhnen is a railway station on the border between Prussia and what was then Russian-occupied Poland.
2. Popular names for various gold coins: "napoleondors" (*Napoléons d'or*) were French coins equal to twenty francs; "friedrichsdors" were Prussian coins equal to five silver thalers; "Dutch yellow boys" (*arapchiki*) were Russian coins, the so-called Dutch *chervonets*, resembling the Dutch ducat, minted in Petersburg.
3. Before the emancipation of 1861, Russian estates were evaluated by the number of adult male serfs ("souls") living on them; they were bound to the land and thus were the property of the landowner.
4. Nikolai Mikhailovich Karamzin (1766–1826) wrote a monumental twelve-volume *History of the Russian State*, the first eight volumes of which were published in 1818, and the remaining four later, the last (reaching the year 1612) appearing posthumously. There is indeed a Myshkin mentioned in the *History*; however, he was not a prince but an architect, who, in 1472, together with a certain Krivtsov, was entrusted by Filipp, the first metropolitan of Moscow, with the construction of a new stone cathedral in Moscow, the Cathedral of the Dormition of the Mother of God; after two years of work, when the vaults were nearly completed, the cathedral collapsed, owing to poor-quality mortar and architectural misjudgment. With Lebedev's strange insistence here, Dostoevsky may have wanted to point readers to that fact.
5. In Russian, the German word *Junker*, meaning "young lord," referred to a lower officer's rank open only to the nobility.
6. The title of "hereditary honorary citizen" was awarded to merchants or other persons not of noble rank for services to the city or the state.

7. A hymn on the words "memory eternal" comes at the end of the Orthodox funeral and memorial services; the prayer is for the person to remain eternally in God's memory.

8. *Menaions* (Greek for "monthly readings") were collections of old Russian spiritual literature, the materials organized day by day and month by month; they contained saints' lives, homilies, explanations of the various feasts, and were often the only reading matter of the uneducated classes.

9. A holy fool (a "fool for God" or "fool in Christ"—*yurodivy* in Russian) might be a harmless village idiot; but there are also saintly persons or ascetics whose saintliness expresses itself as "folly."

10. The Bolshoi (i.e. "Big") Theater in Petersburg, not to be confused with the still-extant Bolshoi Theater in Moscow, stood on Theatralnaya Square from 1783 until 1892, when it was demolished and replaced by the Petersburg Conservatory. The French Theater was a French-language company that performed in the Mikhailovsky Theater (now the Maly, or "Small," Opera Theater). Incidentally, through this company, news from Paris reached Petersburg extraordinarily quickly.

11. A tax farmer was a private person authorized by the government to collect various taxes in exchange for a fixed fee. The practice was obviously open to abuse, and tax farmers could become very rich, though never quite respectable. The practice was abolished by the reforms of the emperor Alexander II in the 1860s.

12. These words were the motto on the coat of arms of Count A. A. Arakcheev (1769–1834), minister of the interior under the emperors Paul I and Alexander I; they were paraphrased by the poet Alexander Pushkin (1799–1837) in his epigram "On Arakcheev."

13. Open courts and trial by jury were first introduced in Russia by the judicial reforms of Alexander II in 1864 and remained controversial for a long time afterwards.

14. The prince's assertion is not quite accurate. In Russia, capital punishment was abolished in 1753–54 under the empress Elizaveta Petrovna (1709–62), but reintroduced by Catherine II (1729–96) as punishment for state, military, and certain other crimes. In the 1860s, owing to the rise of anarchist and terrorist movements, it was resorted to rather frequently. The commentator in the Academy of Sciences edition suggests that Dostoevsky may have introduced the phrase as a blind to keep the censors from interfering with the prince's later discussion.

15. On December 22, 1849, Dostoevsky himself, along with a number of "co-conspirators" from the radical Petrashevsky circle, was subjected to precisely such a mock execution and last-minute reprieve; he "tells us something" about it in more than one of his later works. The prince's account of the experience of "a certain man" in part one, chapter five, reproduces the actual episode in detail. Dostoevsky also draws here and later from *The Last Day of a Man Condemned to Death*, by Victor Hugo (1802–85), which he considered a masterpiece.

16. In 1840–41, the historian and archeologist M. P. Pogodin (1800–75) published an album of *Samples of Old Slavonic-Russian Calligraphy*, containing lithographic reproductions of forty-four samples of handwriting from the tenth to the fourteenth centuries, among them the signature of Pafnuty, a fourteenth-century monk, founder of the Avraamy Monastery, of which he was the hegumen (abbot).

17. Words engraved on a medal awarded by the emperor Nicholas I to Count P. A. Kleinmiechel in 1838, after the reconstruction of the Winter Palace under his supervision.

18. A paraphrase of *Romeo and Juliet*, III, ii, 73: "O serpent heart, hid with a flow'ring face!" which Dostoevsky knew from the translation published by M. N. Katkov in 1841 (he quotes the same line in his *Novel in Nine Letters* written in 1847).

19. It was a custom among young ladies in the nineteenth century to keep personal albums in which friends and visitors would be asked to write witty or sentimental lines or verses; *vers d'album* ("album verse") reached its high point in the verses of the French symbolist Stéphane Mallarmé (1842–98).

20. The Mongol empire, known as the Golden Horde, dominated southern Russia from the thirteenth to the fifteenth century. To "go to the Horde" meant to petition the Mongol rulers on behalf of the subject Russian people.

21. It happens to a rich Corinthian noblewoman in *The Transformations of Lucius*, otherwise known as *The Golden Ass*, by the Latin writer Apuleius (second century A.D.), and to Titania, the queen of the fairies, in Shakespeare's *A Midsummer Night's Dream*—neither case quite belongs to "mythology."

22. An imprecise quotation from the poem "The Journalist, the Reader, and the Writer" (1840), by Mikhail Lermontov (1814–41).

23. Quietism was a form of religious mysticism going back to the writings of the Spanish monk Miguel de Molinos (1628–96), consisting of passive contemplation and a withdrawal from

experiences of the senses; but Aglaya refers more simply to the prince's meekness and passivity.

24. Dostoevsky is probably thinking of "The Beheading of John the Baptist" (1514), by the Swiss painter Hans Fries (*c.* 1460–1520), in the Basel museum, which portrays the face of St. John just as the sword is swung over him.

25. What Dostoevsky refers to as a "cross with four points" is the standard Roman Catholic and Protestant cross with one crossbar; in part two, mention will be made of the "eight-pointed cross" of Byzantine and Russian tradition, which has three crossbars (and thus eight "points" or tips).

26. Dostoevsky saw a copy of *The Madonna with the Family of the Burgomeister Jacob Meyer* (1525–26), by Hans Holbein the Younger (1497–1543), in the Dresden Gallery. The original is in the museum of Darmstadt.

27. In a ukase of April 2, 1837, the emperor Nicholas I forbade the wearing of both moustaches and beards by civil service employees (military officers were allowed moustaches only).

28. An allusion to act IV, scene iii, of the play *Cabal and Love* (1784), by the German poet Friedrich Schiller (1759–1805), in which Ferdinand, suspecting Louisa of unfaithfulness, challenges his rival to a duel "across a handkerchief."

29. The German title *Kammerjunker* ("gentleman of the bedchamber") was adopted by the Russian imperial court; it was a high distinction for a young man.

30. The name of the Novozemlyansky infantry regiment was invented by the poet, playwright, and diplomat Alexander Griboedov (1795–1829) in his comedy *Woe from Wit* (1824), the first real masterpiece of Russian drama, many lines of which have become proverbial.

31. First half of the Italian phrase: *se non è vero è ben trovato* ("if it's not true, it's well invented").

32. The names of the three musketeers in the novel of Alexandre Dumas *père* (1802–70). Porthos, whom General Ivolgin identifies with General Epanchin, was the fat epicure of the three.

33. Kars, in the northeast of Turkey, was besieged by the Russians for many months in 1855, during the Crimean War (1853–56).

34. The *Indépendence Belge* was published in Brussels from 1830 to 1937.

35. See note 22 above. Kolya is thinking of Arbenin insulting Prince Zvezdich (act II, scene iv).

36. Christ is repeatedly referred to in the Gospels as "the king of the Jews," most often as an accusation during his questioning by Pilate, and this mocking "title" was also attached to his cross. Ganya changes it ironically to mean king of the Jewish financiers. Dostoevsky has in mind *The History of Religion and Philosophy in Germany*, a satirical prose text by the poet Heinrich Heine (1797–1856), in which an ironic parallel is drawn between Christ and the banker Meyer Rothschild (1744–1812). Dostoevsky published a Russian translation of Heine's piece in his magazine *Epoch* (Nos. 1–3, 1864); in fact, the Russian censors cut the passage about Christ and Rothschild, but Dostoevsky had of course seen the manuscript intact.

37. The general gives a fantastic interpretation of a real event. The great Russian surgeon N. I. Pirogov (1810–81), who organized medical care for the wounded at the siege of Sevastopol during the Crimean War, left for Petersburg at one point, displeased by the inattention of the high military authorities to problems of medical care. Auguste Nélaton (1807–73), a French surgeon of European repute and member of the Medical Academy of Paris, was the personal surgeon of Garibaldi and Napoleon III; he never set foot in Russia.

38. The reference is to a case that Dostoevsky himself read about in the newspapers: a nineteen-year-old Moscow University student by the name of Danilov was tried for the murder and robbery of the pawnbroker Popov and his maidservant Nordman in January 1866. Dostoevsky was particularly struck by the similarity to Raskolnikov's crime in *Crime and Punishment*, which he had been at work on for several months. During Danilov's trial it came out that the young man, who wanted to get married, had been advised by his father to stop at nothing, not even crime, to achieve his ends.

39. The poet Ivan Krylov (1769–1844) was Russia's greatest fabulist; further on, Ferdyshchenko slightly misquotes from "The Lion and the Ass" (the difference is lost in translation).

40. Provincial marshal of the nobility was the highest elective office in a province before the reforms of Alexander II in 1864.

41. *La Dame aux camélias* ("The Lady with the Camellias"), a novel (1848) and five-act play (1852) by Alexandre Dumas *fils* (1824–95), tells a tragic story of illicit love. The heroine appears at promenades with bouquets of white camellias on certain days of the month and of red camellias on other days; after her death, her lover sees to it that white and red camellias alternate in the same way on her grave.

42. Marlinsky was the pen name of A. A. Bestuzhev (1795–1837), a Romantic writer popular in military circles, to which many of his characters belonged.

43. Russian social thought throughout the nineteenth century was dominated by the dispute between the Westernizers, who favored various degrees of liberal reform to bring Russia into line with developments in Europe, and the Slavophiles, proponents of Russian (and generally Slavic) national culture and Orthodoxy.

44. Dostoevsky drew these details from the case of the Moscow merchant V. F. Mazurin, a young man from a well-off family, who killed the jeweler I. I. Kalmykov with a similarly bound razor. This murder, further details of which will appear later, haunts Nastasya Filippovna throughout the novel.

45. Ekaterinhof, at that time on the southwest periphery of Petersburg, was named in honor of Catherine I (1684–1727), the wife of the emperor Peter the Great (1682–1725), who built a palace there in 1711. In the early nineteenth century, the park surrounding the palace became one of the finest public gardens in the capital and a favorite place for promenades and picnics.

PART TWO

1. The original Vauxhall was a seventeenth-century pleasure garden in London. The word entered Russian as a common noun meaning an outdoor space for concerts and entertainment, with a tearoom, tables, and so on. The vauxhall in Pavlovsk, a suburb of Petersburg where much of the novel is set, was built very near the Pavlovsk railway station, one of the first in Russia—so near, in fact, that *vokzal* also became the Russian word for "railway station."

2. That is, a supporter of the elder branch of the Bourbon family in France, deposed in 1830 in favor of the younger branch of Orléans.

3. The *zemstvo* was an elective provincial council for purposes of local administration, established in 1864 by Alexander II.

4. Tarasov House was the name of the debtors' prison in Petersburg.

5. Holy Week is the week between Palm Sunday and Easter.

6. Pavlovsk, to the south of Petersburg, is a garden suburb named for the emperor Paul I (1754–1801), who had a magnificent palace there. A number of important meetings in the novel take place in the vast, rambling "English" park surrounding the palace. A *dacha* is a summer residence outside the city, anything from a large

separate house to part of a house or one or two rented rooms; the word also summons up a certain summer mode of life, with outings, picnics, and a general air of festivity.

7. The reference is to another notorious murder reported in the newspapers, in which Vitold Gorsky, an eighteen-year-old high-school student from a noble family, killed six members of the merchant Zhemarin's household, including his eleven-year-old son, to whom he gave lessons.

8. These words come from the imperial ukase of November 24, 1864, which promulgated the new judicial statutes; they were carved in gold on a marble plaque in the Petersburg courthouse; the "lawgiver" is the "tsar-reformer" Alexander II.

9. Jeanne Bécu (1743–93), who became the Comtesse du Barry, was the last favorite of Louis XV (1710–74); she was guillotined on the order of the French revolutionary tribunal. The story of her execution and last words is told in the publisher's preface to *Mémoires de madame la comtesse du Barry*, vol. 1 (Paris, 1829).

10. Dostoevsky writes Lebedev's spoken French in Russian transcription, reproducing the speaker's accent. The *levée du roi*, or "king's levee," was a reception that would take place around the king's rising from bed and morning toilet; Lebedev read about it in Mme. du Barry's memoirs.

11. The Apocalypse, or Revelation, of St. John the Theologian is the closing book of the New Testament; balancing the book of Genesis at the beginning of the Old Testament, it contains prophecies of the end of this world and of the Last Judgment. Its visionary, symbolic language has made it subject to many interpretations, often tendentious.

12. The various references in this paragraph are to Revelation 6: 5–8.

13. St. Thomas's Sunday, in the Orthodox Church, is the first Sunday after Easter, named for the apostle who refused to believe in the resurrection until he had ocular and tactile evidence of it (John 20: 24–29).

14. The sect of the castrates (*skoptsi*) in Russia, a reform of the older sect of the flagellants (*khlysti*), was founded in Orlov province in the second half of the eighteenth century by a peasant named Kondraty Selivanov. To combat the promiscuous behavior that generally accompanied the "zeals" of the flagellants, he introduced the practice of self-castration. The sect, which for some reason attracted many rich merchants, moneylenders, and goldsmiths, was condemned by the Church and forbidden by law.

15. Sergei Mikhailovich Solovyov (1820–79), one of the greatest Russian historians, began to publish his *History of Russia from Ancient Times* in 1851; of its twenty-nine volumes, seventeen had appeared by 1867, when Dostoevsky was writing *The Idiot*.

16. In the mid-seventeenth century, the ecclesiastical reforms of the patriarch Nikon caused a schism (*raskol*) in the Russian Orthodox Church. Those who rejected the reforms, led by the archpriest Avvakum, held to the "old belief" and became known as Old Believers.

17. The poem Nastasya Filippovna reads is "Heinrich," by Heinrich Heine, which deals with the famous episode in the history of the Holy Roman Empire when Pope Gregory VII (1020?–1106) forced the emperor Henry IV (1050–1106) to come to the Italian castle of Canossa in 1077 and make humble amends to him. The poem was translated into Russian in 1859 and again in 1862.

18. The prince is referring to the faith of the Old Believers, who did not accept the changes in the church service books instituted in the seventeenth century and made the sign of the cross in the old way, with two fingers, instead of in the three-fingered way introduced by the same reform.

19. See part one, note 26. The painting in question is *Christ's Body in the Tomb* (1521), which Dostoevsky saw in the Basel museum in August 1867, having made a special stop there for that purpose; he even stood on a chair in the museum in order to study the painting more closely. The prince's words further on, "A man can even lose his faith from that painting!" were Dostoevsky's own words to his wife at the time. The painting, which is of central importance to the novel, will be mentioned again later; Dostoevsky first read a description of it in *Letters of a Russian Traveler* (1801), by N. M. Karamzin (see part one, note 4).

20. The details of this murder are again drawn from an actual incident reported in the newspapers—the murder of the tradesman Suslov by a peasant named Balabanov, who repeated the same prayer before taking Suslov's silver watch.

21. The exchanging of crosses was a custom symbolizing spiritual brotherhood.

22. Dostoevsky, who suffered from epilepsy himself, sometimes experienced moments of such "illumination" just before a fit and said that they were "worth a whole life."

23. Cf. Revelation 10: 6: "that there should be time no longer" (King James version).

24. According to Muslim tradition, Muhammad (*c.*570–632) was awakened one night by the archangel Gabriel, who in the process brushed against a jug of water with his wing. Muhammad then traveled to Jerusalem, from there rose into the seven heavens where he spoke with angels, prophets, and Allah, visited the fiery Gehenna, and came back in time to keep the jug from spilling.

25. These confused thoughts are connected with details of the Zhemarin murders (see part two, note 7).

26. The terrace of Lebedev's dacha, as of many country houses, is something between a room and an open veranda: a large, unheated space with many windows, with a door leading to the inner rooms, but also an outside door and steps leading down to the garden. The action of much Russian literature and drama takes place on such terraces.

27. The first Russian state was founded at Novgorod by Rurik, chief of the Scandinavian rovers known as Varangians, in 862, on the invitation of the local Slavic populace. The millennium of Russia was celebrated on September 8, 1862.

28. The poem in question is by Pushkin. The version Dostoevsky quotes is untitled and appears in "Scenes from Knightly Life" (1835), one of Pushkin's "little tragedies." It is Pushkin's revision of a longer version written in 1829.

29. A misquotation from Pushkin's poem "To ***" (1825); it should read "like a genius of pure beauty."

30. "A.N.D." is also incorrect, as we shall see further on. The knight wrote "A.M.D." on his shield, which stood for *Ave Mater Dei* ("Hail Mother of God").

31. The phrase "there's no need to go breaking chairs," which is proverbial in Russia, comes from *The Inspector General* (1836), the famous comedy by Nikolai Gogol (1809–52), in which the mayor says of the schoolteacher, "Of course Alexander the Great is a hero, but why go breaking chairs?"

32. P. V. Annenkov's edition of Pushkin, the first to be based on a study of the poet's manuscripts, was published in seven volumes in 1855–57. Dostoevsky owned it and quotes the verses on the "poor knight" from it.

33. The term "nihilism," first used philosophically in German (*Nihilismus*) to signify annihilation, a reduction to nothing (attributed to Buddha), or the rejection of religious beliefs and moral principles, came via the French *nihilisme* to Russian, where it acquired a political meaning, referring to the doctrines of the

younger generation of socialists of the 1860s, who advocated the destruction of the existing social order without specifying what should replace it. The great nineteenth-century Russian lexicographer Vladimir Ivanovich Dahl (1801–72), normally a model of restraint, defines "nihilism" in his *Interpretive Dictionary of the Living Russian Language* as "an ugly and immoral doctrine which rejects everything that cannot be palpated." The term became current in Russia after it appeared in the novel *Fathers and Sons* (1862), by Ivan Turgenev (1818–83), where it is applied to the hero, Bazarov. The nihilist literary critic D. I. Pisarev (1840–68) was a great disparager of poetry, especially of Pushkin and his "cult of women's little feet."

34. See part two, note 7, and part one, note 38.

35. The opening words in Latin of Psalm 130: "Out of the depths have I cried unto thee, O Lord," sung in Catholic funeral services; the meaning here is "May they rest in peace."

36. The quotation is from Act II, scene ii, of Griboedov's *Woe from Wit* (see part one, note 30).

37. See part one, note 30. "The Stormcloud" was written in 1815.

38. The commentator in the Academy of Sciences edition has established that this epigram is a takeoff on "Self-assured Fedya," by M. E. Saltykov-Shchedrin (1826–89), a satirical epigram on Dostoevsky himself, published in *The Whistle*, No. 9 (1863).

39. The quoted phrase is an allusion to Vera Pavlovna's farewell to her mother, in the radical novel *What Is to Be Done?* (1863), by N. G. Chernyshevsky (1828–89).

40. Probably a reference to the famous doctor S. P. Botkin (1832–89), physician to Alexander II and to Dostoevsky himself.

41. Pierre-Joseph Proudhon (1809–65) was one of the principal French socialist theorists of the nineteenth century, author of the memorable phrase "Property is theft." His libertarian socialism was opposed to Marxism.

42. The line about Princess Marya Alexeevna is a paraphrase of the final line of Famusov's last monologue, in act IV, scene xv, of Griboedov's *Woe from Wit* (see part one, note 30).

43. Ippolit is thinking of Christ.

44. Cf. Revelation 8: 10–11.

45. Keller is referring to a real man: Louis Bourdaloue (1632–1704), a Jesuit and a famous preacher in the age of Louis XIV, though never an archbishop. In the first case, however, he is actually making a pun on bordeaux wine and the Russian word *burda*, which

means "swill"; only in the second case does he come to the more appropriate question of "confession."

1. Russian seminary education was open to the lower classes and was often subsidized by state scholarships. Seminarians were thus not necessarily preparing for the priesthood. Many Russian radicals of the 1860s were former seminarians, like Joseph Stalin later. Dostoevsky wrote in a notebook around this time: "These seminarians have introduced a special negation into our literature, too complete, too hostile, too sharp, and therefore too limited."

2. See part one, note 12, and part two, note 31. Mikhail Vassilievich Lomonosov (1711–65) was a peasant who came on foot from Archangelsk to Petersburg in order to study; he became a great poet and scientist, and, like both Pushkin and Gogol after him, is often called "the father of modern Russian literature."

3. Pavel Afanasyevich Famusov is the father of the heroine in Griboedov's *Woe from Wit* (see part one, note 30).

4. See part one, note 13.

5. Provoked by the young Frenchman's attentions to his wife, Pushkin challenged Georges d'Anthès to a duel; having the first shot, d'Anthès may have fired sooner than he intended to, and his bullet hit Pushkin in the stomach; the wound proved fatal.

6. General Epanchin is trying to use the French expression *ne pas se sentir dans son assiette*, literally "not to feel that you are in your plate," meaning "to be out of sorts."

7. Dueling was forbidden in Russia until 1894, when it was made legal for army officers. Taking part in a duel was severely punishable by law, and a lieutenant like Keller risked being broken to the ranks and thus acquiring the "red cap" of the common foot soldier.

8. Ippolit is recalling the song of the archangel Raphael (ll. 243–244), from the "Prologue in Heaven" that begins the monumental drama *Faust*, by Johann Wolfgang von Goethe (1749–1832): "*Die Sonne tönt nach alter Weise/ In Brudersphären Wettgesang . . .*" ("The sun resounds as of old/In rival-singing with his brother spheres").

9. See part two, note 44.

10. Cf. Revelation 11: 6–7.

11. François-Marie Arouet, known as Voltaire (1694–1778), was a facetious debunker of religious literalism. Dostoevsky especially admired his philosophical novel *Candide* (1759).

12. An ironic reference to Thomas Robert Malthus (1766–1834), English economist, author of *An Essay on the Principle of Population*, who first perceived the threat posed by the geometric increase of the earth's population; he declared that the "superfluous population" of the earth was bound to perish and that all social reforms would fail, and he called for the abolition of falsely philanthropic laws alleviating the condition of the poor. The radical Petrashevsky circle, to which Dostoevsky belonged as a young man, was interested in Malthus's thought and translated some of his writings.

13. See part two, note 23. Ippolit plays on the ambiguity of the Russian translation, which we render here.

14. See part one, notes 2 and 36. An imperial was a Russian gold coin worth ten roubles.

15. Actual state councillor was fourth in the table of fourteen civil service ranks established by Peter the Great, equivalent to the military rank of major general.

16. After his defeat at Waterloo and his second abdication in 1815, Napoleon (1769–1821) wanted to escape to America, but owing to the blockade of the port at Rochefort, he was forced to negotiate with the British, who exiled him to the island of St. Helena.

17. These words come from *Pensées sur la religion et sur quelques autres sujets* ("Thoughts on religion and on several other subjects"), by the French philosopher Blaise Pascal (1623–62).

18. The references are to the raising of Jairus's daughter (Mark 5: 22–43) and the raising of Lazarus (John 11: 1–44). *Talitha cumi* is Aramaic for "Damsel, arise."

19. The lines that follow are not by Charles-Hubert Millevoye (1782–1816), romantic poet, author of "Falling Leaves," but by the satirical poet Nicolas Gilbert (1751–80), from the end of his *Adieux à la vie* ("Farewell to Life"). Dostoevsky misquotes slightly; the first verse should read: "*Ah, puissent voir longtemps votre beauté sacrée . . .*" ("Ah, may they long behold your sacred beauty . . .").

20. In Petersburg during the month of June, the sun rises at between two and three o'clock in the morning; this is the season of the famous "white nights."

21. Pierre-François Lacenaire (1800–36), the subject of a notorious criminal trial in Paris, was a murderer of exceptional vanity and cruelty.

22. The prolific French novelist Paul de Kock (1794–1871) depicted petit bourgeois life, often in rather risqué detail.

23. The name Aglaya comes from the Greek *aglaós*, meaning "splendid, shining, bright, beautiful."

24. Cf. John 8:3–11: "He that is without sin among you, let him first cast a stone at her" (King James version).

25. See part two, note 41, and part three, note 11. Jean-Jacques Rousseau (1712–78), Swiss-born French novelist and philosopher, author of *The Social Contract*, was influential on young Russian radicals like Ippolit and Kolya.

26. The English fraternity of Freemasons reorganized itself in 1717 to form a "grand lodge" in London, with a new constitution and ritual and a system of secret signs; this was to be the parent lodge of all the other lodges in Great Britain and throughout the world. Because of their secrecy and the political role they began to play (for instance, in the French revolution), the Masons were outlawed in some countries, including Russia, where they were forbidden by the emperor Alexander I in 1822. Kolya is probably referring here to the Masons' secrecy and conspiratorial reputation.

27. The French word is *contrecarrer*, "to oppose directly, to thwart."

28. Russian civil servants wore uniforms similar to the military, including hats with cockades.

29. The phrase is proverbial in Russian. In *Anna Karenina*, Leo Tolstoy uses an abbreviated Latin version: "*Quos vult perdere dementat.*" The ultimate source is in a lost Greek tragedy quoted by the Athenian politician and orator Lykurgos (390–24 B.C.).

30. The details come from the Mazurin murder case (see part one, note 44). Zhdanov liquid was a chemical mixture invented in the 1840s by N. I. Zhdanov to eliminate bad odors. Mazurin kept Kalmykov's body for eight months this way.

PART FOUR

1. Podkolesin is one of the suitors in Gogol's play *The Marriage* (1842); at the decisive moment he jumps out of the window and runs away.

2. A line from the comedy *Georges Dandin* (1668), by Molière (1622–73).

3. Lieutenant Pirogov is one of the heroes of Gogol's tale "Nevsky Prospect" (1835); his name, while common in Russia, happens to come from the word for pastry.

4. See part one, note 36.

5. Nozdryov is another of Gogol's heroes, this time from the comic novel-poem *Dead Souls* (1842)—an absurd, blustering liar.

6. See part one, note 5.

7. The year 1812 was the year of Napoleon's disastrous invasion of Russia.

8. This epitaph was actually composed by the Russian writer and historian N. M. Karamzin (see part one, note 4). Dostoevsky and his brother Mikhail had it inscribed on their mother's tombstone in 1837.

9. A panikhida is an Orthodox memorial prayer service for the dead.

10. R. A. Chernosvitov (b. 1810), a member of the Petrashevsky circle (see part one, note 15, and part three, note 12), wrote a book entitled *Instructions for the Designing of an Artificial Leg* (1855).

11. *The Russian Archive* was a highly respected historical review founded in 1863 by P. Bartenev.

12. The reference is to the opening chapter of *From my Past and Thought*, autobiographical reflections by the liberal Russian writer Alexander Herzen (1812–70).

13. Moscow was evacuated at the approach of Napoleon's army and the city was set on fire.

14. The boyars were a privileged rank of the old nobility, the highest in Russia after the rank of prince. Since they were always ready to dispute the absolute power of the tsar, the rank was abolished by Peter the Great.

15. Baron Jean-Baptiste de Bazancourt (1767–1830) was a French general and took part in Napoleon's Russian campaign; he was never a chamber-page and outlived the emperor by nine years.

16. Jean-Baptiste Adolphe Charras (1810–65) was a French politician and military historian. Dostoevsky read his anti-Bonapartist *History of the Campaign of 1815: Waterloo* (1864) while staying in Baden-Baden in 1867; he also had the book in his library.

17. Louis-Nicolas Davout (1770–1823), duke of Auerstaedt, prince of Eckmühl, and *maréchal de France*, was one of Napoleon's best generals. The mameluke Rustan was Napoleon's bodyguard. Constant, one of Napoleon's favorite valets, is often mentioned in memoirs and novels about the emperor.

18. Marie-Josèphe ("Joséphine") Tascher de la Pagerie-Beauharnais (1763–1814) married General Bonaparte in 1796, her first husband, the vicomte de Beauharnais, having been guillotined in 1794. She became empress in 1804, but Napoleon divorced her

in 1809 to marry Marie-Louise de Lorraine-Autriche (1791–1847), daughter of the German emperor Franz II. Thus, in 1812 she was no longer empress.

19. Napoleon's son, François-Charles-Joseph Bonaparte (1811–32), known as Napoleon II, was declared king of Rome at birth. His mother was the empress Marie-Louise, not Josephine.

20. The quotation is from Pushkin's poem "Napoleon" (1821).

21. General Ivolgin quotes imprecisely from the beginning of volume one, chapter six, of *Dead Souls*; Gogol wrote simply: "Oh, my youth! Oh, my freshness!"

22. The Order of St. Anna, named for the mother of the Virgin Mary, was founded in 1735 by Karl Friedrich, Duke of Schleswig-Holstein, in honor of his wife, Anna Petrovna, daughter of Peter the Great. It had four degrees, two civil and two military.

23. The line comes from the unfinished poem "Humor," by the Russian civic poet N. P. Ogaryov (1813–77).

24. Friedrich Christophe Schlosser (1776–1861), German historian, was the author of a *Universal History* (1844–56), which was translated into Russian in 1861–69.

25. An ironic inversion of the apostle Thomas's doubt of Christ's resurrection; see part two, note 13.

26. Stepan Bogdanovich Glebov (c. 1672–1718) was the lover of Peter the Great's repudiated first wife Evdokia Lopukhin. He was accused of conspiring with her and the tsarevich Alexei, was tortured and condemned to this cruel death; Evdokia was sent to a nunnery.

27. Andrei Ivanovich (or Heinrich Johann) Osterman (1686–1747) was a Russian diplomat and statesman.

28. In Russian these words echo proverbial lines from the poem "Borodino" (1837) by Mikhail Lermontov (see part one, note 22); an old man is speaking: "Yes, those were people of our time, / Not to be compared with today's breed . . ."

29. Lebedev makes absurd use of the words about Christ from the Nicene Creed: "the only-begotten, begotten of the Father before all ages."

30. Sir Thomas More (Latin *Morus*) (1478–1535), English humanist, author of *Utopia*, and Lord Chancellor under Henry VIII, was decapitated for refusing to acknowledge the spiritual authority of the king. He was canonized by the Catholic Church in 1935. Lebedev's story is apocryphal, however; on the scaffold, More said to the executioner: "Pluck up thy spirits, man, and be not afraid

to do thine office; my neck is very short; take heed therefore thou strike not awry, for saving of thine honesty" (see the *Lives of Saint Thomas More*, by William Roper and Nicholas Harpsfield).

31. These Latin words from the penitential *confiteor: Mea culpa, mea culpa, mea maxima culpa*, are repeated by Roman Catholic priests before the Mass and by the faithful before communion.

32. In addition to cutting hair, barbers performed other operations, such as letting blood, which might have been thought necessary in the general's case.

33. The Latin words signify papal refusal to satisfy the demands of a secular power. The expression may go back to the Acts of the Apostles (4: 20).

34. *Égalité* is the middle term of the French revolutionary motto: "*Liberté, égalité, fraternité*. In his *Winter Notes from Summer Impressions* (1863), Dostoevsky already cites the motto with *ou la mort* added to the end; his protagonist Kirillov will do the same in *Demons* (1872). The "two million heads" probably come from a reference in part five, chapter thirty-seven, of A. Herzen's *From My Past and Thought* (see part four, note 12) to a German socialist writer who declared that it was enough to destroy two million people and the socialist revolution would go swimmingly. Herzen, a radical himself, called this notion "pernicious rubbish" and traced its origins to the French revolution, describing it as "Marat transformed into a German." Dostoevsky refers to this notion again in *Demons* (1871–72) and in *The Brothers Karamazov* (1879–80).

35. Cf. Matthew 7: 15–16: "Beware of false prophets, which come to you in sheep's clothing, but inwardly they are ravening wolves. Ye shall know them by their fruits" (King James version).

36. That is, the "Pillars of Hercules," the ancient name for the straits of Gibraltar, which marked the boundary of the known world in classical times.

37. The Jesuit order, or Society of Jesus, was founded on Montmartre (Paris) in 1534 by St. Ignatius of Loyola (1491–1556), his friend and follower St. Francis Xavier (1506–52), and four other friends. More militant than contemplative, and with a strict hierarchical administration, the order quickly became very powerful. The Jesuits were eventually expelled from Portugal in 1759 and from France in 1762 (and again in 1880 and 1901). The exiled fathers either went "underground" or dispersed, some even going to Russia, where their influence was not inconsiderable.

38. See part two, note 16.

39. The sect of the flagellants (*khlysti*) emerged among the Russian peasants in the seventeenth century. Its adherents practiced self-flagellation as a means of purification from sin (see part two, note 14).

40. These words echo the words of Christ to the apostles (Mark 9: 35): "If any man desire to be first, the same shall be last of all, and servant of all."

41. Cf. the episode of the healing of the demoniac in Mark 9: 17–27 and Luke 9: 42.

42. See part one, note 43.

43. The lines come from Pushkin's poem "Elegy" (1830).

44. See part two, note 33.

45. In the Orthodox wedding service, one or more "groomsmen" hold crowns above the heads of both bride and groom.

46. The reference is to Christ forgiving the woman taken in adultery (John 8: 3–11); see part three, note 24.

47. The princely family of Rohan is one of the most ancient and illustrious in France; their motto is *"Premier ne puis, second ne daigne, Rohan suis"* ("I cannot be first, I deign not to be second, I am Rohan").

48. Charles-Maurice de Talleyrand-Perigord (1754–1838), prince of Bénévent, bishop of Autun, was one of the most important French statesmen of his time, during which he served under the king, the constitutional assembly, the Directoire, the consulate, the empire, and finally the restoration of the Bourbons; he played a brilliant and skillful role at the Congress of Vienna (1814–15), deciding the fate of post-Napoleonic France and Europe.

49. See part four, note 22. The first degree of the civil order of St. Anna was worn on a ribbon around the neck.

50. The quotation is from a verse fragment about Cleopatra that Pushkin included in his *Egyptian Nights* (1835): Cleopatra addresses the crowd gathered at her feast, asking who would be willing to give his life for a night with her.

51. An imprecise quotation from Matthew 11: 25, Luke 10: 21.

52. *Madame Bovary*, by French novelist Gustave Flaubert (1821–80), caused a scandal when it was first published in 1856 because of its frank treatment of adultery; the heroine commits suicide in the end. Dostoevsky read the novel in the summer of 1867 and admired it.